BATMAN & ROBIN ADVENTURES

VOLUME 1

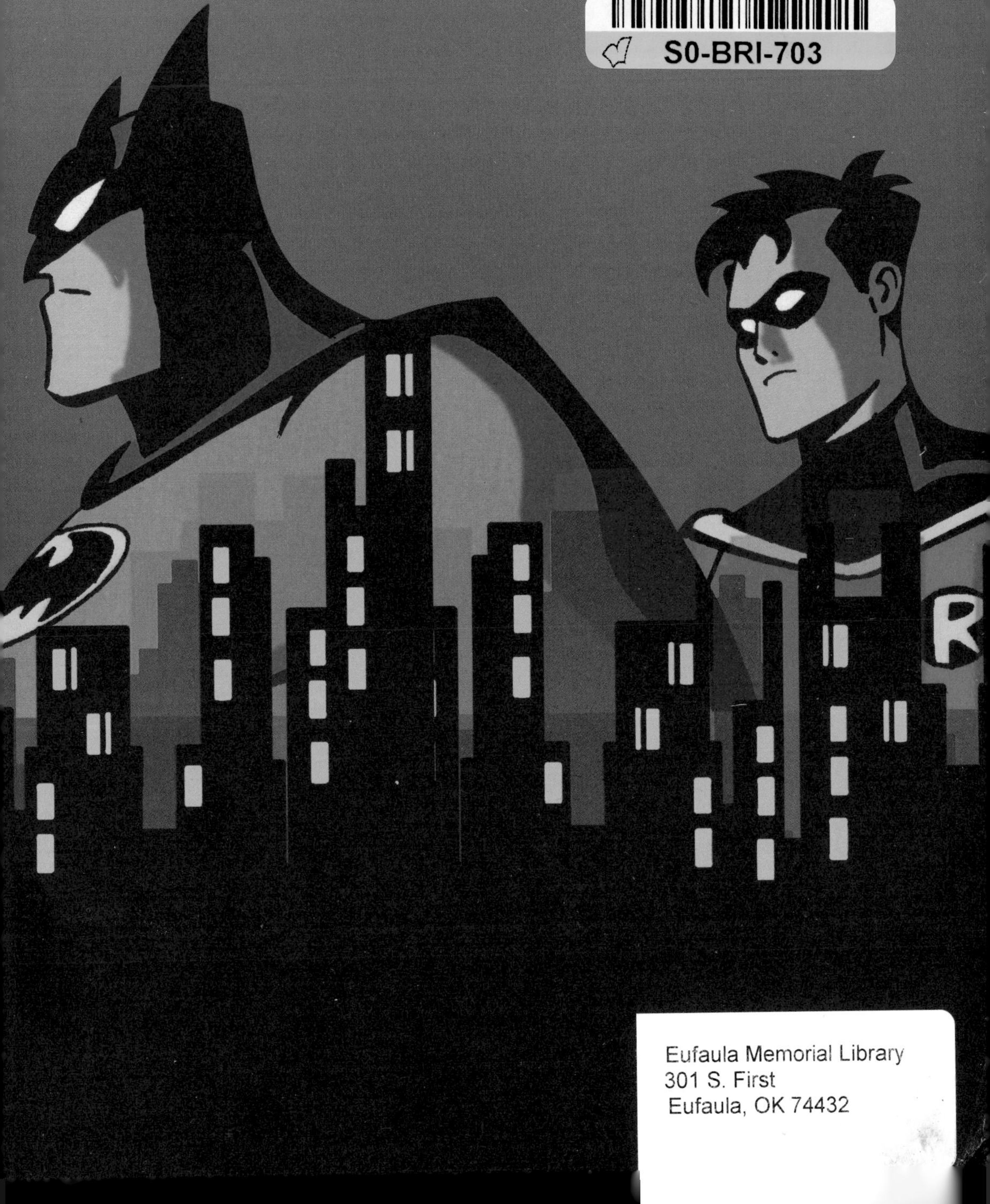

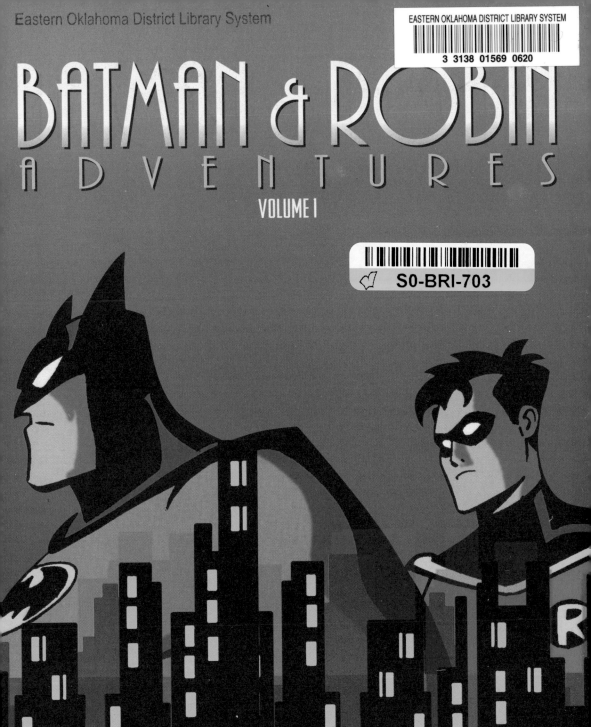

BATMAN & ROBIN ADVENTURES

VOLUME 1

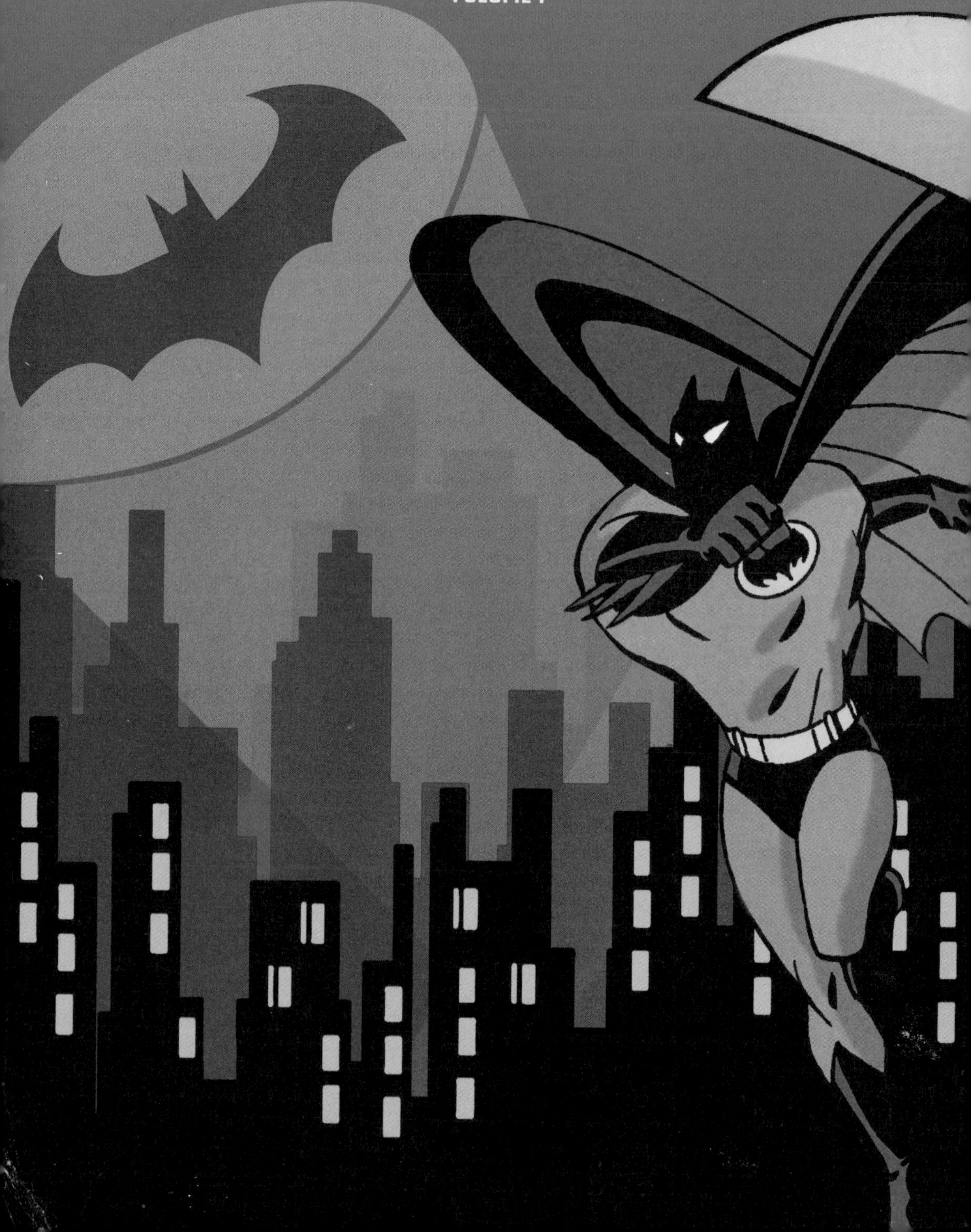

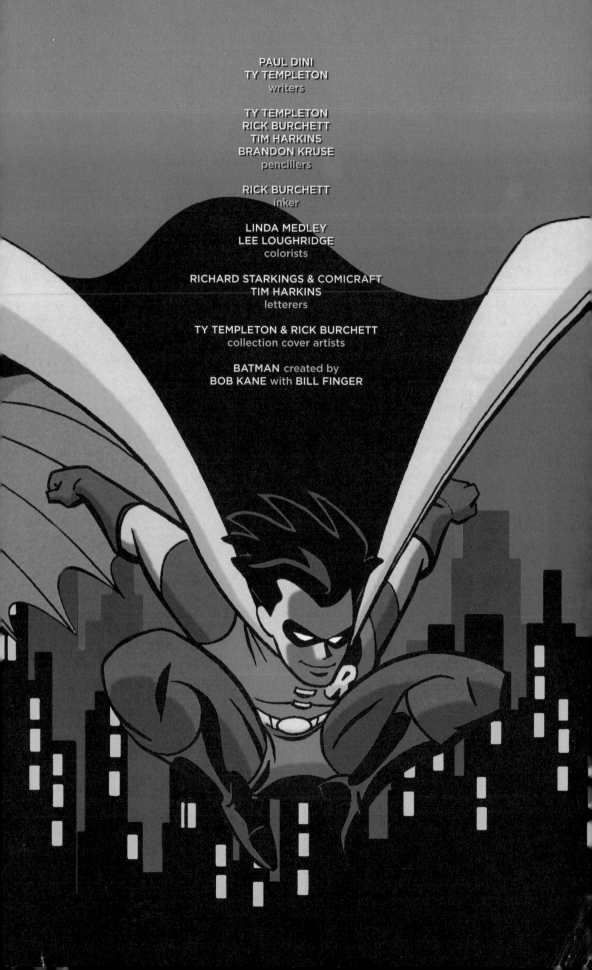

PAUL DINI
TY TEMPLETON
writers

TY TEMPLETON
RICK BURCHETT
TIM HARKINS
BRANDON KRUSE
pencillers

RICK BURCHETT
inker

LINDA MEDLEY
LEE LOUGHRIDGE
colorists

RICHARD STARKINGS & COMICRAFT
TIM HARKINS
letterers

TY TEMPLETON & RICK BURCHETT
collection cover artists

BATMAN created by
BOB KANE with BILL FINGER

Scott Peterson   Editor – Original Series
Darren Vincenzo   Associate Editor – Original Series
Jeb Woodard   Group Editor – Collected Editions
Steve Cook   Design Director – Books
Chris Griggs   Publication Design

Bob Harras   Senior VP – Editor-in-Chief, DC Comics

Diane Nelson   President
Dan DiDio   Publisher
Jim Lee   Publisher
Geoff Johns   President & Chief Creative Officer
Amit Desai   Executive VP – Business & Marketing Strategy,
                        Direct to Consumer & Global Franchise Management
Sam Ades   Senior VP – Direct to Consumer
Bobbie Chase   VP – Talent Development
Mark Chiarello   Senior VP – Art, Design & Collected Editions
John Cunningham   Senior VP – Sales & Trade Marketing
Anne DePies   Senior VP – Business Strategy, Finance & Administration
Don Falletti   VP – Manufacturing Operations
Lawrence Ganem   VP – Editorial Administration & Talent Relations
Alison Gill Senior   VP – Manufacturing & Operations
Hank Kanalz   Senior VP – Editorial Strategy & Administration
Jay Kogan   VP – Legal Affairs
Thomas Loftus   VP – Business Affairs
Jack Mahan   VP – Business Affairs
Nick J. Napolitano   VP – Manufacturing Administration
Eddie Scannell   VP – Consumer Marketing
Courtney Simmons   Senior VP – Publicity & Communications
Jim (Ski) Sokolowski   VP – Comic Book Specialty Sales & Trade Marketing
Nancy Spears   VP – Mass, Book, Digital Sales & Trade Marketing

BATMAN & ROBIN ADVENTURES VOLUME 1

DC Comics, 2900 West Alameda Ave., Burbank, CA 91505
Printed by LSC Communications, Owensville, MO, USA. 11/11/16. First Printing.
ISBN: 978-1-4012-6783-4

Library of Congress Cataloging-in-Publication Data is available.

PEFC Certified

Printed on paper from
sustainably managed
forests and controlled
sources

PEFC/29-31-337   www.pefc.org

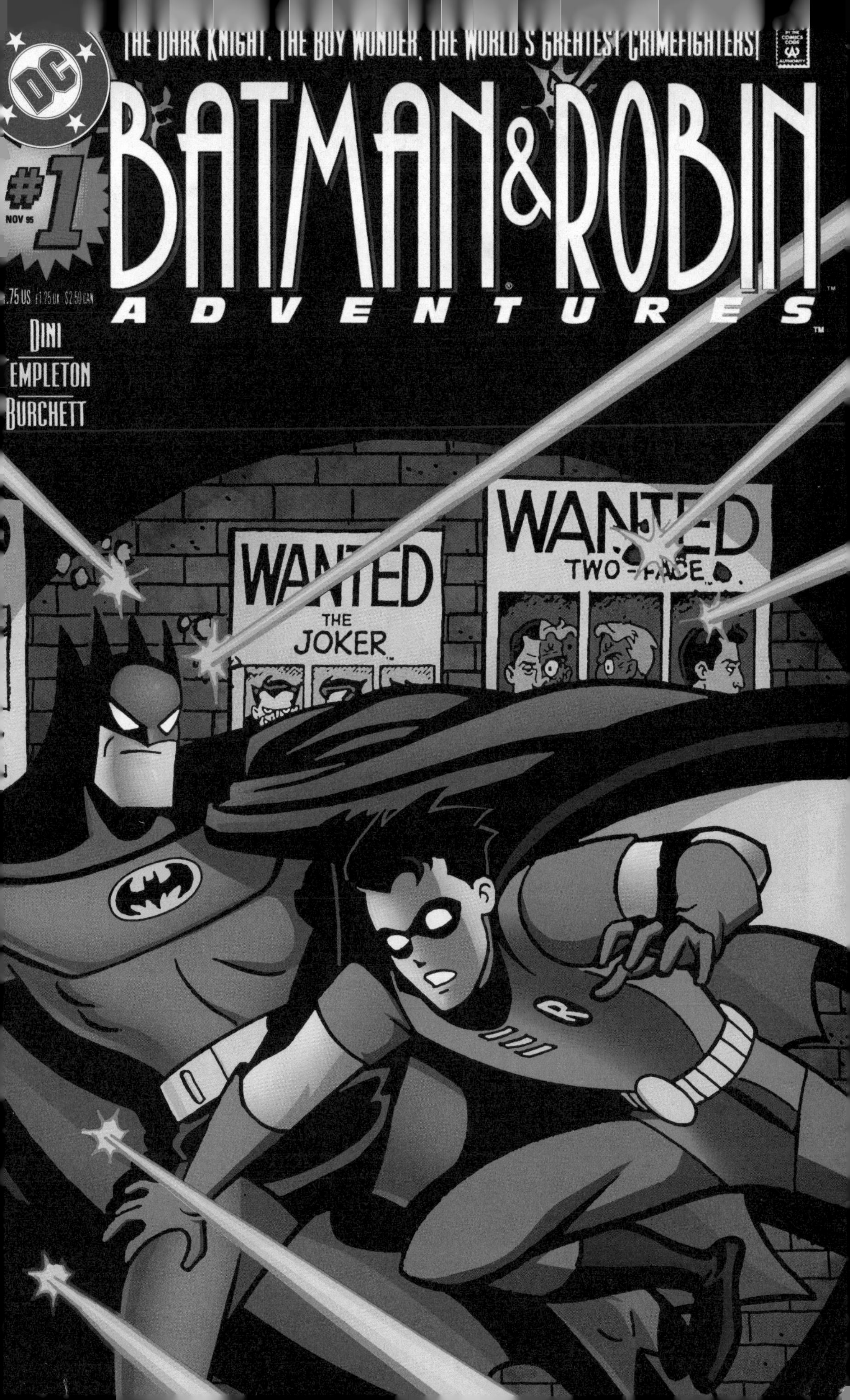
THE DARK KNIGHT, THE BOY WONDER, THE WORLD'S GREATEST CRIMEFIGHTERS!
DC
#1
NOV 95
BATMAN & ROBIN ADVENTURES
.75 US £1.25 UK $2.50 CAN
DINI
EMPLETON
BURCHETT
WANTED
THE JOKER
WANTED
TWO-FACE

TWOTIMER

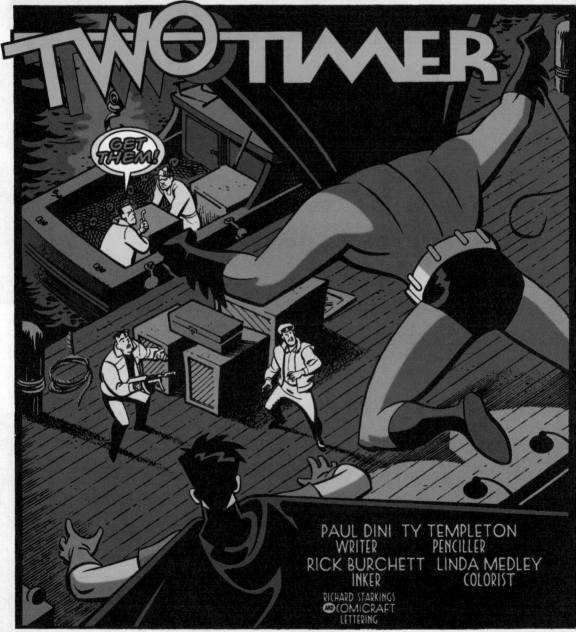

PAUL DINI
WRITER

TY TEMPLETON
PENCILLER

RICK BURCHETT
INKER

LINDA MEDLEY
COLORIST

RICHARD STARKINGS
AND COMICRAFT
LETTERING

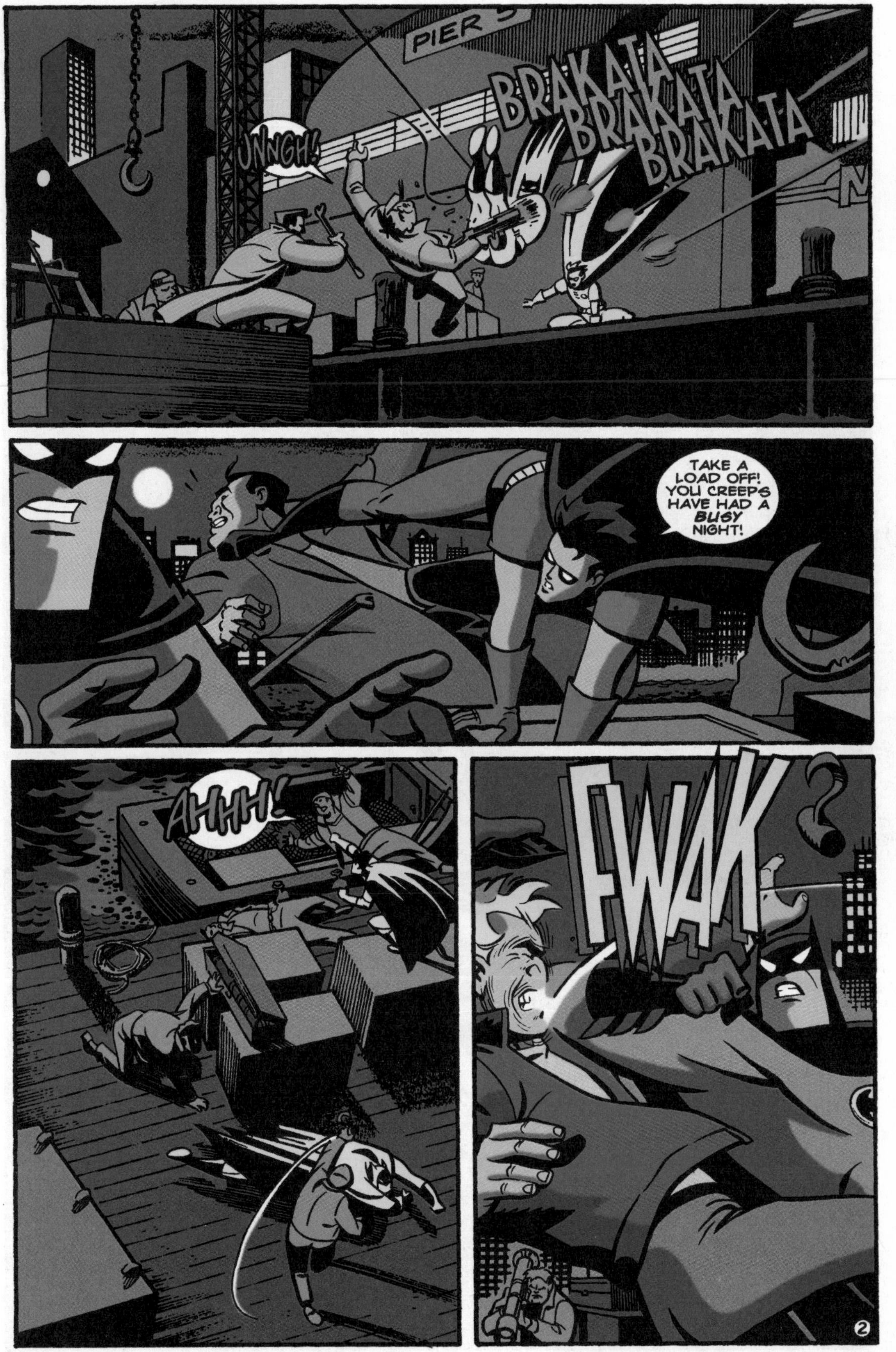
PIER 5
UNNGH!
BRAKATA BRAKATA BRAKATA
TAKE A LOAD OFF! YOU CREEPS HAVE HAD A BUSY NIGHT!
AHHH!
FWAK
2

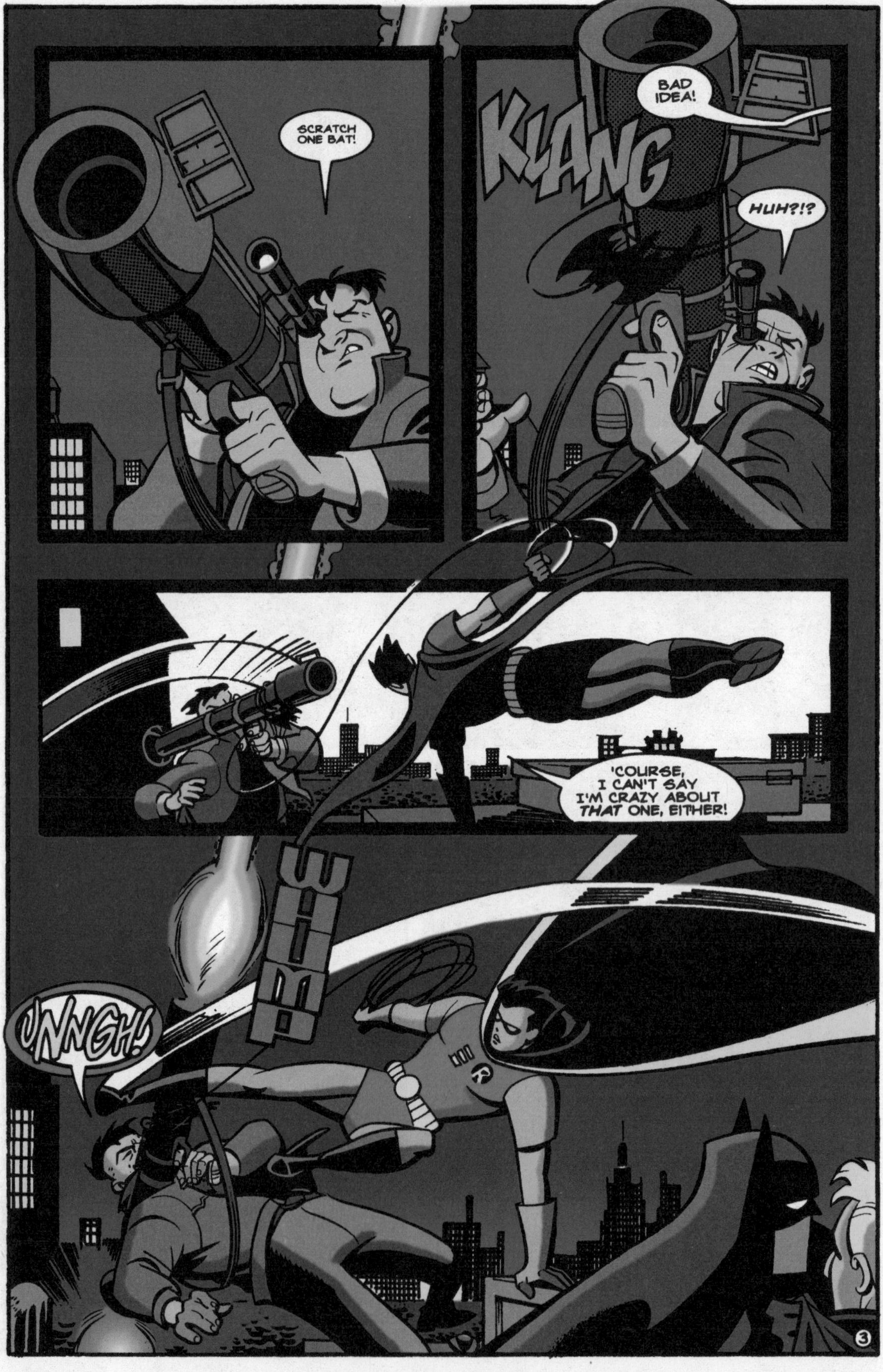
SCRATCH ONE BAT!
KLANG
BAD IDEA!
HUH?!?
'COURSE, I CAN'T SAY I'M CRAZY ABOUT THAT ONE, EITHER!
UNNGH!
3

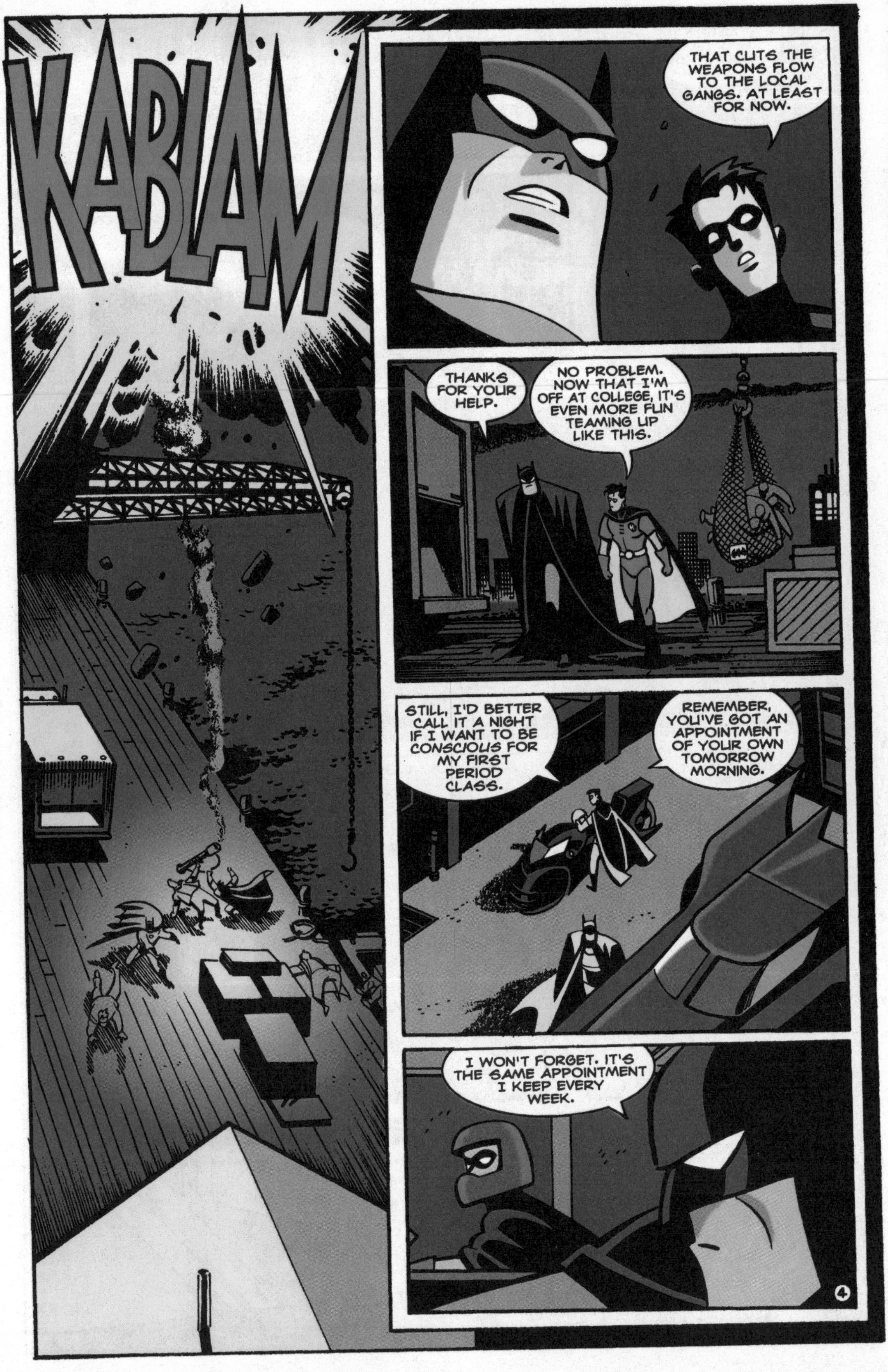
KABLAM
THAT CUTS THE WEAPONS FLOW TO THE LOCAL GANGS. AT LEAST FOR NOW.
THANKS FOR YOUR HELP.
NO PROBLEM. NOW THAT I'M OFF AT COLLEGE, IT'S EVEN MORE FUN TEAMING UP LIKE THIS.
STILL, I'D BETTER CALL IT A NIGHT IF I WANT TO BE CONSCIOUS FOR MY FIRST PERIOD CLASS.
REMEMBER, YOU'VE GOT AN APPOINTMENT OF YOUR OWN TOMORROW MORNING.
I WON'T FORGET. IT'S THE SAME APPOINTMENT I KEEP EVERY WEEK.
4

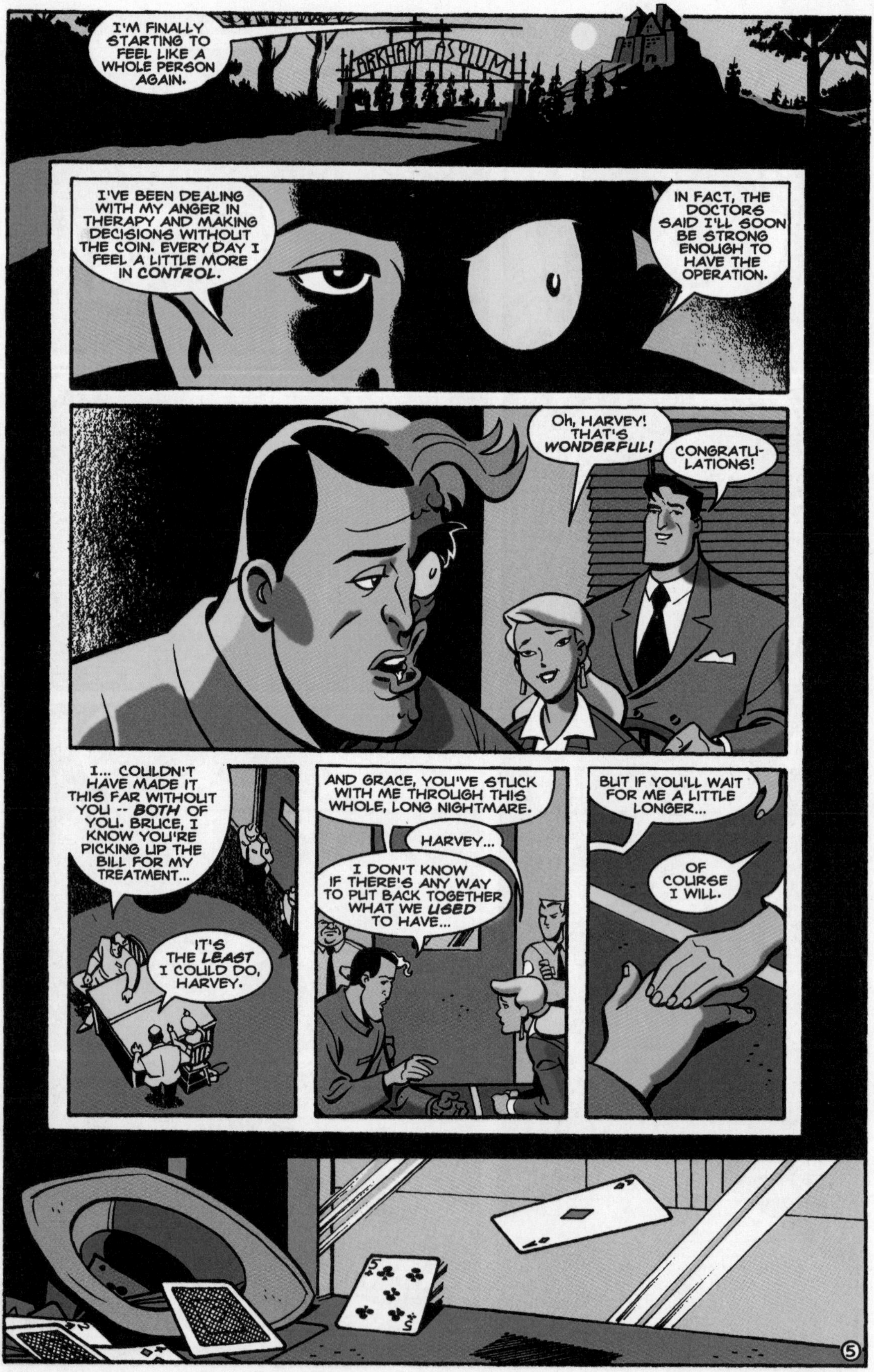

I'M FINALLY STARTING TO FEEL LIKE A WHOLE PERSON AGAIN.
ARKHAM ASYLUM
I'VE BEEN DEALING WITH MY ANGER IN THERAPY AND MAKING DECISIONS WITHOUT THE COIN. EVERY DAY I FEEL A LITTLE MORE IN CONTROL.
IN FACT, THE DOCTORS SAID I'LL SOON BE STRONG ENOUGH TO HAVE THE OPERATION.
Oh, HARVEY! THAT'S WONDERFUL!
CONGRATULATIONS!
I... COULDN'T HAVE MADE IT THIS FAR WITHOUT YOU -- BOTH OF YOU. BRUCE, I KNOW YOU'RE PICKING UP THE BILL FOR MY TREATMENT...
IT'S THE LEAST I COULD DO, HARVEY.
AND GRACE, YOU'VE STUCK WITH ME THROUGH THIS WHOLE, LONG NIGHTMARE.
HARVEY...
I DON'T KNOW IF THERE'S ANY WAY TO PUT BACK TOGETHER WHAT WE USED TO HAVE...
BUT IF YOU'LL WAIT FOR ME A LITTLE LONGER...
OF COURSE I WILL.
5

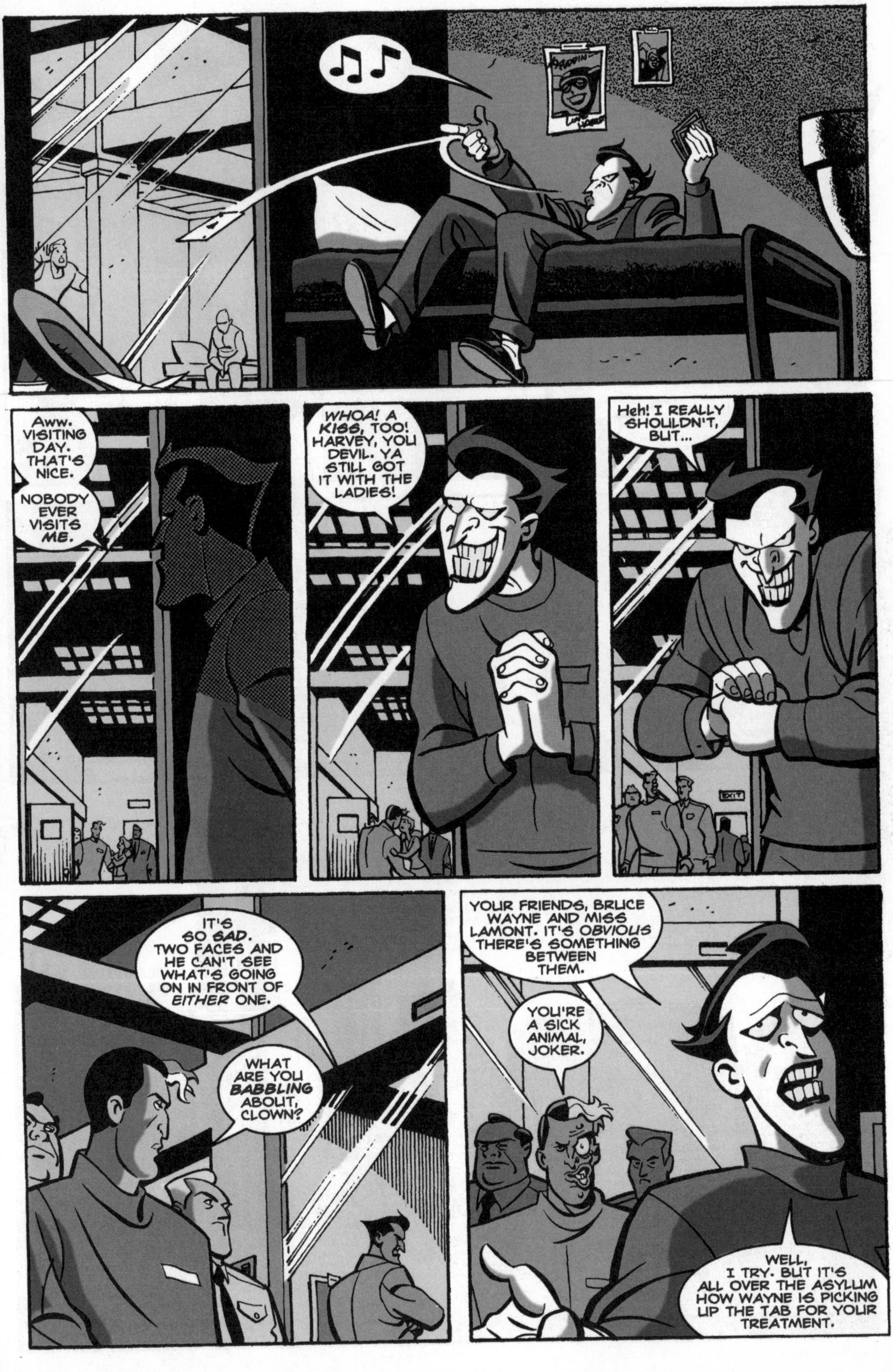
♫♪
Aww. VISITING DAY. THAT'S NICE.
NOBODY EVER VISITS ME.
WHOA! A KISS, TOO! HARVEY, YOU DEVIL. YA STILL GOT IT WITH THE LADIES!
Heh! I REALLY SHOULDN'T, BUT...
EXIT
IT'S SO SAD. TWO FACES AND HE CAN'T SEE WHAT'S GOING ON IN FRONT OF EITHER ONE.
WHAT ARE YOU BABBLING ABOUT, CLOWN?
YOUR FRIENDS, BRUCE WAYNE AND MISS LAMONT. IT'S OBVIOUS THERE'S SOMETHING BETWEEN THEM.
YOU'RE A SICK ANIMAL, JOKER.
WELL, I TRY. BUT IT'S ALL OVER THE ASYLUM HOW WAYNE IS PICKING UP THE TAB FOR YOUR TREATMENT.

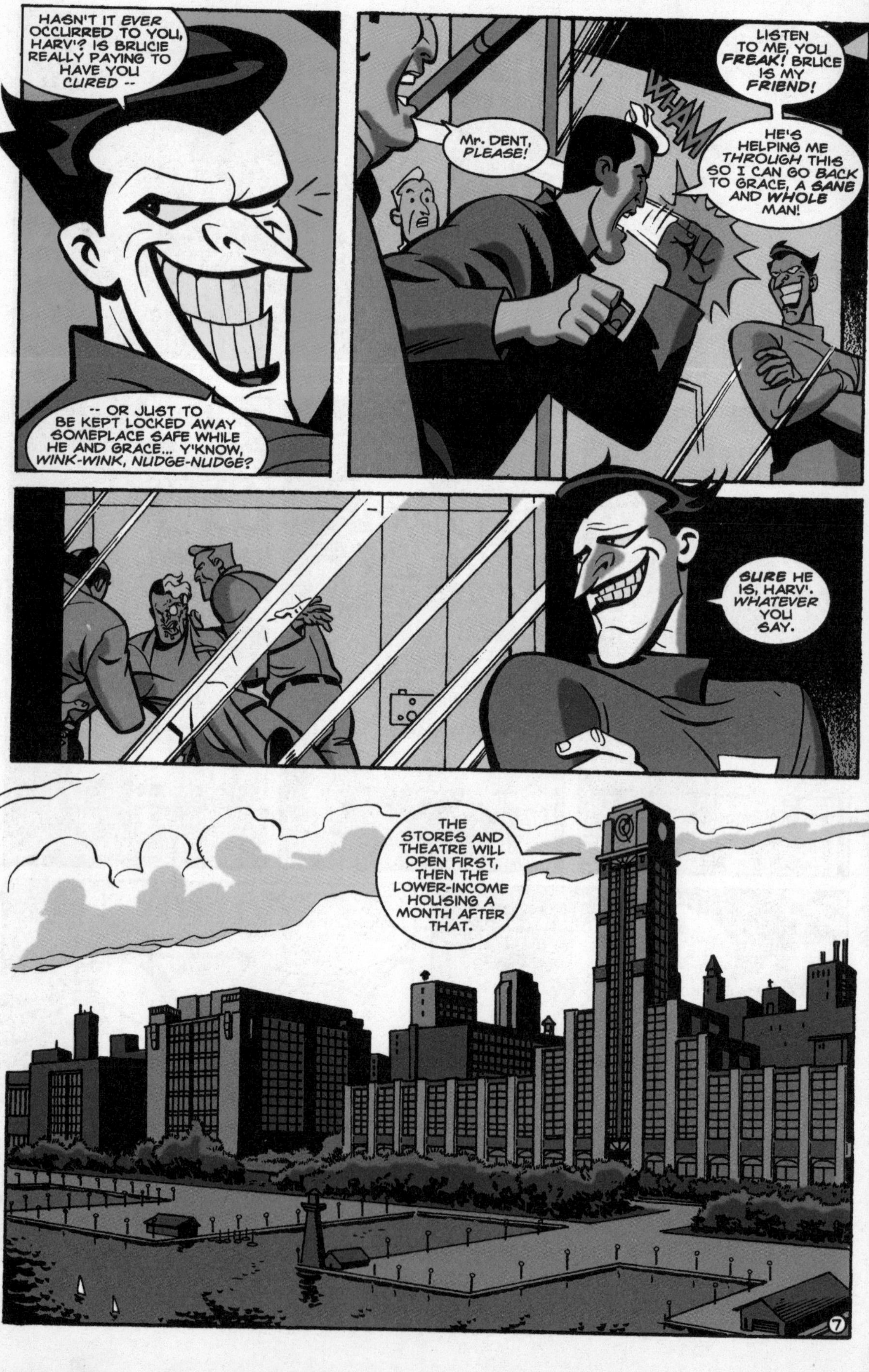
HASN'T IT EVER OCCURRED TO YOU, HARV'? IS BRUCIE REALLY PAYING TO HAVE YOU CURED --
-- OR JUST TO BE KEPT LOCKED AWAY SOMEPLACE SAFE WHILE HE AND GRACE... Y'KNOW, WINK-WINK, NUDGE-NUDGE?
LISTEN TO ME, YOU FREAK! BRUCE IS MY FRIEND!
WHAM
Mr. DENT, PLEASE!
HE'S HELPING ME THROUGH THIS SO I CAN GO BACK TO GRACE, A SANE AND WHOLE MAN!
SURE HE IS, HARV'. WHATEVER YOU SAY.
THE STORES AND THEATRE WILL OPEN FIRST, THEN THE LOWER-INCOME HOUSING A MONTH AFTER THAT.
7

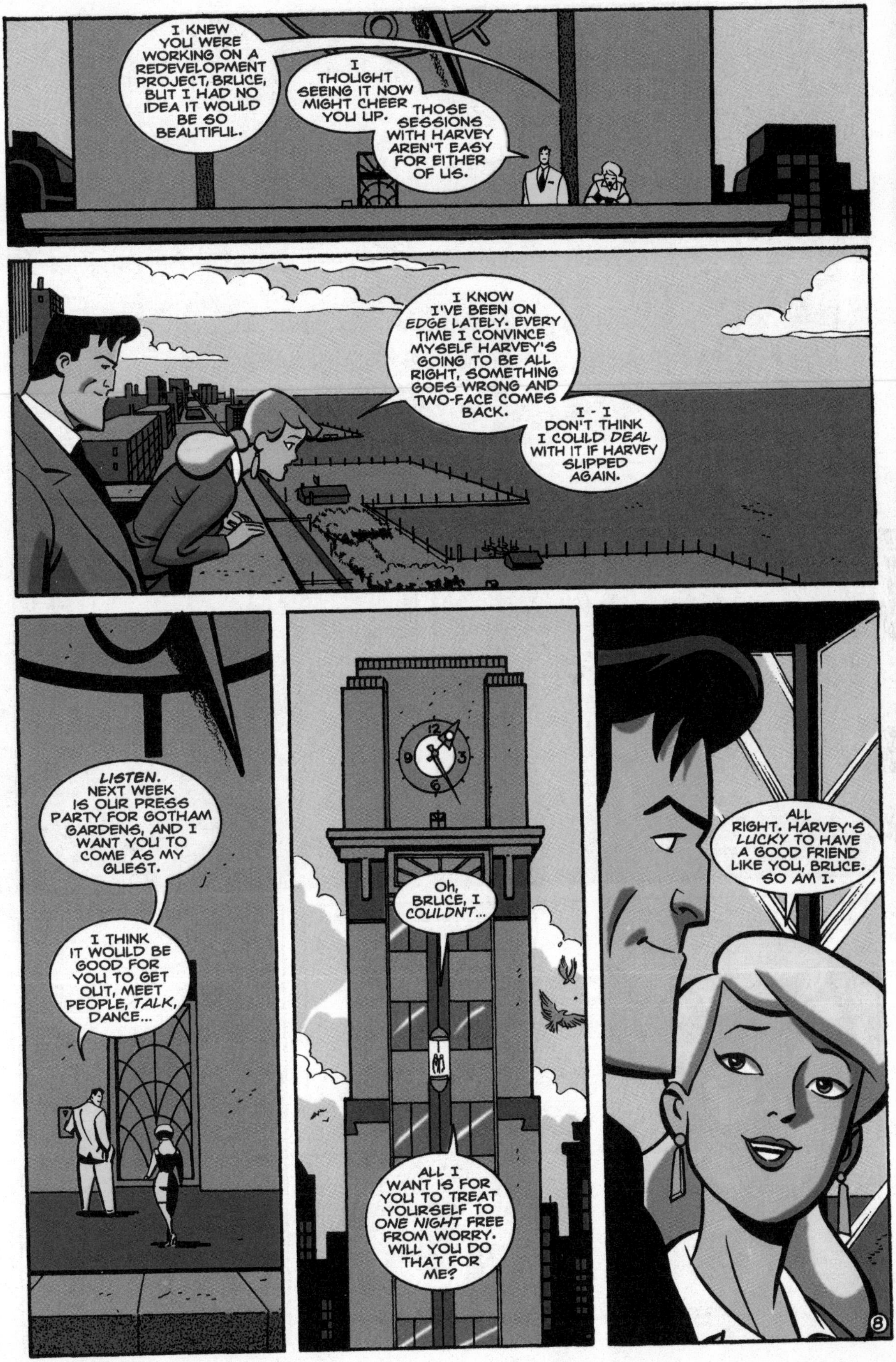
I KNEW YOU WERE WORKING ON A REDEVELOPMENT PROJECT, BRUCE, BUT I HAD NO IDEA IT WOULD BE SO BEAUTIFUL.
I THOUGHT SEEING IT NOW MIGHT CHEER YOU UP.
THOSE SESSIONS WITH HARVEY AREN'T EASY FOR EITHER OF US.
I KNOW I'VE BEEN ON EDGE LATELY. EVERY TIME I CONVINCE MYSELF HARVEY'S GOING TO BE ALL RIGHT, SOMETHING GOES WRONG AND TWO-FACE COMES BACK.
I - I DON'T THINK I COULD DEAL WITH IT IF HARVEY SLIPPED AGAIN.
LISTEN. NEXT WEEK IS OUR PRESS PARTY FOR GOTHAM GARDENS, AND I WANT YOU TO COME AS MY GUEST.
I THINK IT WOULD BE GOOD FOR YOU TO GET OUT, MEET PEOPLE, TALK, DANCE...
Oh, BRUCE, I COULDN'T...
ALL I WANT IS FOR YOU TO TREAT YOURSELF TO ONE NIGHT FREE FROM WORRY. WILL YOU DO THAT FOR ME?
ALL RIGHT. HARVEY'S LUCKY TO HAVE A GOOD FRIEND LIKE YOU, BRUCE. SO AM I.
8

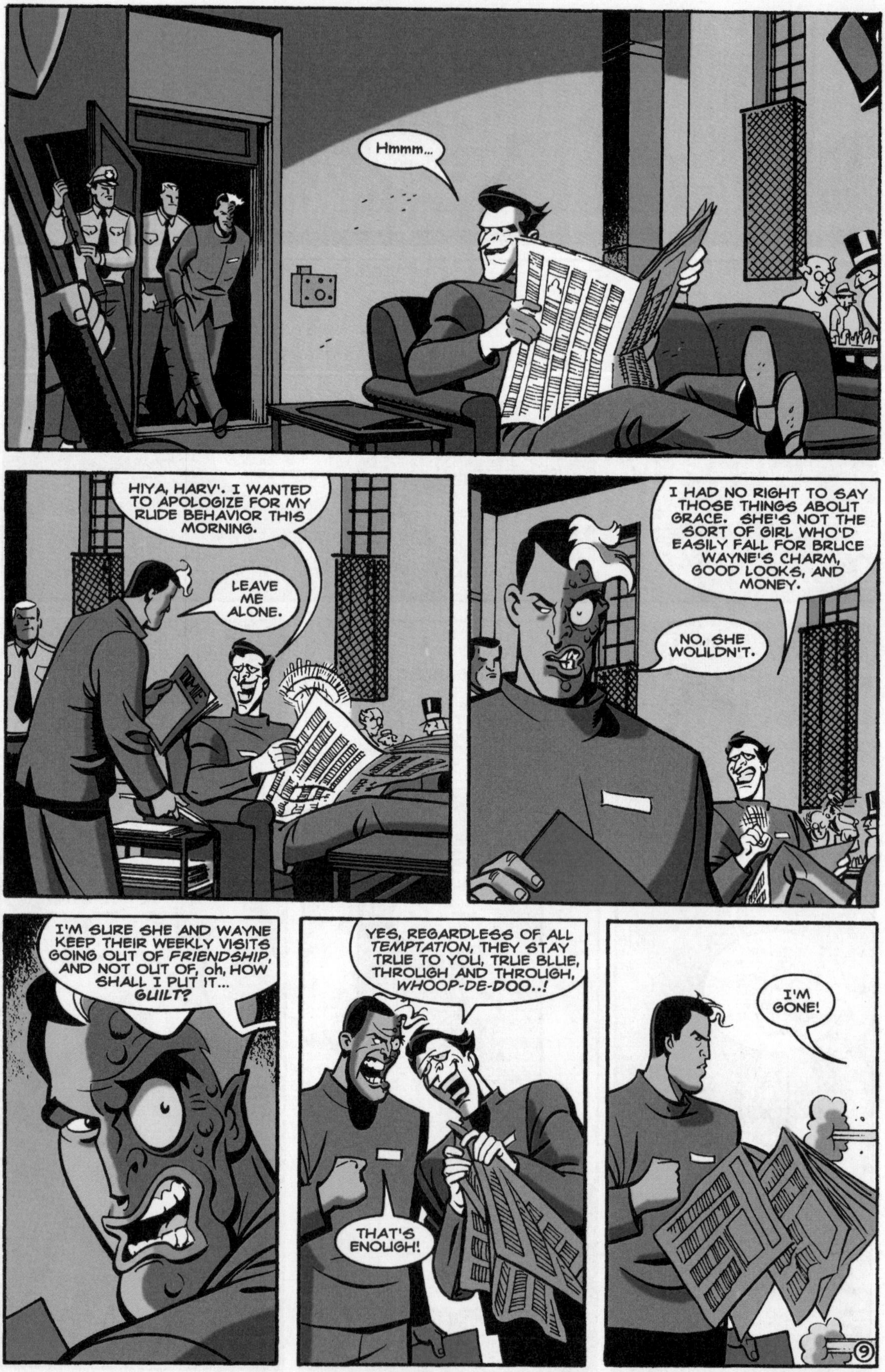
Hmmm...
HIYA, HARV'. I WANTED TO APOLOGIZE FOR MY RUDE BEHAVIOR THIS MORNING.
LEAVE ME ALONE.
I HAD NO RIGHT TO SAY THOSE THINGS ABOUT GRACE. SHE'S NOT THE SORT OF GIRL WHO'D EASILY FALL FOR BRUCE WAYNE'S CHARM, GOOD LOOKS, AND MONEY.
NO, SHE WOULDN'T.
I'M SURE SHE AND WAYNE KEEP THEIR WEEKLY VISITS GOING OUT OF *FRIENDSHIP*, AND NOT OUT OF, oh, HOW SHALL I PUT IT... *GUILT*?
YES, REGARDLESS OF ALL *TEMPTATION*, THEY STAY TRUE TO YOU, TRUE BLUE, THROUGH AND THROUGH, *WHOOP-DE-DOO..!*
THAT'S ENOUGH!
I'M GONE!
9

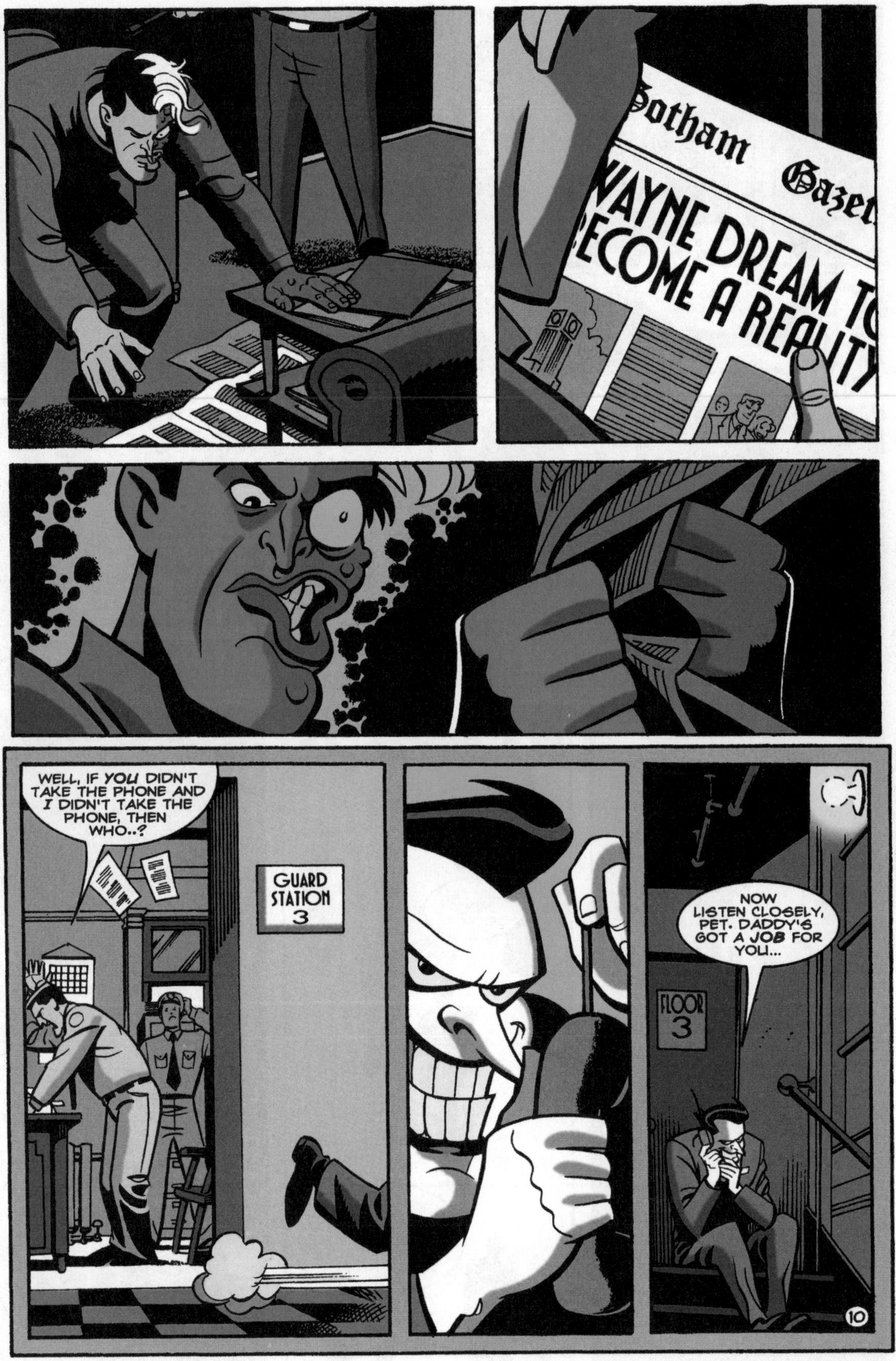
Gotham Gazet
WAYNE DREAM TO
BECOME A REALITY
WELL, IF YOU DIDN'T TAKE THE PHONE AND I DIDN'T TAKE THE PHONE, THEN WHO..?
GUARD STATION 3
NOW LISTEN CLOSELY, PET. DADDY'S GOT A JOB FOR YOU...
FLOOR 3
10

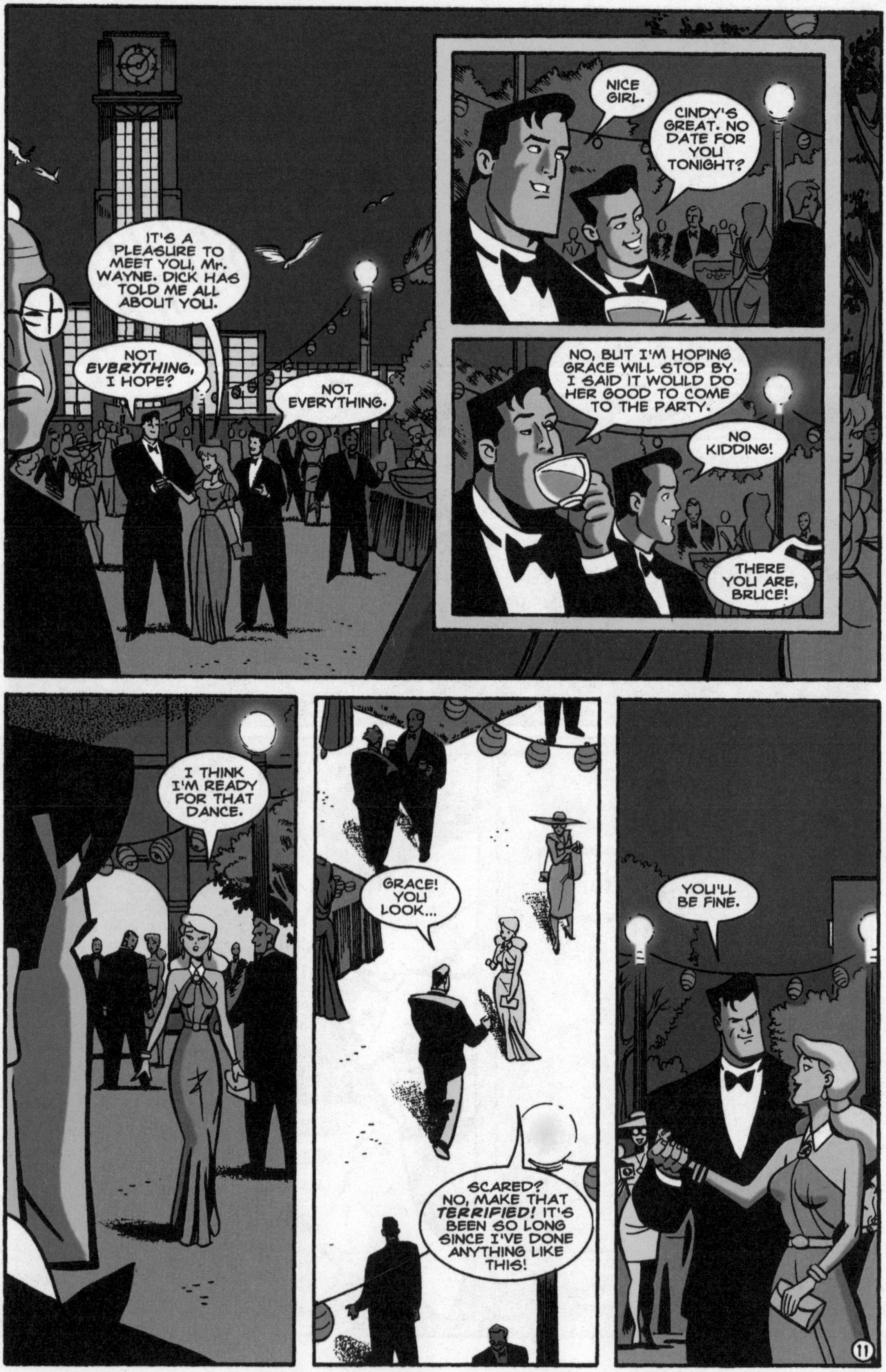
IT'S A PLEASURE TO MEET YOU, Mr. WAYNE. DICK HAS TOLD ME ALL ABOUT YOU.
NOT *EVERYTHING*, I HOPE?
NOT EVERYTHING.
NICE GIRL.
CINDY'S GREAT. NO DATE FOR YOU TONIGHT?
NO, BUT I'M HOPING GRACE WILL STOP BY. I SAID IT WOULD DO HER GOOD TO COME TO THE PARTY.
NO KIDDING!
THERE YOU ARE, BRUCE!
I THINK I'M READY FOR THAT DANCE.
GRACE! YOU LOOK...
SCARED? NO, MAKE THAT *TERRIFIED!* IT'S BEEN SO LONG SINCE I'VE DONE ANYTHING LIKE THIS!
YOU'LL BE FINE.
11

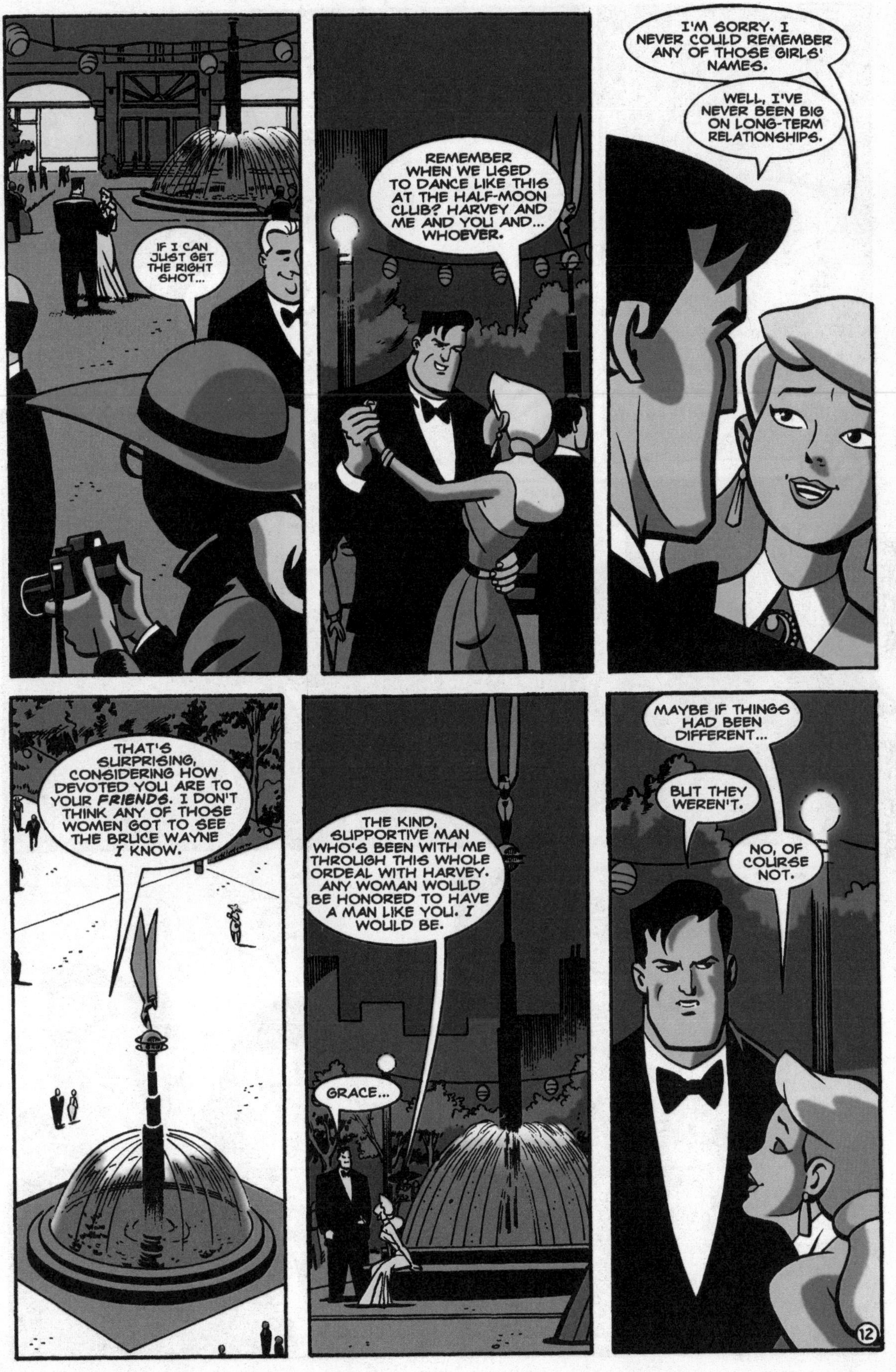
IF I CAN JUST GET THE RIGHT SHOT...
REMEMBER WHEN WE USED TO DANCE LIKE THIS AT THE HALF-MOON CLUB? HARVEY AND ME AND YOU AND... WHOEVER.
I'M SORRY. I NEVER COULD REMEMBER ANY OF THOSE GIRLS' NAMES.
WELL, I'VE NEVER BEEN BIG ON LONG-TERM RELATIONSHIPS.
THAT'S SURPRISING, CONSIDERING HOW DEVOTED YOU ARE TO YOUR *FRIENDS*. I DON'T THINK ANY OF THOSE WOMEN GOT TO SEE THE BRUCE WAYNE *I* KNOW.
THE KIND, SUPPORTIVE MAN WHO'S BEEN WITH ME THROUGH THIS WHOLE ORDEAL WITH HARVEY. ANY WOMAN WOULD BE HONORED TO HAVE A MAN LIKE YOU. *I* WOULD BE.
GRACE...
MAYBE IF THINGS HAD BEEN DIFFERENT...
BUT THEY WEREN'T.
NO, OF COURSE NOT.
12

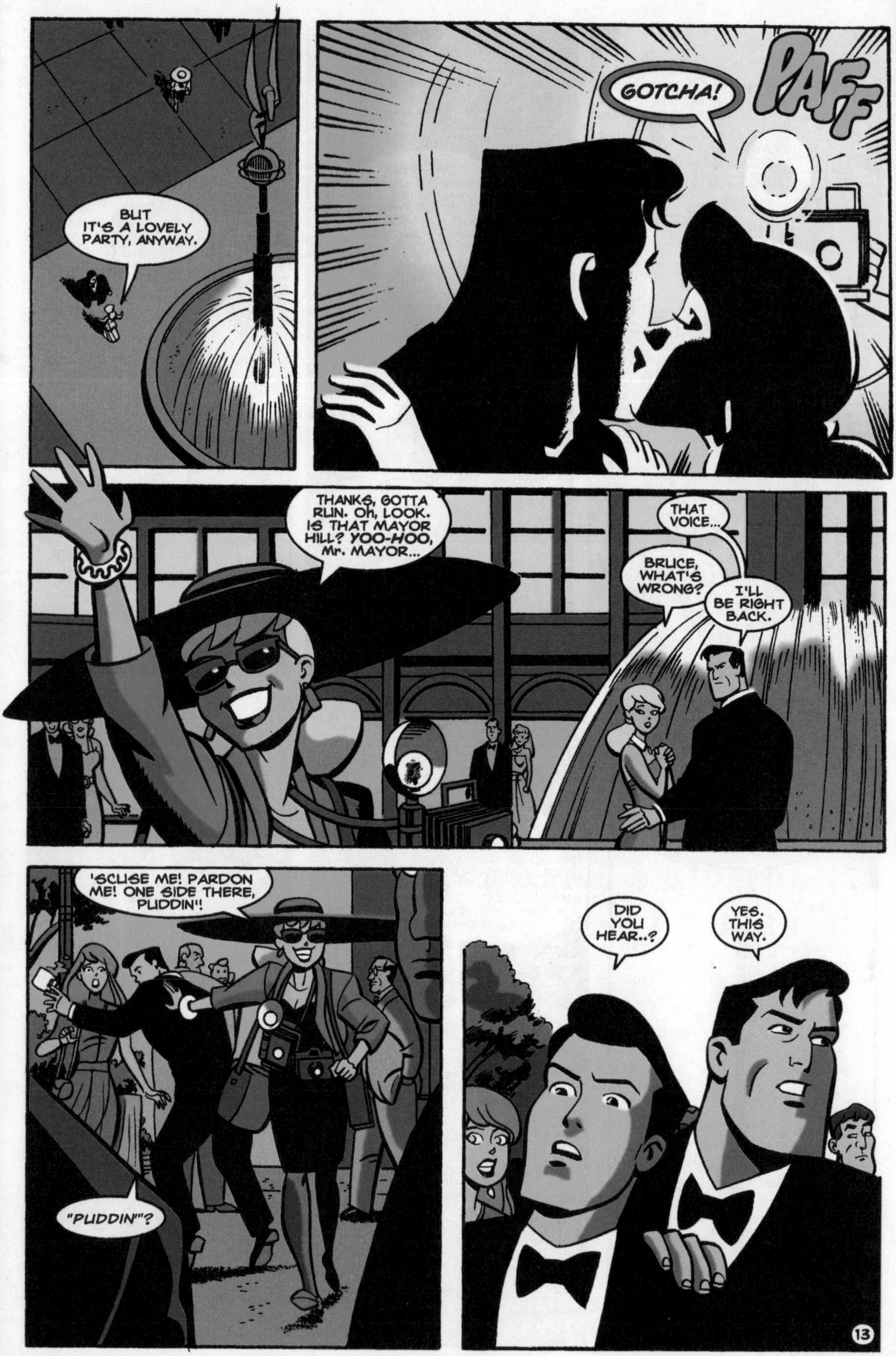
BUT IT'S A LOVELY PARTY, ANYWAY.
GOTCHA!
PAFF
THANKS, GOTTA RUN. OH, LOOK. IS THAT MAYOR HILL? YOO-HOO, Mr. MAYOR...
THAT VOICE...
BRUCE, WHAT'S WRONG?
I'LL BE RIGHT BACK.
'SCUSE ME! PARDON ME! ONE SIDE THERE, PUDDIN'!
"PUDDIN'"?
DID YOU HEAR..?
YES. THIS WAY.
13

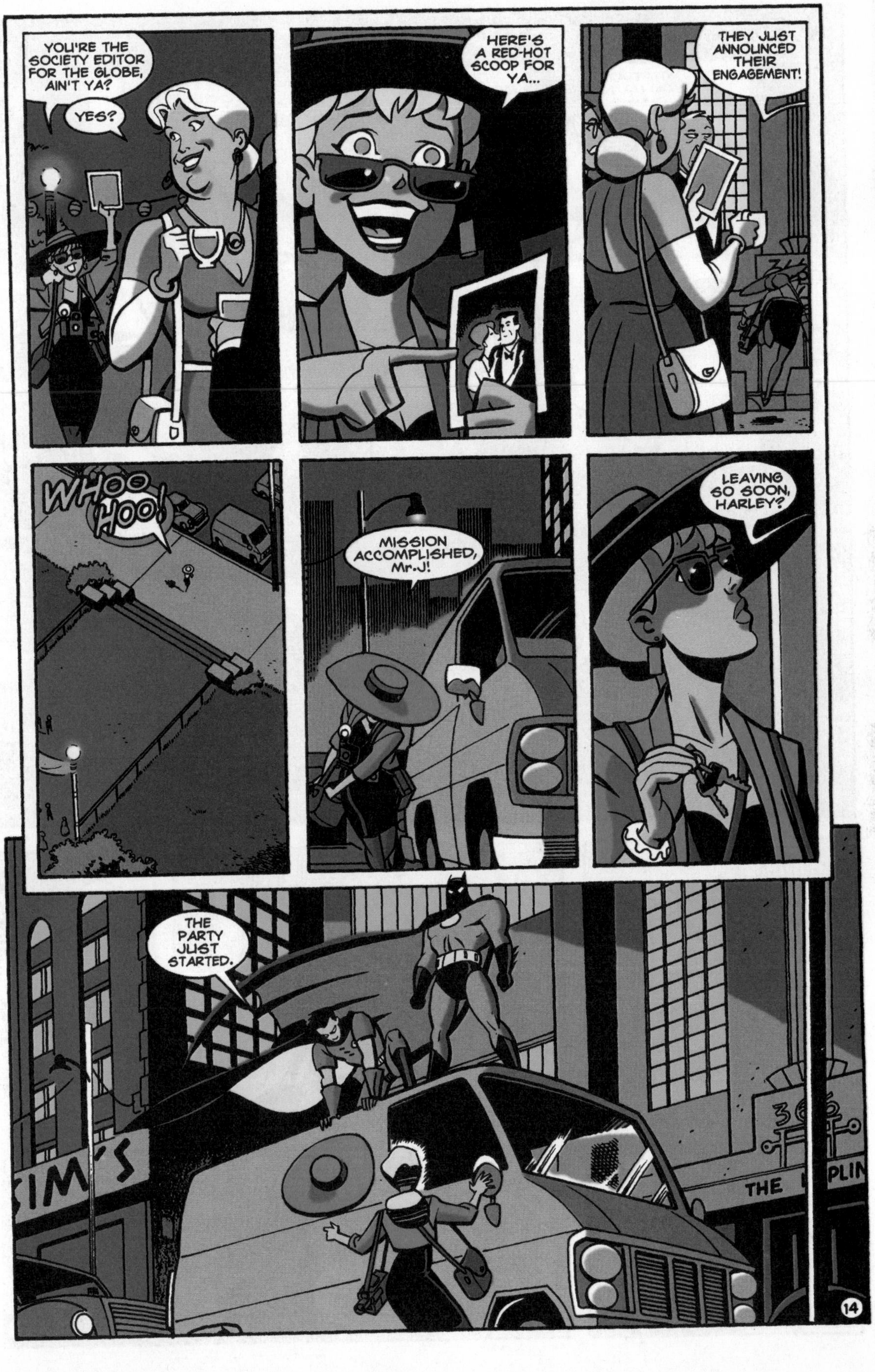
YOU'RE THE SOCIETY EDITOR FOR THE GLOBE, AIN'T YA?
YES?
HERE'S A RED-HOT SCOOP FOR YA...
THEY JUST ANNOUNCED THEIR ENGAGEMENT!
WHOO HOO!
MISSION ACCOMPLISHED, Mr. J!
LEAVING SO SOON, HARLEY?
THE PARTY JUST STARTED.
SIM'S
THE
14

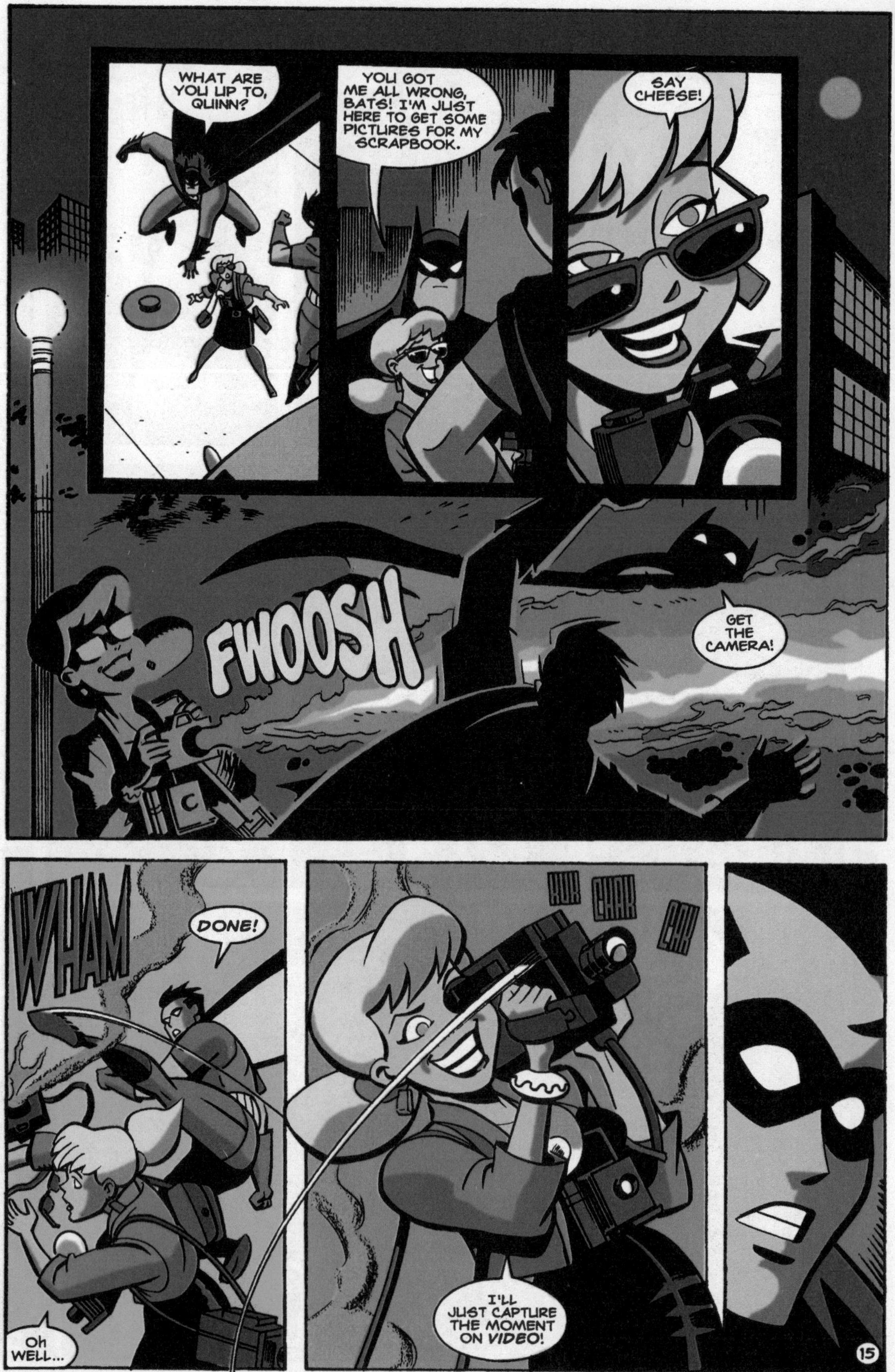
WHAT ARE YOU UP TO, QUINN?
YOU GOT ME ALL WRONG, BATS! I'M JUST HERE TO GET SOME PICTURES FOR MY SCRAPBOOK.
SAY CHEESE!
FWOOSH
GET THE CAMERA!
WHAM
DONE!
Oh WELL...
KLIK
CHAK
CAK
I'LL JUST CAPTURE THE MOMENT ON *VIDEO*!
15

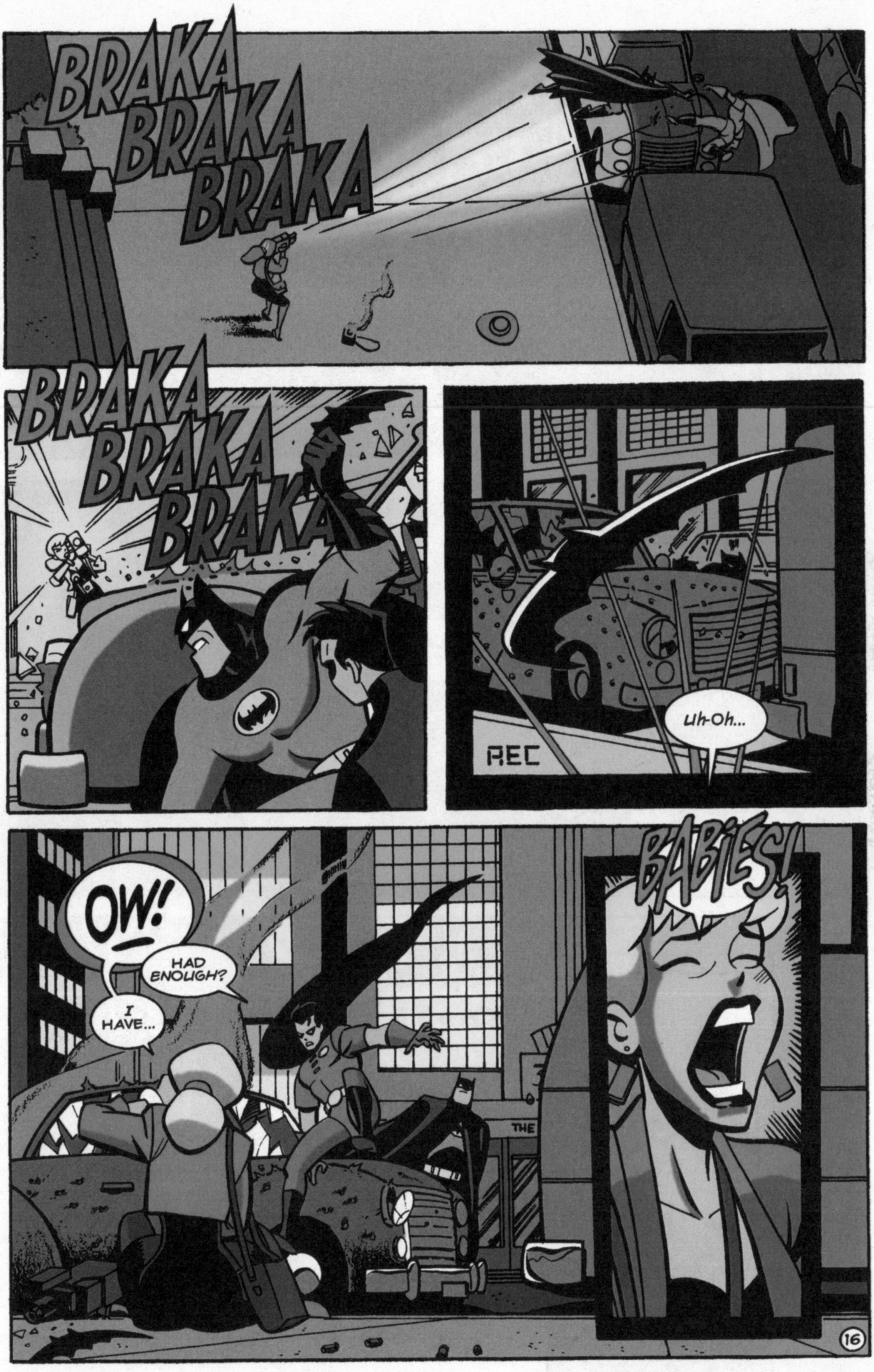
BRAKA
BRAKA
BRAKA
BRAKA
BRAKA
BRAKA
uh-oh...
REC
OW!
HAD ENOUGH?
I HAVE...
BABIES!
THE
16

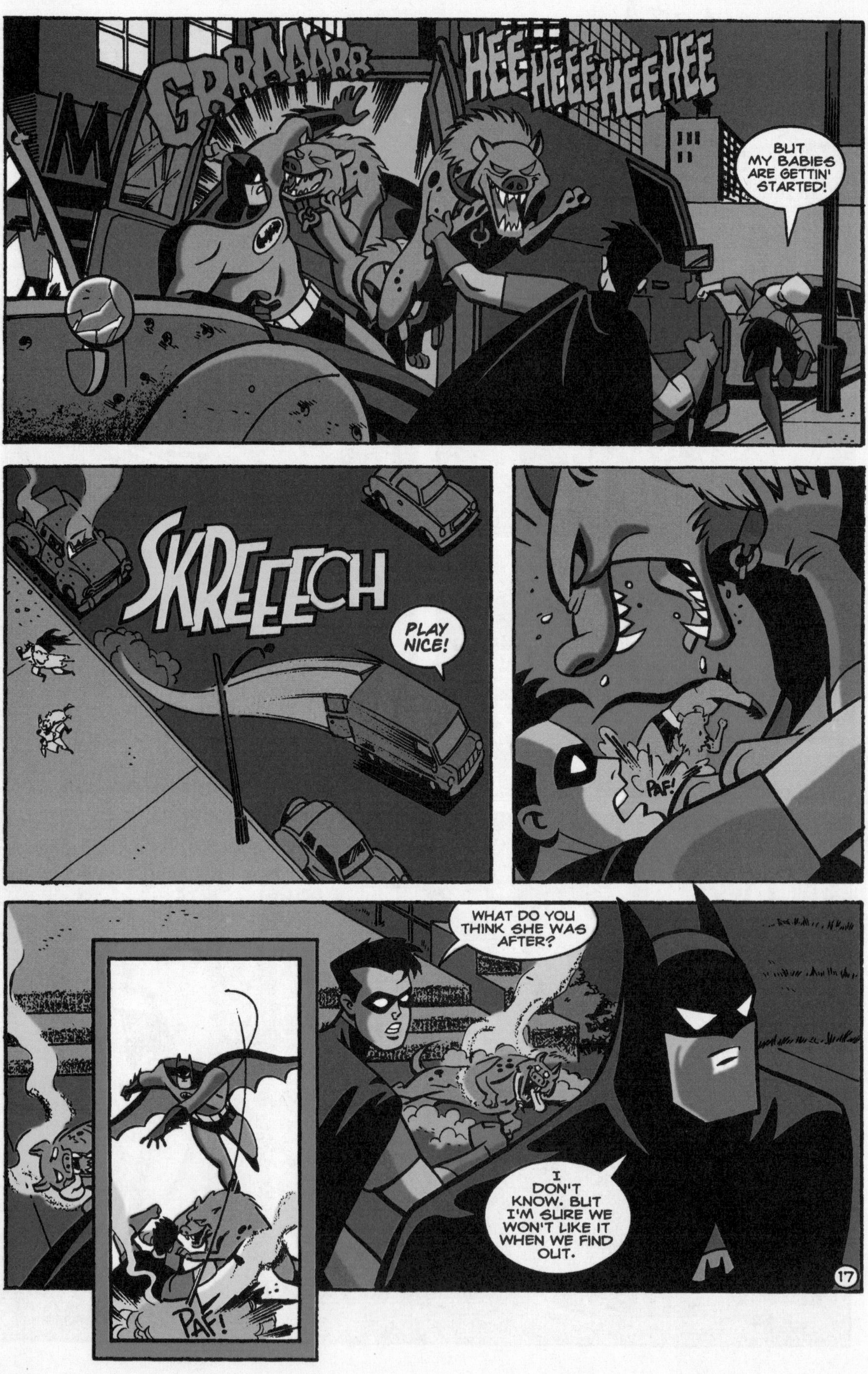

GRRAAARRR
HEE-HEEE-HEEHEE
BUT MY BABIES ARE GETTIN' STARTED!
SKREEECH
PLAY NICE!
PAF!
WHAT DO YOU THINK SHE WAS AFTER?
PAF!
I DON'T KNOW. BUT I'M SURE WE WON'T LIKE IT WHEN WE FIND OUT.
17

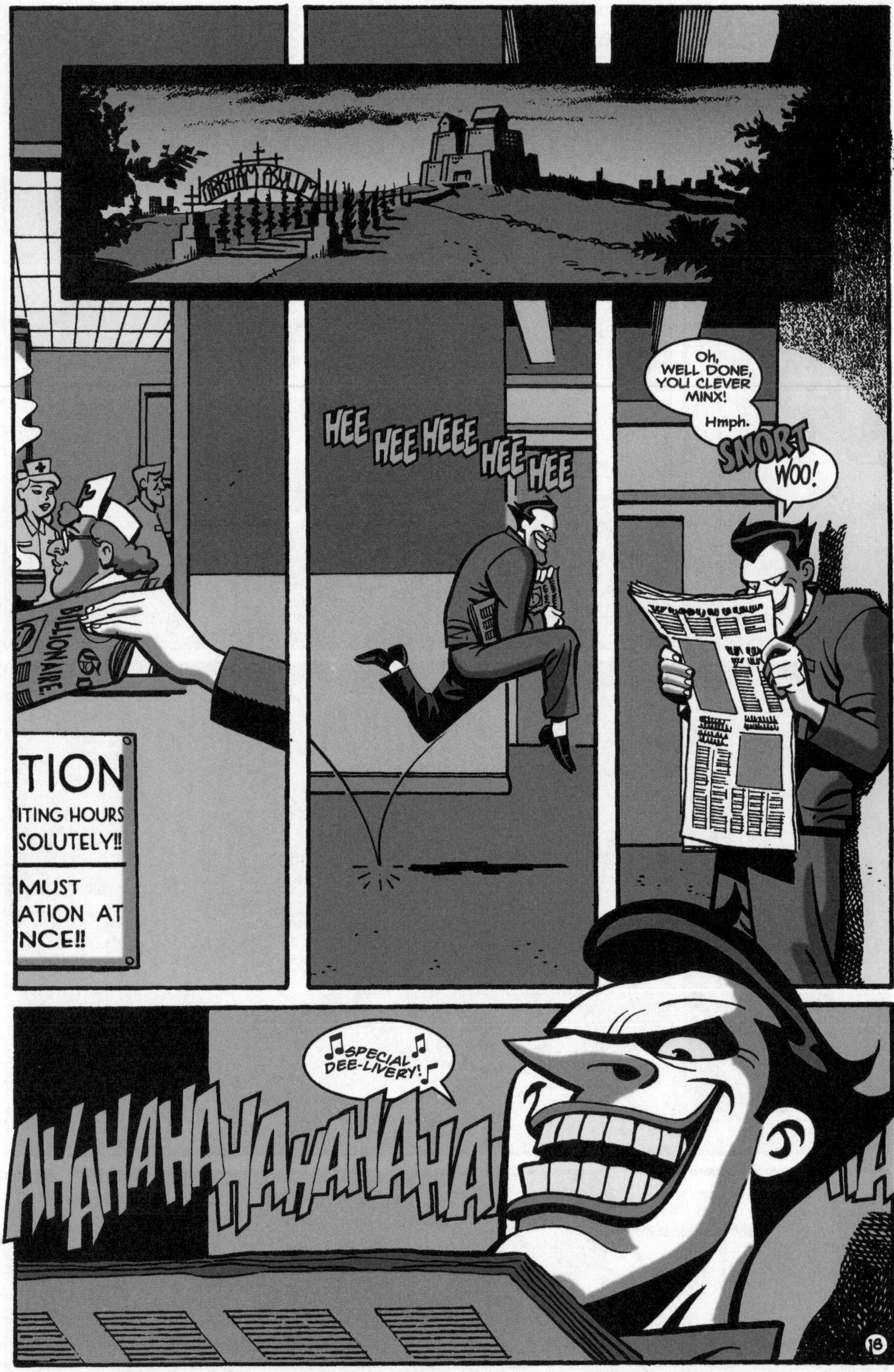
ARKHAM ASYLUM
BILLIONAIRE.
TION
ITING HOURS
SOLUTELY!!
MUST
ATION AT
NCE!!
HEE HEE HEEE HEE HEE
Oh, WELL DONE, YOU CLEVER MINX!
Hmph.
SNORT
WOO!
SPECIAL DEE-LIVERY!
AHAHAHAHAHAHAHAHAHA
18

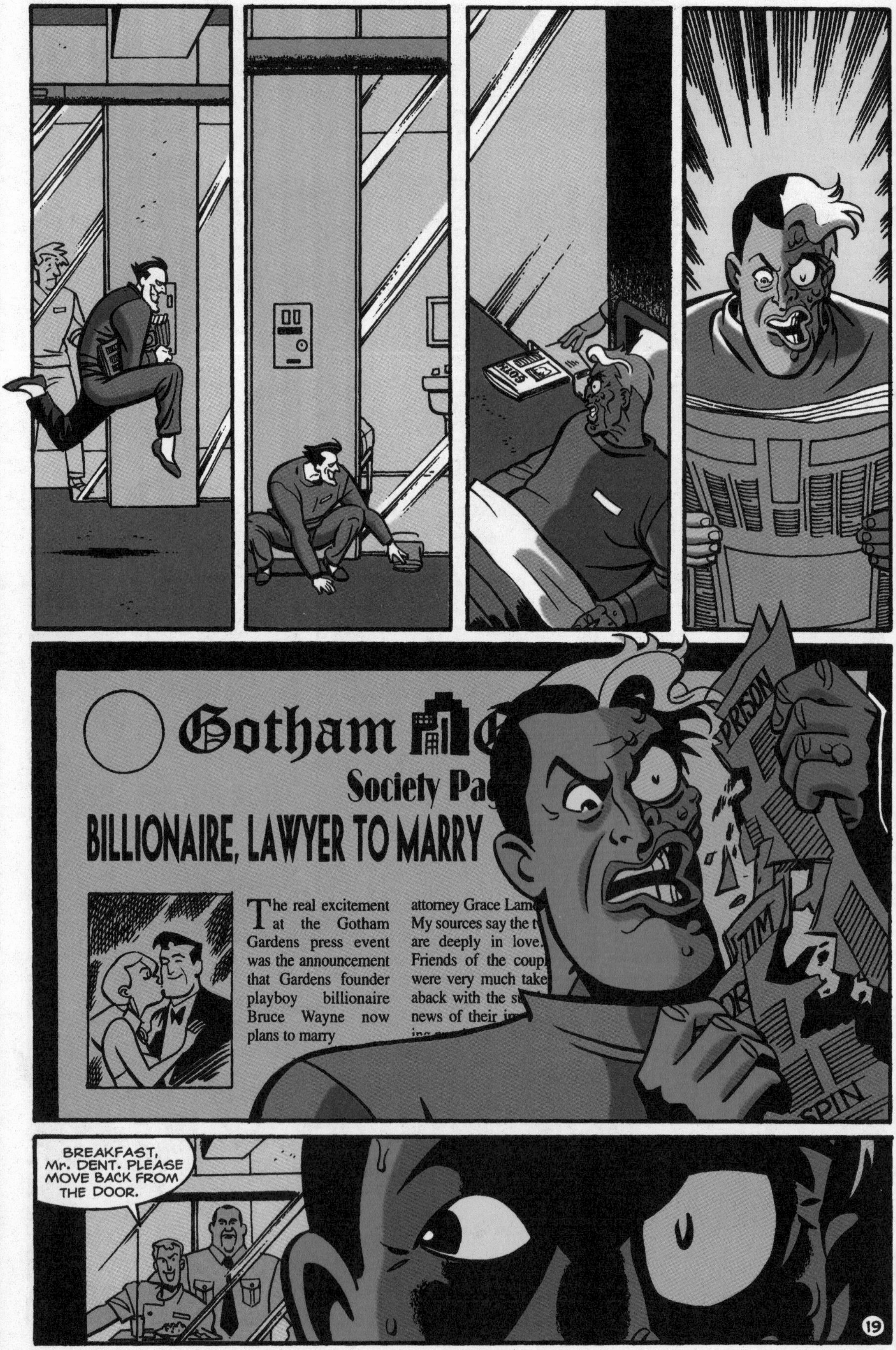
Gotham
Society Pag
BILLIONAIRE, LAWYER TO MARRY
The real excitement at the Gotham Gardens press event was the announcement that Gardens founder playboy billionaire Bruce Wayne now plans to marry
attorney Grace Lam
My sources say the t
are deeply in love.
Friends of the coup
were very much take
aback with the s
news of their i
PRISON
SPIN
BREAKFAST, Mr. DENT. PLEASE MOVE BACK FROM THE DOOR.
19

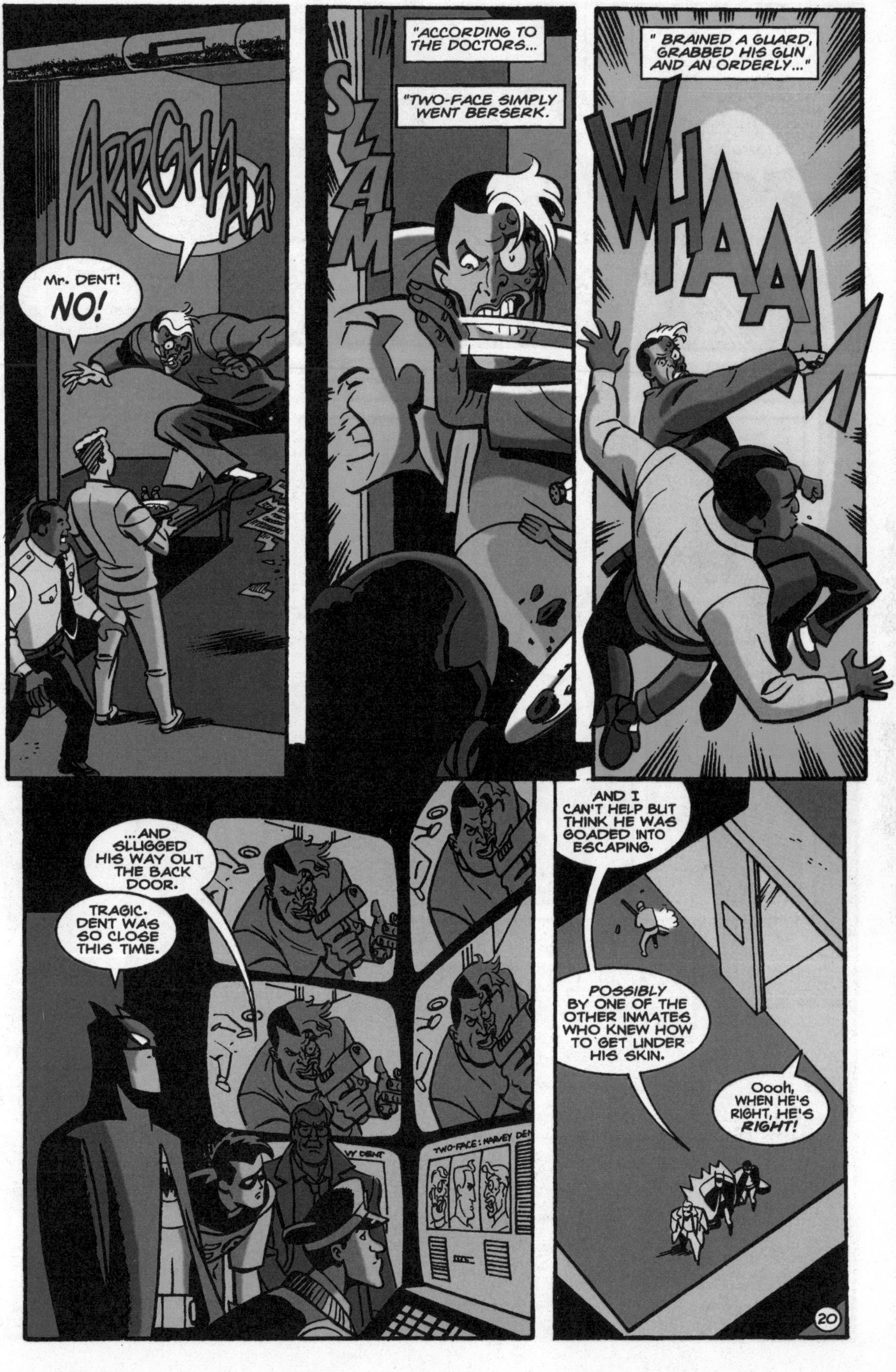
ARRGHAAAA
Mr. DENT! NO!
"ACCORDING TO THE DOCTORS...
"TWO-FACE SIMPLY WENT BERSERK.
SLAM
" BRAINED A GUARD, GRABBED HIS GUN AND AN ORDERLY..."
WHAAAM
...AND SLUGGED HIS WAY OUT THE BACK DOOR.
TRAGIC. DENT WAS SO CLOSE THIS TIME.
TWO-FACE: HARVEY DEN
AND I CAN'T HELP BUT THINK HE WAS GOADED INTO ESCAPING.
POSSIBLY BY ONE OF THE OTHER INMATES WHO KNEW HOW TO GET UNDER HIS SKIN.
Oooh, WHEN HE'S RIGHT, HE'S RIGHT!
20

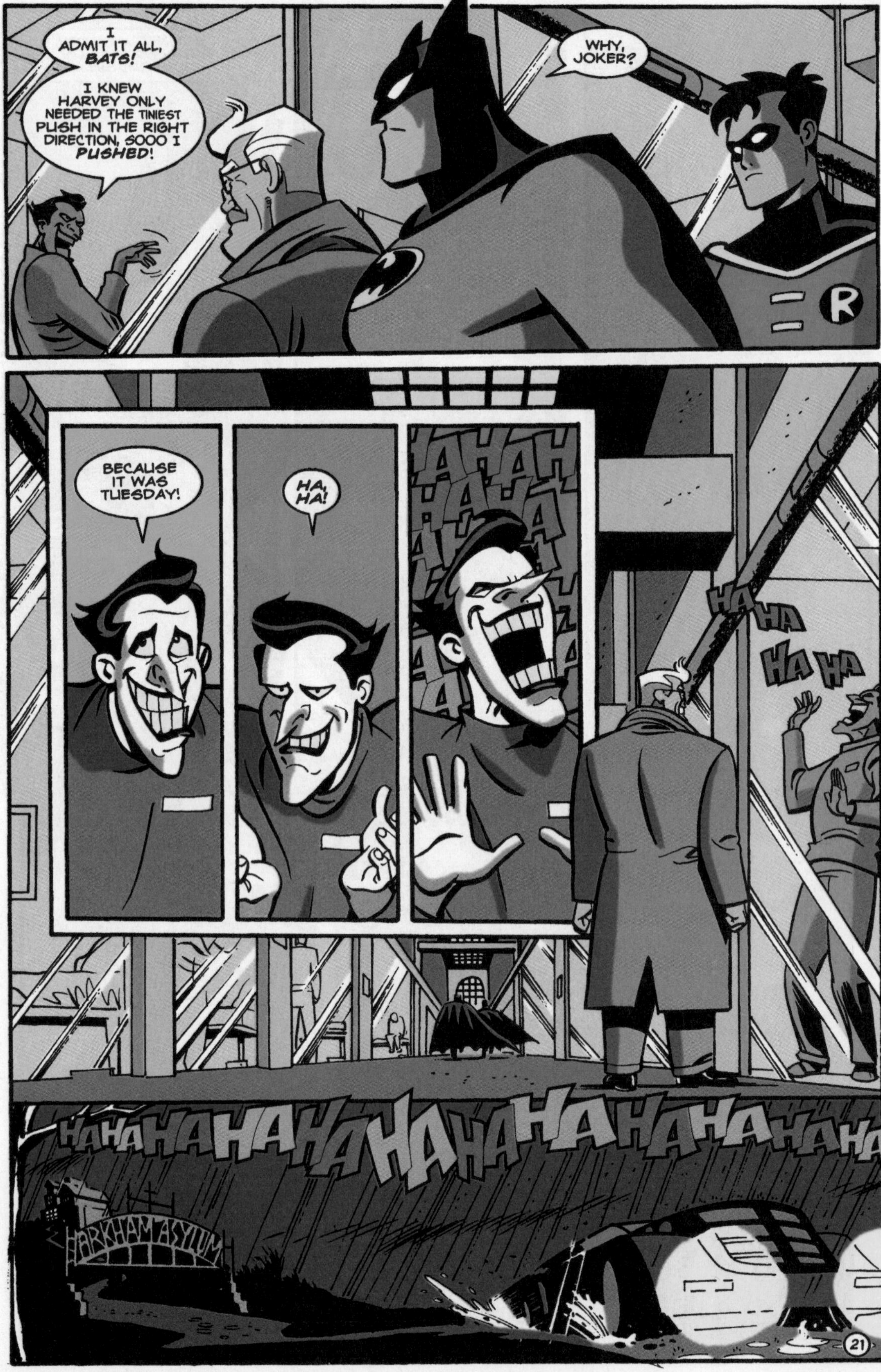
I ADMIT IT ALL, BATS!
I KNEW HARVEY ONLY NEEDED THE TINIEST PUSH IN THE RIGHT DIRECTION, SOOO I PUSHED!
WHY, JOKER?
BECAUSE IT WAS TUESDAY!
HA, HA!
HA HA HA HA HA
HAHAHAHAHAHAHAHAHAHAHAHAHAHAHAHA
ARKHAM ASYLUM
21

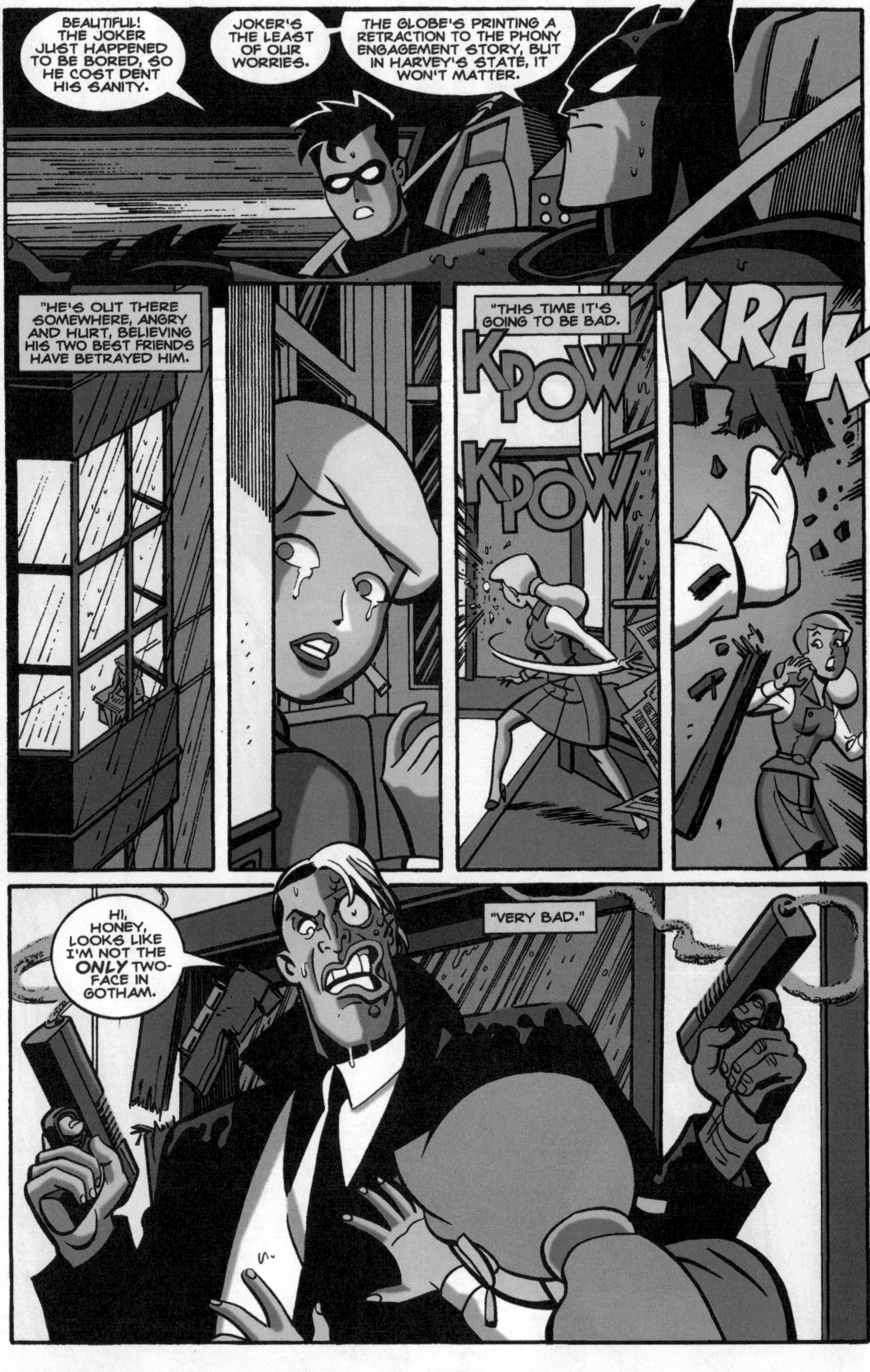
BEAUTIFUL! THE JOKER JUST HAPPENED TO BE BORED, SO HE COST DENT HIS SANITY.
JOKER'S THE LEAST OF OUR WORRIES.
THE GLOBE'S PRINTING A RETRACTION TO THE PHONY ENGAGEMENT STORY, BUT IN HARVEY'S STATE, IT WON'T MATTER.
"HE'S OUT THERE SOMEWHERE, ANGRY AND HURT, BELIEVING HIS TWO BEST FRIENDS HAVE BETRAYED HIM.
"THIS TIME IT'S GOING TO BE BAD.
KPOW
KPOW
KRAK
HI, HONEY, LOOKS LIKE I'M NOT THE ONLY TWO-FACE IN GOTHAM.
"VERY BAD."

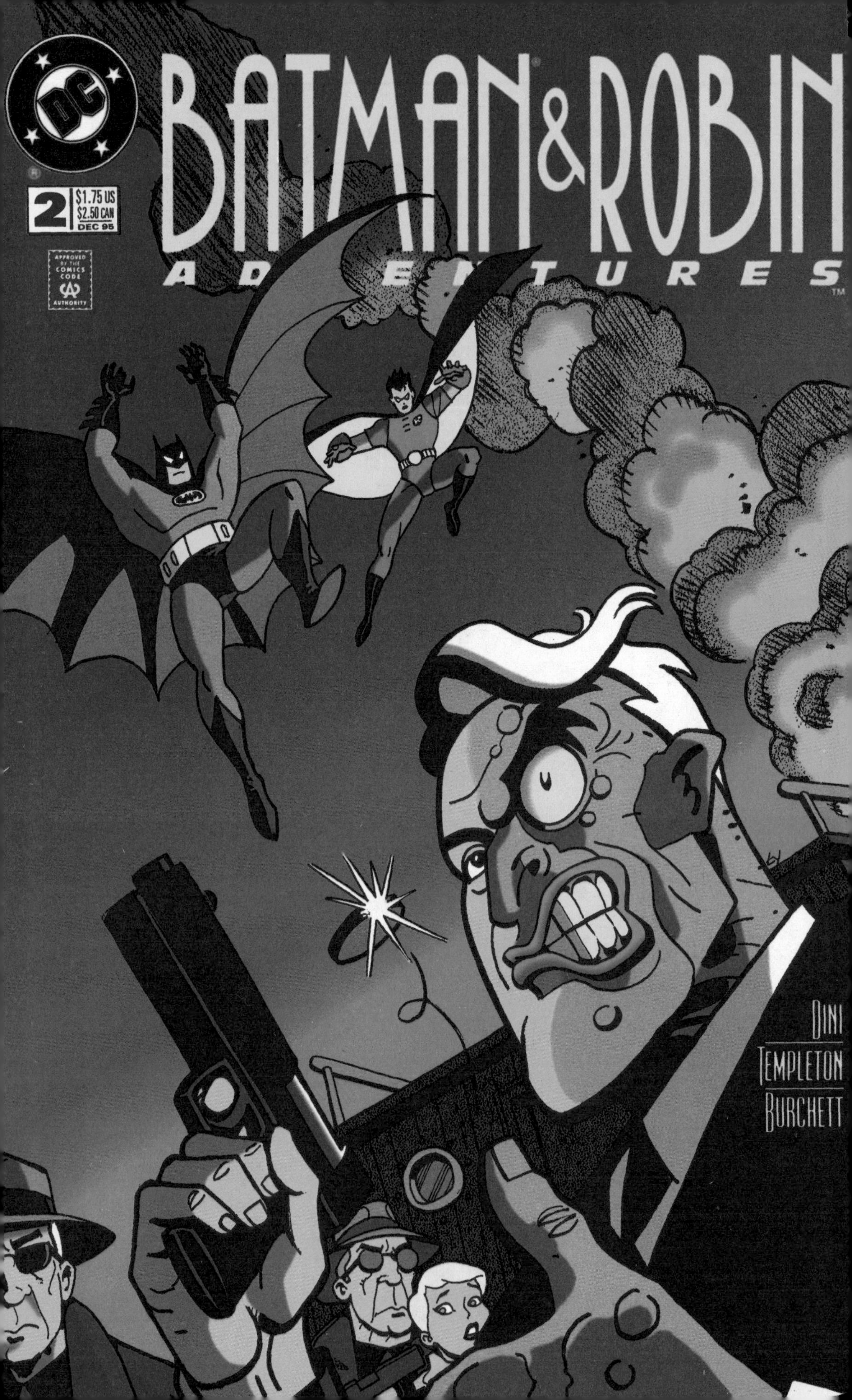
DC
BATMAN & ROBIN
ADVENTURES
2
$1.75 US
$2.50 CAN
DEC 95
APPROVED BY THE COMICS CODE AUTHORITY
DINI
TEMPLETON
BURCHETT

1569-0620

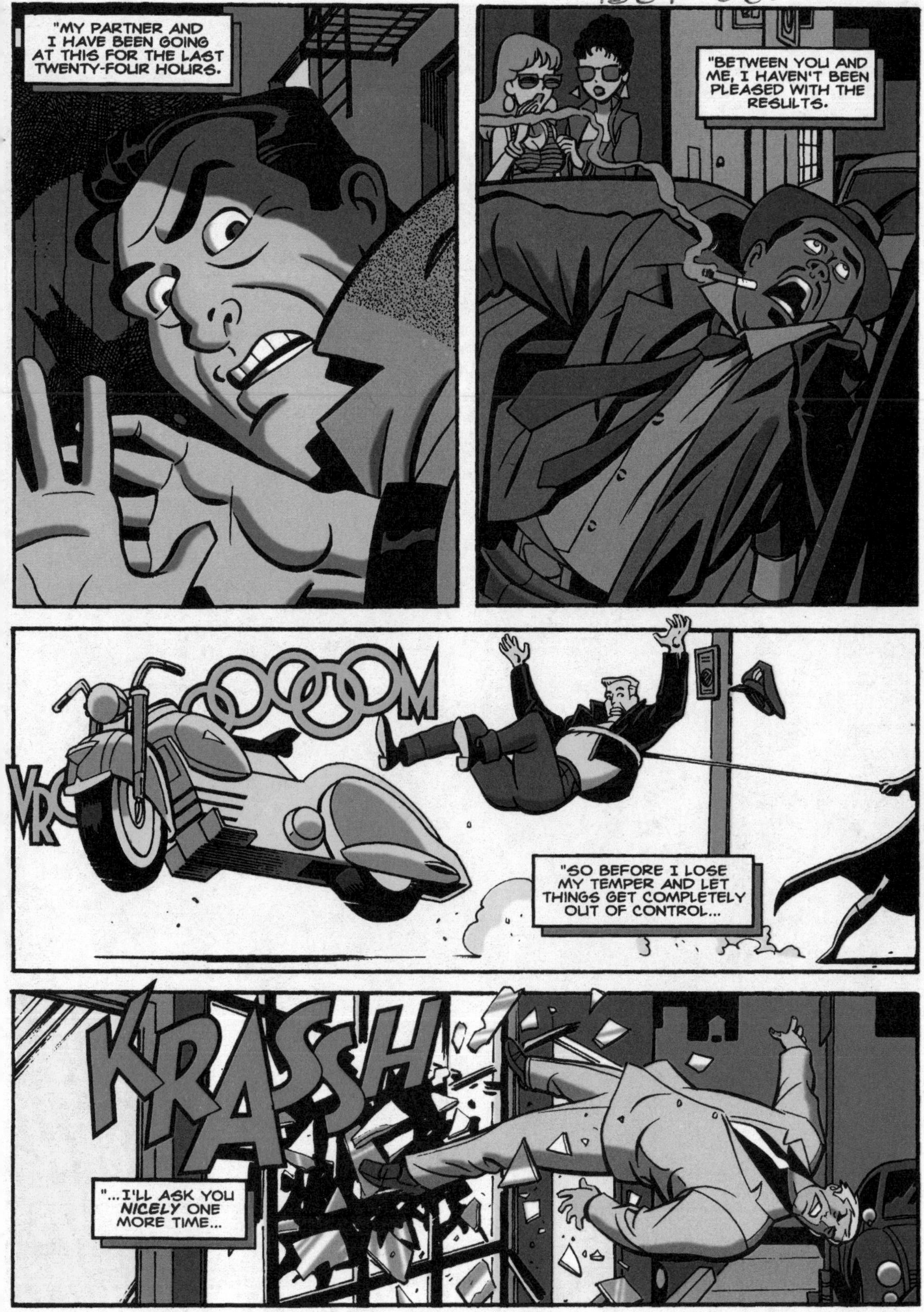
"MY PARTNER AND I HAVE BEEN GOING AT THIS FOR THE LAST TWENTY-FOUR HOURS.
"BETWEEN YOU AND ME, I HAVEN'T BEEN PLEASED WITH THE RESULTS.
VROOOOOOM
"SO BEFORE I LOSE MY TEMPER AND LET THINGS GET COMPLETELY OUT OF CONTROL...
KRASSH
"...I'LL ASK YOU *NICELY* ONE MORE TIME...

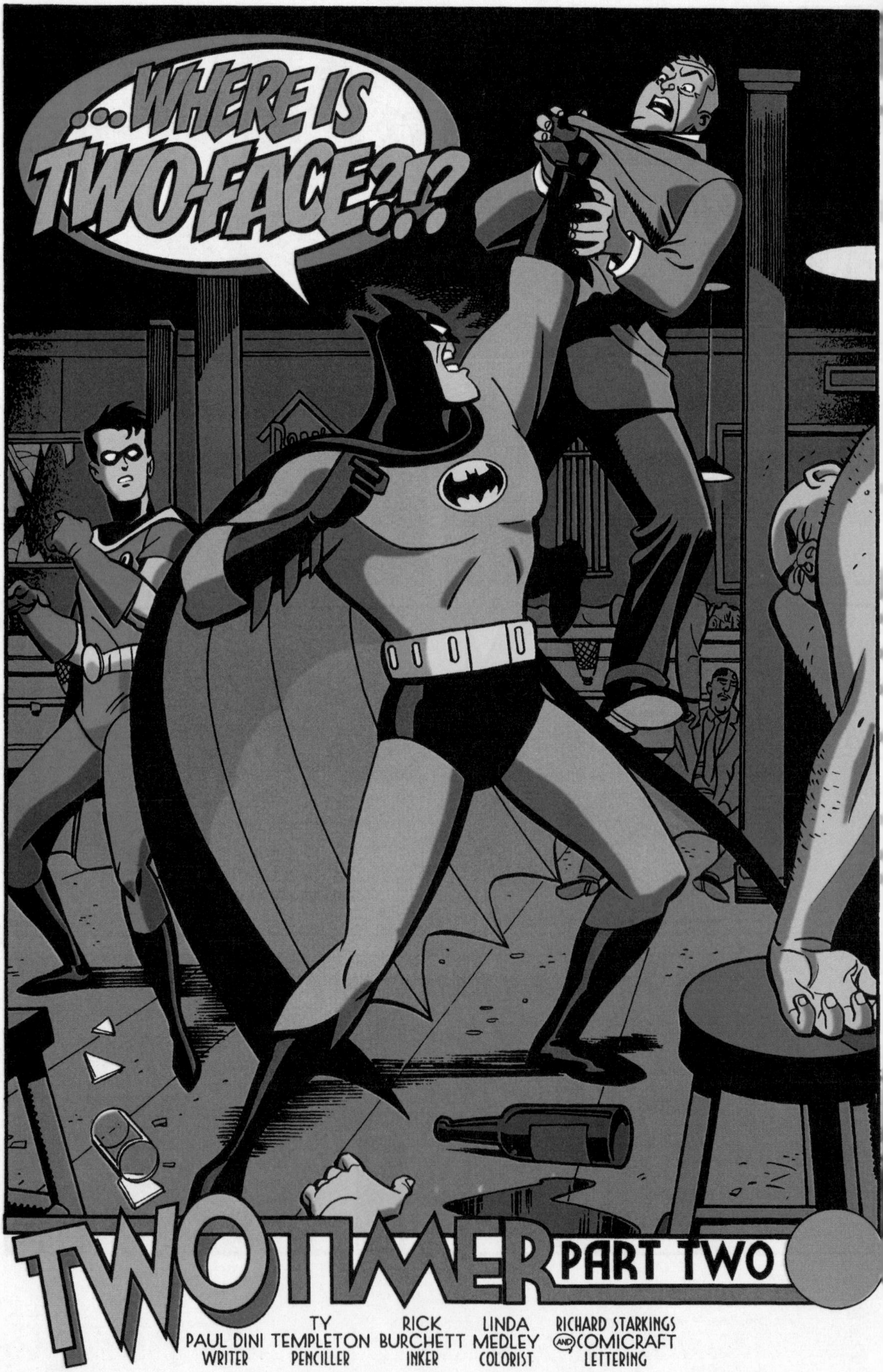
...WHERE IS TWO-FACE?!?
TWO TIMER PART TWO
PAUL DINI WRITER
TY TEMPLETON PENCILLER
RICK BURCHETT INKER
LINDA MEDLEY COLORIST
RICHARD STARKINGS AND COMICRAFT LETTERING

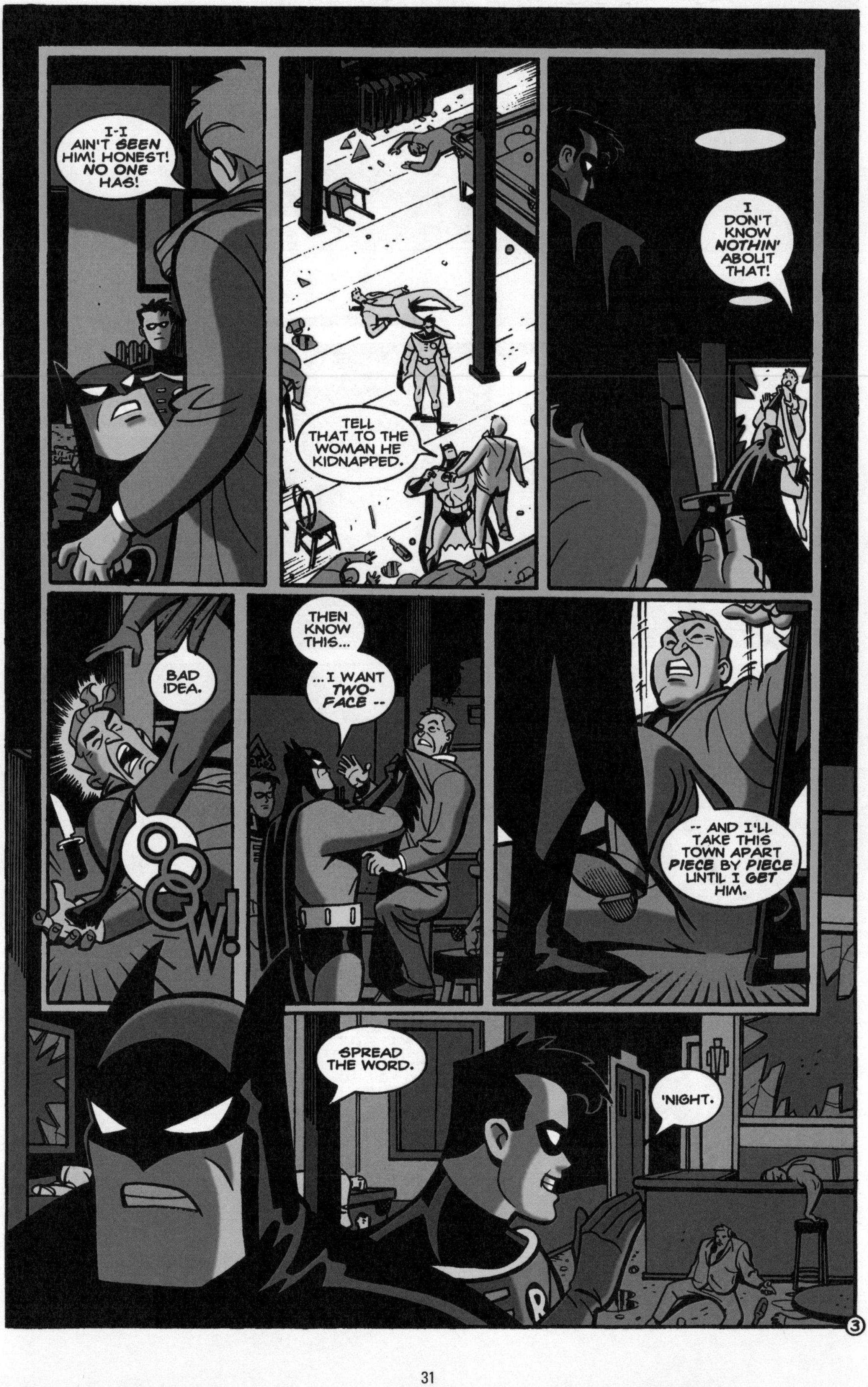

I-I AIN'T SEEN HIM! HONEST! NO ONE HAS!
TELL THAT TO THE WOMAN HE KIDNAPPED.
I DON'T KNOW NOTHIN' ABOUT THAT!
BAD IDEA.
OOOW!
THEN KNOW THIS...
...I WANT TWO-FACE --
-- AND I'LL TAKE THIS TOWN APART PIECE BY PIECE UNTIL I GET HIM.
SPREAD THE WORD.
'NIGHT.
3

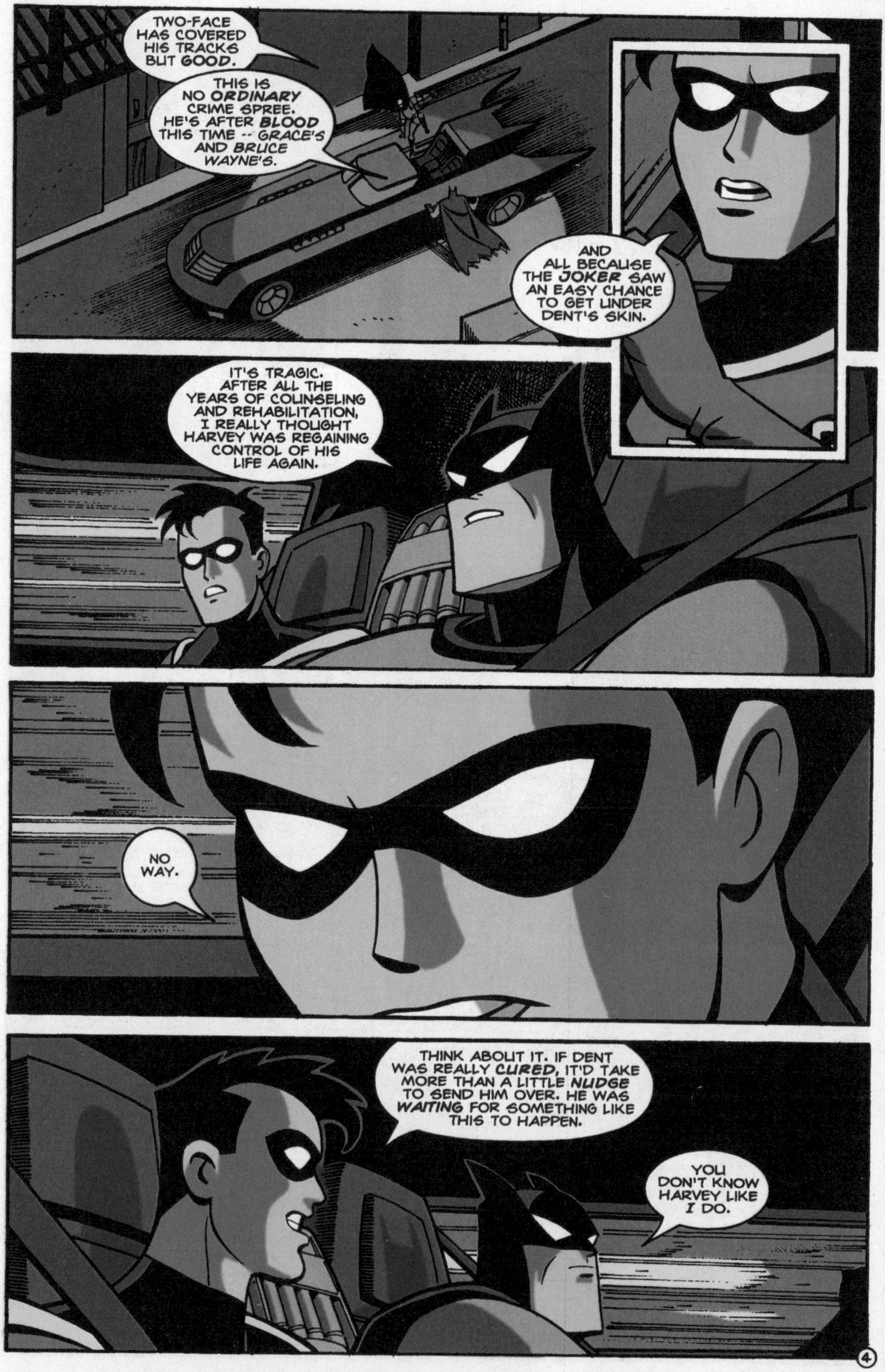
TWO-FACE HAS COVERED HIS TRACKS BUT GOOD.
THIS IS NO ORDINARY CRIME SPREE. HE'S AFTER BLOOD THIS TIME -- GRACE'S AND BRUCE WAYNE'S.
AND ALL BECAUSE THE JOKER SAW AN EASY CHANCE TO GET UNDER DENT'S SKIN.
IT'S TRAGIC. AFTER ALL THE YEARS OF COUNSELING AND REHABILITATION, I REALLY THOUGHT HARVEY WAS REGAINING CONTROL OF HIS LIFE AGAIN.
NO WAY.
THINK ABOUT IT. IF DENT WAS REALLY CURED, IT'D TAKE MORE THAN A LITTLE NUDGE TO SEND HIM OVER. HE WAS WAITING FOR SOMETHING LIKE THIS TO HAPPEN.
YOU DON'T KNOW HARVEY LIKE I DO.
4

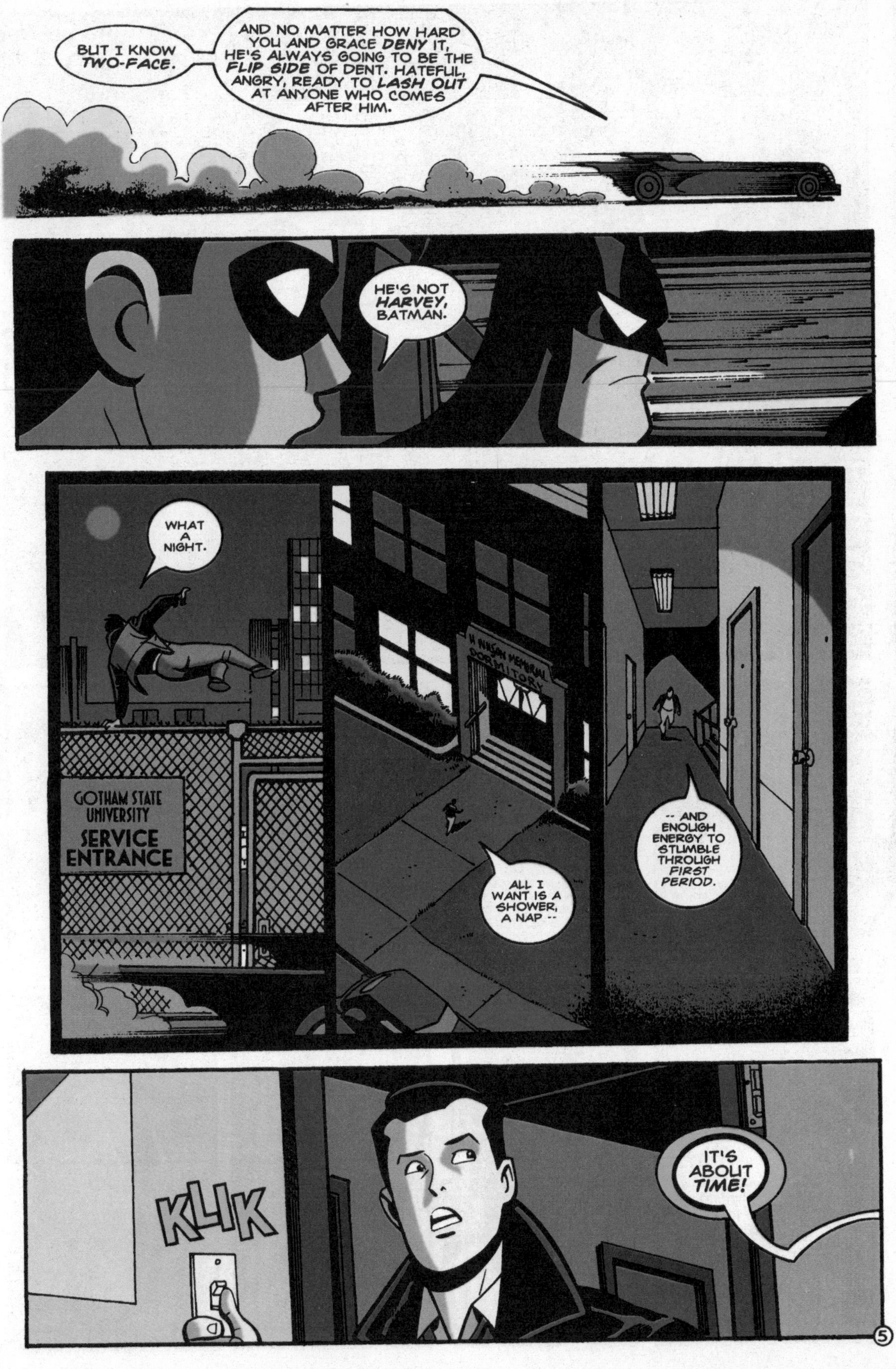
BUT I KNOW TWO-FACE.
AND NO MATTER HOW HARD YOU AND GRACE DENY IT, HE'S ALWAYS GOING TO BE THE FLIP SIDE OF DENT. HATEFUL, ANGRY, READY TO LASH OUT AT ANYONE WHO COMES AFTER HIM.
HE'S NOT HARVEY, BATMAN.
WHAT A NIGHT.
GOTHAM STATE UNIVERSITY
SERVICE ENTRANCE
DORMITORY
ALL I WANT IS A SHOWER, A NAP --
-- AND ENOUGH ENERGY TO STUMBLE THROUGH FIRST PERIOD.
KLIK
IT'S ABOUT TIME!
5

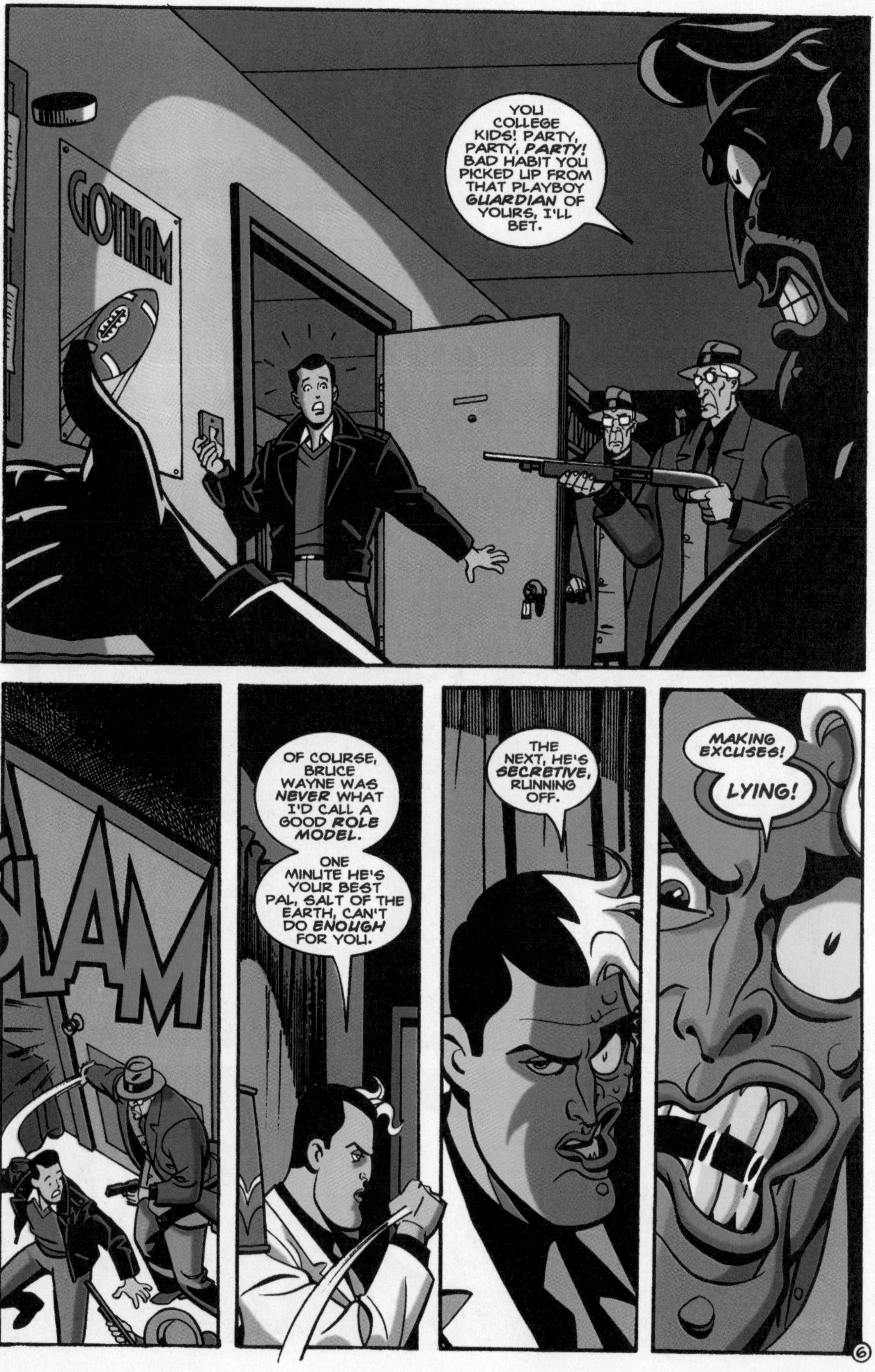
YOU COLLEGE KIDS! PARTY, PARTY, PARTY! BAD HABIT YOU PICKED UP FROM THAT PLAYBOY GUARDIAN OF YOURS, I'LL BET.
GOTHAM
SLAM
OF COURSE, BRUCE WAYNE WAS NEVER WHAT I'D CALL A GOOD ROLE MODEL.
ONE MINUTE HE'S YOUR BEST PAL, SALT OF THE EARTH, CAN'T DO ENOUGH FOR YOU.
THE NEXT, HE'S SECRETIVE, RUNNING OFF.
MAKING EXCUSES!
LYING!
6

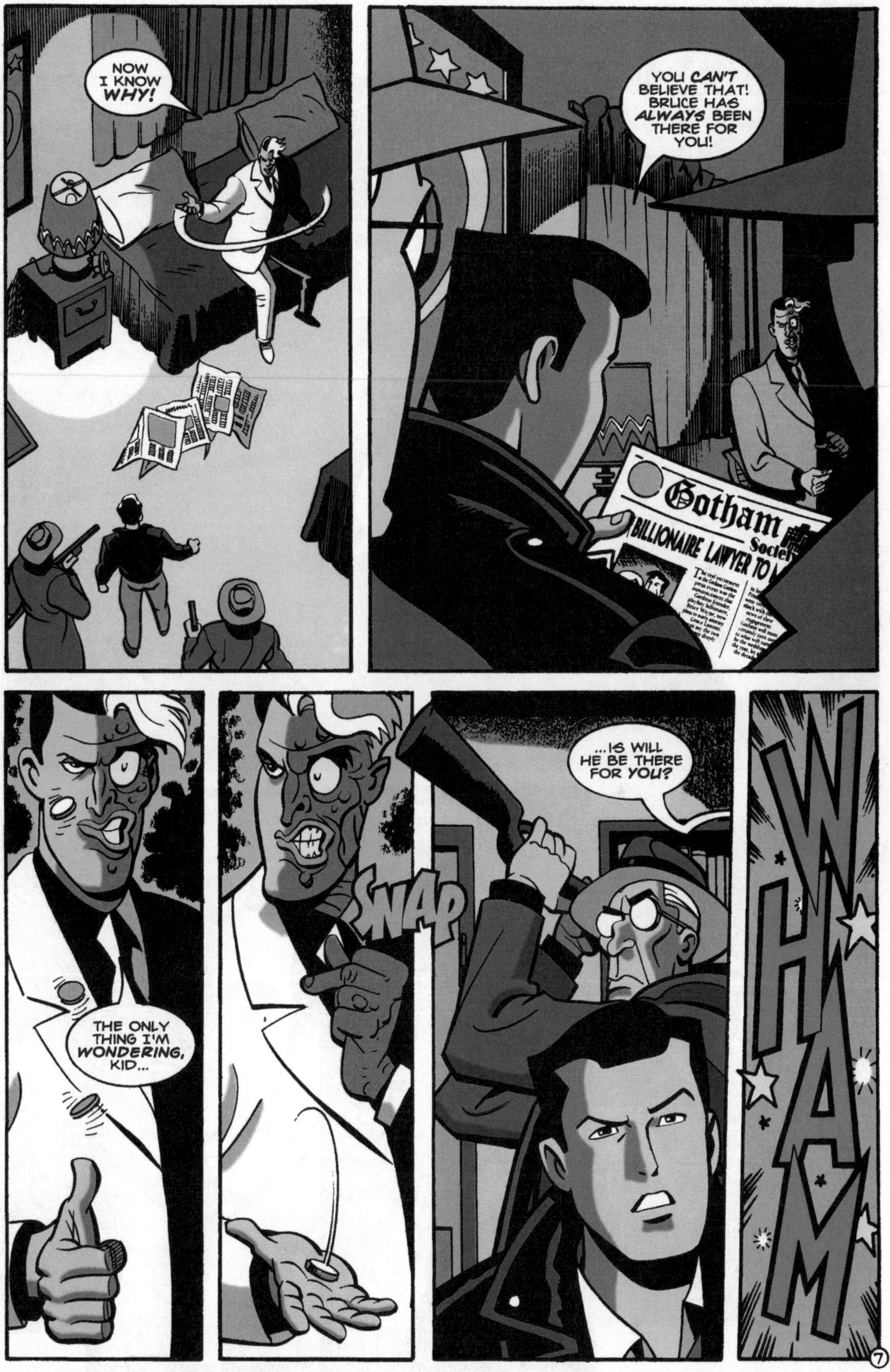
NOW I KNOW WHY!
YOU CAN'T BELIEVE THAT! BRUCE HAS ALWAYS BEEN THERE FOR YOU!
Gotham
BILLIONAIRE LAWYER TO
THE ONLY THING I'M WONDERING, KID...
SNAP
...IS WILL HE BE THERE FOR YOU?
WHAM
7

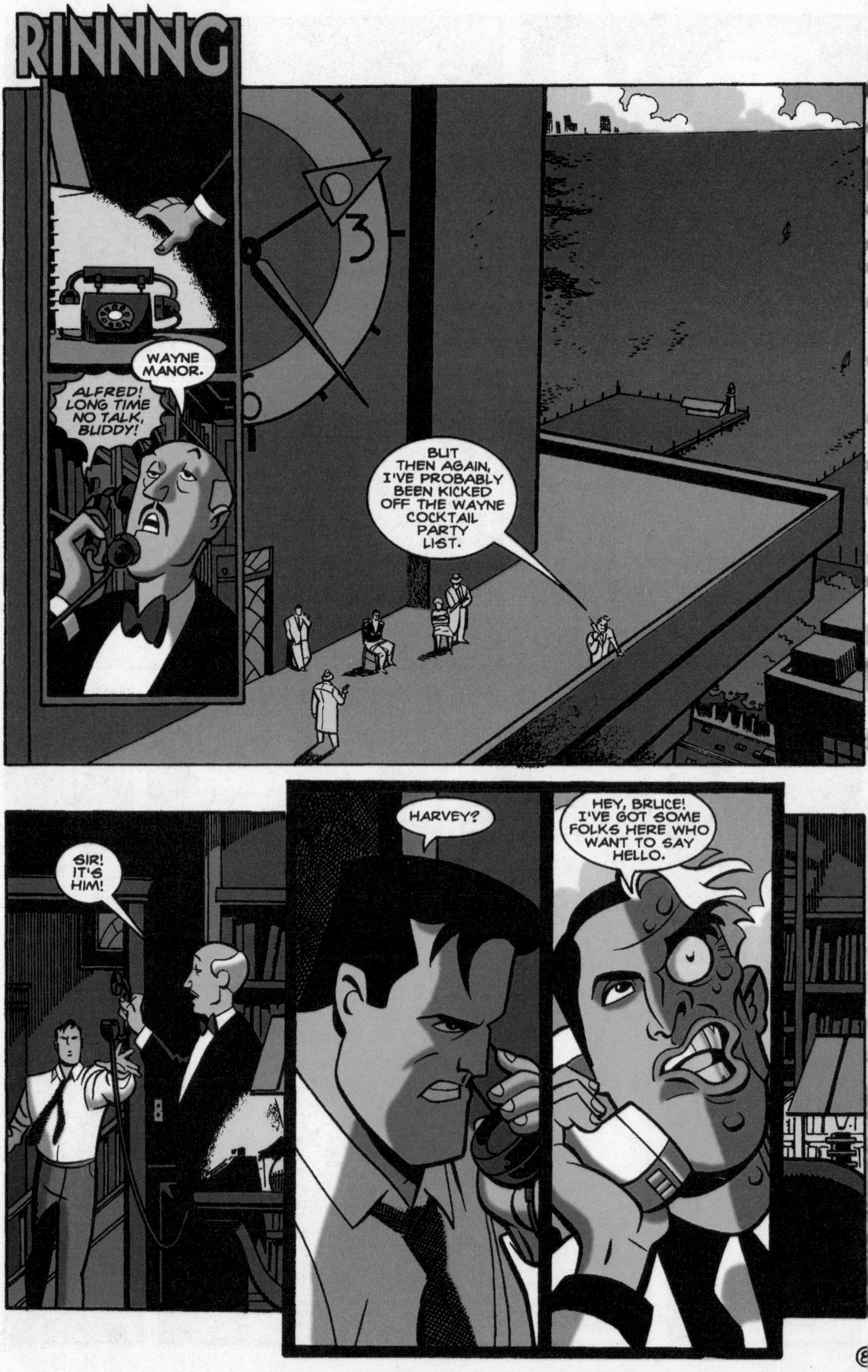
RINNNG
WAYNE MANOR.
ALFRED! LONG TIME NO TALK, BUDDY!
BUT THEN AGAIN, I'VE PROBABLY BEEN KICKED OFF THE WAYNE COCKTAIL PARTY LIST.
SIR! IT'S HIM!
HARVEY?
HEY, BRUCE! I'VE GOT SOME FOLKS HERE WHO WANT TO SAY HELLO.
8

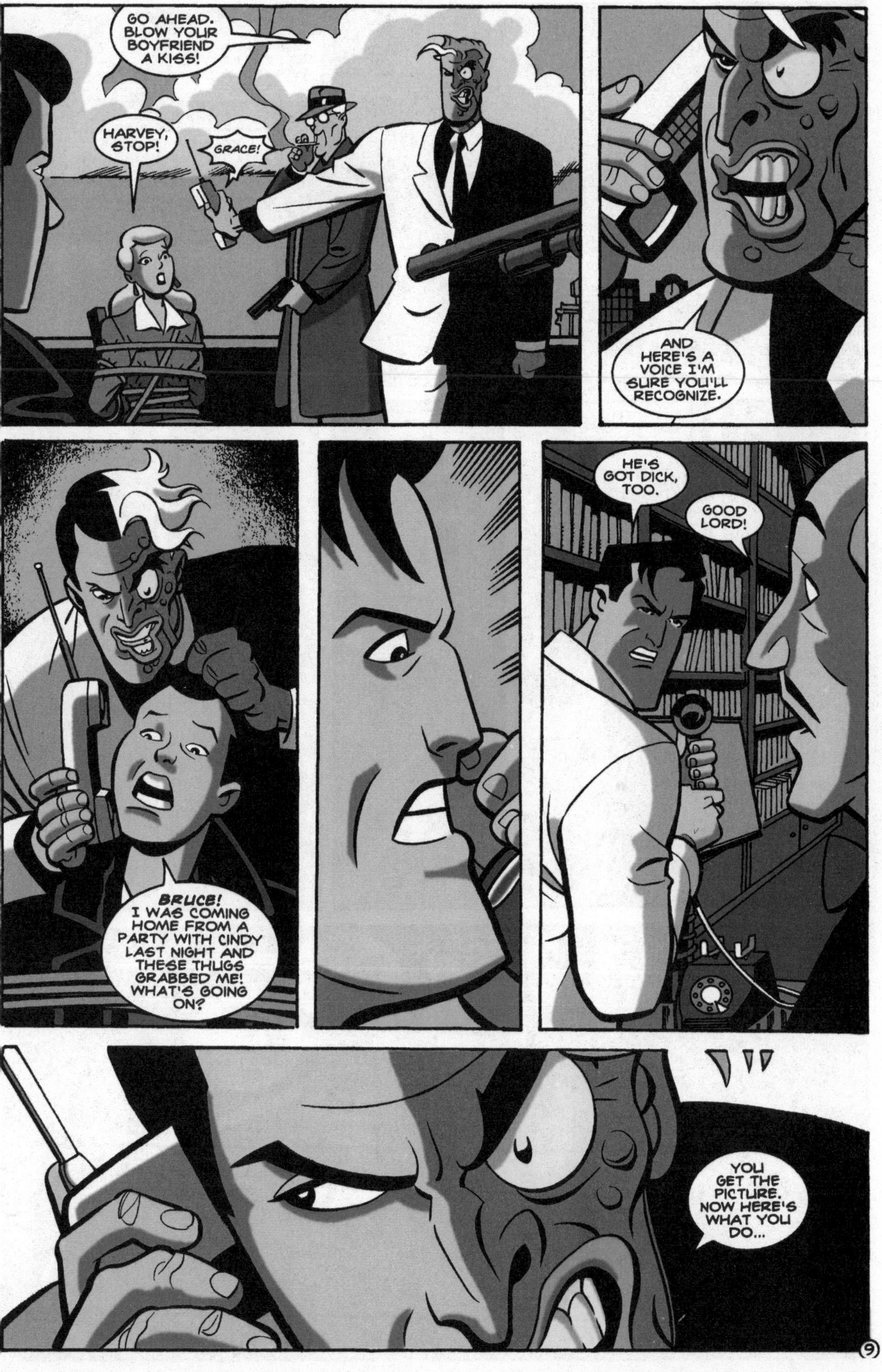
GO AHEAD. BLOW YOUR BOYFRIEND A KISS!
HARVEY, STOP!
GRACE!
AND HERE'S A VOICE I'M SURE YOU'LL RECOGNIZE.
BRUCE! I WAS COMING HOME FROM A PARTY WITH CINDY LAST NIGHT AND THESE THUGS GRABBED ME! WHAT'S GOING ON?
HE'S GOT DICK, TOO.
GOOD LORD!
YOU GET THE PICTURE. NOW HERE'S WHAT YOU DO...
9

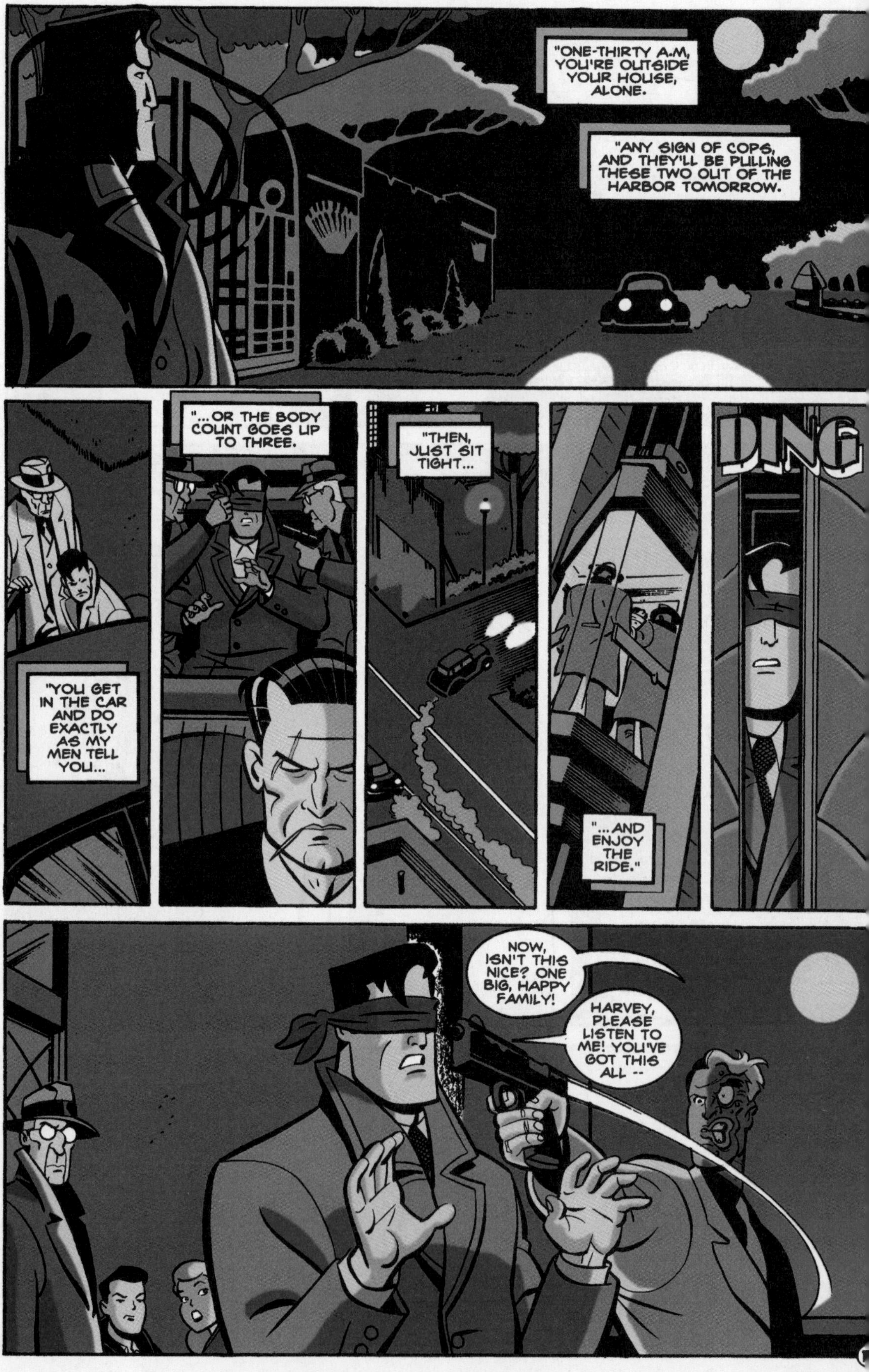
"ONE-THIRTY A.M, YOU'RE OUTSIDE YOUR HOUSE, ALONE.
"ANY SIGN OF COPS, AND THEY'LL BE PULLING THESE TWO OUT OF THE HARBOR TOMORROW.
"YOU GET IN THE CAR AND DO EXACTLY AS MY MEN TELL YOU...
"...OR THE BODY COUNT GOES UP TO THREE.
"THEN, JUST SIT TIGHT...
"...AND ENJOY THE RIDE."
DING
NOW, ISN'T THIS NICE? ONE BIG, HAPPY FAMILY!
HARVEY, PLEASE LISTEN TO ME! YOU'VE GOT THIS ALL --

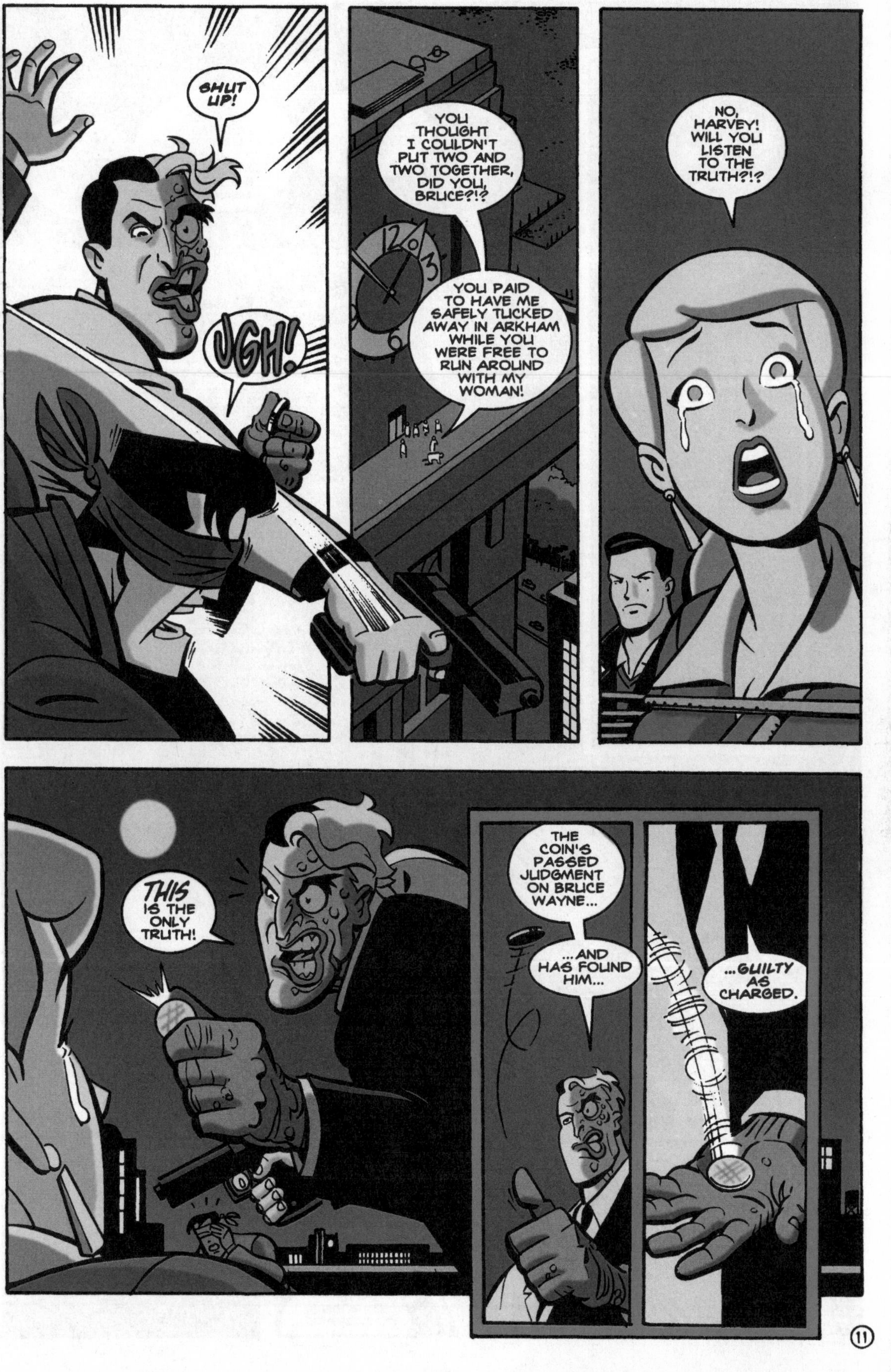
SHUT UP!
UGH!
YOU THOUGHT I COULDN'T PUT TWO AND TWO TOGETHER, DID YOU, BRUCE?!?
YOU PAID TO HAVE ME SAFELY TUCKED AWAY IN ARKHAM WHILE YOU WERE FREE TO RUN AROUND WITH MY WOMAN!
NO, HARVEY! WILL YOU LISTEN TO THE TRUTH?!?
THIS IS THE ONLY TRUTH!
THE COIN'S PASSED JUDGMENT ON BRUCE WAYNE...
...AND HAS FOUND HIM...
...GUILTY AS CHARGED.
11

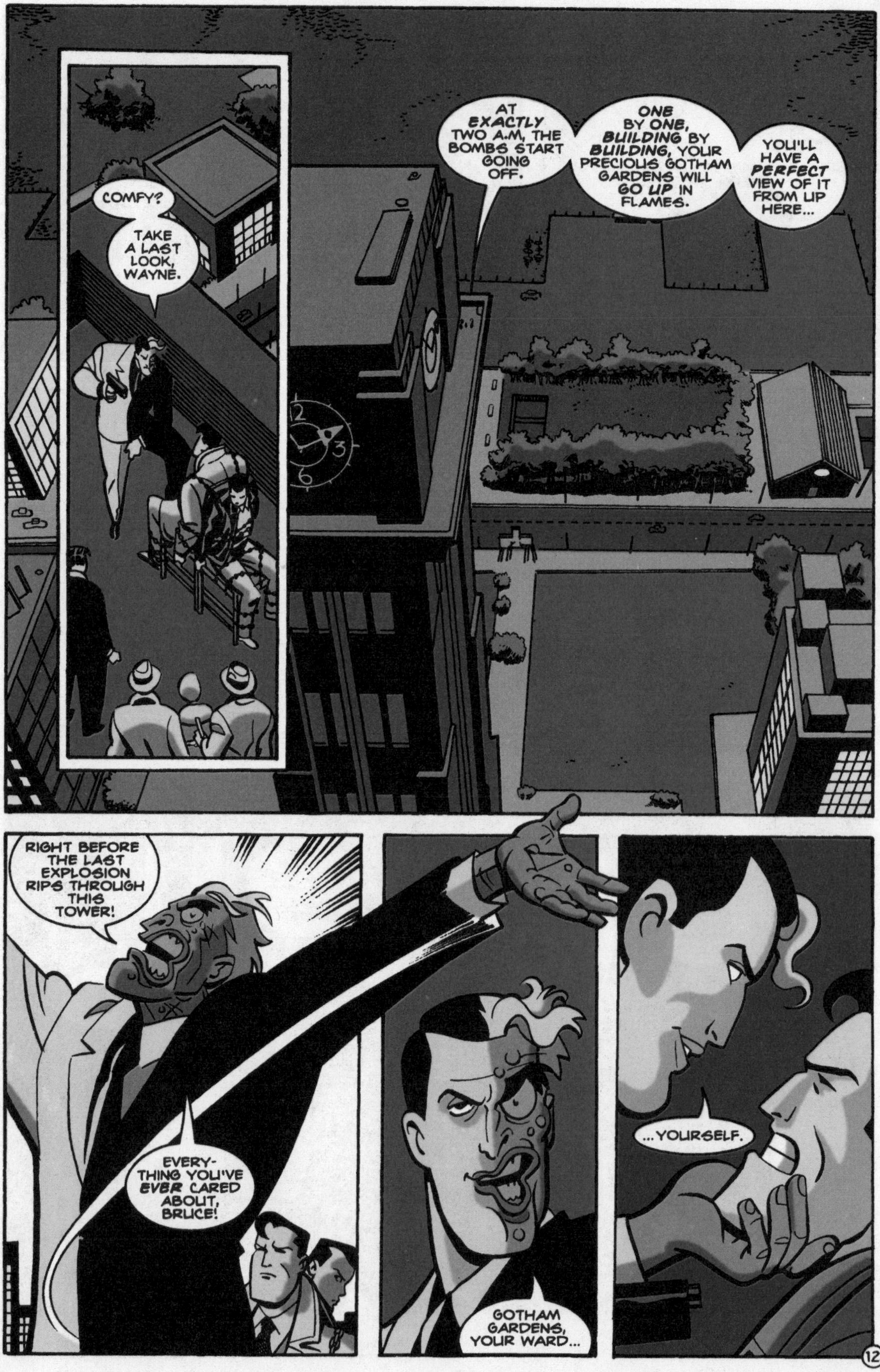
COMFY?
TAKE A LAST LOOK, WAYNE.
AT EXACTLY TWO A.M, THE BOMBS START GOING OFF.
ONE BY ONE, BUILDING BY BUILDING, YOUR PRECIOUS GOTHAM GARDENS WILL GO UP IN FLAMES.
YOU'LL HAVE A PERFECT VIEW OF IT FROM UP HERE...
RIGHT BEFORE THE LAST EXPLOSION RIPS THROUGH THIS TOWER!
EVERY-THING YOU'VE EVER CARED ABOUT, BRUCE!
GOTHAM GARDENS, YOUR WARD...
...YOURSELF.
12

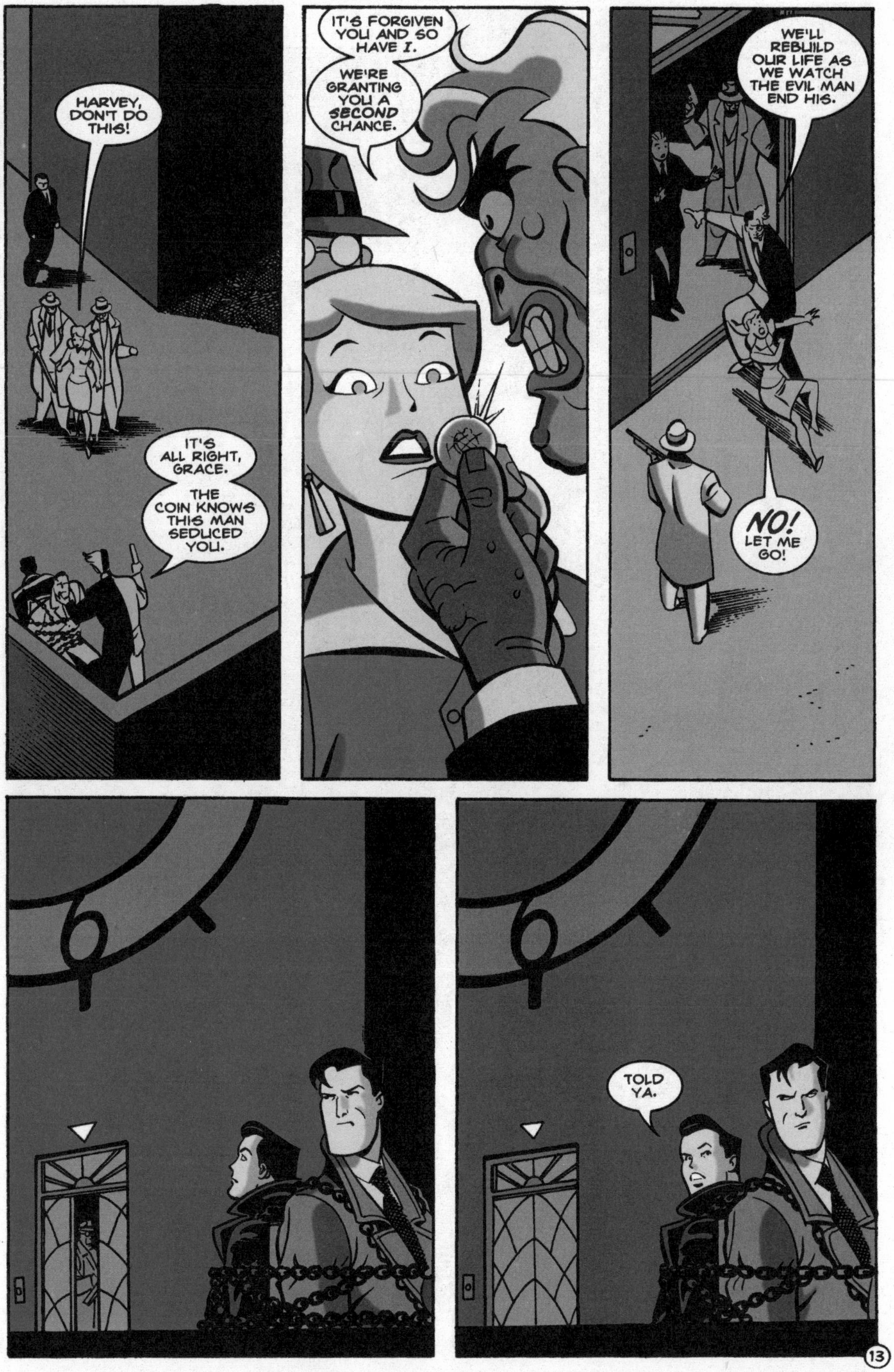
HARVEY, DON'T DO THIS!
IT'S ALL RIGHT, GRACE.
THE COIN KNOWS THIS MAN SEDUCED YOU.
IT'S FORGIVEN YOU AND SO HAVE I.
WE'RE GRANTING YOU A SECOND CHANCE.
WE'LL REBUILD OUR LIFE AS WE WATCH THE EVIL MAN END HIS.
NO! LET ME GO!
TOLD YA.
13

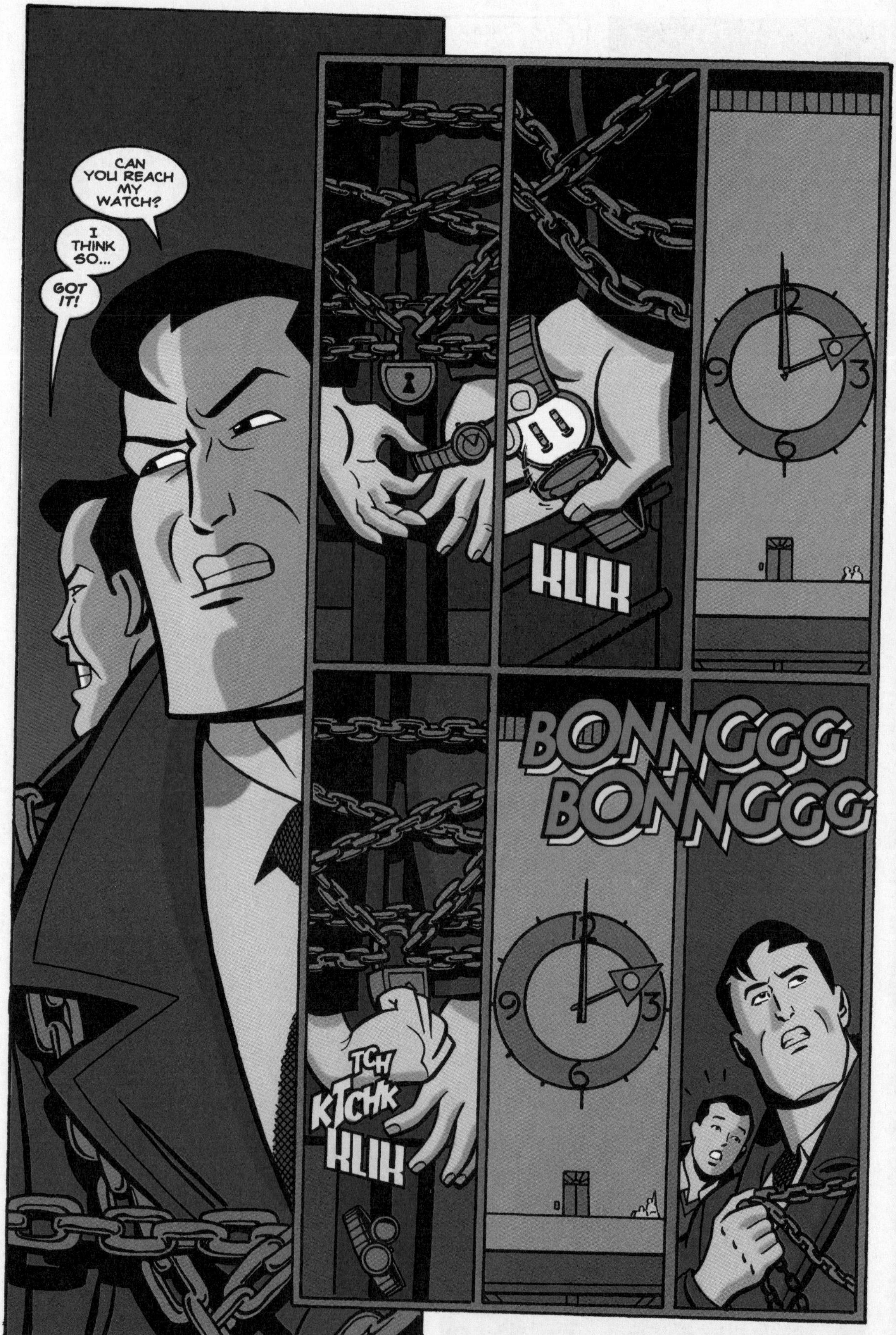
CAN YOU REACH MY WATCH?
I THINK SO...
GOT IT!
KLIK
TCH
KTCHK
KLIK
BONNGGG
BONNGGG

14

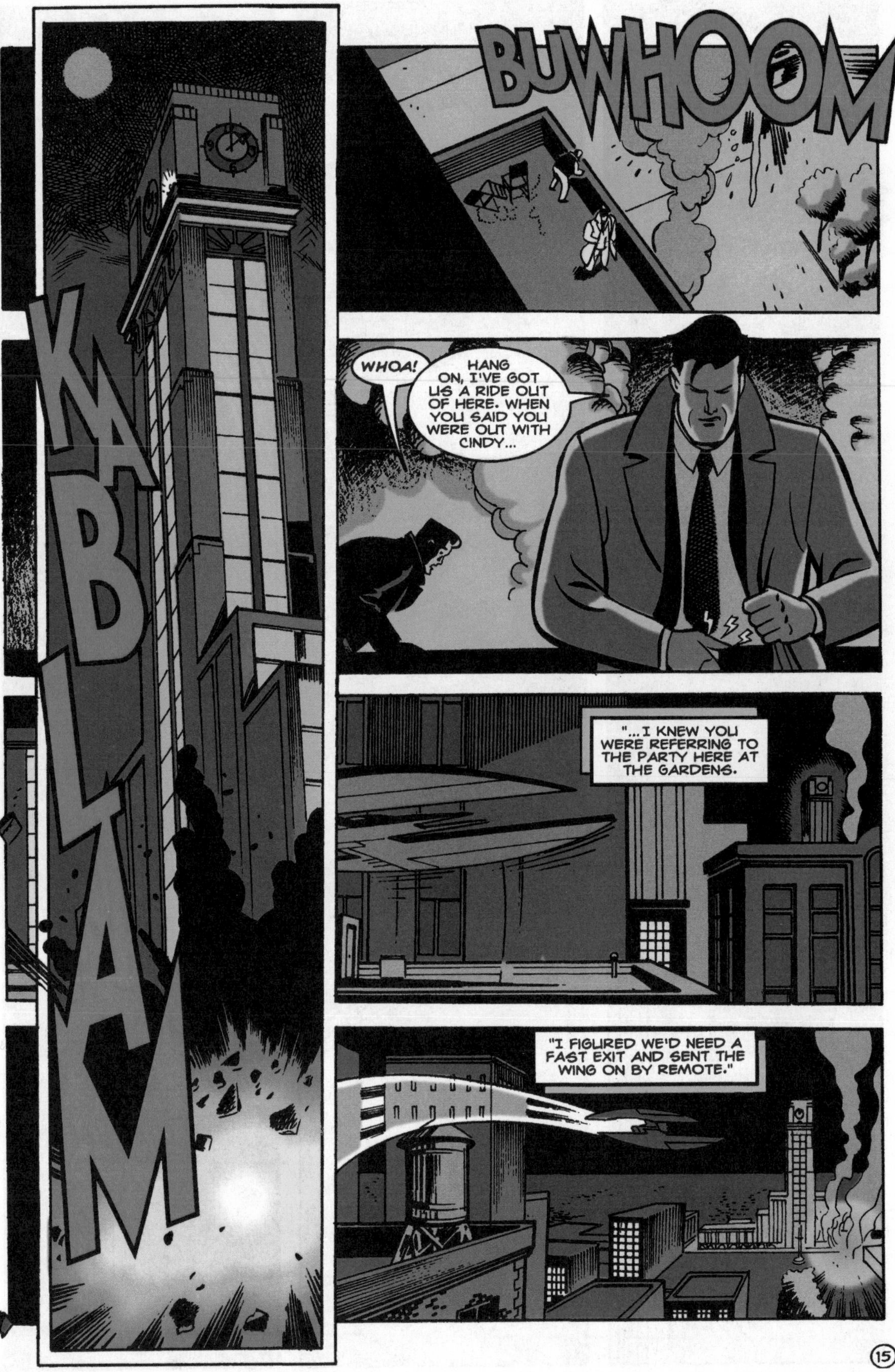
KA-BLAM
BUWHOOM
WHOA!
HANG ON, I'VE GOT US A RIDE OUT OF HERE. WHEN YOU SAID YOU WERE OUT WITH CINDY...
"...I KNEW YOU WERE REFERRING TO THE PARTY HERE AT THE GARDENS.
"I FIGURED WE'D NEED A FAST EXIT AND SENT THE WING ON BY REMOTE."
15

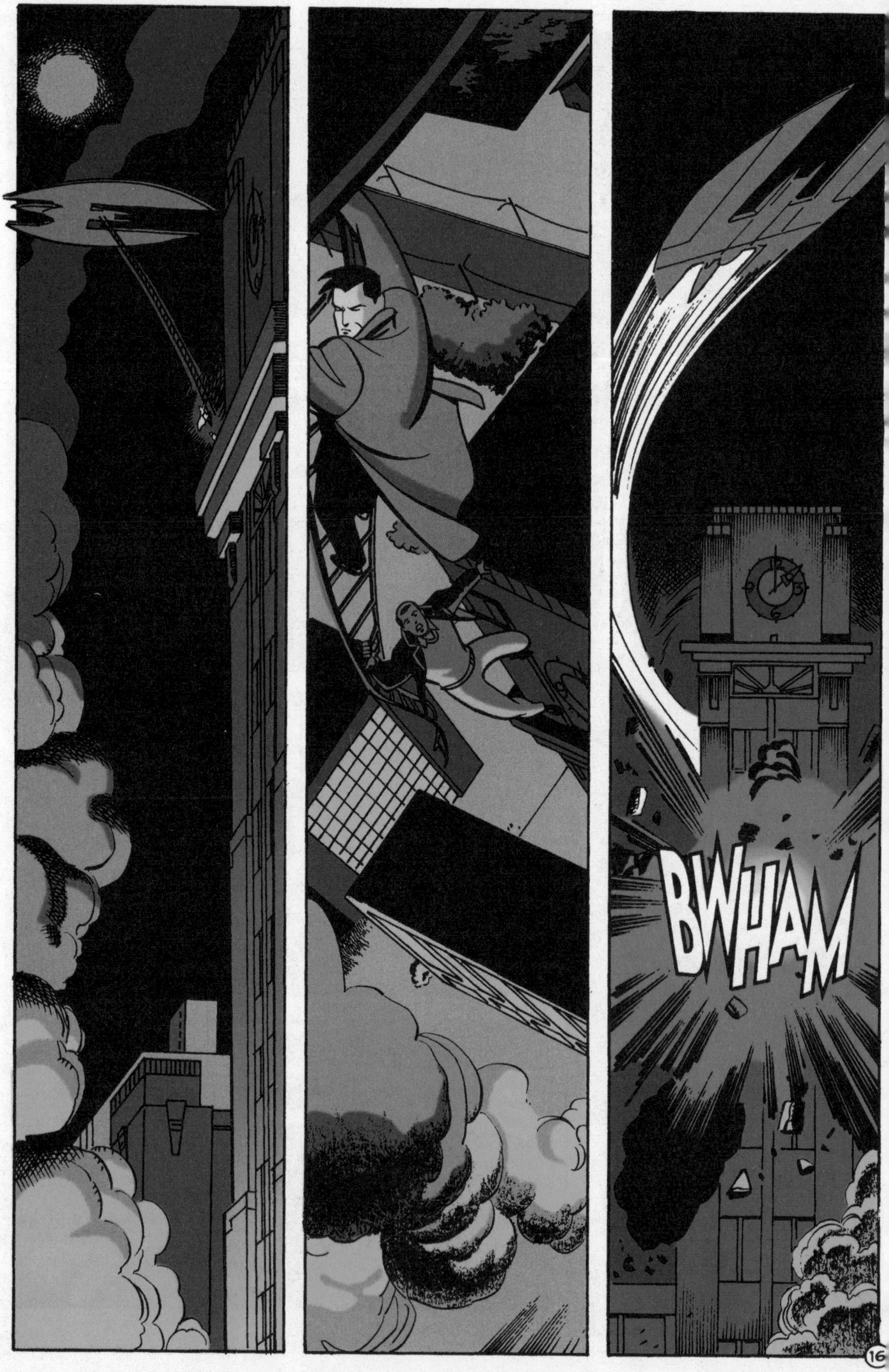
BWHAM
16

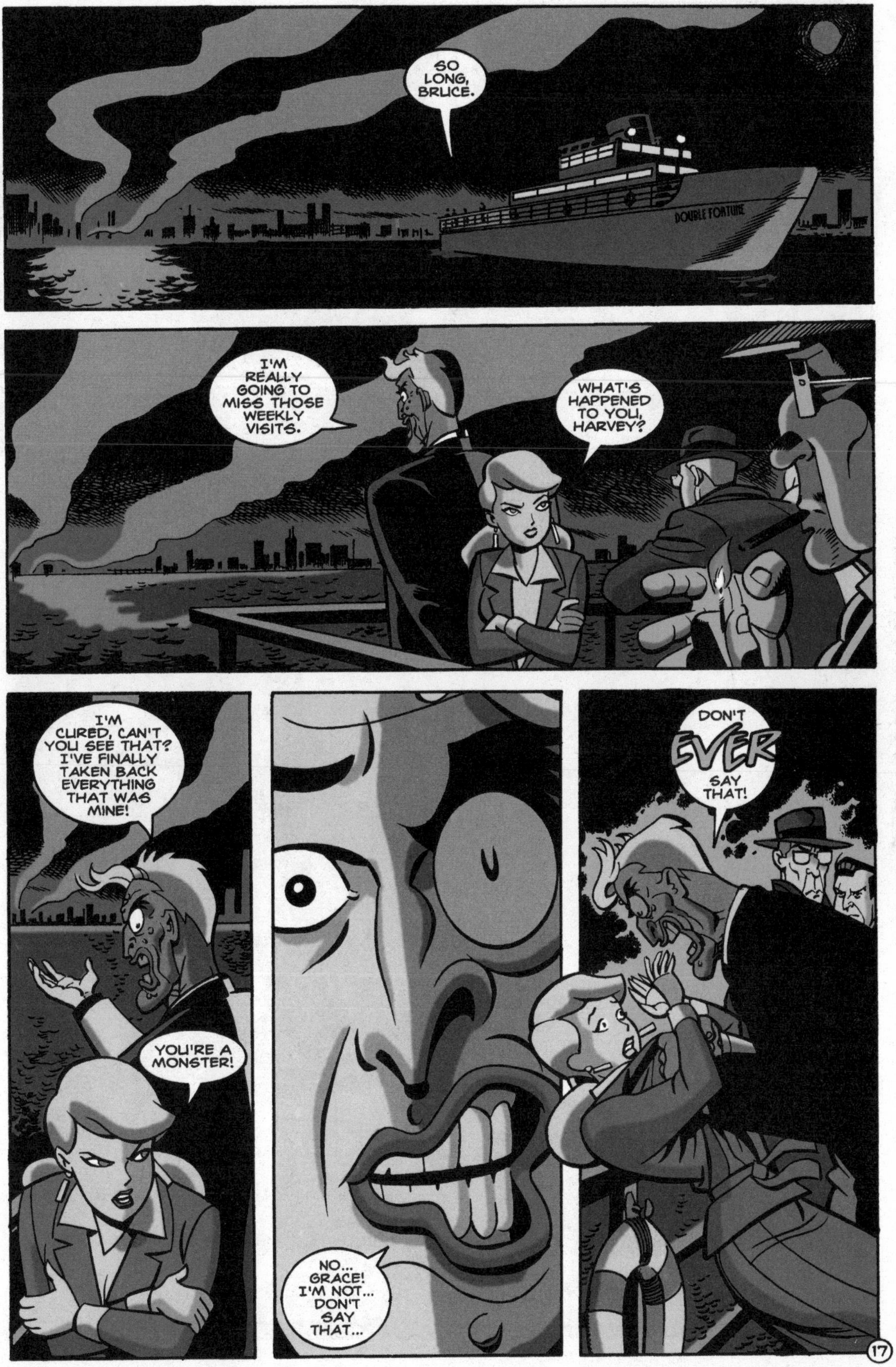

SO LONG, BRUCE.
DOUBLE FORTUNE
I'M REALLY GOING TO MISS THOSE WEEKLY VISITS.
WHAT'S HAPPENED TO YOU, HARVEY?
I'M CURED, CAN'T YOU SEE THAT? I'VE FINALLY TAKEN BACK EVERYTHING THAT WAS MINE!
YOU'RE A MONSTER!
NO... GRACE! I'M NOT... DON'T SAY THAT...
DON'T EVER SAY THAT!
17

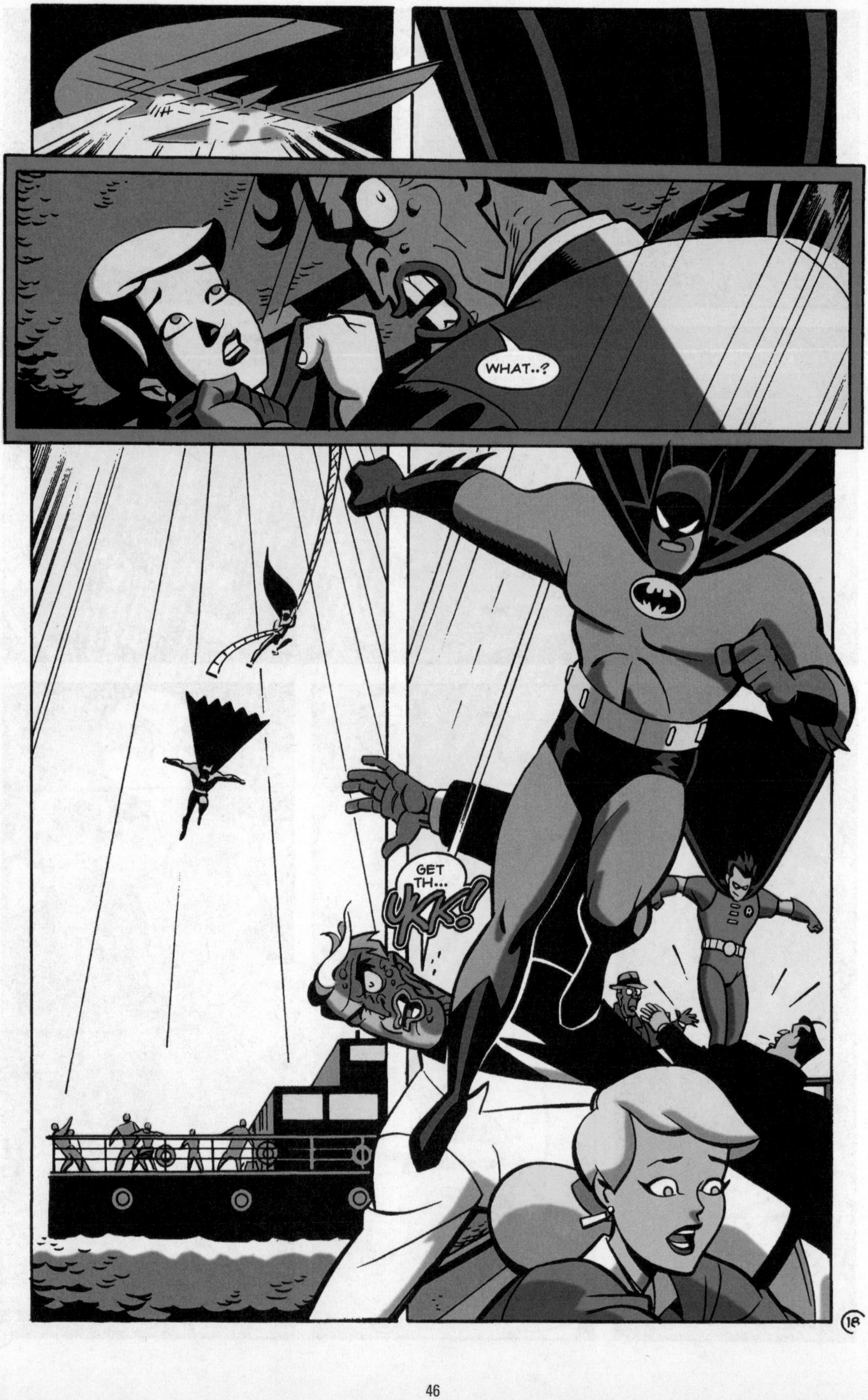

WHAT..?
GET TH...
UKK!
18

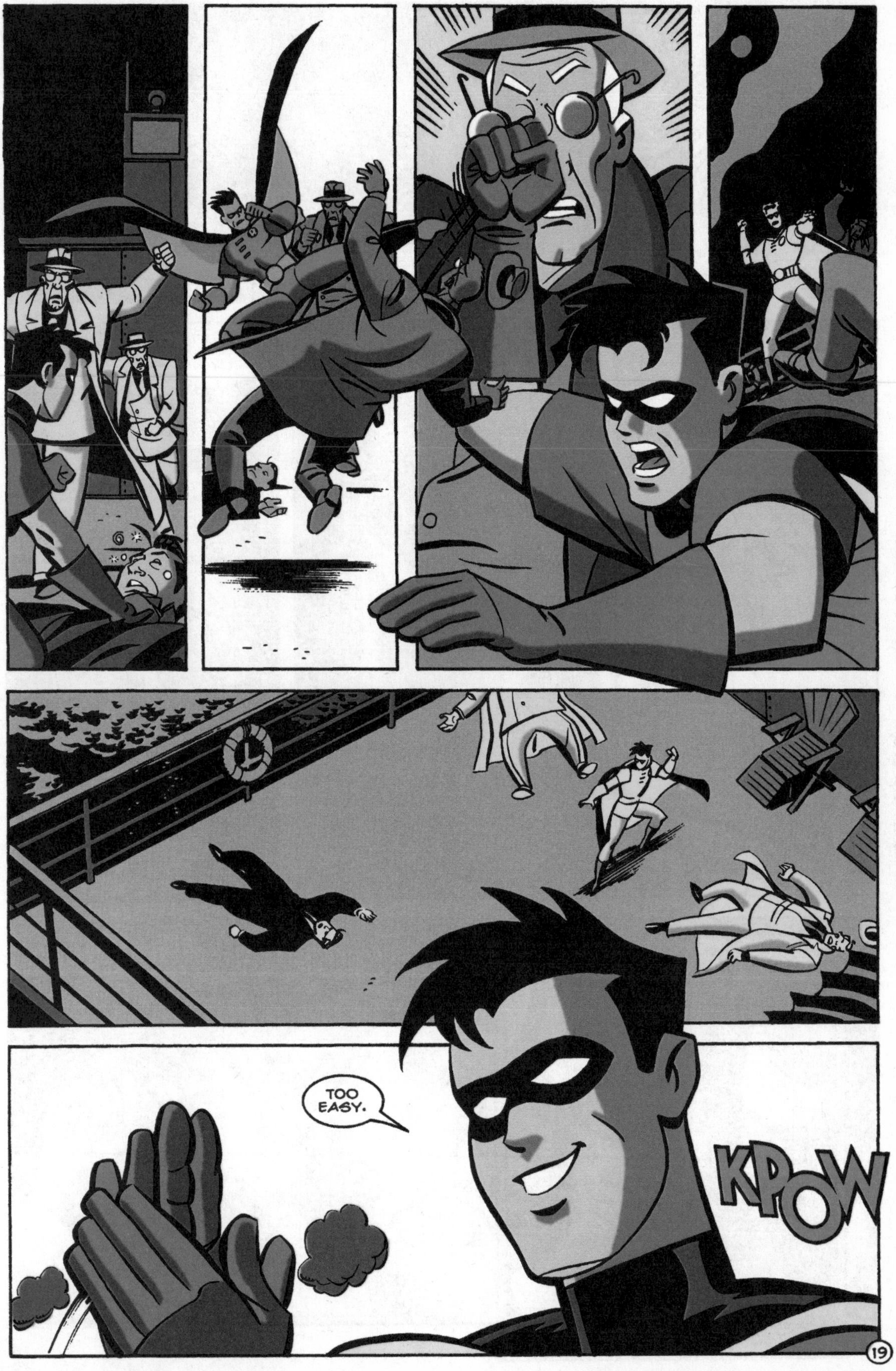
TOO EASY.
KPOW
19

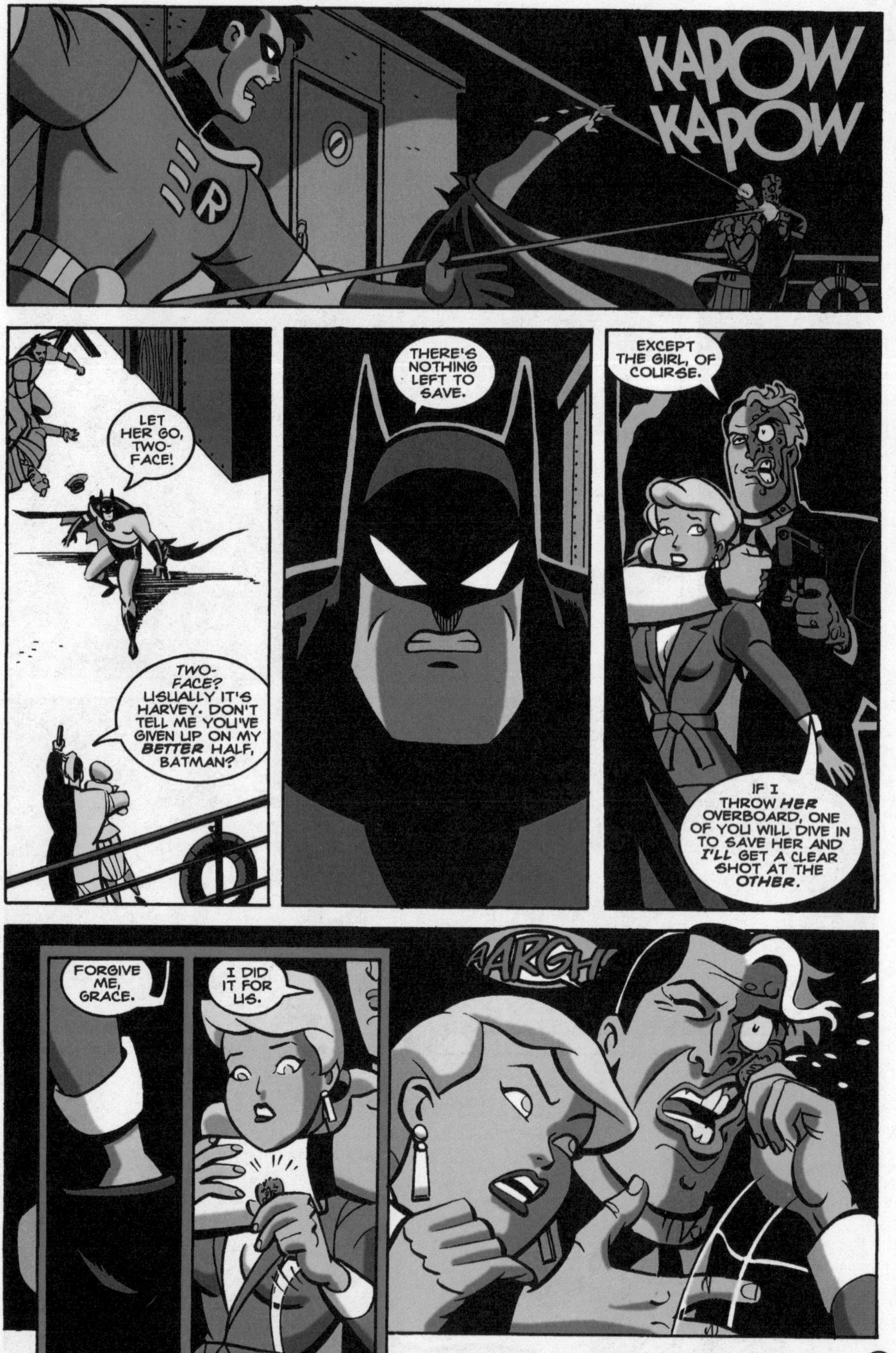
KAPOW
KAPOW
LET HER GO, TWO-FACE!
TWO-FACE? USUALLY IT'S HARVEY. DON'T TELL ME YOU'VE GIVEN UP ON MY *BETTER* HALF, BATMAN?
THERE'S NOTHING LEFT TO SAVE.
EXCEPT THE GIRL, OF COURSE.
IF I THROW *HER* OVERBOARD, ONE OF YOU WILL DIVE IN TO SAVE HER AND *I'LL* GET A CLEAR SHOT AT THE *OTHER*.
FORGIVE ME, GRACE.
I DID IT FOR US.
AARGH!
20

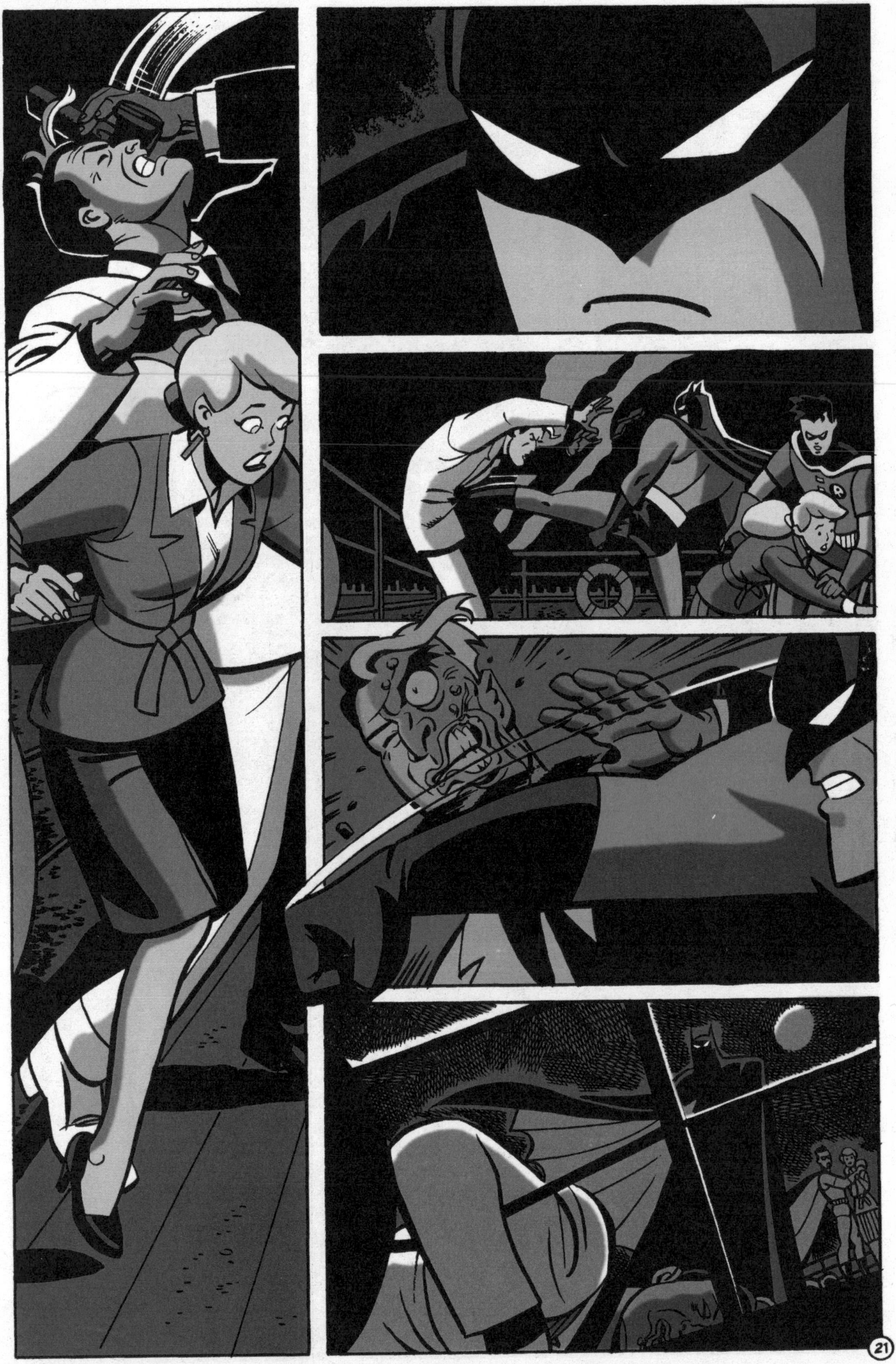
21

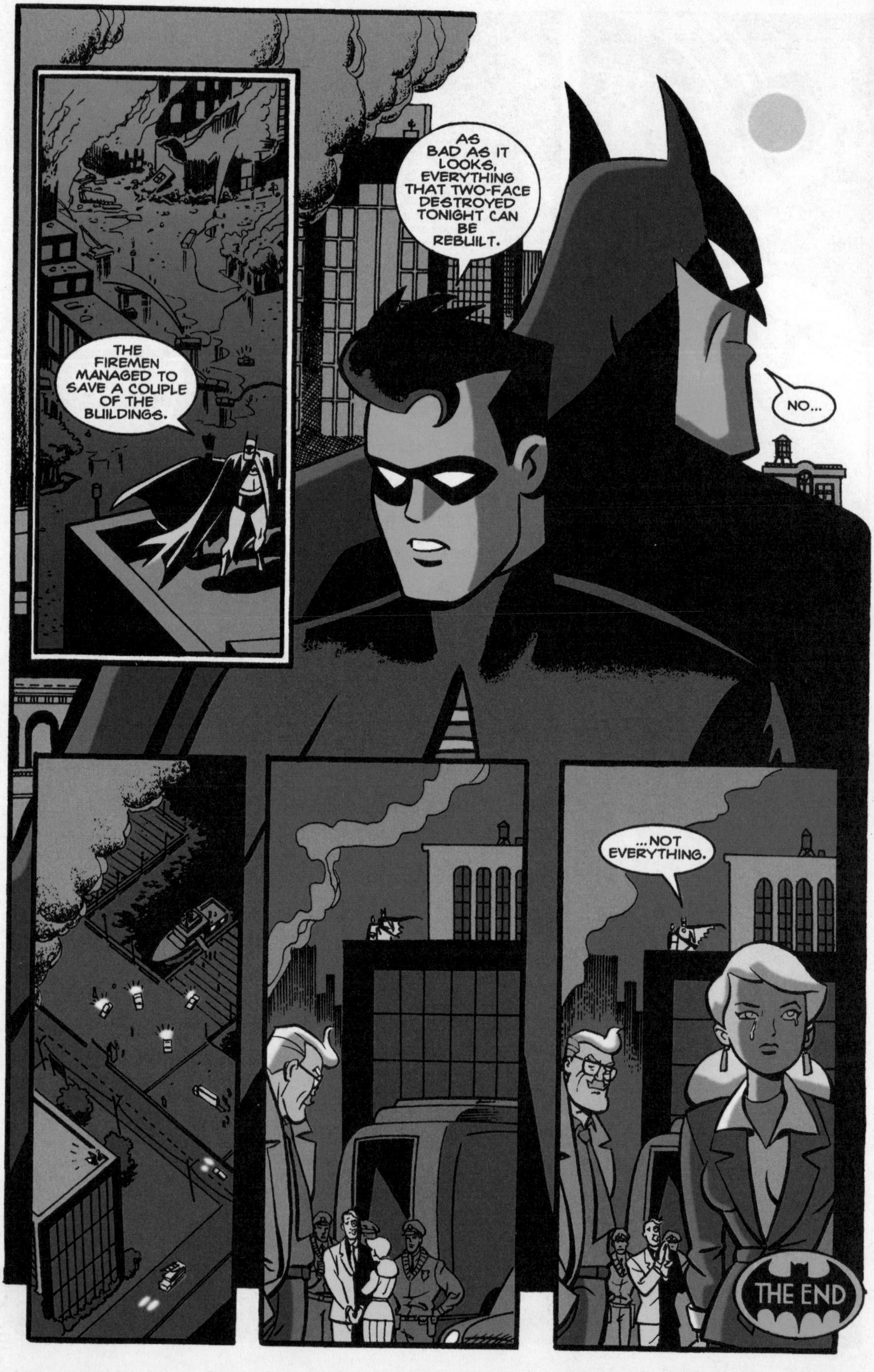
THE FIREMEN MANAGED TO SAVE A COUPLE OF THE BUILDINGS.
AS BAD AS IT LOOKS, EVERYTHING THAT TWO-FACE DESTROYED TONIGHT CAN BE REBUILT.
NO...
...NOT EVERYTHING.
THE END

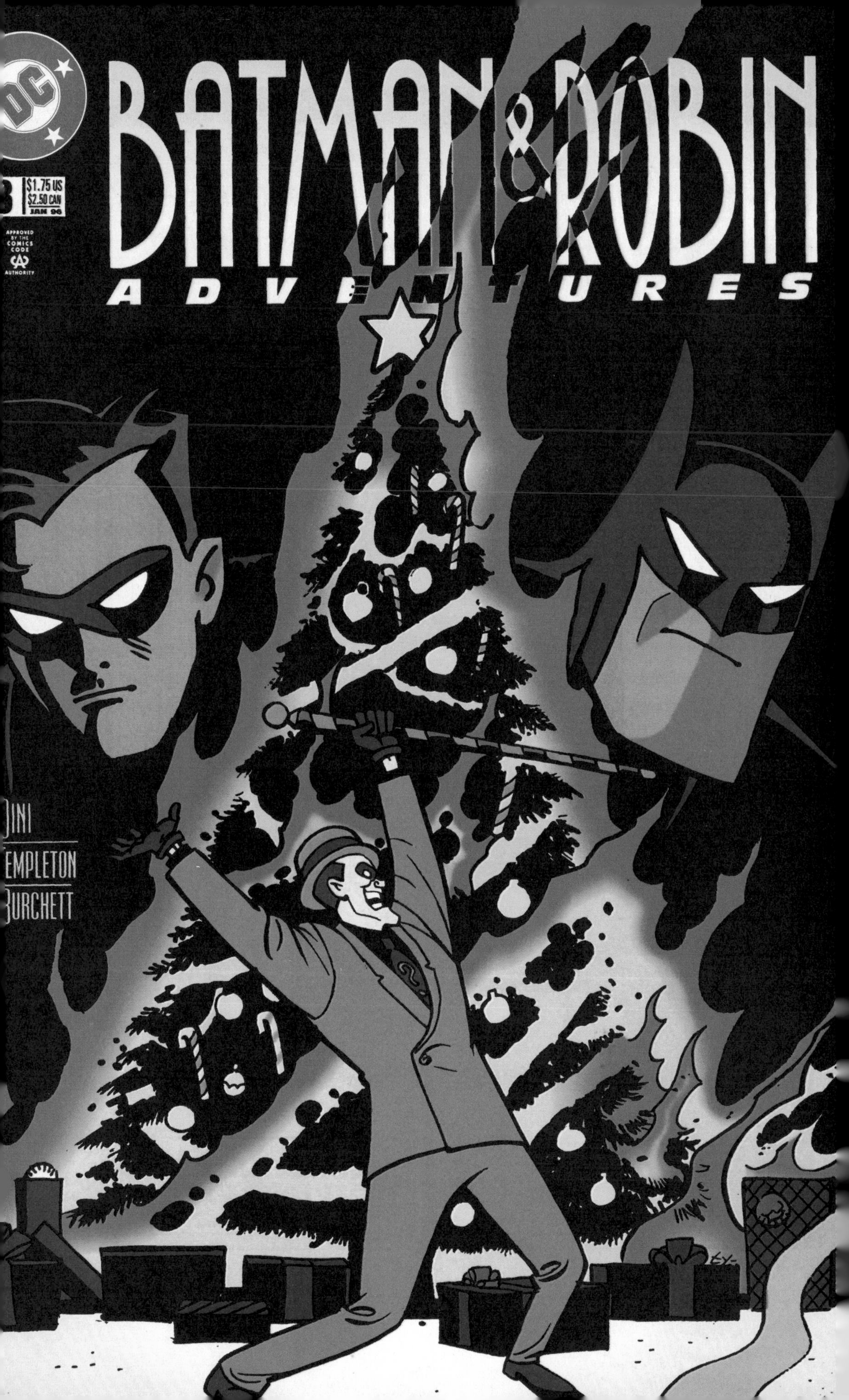

BATMAN & ROBIN
ADVENTURES
$1.75 US
$2.50 CAN
JAN 96
APPROVED BY THE COMICS CODE AUTHORITY
INI
EMPLETON
URCHETT

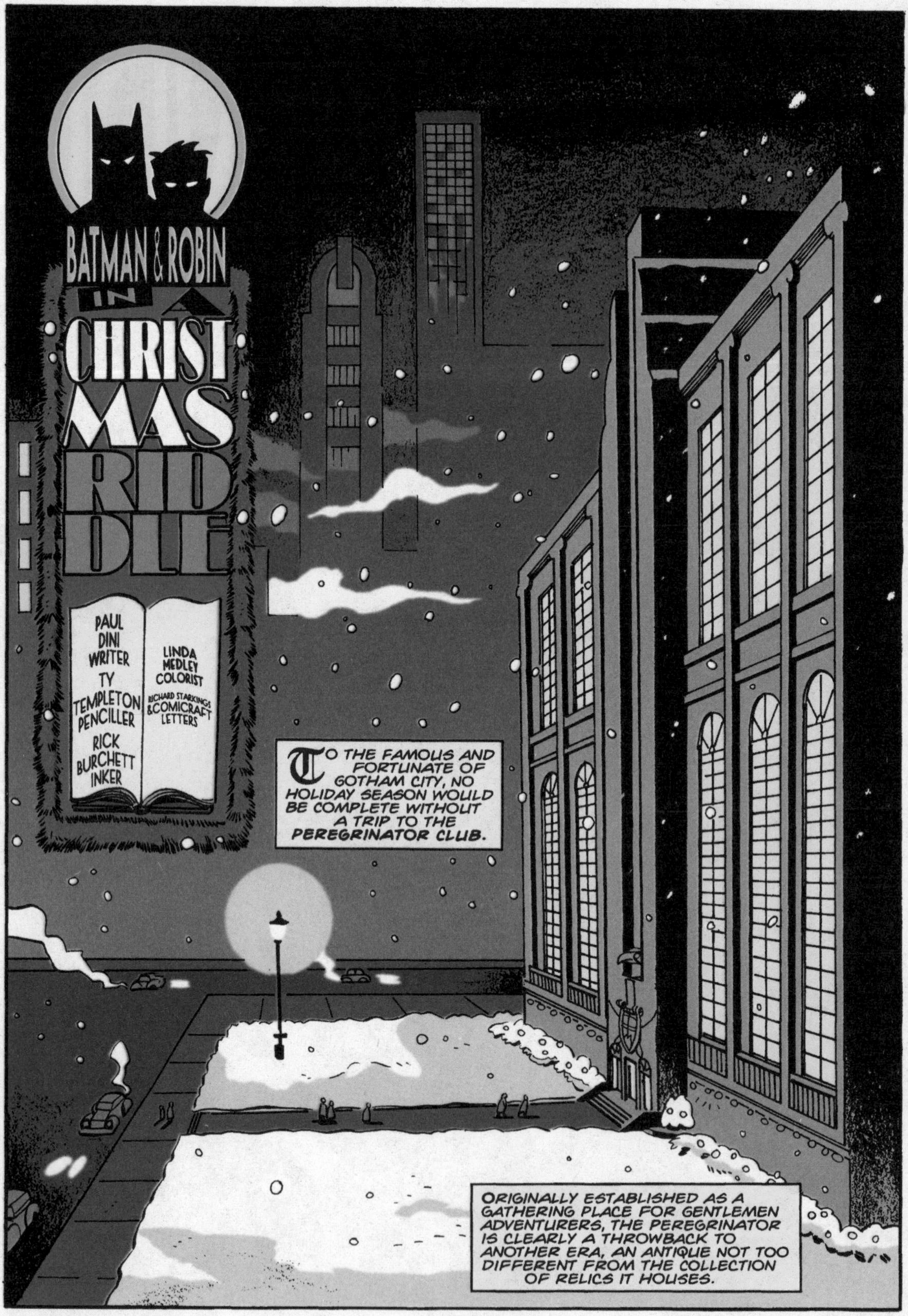
BATMAN & ROBIN
IN
CHRISTMAS RIDDLE
PAUL DINI WRITER
TY TEMPLETON PENCILLER
RICK BURCHETT INKER
LINDA MEDLEY COLORIST
RICHARD STARKINGS & COMICRAFT LETTERS
TO THE FAMOUS AND FORTUNATE OF GOTHAM CITY, NO HOLIDAY SEASON WOULD BE COMPLETE WITHOUT A TRIP TO THE PEREGRINATOR CLUB.
ORIGINALLY ESTABLISHED AS A GATHERING PLACE FOR GENTLEMEN ADVENTURERS, THE PEREGRINATOR IS CLEARLY A THROWBACK TO ANOTHER ERA, AN ANTIQUE NOT TOO DIFFERENT FROM THE COLLECTION OF RELICS IT HOUSES.

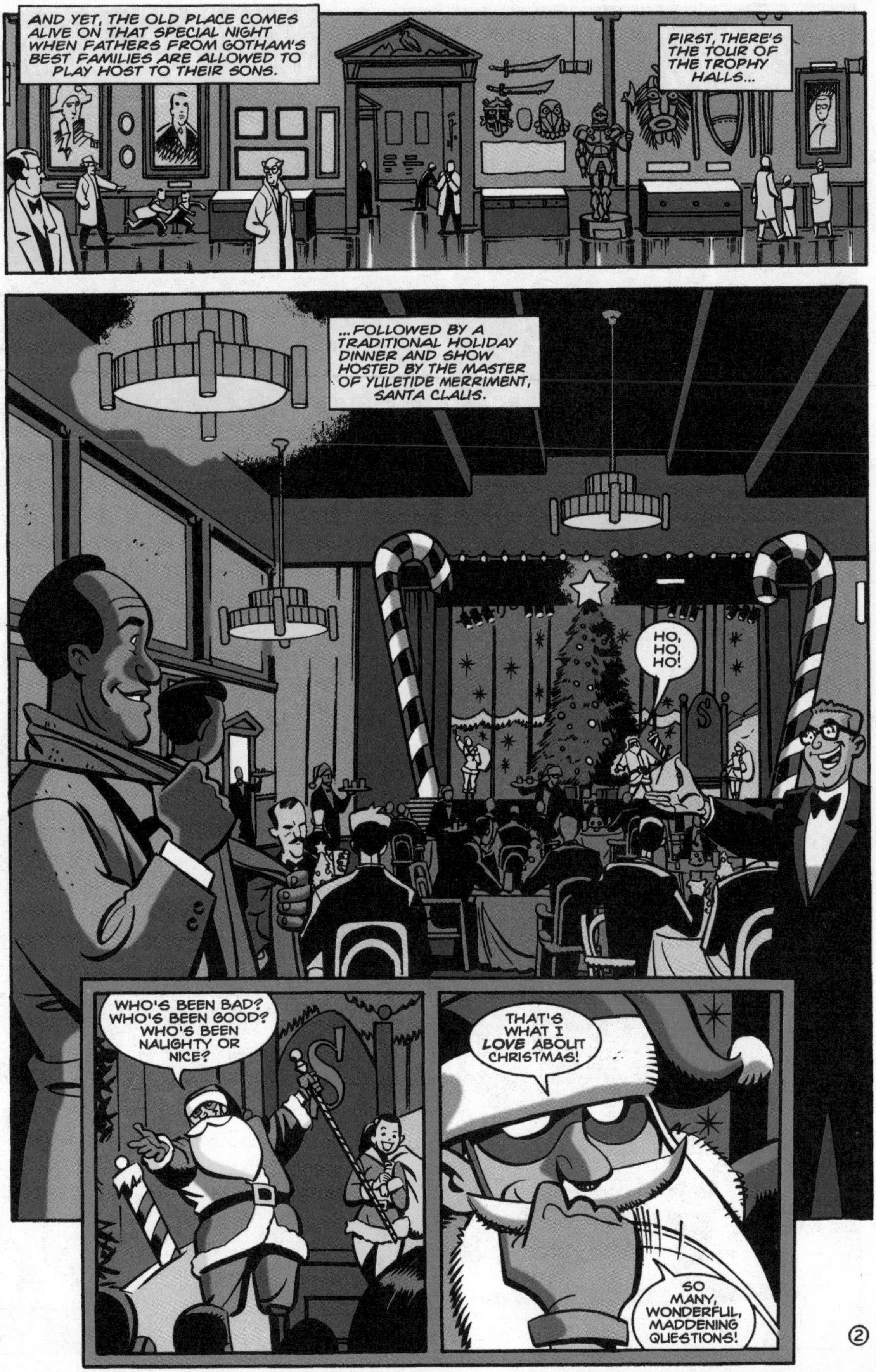
AND YET, THE OLD PLACE COMES ALIVE ON THAT SPECIAL NIGHT WHEN FATHERS FROM GOTHAM'S BEST FAMILIES ARE ALLOWED TO PLAY HOST TO THEIR SONS.
FIRST, THERE'S THE TOUR OF THE TROPHY HALLS...
...FOLLOWED BY A TRADITIONAL HOLIDAY DINNER AND SHOW HOSTED BY THE MASTER OF YULETIDE MERRIMENT, SANTA CLAUS.
HO, HO, HO!
WHO'S BEEN BAD? WHO'S BEEN GOOD? WHO'S BEEN NAUGHTY OR NICE?
THAT'S WHAT I LOVE ABOUT CHRISTMAS!
SO MANY, WONDERFUL, MADDENING QUESTIONS!
2

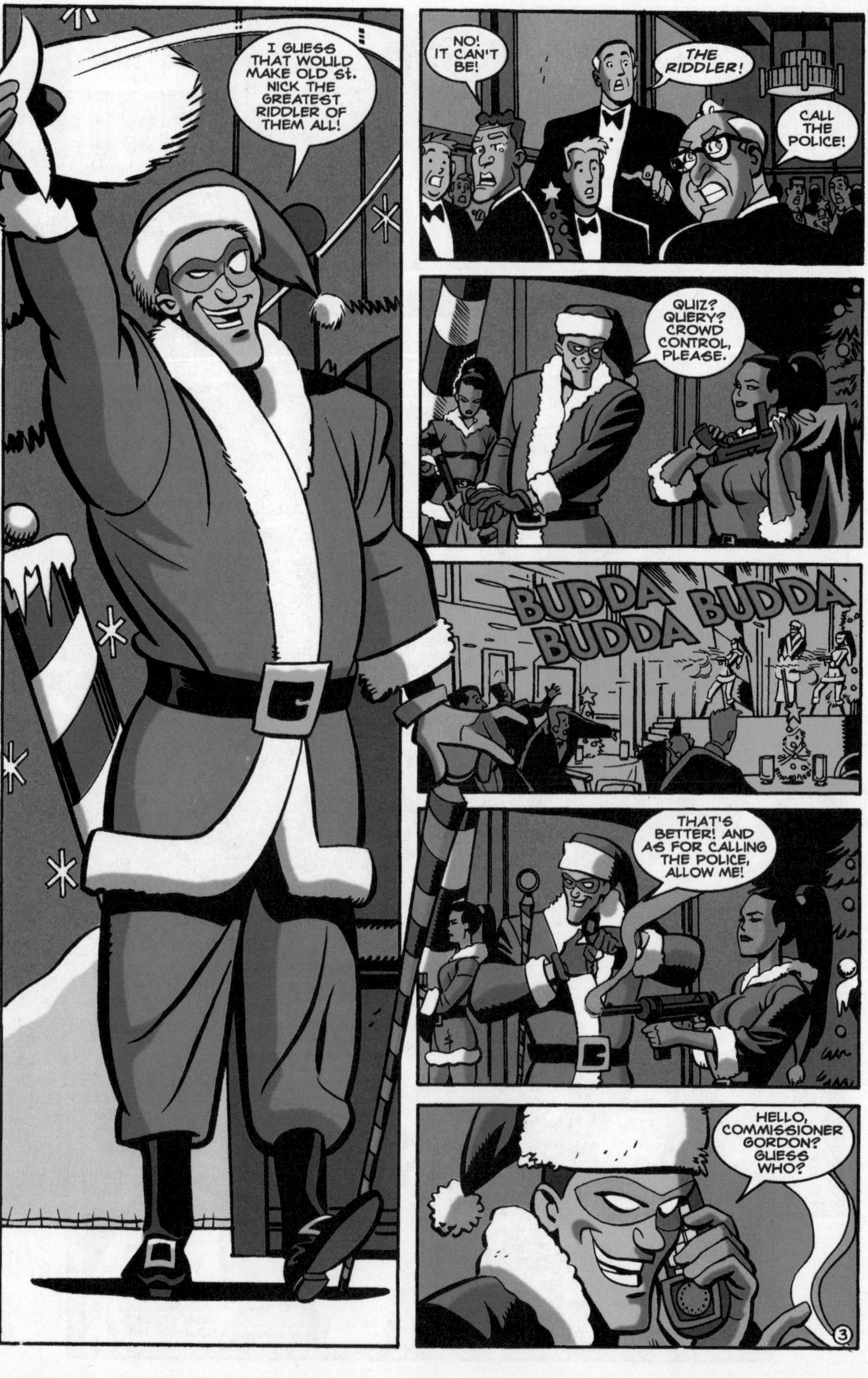
I GUESS THAT WOULD MAKE OLD St. NICK THE GREATEST RIDDLER OF THEM ALL!
NO! IT CAN'T BE!
THE RIDDLER!
CALL THE POLICE!
QUIZ? QUERY? CROWD CONTROL, PLEASE.
BUDDA BUDDA BUDDA
THAT'S BETTER! AND AS FOR CALLING THE POLICE, ALLOW ME!
HELLO, COMMISSIONER GORDON? GUESS WHO?
3

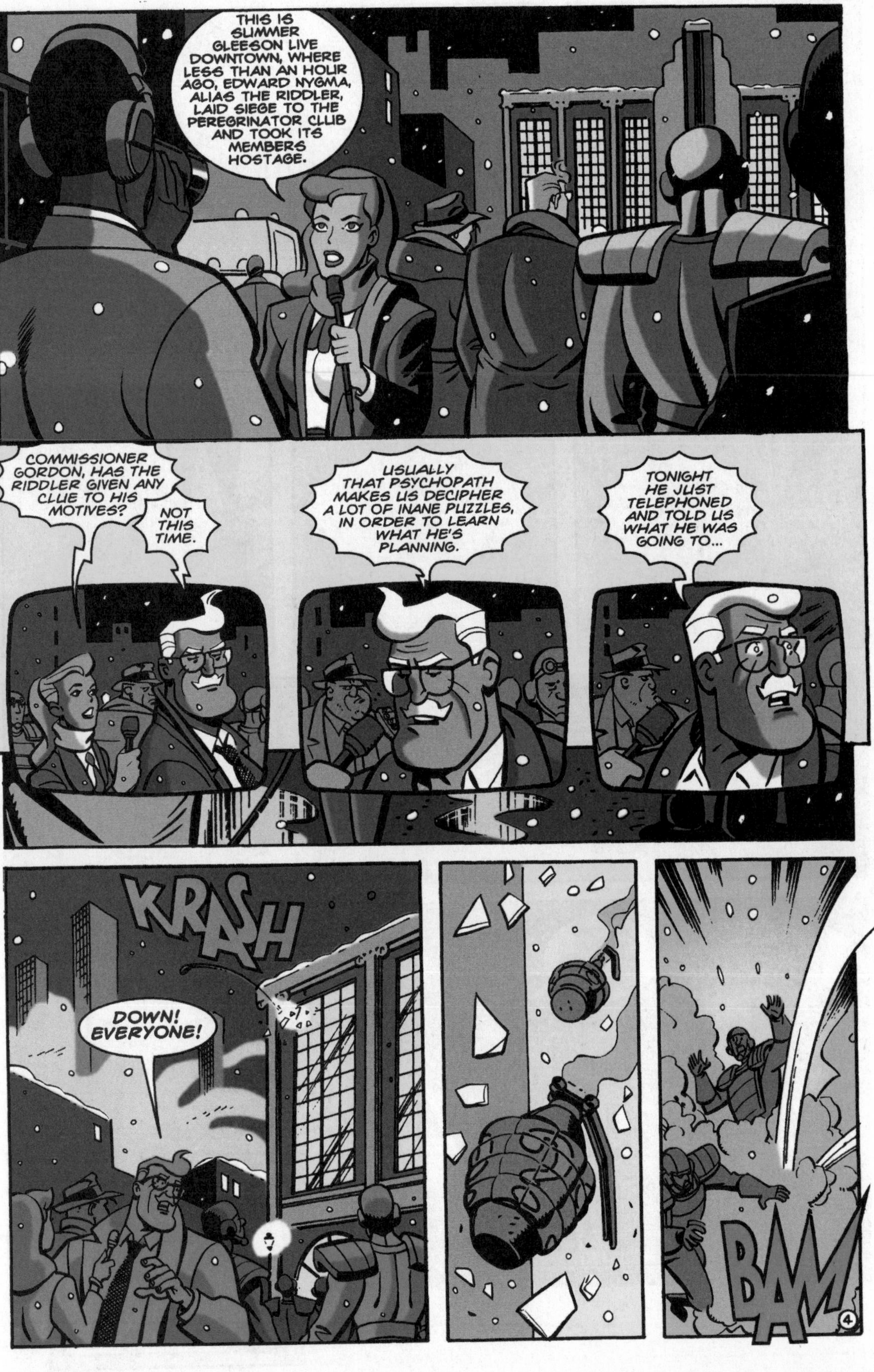
THIS IS SUMMER GLEESON LIVE DOWNTOWN, WHERE LESS THAN AN HOUR AGO, EDWARD NYGMA, ALIAS THE RIDDLER, LAID SIEGE TO THE PEREGRINATOR CLUB AND TOOK ITS MEMBERS HOSTAGE.
COMMISSIONER GORDON, HAS THE RIDDLER GIVEN ANY CLUE TO HIS MOTIVES?
NOT THIS TIME.
USUALLY THAT PSYCHOPATH MAKES US DECIPHER A LOT OF INANE PUZZLES, IN ORDER TO LEARN WHAT HE'S PLANNING.
TONIGHT HE JUST TELEPHONED AND TOLD US WHAT HE WAS GOING TO...
KRASH
DOWN! EVERYONE!
BAM
4

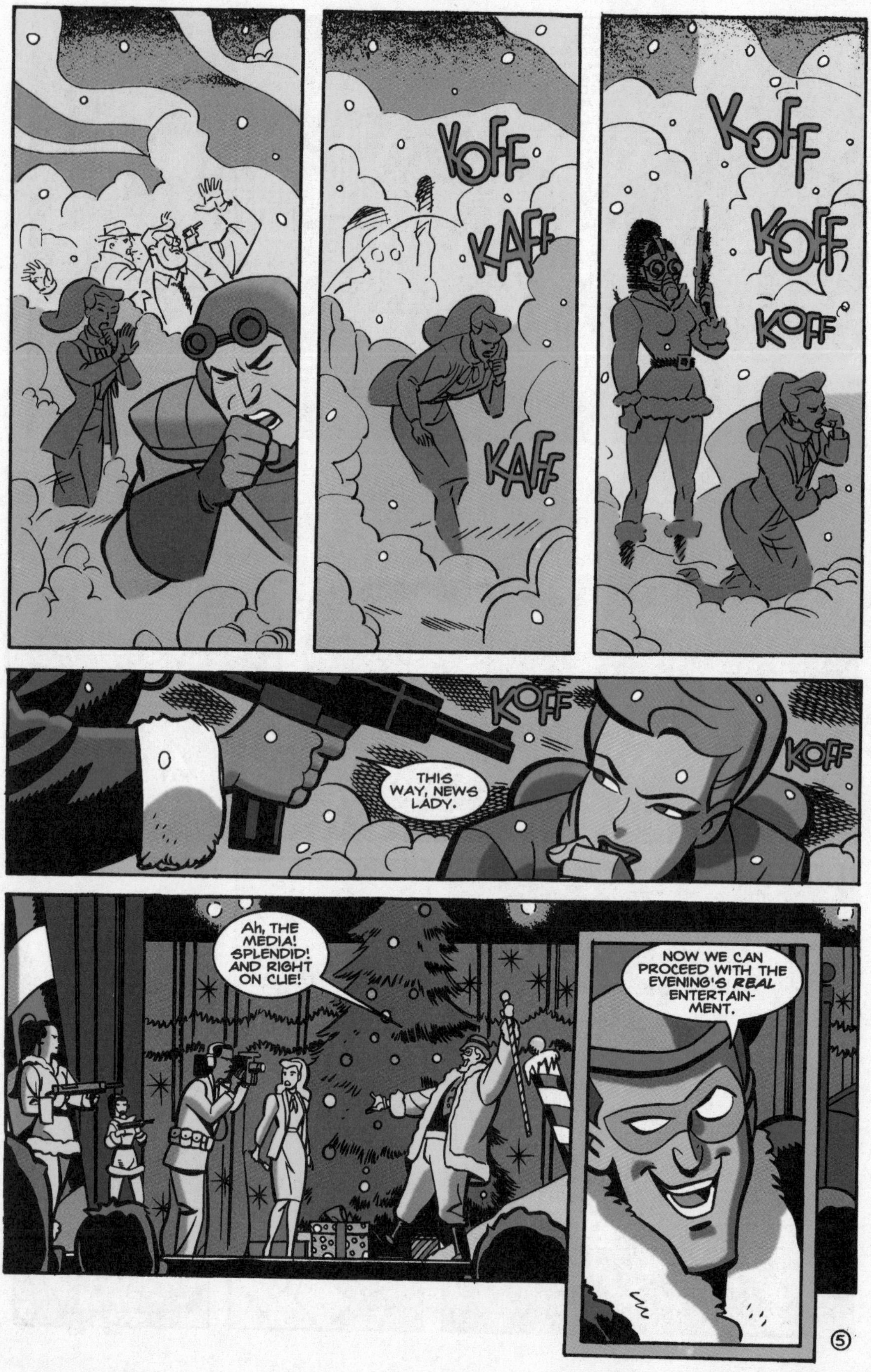
KOFF
KAFF
KAFF
KOFF
KOFF
KOFF
KOFF
KOFF
THIS WAY, NEWS LADY.
Ah, THE MEDIA! SPLENDID! AND RIGHT ON CUE!
NOW WE CAN PROCEED WITH THE EVENING'S *REAL* ENTERTAINMENT.
5

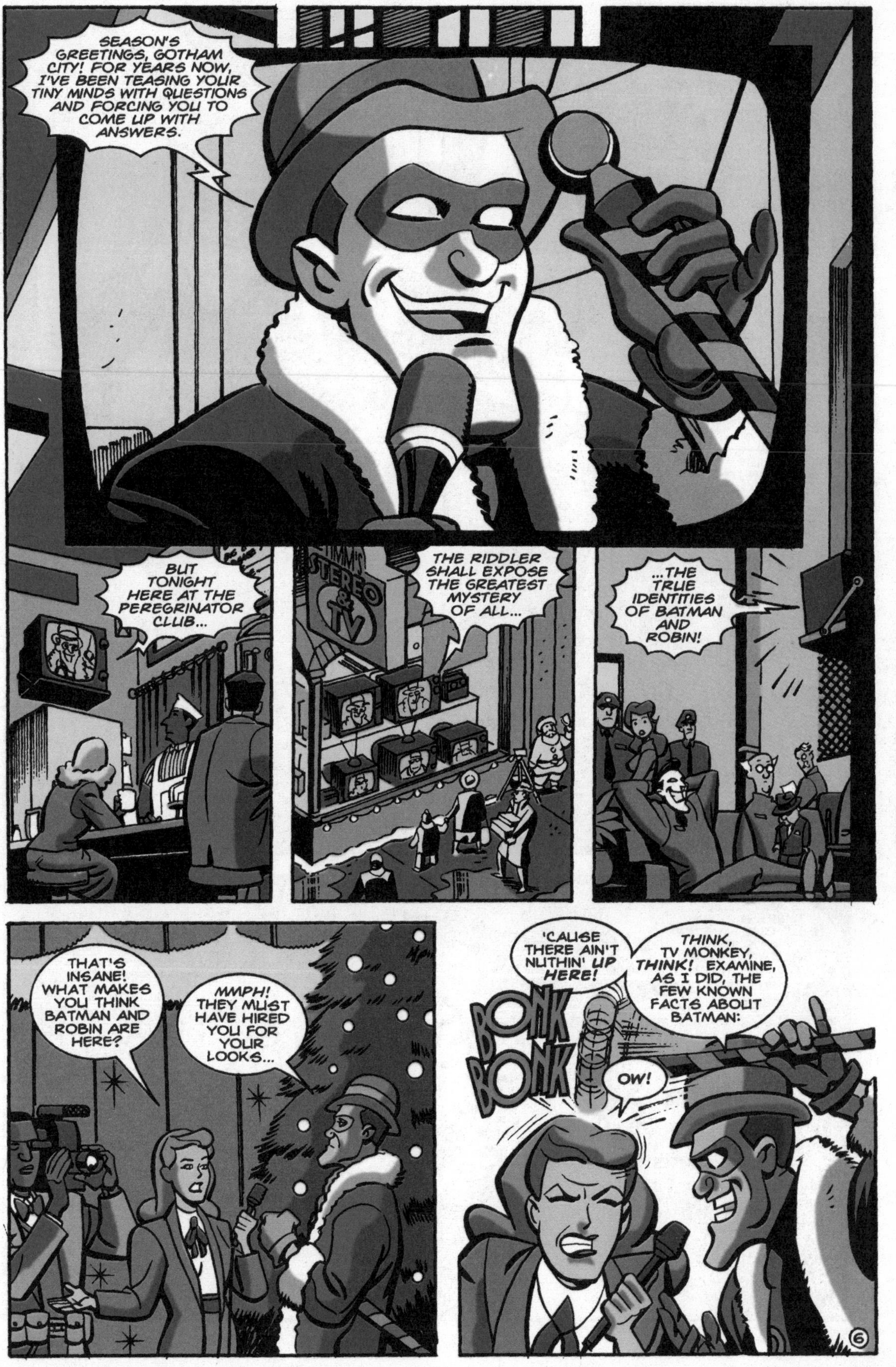
SEASON'S GREETINGS, GOTHAM CITY! FOR YEARS NOW, I'VE BEEN TEASING YOUR TINY MINDS WITH QUESTIONS AND FORCING YOU TO COME UP WITH ANSWERS.
BUT TONIGHT HERE AT THE PEREGRINATOR CLUB...
STEREO & TV
THE RIDDLER SHALL EXPOSE THE GREATEST MYSTERY OF ALL...
...THE TRUE IDENTITIES OF BATMAN AND ROBIN!
THAT'S INSANE! WHAT MAKES YOU THINK BATMAN AND ROBIN ARE HERE?
MMPH! THEY MUST HAVE HIRED YOU FOR YOUR LOOKS...
'CAUSE THERE AIN'T NUTHIN' UP HERE!
BONK BONK
OW!
THINK, TV MONKEY, THINK! EXAMINE, AS I DID, THE FEW KNOWN FACTS ABOUT BATMAN:

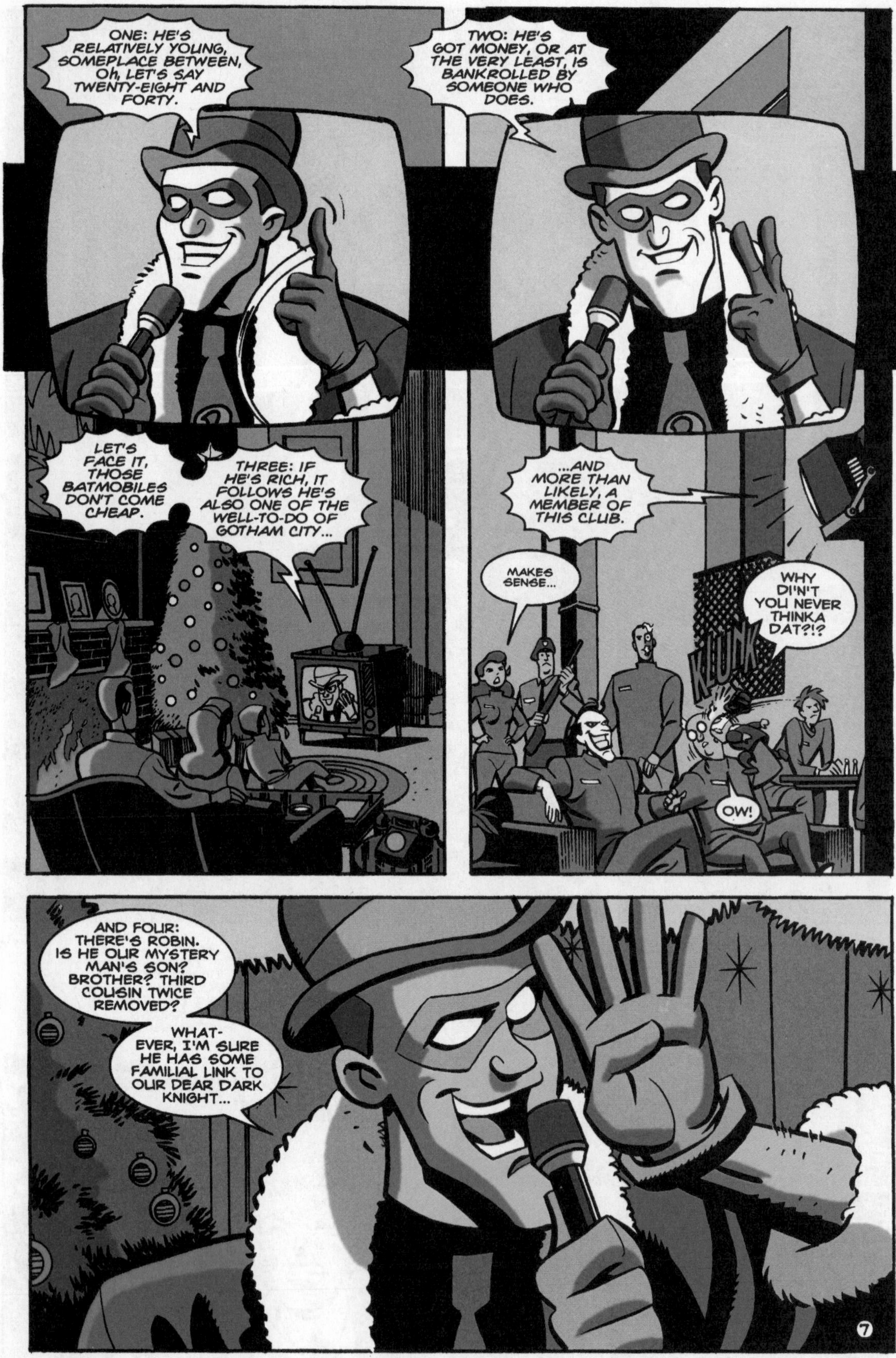
ONE: HE'S RELATIVELY YOUNG, SOMEPLACE BETWEEN, Oh, LET'S SAY TWENTY-EIGHT AND FORTY.
TWO: HE'S GOT MONEY, OR AT THE VERY LEAST, IS BANKROLLED BY SOMEONE WHO DOES.
LET'S FACE IT, THOSE BATMOBILES DON'T COME CHEAP.
THREE: IF HE'S RICH, IT FOLLOWS HE'S ALSO ONE OF THE WELL-TO-DO OF GOTHAM CITY...
...AND MORE THAN LIKELY, A MEMBER OF THIS CLUB.
MAKES SENSE...
WHY DI'N'T YOU NEVER THINKA DAT?!?
KLUNK
OW!
AND FOUR: THERE'S ROBIN. IS HE OUR MYSTERY MAN'S SON? BROTHER? THIRD COUSIN TWICE REMOVED?
WHAT-EVER, I'M SURE HE HAS SOME FAMILIAL LINK TO OUR DEAR DARK KNIGHT...
7

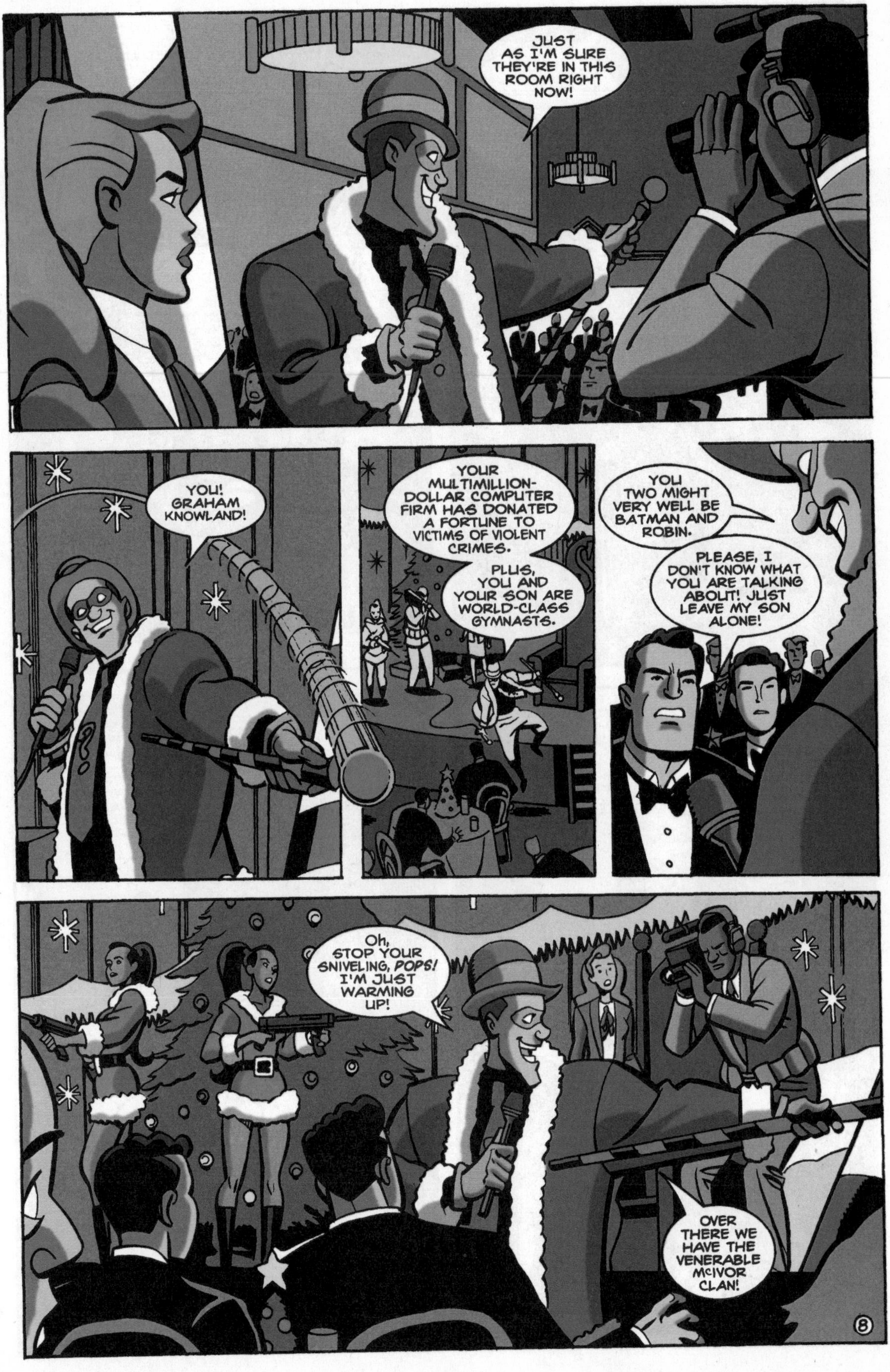
JUST AS I'M SURE THEY'RE IN THIS ROOM RIGHT NOW!
YOU! GRAHAM KNOWLAND!
YOUR MULTIMILLION-DOLLAR COMPUTER FIRM HAS DONATED A FORTUNE TO VICTIMS OF VIOLENT CRIMES.
PLUS, YOU AND YOUR SON ARE WORLD-CLASS GYMNASTS.
YOU TWO MIGHT VERY WELL BE BATMAN AND ROBIN.
PLEASE, I DON'T KNOW WHAT YOU ARE TALKING ABOUT! JUST LEAVE MY SON ALONE!
Oh, STOP YOUR SNIVELING, *POPS!* I'M JUST WARMING UP!
OVER THERE WE HAVE THE VENERABLE McIVOR CLAN!
8

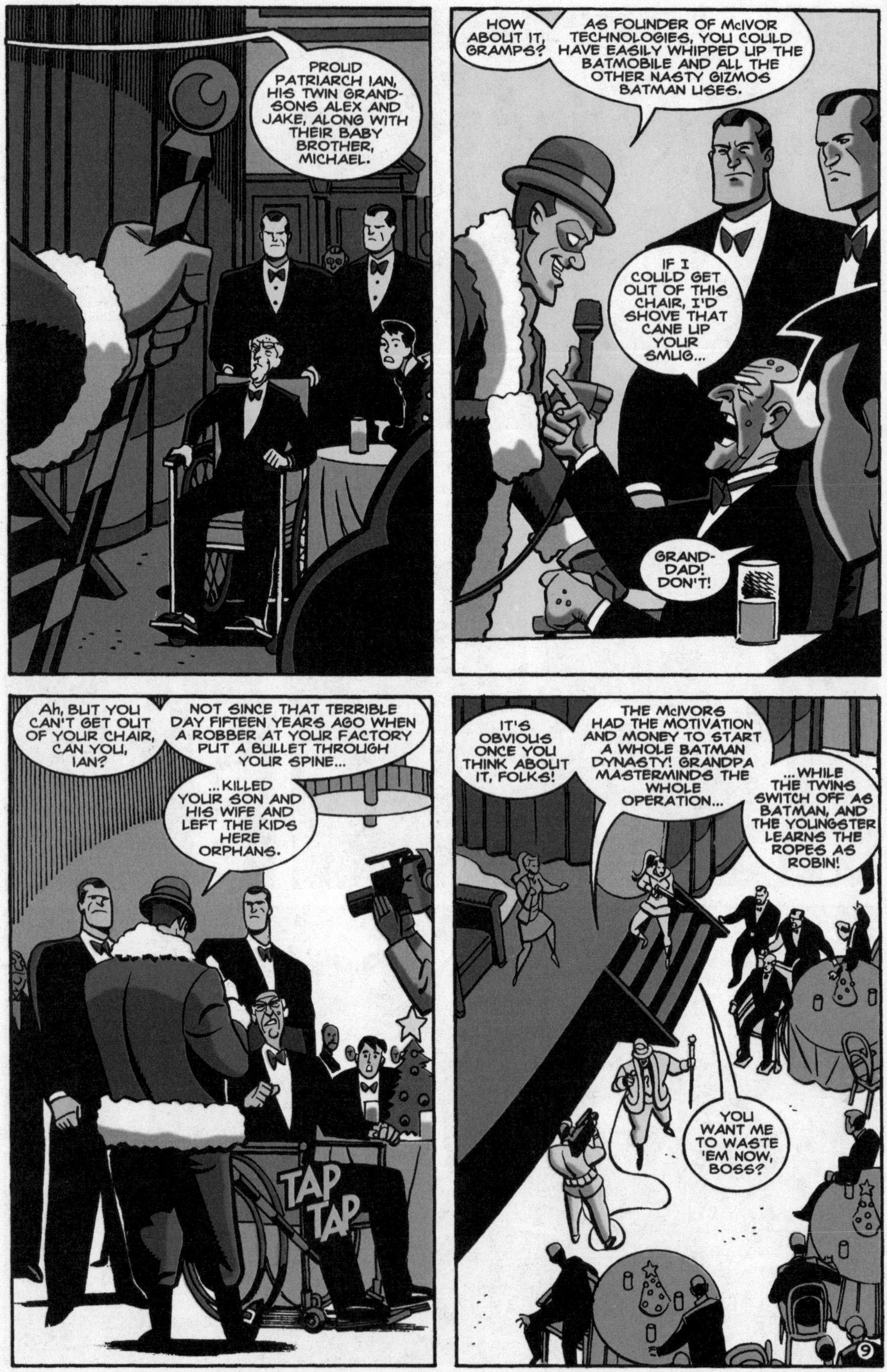
PROUD PATRIARCH IAN, HIS TWIN GRAND-SONS ALEX AND JAKE, ALONG WITH THEIR BABY BROTHER, MICHAEL.
HOW ABOUT IT, GRAMPS?
AS FOUNDER OF McIVOR TECHNOLOGIES, YOU COULD HAVE EASILY WHIPPED UP THE BATMOBILE AND ALL THE OTHER NASTY GIZMOS BATMAN USES.
IF I COULD GET OUT OF THIS CHAIR, I'D SHOVE THAT CANE UP YOUR SMUG...
GRAND-DAD! DON'T!
Ah, BUT YOU CAN'T GET OUT OF YOUR CHAIR, CAN YOU, IAN?
NOT SINCE THAT TERRIBLE DAY FIFTEEN YEARS AGO WHEN A ROBBER AT YOUR FACTORY PUT A BULLET THROUGH YOUR SPINE...
...KILLED YOUR SON AND HIS WIFE AND LEFT THE KIDS HERE ORPHANS.
TAP TAP
IT'S OBVIOUS ONCE YOU THINK ABOUT IT, FOLKS!
THE McIVORS HAD THE MOTIVATION AND MONEY TO START A WHOLE BATMAN DYNASTY! GRANDPA MASTERMINDS THE WHOLE OPERATION...
...WHILE THE TWINS SWITCH OFF AS BATMAN, AND THE YOUNGSTER LEARNS THE ROPES AS ROBIN!
YOU WANT ME TO WASTE 'EM NOW, BOSS?
9

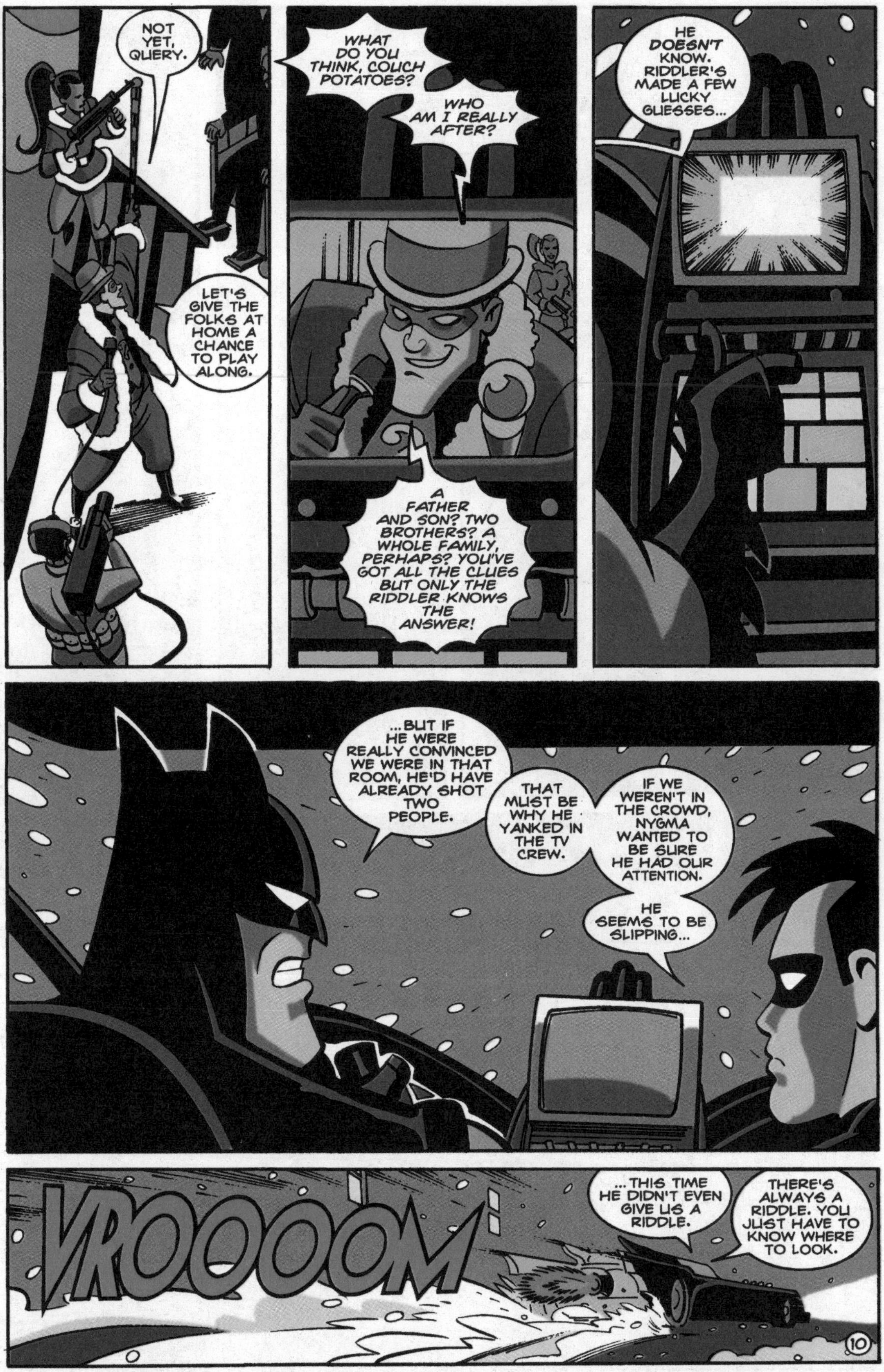
NOT YET, QUERY.
LET'S GIVE THE FOLKS AT HOME A CHANCE TO PLAY ALONG.
WHAT DO YOU THINK, COUCH POTATOES?
WHO AM I REALLY AFTER?
A FATHER AND SON? TWO BROTHERS? A WHOLE FAMILY, PERHAPS? YOU'VE GOT ALL THE CLUES BUT ONLY THE RIDDLER KNOWS THE ANSWER!
HE DOESN'T KNOW. RIDDLER'S MADE A FEW LUCKY GUESSES...
...BUT IF HE WERE REALLY CONVINCED WE WERE IN THAT ROOM, HE'D HAVE ALREADY SHOT TWO PEOPLE.
THAT MUST BE WHY HE YANKED IN THE TV CREW.
IF WE WEREN'T IN THE CROWD, NYGMA WANTED TO BE SURE HE HAD OUR ATTENTION.
HE SEEMS TO BE SLIPPING...
VROOOOM
...THIS TIME HE DIDN'T EVEN GIVE US A RIDDLE.
THERE'S ALWAYS A RIDDLE. YOU JUST HAVE TO KNOW WHERE TO LOOK.
10

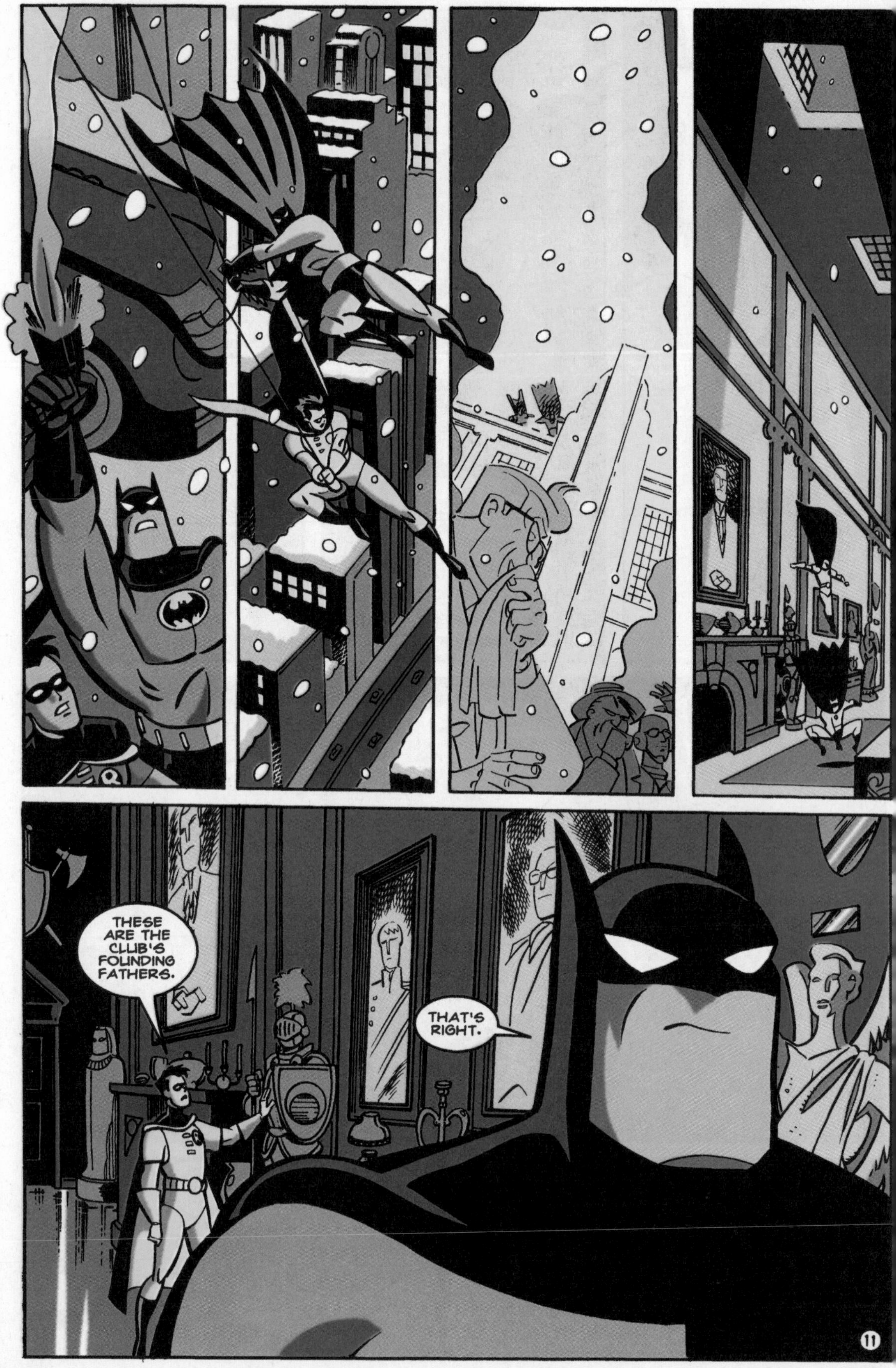
THESE ARE THE CLUB'S FOUNDING FATHERS.
THAT'S RIGHT.
11

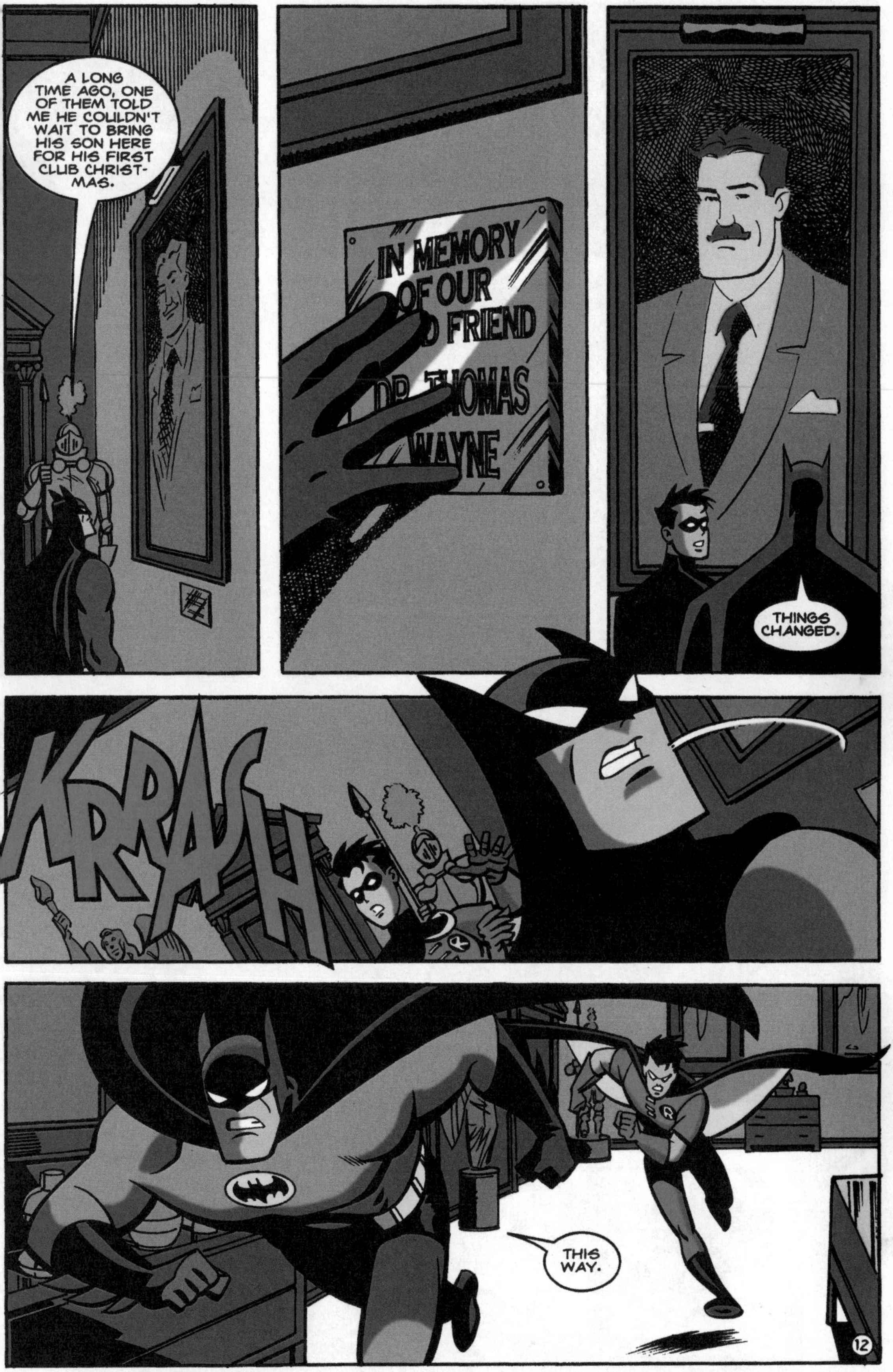
A LONG TIME AGO, ONE OF THEM TOLD ME HE COULDN'T WAIT TO BRING HIS SON HERE FOR HIS FIRST CLUB CHRIST-MAS.
IN MEMORY OF OUR
FRIEND
DR. THOMAS WAYNE
THINGS CHANGED.
KRRASH
THIS WAY.
12

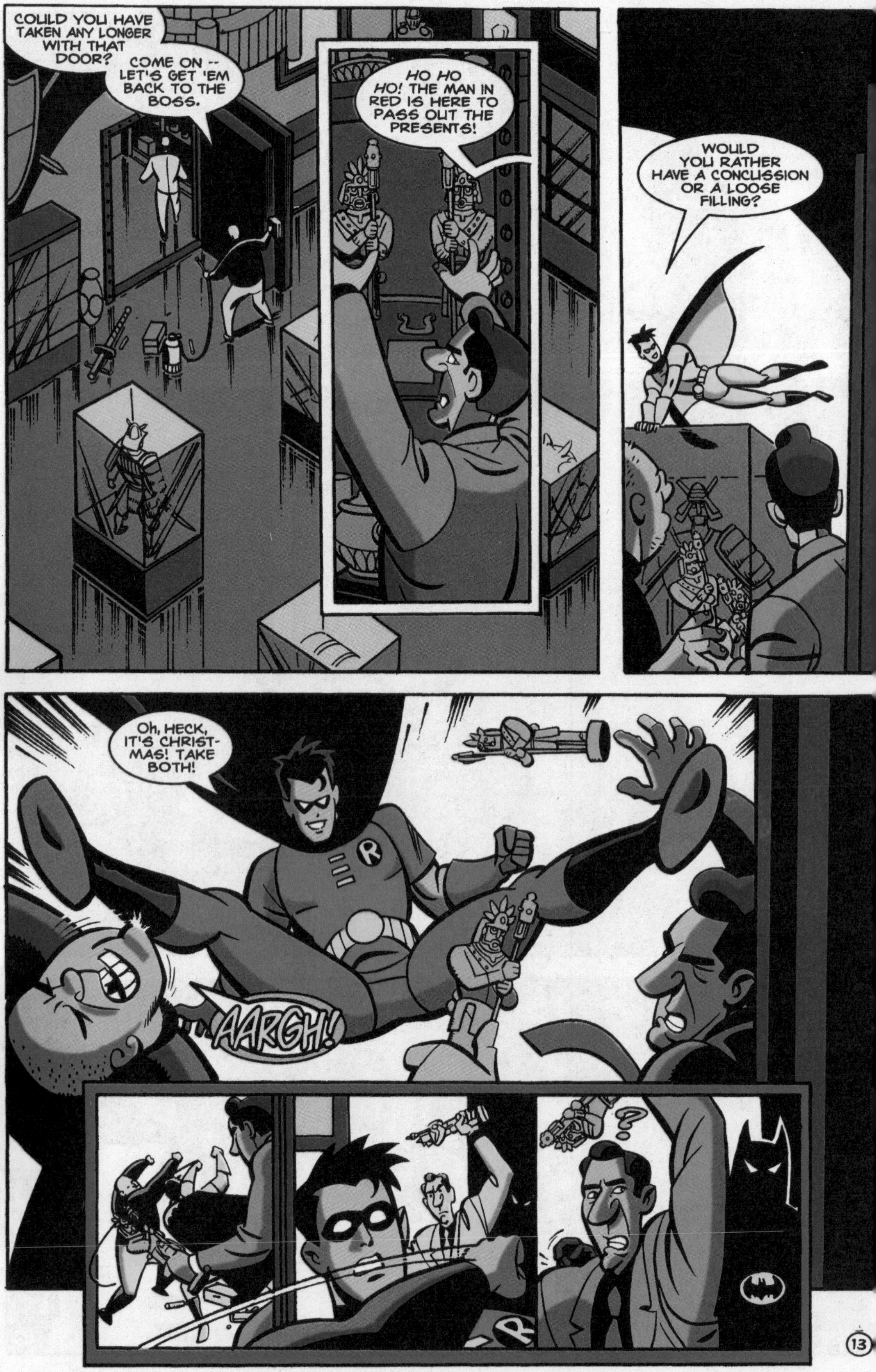

COULD YOU HAVE TAKEN ANY LONGER WITH THAT DOOR?
COME ON -- LET'S GET 'EM BACK TO THE BOSS.
HO HO HO! THE MAN IN RED IS HERE TO PASS OUT THE PRESENTS!
WOULD YOU RATHER HAVE A CONCUSSION OR A LOOSE FILLING?
Oh, HECK, IT'S CHRIST-MAS! TAKE BOTH!
AARGH!
?
13

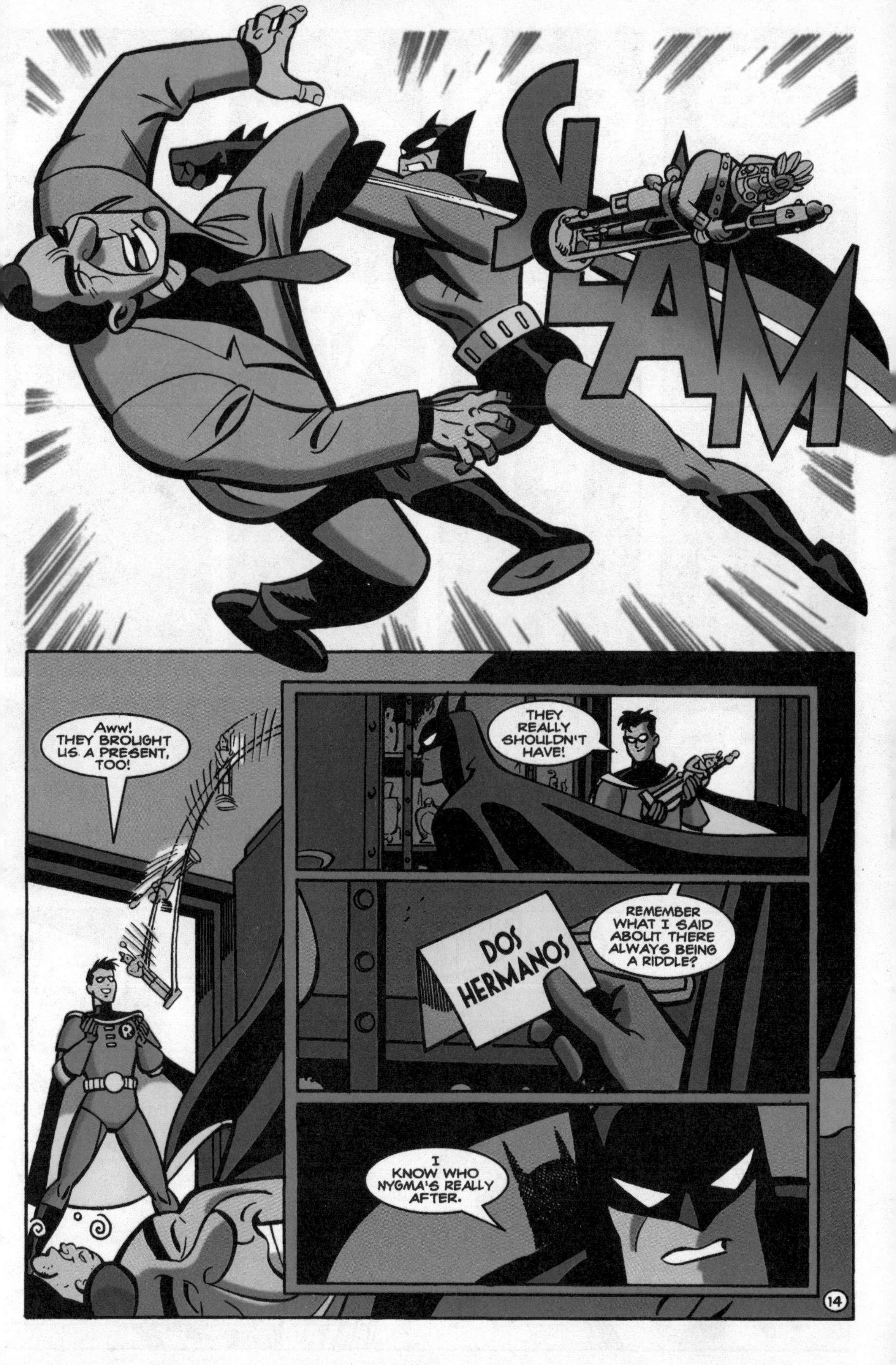
SLAM
Aww! THEY BROUGHT US A PRESENT, TOO!
THEY REALLY SHOULDN'T HAVE!
DOS HERMANOS
REMEMBER WHAT I SAID ABOUT THERE ALWAYS BEING A RIDDLE?
I KNOW WHO NYGMA'S REALLY AFTER.
14

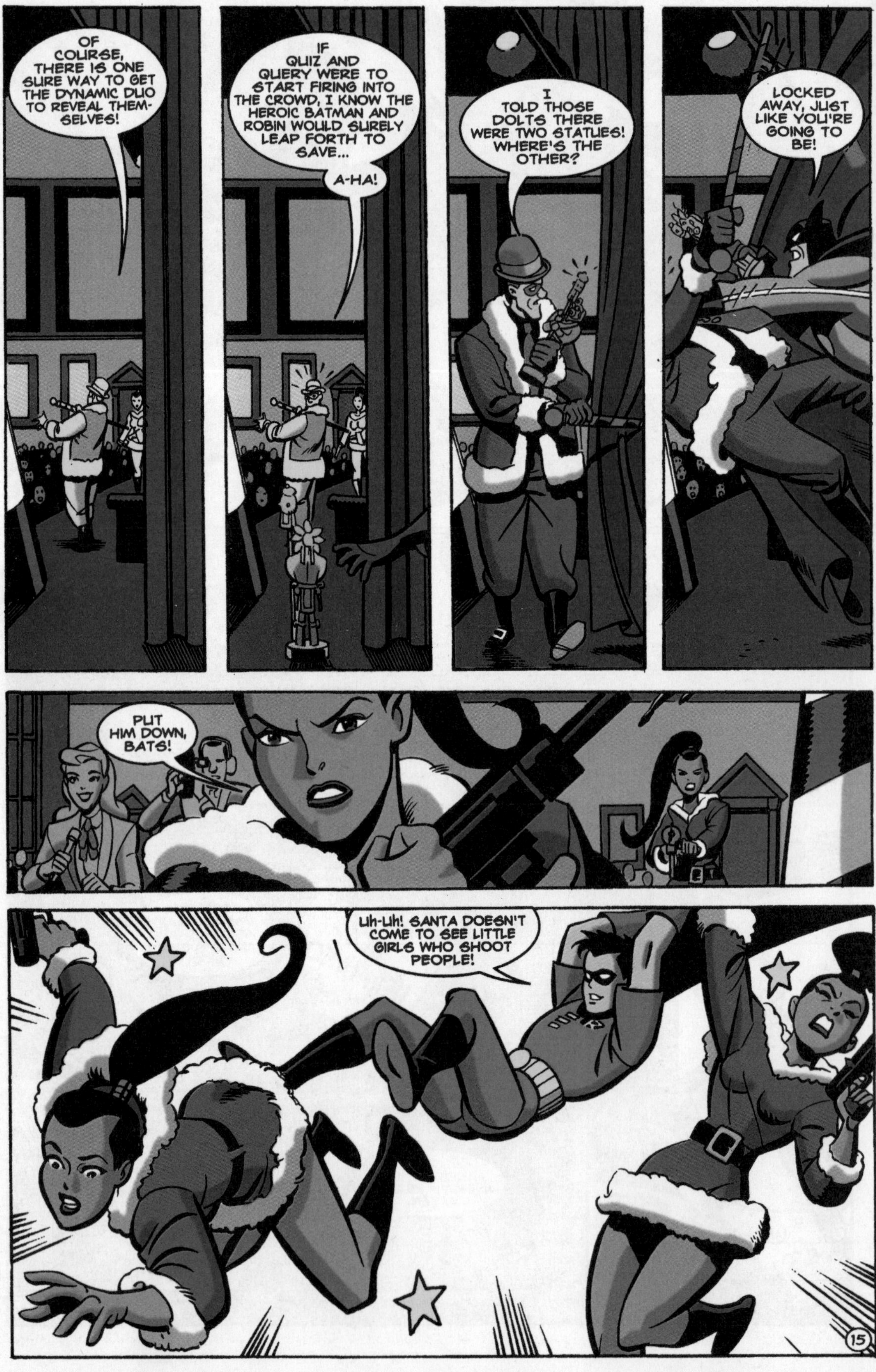
OF COURSE, THERE IS ONE SURE WAY TO GET THE DYNAMIC DUO TO REVEAL THEM-SELVES!
IF QUIZ AND QUERY WERE TO START FIRING INTO THE CROWD, I KNOW THE HEROIC BATMAN AND ROBIN WOULD SURELY LEAP FORTH TO SAVE...
A-HA!
I TOLD THOSE DOLTS THERE WERE TWO STATUES! WHERE'S THE OTHER?
LOCKED AWAY, JUST LIKE YOU'RE GOING TO BE!
PUT HIM DOWN, BATS!
Uh-Uh! SANTA DOESN'T COME TO SEE LITTLE GIRLS WHO SHOOT PEOPLE!
15

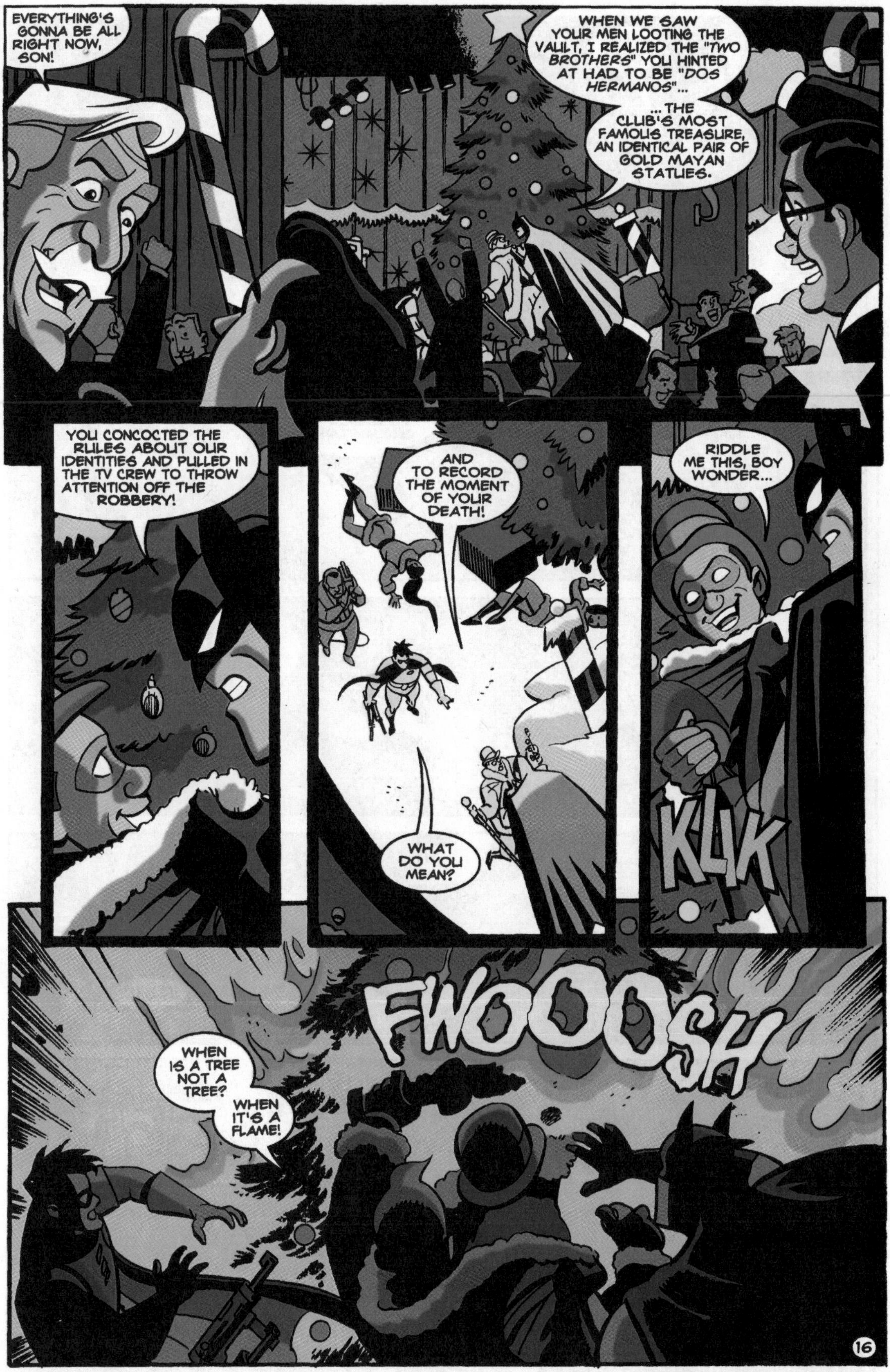
EVERYTHING'S GONNA BE ALL RIGHT NOW, SON!
WHEN WE SAW YOUR MEN LOOTING THE VAULT, I REALIZED THE "TWO BROTHERS" YOU HINTED AT HAD TO BE "DOS HERMANOS"...
...THE CLUB'S MOST FAMOUS TREASURE, AN IDENTICAL PAIR OF GOLD MAYAN STATUES.
YOU CONCOCTED THE RULES ABOUT OUR IDENTITIES AND PULLED IN THE TV CREW TO THROW ATTENTION OFF THE ROBBERY!
AND TO RECORD THE MOMENT OF YOUR DEATH!
WHAT DO YOU MEAN?
RIDDLE ME THIS, BOY WONDER...
KLIK
FWOOOSH
WHEN IS A TREE NOT A TREE?
WHEN IT'S A FLAME!
16

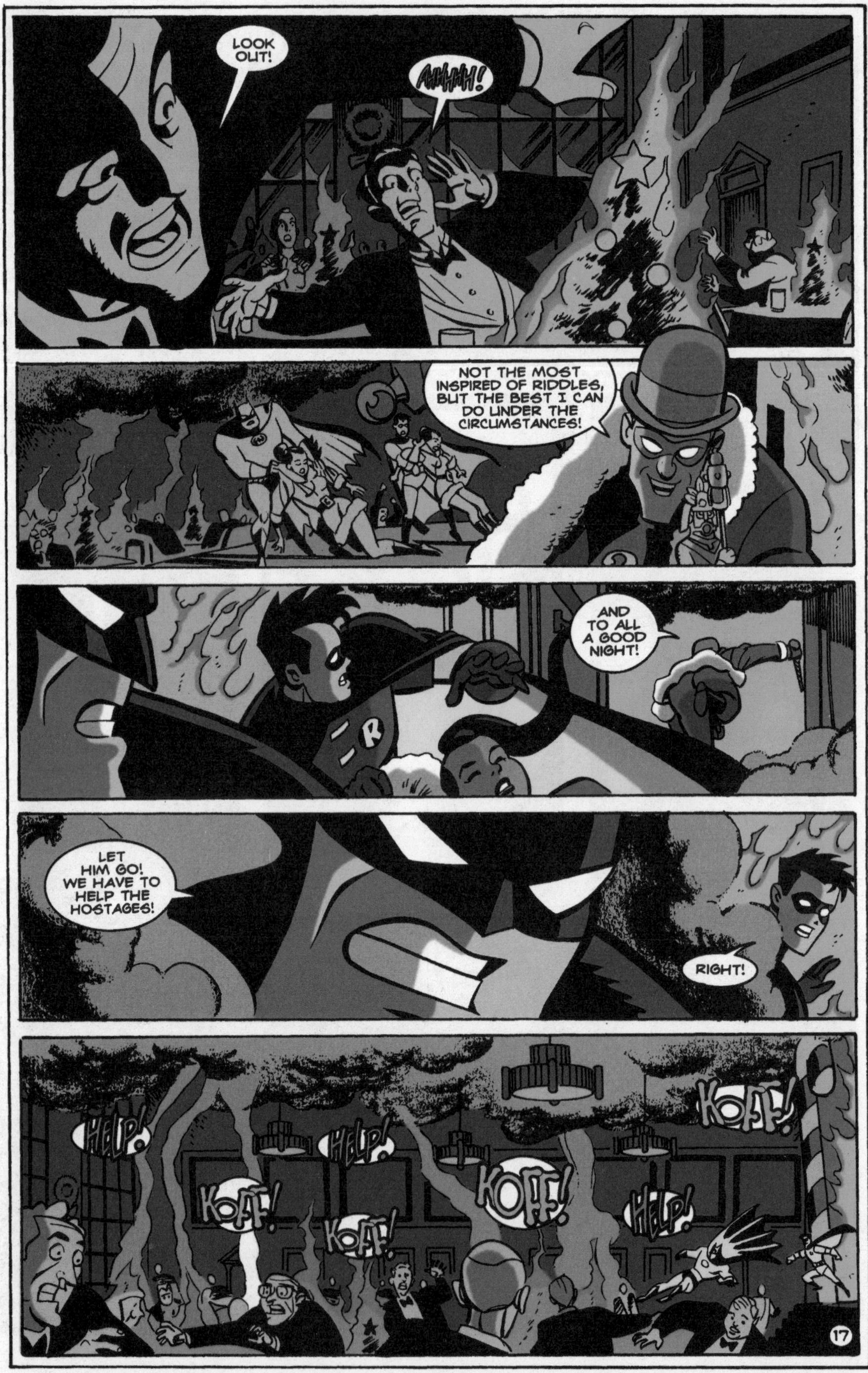
LOOK OUT!
AHHHH!
NOT THE MOST INSPIRED OF RIDDLES, BUT THE BEST I CAN DO UNDER THE CIRCUMSTANCES!
AND TO ALL A GOOD NIGHT!
LET HIM GO! WE HAVE TO HELP THE HOSTAGES!
RIGHT!
HELP!
HELP!
KOFF!
KOFF!
KOFF!
HELP!
KOFF!
17

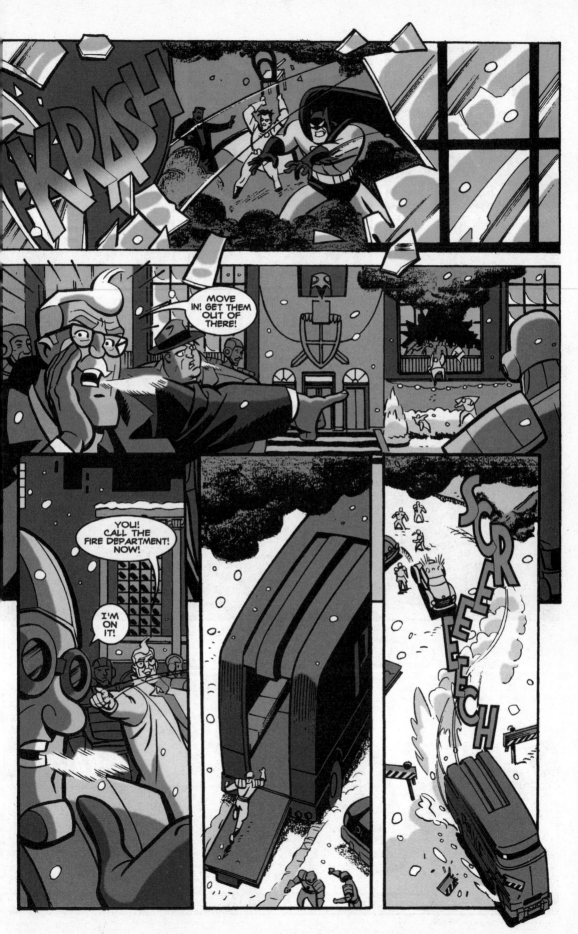

KRASH

MOVE IN! GET THEM OUT OF THERE!

YOU! CALL THE FIRE DEPARTMENT! NOW!

I'M ON IT!

SCREEECH

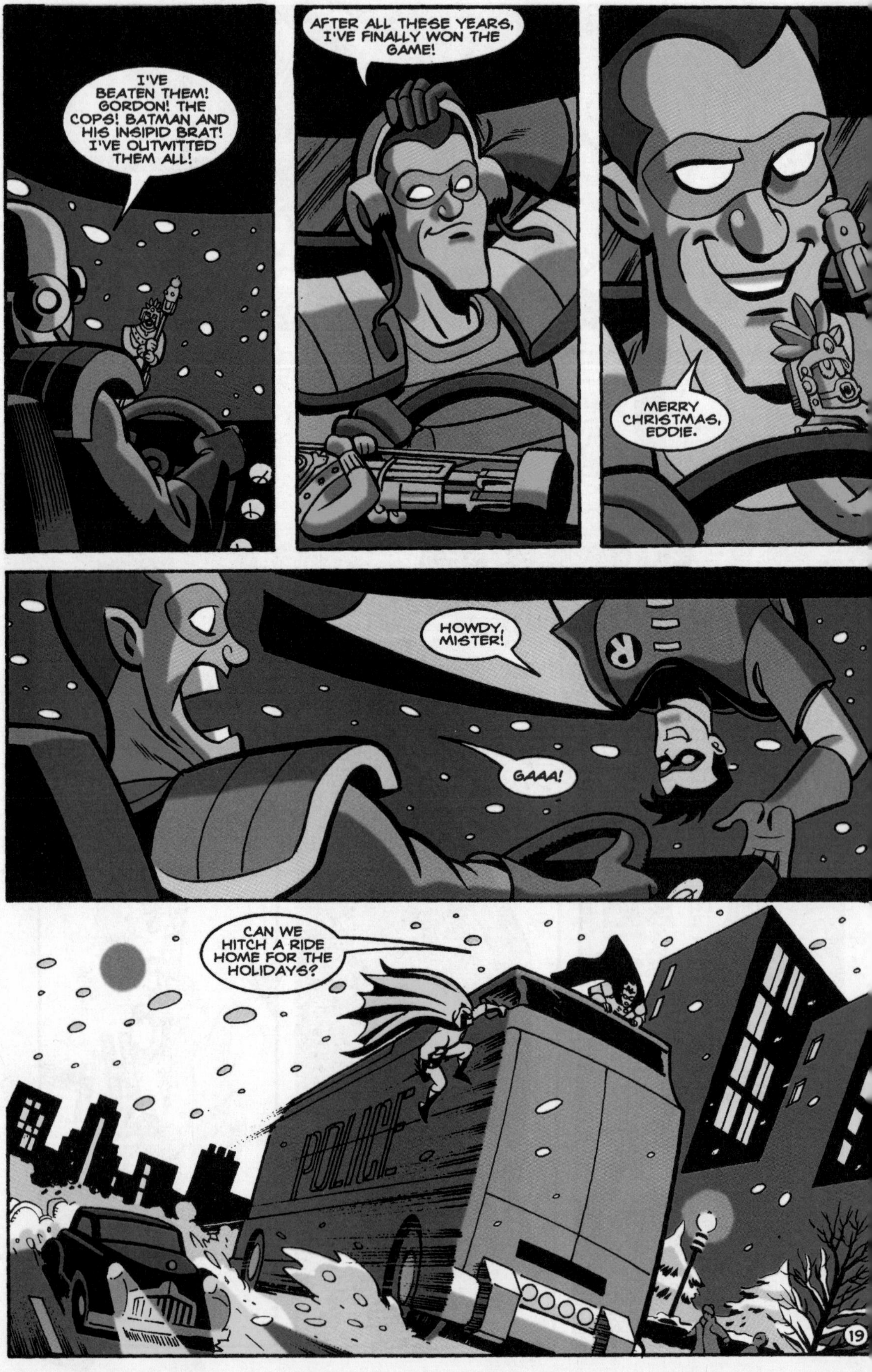
I'VE BEATEN THEM! GORDON! THE COPS! BATMAN AND HIS INSIPID BRAT! I'VE OUTWITTED THEM ALL!
AFTER ALL THESE YEARS, I'VE FINALLY WON THE GAME!
MERRY CHRISTMAS, EDDIE.
HOWDY, MISTER!
GAAA!
CAN WE HITCH A RIDE HOME FOR THE HOLIDAYS?
POLICE

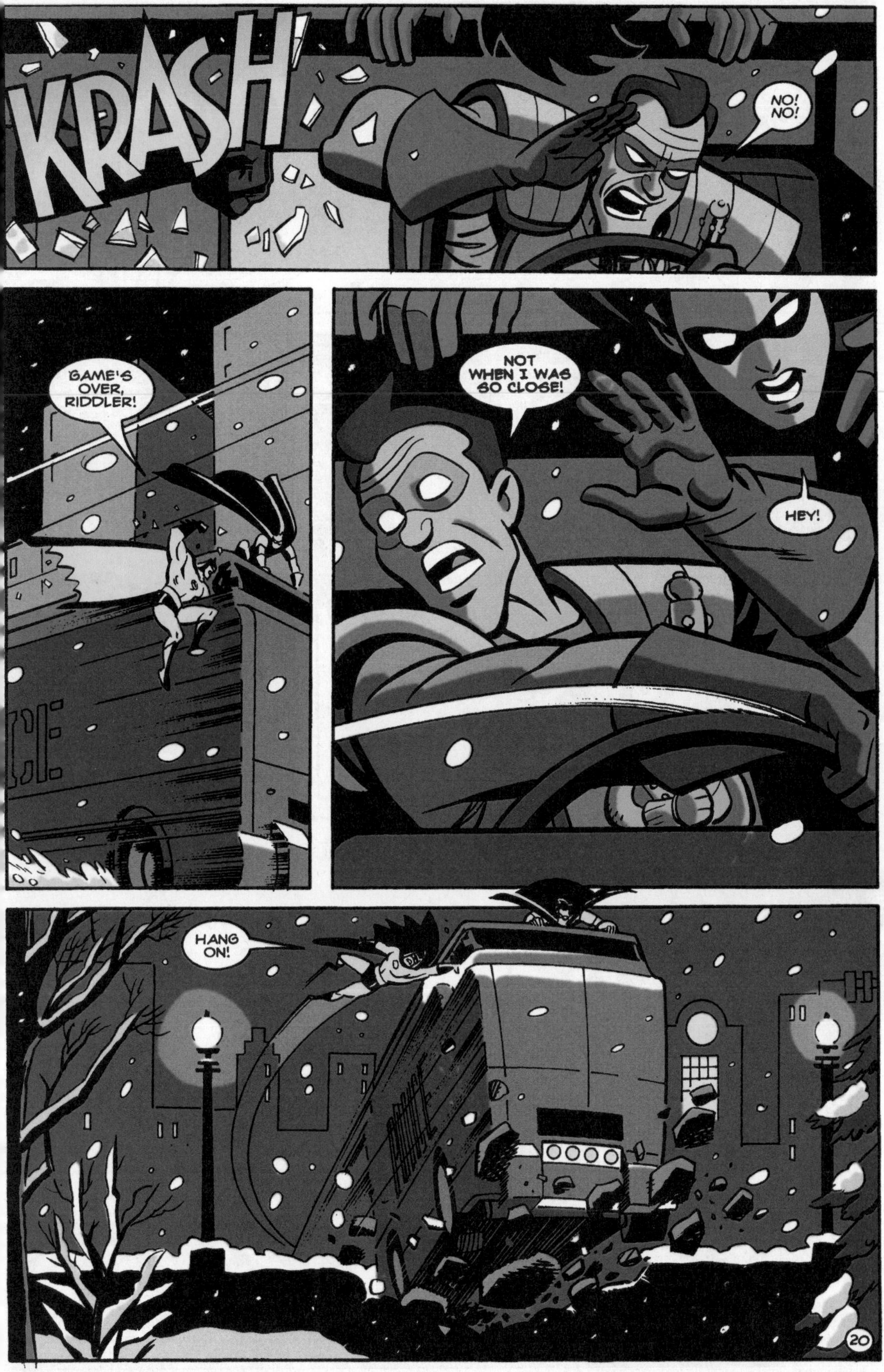
KRASH
NO! NO!
GAME'S OVER, RIDDLER!
NOT WHEN I WAS SO CLOSE!
HEY!
HANG ON!
20

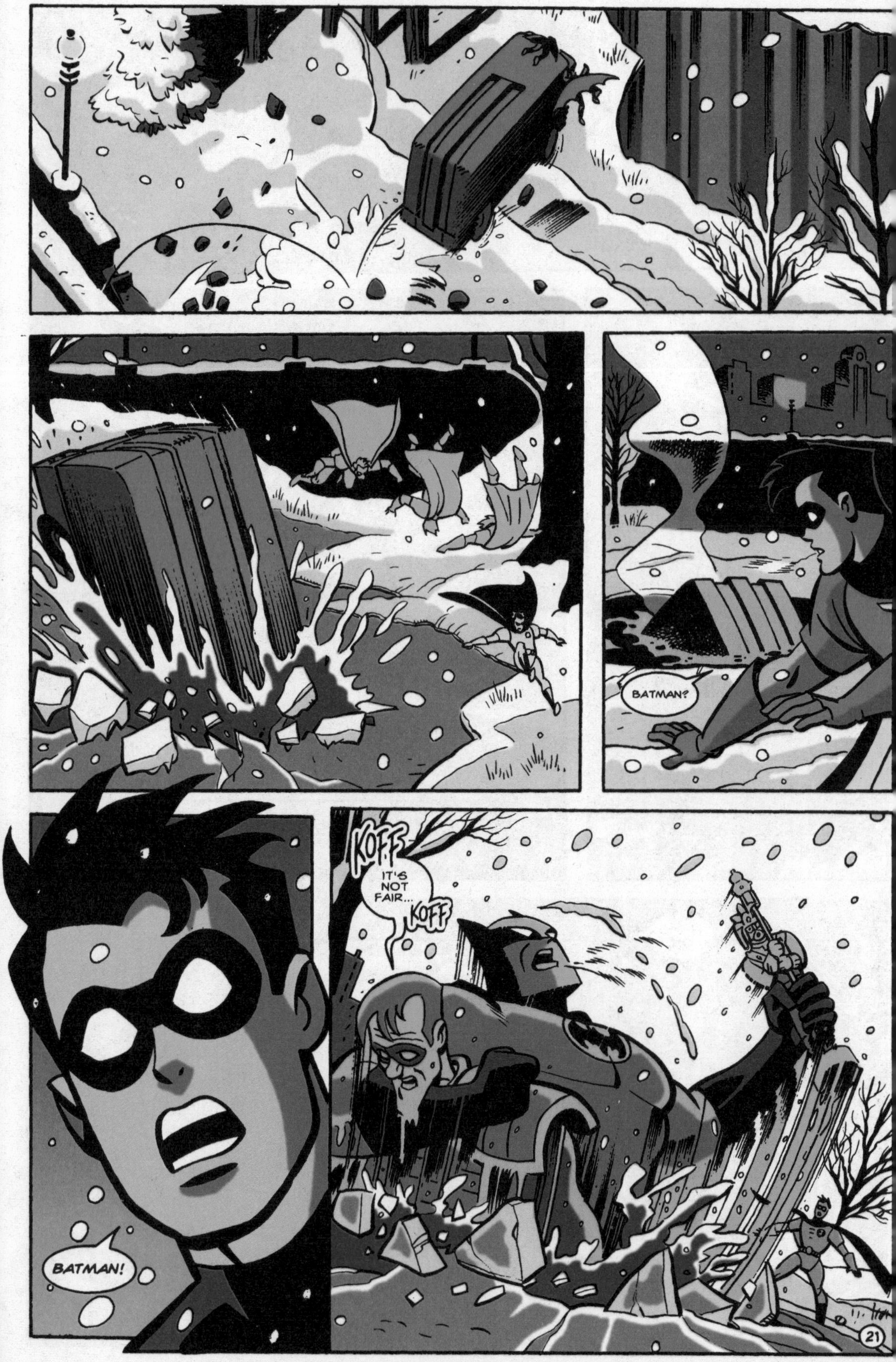
BATMAN?
BATMAN!
KOFF
IT'S NOT FAIR...
KOFF
21

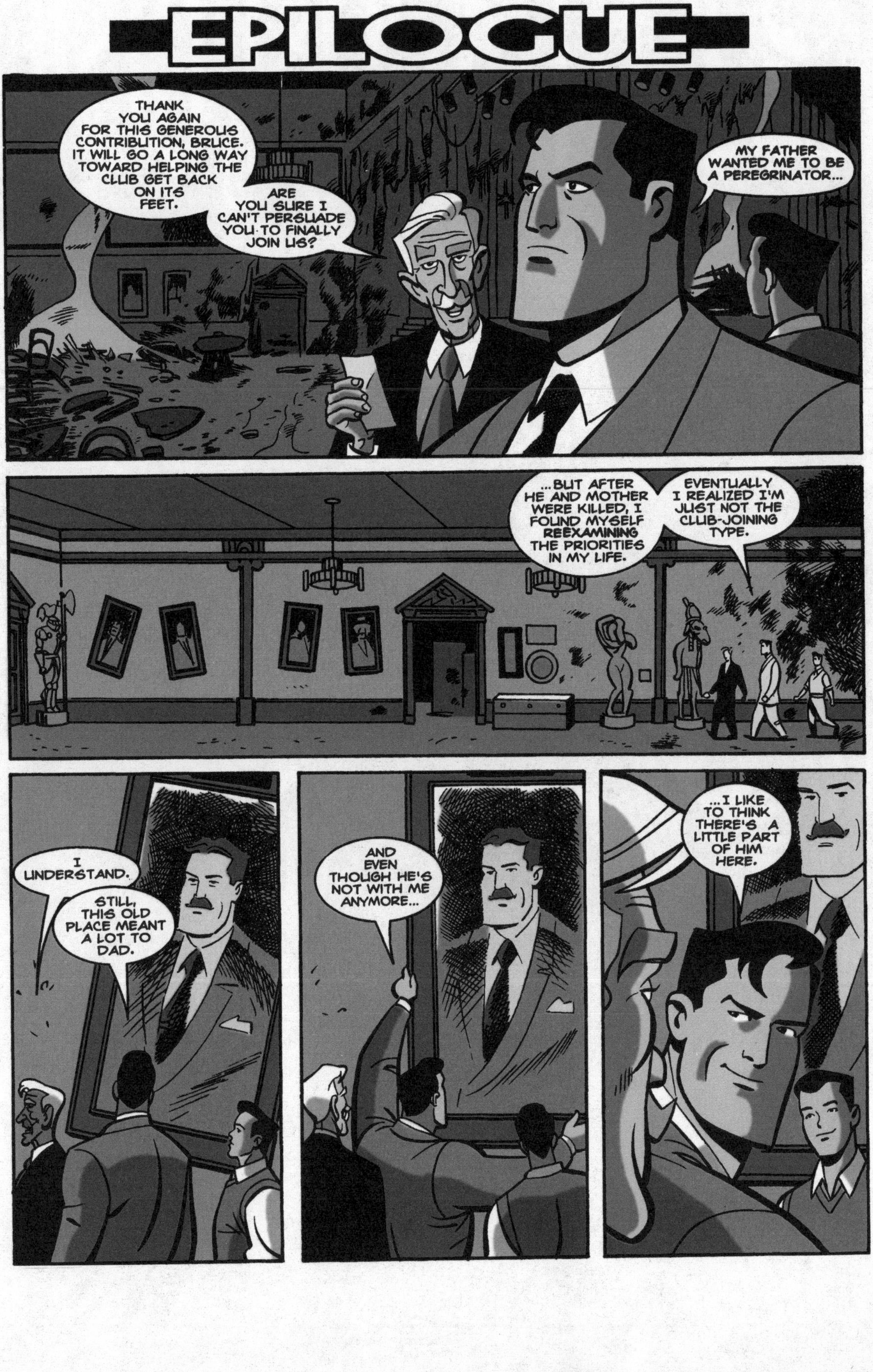
EPILOGUE
THANK YOU AGAIN FOR THIS GENEROUS CONTRIBUTION, BRUCE. IT WILL GO A LONG WAY TOWARD HELPING THE CLUB GET BACK ON ITS FEET.
ARE YOU SURE I CAN'T PERSUADE YOU TO FINALLY JOIN US?
MY FATHER WANTED ME TO BE A PEREGRINATOR...
...BUT AFTER HE AND MOTHER WERE KILLED, I FOUND MYSELF REEXAMINING THE PRIORITIES IN MY LIFE.
EVENTUALLY I REALIZED I'M JUST NOT THE CLUB-JOINING TYPE.
I UNDERSTAND.
STILL, THIS OLD PLACE MEANT A LOT TO DAD.
AND EVEN THOUGH HE'S NOT WITH ME ANYMORE...
...I LIKE TO THINK THERE'S A LITTLE PART OF HIM HERE.

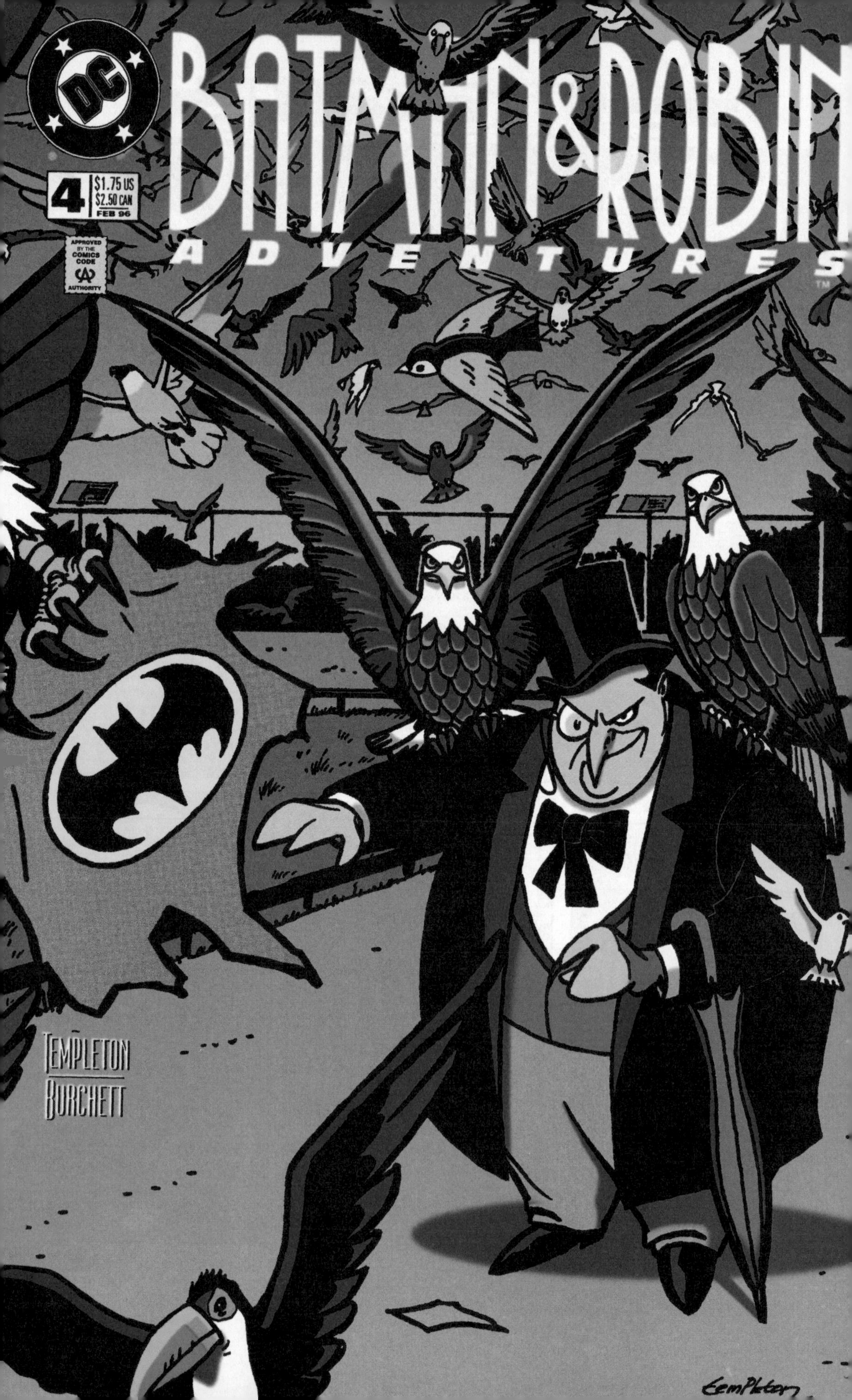
DC
BATMAN & ROBIN
ADVENTURES
4
$1.75 US
$2.50 CAN
FEB 96
APPROVED BY THE COMICS CODE AUTHORITY
TEMPLETON
BURCHETT
Templeton

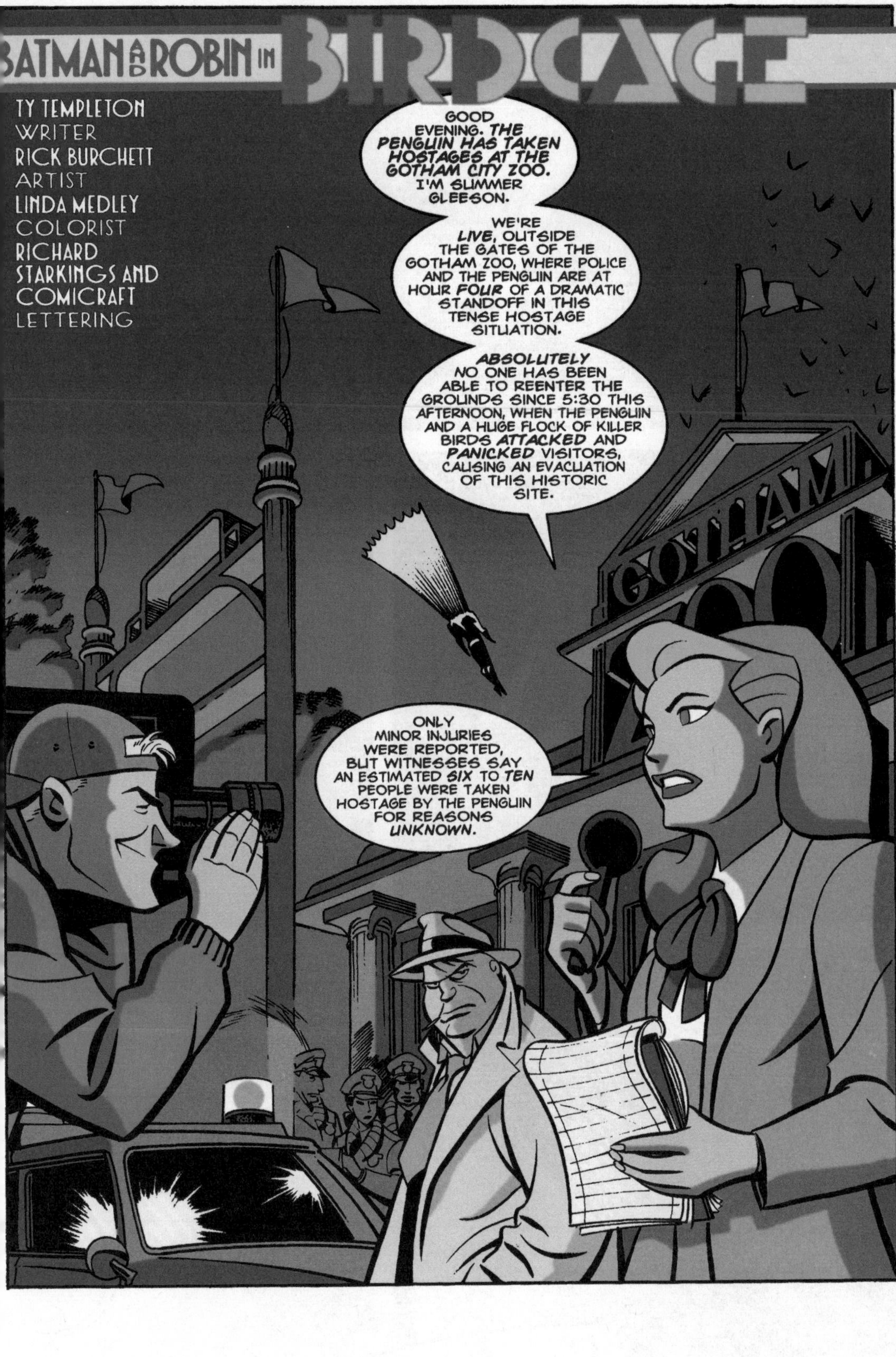
BATMAN AND ROBIN IN
BIRDCAGE
TY TEMPLETON WRITER
RICK BURCHETT ARTIST
LINDA MEDLEY COLORIST
RICHARD STARKINGS AND COMICRAFT LETTERING
GOOD EVENING. THE PENGUIN HAS TAKEN HOSTAGES AT THE GOTHAM CITY ZOO. I'M SUMMER GLEESON.
WE'RE LIVE, OUTSIDE THE GATES OF THE GOTHAM ZOO, WHERE POLICE AND THE PENGUIN ARE AT HOUR FOUR OF A DRAMATIC STANDOFF IN THIS TENSE HOSTAGE SITUATION.
ABSOLUTELY NO ONE HAS BEEN ABLE TO REENTER THE GROUNDS SINCE 5:30 THIS AFTERNOON, WHEN THE PENGUIN AND A HUGE FLOCK OF KILLER BIRDS ATTACKED AND PANICKED VISITORS, CAUSING AN EVACUATION OF THIS HISTORIC SITE.
GOTHAM ZOO
ONLY MINOR INJURIES WERE REPORTED, BUT WITNESSES SAY AN ESTIMATED SIX TO TEN PEOPLE WERE TAKEN HOSTAGE BY THE PENGUIN FOR REASONS UNKNOWN.

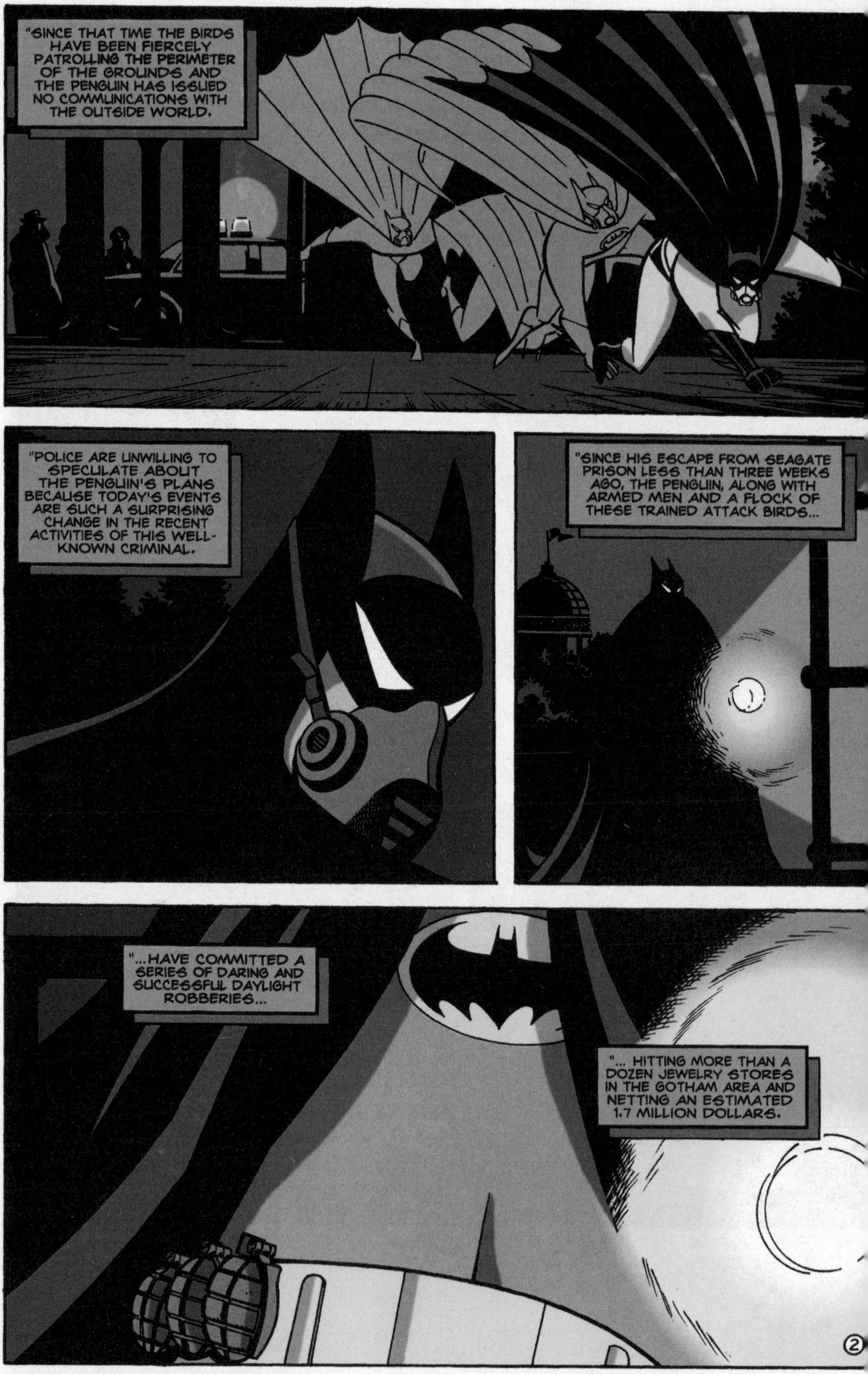
"SINCE THAT TIME THE BIRDS HAVE BEEN FIERCELY PATROLLING THE PERIMETER OF THE GROUNDS AND THE PENGUIN HAS ISSUED NO COMMUNICATIONS WITH THE OUTSIDE WORLD.
"POLICE ARE UNWILLING TO SPECULATE ABOUT THE PENGUIN'S PLANS BECAUSE TODAY'S EVENTS ARE SUCH A SURPRISING CHANGE IN THE RECENT ACTIVITIES OF THIS WELL-KNOWN CRIMINAL.
"SINCE HIS ESCAPE FROM SEAGATE PRISON LESS THAN THREE WEEKS AGO, THE PENGUIN, ALONG WITH ARMED MEN AND A FLOCK OF THESE TRAINED ATTACK BIRDS...
"...HAVE COMMITTED A SERIES OF DARING AND SUCCESSFUL DAYLIGHT ROBBERIES...
"... HITTING MORE THAN A DOZEN JEWELRY STORES IN THE GOTHAM AREA AND NETTING AN ESTIMATED 1.7 MILLION DOLLARS.
2

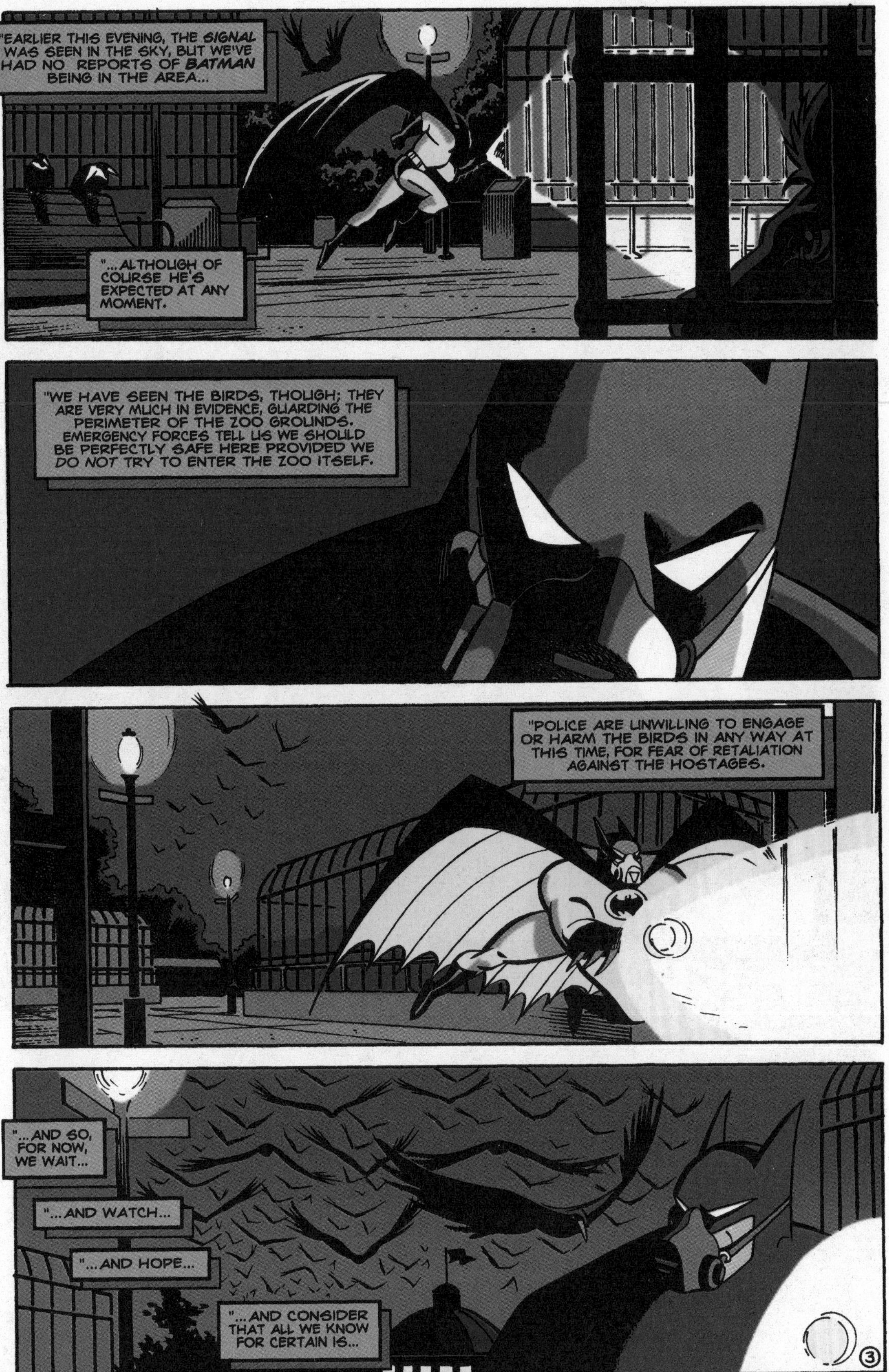
"EARLIER THIS EVENING, THE SIGNAL WAS SEEN IN THE SKY, BUT WE'VE HAD NO REPORTS OF BATMAN BEING IN THE AREA...
"...ALTHOUGH OF COURSE HE'S EXPECTED AT ANY MOMENT.
"WE HAVE SEEN THE BIRDS, THOUGH; THEY ARE VERY MUCH IN EVIDENCE, GUARDING THE PERIMETER OF THE ZOO GROUNDS. EMERGENCY FORCES TELL US WE SHOULD BE PERFECTLY SAFE HERE PROVIDED WE DO NOT TRY TO ENTER THE ZOO ITSELF.
"POLICE ARE UNWILLING TO ENGAGE OR HARM THE BIRDS IN ANY WAY AT THIS TIME, FOR FEAR OF RETALIATION AGAINST THE HOSTAGES.
"...AND SO, FOR NOW, WE WAIT...
"...AND WATCH...
"...AND HOPE...
"...AND CONSIDER THAT ALL WE KNOW FOR CERTAIN IS...
3

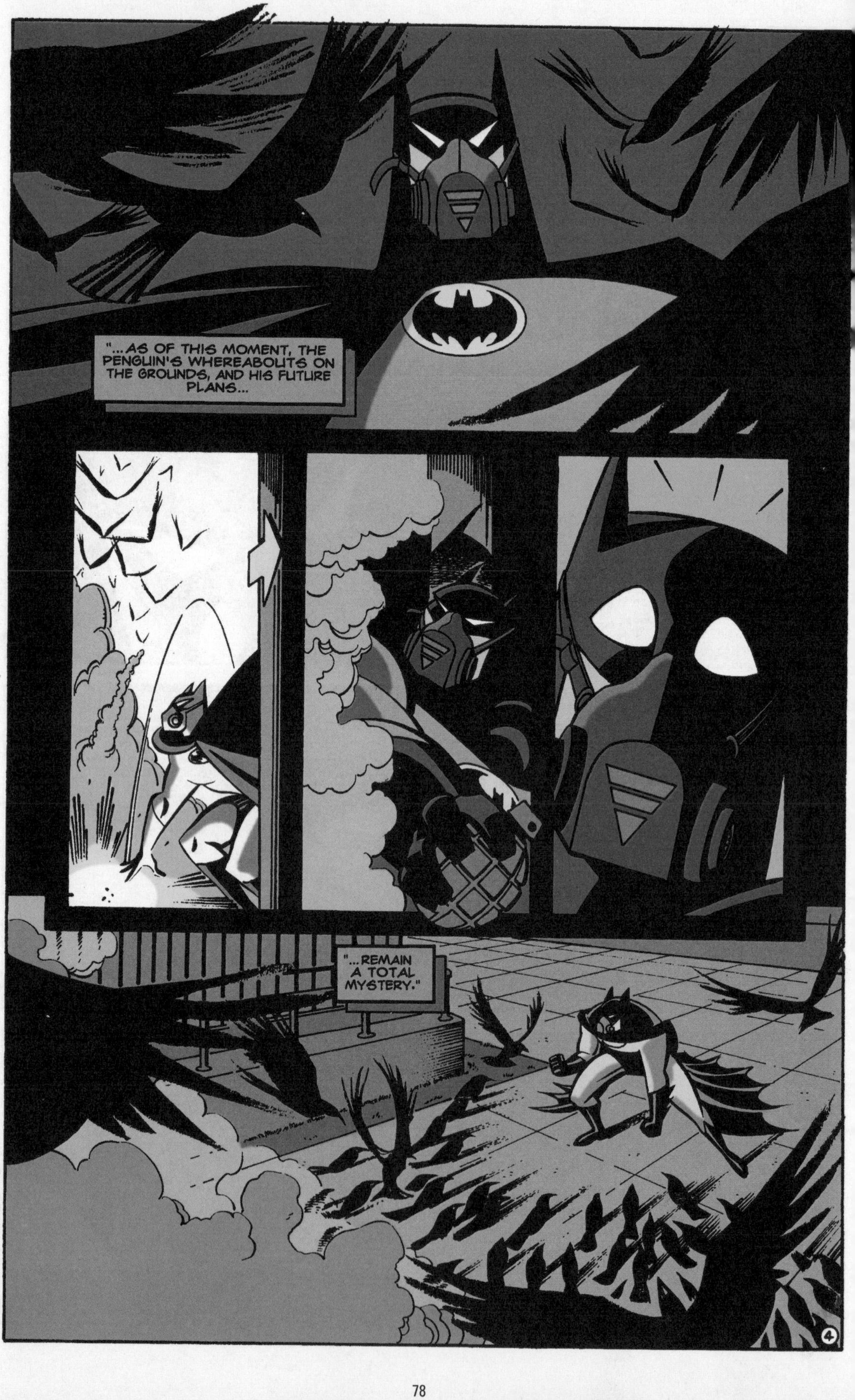
"...AS OF THIS MOMENT, THE PENGUIN'S WHEREABOUTS ON THE GROUNDS, AND HIS FUTURE PLANS...
"...REMAIN A TOTAL MYSTERY."
4

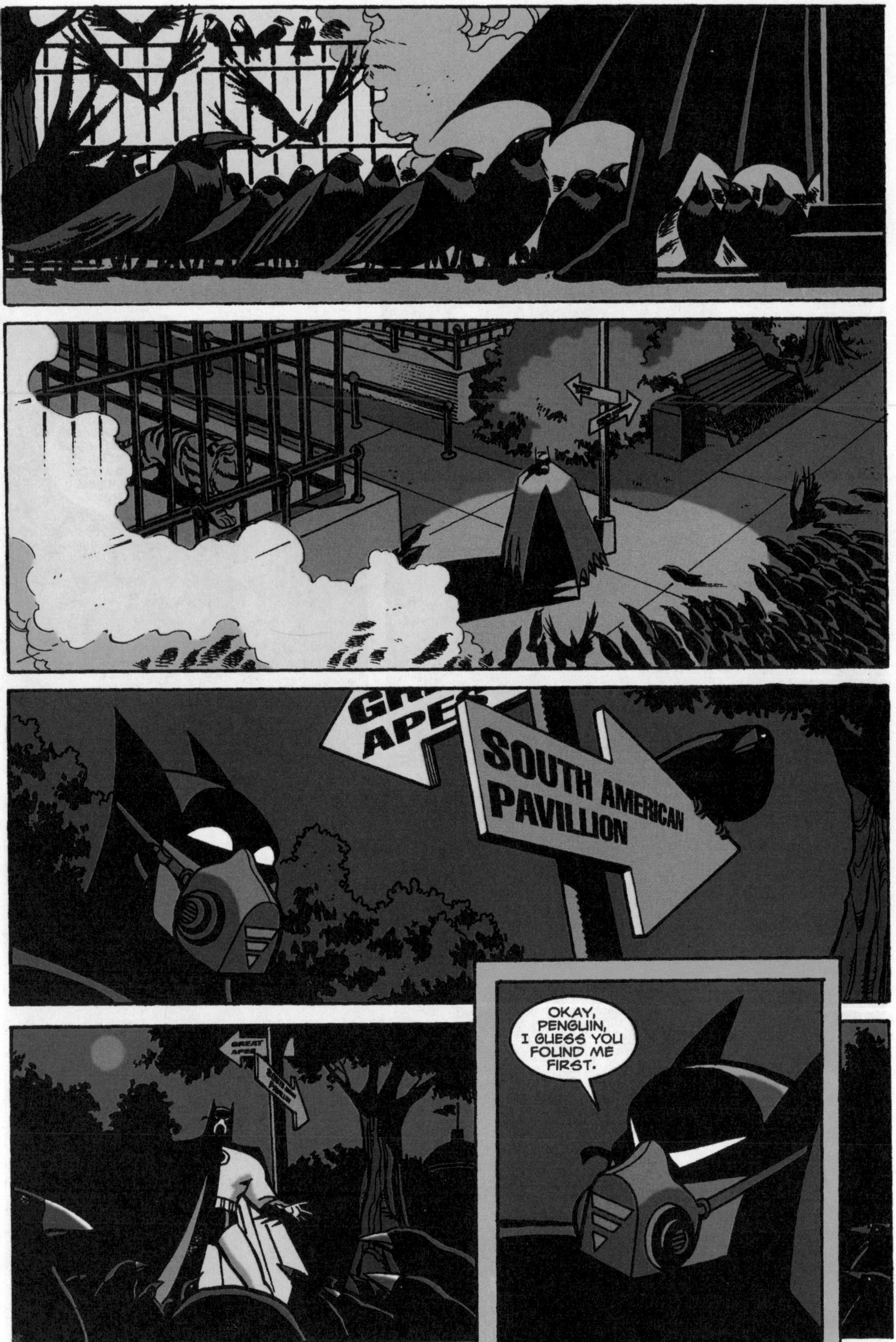
GREAT APES
SOUTH AMERICAN PAVILLION
OKAY, PENGUIN, I GUESS YOU FOUND ME FIRST.
5

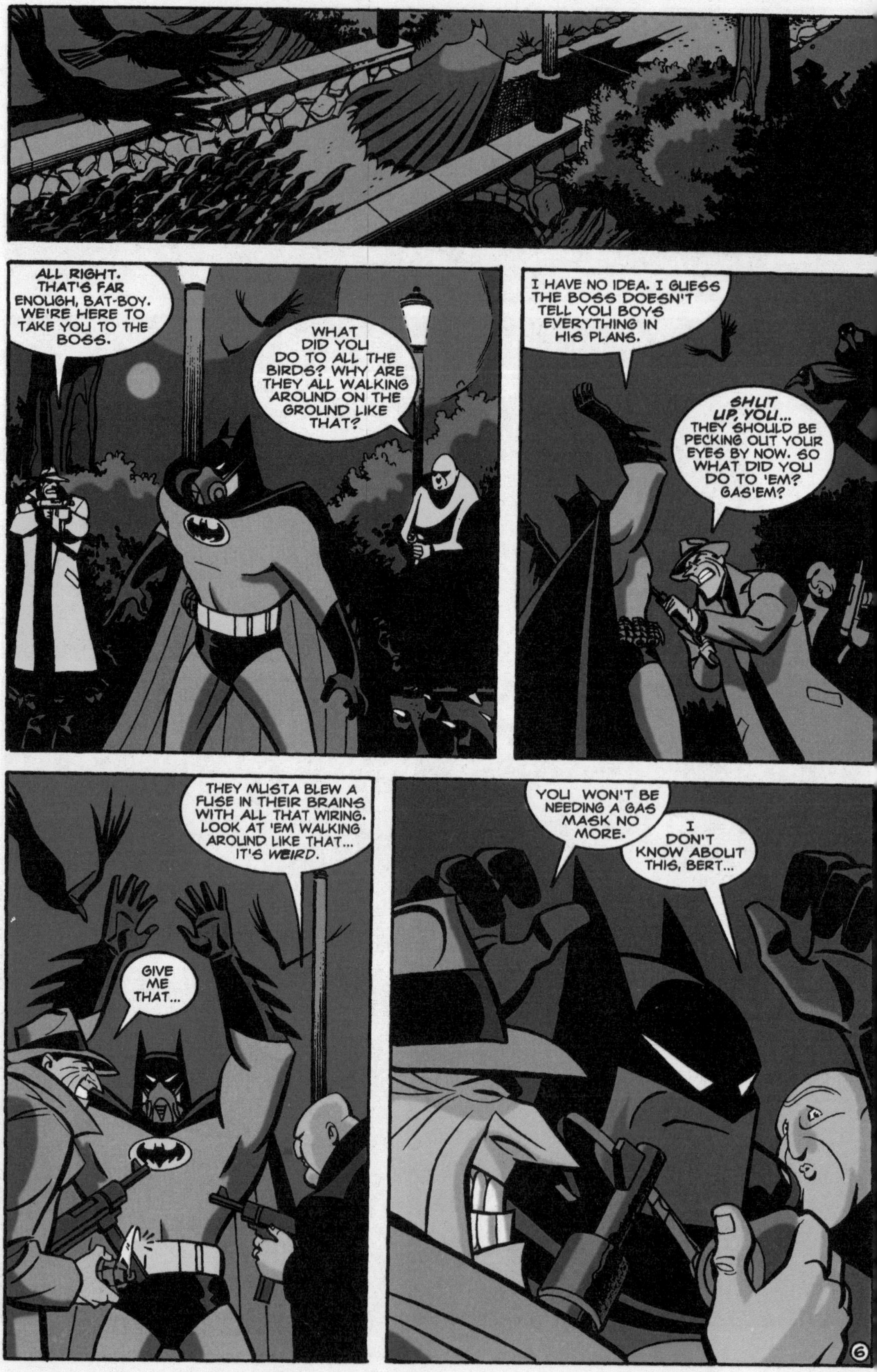
ALL RIGHT. THAT'S FAR ENOUGH, BAT-BOY. WE'RE HERE TO TAKE YOU TO THE BOSS.
WHAT DID YOU DO TO ALL THE BIRDS? WHY ARE THEY ALL WALKING AROUND ON THE GROUND LIKE THAT?
I HAVE NO IDEA. I GUESS THE BOSS DOESN'T TELL YOU BOYS EVERYTHING IN HIS PLANS.
SHUT UP, YOU... THEY SHOULD BE PECKING OUT YOUR EYES BY NOW. SO WHAT DID YOU DO TO 'EM? GAS'EM?
THEY MUSTA BLEW A FUSE IN THEIR BRAINS WITH ALL THAT WIRING. LOOK AT 'EM WALKING AROUND LIKE THAT... IT'S WEIRD.
GIVE ME THAT...
YOU WON'T BE NEEDING A GAS MASK NO MORE.
I DON'T KNOW ABOUT THIS, BERT...
6

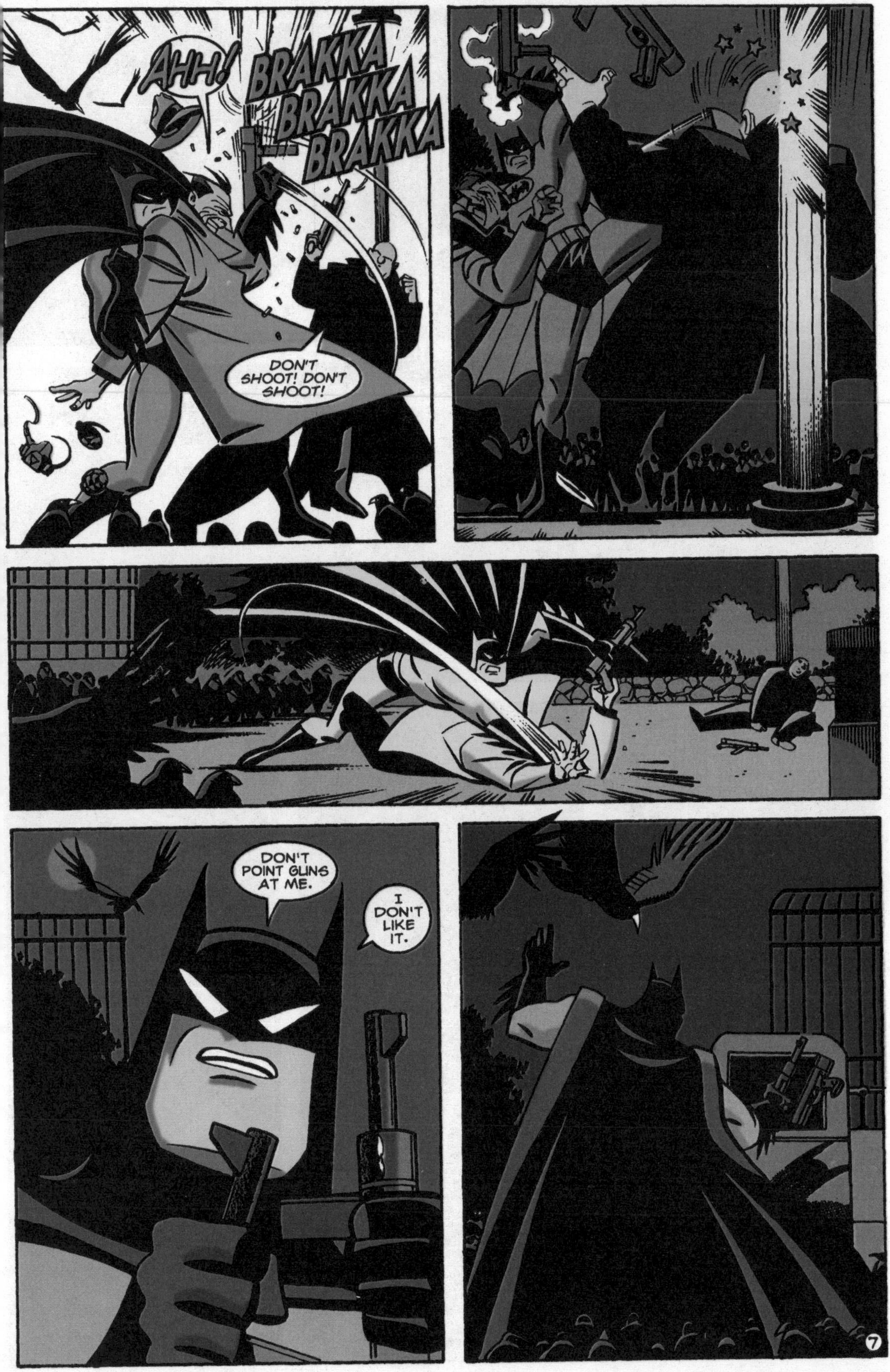
AHH!
BRAKKA
BRAKKA
BRAKKA
DON'T SHOOT! DON'T SHOOT!
DON'T POINT GUNS AT ME.
I DON'T LIKE IT.
7

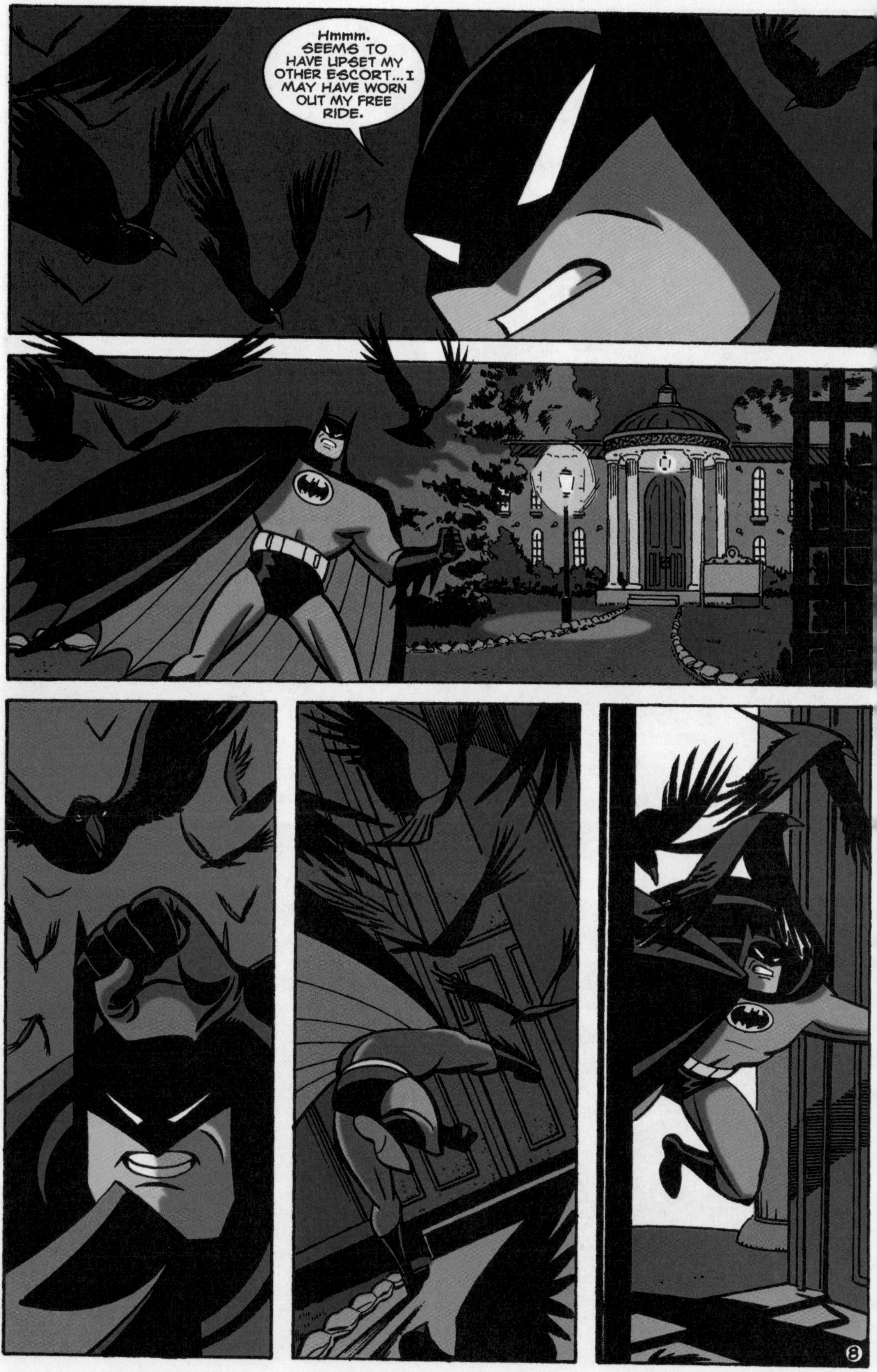
Hmmm. SEEMS TO HAVE UPSET MY OTHER ESCORT... I MAY HAVE WORN OUT MY FREE RIDE.
8

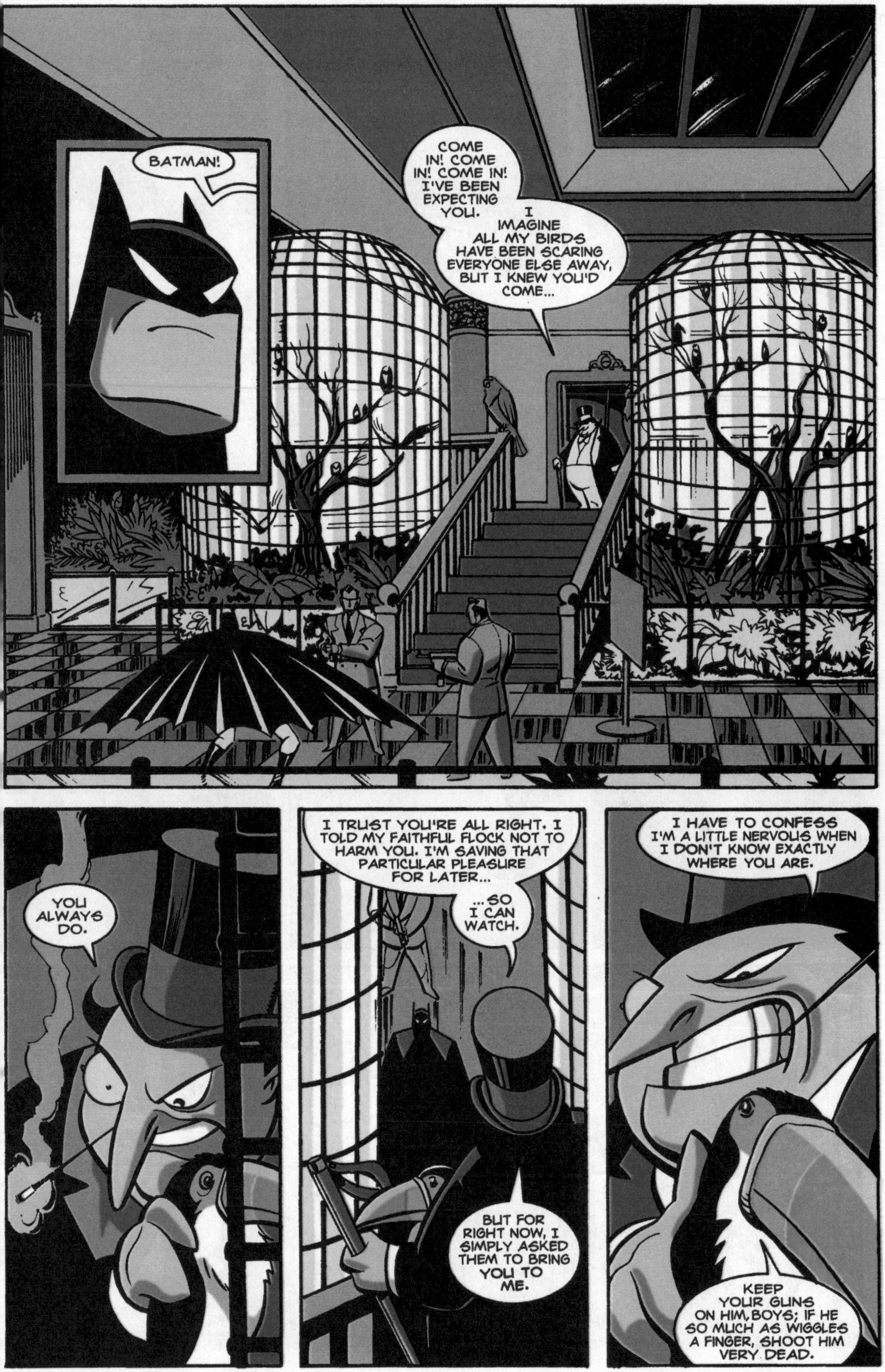
BATMAN!
COME IN! COME IN! COME IN! I'VE BEEN EXPECTING YOU.
I IMAGINE ALL MY BIRDS HAVE BEEN SCARING EVERYONE ELSE AWAY, BUT I KNEW YOU'D COME...
YOU ALWAYS DO.
I TRUST YOU'RE ALL RIGHT. I TOLD MY FAITHFUL FLOCK NOT TO HARM YOU. I'M SAVING THAT PARTICULAR PLEASURE FOR LATER...
...SO I CAN WATCH.
BUT FOR RIGHT NOW, I SIMPLY ASKED THEM TO BRING YOU TO ME.
I HAVE TO CONFESS I'M A LITTLE NERVOUS WHEN I DON'T KNOW EXACTLY WHERE YOU ARE.
KEEP YOUR GUNS ON HIM, BOYS; IF HE SO MUCH AS WIGGLES A FINGER, SHOOT HIM VERY DEAD.

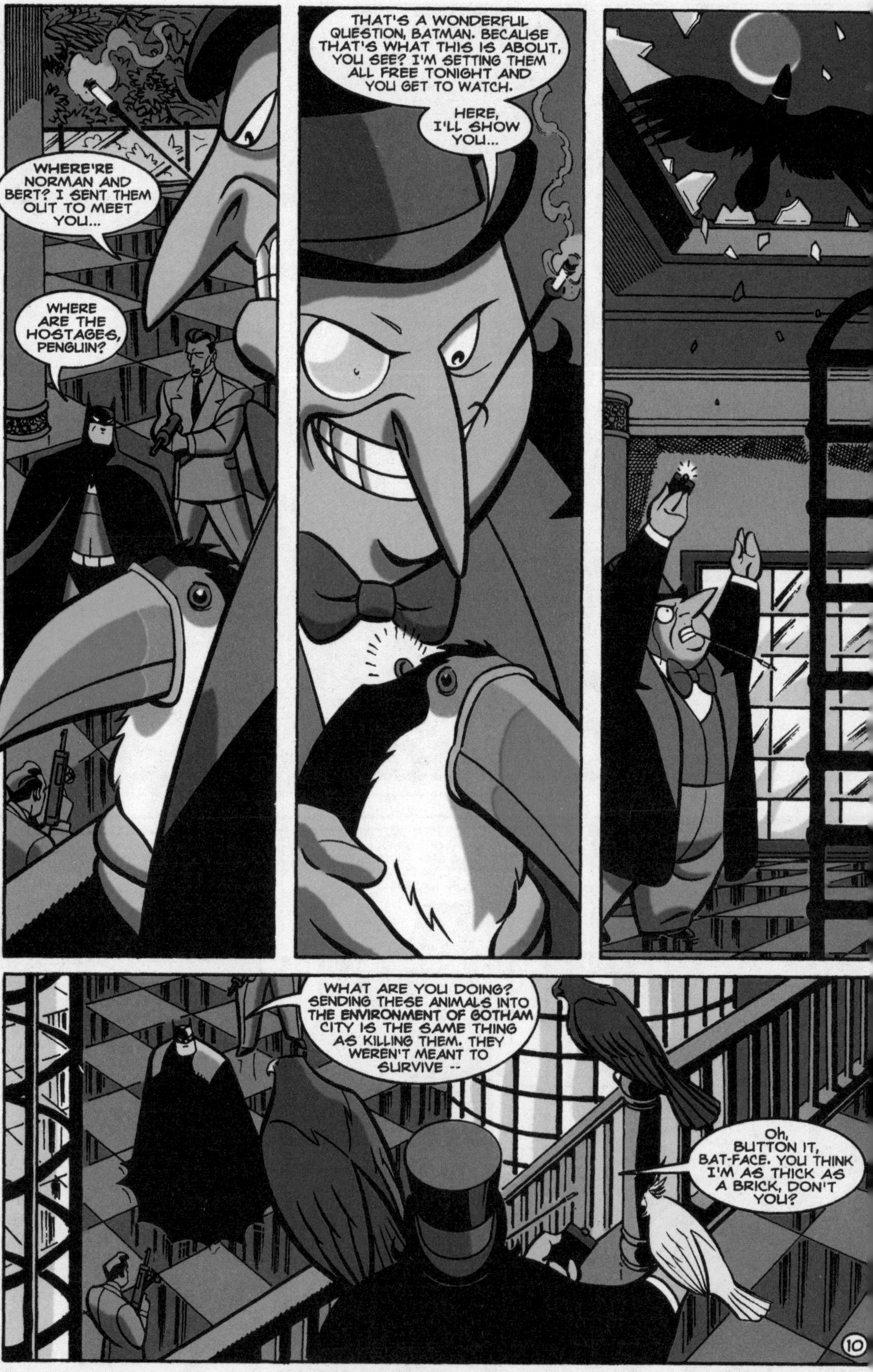

WHERE'RE NORMAN AND BERT? I SENT THEM OUT TO MEET YOU...
WHERE ARE THE HOSTAGES, PENGUIN?
THAT'S A WONDERFUL QUESTION, BATMAN. BECAUSE THAT'S WHAT THIS IS ABOUT, YOU SEE? I'M SETTING THEM ALL FREE TONIGHT AND YOU GET TO WATCH.
HERE, I'LL SHOW YOU...
WHAT ARE YOU DOING? SENDING THESE ANIMALS INTO THE ENVIRONMENT OF GOTHAM CITY IS THE SAME THING AS KILLING THEM. THEY WEREN'T MEANT TO SURVIVE --
Oh, BUTTON IT, BAT-FACE. YOU THINK I'M AS THICK AS A BRICK, DON'T YOU?
10

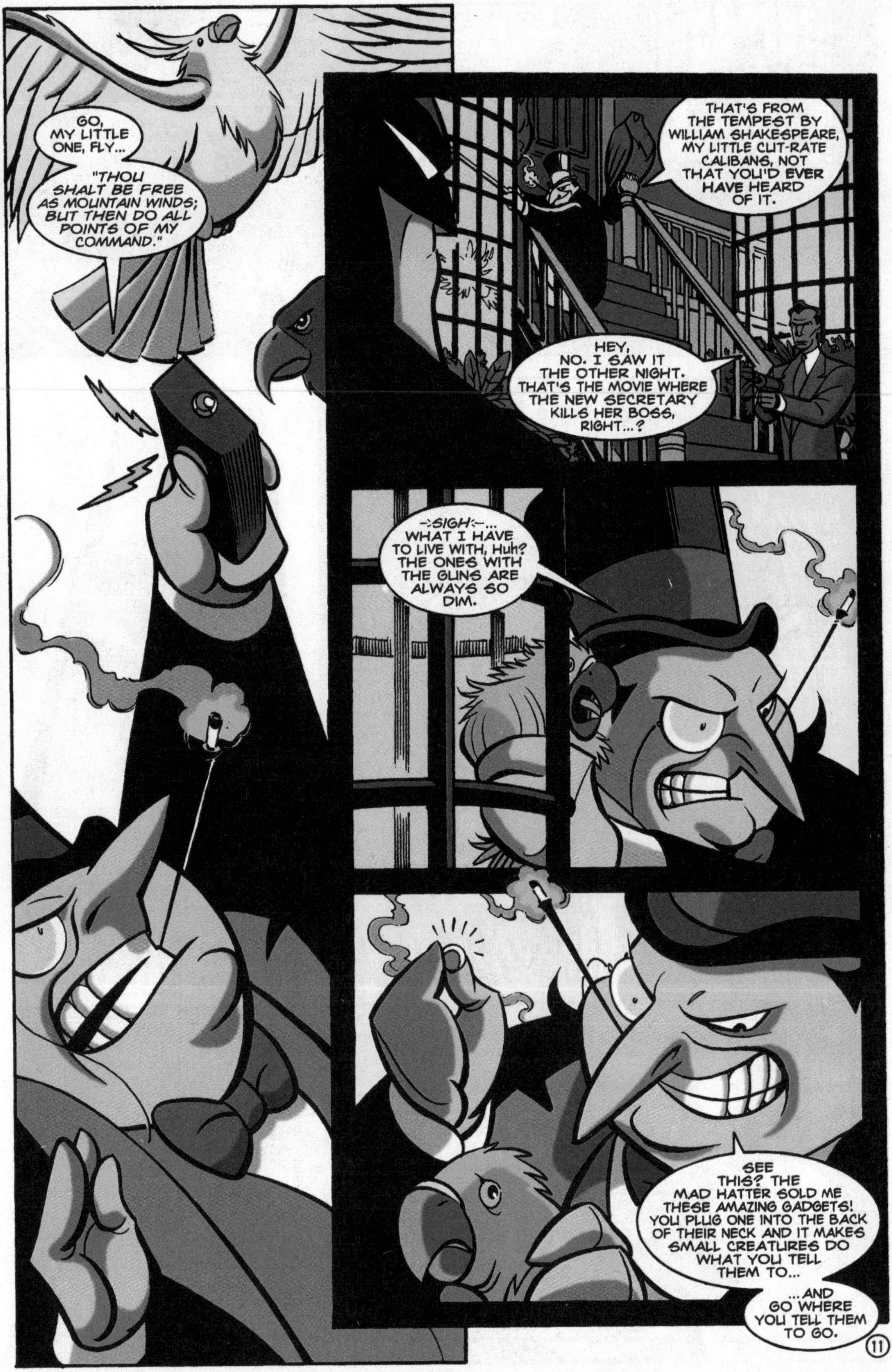
GO, MY LITTLE ONE, FLY...
"THOU SHALT BE FREE AS MOUNTAIN WINDS; BUT THEN DO ALL POINTS OF MY COMMAND."
THAT'S FROM THE TEMPEST BY WILLIAM SHAKESPEARE, MY LITTLE CUT-RATE CALIBANS, NOT THAT YOU'D EVER HAVE HEARD OF IT.
HEY, NO. I SAW IT THE OTHER NIGHT. THAT'S THE MOVIE WHERE THE NEW SECRETARY KILLS HER BOSS, RIGHT...?
-SIGH-... WHAT I HAVE TO LIVE WITH, Huh? THE ONES WITH THE GUNS ARE ALWAYS SO DIM.
SEE THIS? THE MAD HATTER SOLD ME THESE AMAZING GADGETS! YOU PLUG ONE INTO THE BACK OF THEIR NECK AND IT MAKES SMALL CREATURES DO WHAT YOU TELL THEM TO...
...AND GO WHERE YOU TELL THEM TO GO.
11

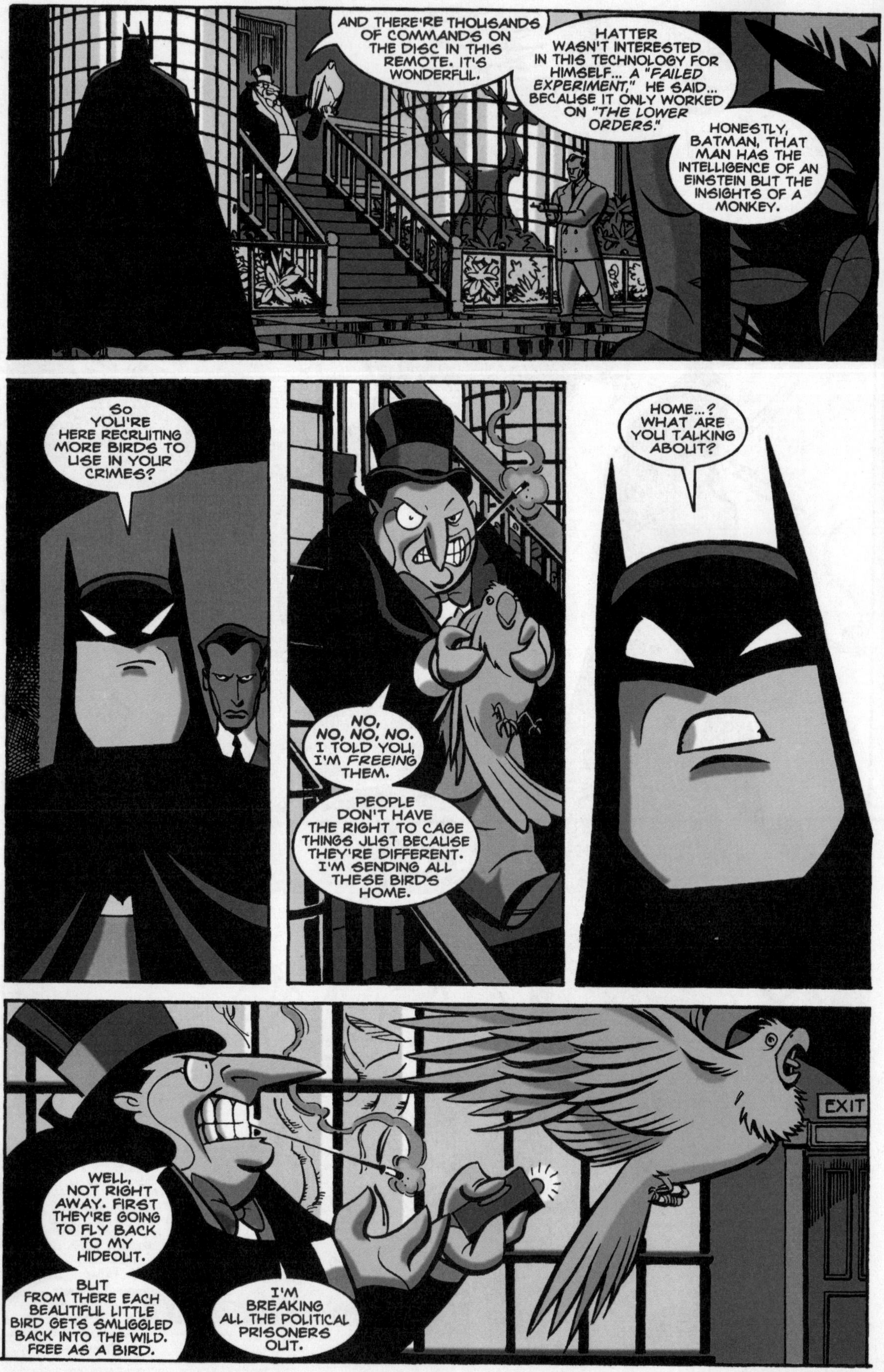
AND THERE'RE THOUSANDS OF COMMANDS ON THE DISC IN THIS REMOTE. IT'S WONDERFUL.
HATTER WASN'T INTERESTED IN THIS TECHNOLOGY FOR HIMSELF... A "FAILED EXPERIMENT," HE SAID... BECAUSE IT ONLY WORKED ON "THE LOWER ORDERS."
HONESTLY, BATMAN, THAT MAN HAS THE INTELLIGENCE OF AN EINSTEIN BUT THE INSIGHTS OF A MONKEY.
SO YOU'RE HERE RECRUITING MORE BIRDS TO USE IN YOUR CRIMES?
NO, NO, NO, NO. I TOLD YOU, I'M FREEING THEM.
PEOPLE DON'T HAVE THE RIGHT TO CAGE THINGS JUST BECAUSE THEY'RE DIFFERENT. I'M SENDING ALL THESE BIRDS HOME.
HOME...? WHAT ARE YOU TALKING ABOUT?
WELL, NOT RIGHT AWAY. FIRST THEY'RE GOING TO FLY BACK TO MY HIDEOUT.
BUT FROM THERE EACH BEAUTIFUL LITTLE BIRD GETS SMUGGLED BACK INTO THE WILD. FREE AS A BIRD.
I'M BREAKING ALL THE POLITICAL PRISONERS OUT.
EXIT

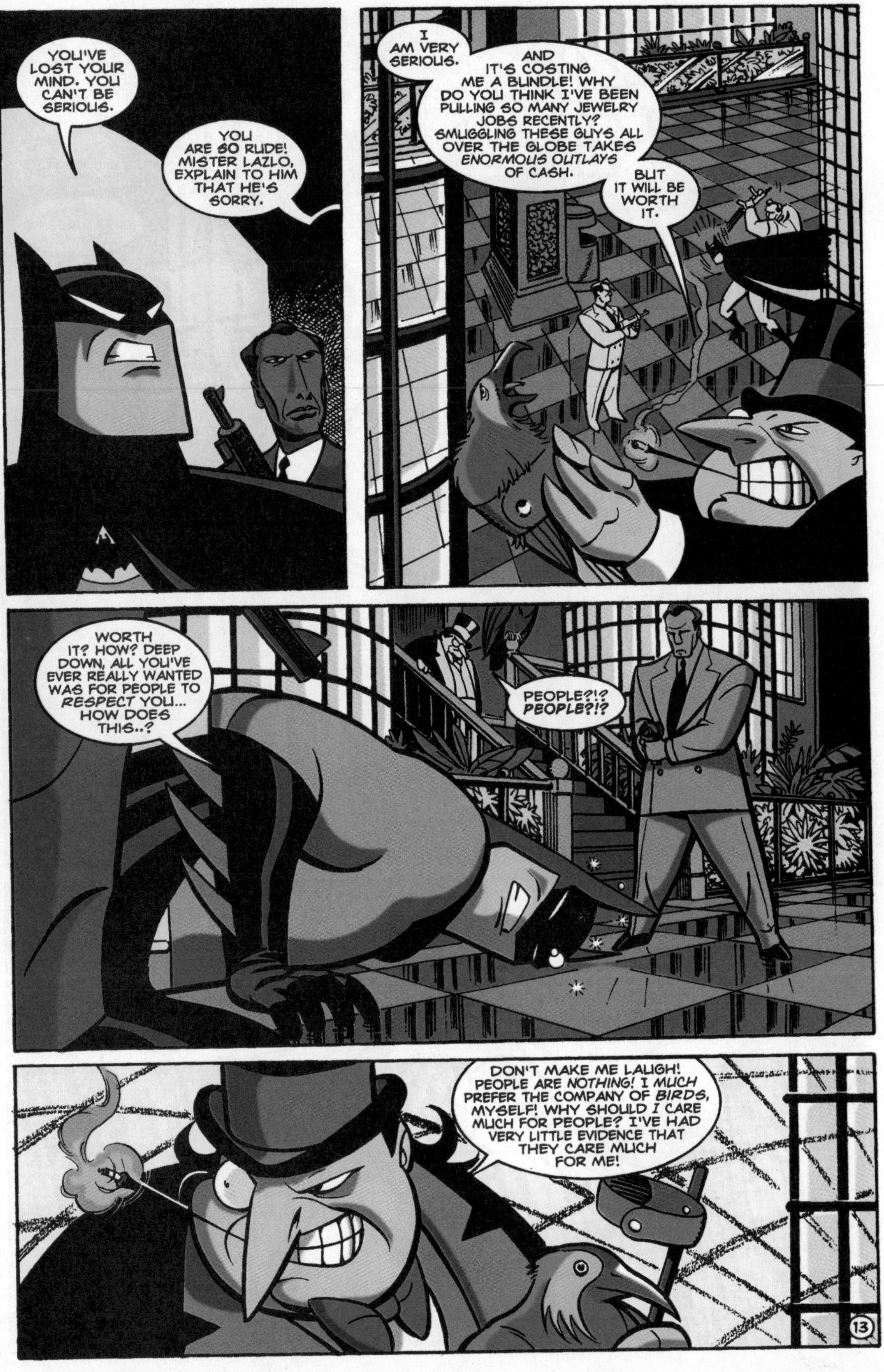
YOU'VE LOST YOUR MIND. YOU CAN'T BE SERIOUS.
YOU ARE SO RUDE! MISTER LAZLO, EXPLAIN TO HIM THAT HE'S SORRY.
I AM VERY SERIOUS.
AND IT'S COSTING ME A BUNDLE! WHY DO YOU THINK I'VE BEEN PULLING SO MANY JEWELRY JOBS RECENTLY? SMUGGLING THESE GUYS ALL OVER THE GLOBE TAKES *ENORMOUS OUTLAYS* OF CASH.
BUT IT WILL BE WORTH IT.
WORTH IT? HOW? DEEP DOWN, ALL YOU'VE EVER REALLY WANTED WAS FOR PEOPLE TO *RESPECT* YOU... HOW DOES THIS..?
PEOPLE?!? *PEOPLE?!?*
DON'T MAKE ME LAUGH! PEOPLE ARE *NOTHING*! I *MUCH* PREFER THE COMPANY OF *BIRDS*, MYSELF! WHY SHOULD *I* CARE MUCH FOR PEOPLE? I'VE HAD VERY LITTLE EVIDENCE THAT THEY CARE MUCH FOR ME!
13

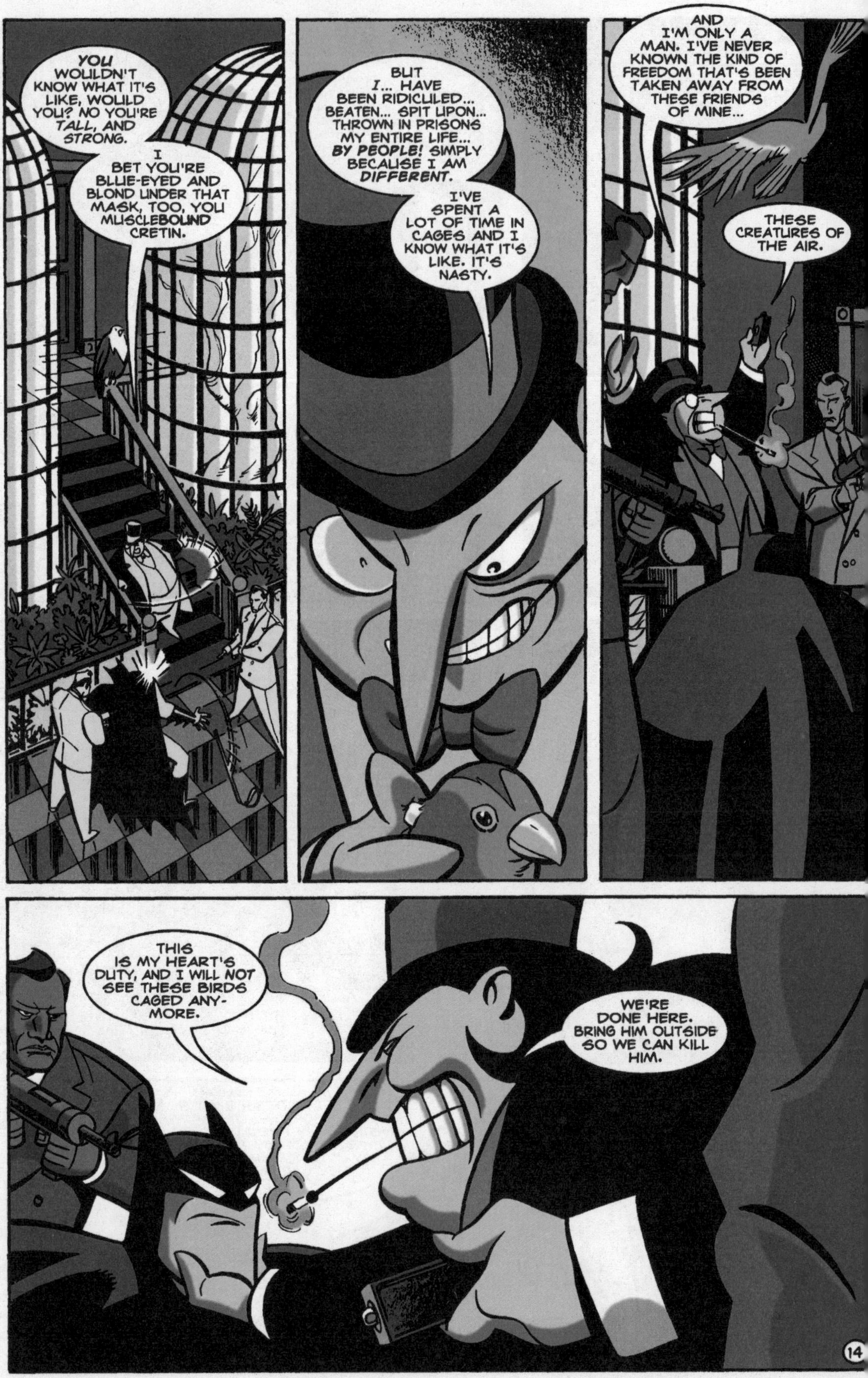
YOU WOULDN'T KNOW WHAT IT'S LIKE, WOULD YOU? NO YOU'RE TALL, AND STRONG.
I BET YOU'RE BLUE-EYED AND BLOND UNDER THAT MASK, TOO, YOU MUSCLEBOUND CRETIN.
BUT I... HAVE BEEN RIDICULED... BEATEN... SPIT UPON... THROWN IN PRISONS MY ENTIRE LIFE... BY PEOPLE! SIMPLY BECAUSE I AM DIFFERENT.
I'VE SPENT A LOT OF TIME IN CAGES AND I KNOW WHAT IT'S LIKE. IT'S NASTY.
AND I'M ONLY A MAN. I'VE NEVER KNOWN THE KIND OF FREEDOM THAT'S BEEN TAKEN AWAY FROM THESE FRIENDS OF MINE...
THESE CREATURES OF THE AIR.
THIS IS MY HEART'S DUTY, AND I WILL NOT SEE THESE BIRDS CAGED ANY-MORE.
WE'RE DONE HERE. BRING HIM OUTSIDE SO WE CAN KILL HIM.
14

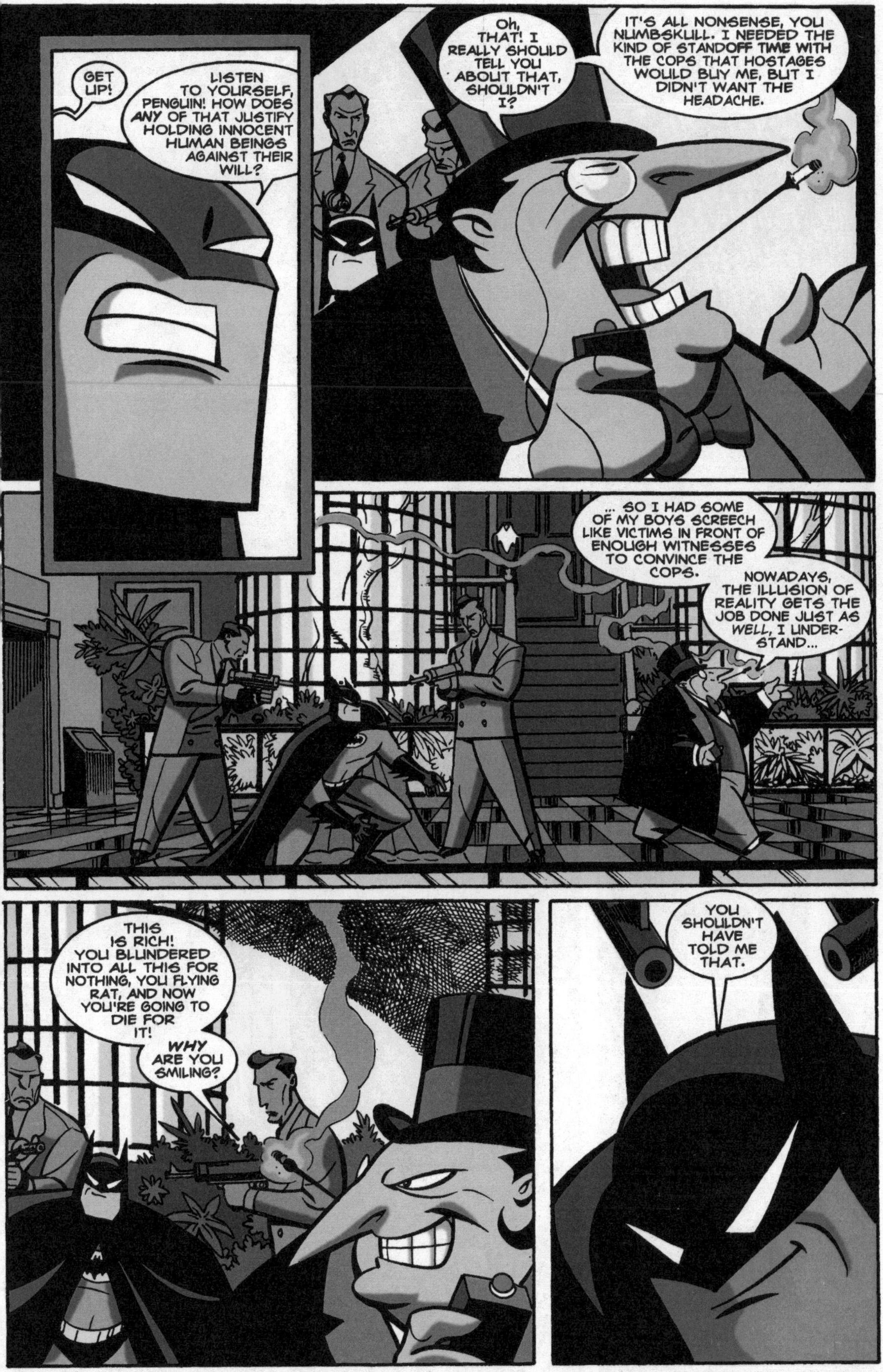
GET UP!
LISTEN TO YOURSELF, PENGUIN! HOW DOES ANY OF THAT JUSTIFY HOLDING INNOCENT HUMAN BEINGS AGAINST THEIR WILL?
Oh, THAT! I REALLY SHOULD TELL YOU ABOUT THAT, SHOULDN'T I?
IT'S ALL NONSENSE, YOU NUMBSKULL. I NEEDED THE KIND OF STANDOFF TIME WITH THE COPS THAT HOSTAGES WOULD BUY ME, BUT I DIDN'T WANT THE HEADACHE.
... SO I HAD SOME OF MY BOYS SCREECH LIKE VICTIMS IN FRONT OF ENOUGH WITNESSES TO CONVINCE THE COPS.
NOWADAYS, THE ILLUSION OF REALITY GETS THE JOB DONE JUST AS WELL, I UNDER-STAND...
THIS IS RICH! YOU BLUNDERED INTO ALL THIS FOR NOTHING, YOU FLYING RAT, AND NOW YOU'RE GOING TO DIE FOR IT!
WHY ARE YOU SMILING?
YOU SHOULDN'T HAVE TOLD ME THAT.

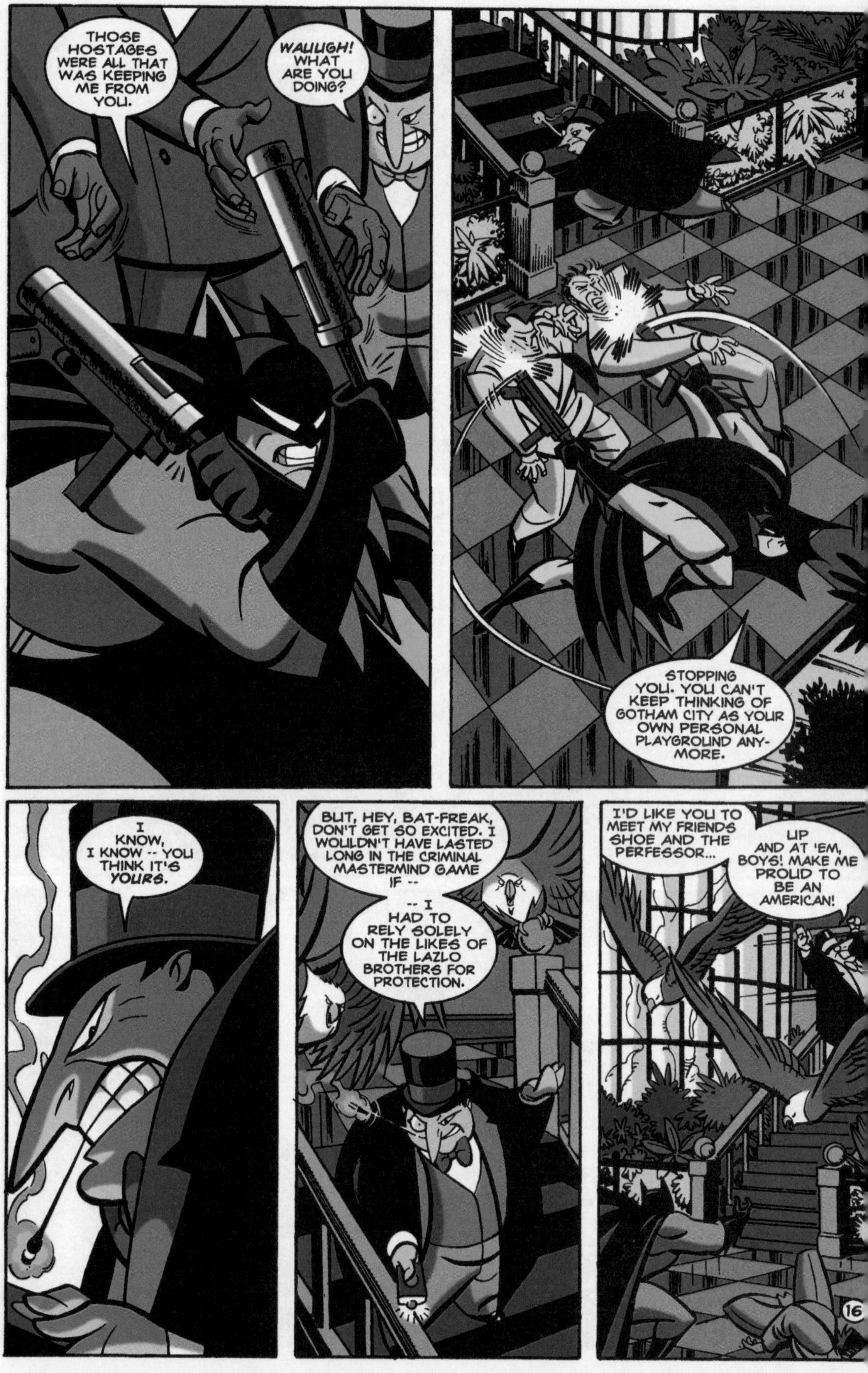
THOSE HOSTAGES WERE ALL THAT WAS KEEPING ME FROM YOU.
WAUUGH! WHAT ARE YOU DOING?
STOPPING YOU. YOU CAN'T KEEP THINKING OF GOTHAM CITY AS YOUR OWN PERSONAL PLAYGROUND ANY-MORE.
I KNOW, I KNOW -- YOU THINK IT'S YOURS.
BUT, HEY, BAT-FREAK, DON'T GET SO EXCITED. I WOULDN'T HAVE LASTED LONG IN THE CRIMINAL MASTERMIND GAME IF --
-- I HAD TO RELY SOLELY ON THE LIKES OF THE LAZLO BROTHERS FOR PROTECTION.
I'D LIKE YOU TO MEET MY FRIENDS SHOE AND THE PERFESSOR...
UP AND AT 'EM, BOYS! MAKE ME PROUD TO BE AN AMERICAN!
16

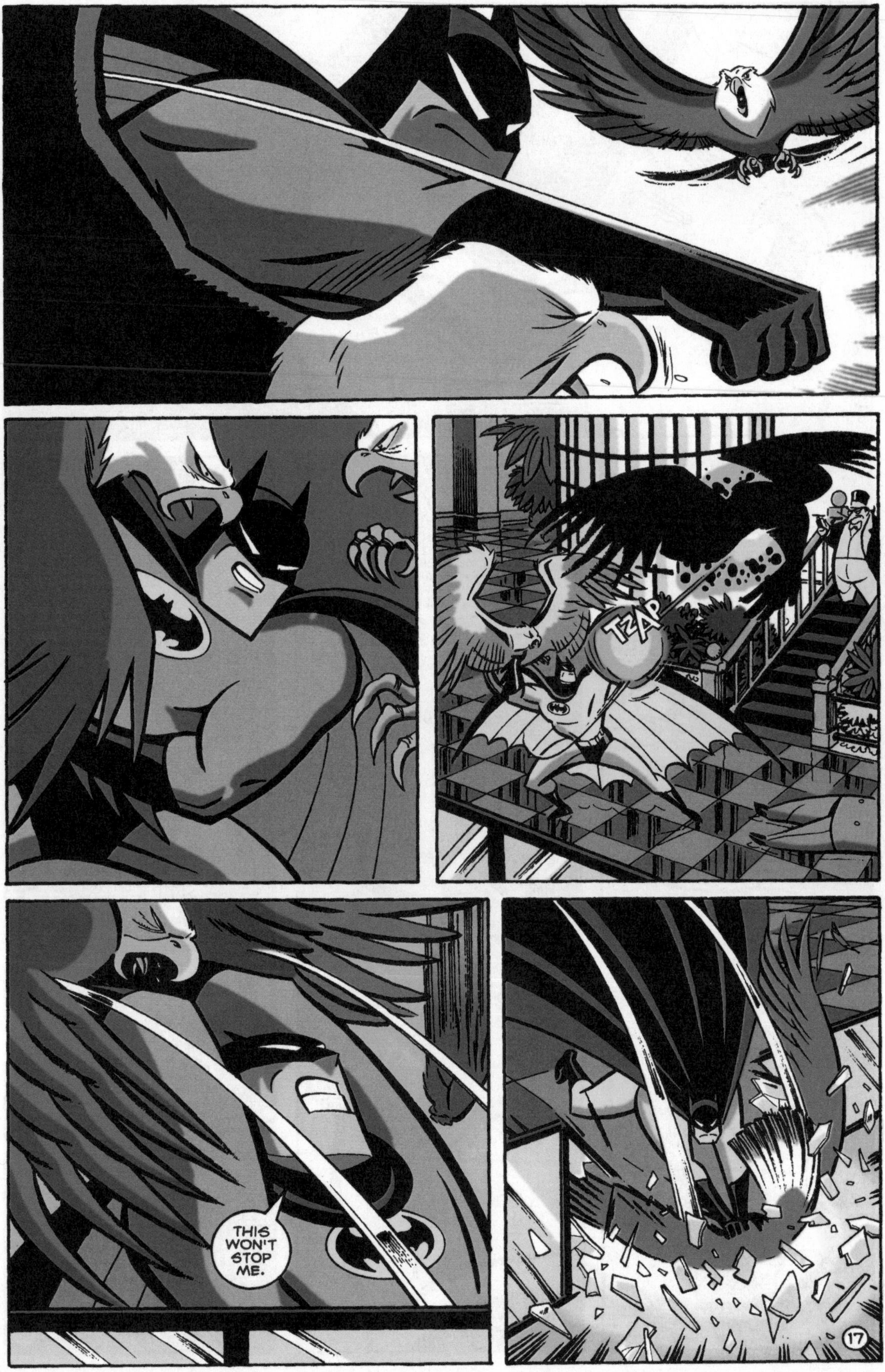
TZAP
THIS WON'T STOP ME.
17

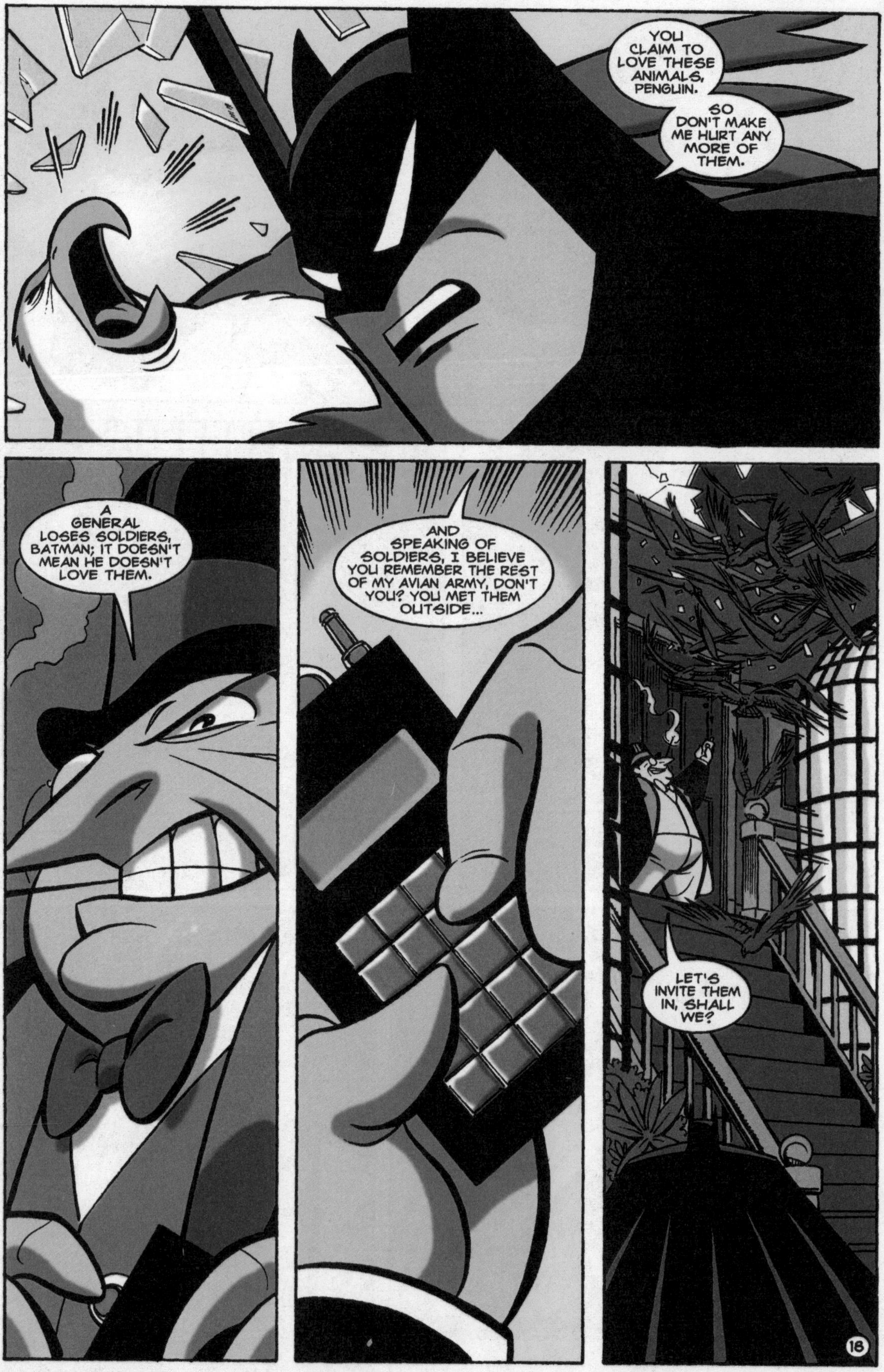
YOU CLAIM TO LOVE THESE ANIMALS, PENGUIN.
SO DON'T MAKE ME HURT ANY MORE OF THEM.
A GENERAL LOSES SOLDIERS, BATMAN; IT DOESN'T MEAN HE DOESN'T LOVE THEM.
AND SPEAKING OF SOLDIERS, I BELIEVE YOU REMEMBER THE REST OF MY AVIAN ARMY, DON'T YOU? YOU MET THEM OUTSIDE...
LET'S INVITE THEM IN, SHALL WE?
18

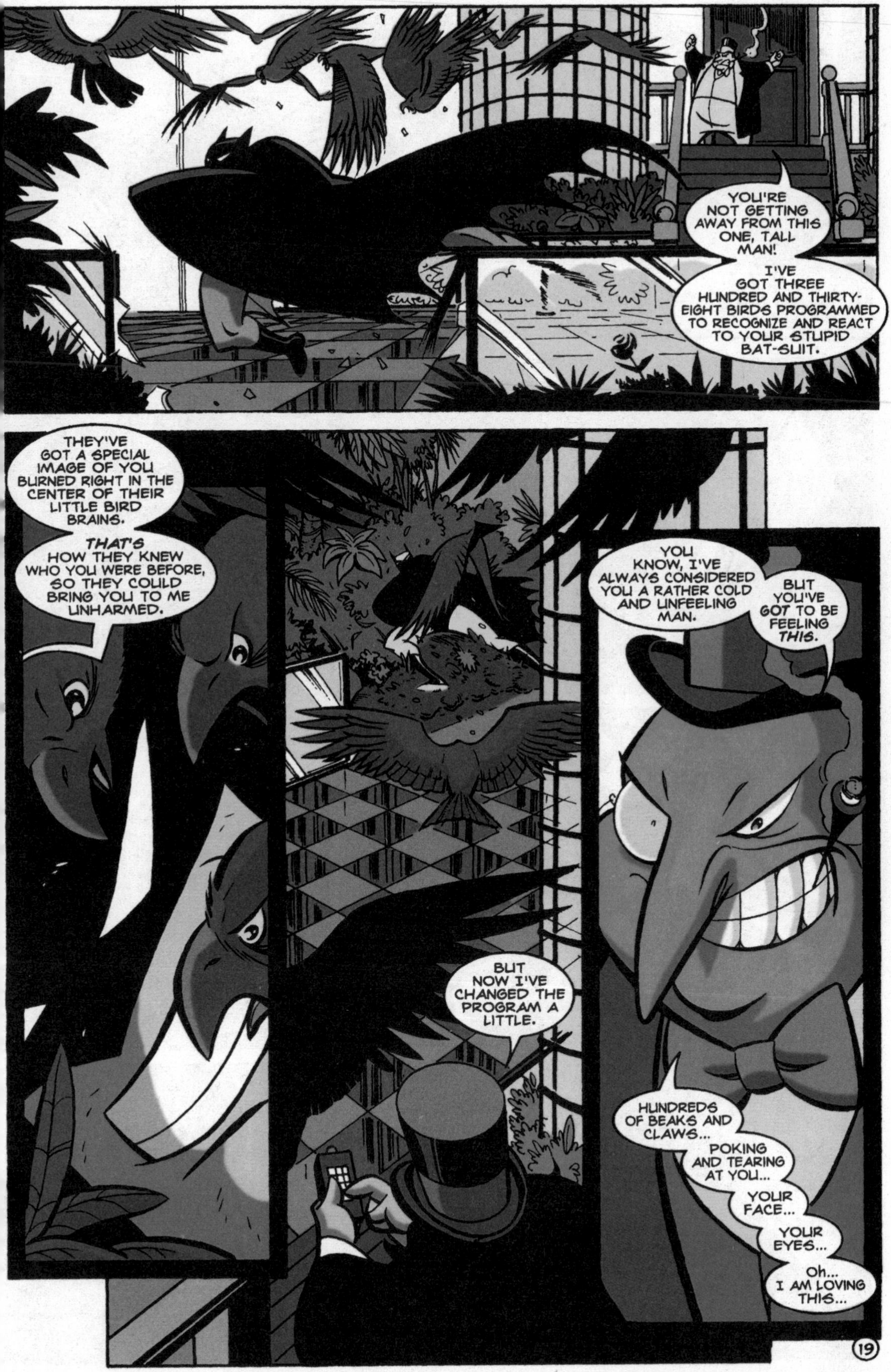
YOU'RE NOT GETTING AWAY FROM THIS ONE, TALL MAN!
I'VE GOT THREE HUNDRED AND THIRTY-EIGHT BIRDS PROGRAMMED TO RECOGNIZE AND REACT TO YOUR STUPID BAT-SUIT.
THEY'VE GOT A SPECIAL IMAGE OF YOU BURNED RIGHT IN THE CENTER OF THEIR LITTLE BIRD BRAINS.
THAT'S HOW THEY KNEW WHO YOU WERE BEFORE, SO THEY COULD BRING YOU TO ME UNHARMED.
BUT NOW I'VE CHANGED THE PROGRAM A LITTLE.
YOU KNOW, I'VE ALWAYS CONSIDERED YOU A RATHER COLD AND UNFEELING MAN.
BUT YOU'VE GOT TO BE FEELING *THIS.*
HUNDREDS OF BEAKS AND CLAWS...
POKING AND TEARING AT YOU...
YOUR FACE...
YOUR EYES...
Oh... I AM LOVING THIS...
19

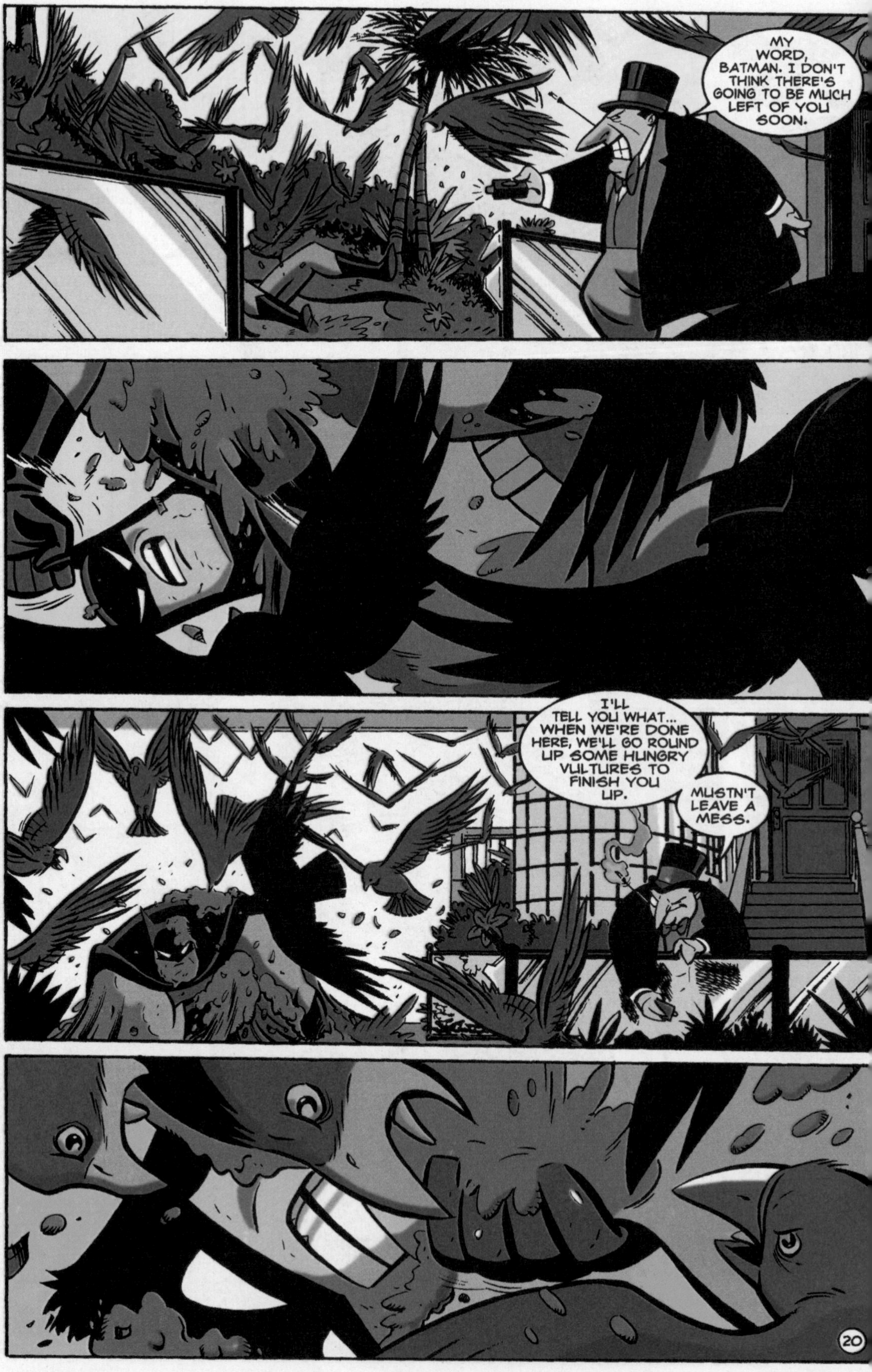
MY WORD, BATMAN. I DON'T THINK THERE'S GOING TO BE MUCH LEFT OF YOU SOON.
I'LL TELL YOU WHAT... WHEN WE'RE DONE HERE, WE'LL GO ROUND UP SOME HUNGRY VULTURES TO FINISH YOU UP.
MUSTN'T LEAVE A MESS.
20

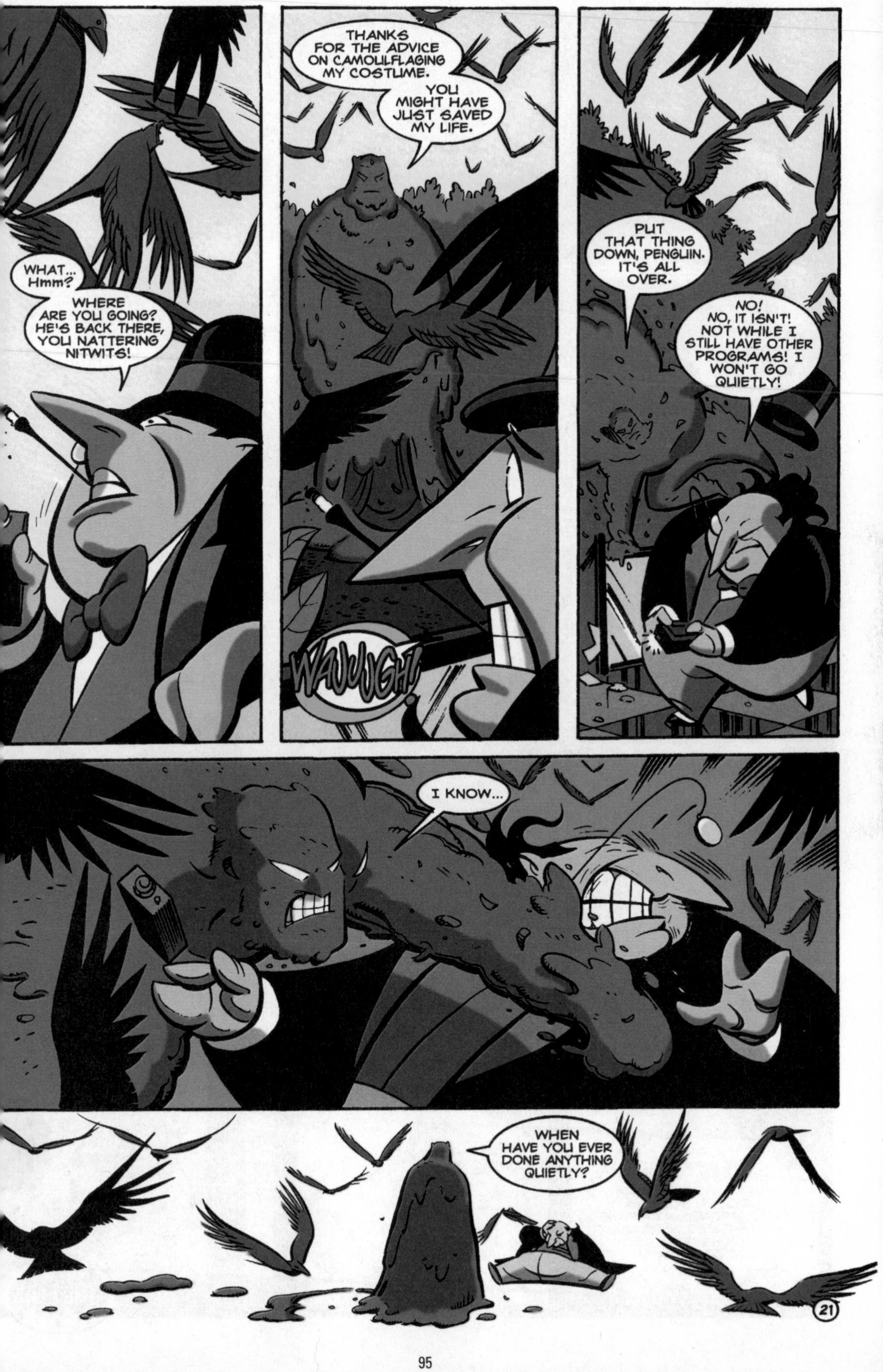
WHAT... Hmm?
WHERE ARE YOU GOING? HE'S BACK THERE, YOU NATTERING NITWITS!
THANKS FOR THE ADVICE ON CAMOUFLAGING MY COSTUME.
YOU MIGHT HAVE JUST SAVED MY LIFE.
WAUUUGH!
PUT THAT THING DOWN, PENGUIN. IT'S ALL OVER.
NO! NO, IT ISN'T! NOT WHILE I STILL HAVE OTHER PROGRAMS! I WON'T GO QUIETLY!
I KNOW...
WHEN HAVE YOU EVER DONE ANYTHING QUIETLY?
21

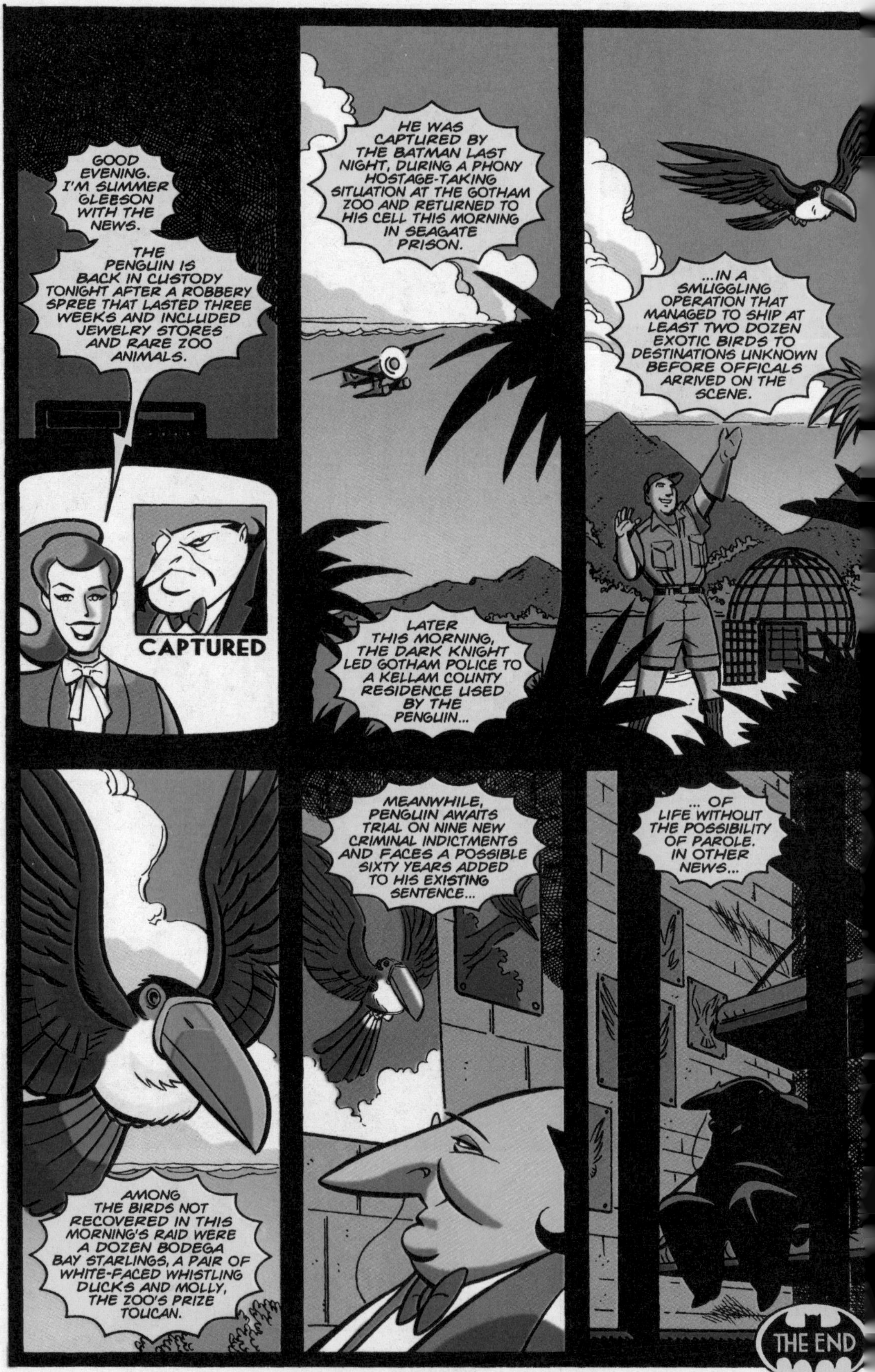
GOOD EVENING. I'M SUMMER GLEESON WITH THE NEWS.
THE PENGUIN IS BACK IN CUSTODY TONIGHT AFTER A ROBBERY SPREE THAT LASTED THREE WEEKS AND INCLUDED JEWELRY STORES AND RARE ZOO ANIMALS.
CAPTURED
HE WAS CAPTURED BY THE BATMAN LAST NIGHT, DURING A PHONY HOSTAGE-TAKING SITUATION AT THE GOTHAM ZOO AND RETURNED TO HIS CELL THIS MORNING IN SEAGATE PRISON.
LATER THIS MORNING, THE DARK KNIGHT LED GOTHAM POLICE TO A KELLAM COUNTY RESIDENCE USED BY THE PENGUIN...
...IN A SMUGGLING OPERATION THAT MANAGED TO SHIP AT LEAST TWO DOZEN EXOTIC BIRDS TO DESTINATIONS UNKNOWN BEFORE OFFICALS ARRIVED ON THE SCENE.
AMONG THE BIRDS NOT RECOVERED IN THIS MORNING'S RAID WERE A DOZEN BODEGA BAY STARLINGS, A PAIR OF WHITE-FACED WHISTLING DUCKS AND MOLLY, THE ZOO'S PRIZE TOUCAN.
MEANWHILE, PENGUIN AWAITS TRIAL ON NINE NEW CRIMINAL INDICTMENTS AND FACES A POSSIBLE SIXTY YEARS ADDED TO HIS EXISTING SENTENCE...
... OF LIFE WITHOUT THE POSSIBILITY OF PAROLE. IN OTHER NEWS...
THE END

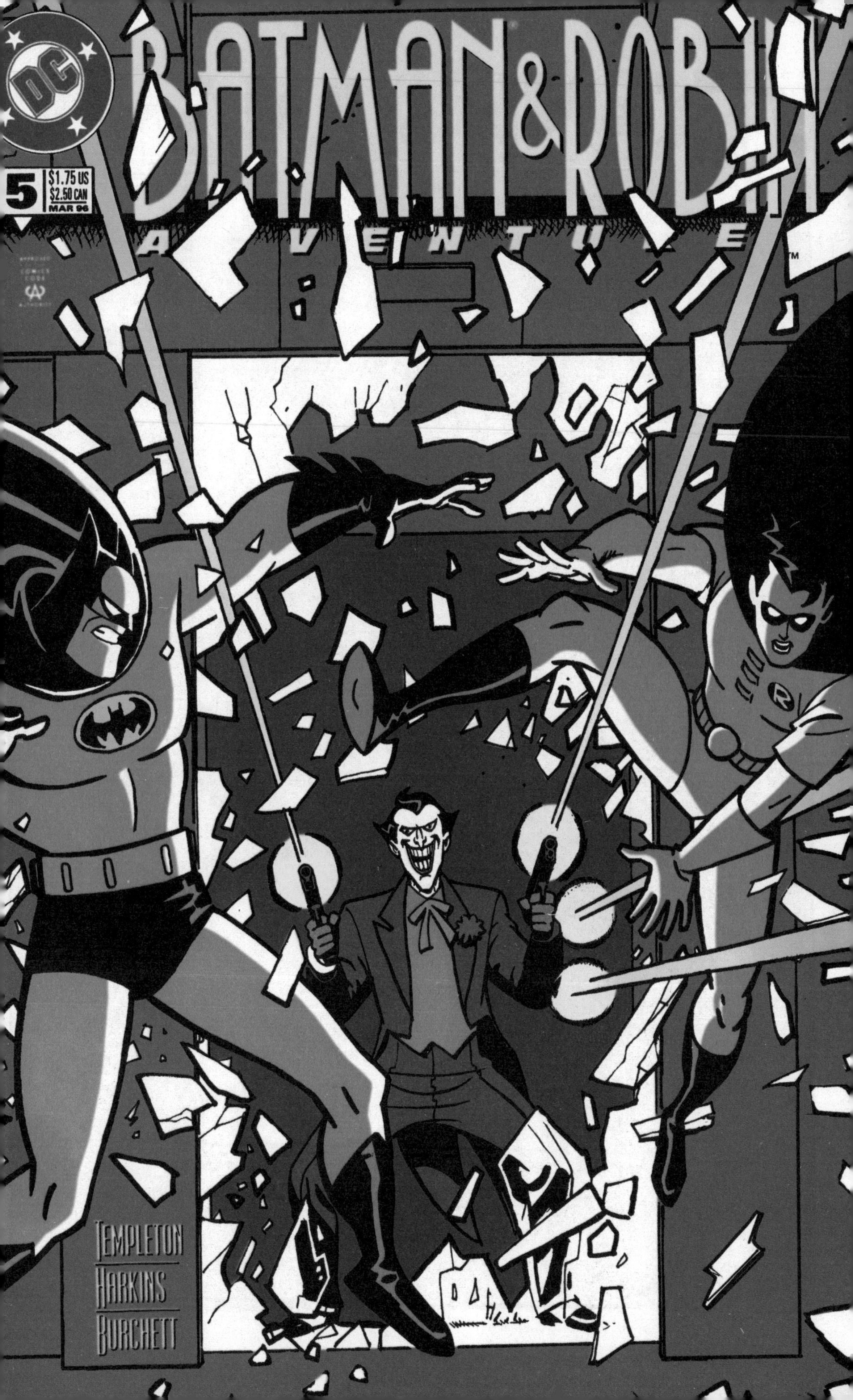
DC
BATMAN & ROBIN
5
$1.75 US
$2.50 CAN
MAR 96
TEMPLETON
HARKINS
BURCHETT

SECOND BANANA

TY TEMPLETON WRITER
TIM HARKINS PENCILLER
RICK BURCHETT INKER
LINDA MEDLEY COLORIST
RICHARD STARKINGS AND COMICRAFT LETTERS

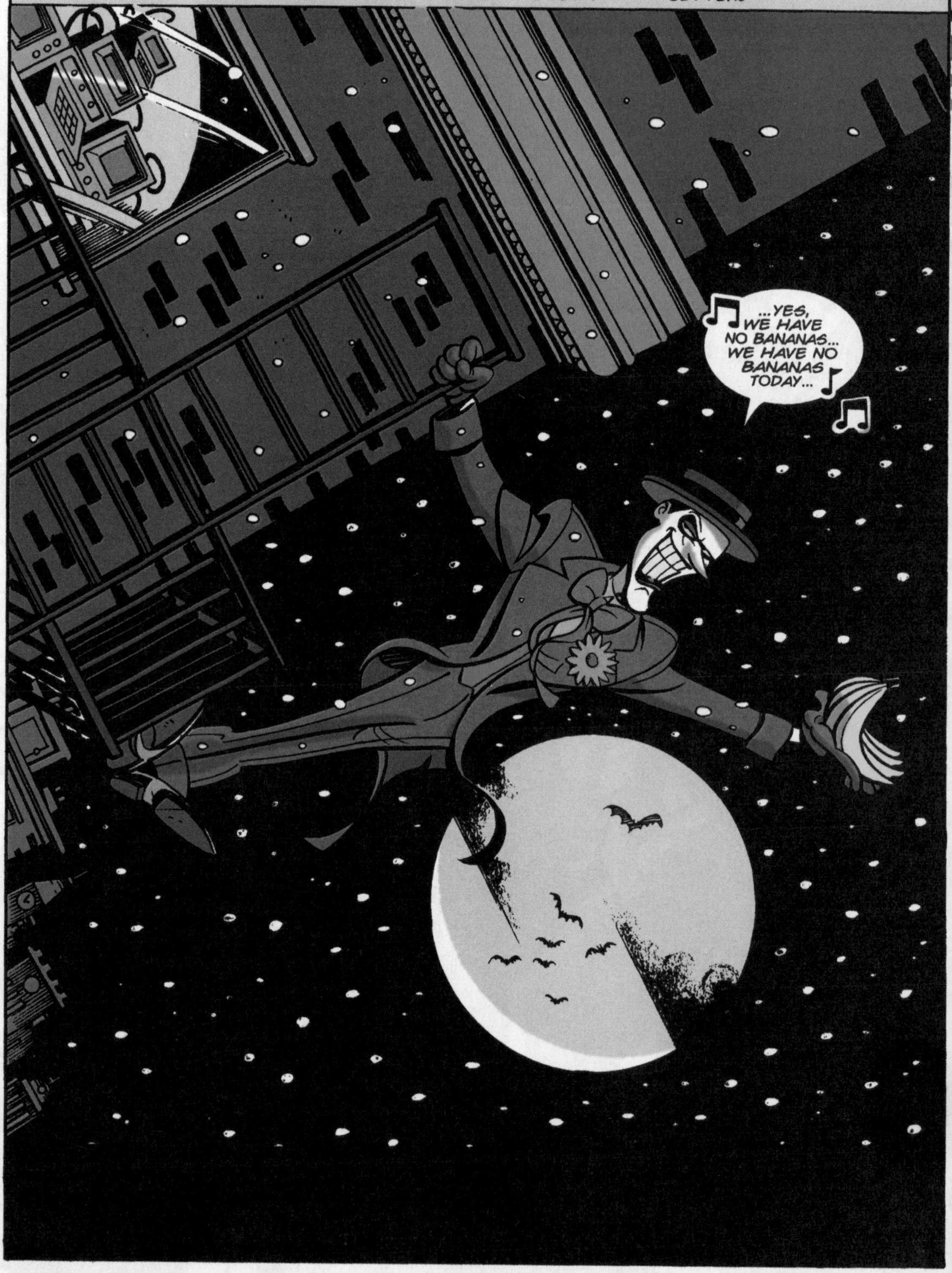
...YES, WE HAVE NO BANANAS... WE HAVE NO BANANAS TODAY...

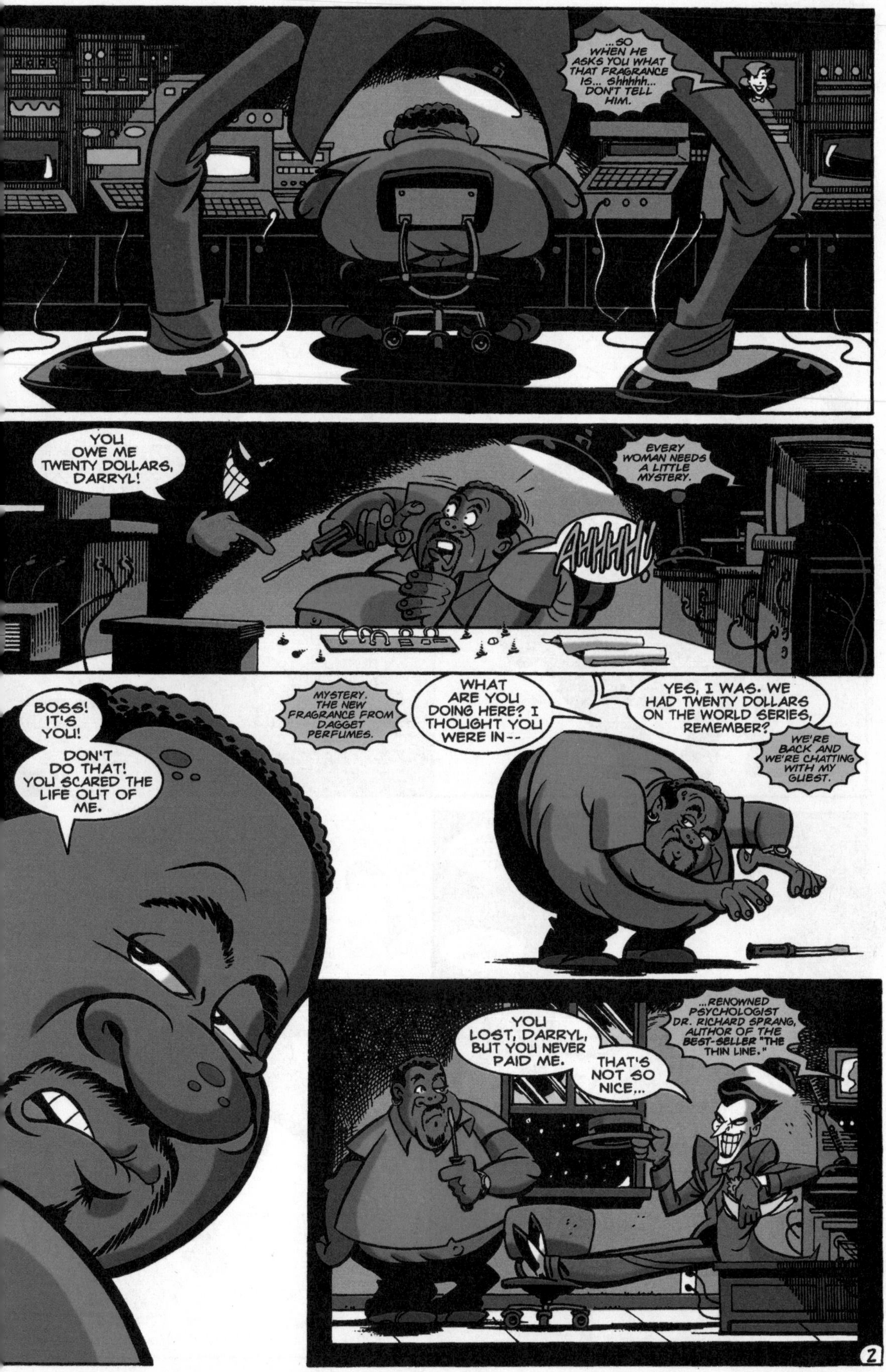
...SO WHEN HE ASKS YOU WHAT THAT FRAGRANCE IS... Shhhhh... DON'T TELL HIM.
YOU OWE ME TWENTY DOLLARS, DARRYL!
EVERY WOMAN NEEDS A LITTLE MYSTERY.
AHHHH!
BOSS! IT'S YOU!
DON'T DO THAT! YOU SCARED THE LIFE OUT OF ME.
MYSTERY. THE NEW FRAGRANCE FROM DAGGET PERFUMES.
WHAT ARE YOU DOING HERE? I THOUGHT YOU WERE IN--
YES, I WAS. WE HAD TWENTY DOLLARS ON THE WORLD SERIES, REMEMBER?
WE'RE BACK AND WE'RE CHATTING WITH MY GUEST.
YOU LOST, DARRYL, BUT YOU NEVER PAID ME.
THAT'S NOT SO NICE,...
...RENOWNED PSYCHOLOGIST DR. RICHARD SPRANG, AUTHOR OF THE BEST-SELLER "THE THIN LINE."
2

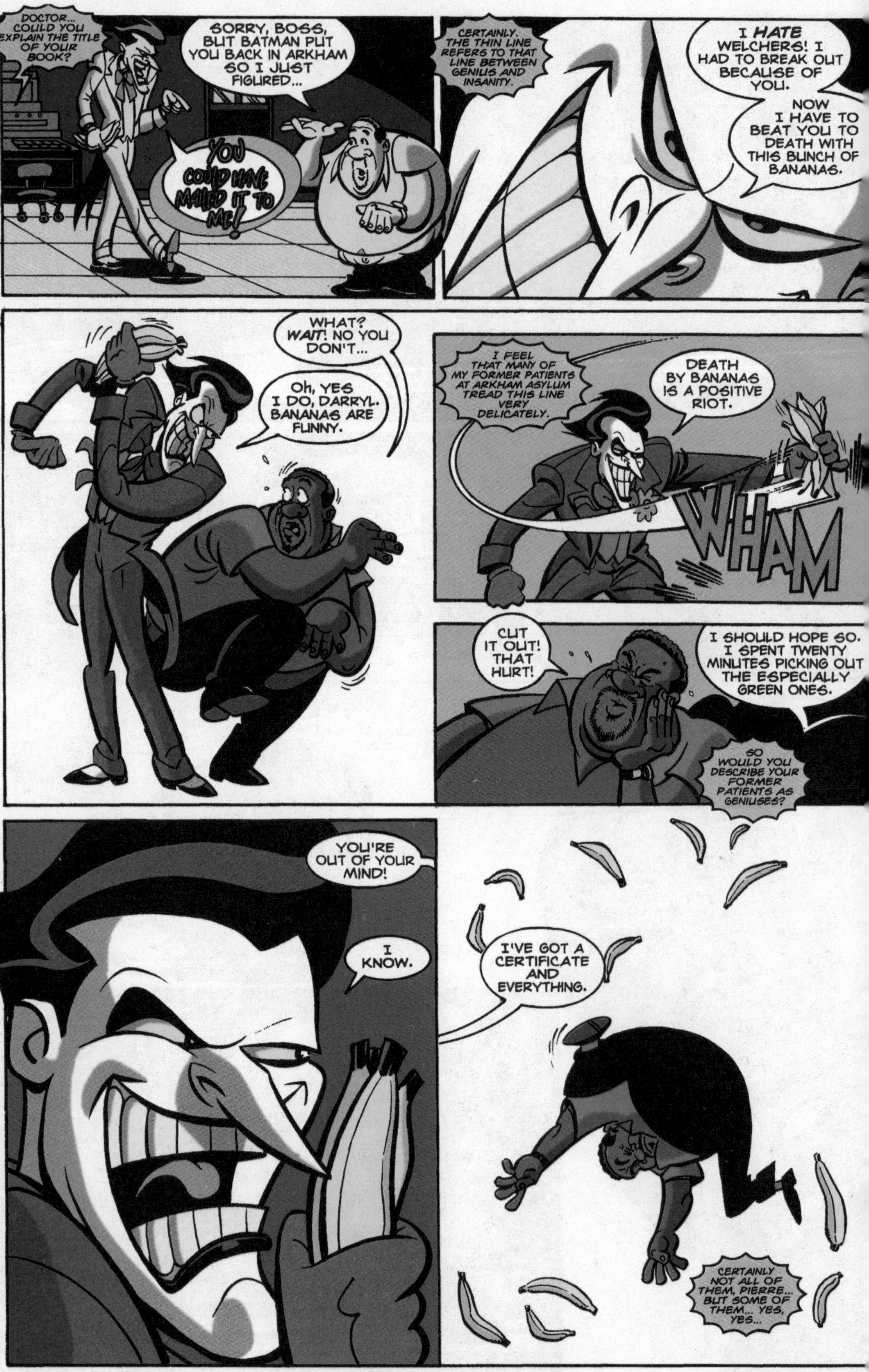
DOCTOR... COULD YOU EXPLAIN THE TITLE OF YOUR BOOK?
SORRY, BOSS, BUT BATMAN PUT YOU BACK IN ARKHAM SO I JUST FIGURED...
YOU COULD HAVE MAILED IT TO ME!
CERTAINLY. THE THIN LINE REFERS TO THAT LINE BETWEEN GENIUS AND INSANITY.
I HATE WELCHERS! I HAD TO BREAK OUT BECAUSE OF YOU.
NOW I HAVE TO BEAT YOU TO DEATH WITH THIS BUNCH OF BANANAS.
WHAT? WAIT! NO YOU DON'T...
Oh, YES I DO, DARRYL. BANANAS ARE FUNNY.
I FEEL THAT MANY OF MY FORMER PATIENTS AT ARKHAM ASYLUM TREAD THIS LINE VERY DELICATELY.
DEATH BY BANANAS IS A POSITIVE RIOT.
WHAM
CUT IT OUT! THAT HURT!
I SHOULD HOPE SO. I SPENT TWENTY MINUTES PICKING OUT THE ESPECIALLY GREEN ONES.
SO WOULD YOU DESCRIBE YOUR FORMER PATIENTS AS GENIUSES?
YOU'RE OUT OF YOUR MIND!
I KNOW.
I'VE GOT A CERTIFICATE AND EVERYTHING.
CERTAINLY NOT ALL OF THEM, PIERRE... BUT SOME OF THEM... YES, YES...

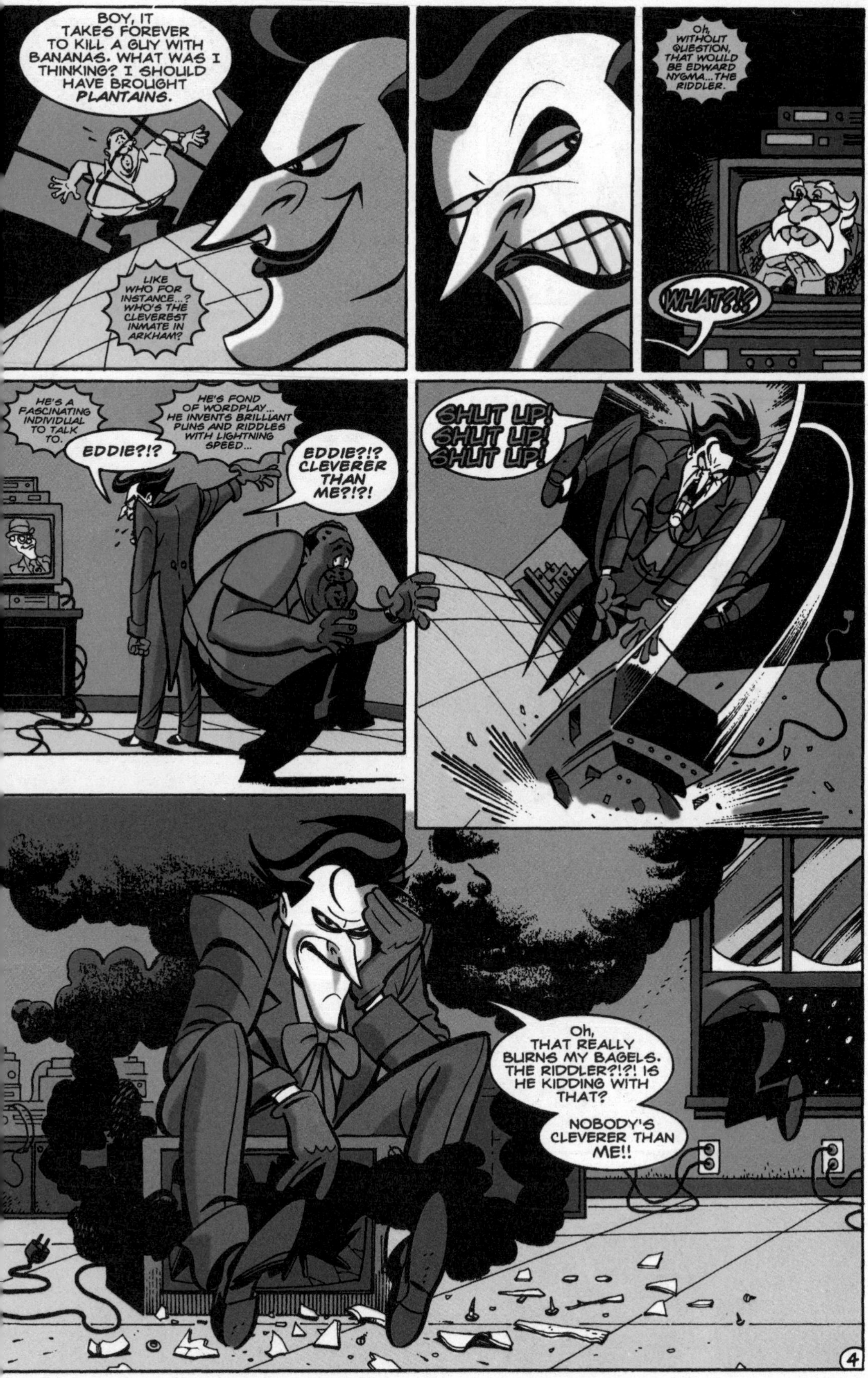

BOY, IT TAKES FOREVER TO KILL A GUY WITH BANANAS. WHAT WAS I THINKING? I SHOULD HAVE BROUGHT PLANTAINS.
LIKE WHO FOR INSTANCE...? WHO'S THE CLEVEREST INMATE IN ARKHAM?
Oh, WITHOUT QUESTION, THAT WOULD BE EDWARD NYGMA...THE RIDDLER.
WHAT?!?
HE'S A FASCINATING INDIVIDUAL TO TALK TO.
HE'S FOND OF WORDPLAY... HE INVENTS BRILLIANT PUNS AND RIDDLES WITH LIGHTNING SPEED...
EDDIE?!?
EDDIE?!? CLEVERER THAN ME?!?!
SHUT UP! SHUT UP! SHUT UP!
Oh, THAT REALLY BURNS MY BAGELS. THE RIDDLER?!?! IS HE KIDDING WITH THAT?
NOBODY'S CLEVERER THAN ME!!
4

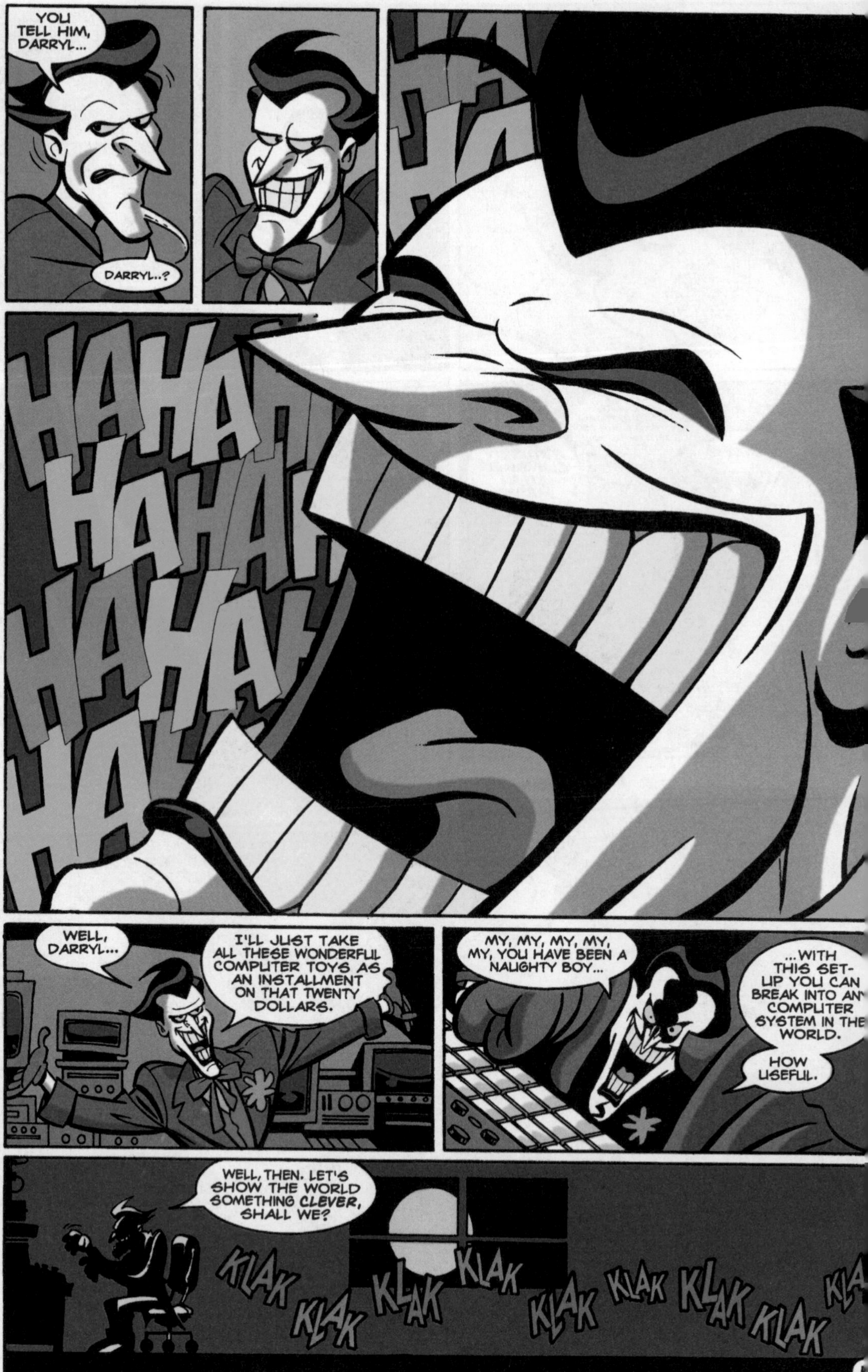
YOU TELL HIM, DARRYL...
DARRYL..?
HAHAHAHA
WELL, DARRYL...
I'LL JUST TAKE ALL THESE WONDERFUL COMPUTER TOYS AS AN INSTALLMENT ON THAT TWENTY DOLLARS.
MY, MY, MY, MY, MY, YOU HAVE BEEN A NAUGHTY BOY...
...WITH THIS SET-UP YOU CAN BREAK INTO AN COMPUTER SYSTEM IN THE WORLD.
HOW USEFUL.
WELL, THEN. LET'S SHOW THE WORLD SOMETHING CLEVER, SHALL WE?
KLAK KLAK KLAK KLAK KLAK KLAK KLAK KLAK

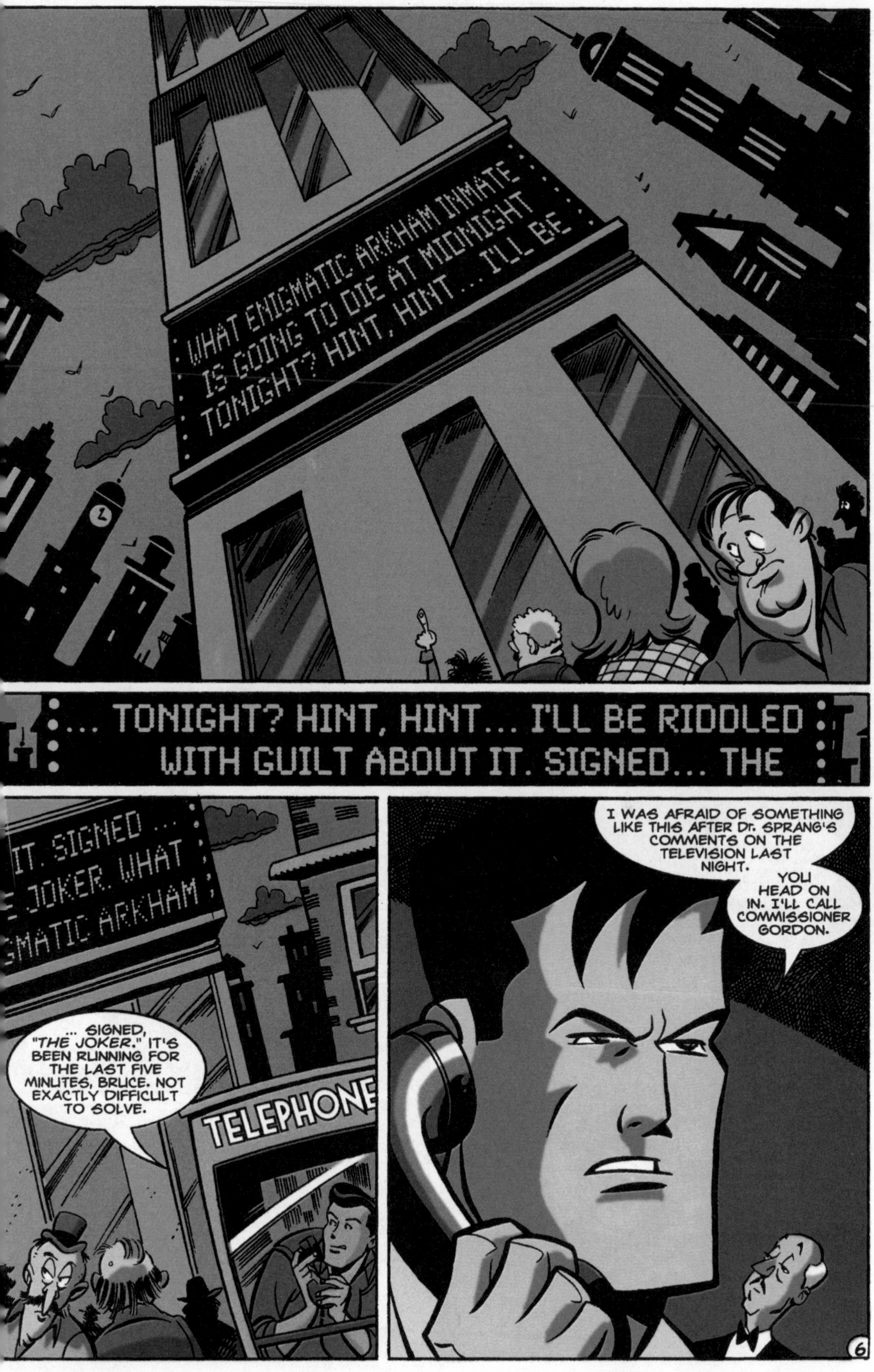
WHAT ENIGMATIC ARKHAM INMATE IS GOING TO DIE AT MIDNIGHT TONIGHT? HINT, HINT... I'LL BE
... TONIGHT? HINT, HINT... I'LL BE RIDDLED WITH GUILT ABOUT IT. SIGNED... THE
IT. SIGNED... JOKER. WHAT MATIC ARKHAM
... SIGNED, "THE JOKER." IT'S BEEN RUNNING FOR THE LAST FIVE MINUTES, BRUCE. NOT EXACTLY DIFFICULT TO SOLVE.
TELEPHONE
I WAS AFRAID OF SOMETHING LIKE THIS AFTER Dr. SPRANG'S COMMENTS ON THE TELEVISION LAST NIGHT.
YOU HEAD ON IN. I'LL CALL COMMISSIONER GORDON.
6

WELL, THE LAB JUST REPORTED IN, NYGMA, AND YOU'RE CLEAN FOR POISONS.

WHATEVER THE JOKER'S GOING TO DO, AT LEAST WE KNOW HE HASN'T DONE IT YET.

I'M GIDDY WITH RELIEF.

BULLOCK, THIS IS GORDON. HOW ARE THINGS ON YOUR END?

TIGHT AS A DRUM, COMMISSIONER. A COCKROACH COULDN'T GET INTO THIS BUILDING WITHOUT MY SAY-SO.

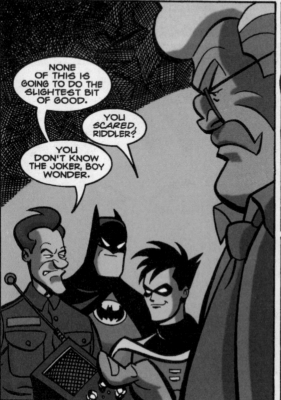

NONE OF THIS IS GOING TO DO THE SLIGHTEST BIT OF GOOD.

YOU SCARED, RIDDLER?

YOU DON'T KNOW THE JOKER, BOY WONDER.

OH, YOU AND BATMAN MIGHT CATCH HIM FROM TIME TO TIME, BUT YOU DON'T LIVE WITH HIM LIKE I DO. HE'S A MANIAC.

AND WHEN THAT MANIAC GETS IT INTO HIS MIND TO DO SOMETHING, HE'S UNSTOPPABLE. EVEN BY YOU.

NO, I'M NOT SCARED.

WITH THREE MINUTES LEFT UNTIL MIDNIGHT, I'M JUST RESIGNED.

7

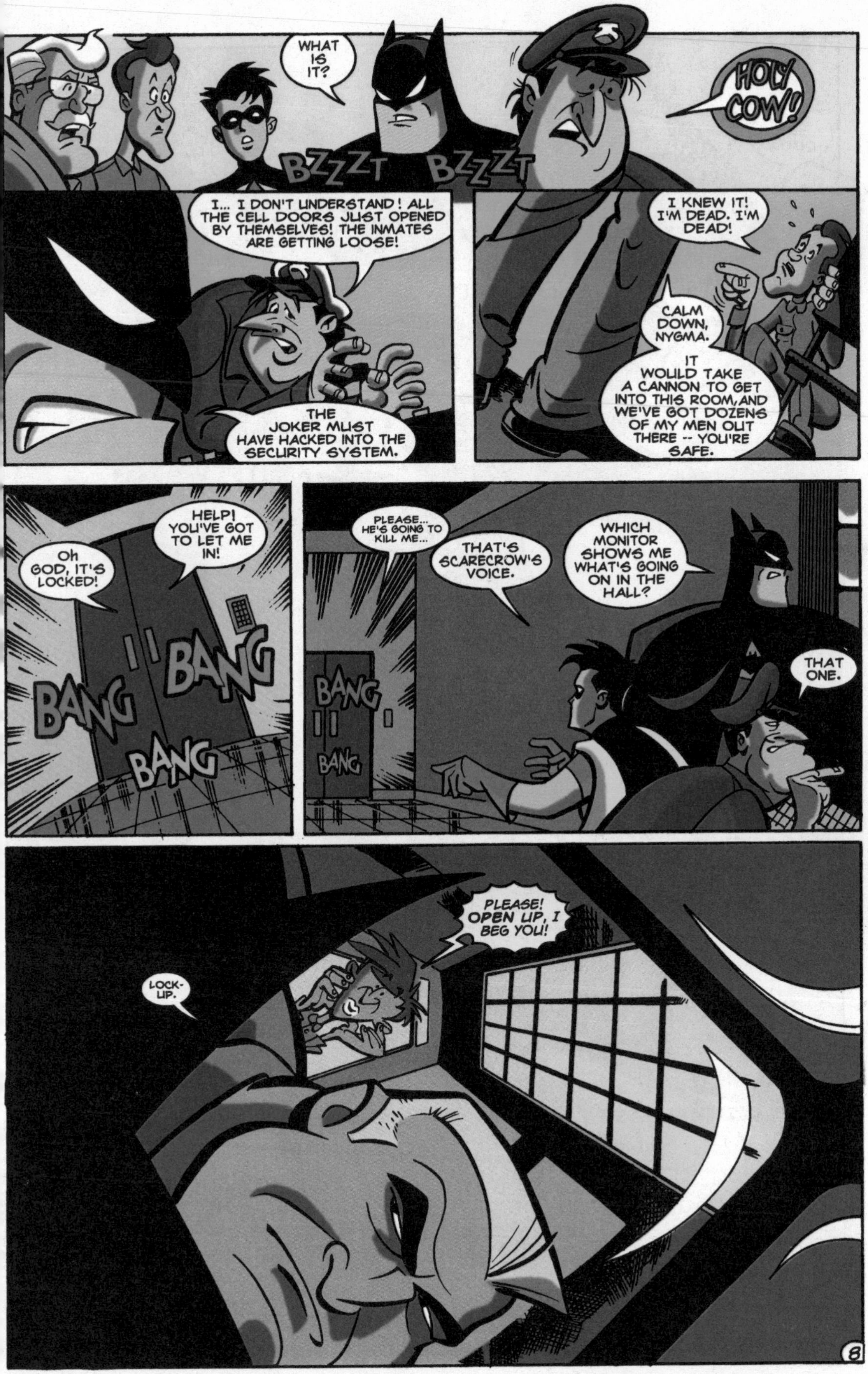
WHAT IS IT?
BZZZT BZZZT
HOLY COW!
I... I DON'T UNDERSTAND! ALL THE CELL DOORS JUST OPENED BY THEMSELVES! THE INMATES ARE GETTING LOOSE!
THE JOKER MUST HAVE HACKED INTO THE SECURITY SYSTEM.
I KNEW IT! I'M DEAD. I'M DEAD!
CALM DOWN, NYGMA.
IT WOULD TAKE A CANNON TO GET INTO THIS ROOM, AND WE'VE GOT DOZENS OF MY MEN OUT THERE -- YOU'RE SAFE.
Oh GOD, IT'S LOCKED!
HELP! YOU'VE GOT TO LET ME IN!
BANG BANG BANG
PLEASE... HE'S GOING TO KILL ME...
THAT'S SCARECROW'S VOICE.
WHICH MONITOR SHOWS ME WHAT'S GOING ON IN THE HALL?
BANG BANG
THAT ONE.
PLEASE! OPEN UP, I BEG YOU!
LOCK-UP.
8

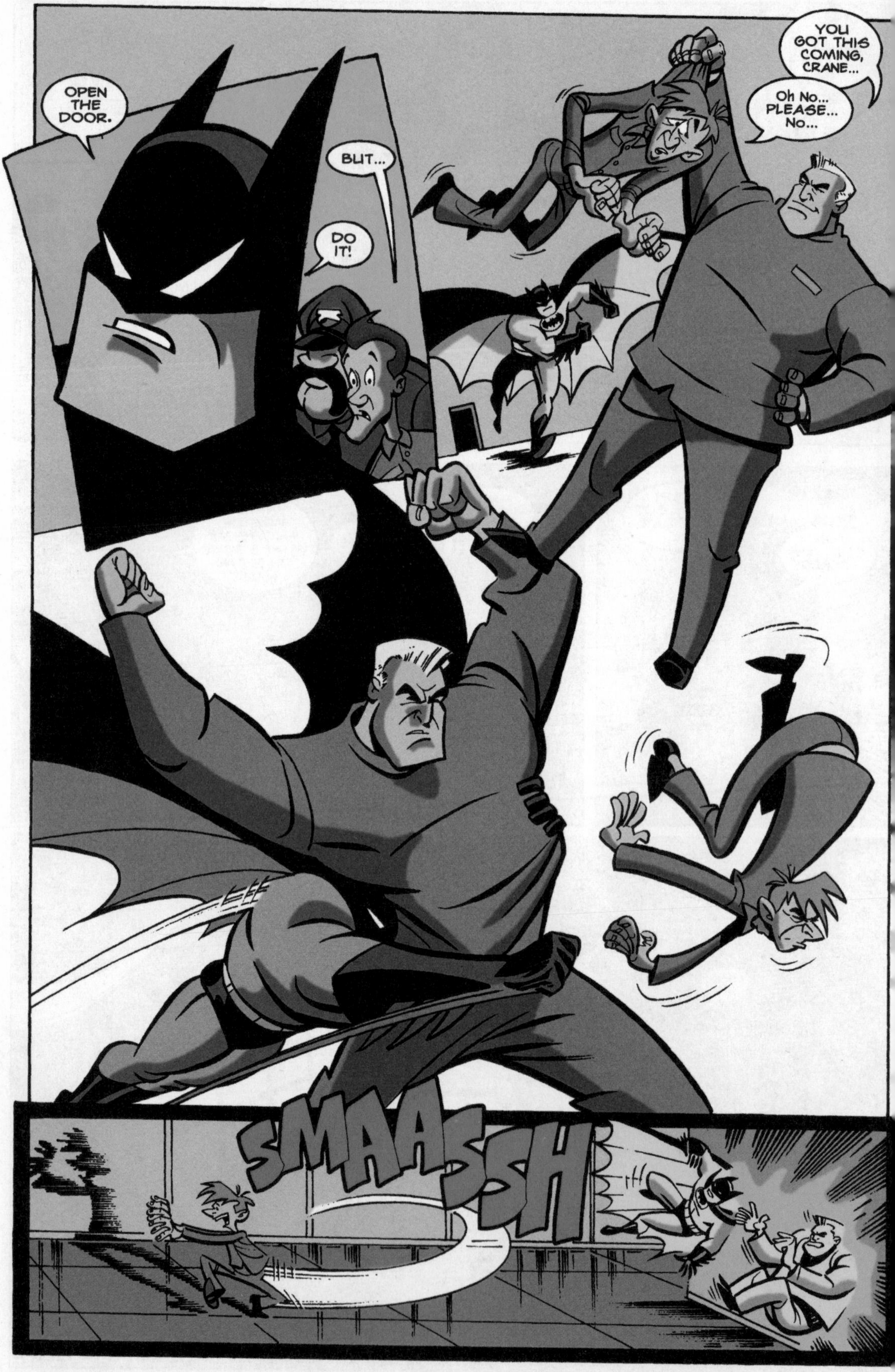
OPEN THE DOOR.
BUT...
DO IT!
YOU GOT THIS COMING, CRANE...
Oh No... PLEASE... No...
SMAASSH

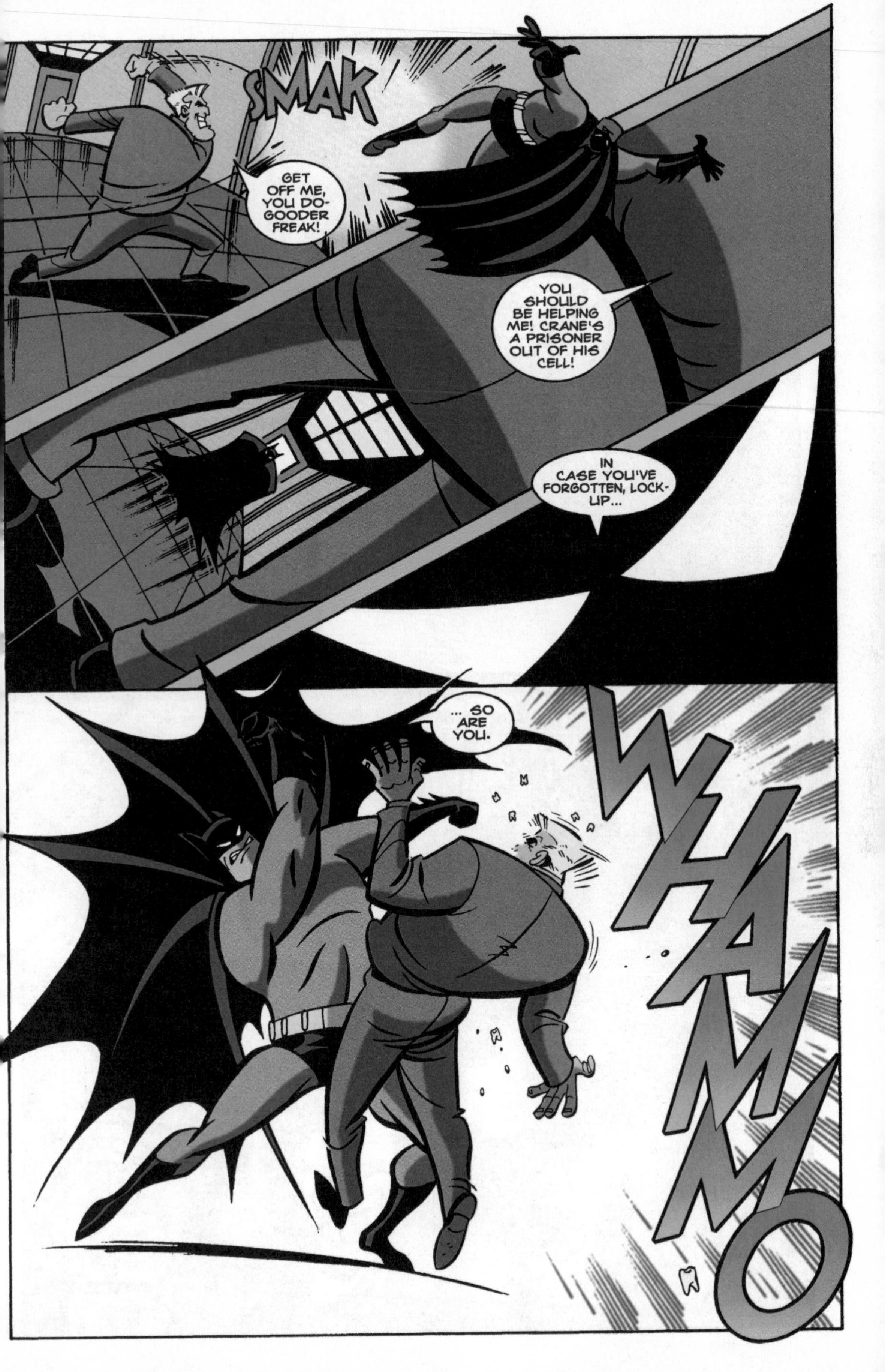
SMAK
GET OFF ME, YOU DO-GOODER FREAK!
YOU SHOULD BE HELPING ME! CRANE'S A PRISONER OUT OF HIS CELL!
IN CASE YOU'VE FORGOTTEN, LOCK-UP...
... SO ARE YOU.
WHAMMO

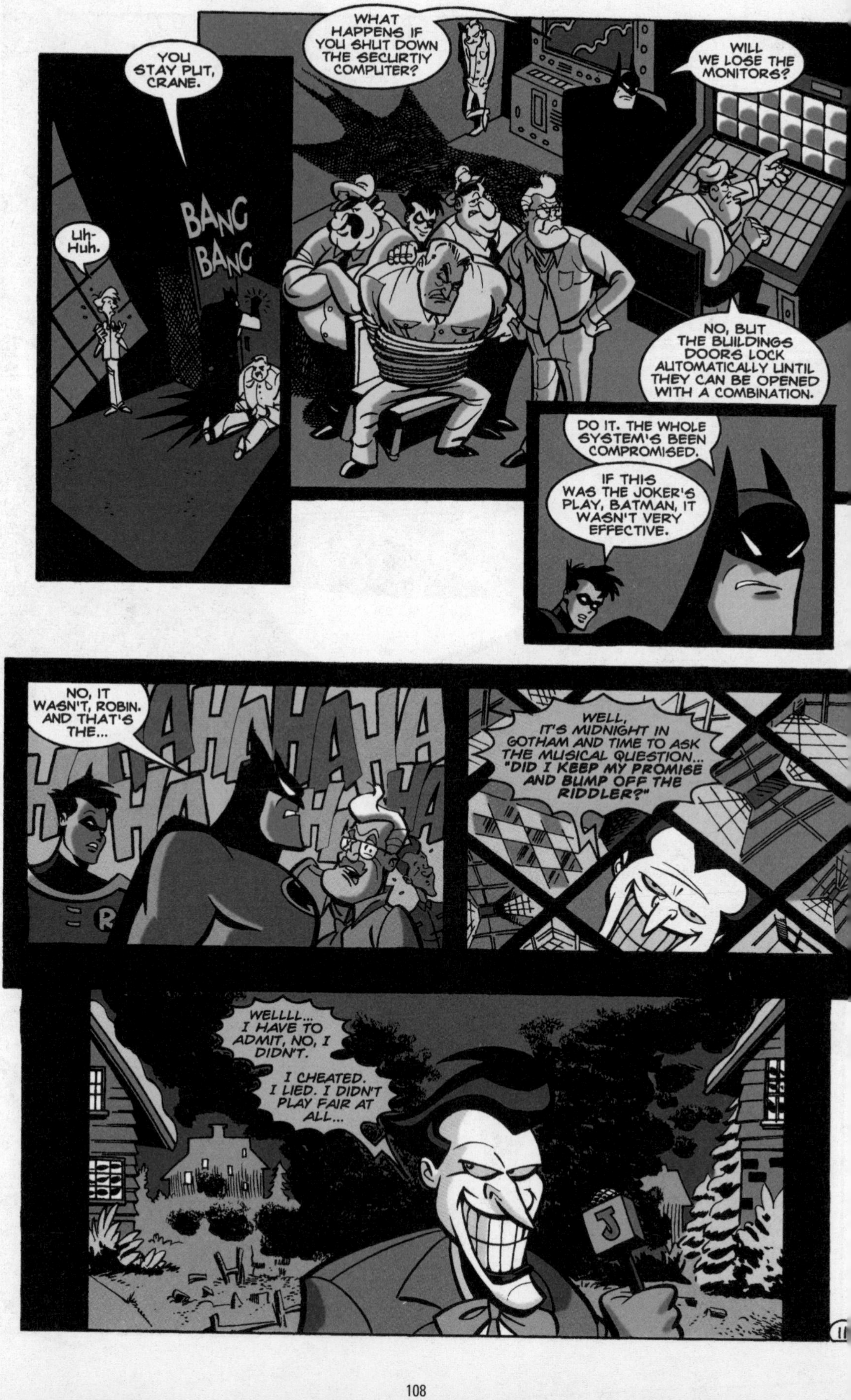
YOU STAY PUT, CRANE.
UH-HUH.
BANG
BANG
WHAT HAPPENS IF YOU SHUT DOWN THE SECURTIY COMPUTER?
WILL WE LOSE THE MONITORS?
NO, BUT THE BUILDINGS DOORS LOCK AUTOMATICALLY UNTIL THEY CAN BE OPENED WITH A COMBINATION.
DO IT. THE WHOLE SYSTEM'S BEEN COMPROMISED.
IF THIS WAS THE JOKER'S PLAY, BATMAN, IT WASN'T VERY EFFECTIVE.
NO, IT WASN'T, ROBIN. AND THAT'S THE...
WELL, IT'S MIDNIGHT IN GOTHAM AND TIME TO ASK THE MUSICAL QUESTION... "DID I KEEP MY PROMISE AND BUMP OFF THE RIDDLER?"
WELLLL... I HAVE TO ADMIT, NO, I DIDN'T.
I CHEATED. I LIED. I DIDN'T PLAY FAIR AT ALL...
J
11

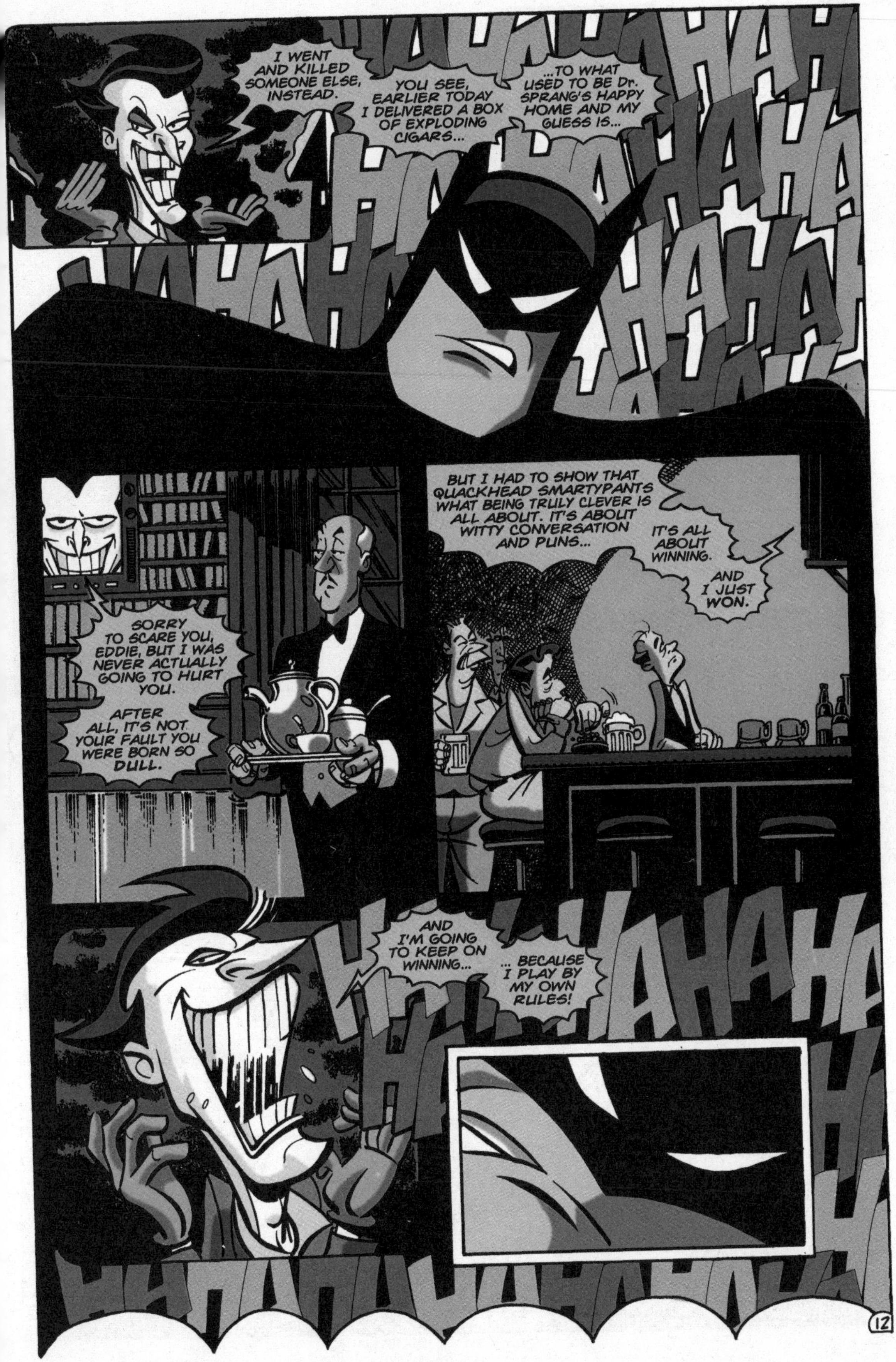
I WENT AND KILLED SOMEONE ELSE, INSTEAD.
YOU SEE, EARLIER TODAY I DELIVERED A BOX OF EXPLODING CIGARS...
...TO WHAT USED TO BE Dr. SPRANG'S HAPPY HOME AND MY GUESS IS...
SORRY TO SCARE YOU, EDDIE, BUT I WAS NEVER ACTUALLY GOING TO HURT YOU.
AFTER ALL, IT'S NOT YOUR FAULT YOU WERE BORN SO DULL.
BUT I HAD TO SHOW THAT QUACKHEAD SMARTYPANTS WHAT BEING TRULY CLEVER IS ALL ABOUT. IT'S ABOUT WITTY CONVERSATION AND PUNS...
IT'S ALL ABOUT WINNING.
AND I JUST WON.
AND I'M GOING TO KEEP ON WINNING...
... BECAUSE I PLAY BY MY OWN RULES!
12

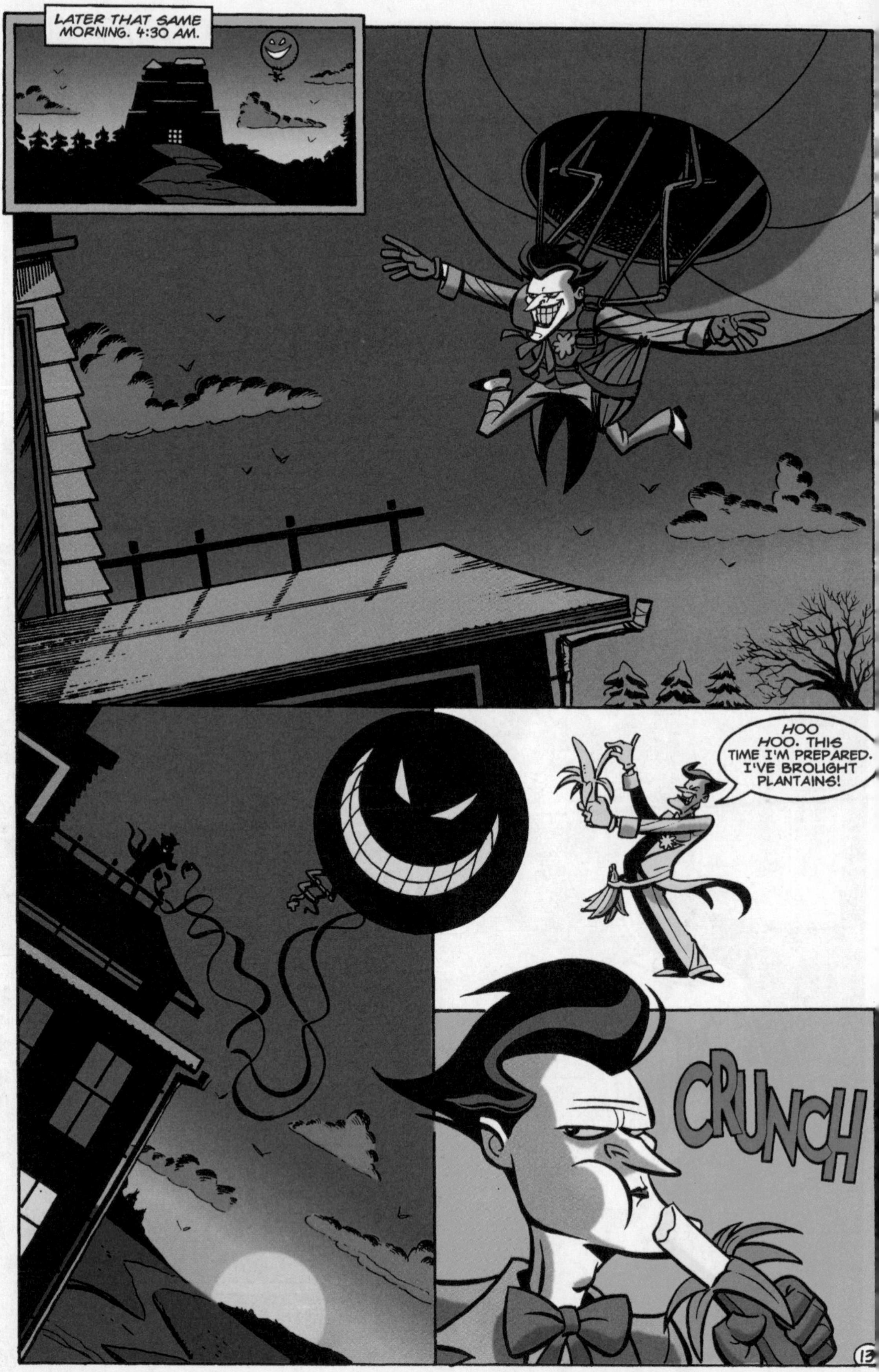
LATER THAT SAME MORNING. 4:30 AM.
HOO HOO. THIS TIME I'M PREPARED. I'VE BROUGHT PLANTAINS!
CRUNCH
13

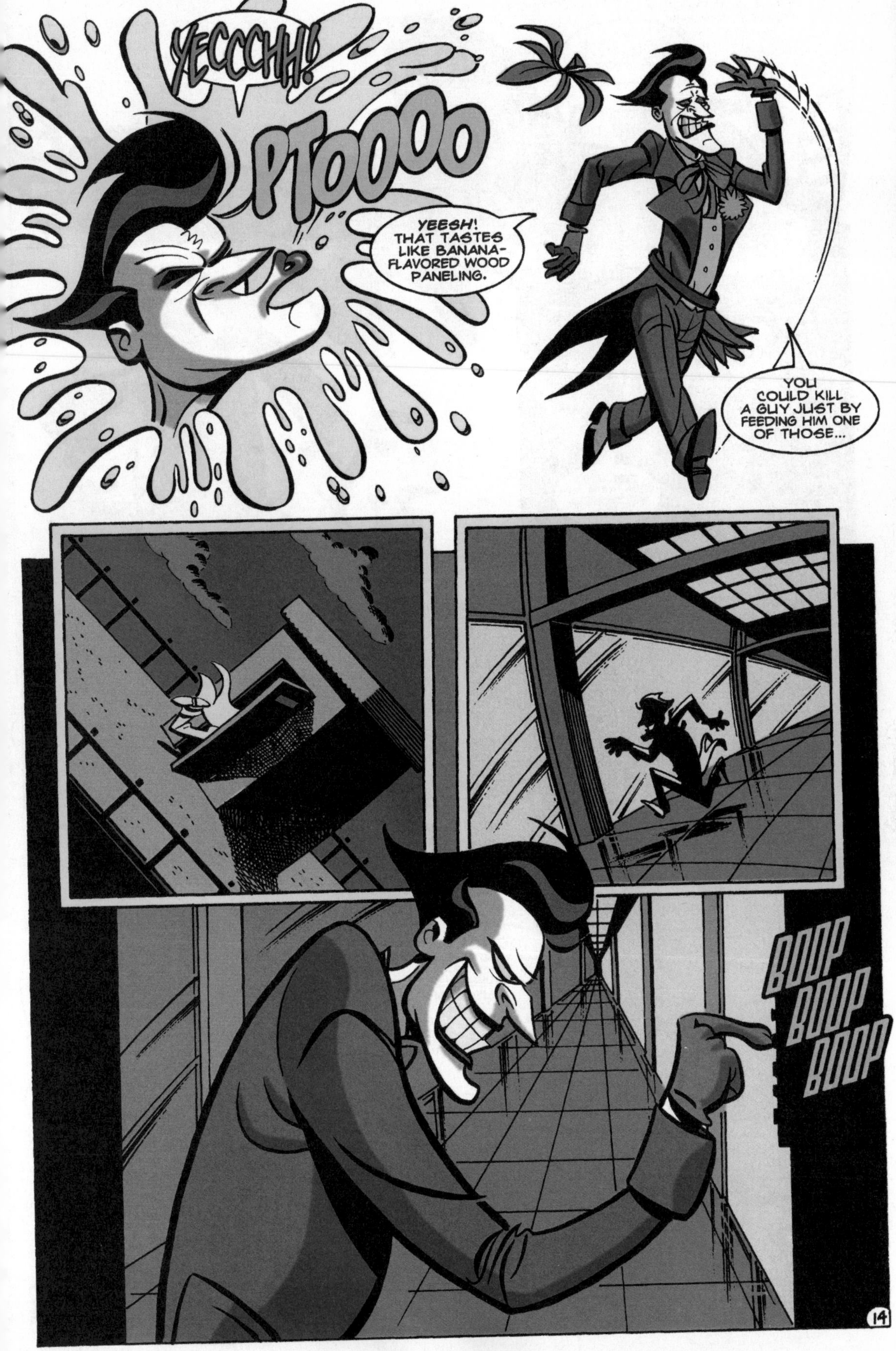
YECCCHH!
PTOOOO
YEESH! THAT TASTES LIKE BANANA-FLAVORED WOOD PANELING.
YOU COULD KILL A GUY JUST BY FEEDING HIM ONE OF THOSE...
BOOP BOOP BOOP
14

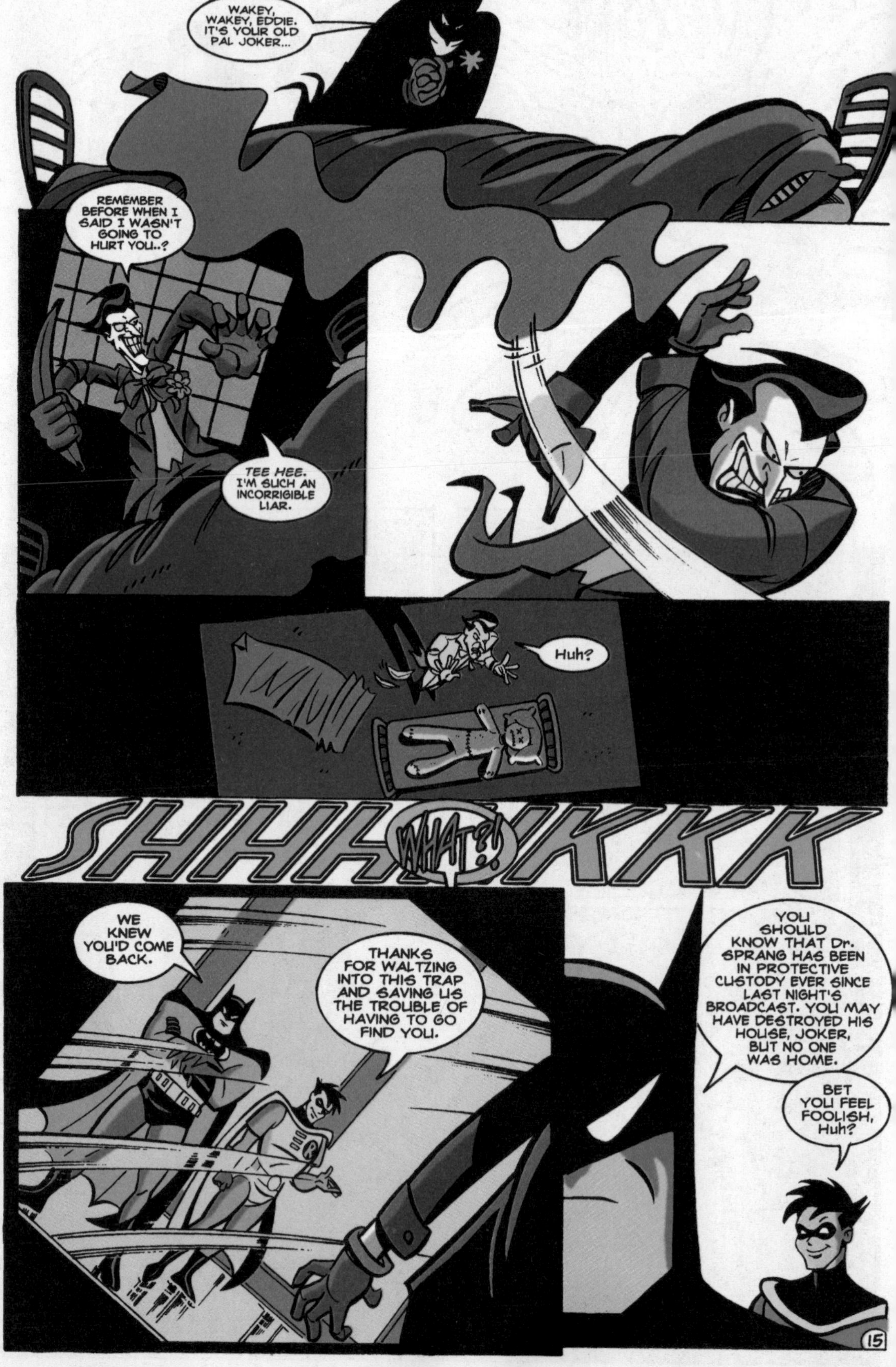
WAKEY, WAKEY, EDDIE. IT'S YOUR OLD PAL JOKER...
REMEMBER BEFORE WHEN I SAID I WASN'T GOING TO HURT YOU..?
TEE HEE. I'M SUCH AN INCORRIGIBLE LIAR.
Huh?
SHHHKKKK
WHAT?!
WE KNEW YOU'D COME BACK.
THANKS FOR WALTZING INTO THIS TRAP AND SAVING US THE TROUBLE OF HAVING TO GO FIND YOU.
YOU SHOULD KNOW THAT Dr. SPRANG HAS BEEN IN PROTECTIVE CUSTODY EVER SINCE LAST NIGHT'S BROADCAST. YOU MAY HAVE DESTROYED HIS HOUSE, JOKER, BUT NO ONE WAS HOME.
BET YOU FEEL FOOLISH, Huh?
15

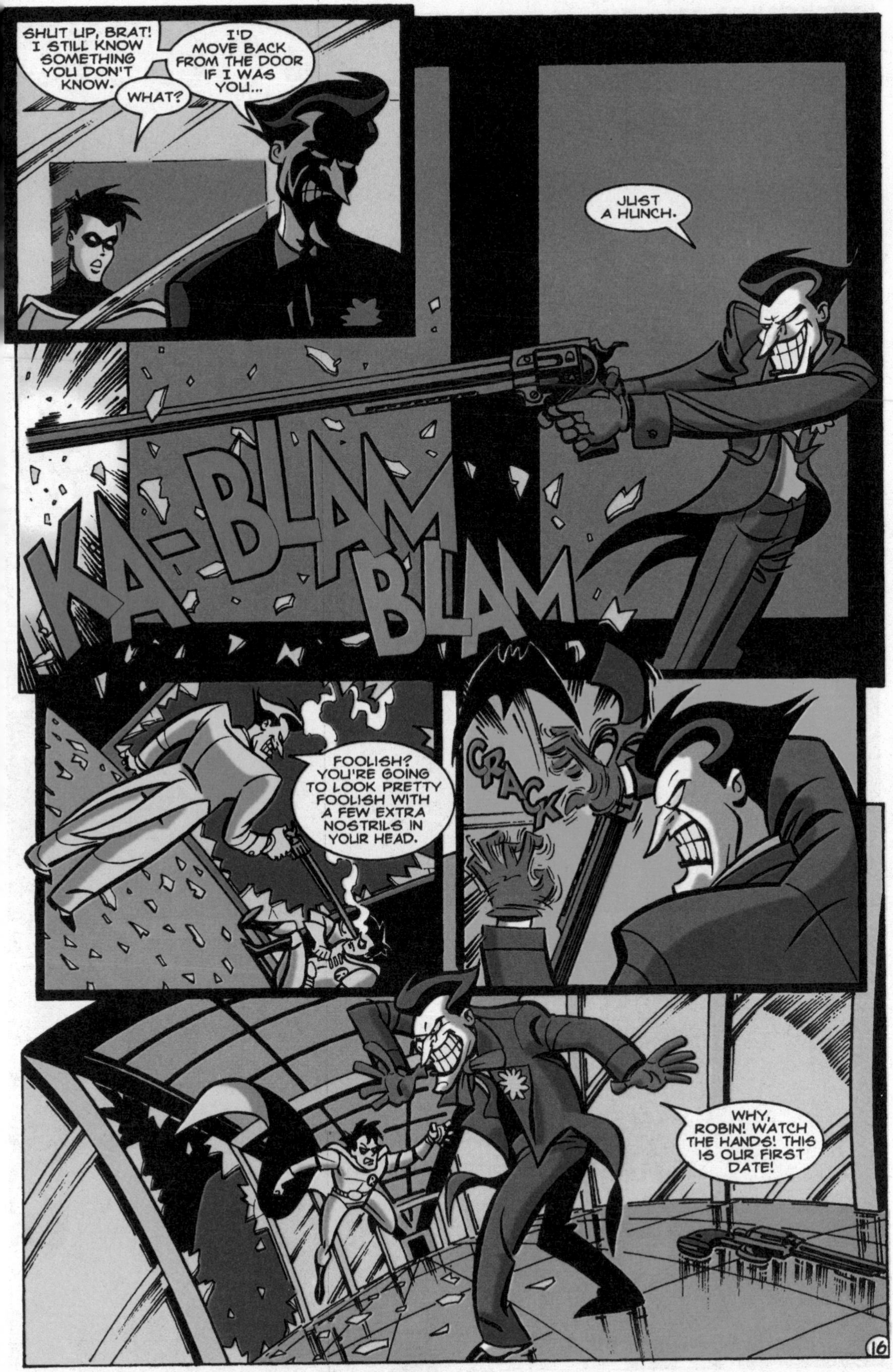
SHUT UP, BRAT! I STILL KNOW SOMETHING YOU DON'T KNOW.
WHAT?
I'D MOVE BACK FROM THE DOOR IF I WAS YOU...
JUST A HUNCH.
KA-BLAM BLAM
FOOLISH? YOU'RE GOING TO LOOK PRETTY FOOLISH WITH A FEW EXTRA NOSTRILS IN YOUR HEAD.
CRACK
WHY, ROBIN! WATCH THE HANDS! THIS IS OUR FIRST DATE!
16

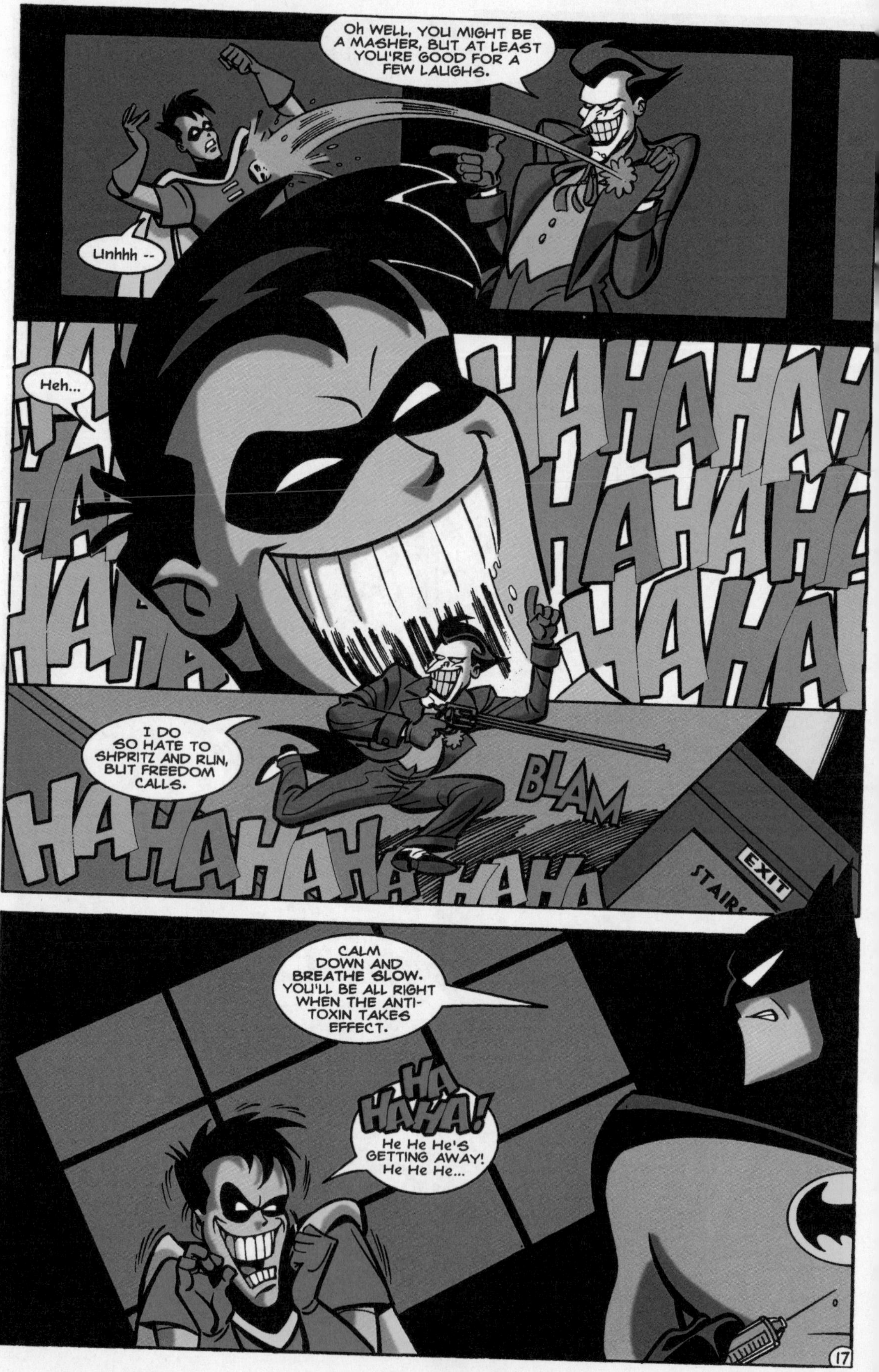
Oh WELL, YOU MIGHT BE A MASHER, BUT AT LEAST YOU'RE GOOD FOR A FEW LAUGHS.
Unhhh --
Heh...
HAHAHAHAHAHAHAHAHA
I DO SO HATE TO SHPRITZ AND RUN, BUT FREEDOM CALLS.
BLAM
HAHAHAHAHAHAHA
EXIT
STAIRS
CALM DOWN AND BREATHE SLOW. YOU'LL BE ALL RIGHT WHEN THE ANTI-TOXIN TAKES EFFECT.
HA HAHA!
He He He's GETTING AWAY! He He He...
17

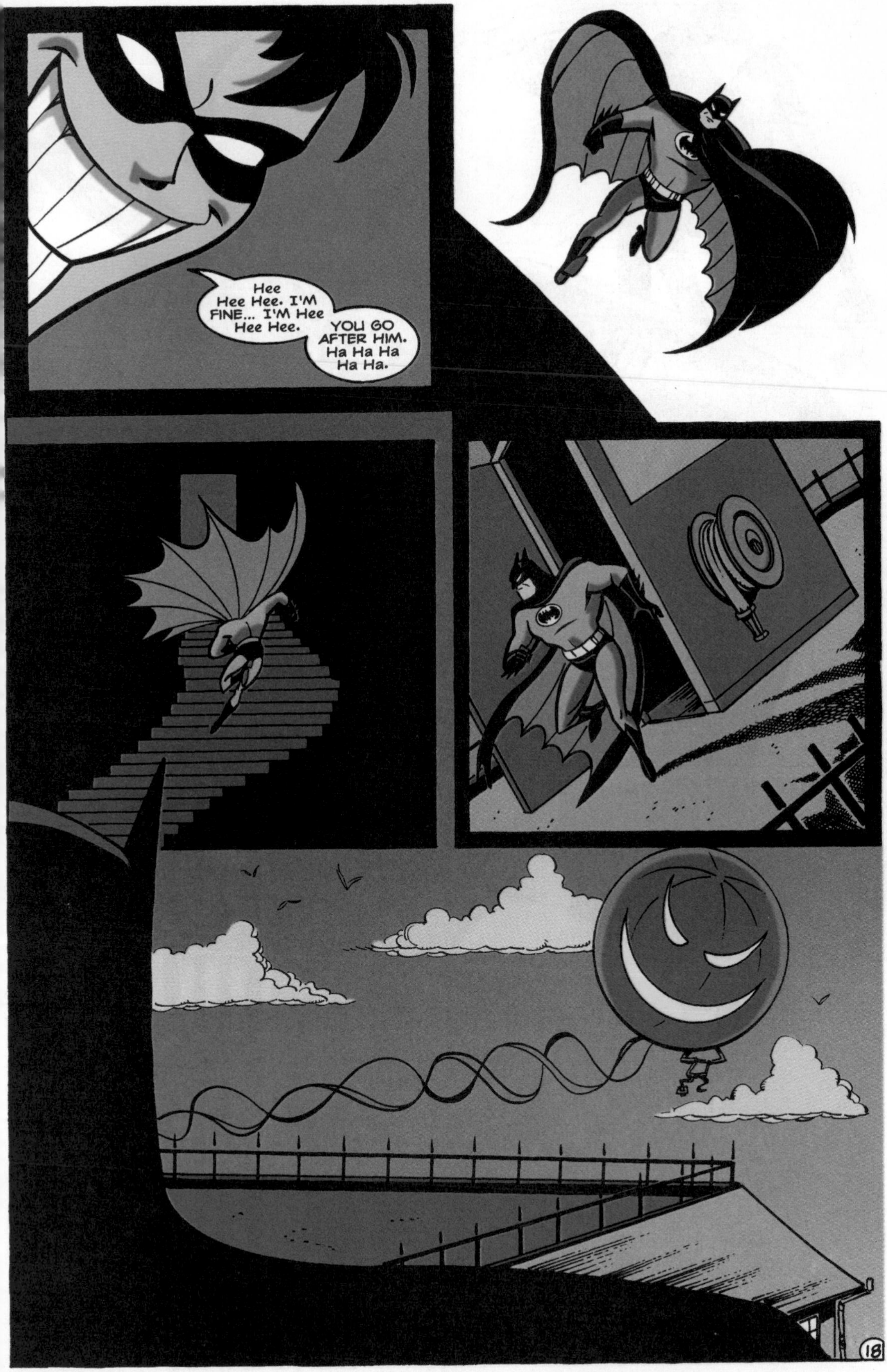
Hee Hee Hee. I'M FINE... I'M Hee Hee Hee.
YOU GO AFTER HIM. Ha Ha Ha Ha Ha.
18

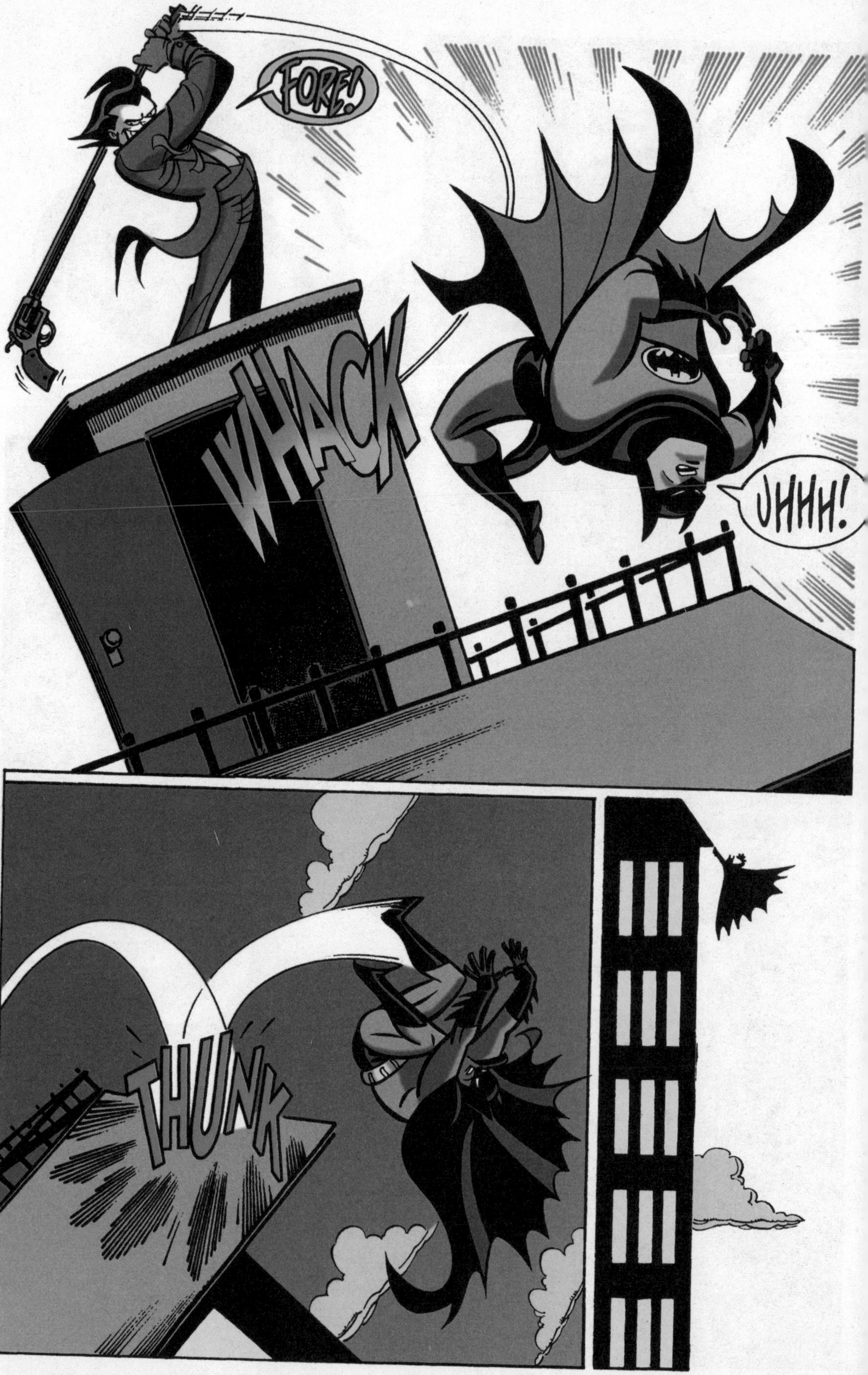
FORE!
WHACK
UHHH!
THUNK

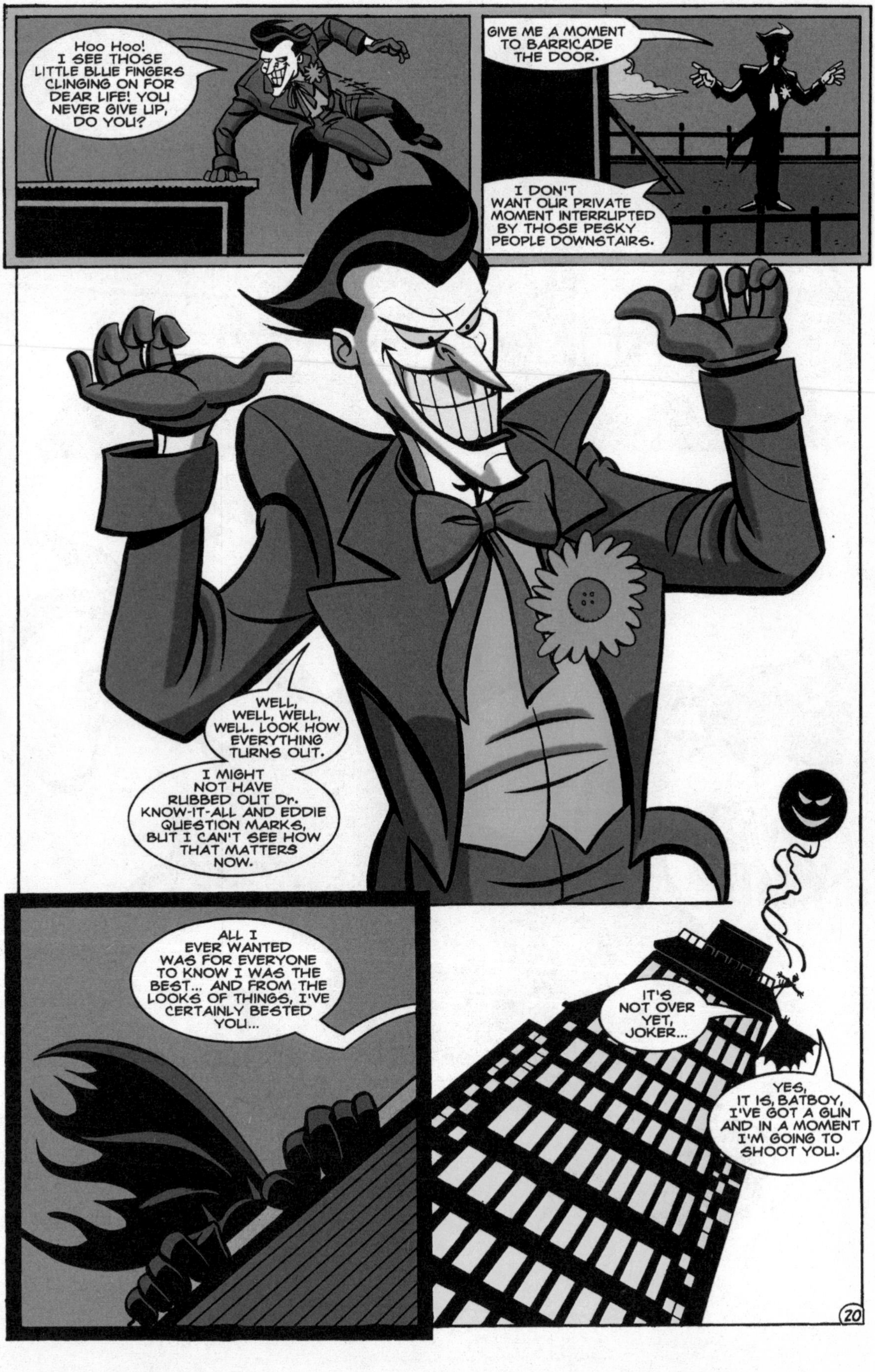
Hoo Hoo! I SEE THOSE LITTLE BLUE FINGERS CLINGING ON FOR DEAR LIFE! YOU NEVER GIVE UP, DO YOU?
GIVE ME A MOMENT TO BARRICADE THE DOOR.
I DON'T WANT OUR PRIVATE MOMENT INTERRUPTED BY THOSE PESKY PEOPLE DOWNSTAIRS.
WELL, WELL, WELL, WELL. LOOK HOW EVERYTHING TURNS OUT.
I MIGHT NOT HAVE RUBBED OUT Dr. KNOW-IT-ALL AND EDDIE QUESTION MARKS, BUT I CAN'T SEE HOW THAT MATTERS NOW.
ALL I EVER WANTED WAS FOR EVERYONE TO KNOW I WAS THE BEST... AND FROM THE LOOKS OF THINGS, I'VE CERTAINLY BESTED YOU...
IT'S NOT OVER YET, JOKER...
YES, IT IS, BATBOY, I'VE GOT A GUN AND IN A MOMENT I'M GOING TO SHOOT YOU.
20

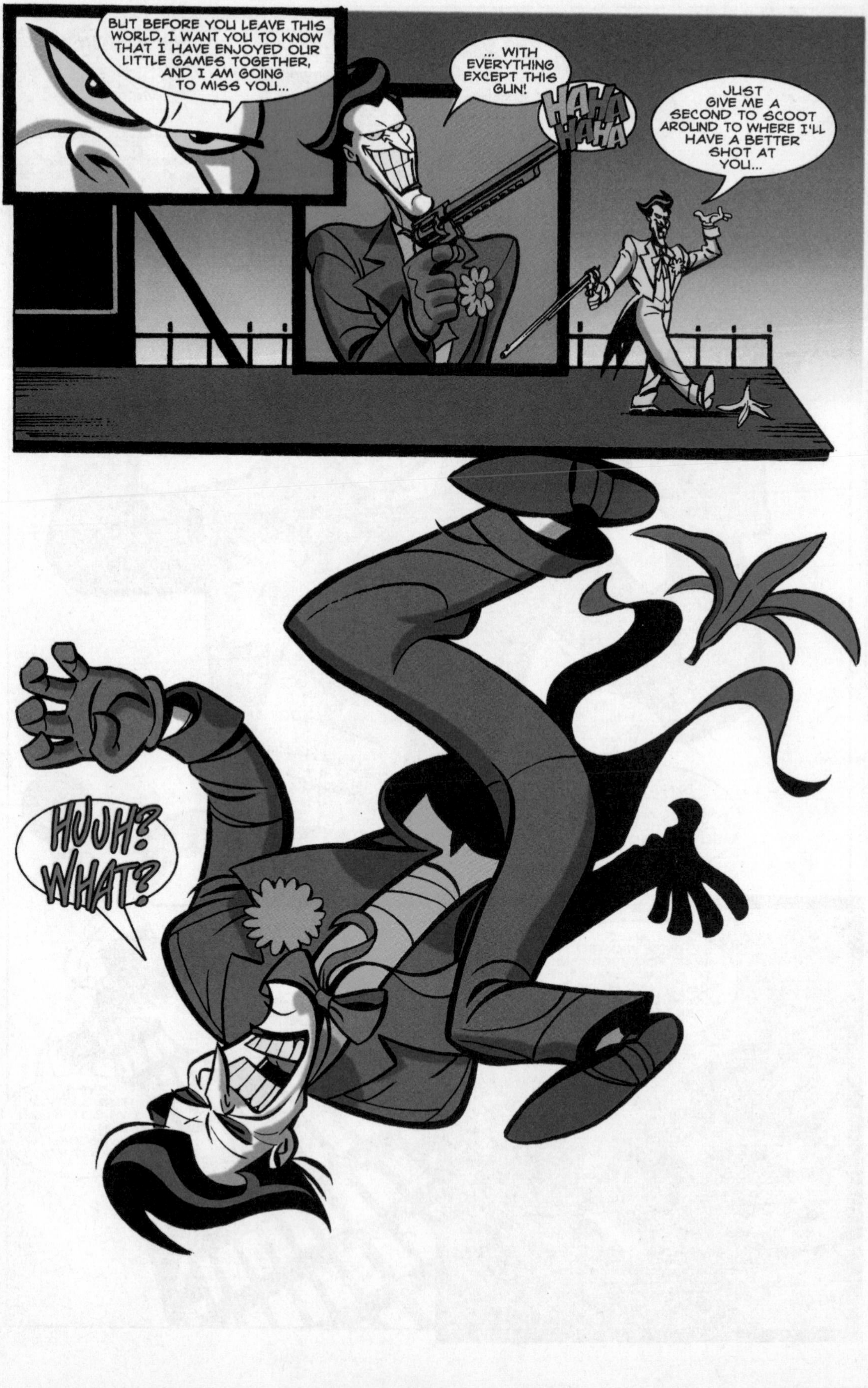
BUT BEFORE YOU LEAVE THIS WORLD, I WANT YOU TO KNOW THAT I HAVE ENJOYED OUR LITTLE GAMES TOGETHER, AND I AM GOING TO MISS YOU...
... WITH EVERYTHING EXCEPT THIS GUN!
HAHA HAHA
JUST GIVE ME A SECOND TO SCOOT AROUND TO WHERE I'LL HAVE A BETTER SHOT AT YOU...
HUJH? WHAT?

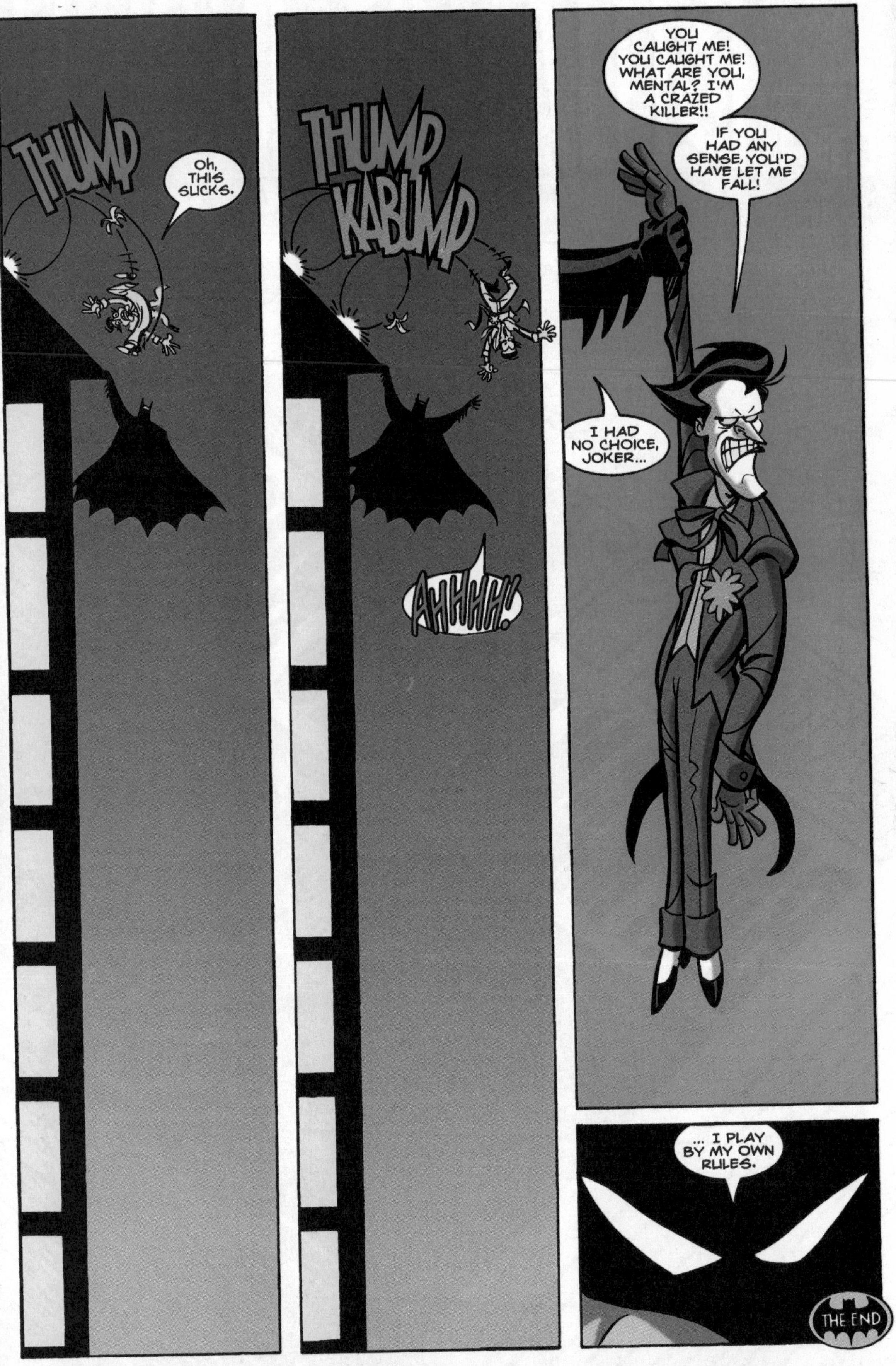
THUMP
Oh, THIS SUCKS.
THUMP
KABUMP
AHHHH!
YOU CAUGHT ME! YOU CAUGHT ME! WHAT ARE YOU, MENTAL? I'M A CRAZED KILLER!!
IF YOU HAD ANY SENSE, YOU'D HAVE LET ME FALL!
I HAD NO CHOICE, JOKER...
... I PLAY BY MY OWN RULES.
THE END

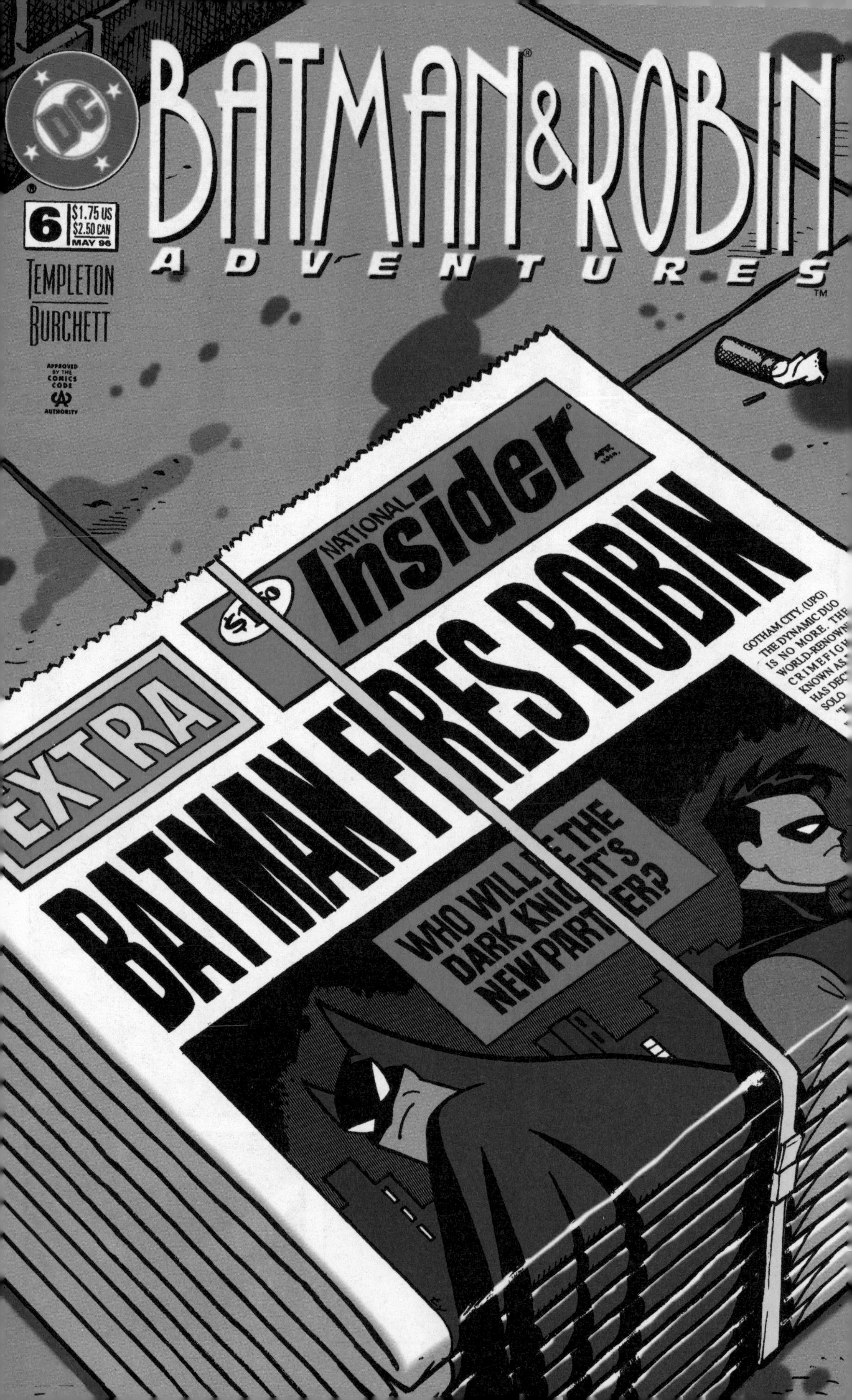
BATMAN® & ROBIN®
ADVENTURES™
DC
6 $1.75 US $2.50 CAN MAY 96
TEMPLETON
BURCHETT
APPROVED BY THE COMICS CODE AUTHORITY
NATIONAL Insider®
EXTRA
BATMAN FIRES ROBIN
GOTHAM CITY. (UPG) THE DYNAMIC DUO IS NO MORE. THE WORLD-RENOWN CRIMEFIGH KNOWN AS HAS DEC SOLO
WHO WILL E THE DARK KNIG T'S NEW PART ER?

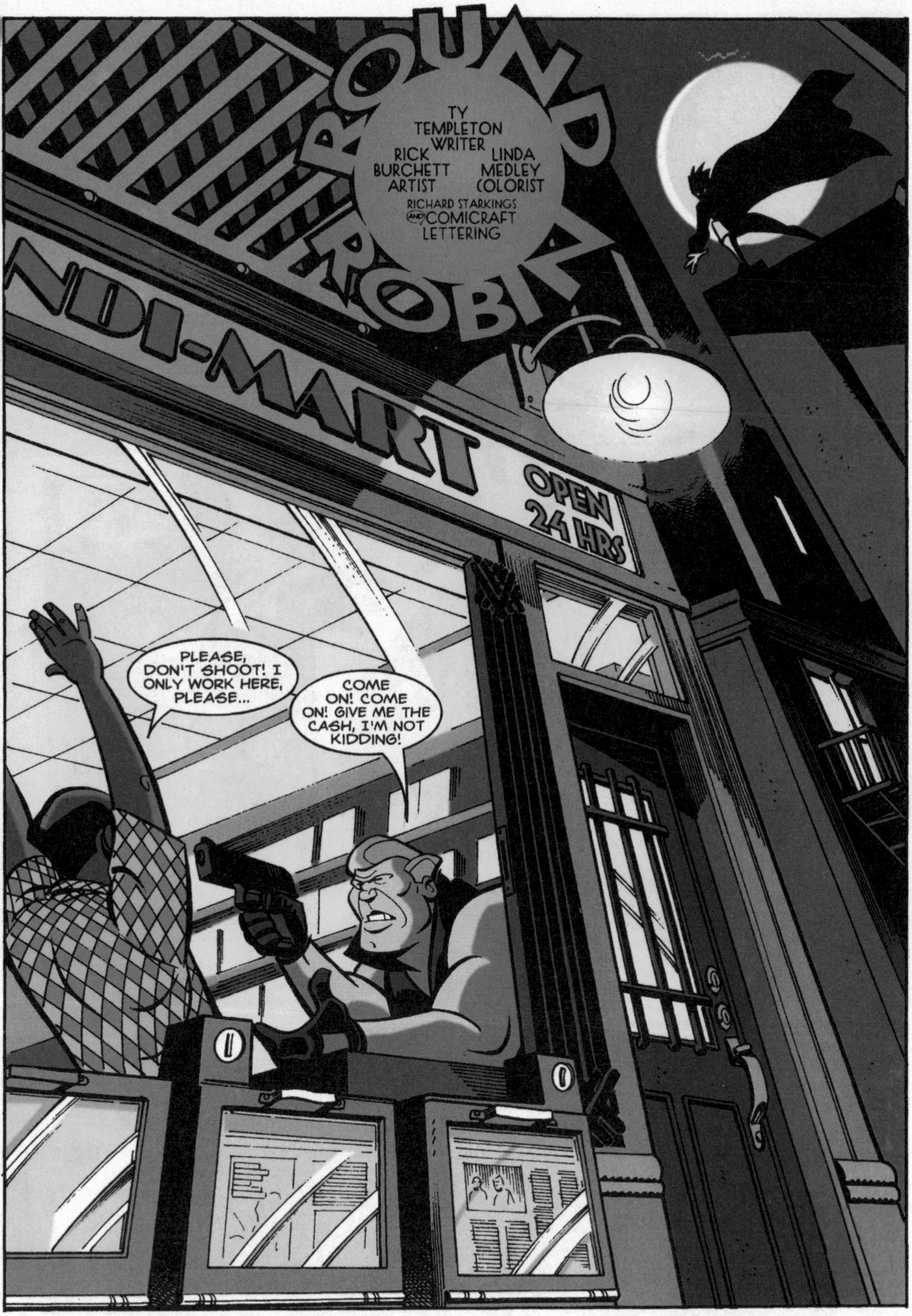
ROUND ROBIN
TY TEMPLETON WRITER
RICK BURCHETT ARTIST
LINDA MEDLEY COLORIST
RICHARD STARKINGS AND COMICRAFT LETTERING
NDI-MART
OPEN 24 HRS
PLEASE, DON'T SHOOT! I ONLY WORK HERE, PLEASE...
COME ON! COME ON! GIVE ME THE CASH, I'M NOT KIDDING!

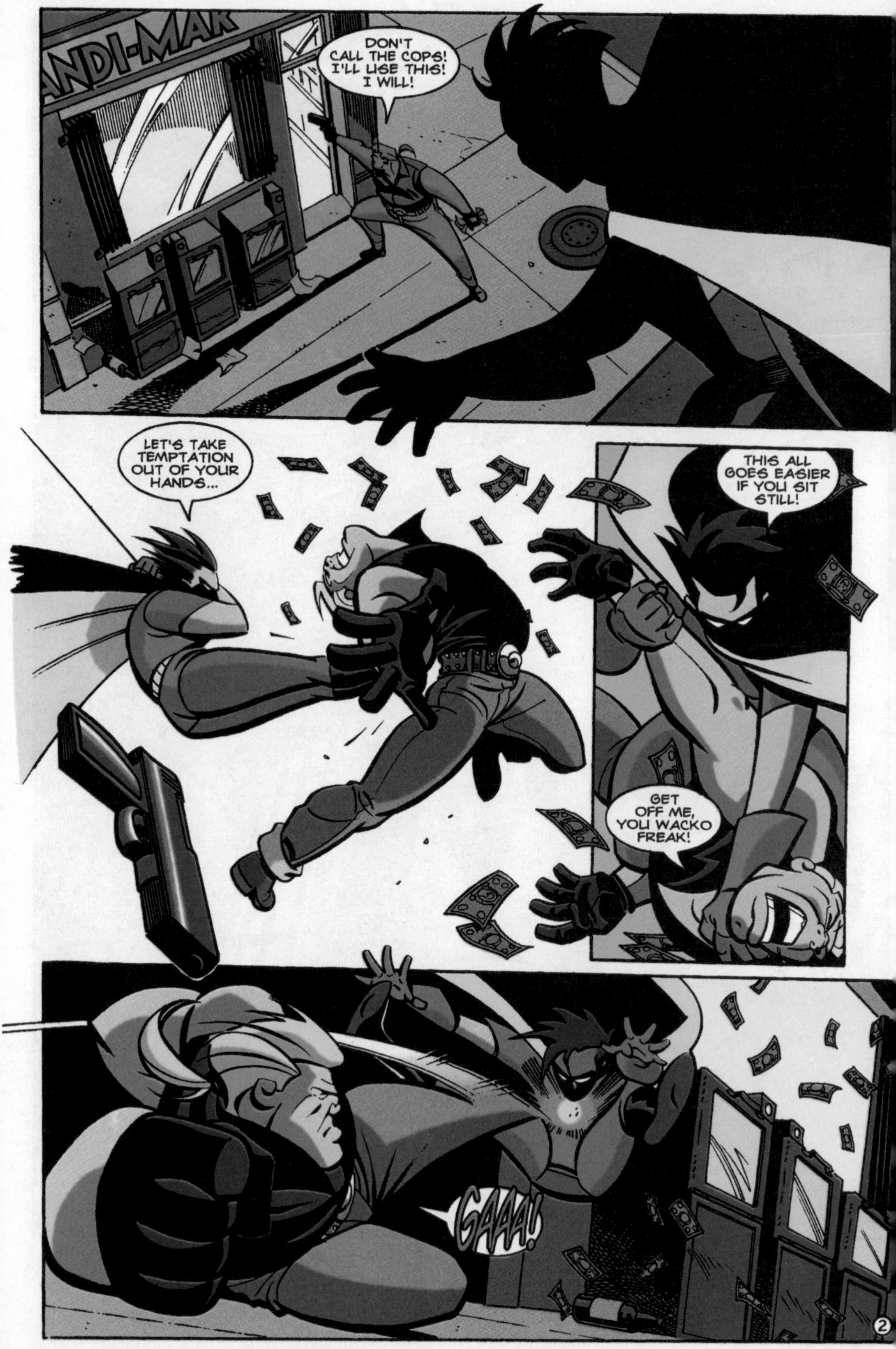
ANDI-MAK
DON'T CALL THE COPS! I'LL USE THIS! I WILL!
LET'S TAKE TEMPTATION OUT OF YOUR HANDS...
THIS ALL GOES EASIER IF YOU SIT STILL!
GET OFF ME, YOU WACKO FREAK!
GAAA!
2

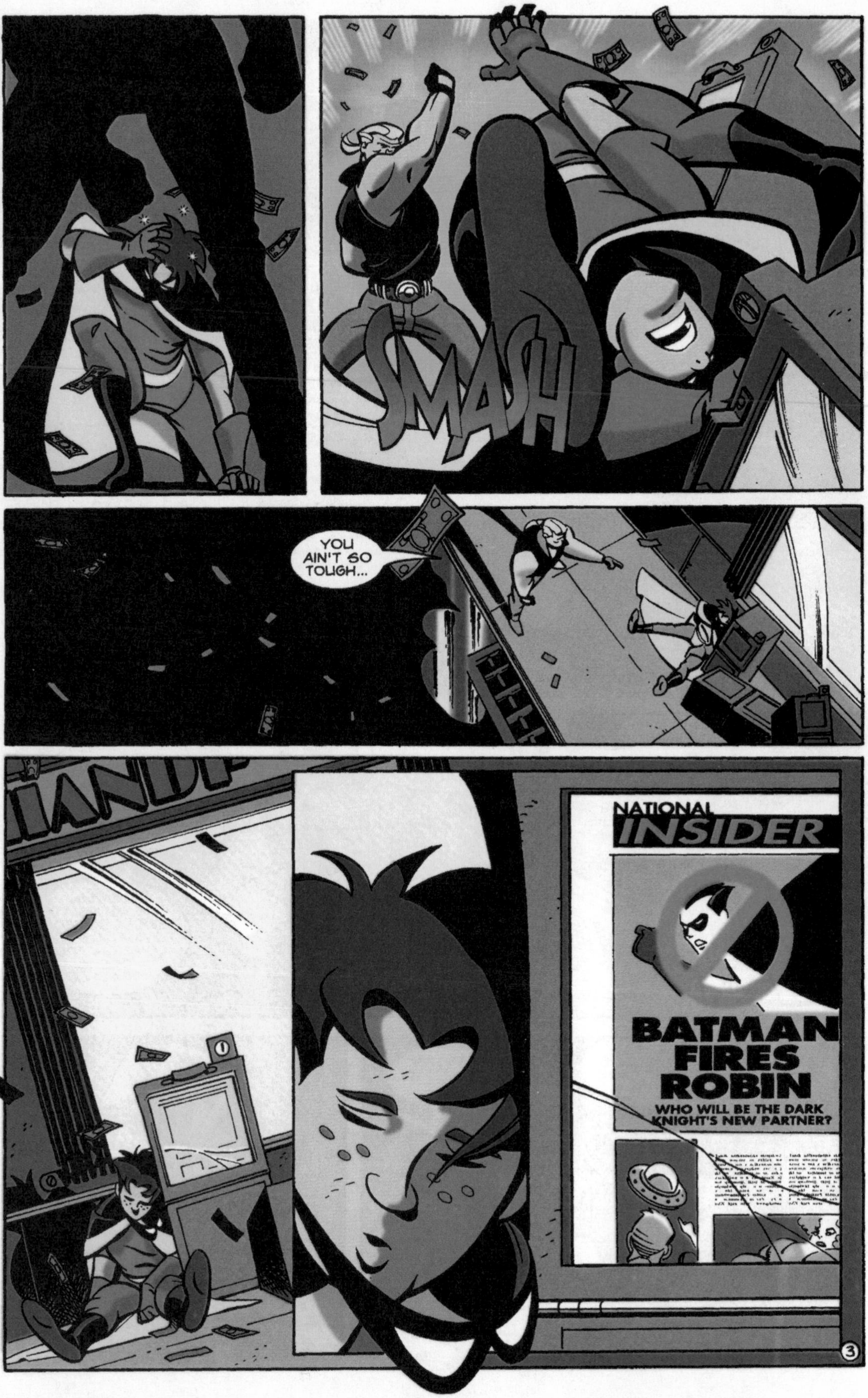
SMASH
YOU AIN'T SO TOUGH...
NATIONAL INSIDER
BATMAN FIRES ROBIN
WHO WILL BE THE DARK KNIGHT'S NEW PARTNER?
3

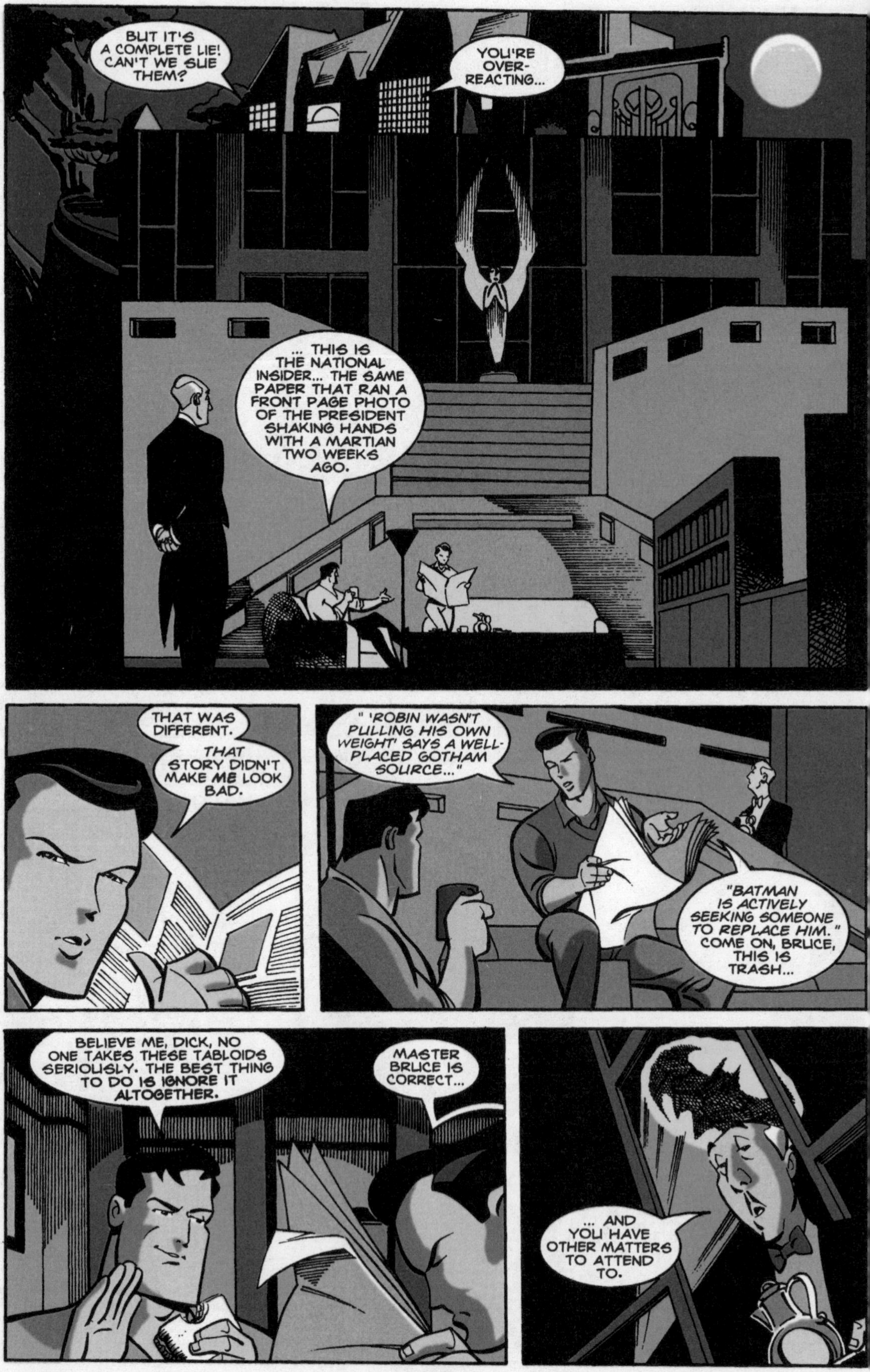
BUT IT'S A COMPLETE LIE! CAN'T WE SUE THEM?
YOU'RE OVER-REACTING...
... THIS IS THE NATIONAL INSIDER... THE SAME PAPER THAT RAN A FRONT PAGE PHOTO OF THE PRESIDENT SHAKING HANDS WITH A MARTIAN TWO WEEKS AGO.
THAT WAS DIFFERENT.
THAT STORY DIDN'T MAKE ME LOOK BAD.
" 'ROBIN WASN'T PULLING HIS OWN WEIGHT' SAYS A WELL-PLACED GOTHAM SOURCE..."
"BATMAN IS ACTIVELY SEEKING SOMEONE TO REPLACE HIM." COME ON, BRUCE, THIS IS TRASH...
BELIEVE ME, DICK, NO ONE TAKES THESE TABLOIDS SERIOUSLY. THE BEST THING TO DO IS IGNORE IT ALTOGETHER.
MASTER BRUCE IS CORRECT...
... AND YOU HAVE OTHER MATTERS TO ATTEND TO.

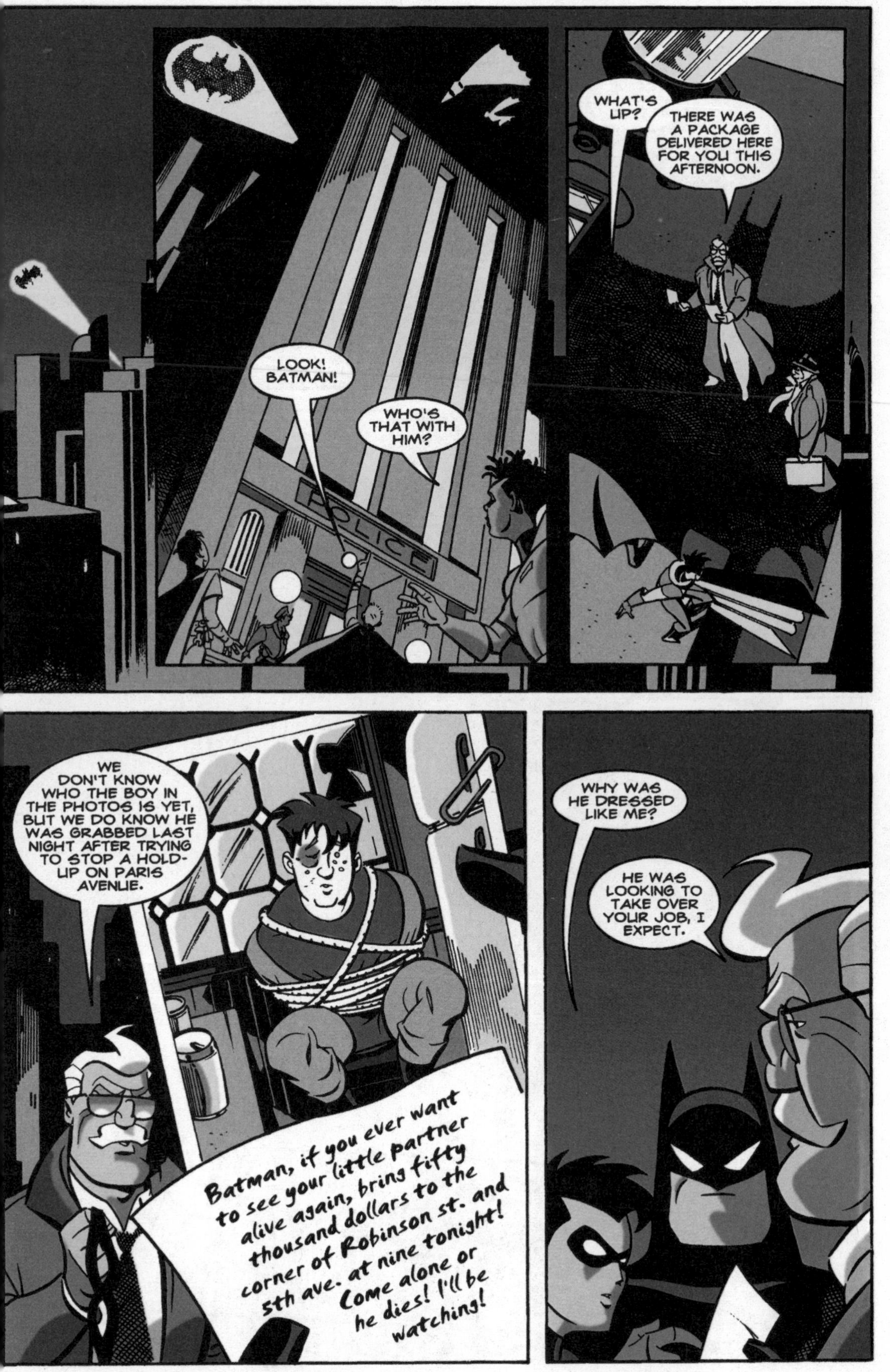
LOOK! BATMAN!
WHO'S THAT WITH HIM?
WHAT'S UP?
THERE WAS A PACKAGE DELIVERED HERE FOR YOU THIS AFTERNOON.
WE DON'T KNOW WHO THE BOY IN THE PHOTOS IS YET, BUT WE DO KNOW HE WAS GRABBED LAST NIGHT AFTER TRYING TO STOP A HOLD-UP ON PARIS AVENUE.
Batman, if you ever want to see your little partner alive again, bring fifty thousand dollars to the corner of Robinson st. and 5th ave. at nine tonight! Come alone or he dies! I'll be watching!
WHY WAS HE DRESSED LIKE ME?
HE WAS LOOKING TO TAKE OVER YOUR JOB, I EXPECT.

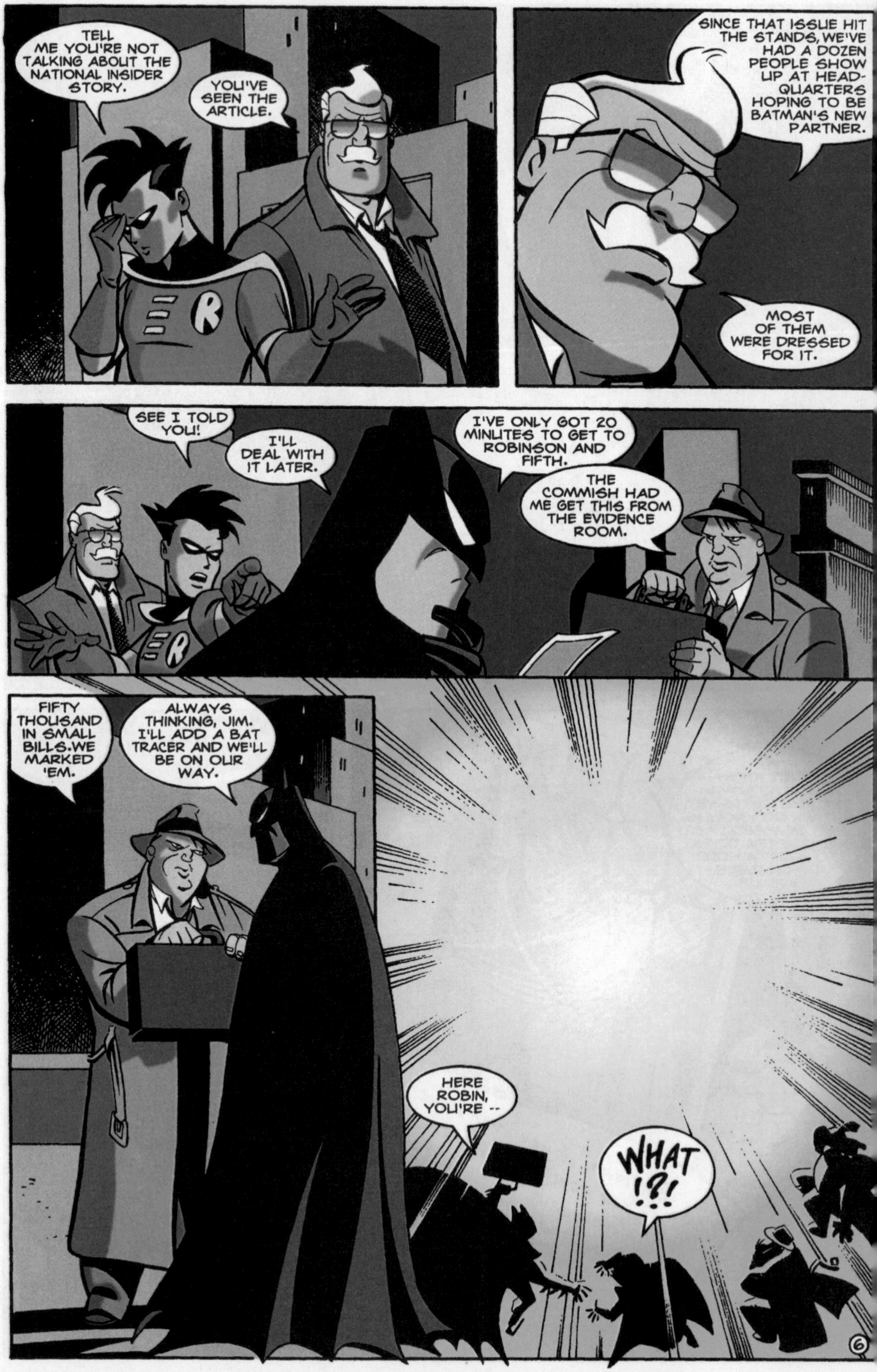
TELL ME YOU'RE NOT TALKING ABOUT THE NATIONAL INSIDER STORY.
YOU'VE SEEN THE ARTICLE.
SINCE THAT ISSUE HIT THE STANDS, WE'VE HAD A DOZEN PEOPLE SHOW UP AT HEAD-QUARTERS HOPING TO BE BATMAN'S NEW PARTNER.
MOST OF THEM WERE DRESSED FOR IT.
SEE I TOLD YOU!
I'LL DEAL WITH IT LATER.
I'VE ONLY GOT 20 MINUTES TO GET TO ROBINSON AND FIFTH.
THE COMMISH HAD ME GET THIS FROM THE EVIDENCE ROOM.
FIFTY THOUSAND IN SMALL BILLS. WE MARKED 'EM.
ALWAYS THINKING, JIM. I'LL ADD A BAT TRACER AND WE'LL BE ON OUR WAY.
HERE ROBIN, YOU'RE --
WHAT !?!
6

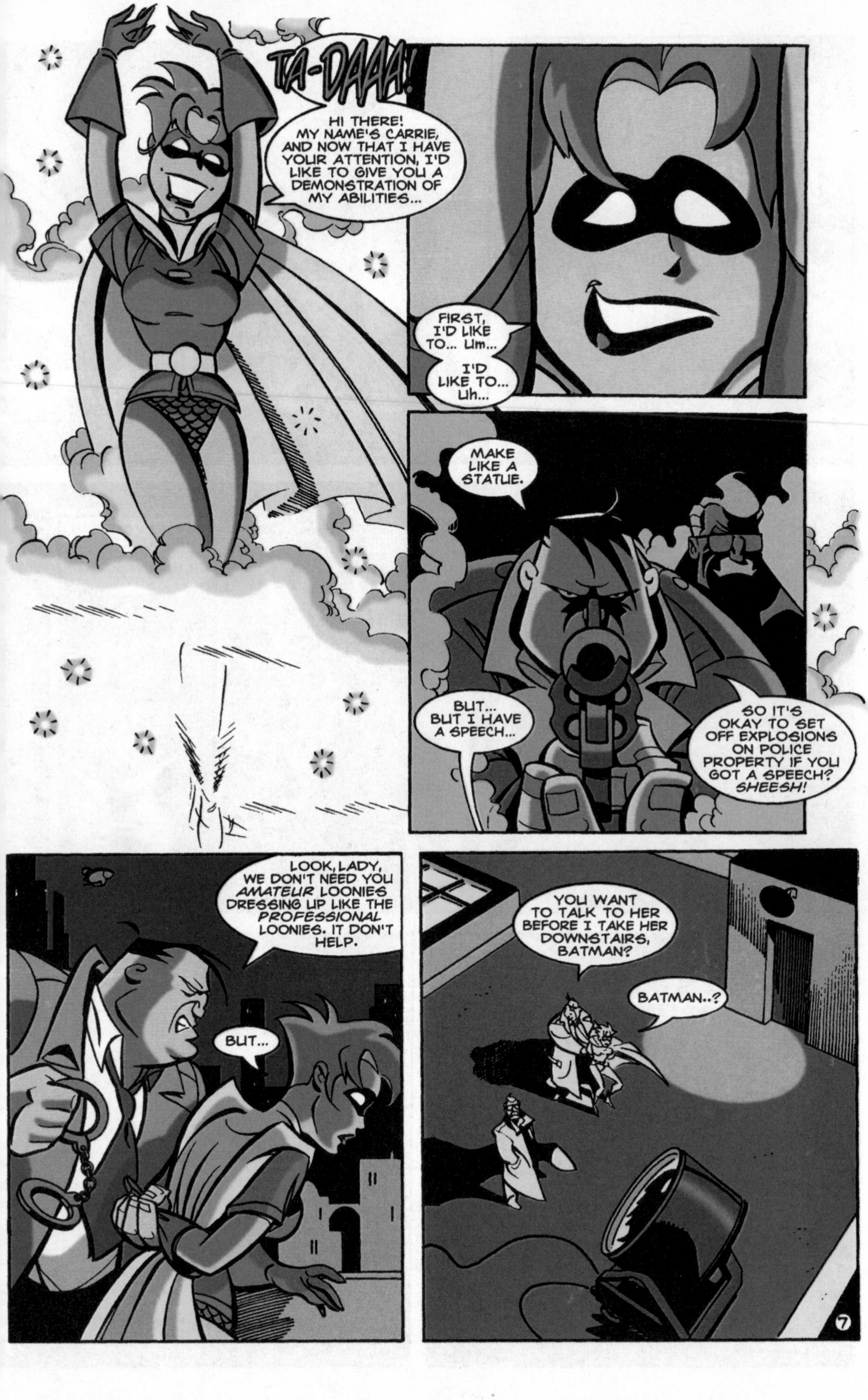
TA-DAAA!
HI THERE! MY NAME'S CARRIE, AND NOW THAT I HAVE YOUR ATTENTION, I'D LIKE TO GIVE YOU A DEMONSTRATION OF MY ABILITIES...
FIRST, I'D LIKE TO... UM...
I'D LIKE TO... UH...
MAKE LIKE A STATUE.
BUT... BUT I HAVE A SPEECH...
SO IT'S OKAY TO SET OFF EXPLOSIONS ON POLICE PROPERTY IF YOU GOT A SPEECH? SHEESH!
LOOK, LADY, WE DON'T NEED YOU AMATEUR LOONIES DRESSING UP LIKE THE PROFESSIONAL LOONIES. IT DON'T HELP.
BUT...
YOU WANT TO TALK TO HER BEFORE I TAKE HER DOWNSTAIRS, BATMAN?
BATMAN..?
7

THERE THEY GO!

COME ON!

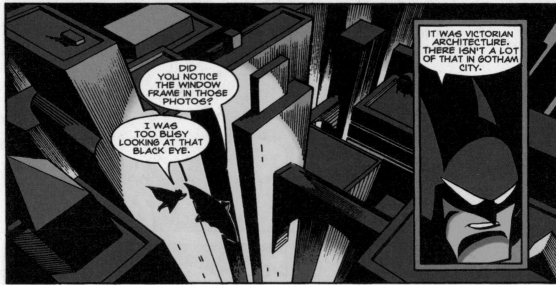

DID YOU NOTICE THE WINDOW FRAME IN THOSE PHOTOS?

I WAS TOO BUSY LOOKING AT THAT BLACK EYE.

IT WAS VICTORIAN ARCHITECTURE. THERE ISN'T A LOT OF THAT IN GOTHAM CITY.

AND ALL OF IT IN THE CABBAGETOWN DISTRICT, SOUTH OF THE PARK.

THERE'RE HUNDREDS OF WINDOWS IN CABBAGE-TOWN --

BUT ONLY ONE LIKE THAT WITH A BROKEN PANE IN THE UPPER RIGHT CORNER.

GET ON IT. I'M GOING TO THE RENDEZVOUS.

CALL ME ON YOUR RADIO IF YOU FIND ANYTHING.

8

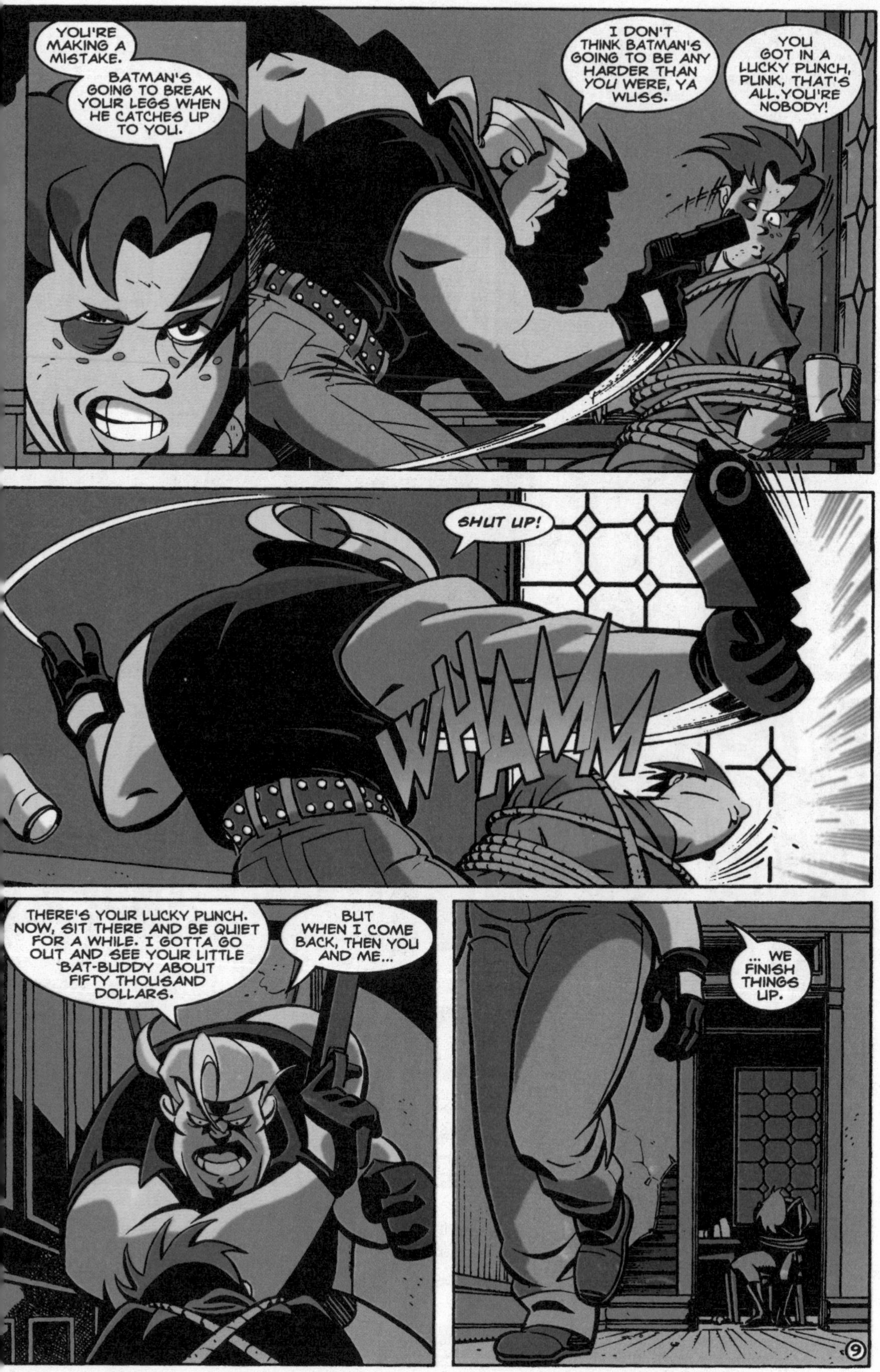
YOU'RE MAKING A MISTAKE.
BATMAN'S GOING TO BREAK YOUR LEGS WHEN HE CATCHES UP TO YOU.
I DON'T THINK BATMAN'S GOING TO BE ANY HARDER THAN YOU WERE, YA WUSS.
YOU GOT IN A LUCKY PUNCH, PUNK, THAT'S ALL. YOU'RE NOBODY!
SHUT UP!
WHAMM
THERE'S YOUR LUCKY PUNCH. NOW, SIT THERE AND BE QUIET FOR A WHILE. I GOTTA GO OUT AND SEE YOUR LITTLE BAT-BUDDY ABOUT FIFTY THOUSAND DOLLARS.
BUT WHEN I COME BACK, THEN YOU AND ME...
... WE FINISH THINGS UP.
9

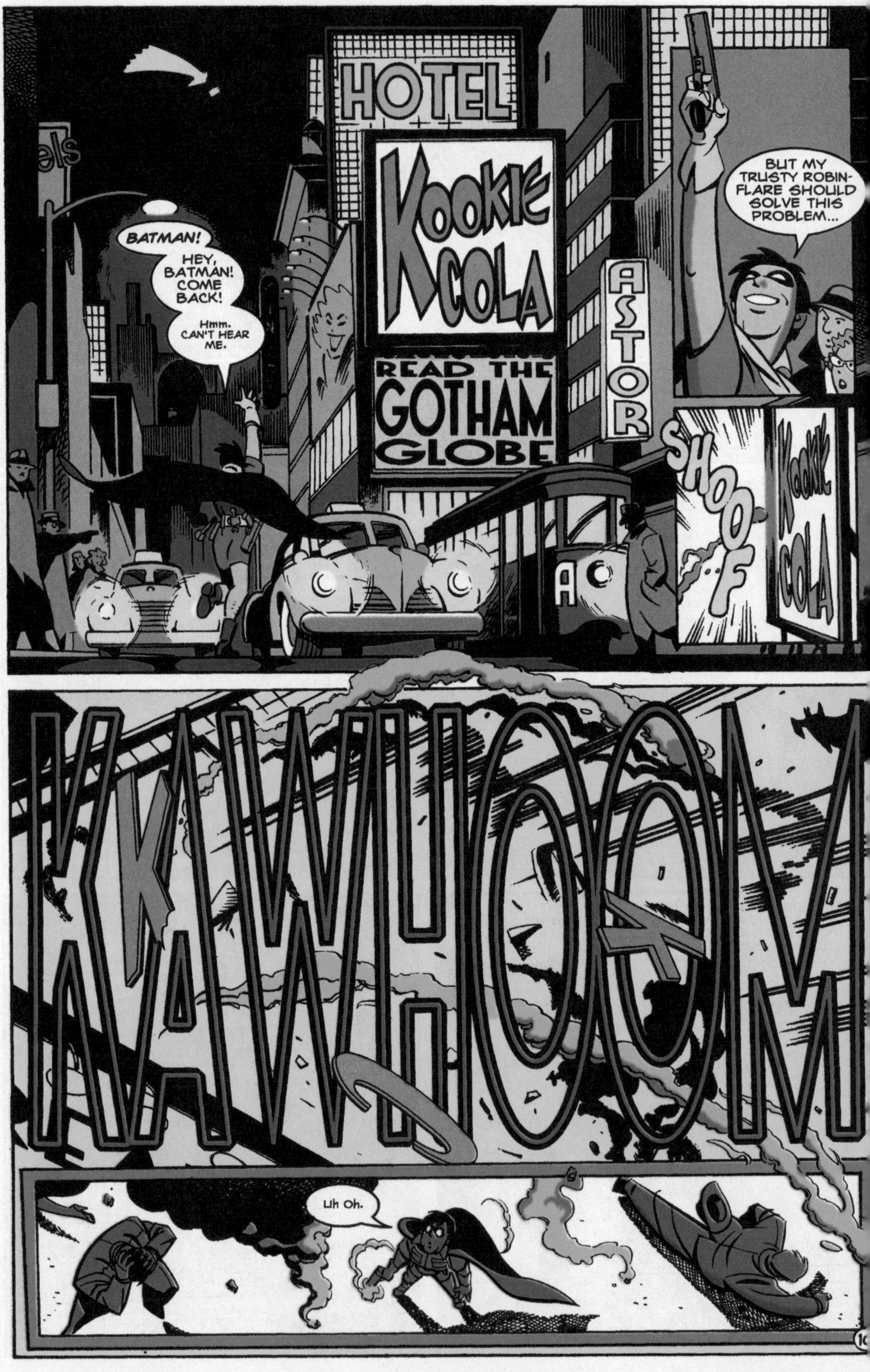
HOTEL
KOOKIE COLA
READ THE GOTHAM GLOBE
ASTOR
BATMAN!
HEY, BATMAN! COME BACK!
Hmm. CAN'T HEAR ME.
BUT MY TRUSTY ROBIN-FLARE SHOULD SOLVE THIS PROBLEM...
SHOOOF
KOOKIE COLA
KAWHOOM
Uh Oh.

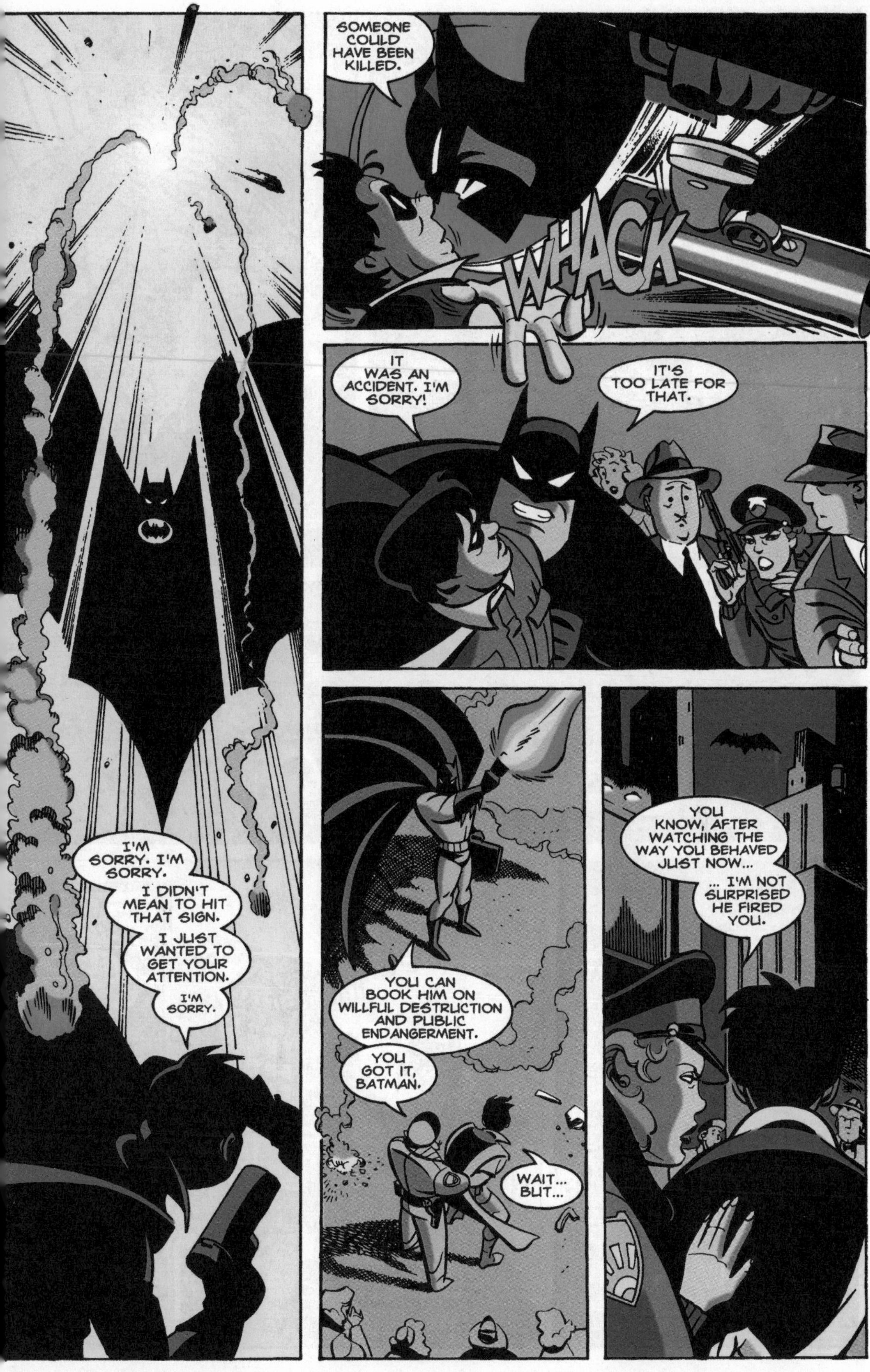
I'M SORRY. I'M SORRY.
I DIDN'T MEAN TO HIT THAT SIGN.
I JUST WANTED TO GET YOUR ATTENTION.
I'M SORRY.
SOMEONE COULD HAVE BEEN KILLED.
WHACK
IT WAS AN ACCIDENT. I'M SORRY!
IT'S TOO LATE FOR THAT.
YOU CAN BOOK HIM ON WILLFUL DESTRUCTION AND PUBLIC ENDANGERMENT.
YOU GOT IT, BATMAN.
WAIT... BUT...
YOU KNOW, AFTER WATCHING THE WAY YOU BEHAVED JUST NOW...
... I'M NOT SURPRISED HE FIRED YOU.

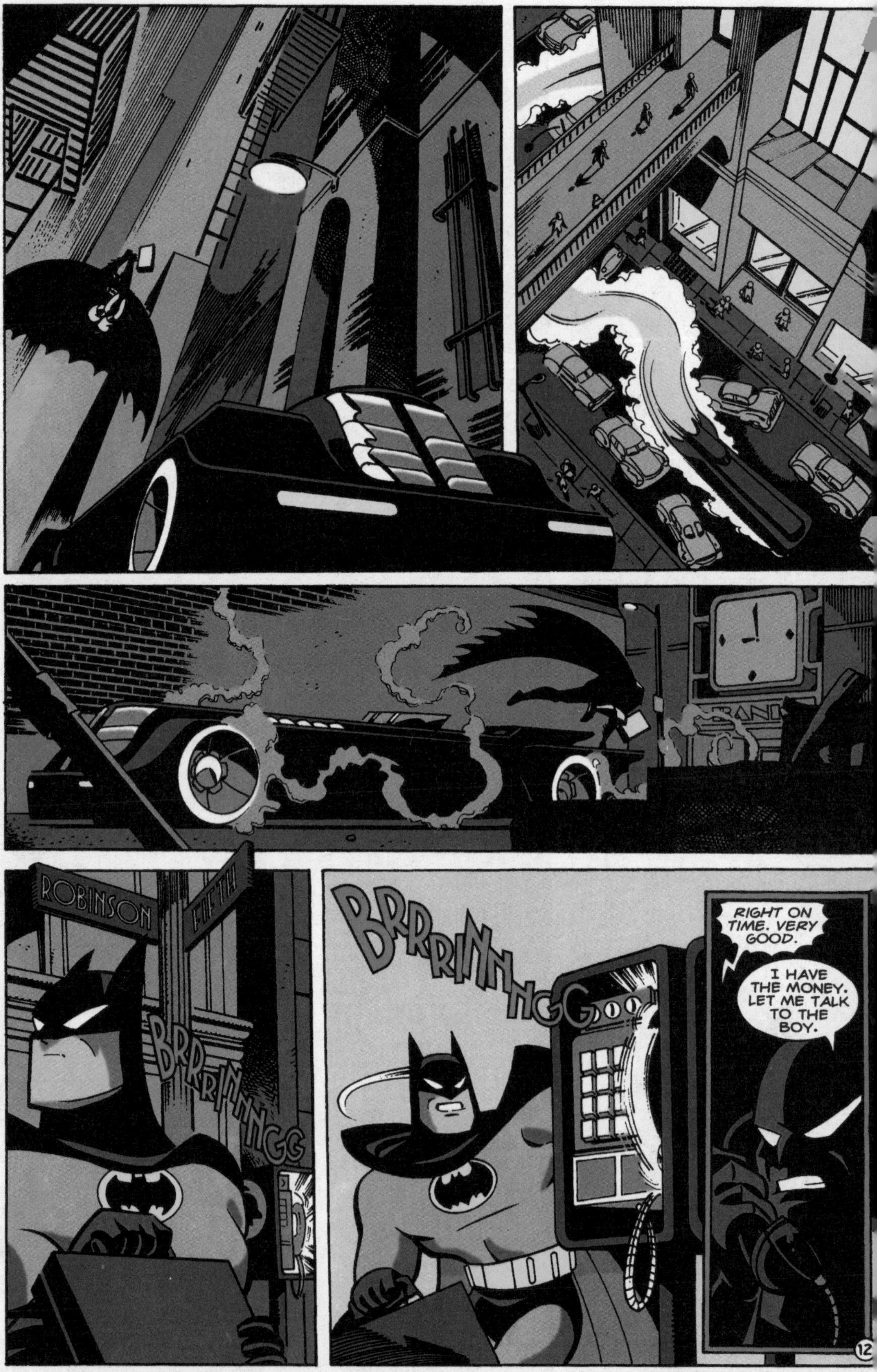
ROBINSON
FIFTH
BRRRINNNGG
BRRRINNNGG
RIGHT ON TIME. VERY GOOD.
I HAVE THE MONEY. LET ME TALK TO THE BOY.
12

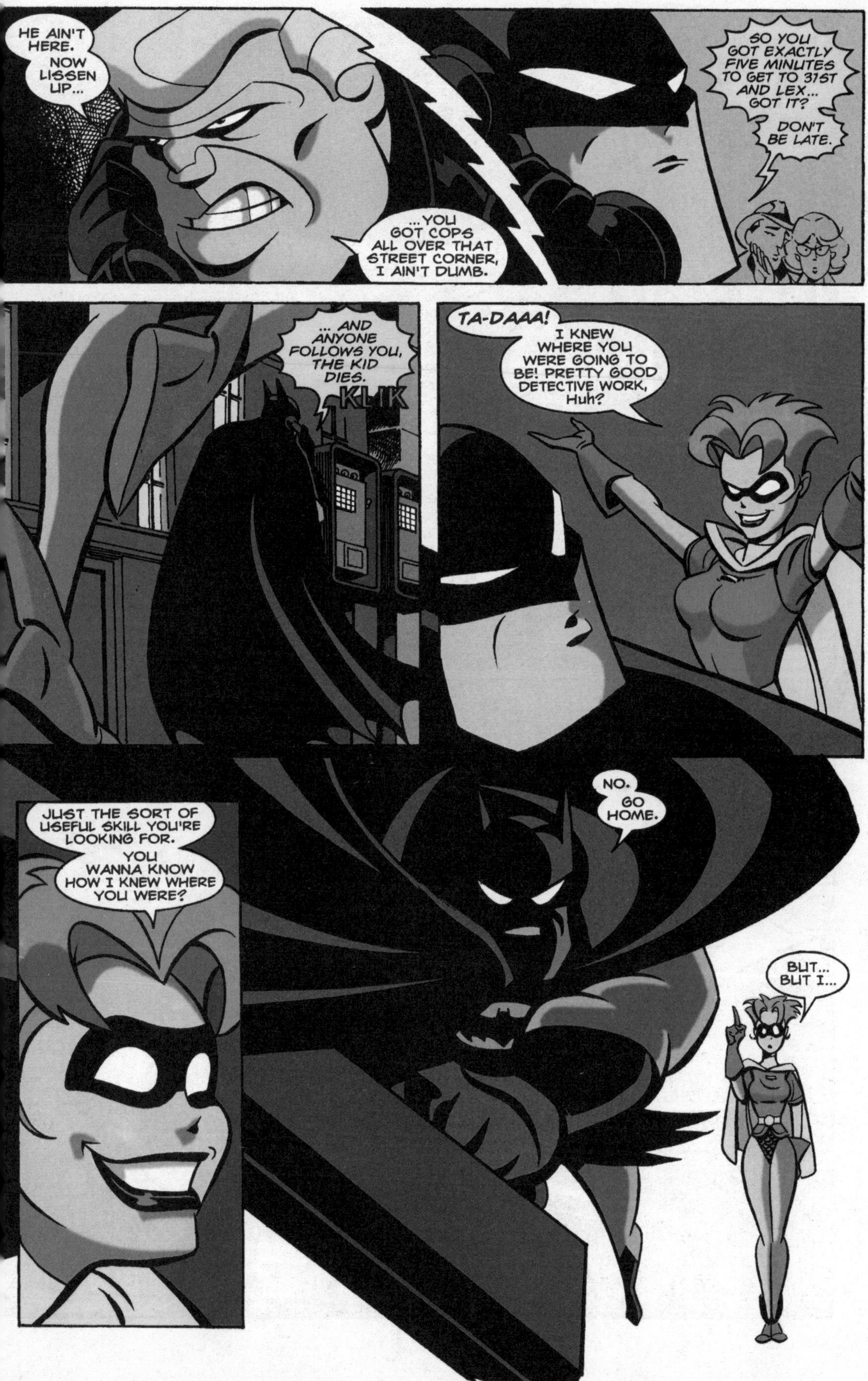
HE AIN'T HERE. NOW LISSEN UP...
...YOU GOT COPS ALL OVER THAT STREET CORNER, I AIN'T DUMB.
SO YOU GOT EXACTLY FIVE MINUTES TO GET TO 31ST AND LEX... GOT IT?
DON'T BE LATE.
... AND ANYONE FOLLOWS YOU, THE KID DIES.
KLIK
TA-DAAA!
I KNEW WHERE YOU WERE GOING TO BE! PRETTY GOOD DETECTIVE WORK, Huh?
JUST THE SORT OF USEFUL SKILL YOU'RE LOOKING FOR.
YOU WANNA KNOW HOW I KNEW WHERE YOU WERE?
NO. GO HOME.
BUT... BUT I...

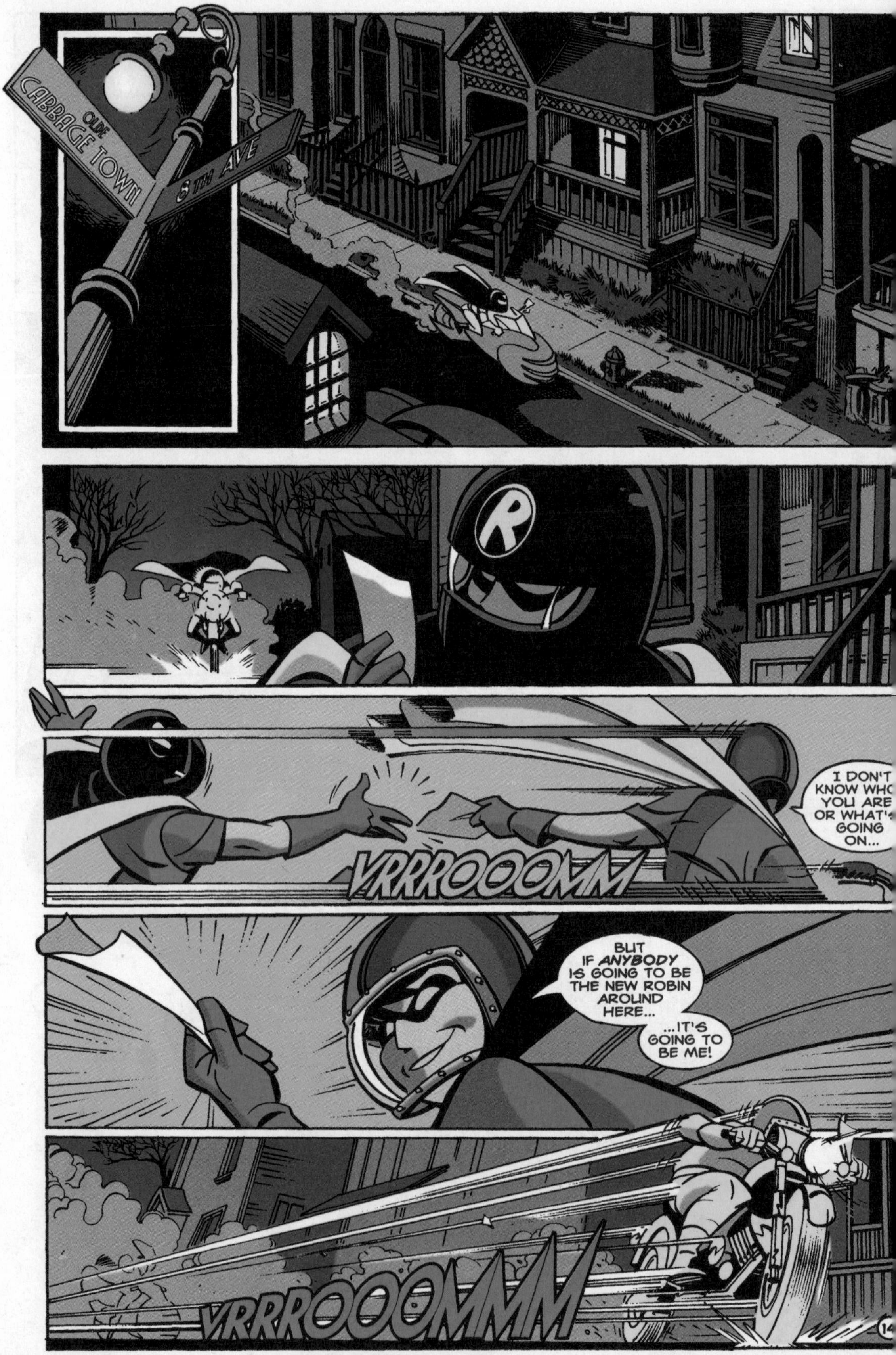

OLDE CABBAGE TOWN
8TH AVE
I DON'T KNOW WHO YOU ARE OR WHAT'S GOING ON...
VRRROOOMM
BUT IF *ANYBODY* IS GOING TO BE THE NEW ROBIN AROUND HERE...
...IT'S GOING TO BE ME!
VRRROOOMMM
14

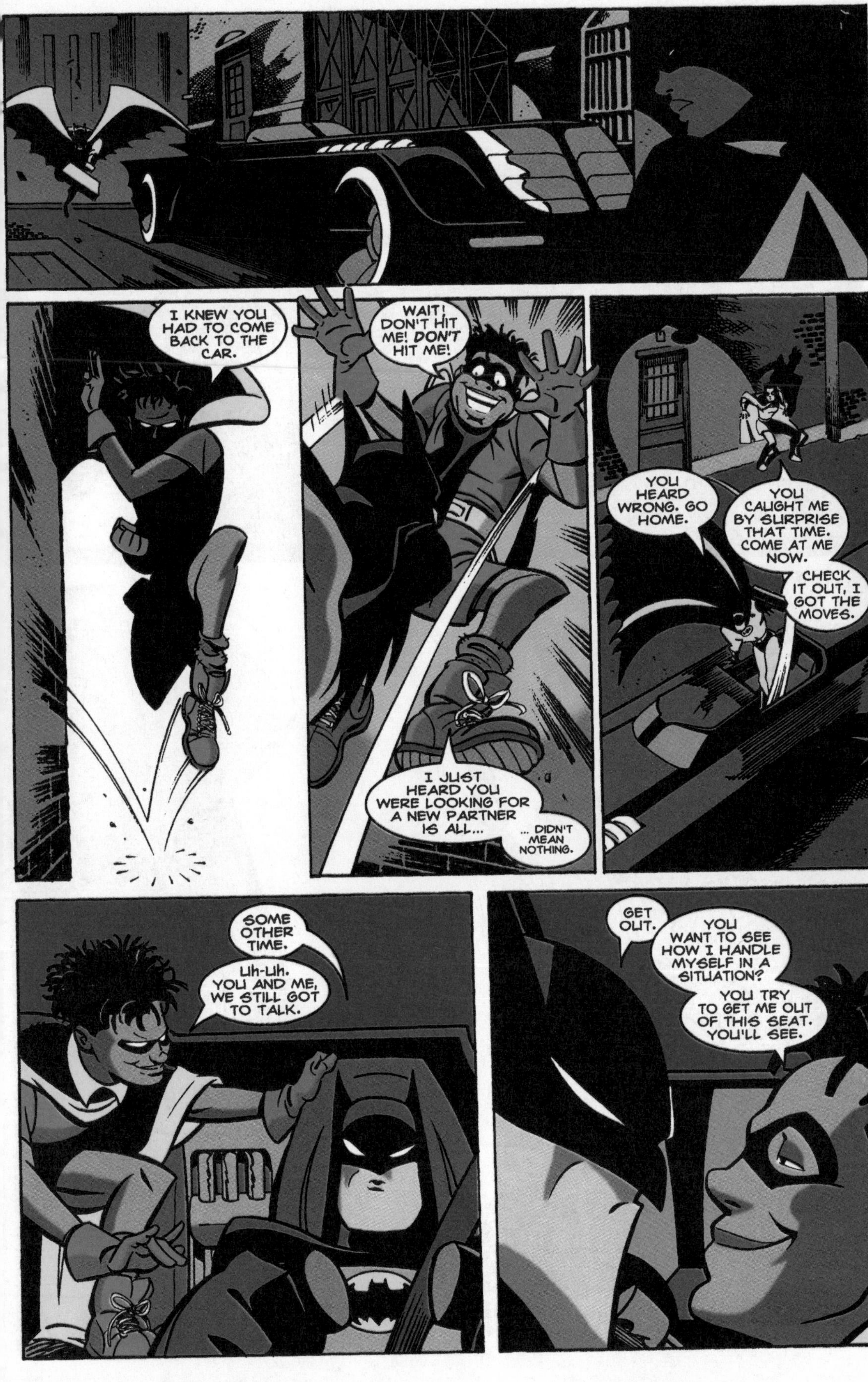

I KNEW YOU HAD TO COME BACK TO THE CAR.
WAIT! DON'T HIT ME! DON'T HIT ME!
I JUST HEARD YOU WERE LOOKING FOR A NEW PARTNER IS ALL...
... DIDN'T MEAN NOTHING.
YOU HEARD WRONG. GO HOME.
YOU CAUGHT ME BY SURPRISE THAT TIME. COME AT ME NOW.
CHECK IT OUT, I GOT THE MOVES.
SOME OTHER TIME.
UH-UH. YOU AND ME, WE STILL GOT TO TALK.
GET OUT.
YOU WANT TO SEE HOW I HANDLE MYSELF IN A SITUATION?
YOU TRY TO GET ME OUT OF THIS SEAT. YOU'LL SEE.

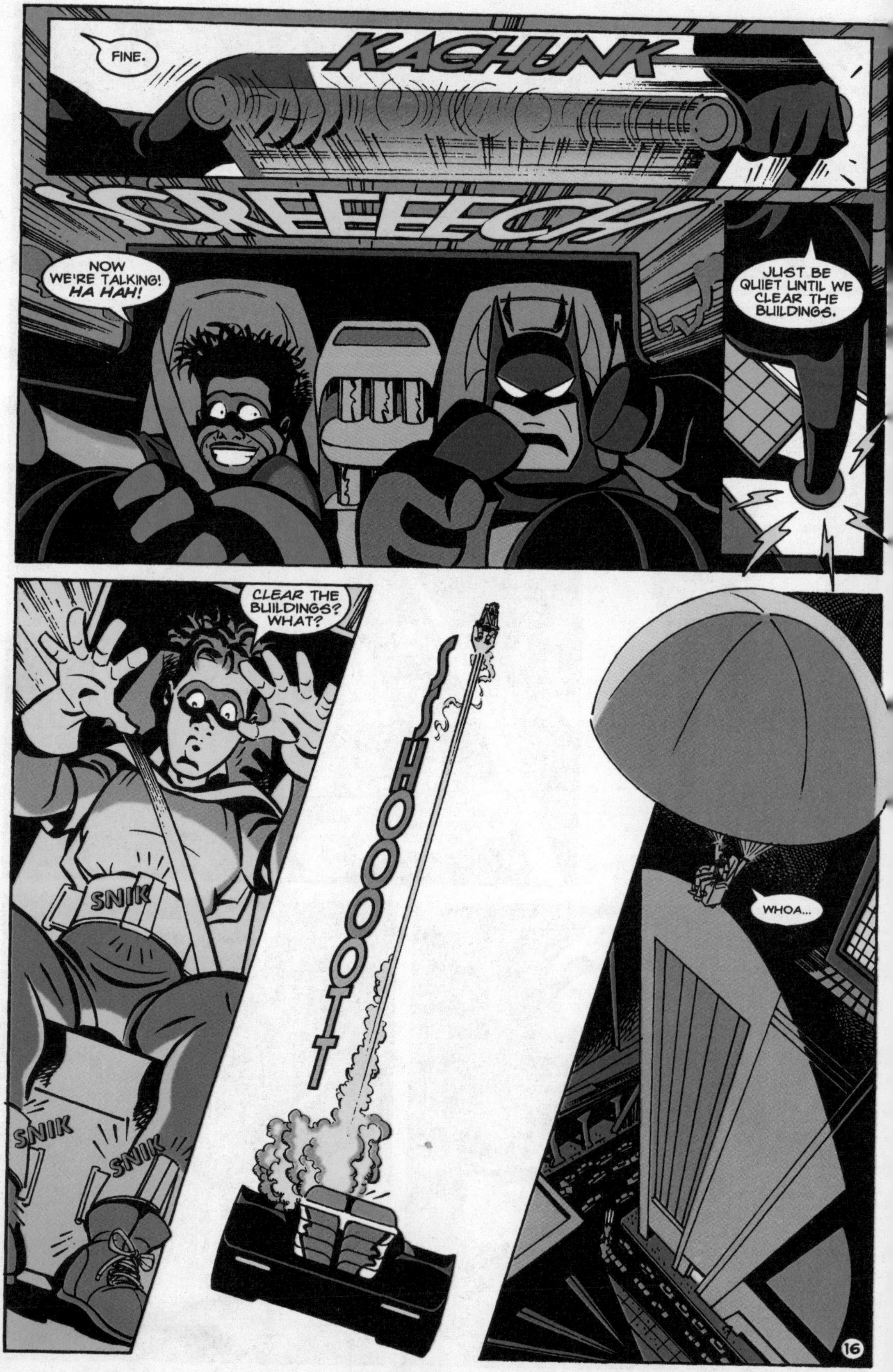
FINE.
KACHUNK
SCREEEECH
NOW WE'RE TALKING! HA HAH!
JUST BE QUIET UNTIL WE CLEAR THE BUILDINGS.
CLEAR THE BUILDINGS? WHAT?
SNIK
SNIK
SNIK
TOOOOOOOOSH
WHOA...
16

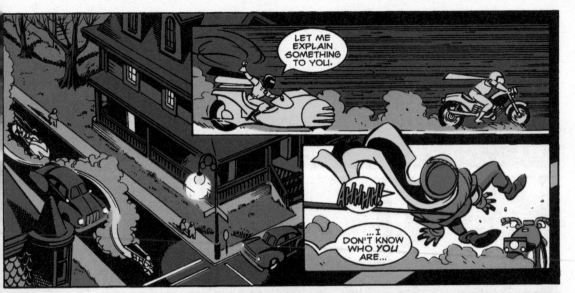

LET ME EXPLAIN SOMETHING TO YOU.

AHHHH!

...I DON'T KNOW WHO *YOU* ARE...

...BUT YOU ARE DEALING WITH THE ONE...

...THE ONLY... ...ACCEPT NO SUBSTITUTES...

...ROBIN!

WHUMP

AND IN CASE YOU HAVEN'T HEARD, THERE ARE NO MARTIANS IN THE WHITE HOUSE, DUMMY.

HEY...

COOL.

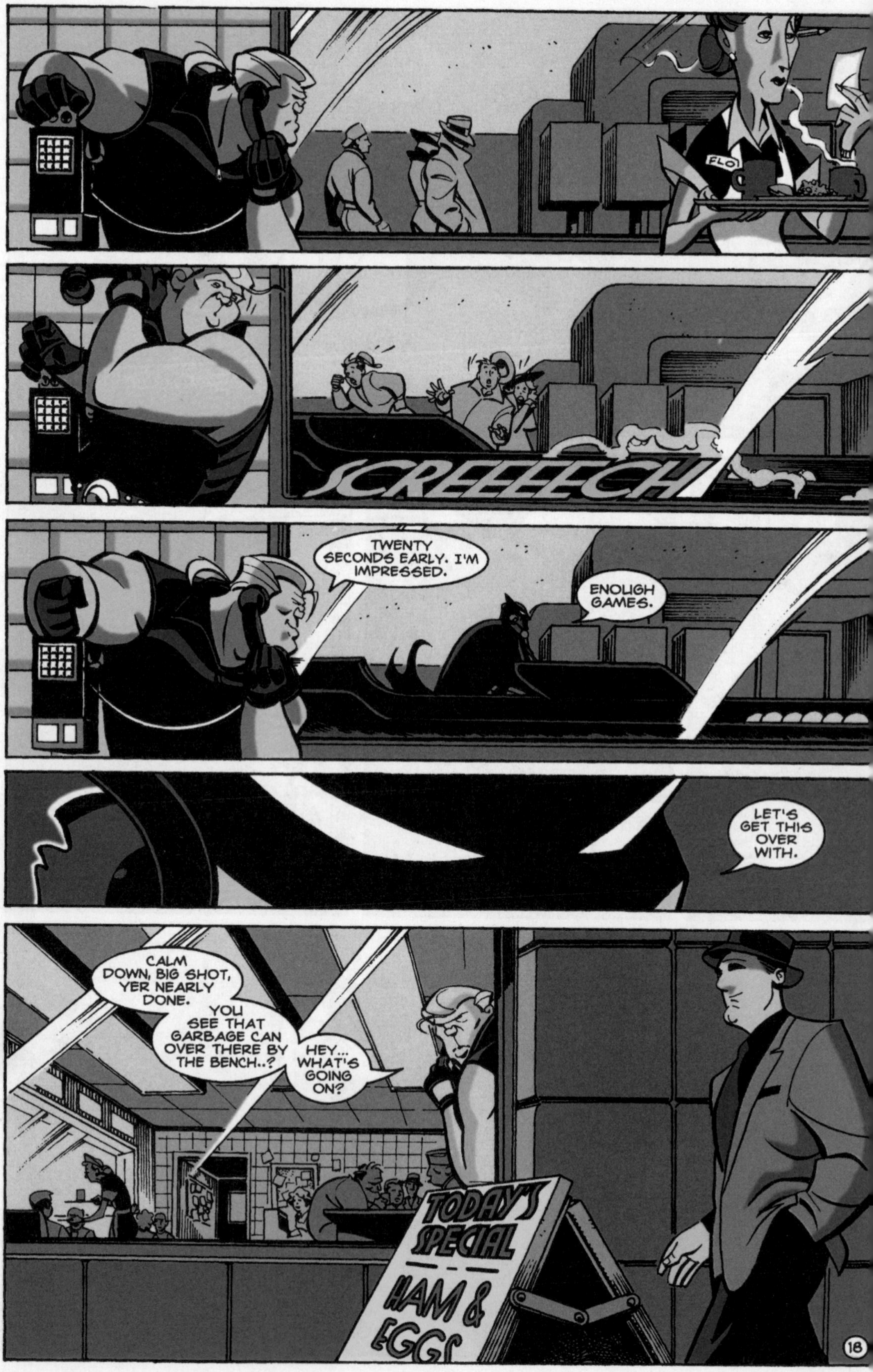
FLO
SCREEEEECH
TWENTY SECONDS EARLY. I'M IMPRESSED.
ENOUGH GAMES.
LET'S GET THIS OVER WITH.
CALM DOWN, BIG SHOT, YER NEARLY DONE.
YOU SEE THAT GARBAGE CAN OVER THERE BY THE BENCH..?
HEY... WHAT'S GOING ON?
TODAY'S SPECIAL
HAM & EGGS
18

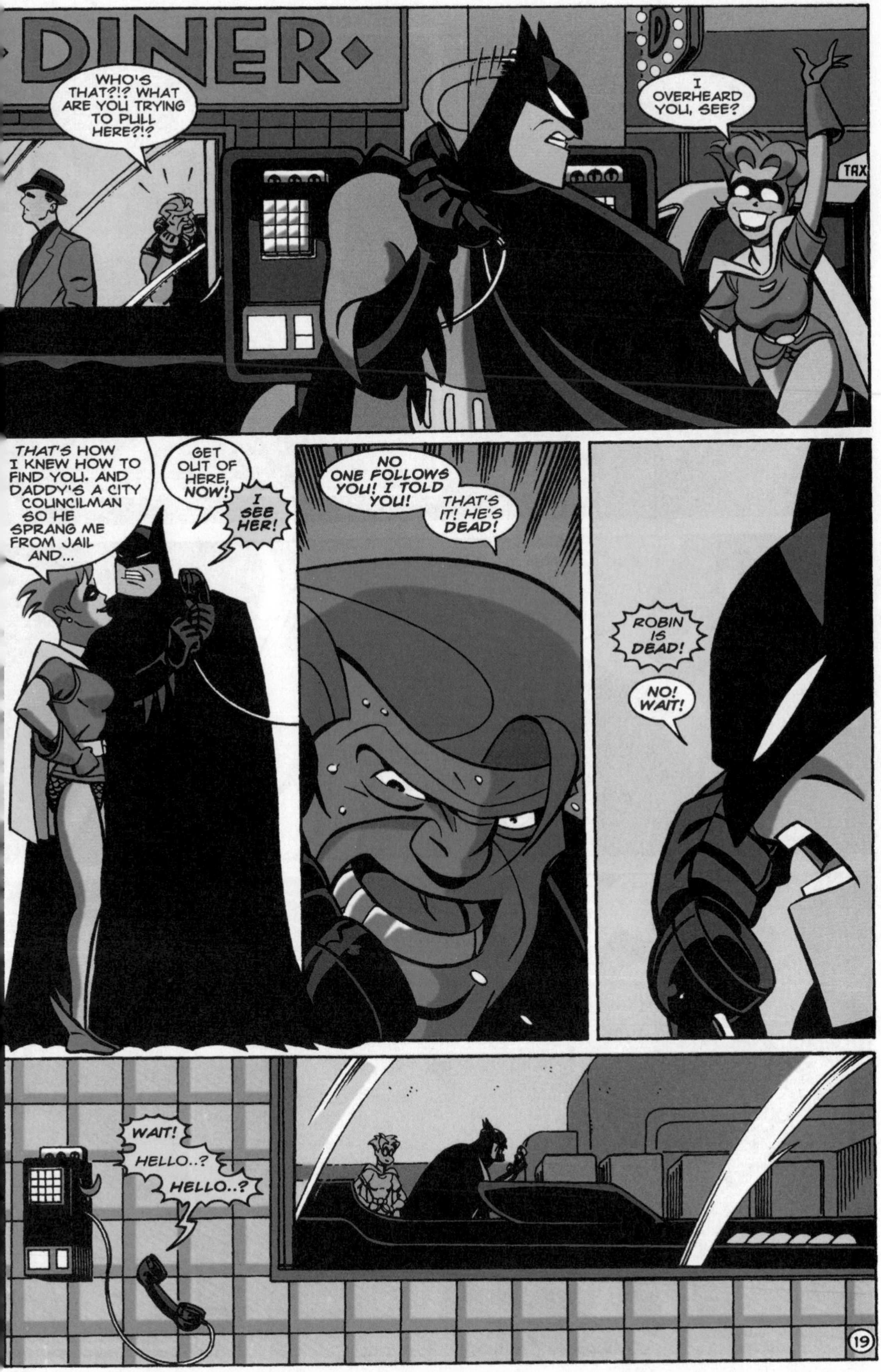
DINER
WHO'S THAT?!? WHAT ARE YOU TRYING TO PULL HERE?!?
I OVERHEARD YOU, SEE?
TAX
THAT'S HOW I KNEW HOW TO FIND YOU. AND DADDY'S A CITY COUNCILMAN SO HE SPRANG ME FROM JAIL AND...
GET OUT OF HERE, NOW!
I SEE HER!
NO ONE FOLLOWS YOU! I TOLD YOU!
THAT'S IT! HE'S DEAD!
ROBIN IS DEAD!
NO! WAIT!
WAIT!
HELLO..?
HELLO..?
19

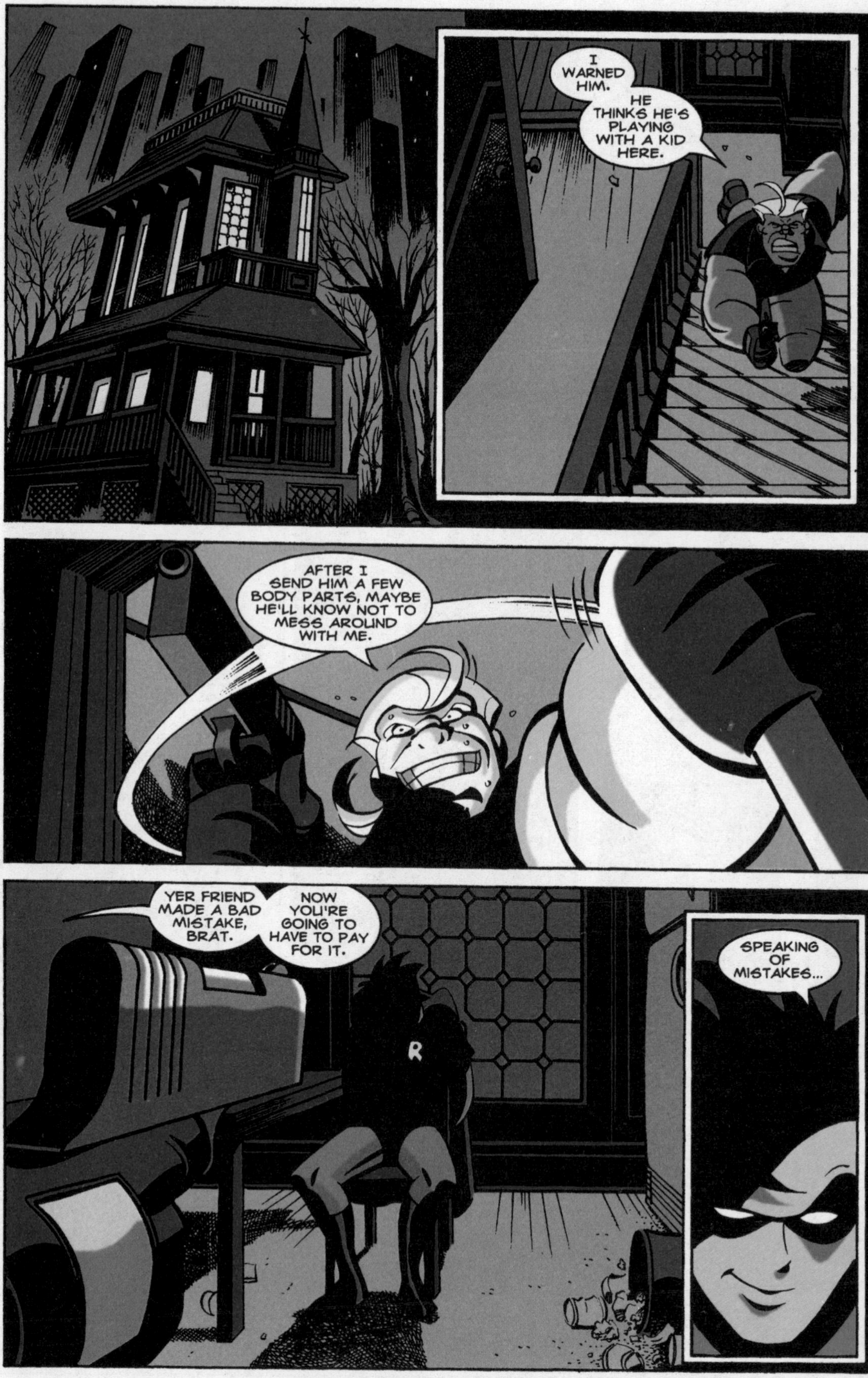
I WARNED HIM.
HE THINKS HE'S PLAYING WITH A KID HERE.
AFTER I SEND HIM A FEW BODY PARTS, MAYBE HE'LL KNOW NOT TO MESS AROUND WITH ME.
YER FRIEND MADE A BAD MISTAKE, BRAT.
NOW YOU'RE GOING TO HAVE TO PAY FOR IT.
SPEAKING OF MISTAKES...

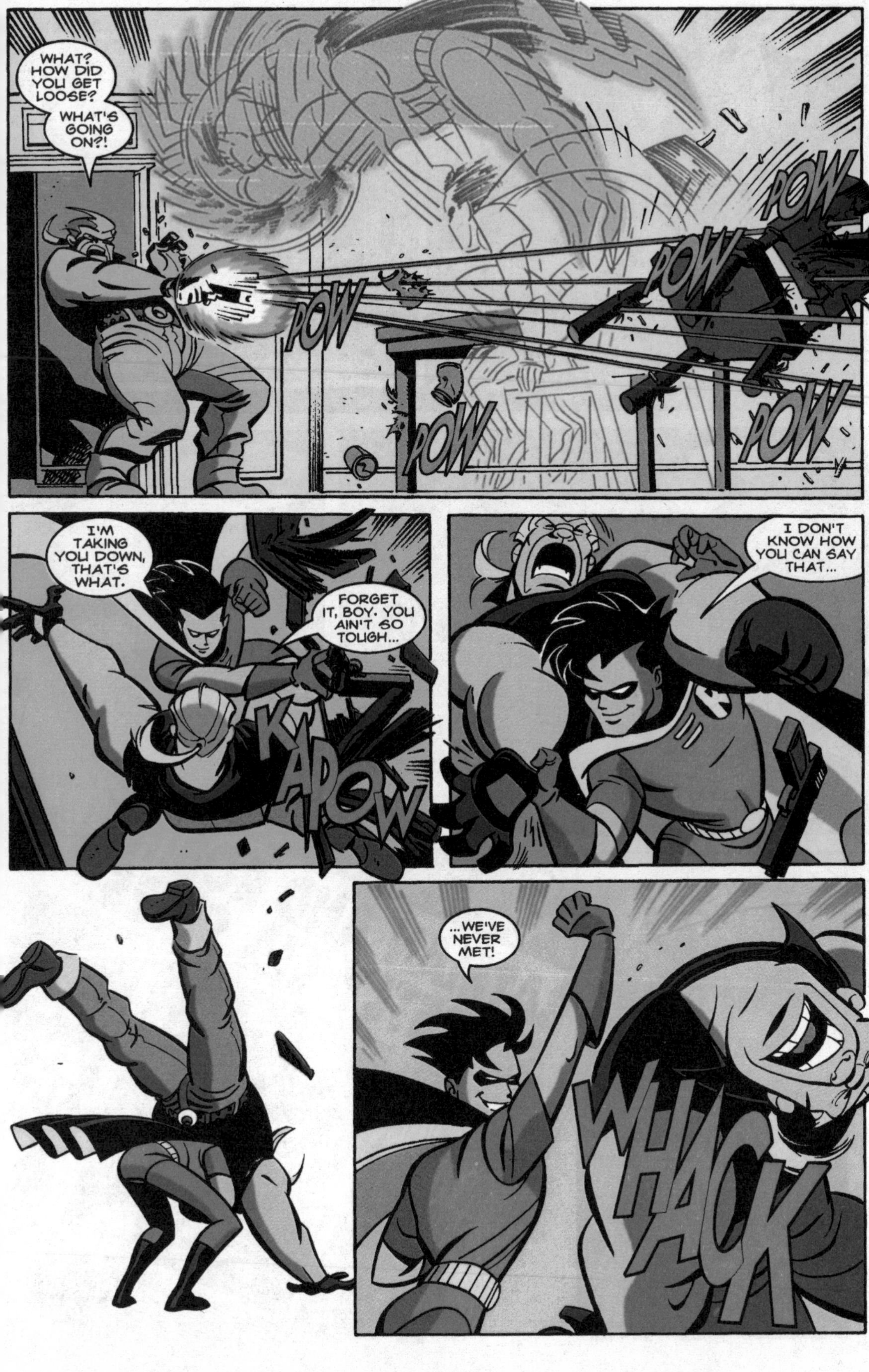
WHAT? HOW DID YOU GET LOOSE?
WHAT'S GOING ON?!
POW
POW
POW
POW
POW
I'M TAKING YOU DOWN, THAT'S WHAT.
FORGET IT, BOY. YOU AIN'T SO TOUGH...
KAPOW
I DON'T KNOW HOW YOU CAN SAY THAT...
...WE'VE NEVER MET!
WHACK

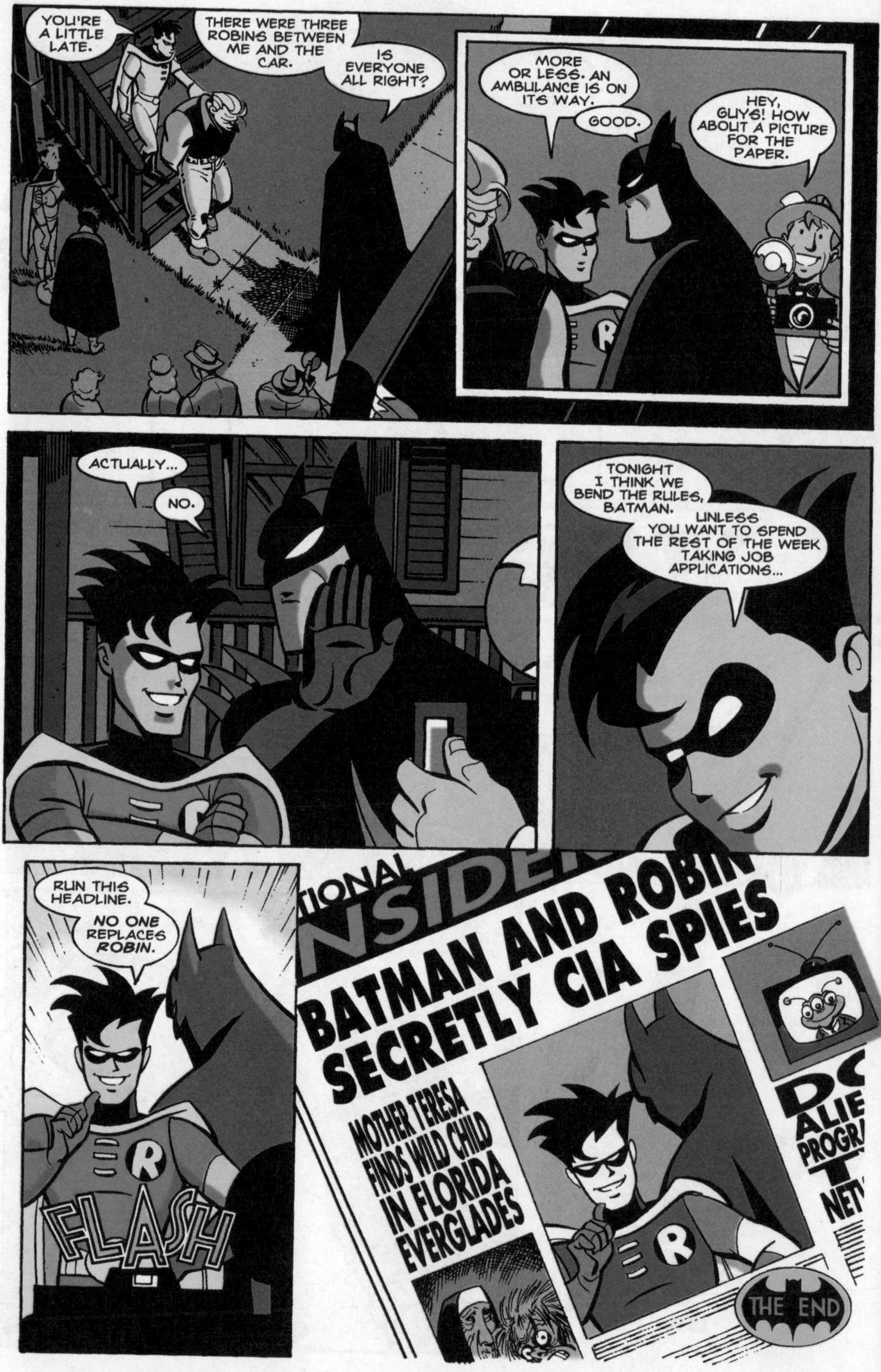

YOU'RE A LITTLE LATE.
THERE WERE THREE ROBINS BETWEEN ME AND THE CAR.
IS EVERYONE ALL RIGHT?
MORE OR LESS. AN AMBULANCE IS ON ITS WAY.
GOOD.
HEY, GUYS! HOW ABOUT A PICTURE FOR THE PAPER.
ACTUALLY...
NO.
TONIGHT I THINK WE BEND THE RULES, BATMAN.
UNLESS YOU WANT TO SPEND THE REST OF THE WEEK TAKING JOB APPLICATIONS...
RUN THIS HEADLINE.
NO ONE REPLACES ROBIN.
FLASH
BATMAN AND ROBIN SECRETLY CIA SPIES
MOTHER TERESA FINDS WILD CHILD IN FLORIDA EVERGLADES
THE END

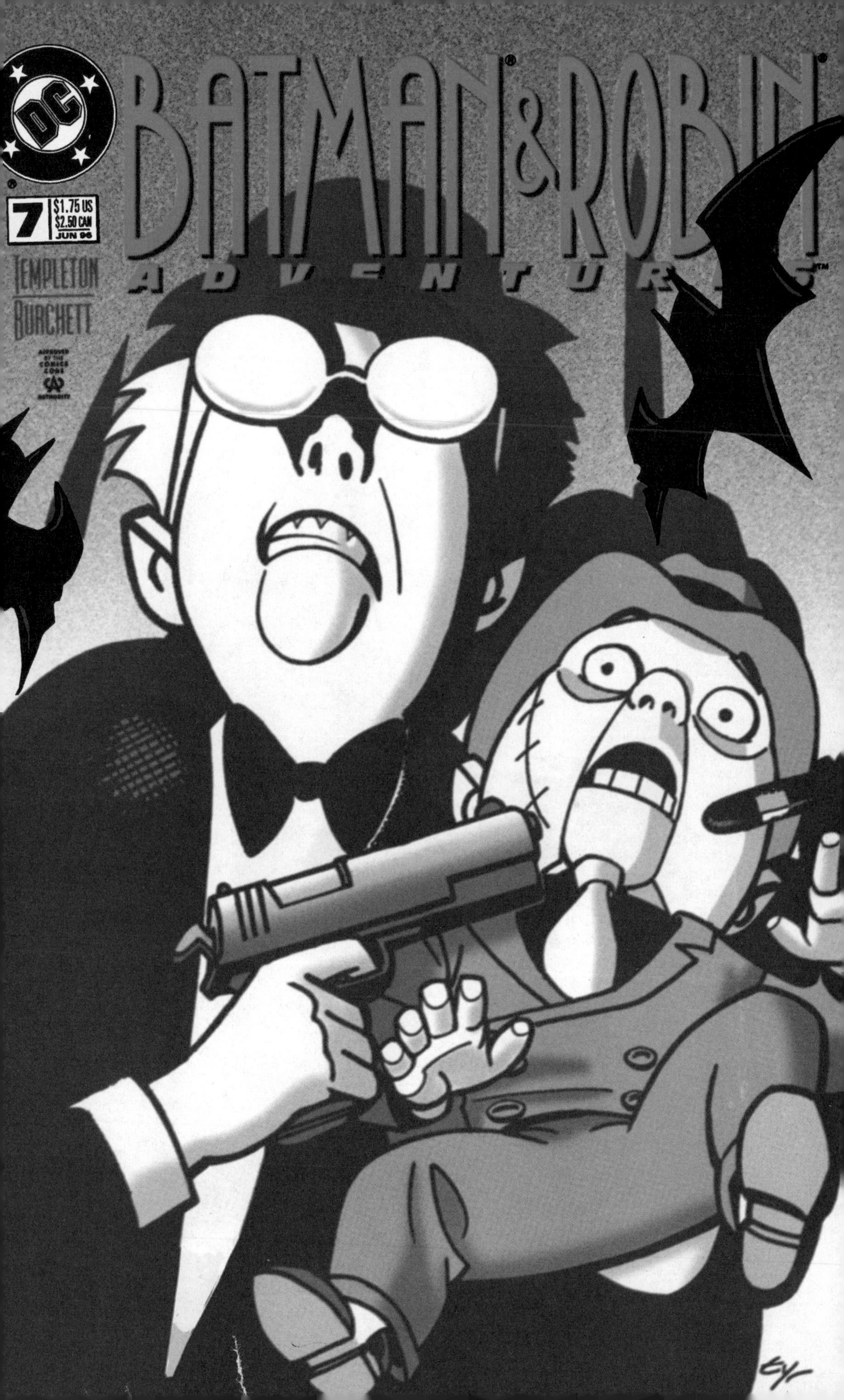
DC
BATMAN & ROBIN
ADVENTURES
7
$1.75 US
$2.50 CAN
JUN 96
TEMPLETON
BURCHETT

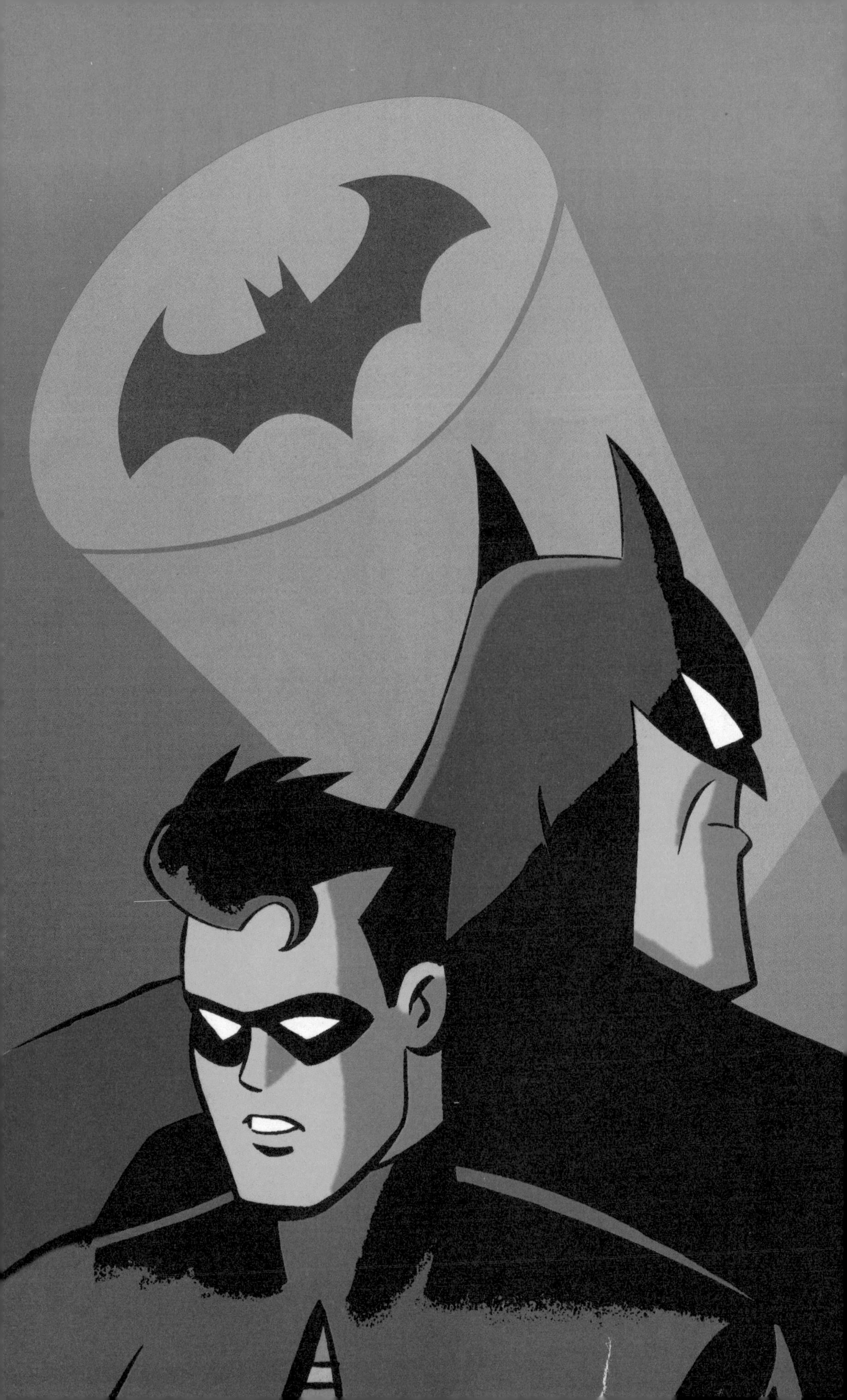

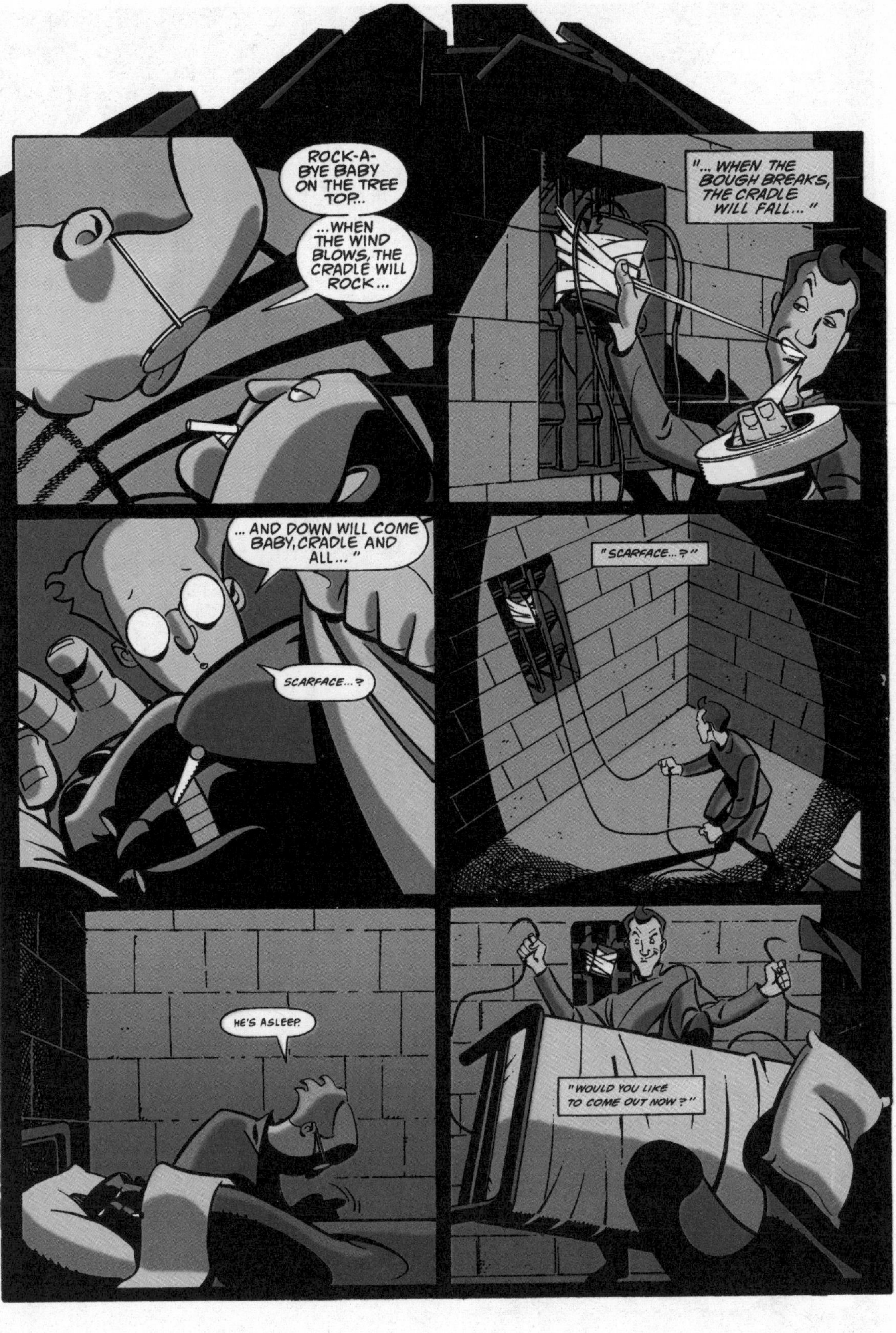
ROCK-A-BYE BABY ON THE TREE TOP...
...WHEN THE WIND BLOWS, THE CRADLE WILL ROCK...
"... WHEN THE BOUGH BREAKS, THE CRADLE WILL FALL..."
... AND DOWN WILL COME BABY, CRADLE AND ALL..."
SCARFACE...?
"SCARFACE...?"
HE'S ASLEEP.
"WOULD YOU LIKE TO COME OUT NOW?"

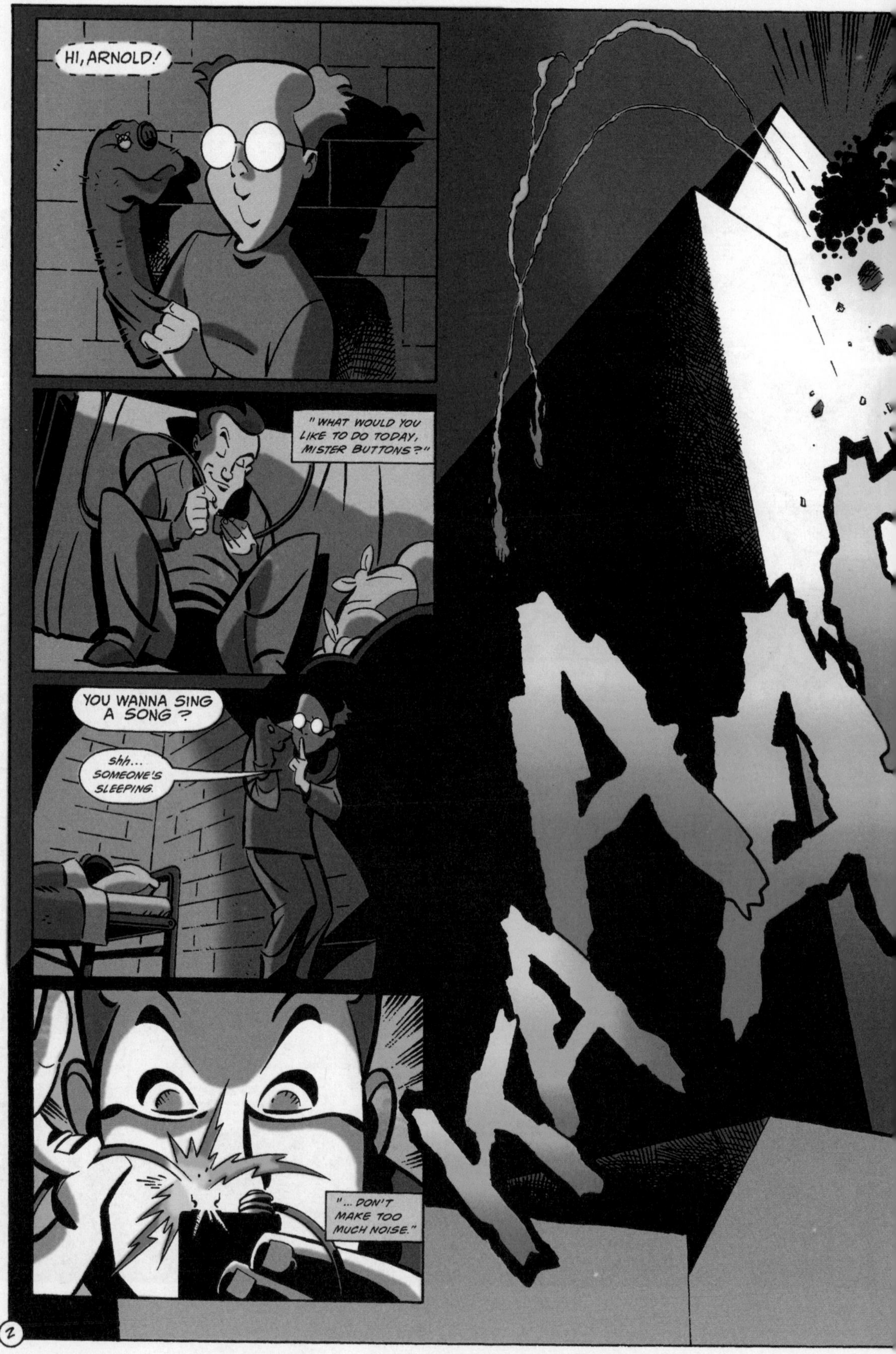
HI, ARNOLD!
"WHAT WOULD YOU LIKE TO DO TODAY, MISTER BUTTONS?"
YOU WANNA SING A SONG?
Shh... SOMEONE'S SLEEPING.
"...DON'T MAKE TOO MUCH NOISE."

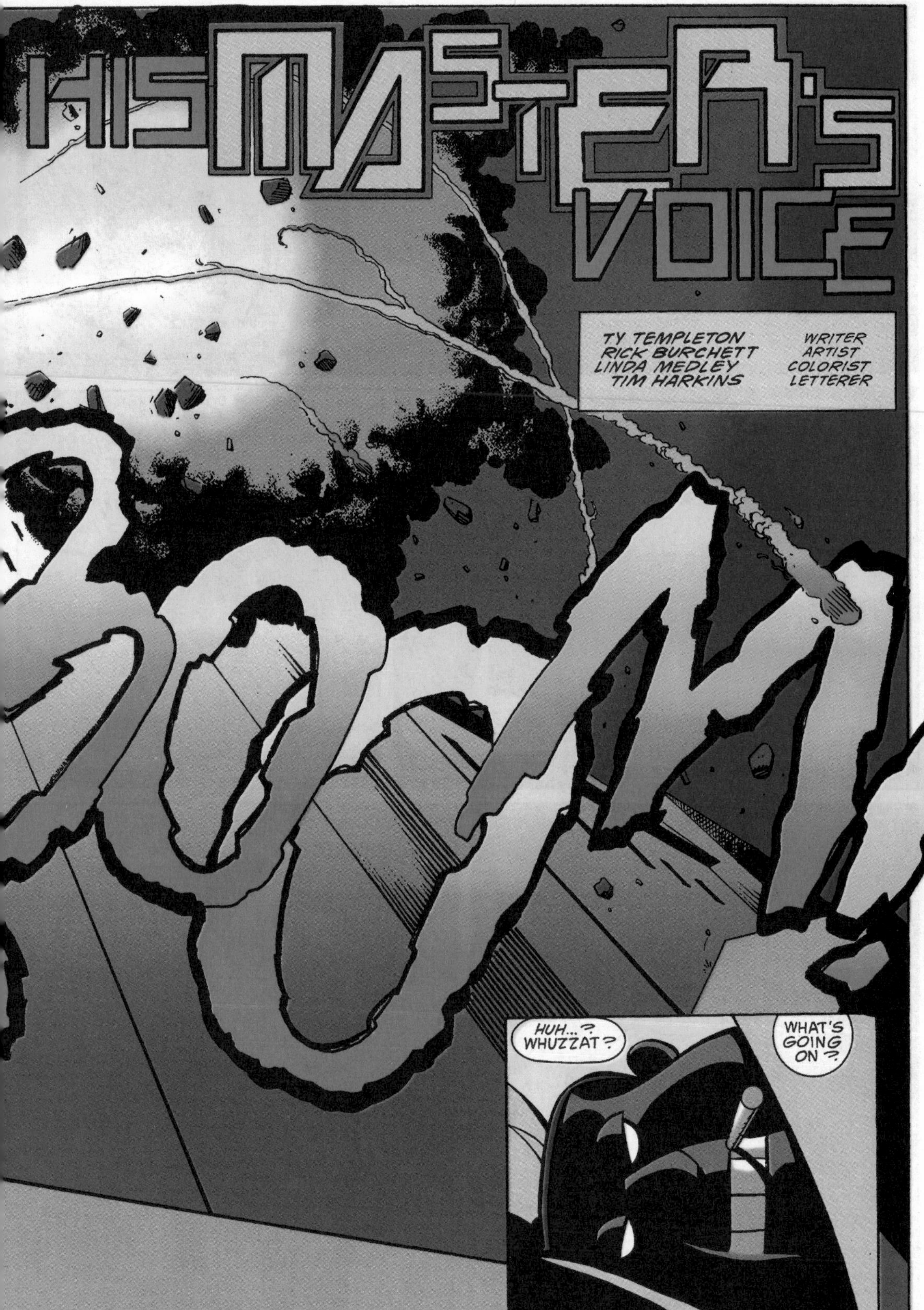
HIS MASTER'S VOICE
TY TEMPLETON WRITER
RICK BURCHETT ARTIST
LINDA MEDLEY COLORIST
TIM HARKINS LETTERER
BOOM!
HUH...? WHUZZAT?
WHAT'S GOING ON?
3

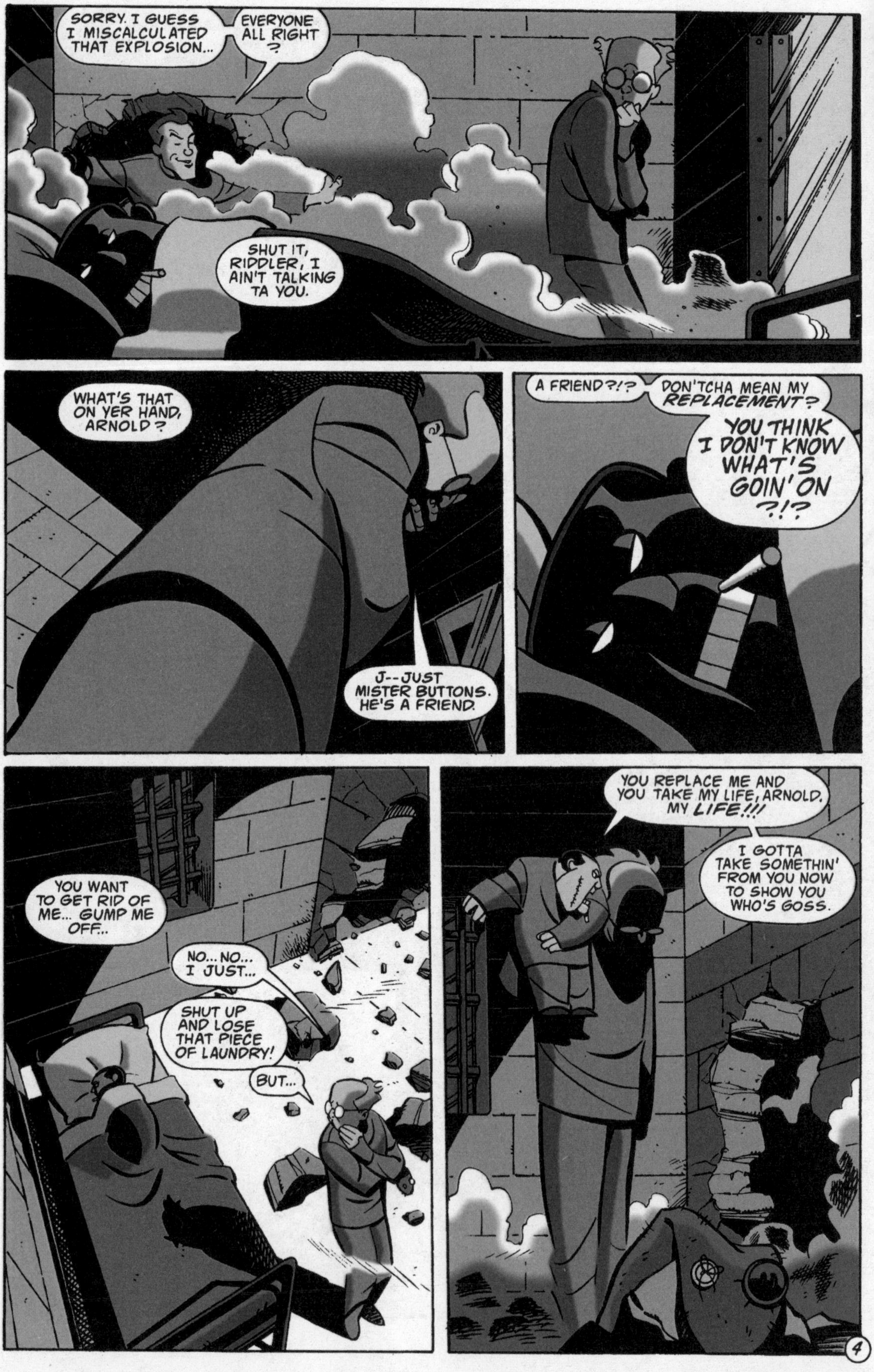

SORRY. I GUESS I MISCALCULATED THAT EXPLOSION...
EVERYONE ALL RIGHT ?
SHUT IT, RIDDLER, I AIN'T TALKING TA YOU.
WHAT'S THAT ON YER HAND, ARNOLD ?
J--JUST MISTER BUTTONS. HE'S A FRIEND.
A FRIEND?!?
DON'TCHA MEAN MY REPLACEMENT?
YOU THINK I DON'T KNOW WHAT'S GOIN' ON ?!?
YOU WANT TO GET RID OF ME... GUMP ME OFF...
NO... NO... I JUST...
SHUT UP AND LOSE THAT PIECE OF LAUNDRY!
BUT...
YOU REPLACE ME AND YOU TAKE MY LIFE, ARNOLD. MY LIFE!!!
I GOTTA TAKE SOMETHIN' FROM YOU NOW TO SHOW YOU WHO'S GOSS.
4

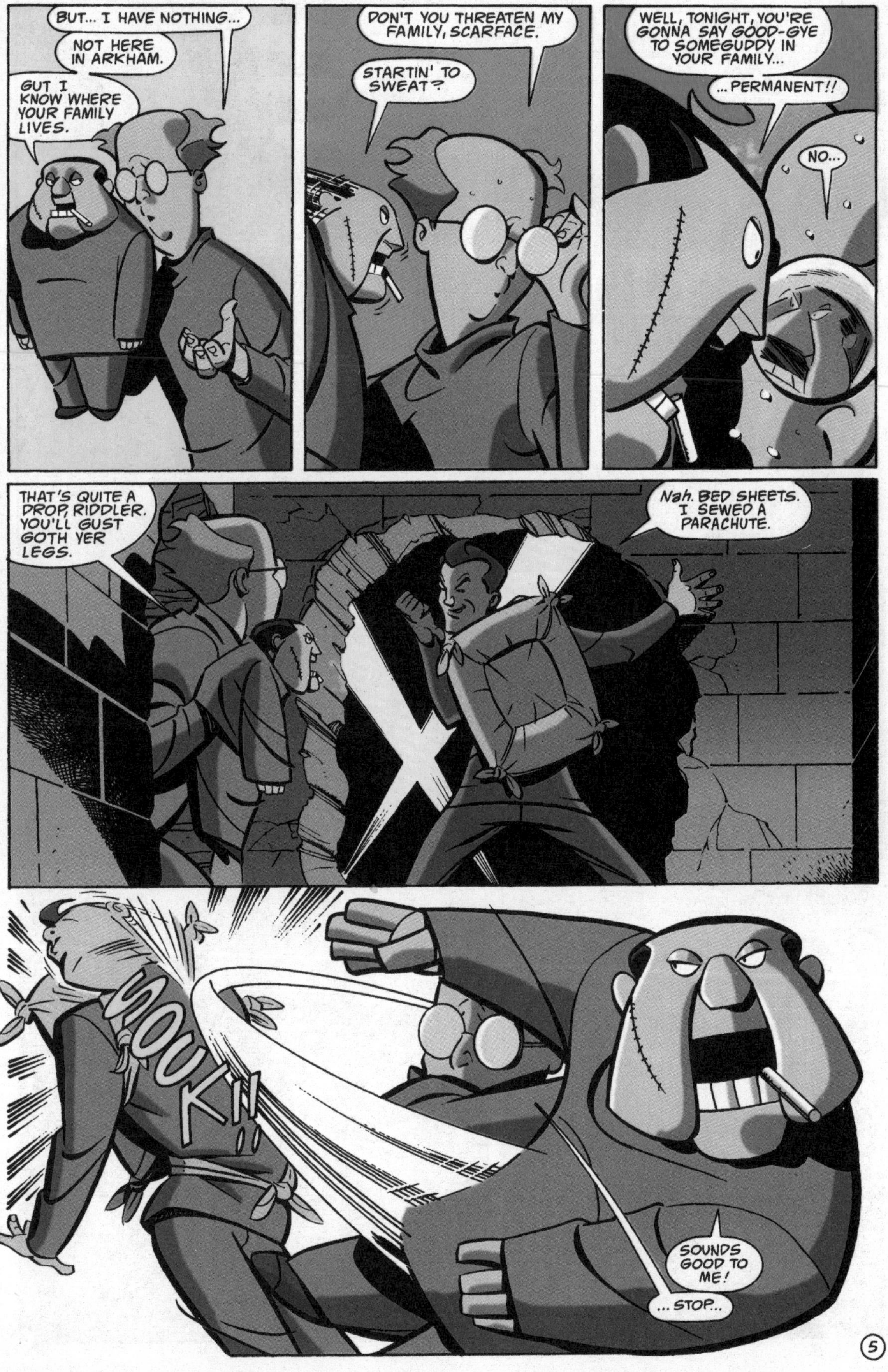
BUT... I HAVE NOTHING...
NOT HERE IN ARKHAM.
GUT I KNOW WHERE YOUR FAMILY LIVES.
DON'T YOU THREATEN MY FAMILY, SCARFACE.
STARTIN' TO SWEAT?
WELL, TONIGHT, YOU'RE GONNA SAY GOOD-GYE TO SOMEGUDDY IN YOUR FAMILY...
...PERMANENT!!
NO...
THAT'S QUITE A DROP, RIDDLER. YOU'LL GUST GOTH YER LEGS.
Nah. BED SHEETS. I SEWED A PARACHUTE.
SOUK!!
SOUNDS GOOD TO ME!
...STOP...
5

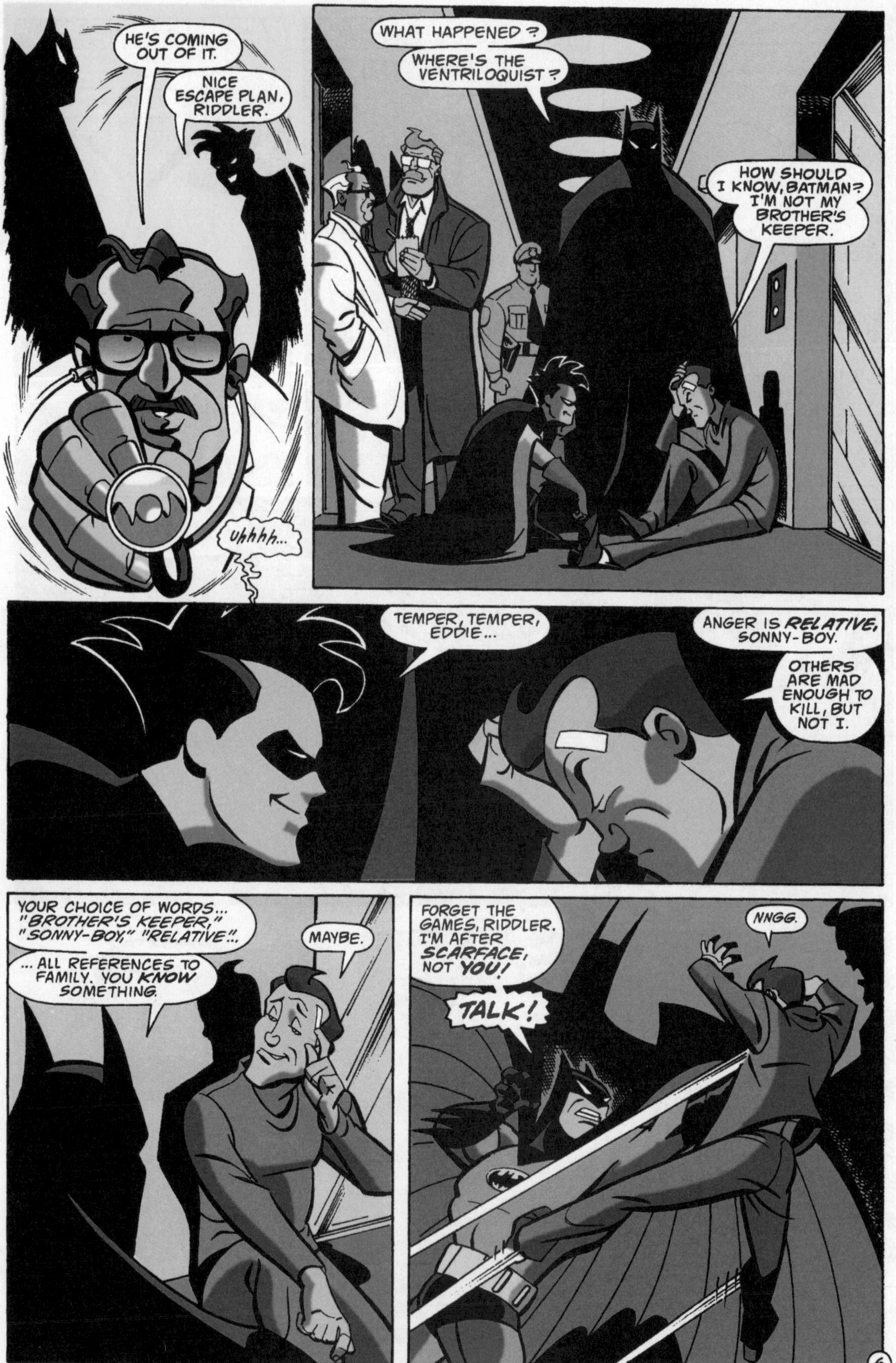
HE'S COMING OUT OF IT.
NICE ESCAPE PLAN, RIDDLER.
uhhhh...
WHAT HAPPENED ?
WHERE'S THE VENTRILOQUIST ?
HOW SHOULD I KNOW, BATMAN? I'M NOT MY BROTHER'S KEEPER.
TEMPER, TEMPER, EDDIE...
ANGER IS *RELATIVE,* SONNY-BOY.
OTHERS ARE MAD ENOUGH TO KILL, BUT NOT I.
YOUR CHOICE OF WORDS... "*BROTHER'S KEEPER,*" "*SONNY-BOY,*" "*RELATIVE*"...
... ALL REFERENCES TO FAMILY. YOU *KNOW* SOMETHING.
MAYBE.
FORGET THE GAMES, RIDDLER. I'M AFTER *SCARFACE,* NOT *YOU!*
TALK!
NNGG.
6

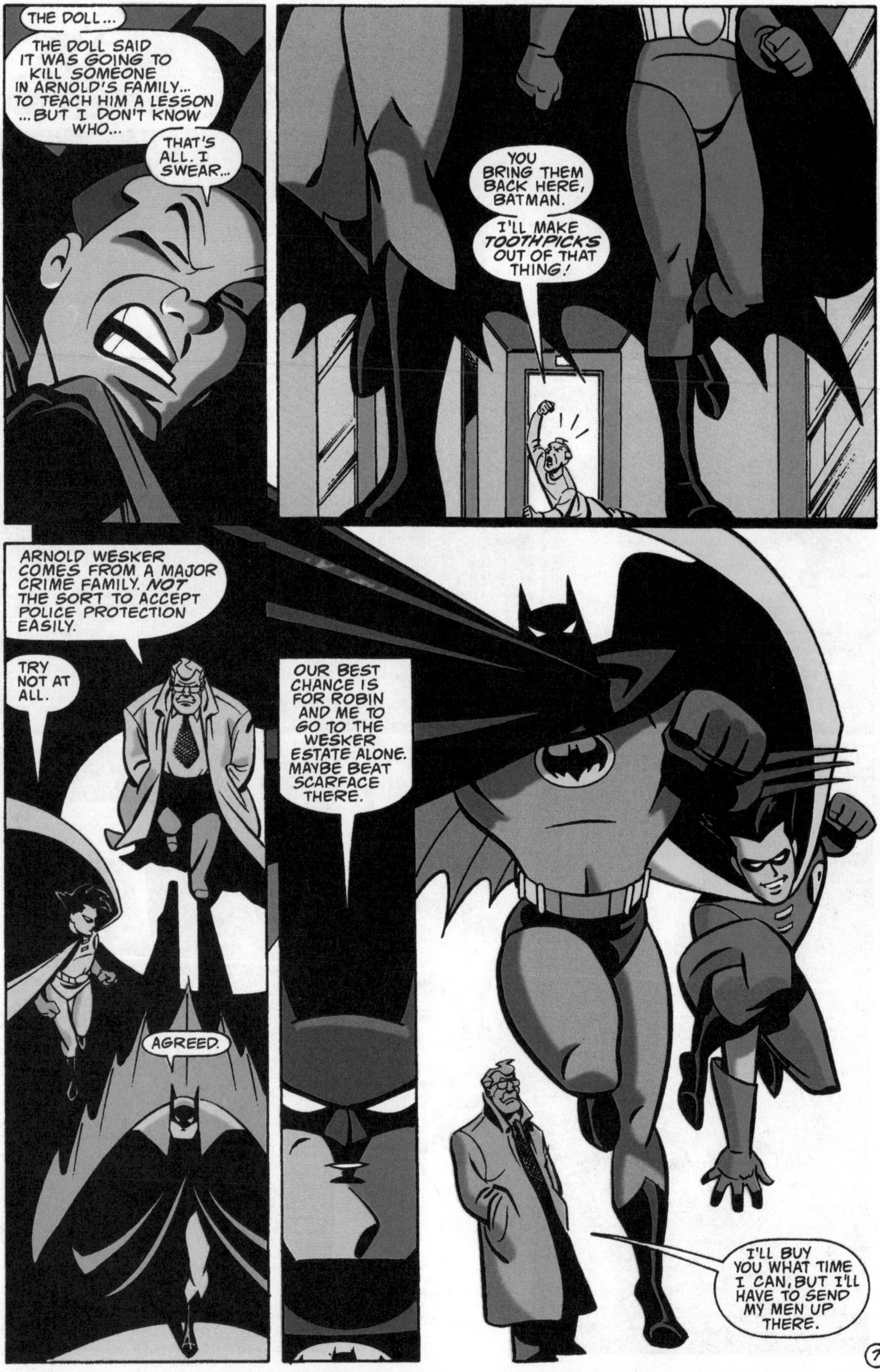
THE DOLL...
THE DOLL SAID IT WAS GOING TO KILL SOMEONE IN ARNOLD'S FAMILY... TO TEACH HIM A LESSON ...BUT I DON'T KNOW WHO...
THAT'S ALL. I SWEAR...
YOU BRING THEM BACK HERE, BATMAN.
I'LL MAKE TOOTHPICKS OUT OF THAT THING!
ARNOLD WESKER COMES FROM A MAJOR CRIME FAMILY. NOT THE SORT TO ACCEPT POLICE PROTECTION EASILY.
TRY NOT AT ALL.
AGREED.
OUR BEST CHANCE IS FOR ROBIN AND ME TO GO TO THE WESKER ESTATE ALONE. MAYBE BEAT SCARFACE THERE.
I'LL BUY YOU WHAT TIME I CAN, BUT I'LL HAVE TO SEND MY MEN UP THERE.
7

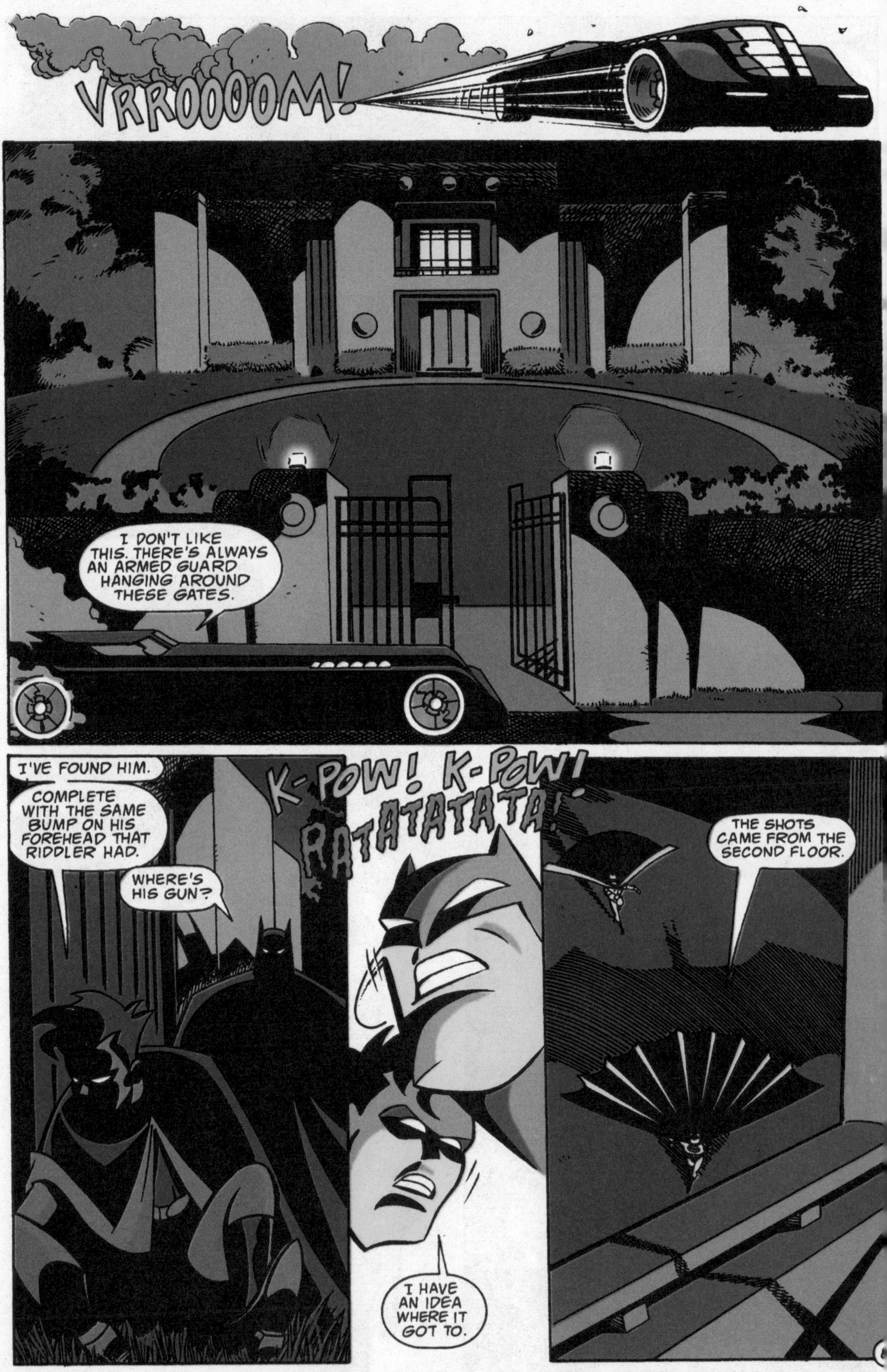
VRROOOOM!
I DON'T LIKE THIS. THERE'S ALWAYS AN ARMED GUARD HANGING AROUND THESE GATES.
I'VE FOUND HIM.
COMPLETE WITH THE SAME BUMP ON HIS FOREHEAD THAT RIDDLER HAD.
WHERE'S HIS GUN?
K-POW! K-POW! RATATATATA!
I HAVE AN IDEA WHERE IT GOT TO.
THE SHOTS CAME FROM THE SECOND FLOOR.

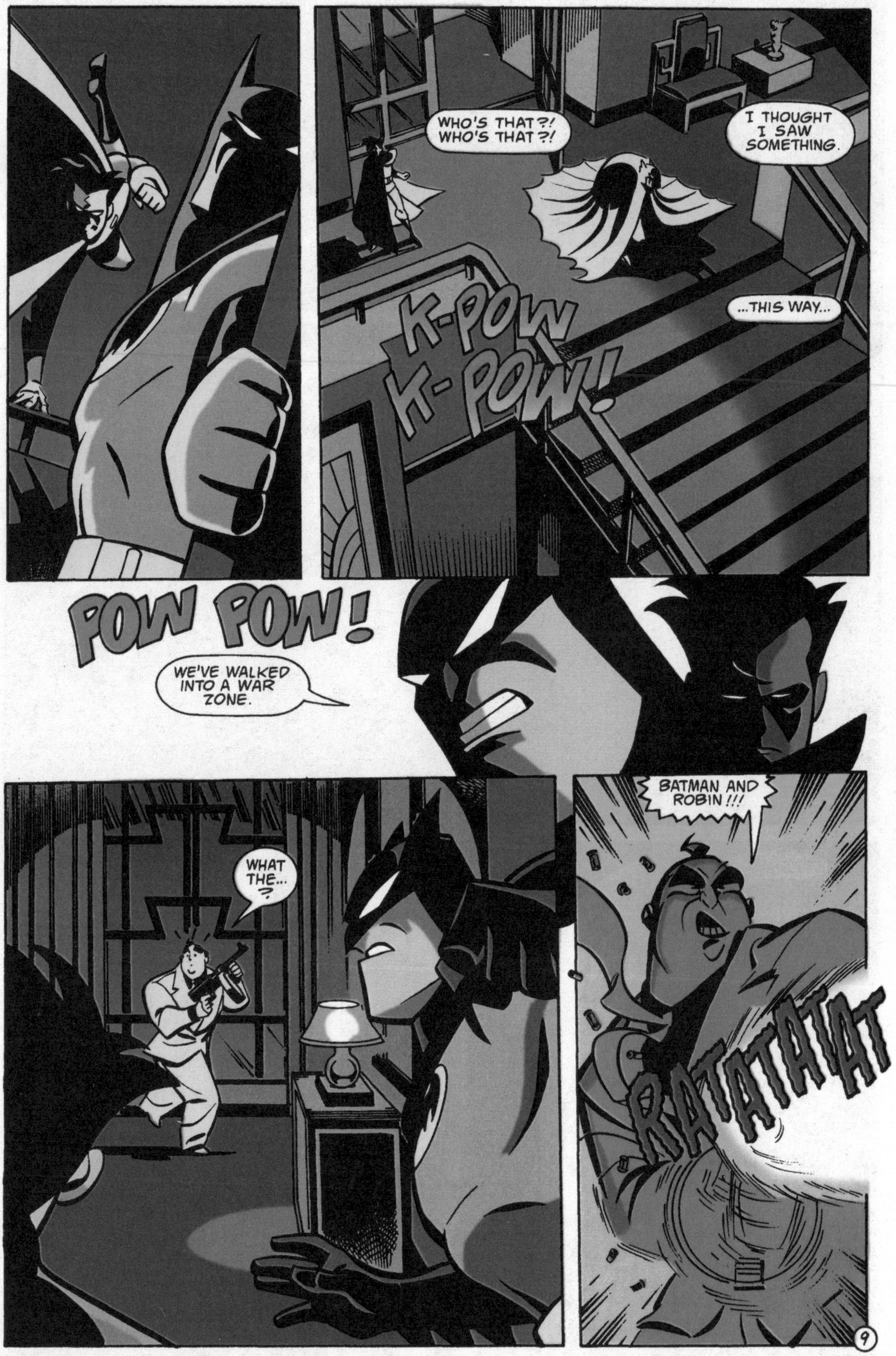
WHO'S THAT?! WHO'S THAT?!
I THOUGHT I SAW SOMETHING.
...THIS WAY...
K-POW K-POW!
POW POW!
WE'VE WALKED INTO A WAR ZONE.
WHAT THE... ?
BATMAN AND ROBIN!!!
RATATATAT
9

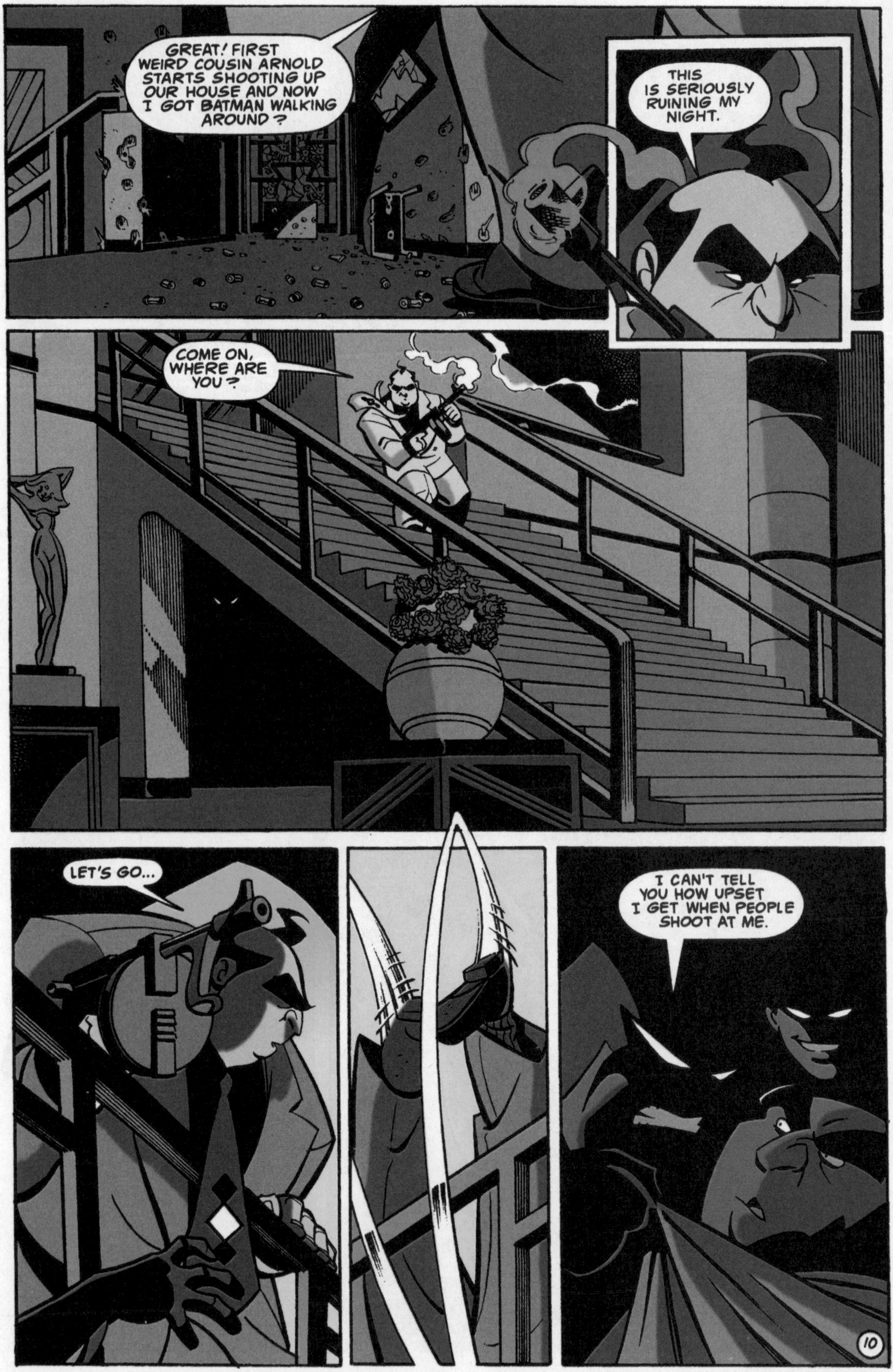
GREAT! FIRST WEIRD COUSIN ARNOLD STARTS SHOOTING UP OUR HOUSE AND NOW I GOT BATMAN WALKING AROUND?
THIS IS SERIOUSLY RUINING MY NIGHT.
COME ON, WHERE ARE YOU?
LET'S GO...
I CAN'T TELL YOU HOW UPSET I GET WHEN PEOPLE SHOOT AT ME.
10

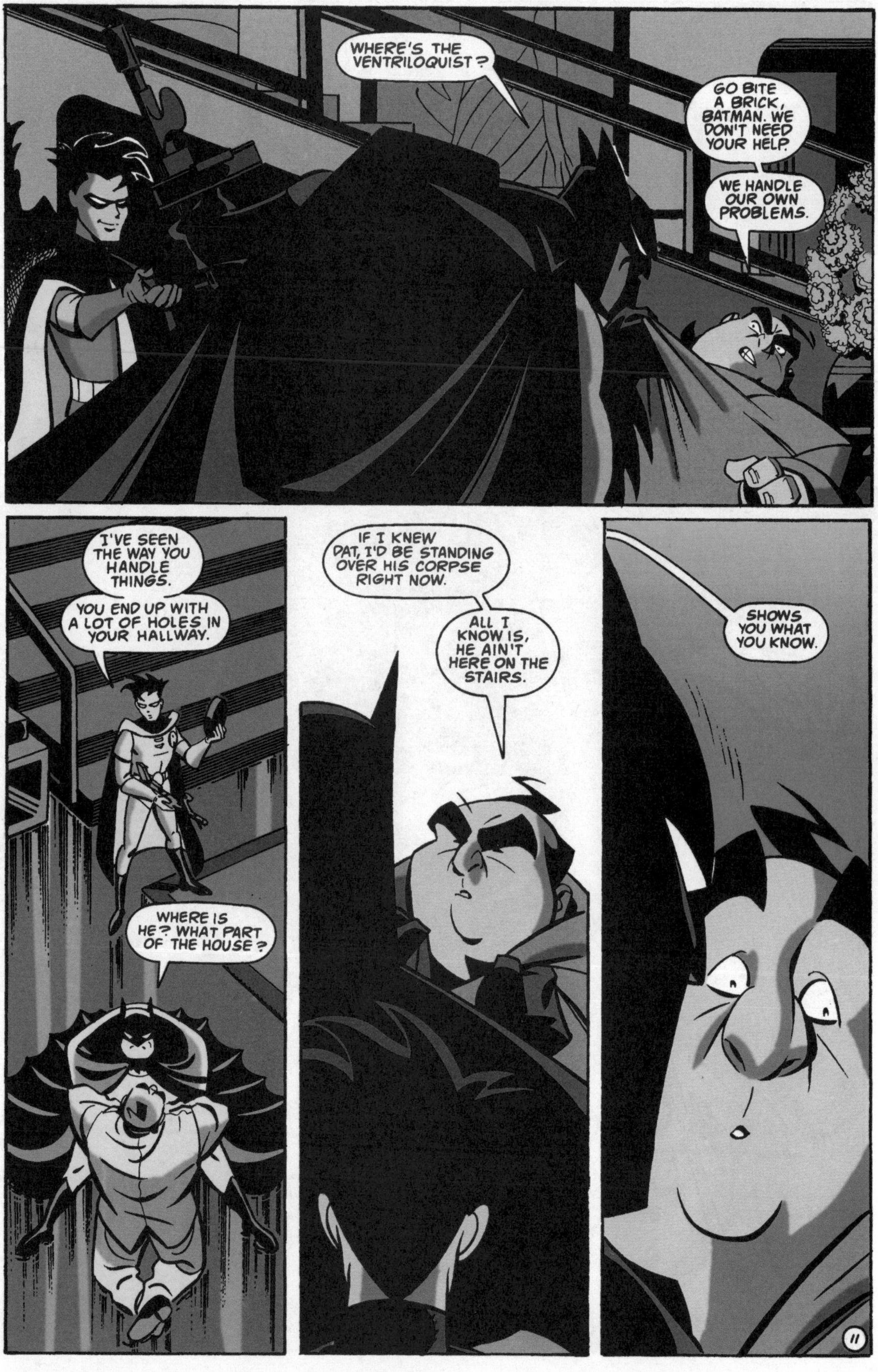
WHERE'S THE VENTRILOQUIST?
GO BITE A BRICK, BATMAN. WE DON'T NEED YOUR HELP.
WE HANDLE OUR OWN PROBLEMS.
I'VE SEEN THE WAY YOU HANDLE THINGS.
YOU END UP WITH A LOT OF HOLES IN YOUR HALLWAY.
WHERE IS HE? WHAT PART OF THE HOUSE?
IF I KNEW DAT, I'D BE STANDING OVER HIS CORPSE RIGHT NOW.
ALL I KNOW IS, HE AIN'T HERE ON THE STAIRS.
SHOWS YOU WHAT YOU KNOW.
11

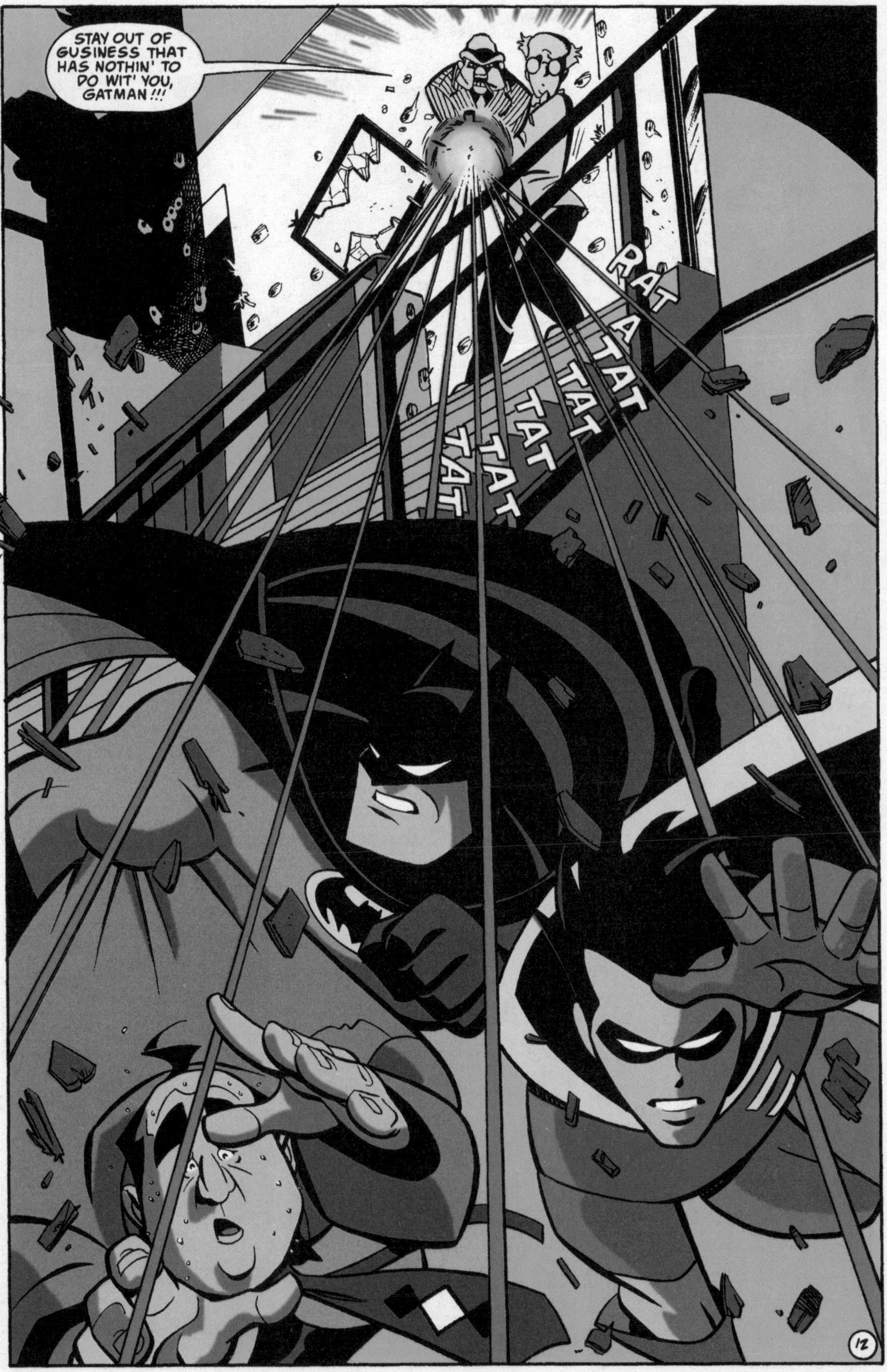
STAY OUT OF GUSINESS THAT HAS NOTHIN' TO DO WIT' YOU, GATMAN!!!
RAT A TAT TAT TAT TAT TAT
12

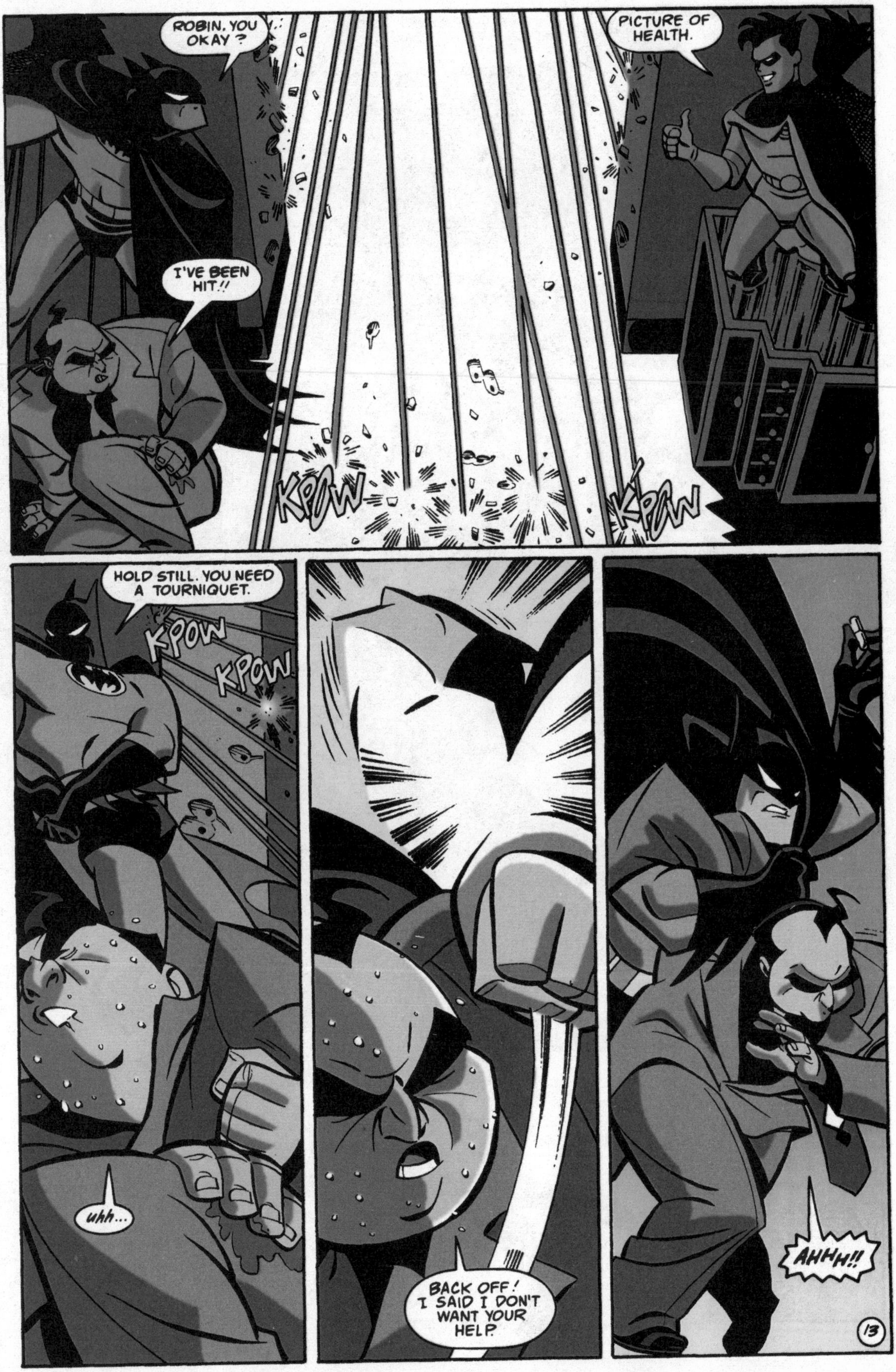
ROBIN, YOU OKAY?
PICTURE OF HEALTH.
I'VE BEEN HIT!!
KPOW
KPOW
HOLD STILL. YOU NEED A TOURNIQUET.
KPOW
KPOW!
uhh...
BACK OFF! I SAID I DON'T WANT YOUR HELP.
AHHH!!
13

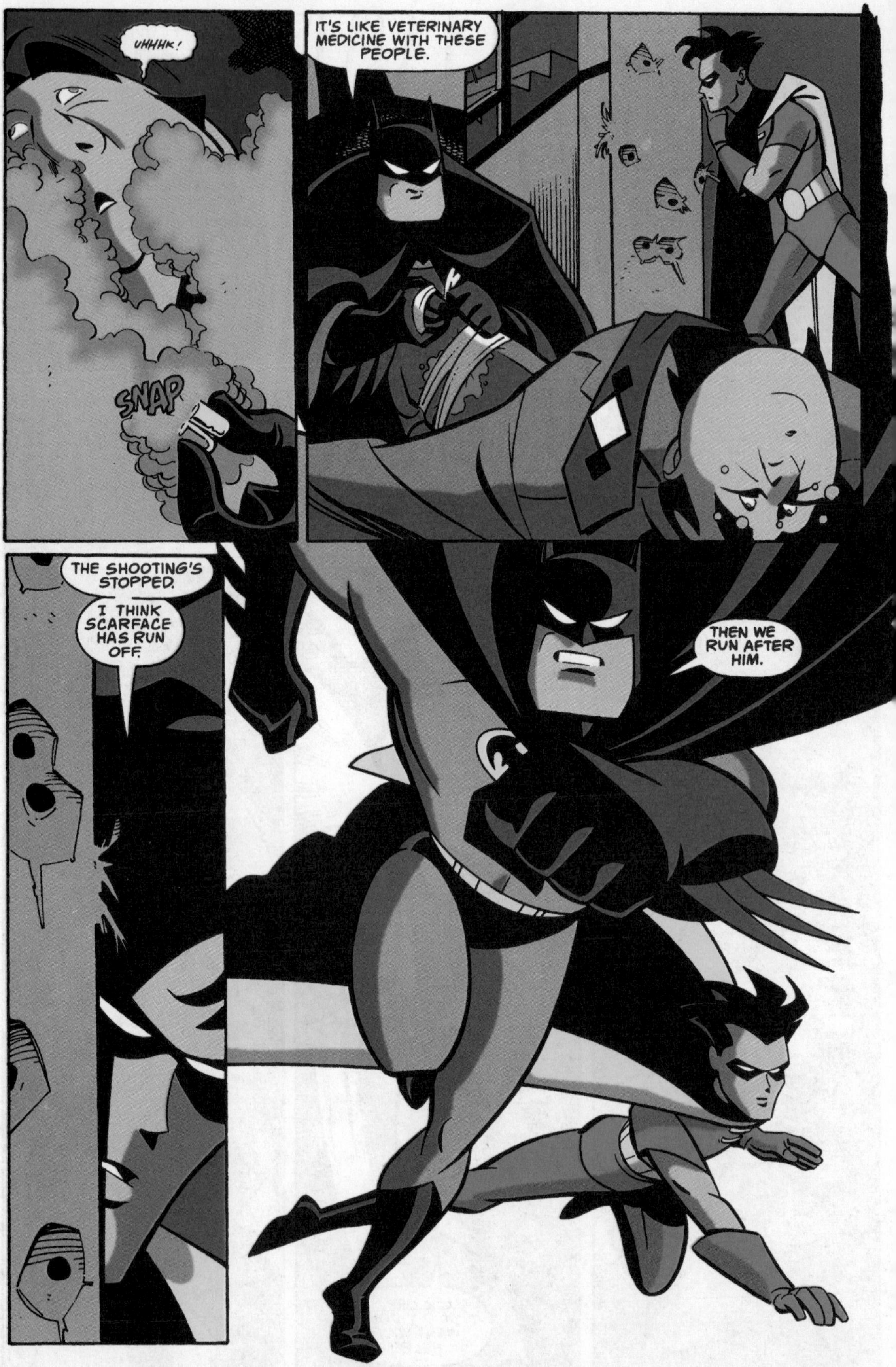
UHHHK!
SNAP
IT'S LIKE VETERINARY MEDICINE WITH THESE PEOPLE.
THE SHOOTING'S STOPPED.
I THINK SCARFACE HAS RUN OFF.
THEN WE RUN AFTER HIM.

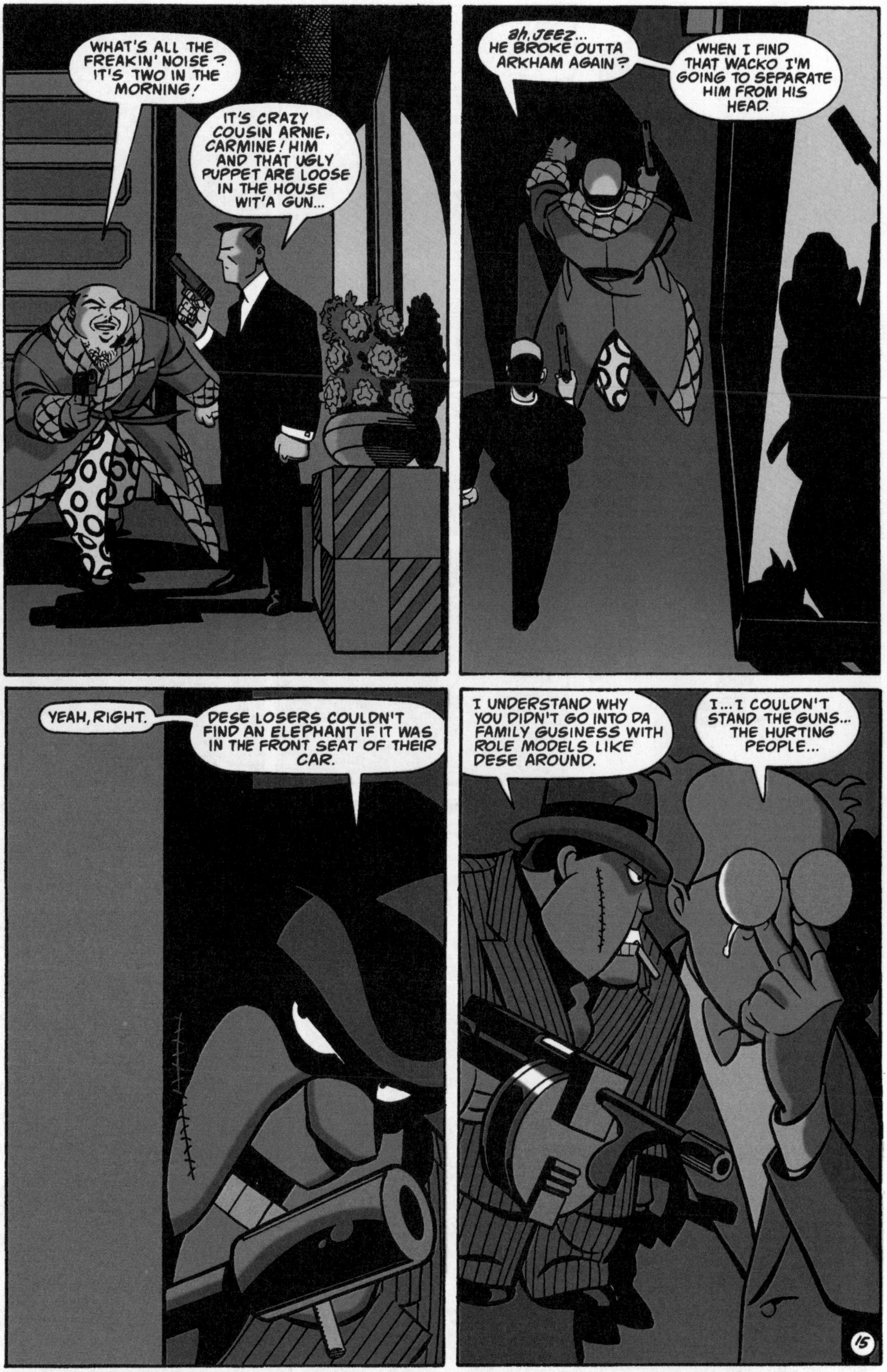
WHAT'S ALL THE FREAKIN' NOISE? IT'S TWO IN THE MORNING!
IT'S CRAZY COUSIN ARNIE, CARMINE! HIM AND THAT UGLY PUPPET ARE LOOSE IN THE HOUSE WIT'A GUN...
ah, JEEZ... HE BROKE OUTTA ARKHAM AGAIN?
WHEN I FIND THAT WACKO I'M GOING TO SEPARATE HIM FROM HIS HEAD.
YEAH, RIGHT.
DESE LOSERS COULDN'T FIND AN ELEPHANT IF IT WAS IN THE FRONT SEAT OF THEIR CAR.
I UNDERSTAND WHY YOU DIDN'T GO INTO DA FAMILY GUSINESS WITH ROLE MODELS LIKE DESE AROUND.
I... I COULDN'T STAND THE GUNS... THE HURTING PEOPLE...
15

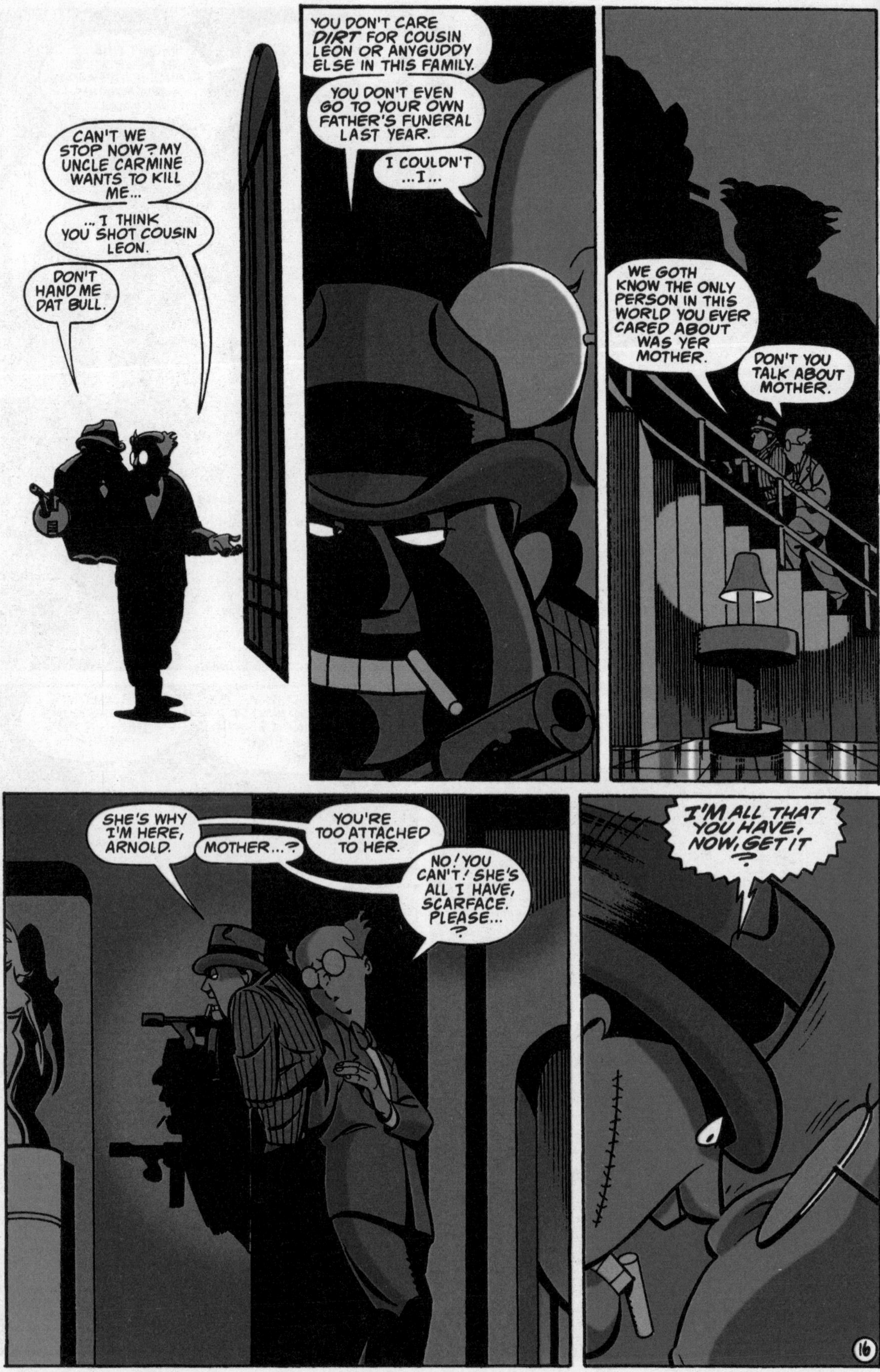
CAN'T WE STOP NOW? MY UNCLE CARMINE WANTS TO KILL ME...
...I THINK YOU SHOT COUSIN LEON.
DON'T HAND ME DAT BULL.
YOU DON'T CARE DIRT FOR COUSIN LEON OR ANYGUDDY ELSE IN THIS FAMILY.
YOU DON'T EVEN GO TO YOUR OWN FATHER'S FUNERAL LAST YEAR.
I COULDN'T ...I...
WE GOTH KNOW THE ONLY PERSON IN THIS WORLD YOU EVER CARED ABOUT WAS YER MOTHER.
DON'T YOU TALK ABOUT MOTHER.
SHE'S WHY I'M HERE, ARNOLD.
MOTHER...?
YOU'RE TOO ATTACHED TO HER.
NO! YOU CAN'T! SHE'S ALL I HAVE, SCARFACE. PLEASE...?
I'M ALL THAT YOU HAVE, NOW, GET IT?
16

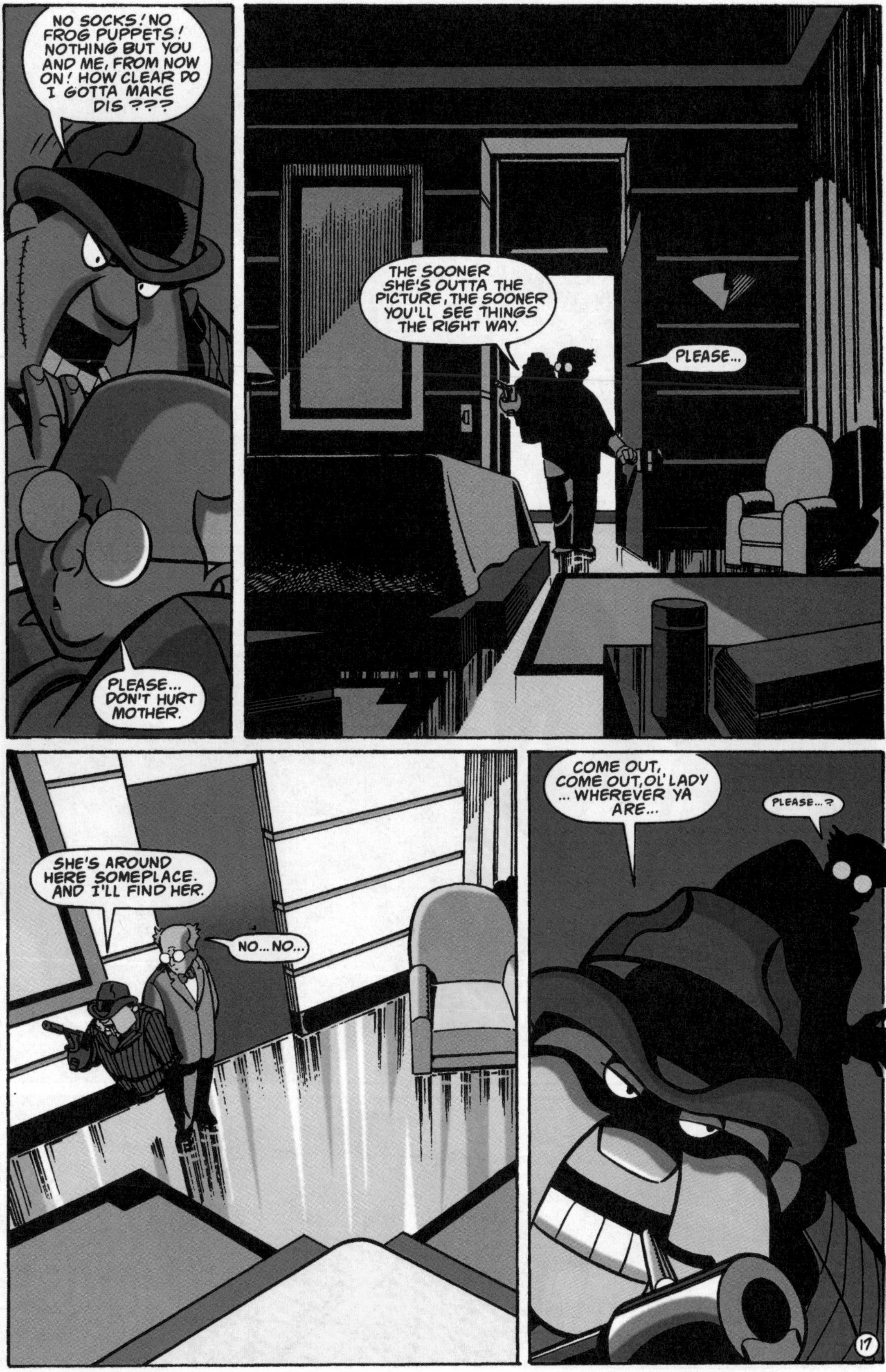
NO SOCKS! NO FROG PUPPETS! NOTHING BUT YOU AND ME, FROM NOW ON! HOW CLEAR DO I GOTTA MAKE DIS???
PLEASE... DON'T HURT MOTHER.
THE SOONER SHE'S OUTTA THE PICTURE, THE SOONER YOU'LL SEE THINGS THE RIGHT WAY.
PLEASE...
SHE'S AROUND HERE SOMEPLACE. AND I'LL FIND HER.
NO... NO...
COME OUT, COME OUT, OL' LADY ... WHEREVER YA ARE...
PLEASE...?
17

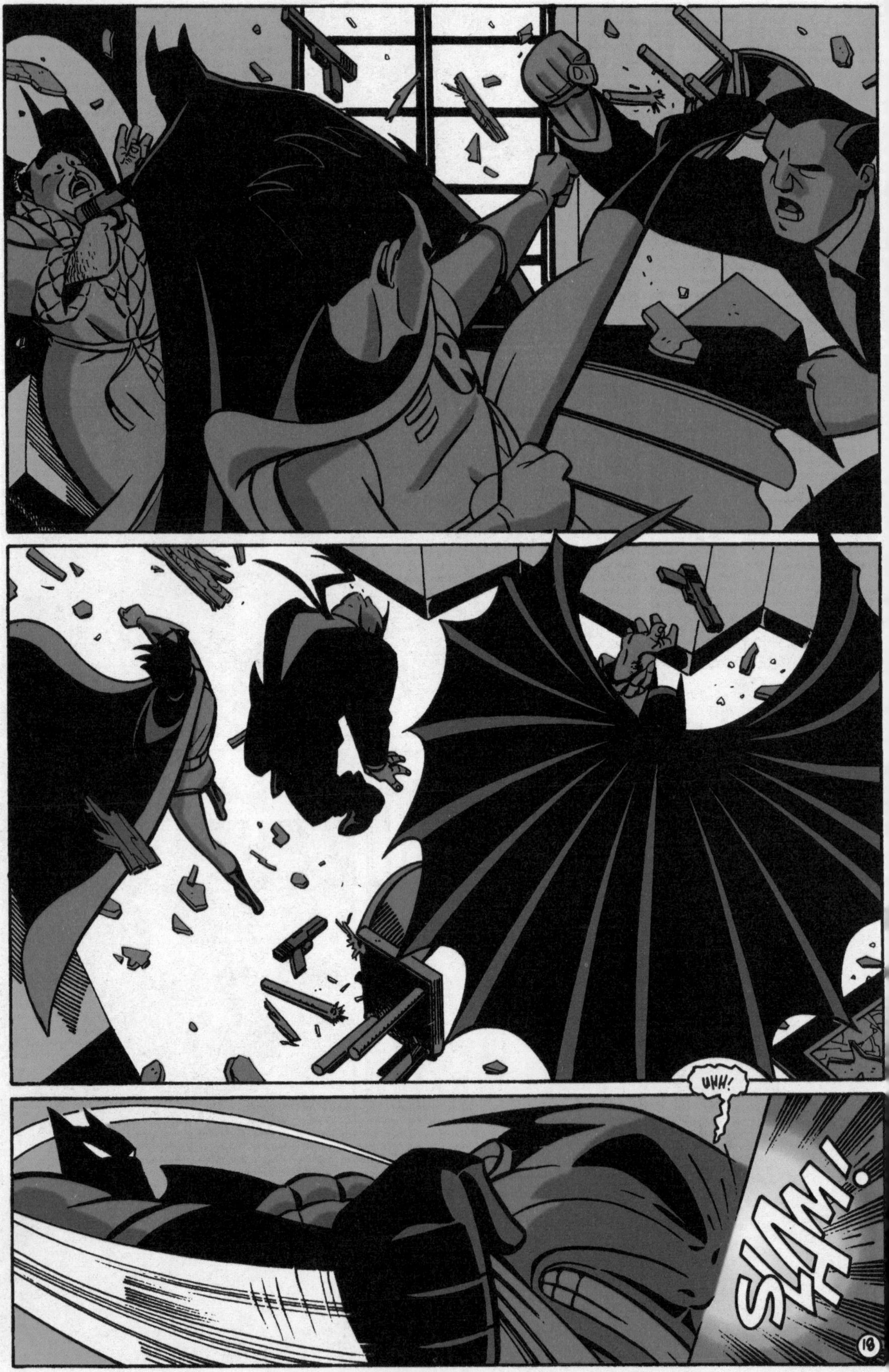
UNH!
SLAM!
18

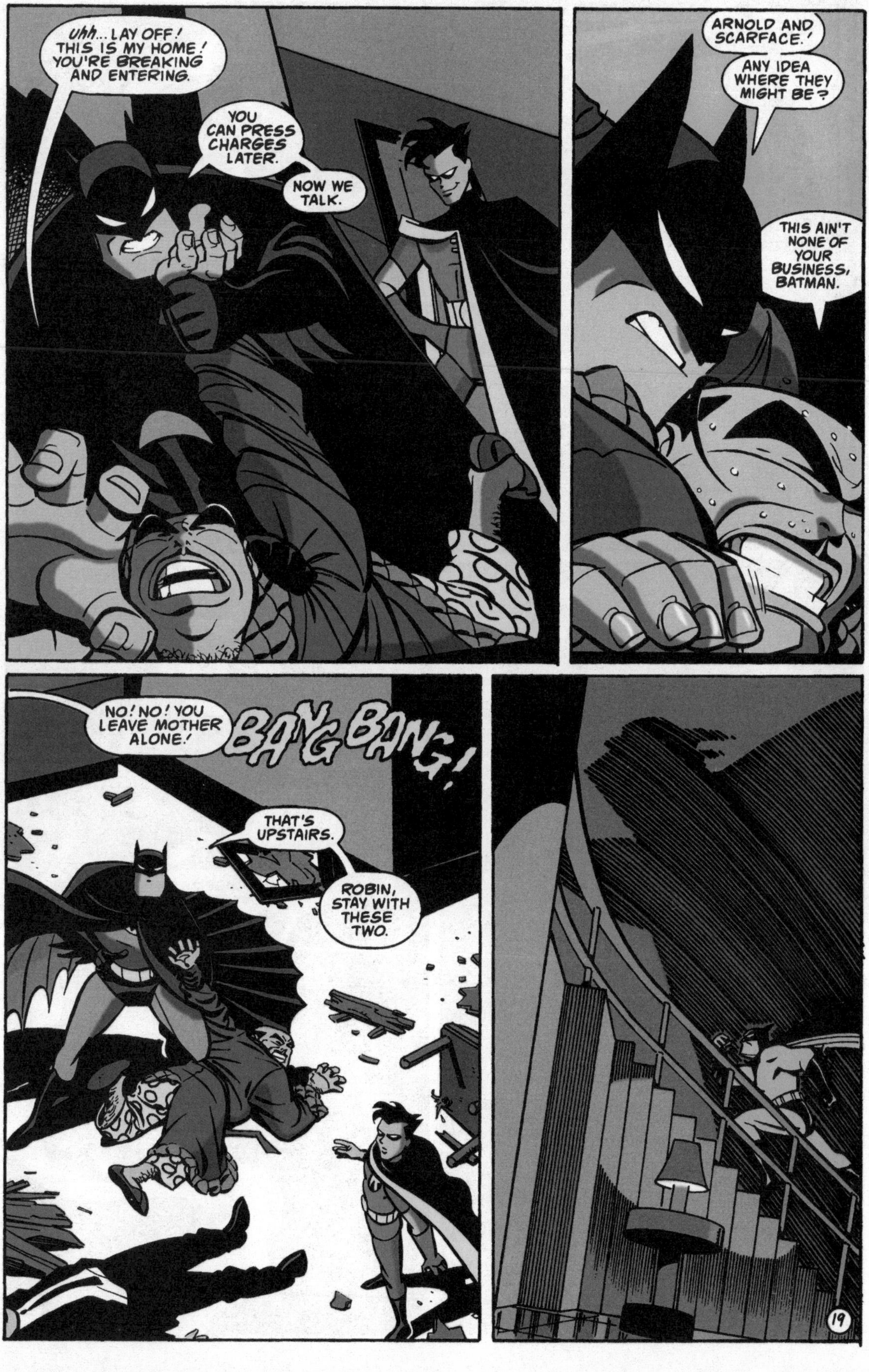

UHH... LAY OFF! THIS IS MY HOME! YOU'RE BREAKING AND ENTERING.
YOU CAN PRESS CHARGES LATER.
NOW WE TALK.
ARNOLD AND SCARFACE.'
ANY IDEA WHERE THEY MIGHT BE?
THIS AIN'T NONE OF YOUR BUSINESS, BATMAN.
NO! NO! YOU LEAVE MOTHER ALONE!
BANG BANG!
THAT'S UPSTAIRS.
ROBIN, STAY WITH THESE TWO.
19

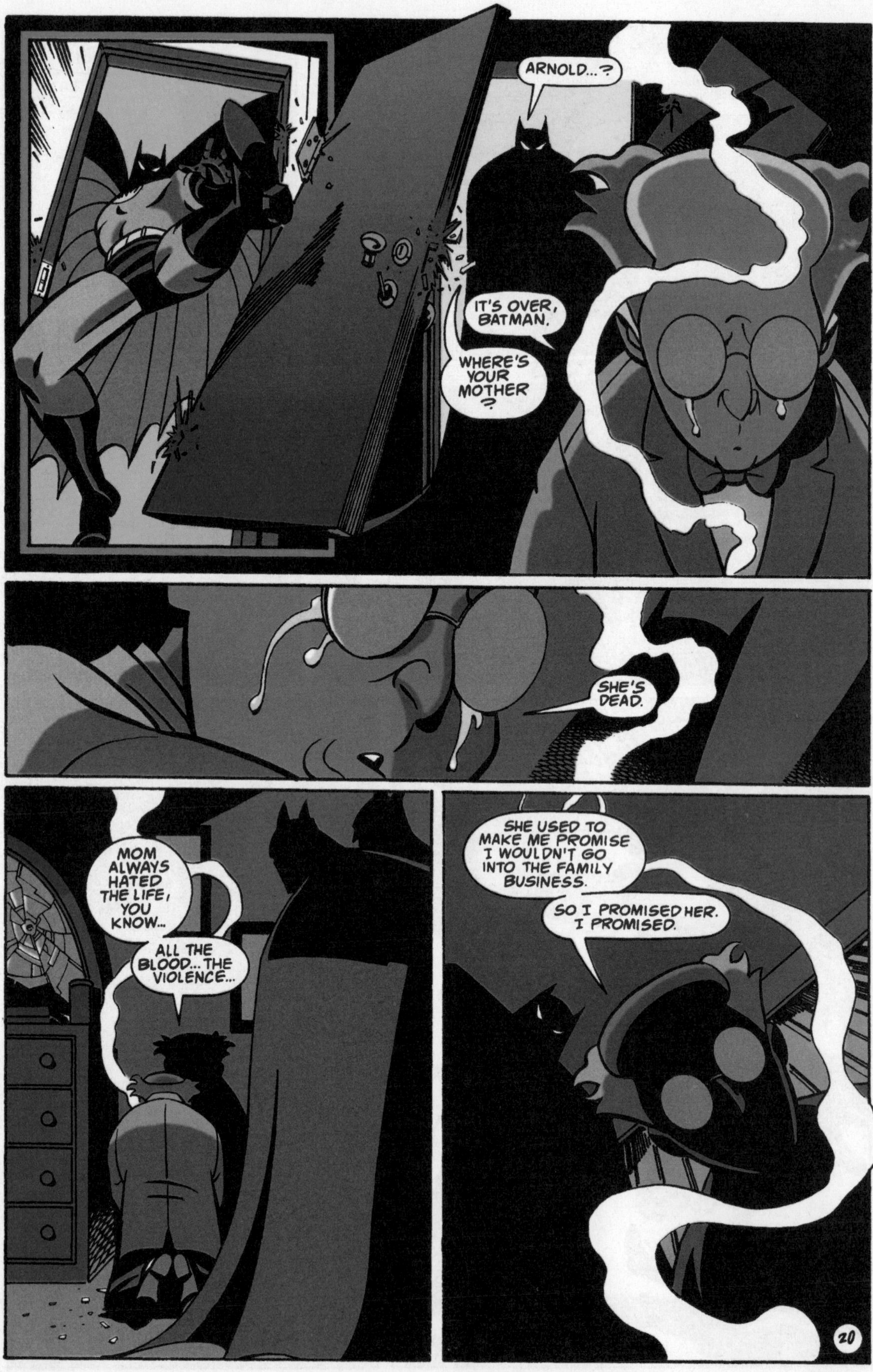
ARNOLD...?
IT'S OVER, BATMAN.
WHERE'S YOUR MOTHER?
SHE'S DEAD.
MOM ALWAYS HATED THE LIFE, YOU KNOW...
ALL THE BLOOD... THE VIOLENCE...
SHE USED TO MAKE ME PROMISE I WOULDN'T GO INTO THE FAMILY BUSINESS.
SO I PROMISED HER. I PROMISED.
20

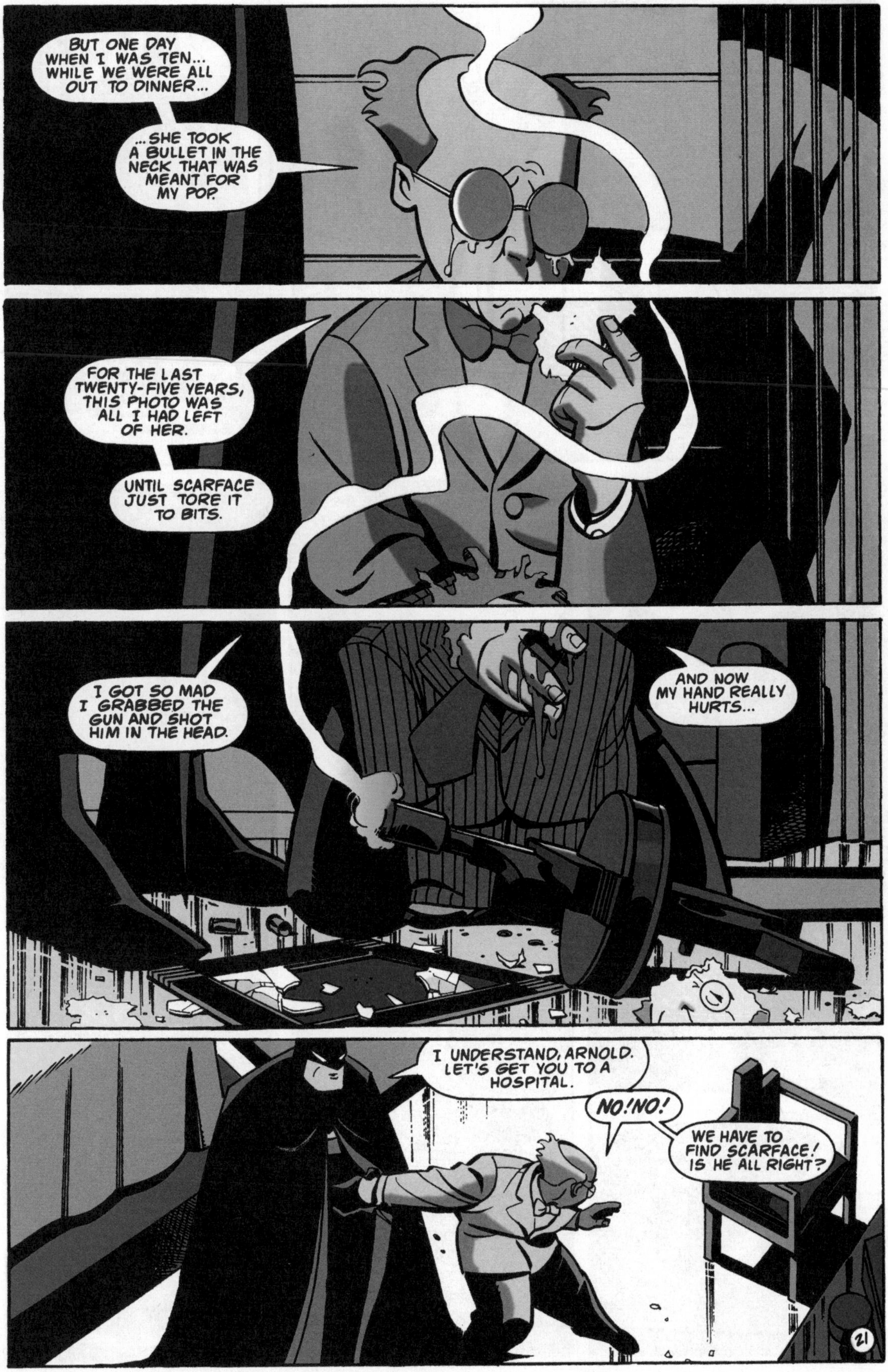
BUT ONE DAY WHEN I WAS TEN... WHILE WE WERE ALL OUT TO DINNER...
...SHE TOOK A BULLET IN THE NECK THAT WAS MEANT FOR MY POP.
FOR THE LAST TWENTY-FIVE YEARS, THIS PHOTO WAS ALL I HAD LEFT OF HER.
UNTIL SCARFACE JUST TORE IT TO BITS.
I GOT SO MAD I GRABBED THE GUN AND SHOT HIM IN THE HEAD.
AND NOW MY HAND REALLY HURTS...
I UNDERSTAND, ARNOLD. LET'S GET YOU TO A HOSPITAL.
NO! NO!
WE HAVE TO FIND SCARFACE! IS HE ALL RIGHT?
21

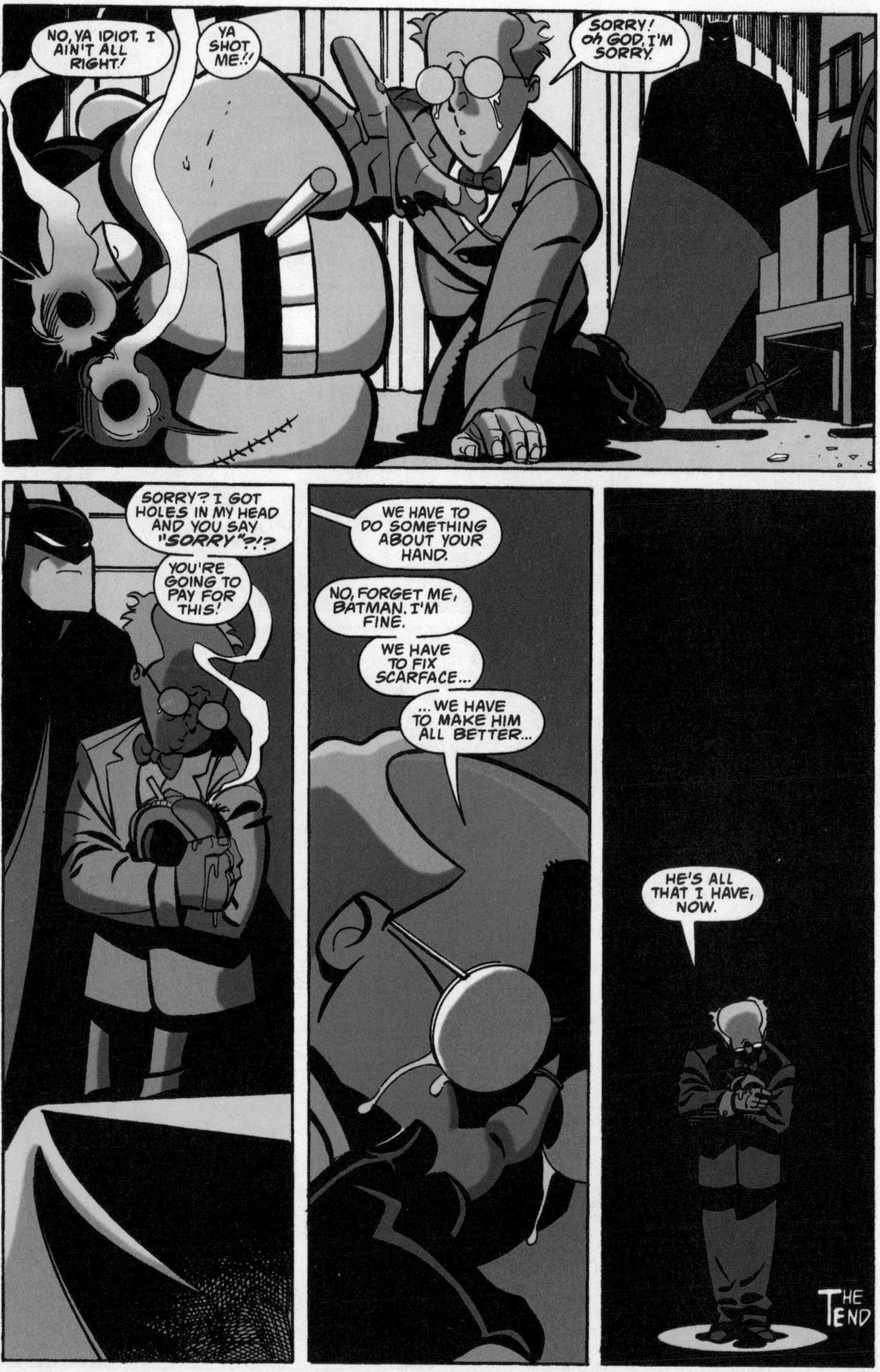
NO, YA IDIOT, I AIN'T ALL RIGHT!
YA SHOT ME!!
SORRY! oh GOD, I'M SORRY.
SORRY? I GOT HOLES IN MY HEAD AND YOU SAY "SORRY"?!?
YOU'RE GOING TO PAY FOR THIS!
WE HAVE TO DO SOMETHING ABOUT YOUR HAND.
NO, FORGET ME, BATMAN. I'M FINE.
WE HAVE TO FIX SCARFACE...
...WE HAVE TO MAKE HIM ALL BETTER...
HE'S ALL THAT I HAVE, NOW.
THE END

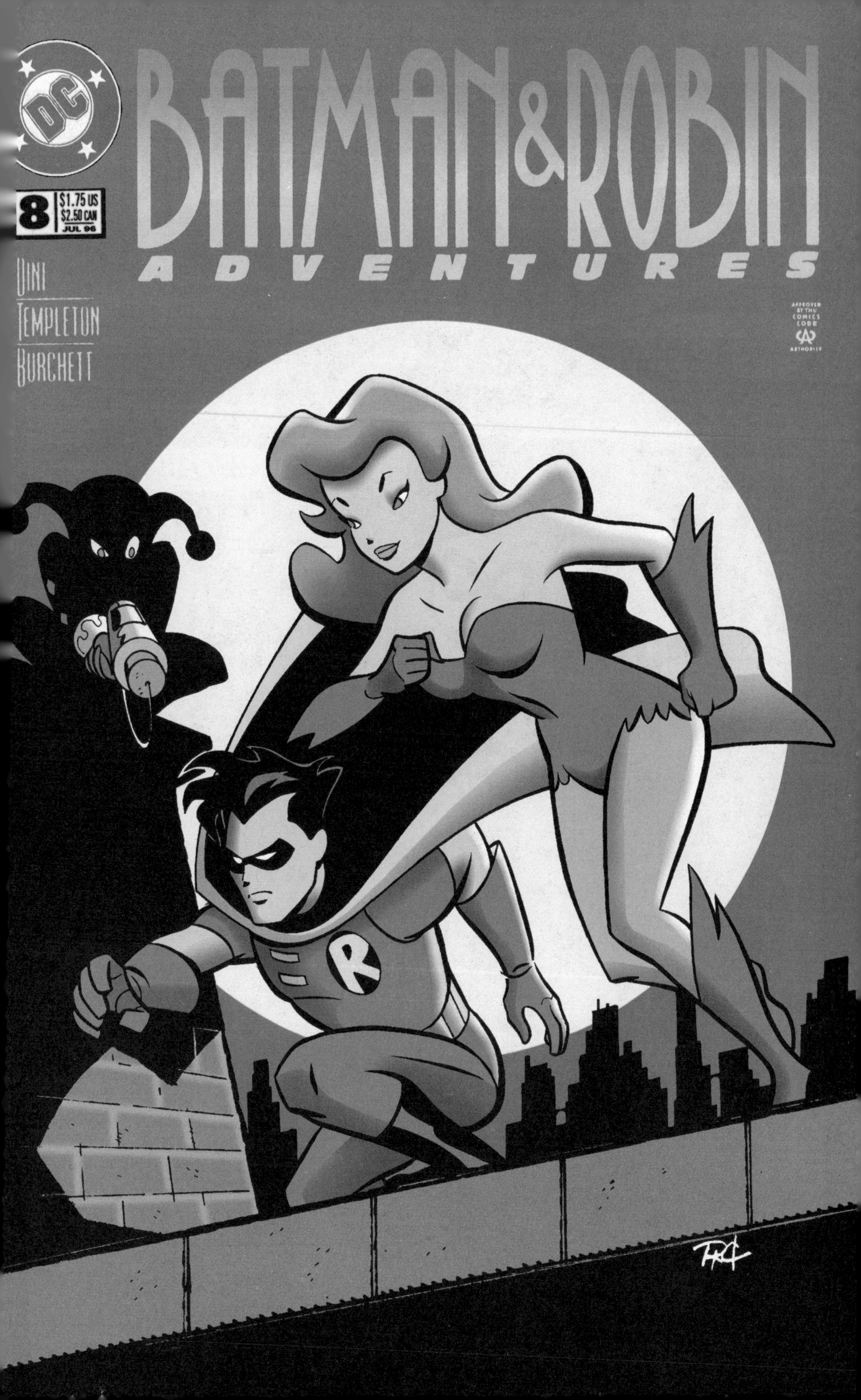

BATMAN & ROBIN
ADVENTURES
8
$1.75 US
$2.50 CAN
JUL 96
DINI
TEMPLETON
BURCHETT

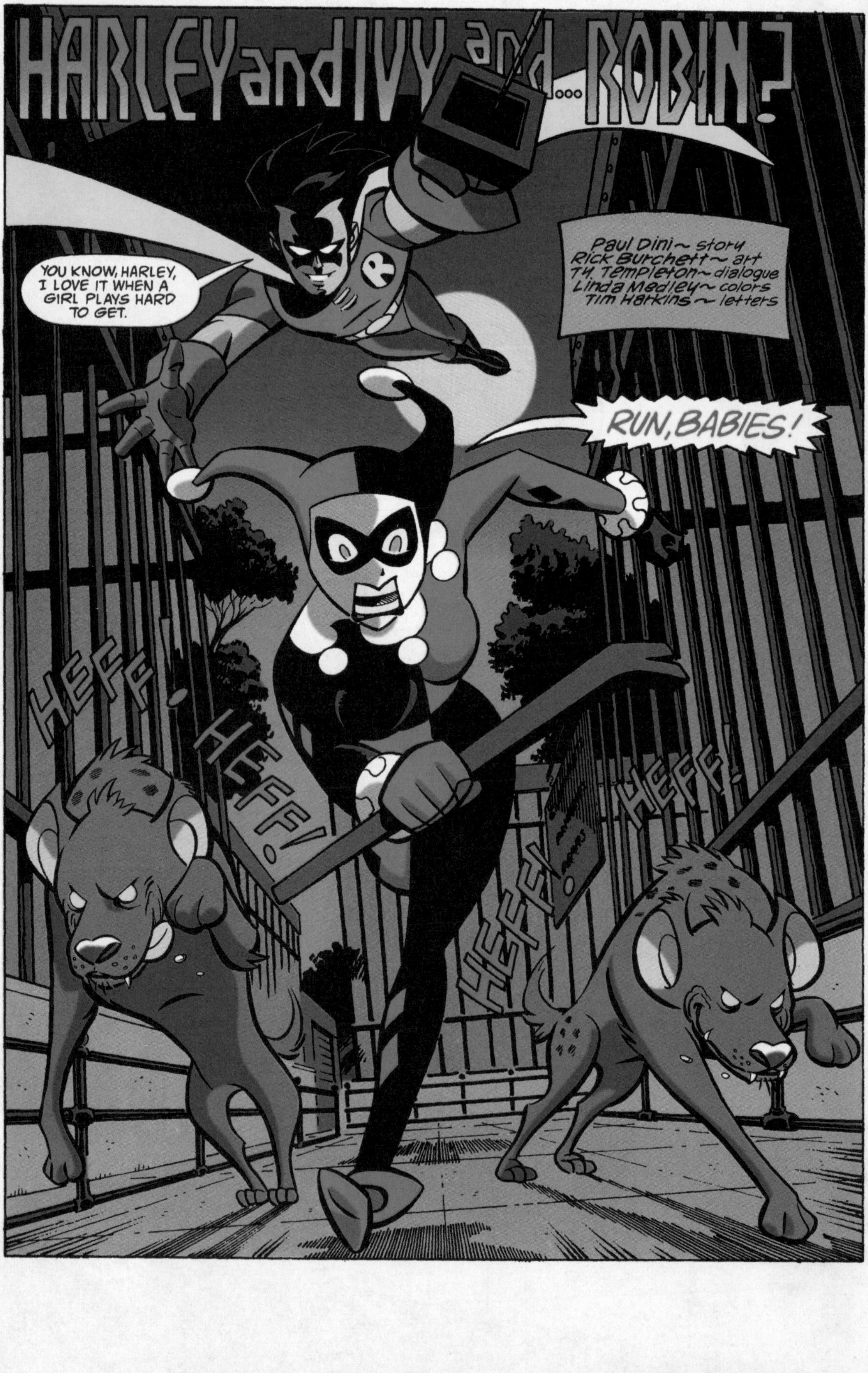
HARLEY and IVY and... ROBIN?
YOU KNOW, HARLEY, I LOVE IT WHEN A GIRL PLAYS HARD TO GET.
Paul Dini ~ story
Rick Burchett ~ art
Ty Templeton ~ dialogue
Linda Medley ~ colors
Tim Harkins ~ letters
RUN, BABIES!
HEFF! HEFF!
HEFF! HEFF!

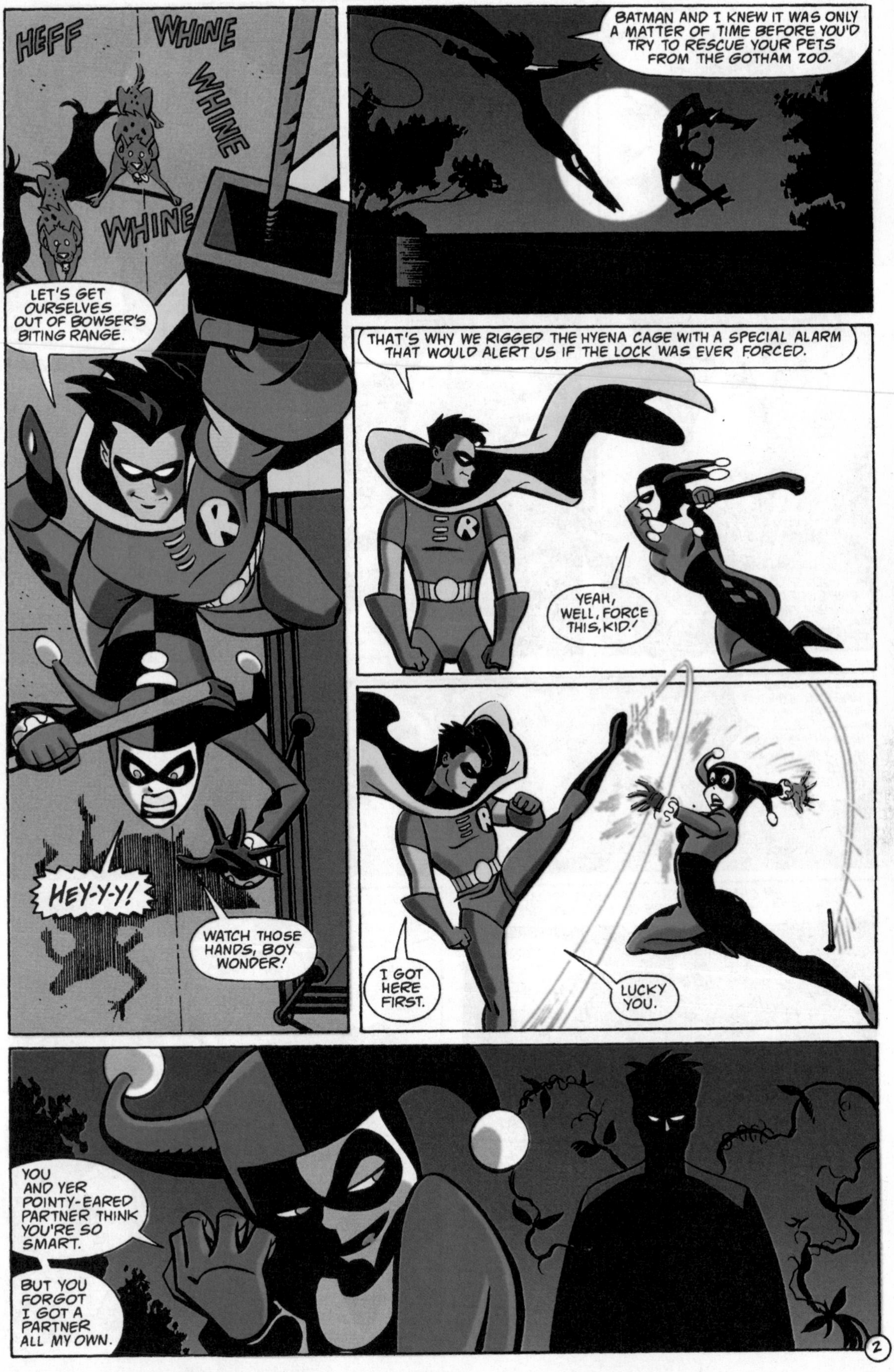
HEFF
WHINE
WHINE
WHINE
LET'S GET OURSELVES OUT OF BOWSER'S BITING RANGE.
HEY-Y-Y!
WATCH THOSE HANDS, BOY WONDER!
BATMAN AND I KNEW IT WAS ONLY A MATTER OF TIME BEFORE YOU'D TRY TO RESCUE YOUR PETS FROM THE GOTHAM ZOO.
THAT'S WHY WE RIGGED THE HYENA CAGE WITH A SPECIAL ALARM THAT WOULD ALERT US IF THE LOCK WAS EVER FORCED.
YEAH, WELL, FORCE THIS, KID!
I GOT HERE FIRST.
LUCKY YOU.
YOU AND YER POINTY-EARED PARTNER THINK YOU'RE SO SMART.
BUT YOU FORGOT I GOT A PARTNER ALL MY OWN.
2

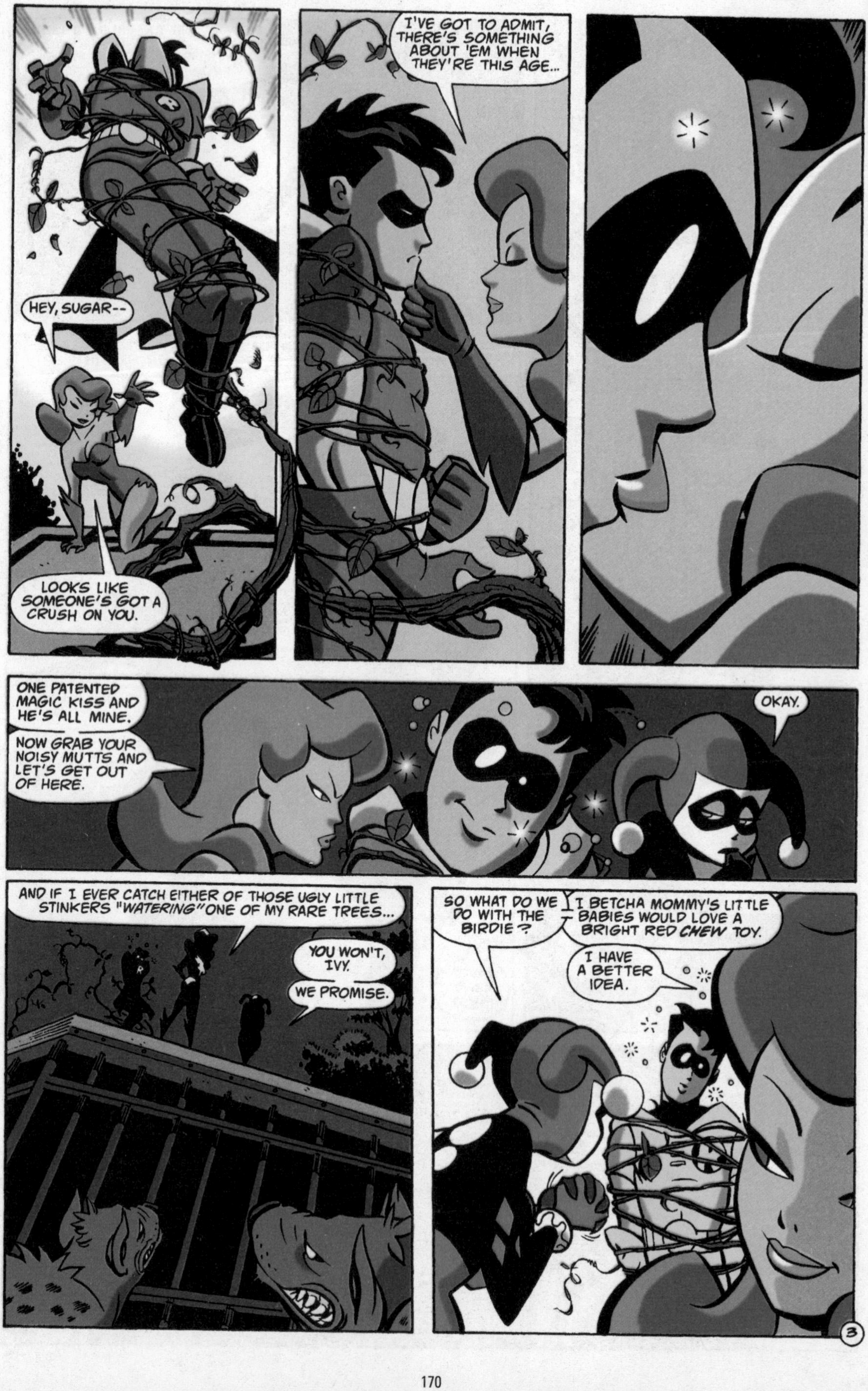
I'VE GOT TO ADMIT, THERE'S SOMETHING ABOUT 'EM WHEN THEY'RE THIS AGE...
HEY, SUGAR--
LOOKS LIKE SOMEONE'S GOT A CRUSH ON YOU.
ONE PATENTED MAGIC KISS AND HE'S ALL MINE.
NOW GRAB YOUR NOISY MUTTS AND LET'S GET OUT OF HERE.
OKAY.
AND IF I EVER CATCH EITHER OF THOSE UGLY LITTLE STINKERS "WATERING" ONE OF MY RARE TREES...
YOU WON'T, IVY.
WE PROMISE.
SO WHAT DO WE DO WITH THE BIRDIE?
I BETCHA MOMMY'S LITTLE BABIES WOULD LOVE A BRIGHT RED CHEW TOY.
I HAVE A BETTER IDEA.
3

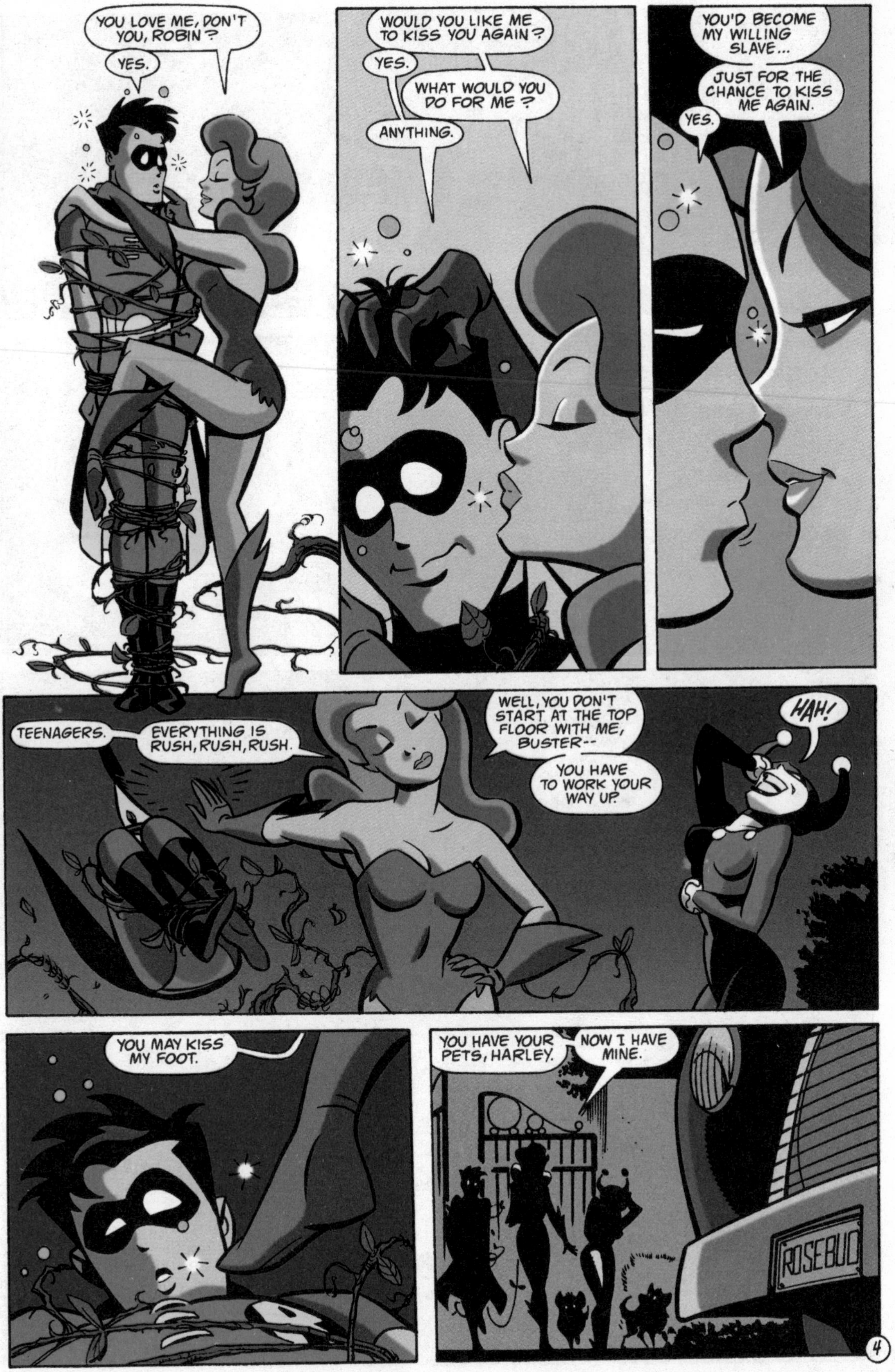
YOU LOVE ME, DON'T YOU, ROBIN?
YES.
WOULD YOU LIKE ME TO KISS YOU AGAIN?
YES.
WHAT WOULD YOU DO FOR ME?
ANYTHING.
YOU'D BECOME MY WILLING SLAVE...
JUST FOR THE CHANCE TO KISS ME AGAIN.
YES.
TEENAGERS.
EVERYTHING IS RUSH, RUSH, RUSH.
WELL, YOU DON'T START AT THE TOP FLOOR WITH ME, BUSTER--
YOU HAVE TO WORK YOUR WAY UP.
HAH!
YOU MAY KISS MY FOOT.
YOU HAVE YOUR PETS, HARLEY.
NOW I HAVE MINE.
ROSEBUD
4

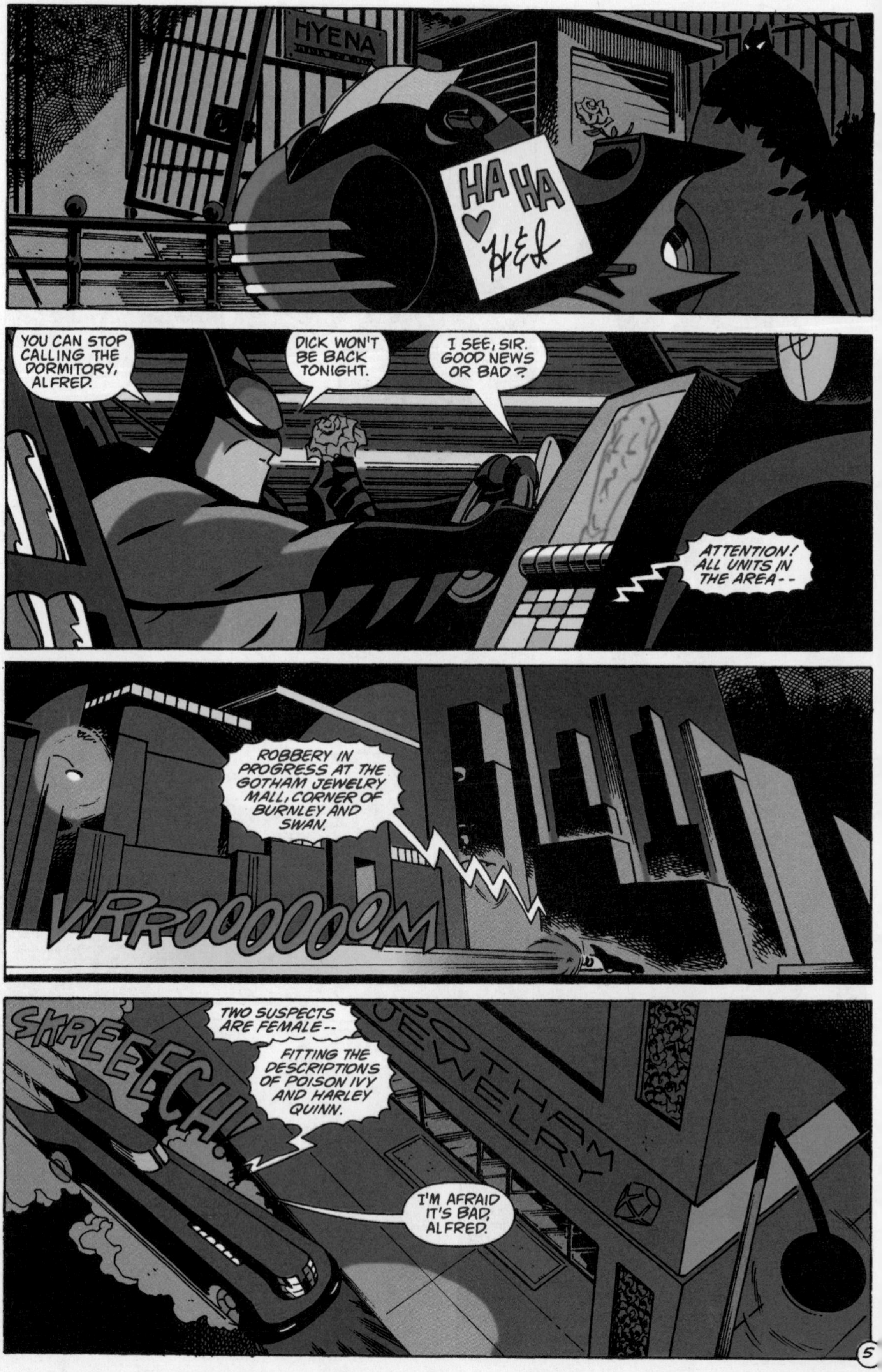
HYENA
HA HA
YOU CAN STOP CALLING THE DORMITORY, ALFRED.
DICK WON'T BE BACK TONIGHT.
I SEE, SIR. GOOD NEWS OR BAD?
ATTENTION! ALL UNITS IN THE AREA--
ROBBERY IN PROGRESS AT THE GOTHAM JEWELRY MALL, CORNER OF BURNLEY AND SWAN.
VRROOOOOOOM
SKREEEECH!
TWO SUSPECTS ARE FEMALE--
FITTING THE DESCRIPTIONS OF POISON IVY AND HARLEY QUINN.
GOTHAM JEWELRY
I'M AFRAID IT'S BAD, ALFRED.
5

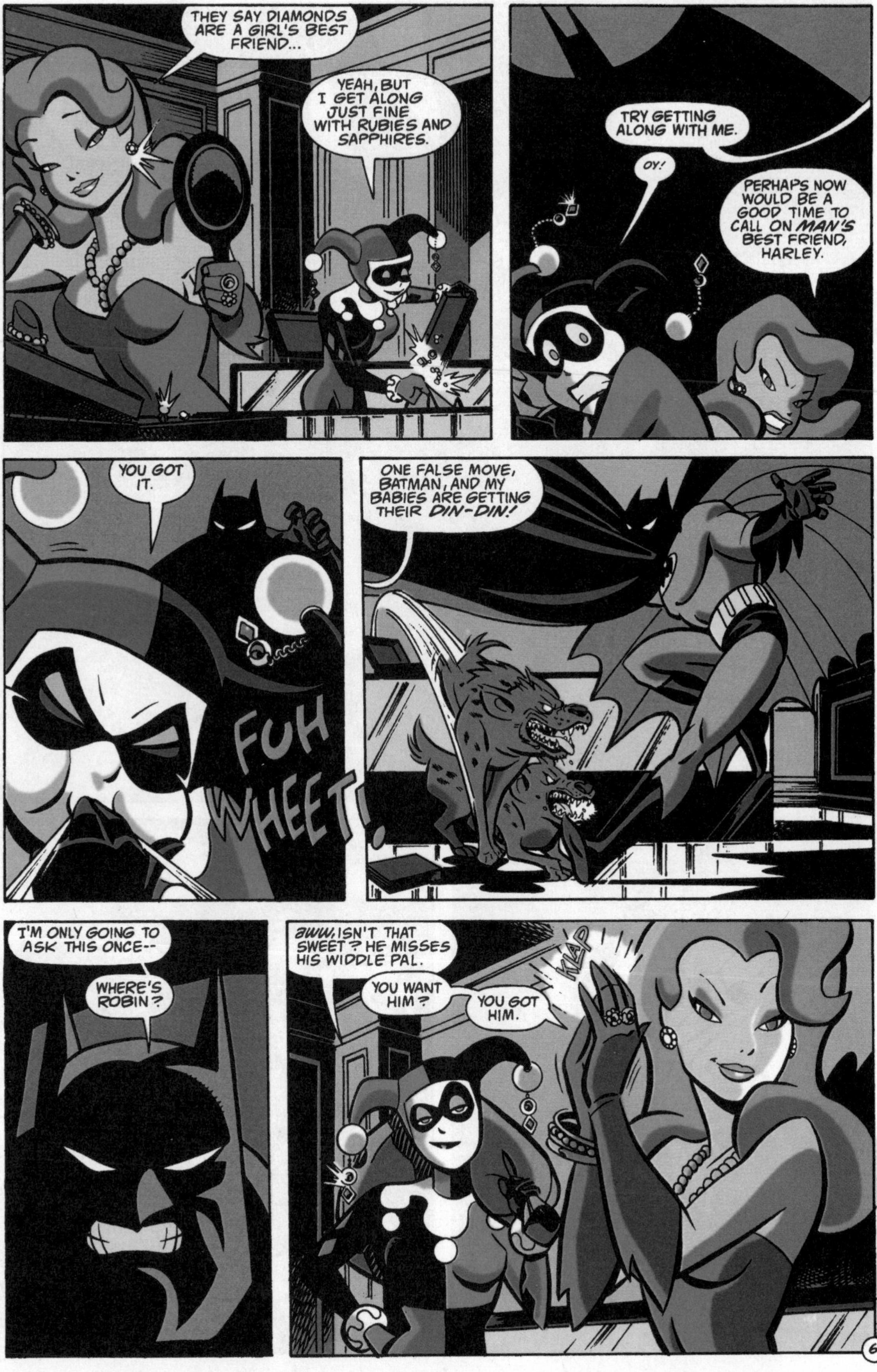

THEY SAY DIAMONDS ARE A GIRL'S BEST FRIEND...
YEAH, BUT I GET ALONG JUST FINE WITH RUBIES AND SAPPHIRES.
TRY GETTING ALONG WITH ME.
OY!
PERHAPS NOW WOULD BE A GOOD TIME TO CALL ON MAN'S BEST FRIEND, HARLEY.
YOU GOT IT.
FUH WHEET!
ONE FALSE MOVE, BATMAN, AND MY BABIES ARE GETTING THEIR DIN-DIN!
I'M ONLY GOING TO ASK THIS ONCE--
WHERE'S ROBIN?
AWW, ISN'T THAT SWEET? HE MISSES HIS WIDDLE PAL.
YOU WANT HIM?
YOU GOT HIM.
KLAP
6

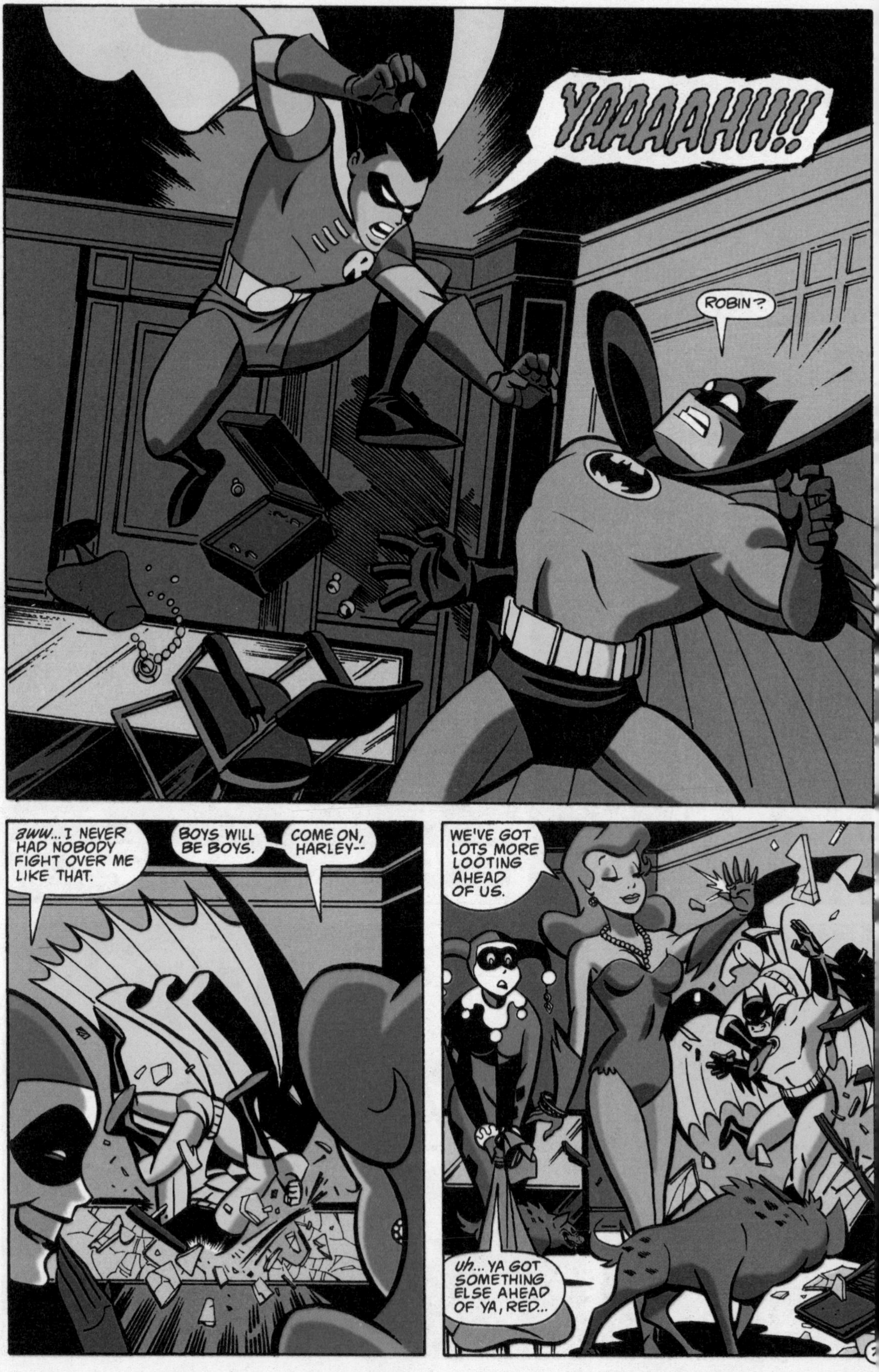
YAAAAHH!!
ROBIN?
aww... I NEVER HAD NOBODY FIGHT OVER ME LIKE THAT.
BOYS WILL BE BOYS.
COME ON, HARLEY--
WE'VE GOT LOTS MORE LOOTING AHEAD OF US.
uh... YA GOT SOMETHING ELSE AHEAD OF YA, RED...

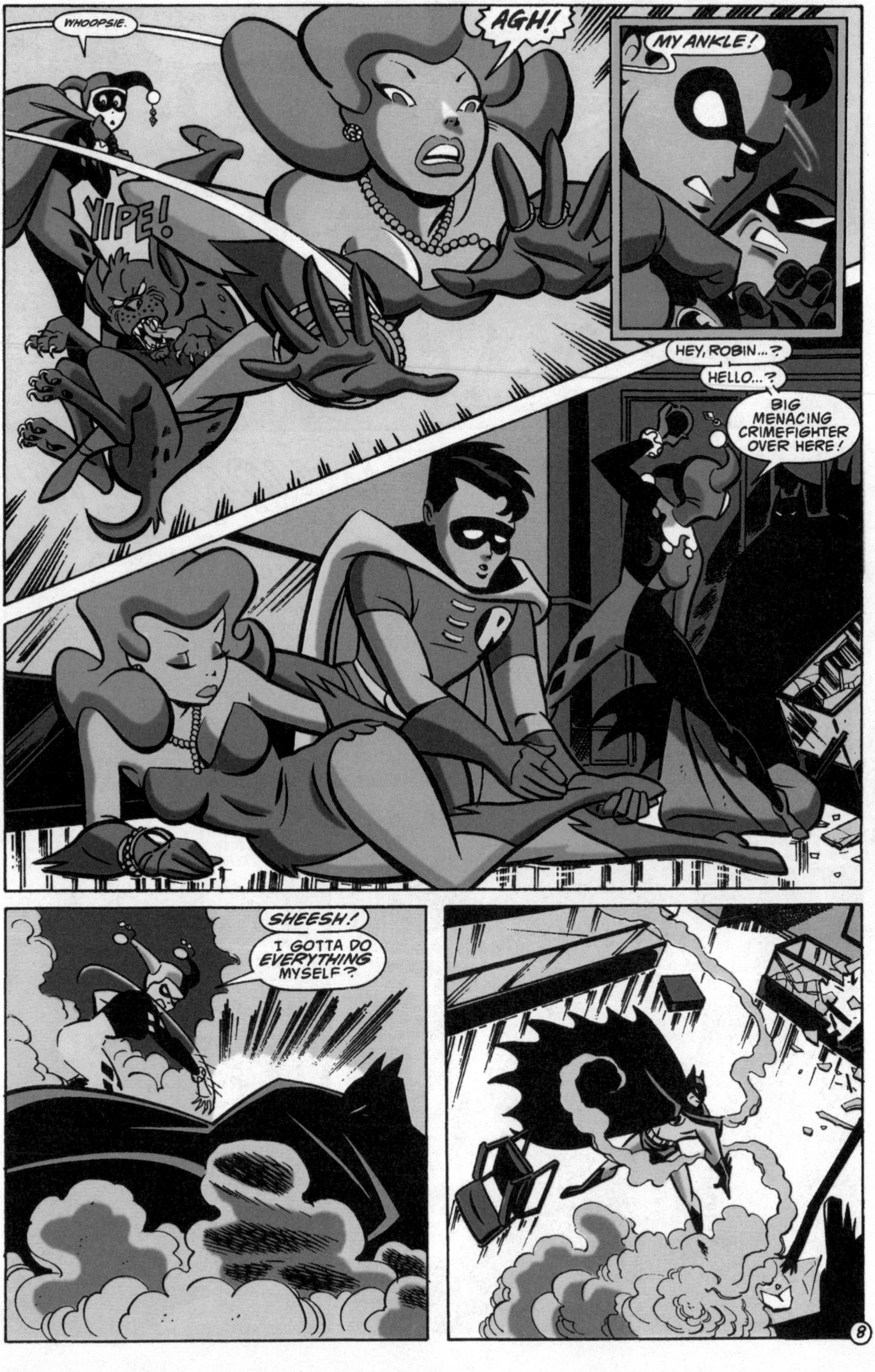
WHOOPSIE.
AGH!
MY ANKLE!
YIPE!
HEY, ROBIN...?
HELLO...?
BIG MENACING CRIMEFIGHTER OVER HERE!
SHEESH!
I GOTTA DO EVERYTHING MYSELF?
8

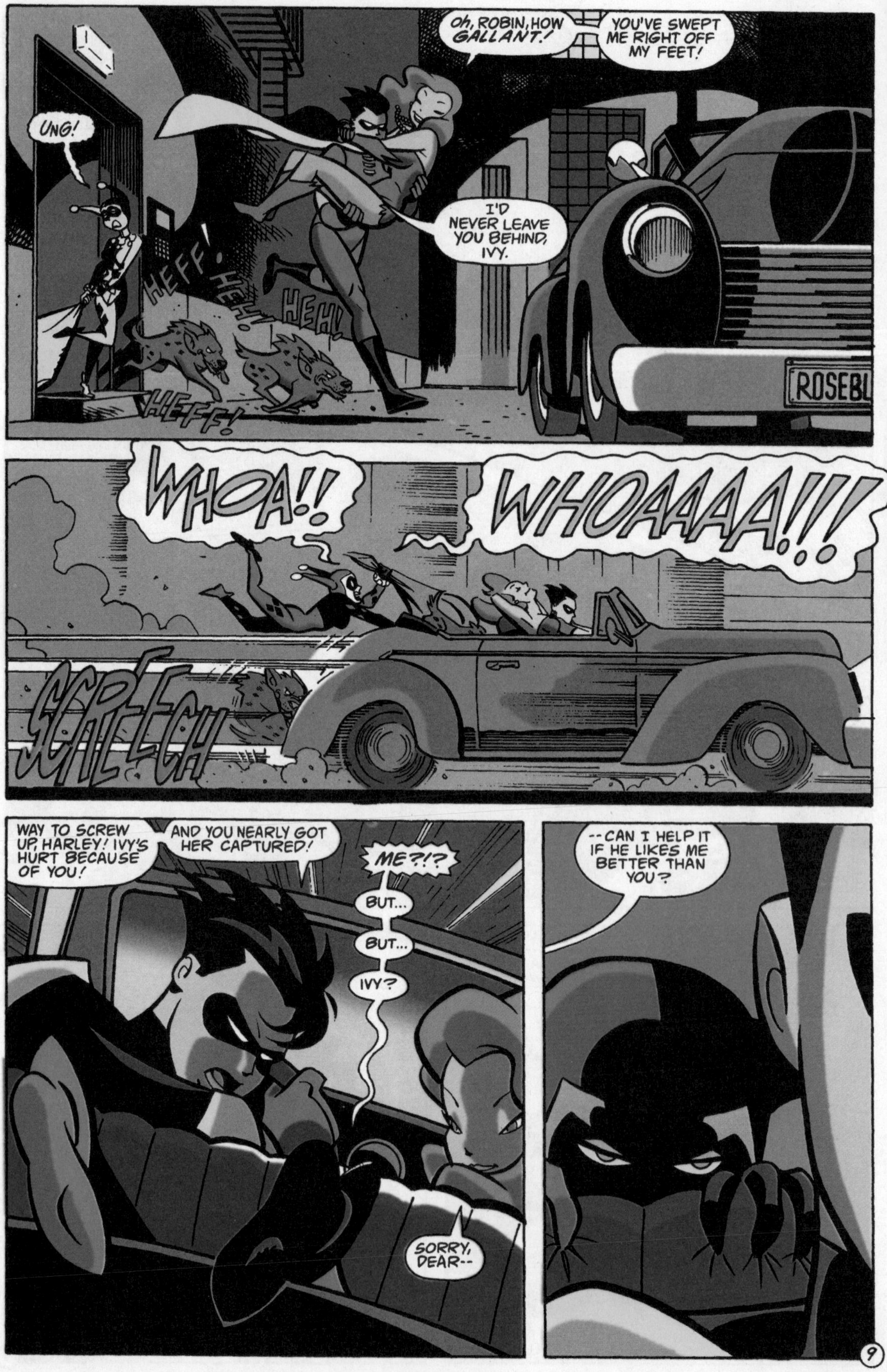
Oh, ROBIN, HOW GALLANT!
YOU'VE SWEPT ME RIGHT OFF MY FEET!
UNG!
I'D NEVER LEAVE YOU BEHIND, IVY.
HEFF!
HEH!
HEH!
HEFF!
ROSEBL
WHOA!!
WHOAAAA!!!
SCREECH
WAY TO SCREW UP, HARLEY! IVY'S HURT BECAUSE OF YOU!
AND YOU NEARLY GOT HER CAPTURED!
ME?!?
BUT...
BUT...
IVY?
SORRY, DEAR--
--CAN I HELP IT IF HE LIKES ME BETTER THAN YOU?
9

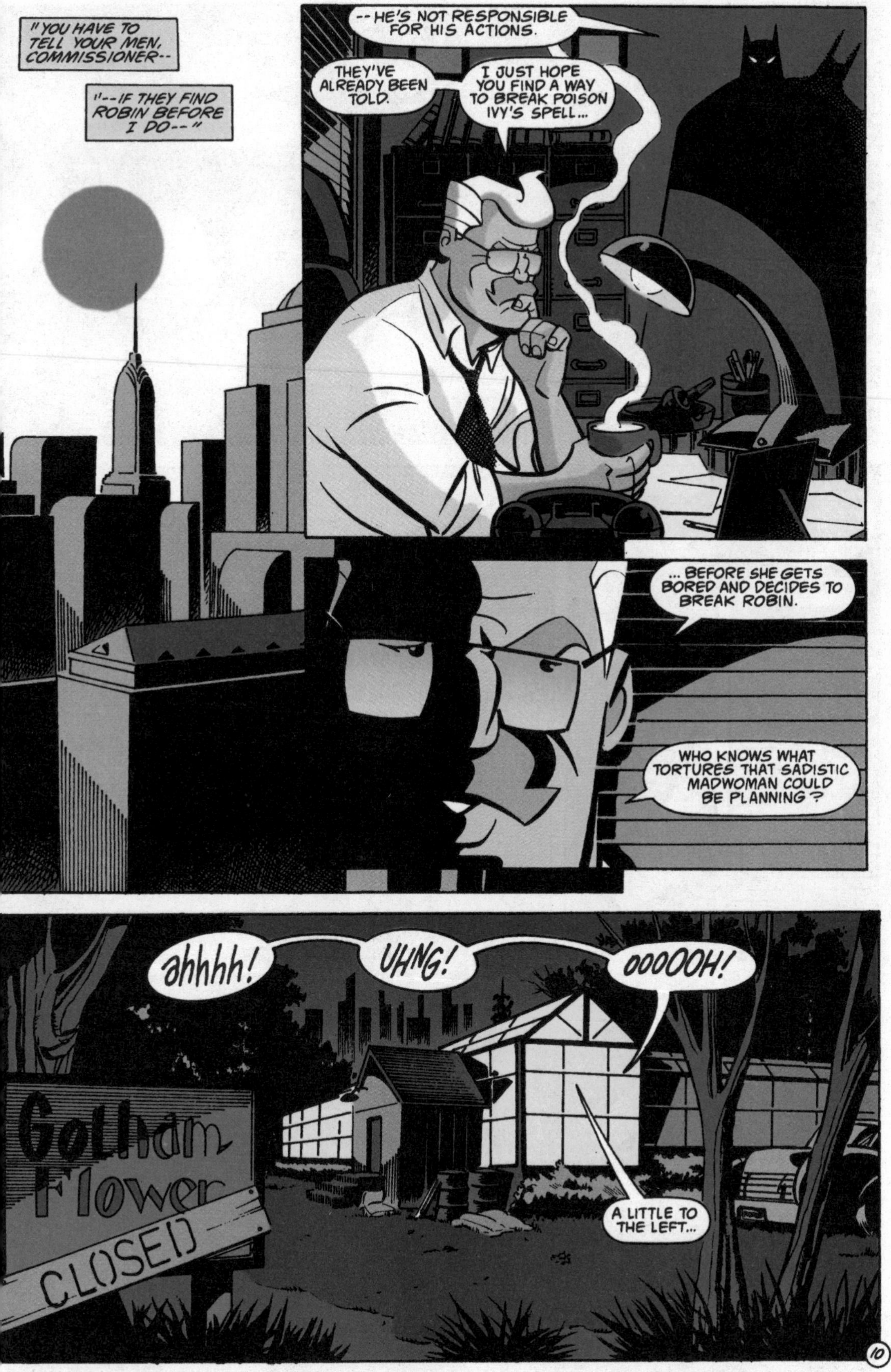
"YOU HAVE TO TELL YOUR MEN, COMMISSIONER--
"--IF THEY FIND ROBIN BEFORE I DO--"
--HE'S NOT RESPONSIBLE FOR HIS ACTIONS.
THEY'VE ALREADY BEEN TOLD.
I JUST HOPE YOU FIND A WAY TO BREAK POISON IVY'S SPELL...
... BEFORE SHE GETS BORED AND DECIDES TO BREAK ROBIN.
WHO KNOWS WHAT TORTURES THAT SADISTIC MADWOMAN COULD BE PLANNING?
ahhhh!
UHNG!
OOOOOH!
A LITTLE TO THE LEFT...
Gotham Flower
CLOSED
10

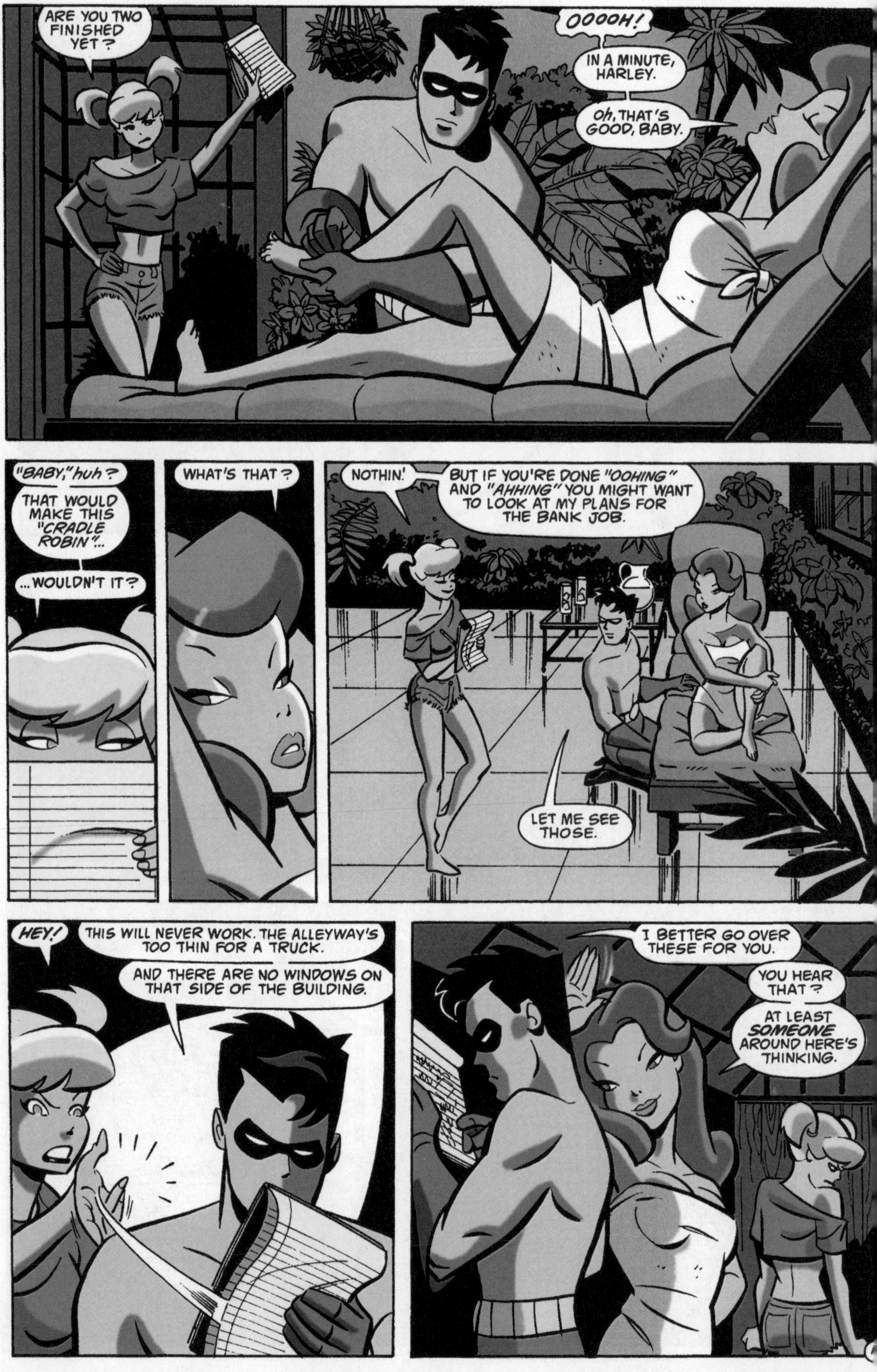
ARE YOU TWO FINISHED YET?
OOOOH!
IN A MINUTE, HARLEY.
OH, THAT'S GOOD, BABY.
"BABY," huh?
THAT WOULD MAKE THIS "CRADLE ROBIN"...
...WOULDN'T IT?
WHAT'S THAT?
NOTHIN'.
BUT IF YOU'RE DONE "OOHING" AND "AHHING" YOU MIGHT WANT TO LOOK AT MY PLANS FOR THE BANK JOB.
LET ME SEE THOSE.
HEY!
THIS WILL NEVER WORK. THE ALLEYWAY'S TOO THIN FOR A TRUCK.
AND THERE ARE NO WINDOWS ON THAT SIDE OF THE BUILDING.
I BETTER GO OVER THESE FOR YOU.
YOU HEAR THAT?
AT LEAST SOMEONE AROUND HERE'S THINKING.

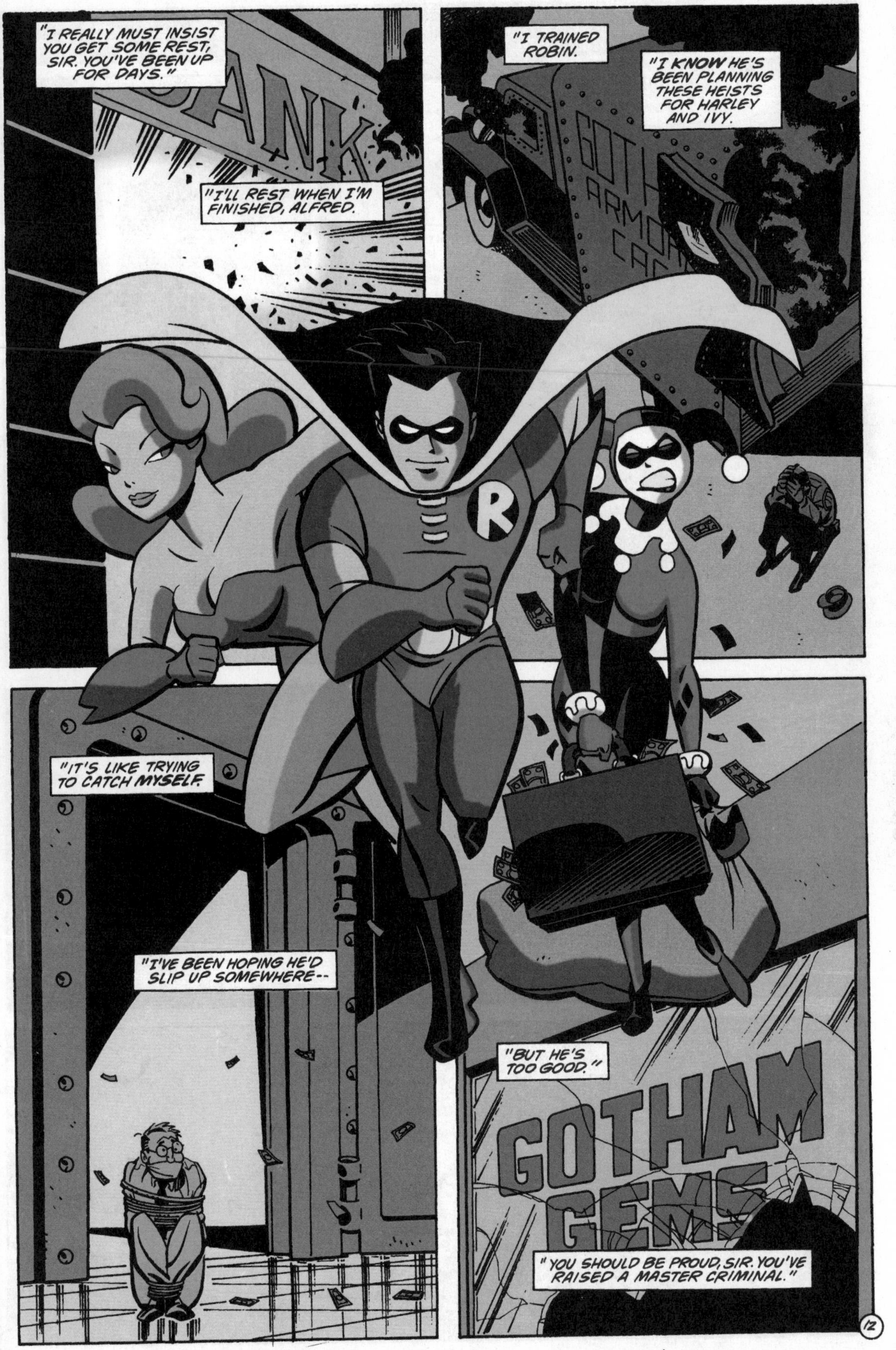
"I REALLY MUST INSIST YOU GET SOME REST, SIR. YOU'VE BEEN UP FOR DAYS."
"I'LL REST WHEN I'M FINISHED, ALFRED.
"I TRAINED ROBIN.
"I KNOW HE'S BEEN PLANNING THESE HEISTS FOR HARLEY AND IVY.
"IT'S LIKE TRYING TO CATCH MYSELF.
"I'VE BEEN HOPING HE'D SLIP UP SOMEWHERE--
"BUT HE'S TOO GOOD."
GOTHAM GEMS
"YOU SHOULD BE PROUD, SIR. YOU'VE RAISED A MASTER CRIMINAL."
12

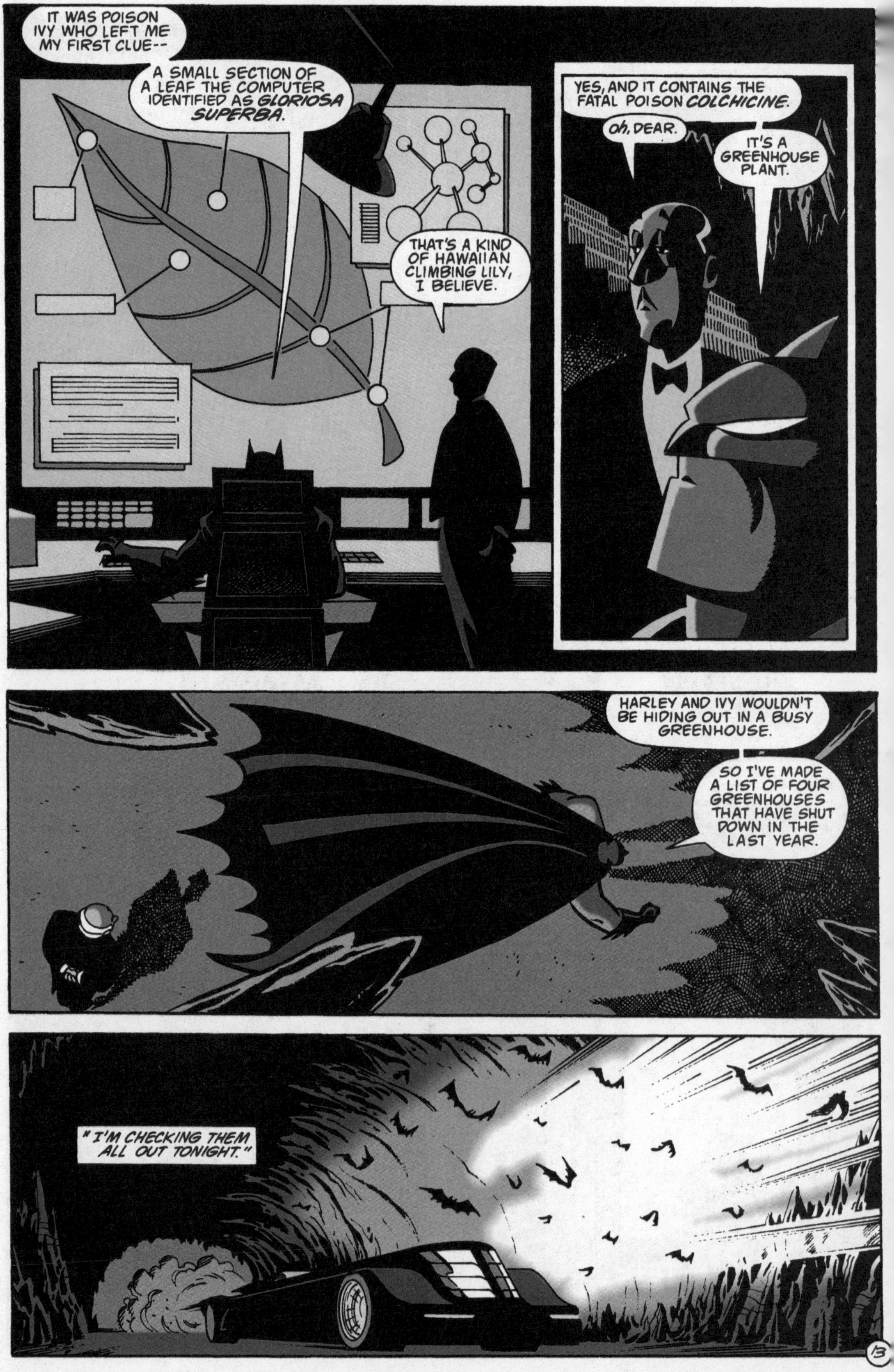
IT WAS POISON IVY WHO LEFT ME MY FIRST CLUE--
A SMALL SECTION OF A LEAF THE COMPUTER IDENTIFIED AS GLORIOSA SUPERBA.
THAT'S A KIND OF HAWAIIAN CLIMBING LILY, I BELIEVE.
YES, AND IT CONTAINS THE FATAL POISON COLCHICINE.
Oh, DEAR.
IT'S A GREENHOUSE PLANT.
HARLEY AND IVY WOULDN'T BE HIDING OUT IN A BUSY GREENHOUSE.
SO I'VE MADE A LIST OF FOUR GREENHOUSES THAT HAVE SHUT DOWN IN THE LAST YEAR.
"I'M CHECKING THEM ALL OUT TONIGHT."
13

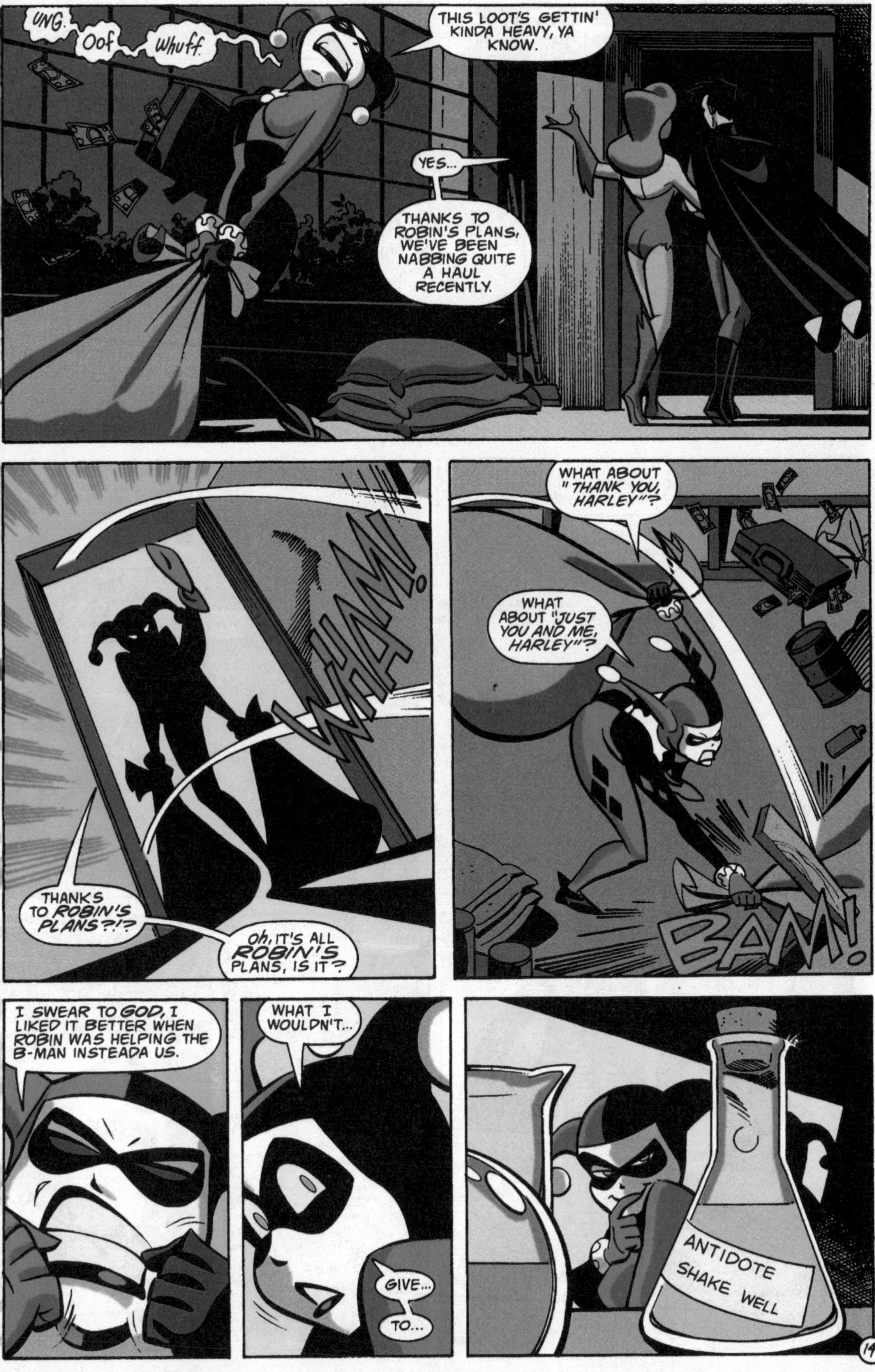
UNG.
Oof
Whuff.
THIS LOOT'S GETTIN' KINDA HEAVY, YA KNOW.
YES...
THANKS TO ROBIN'S PLANS, WE'VE BEEN NABBING QUITE A HAUL RECENTLY.
WHAM!
THANKS TO ROBIN'S PLANS?!?
Oh, IT'S ALL ROBIN'S PLANS, IS IT?
WHAT ABOUT "THANK YOU, HARLEY"?
WHAT ABOUT "JUST YOU AND ME, HARLEY"?
BAM!
I SWEAR TO GOD, I LIKED IT BETTER WHEN ROBIN WAS HELPING THE B-MAN INSTEADA US.
WHAT I WOULDN'T...
GIVE...
TO...
ANTIDOTE
SHAKE WELL
14

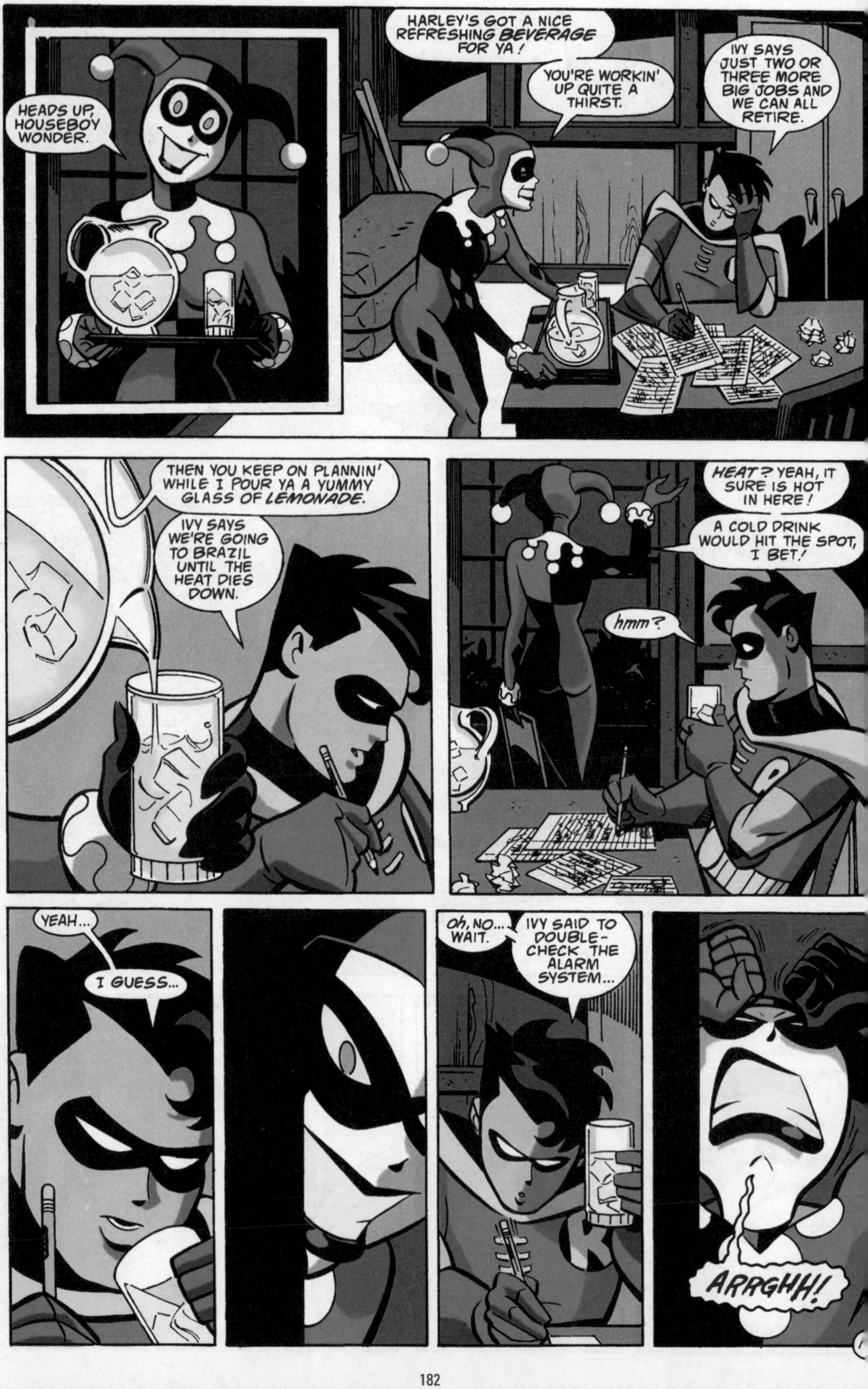
HEADS UP, HOUSEBOY WONDER.
HARLEY'S GOT A NICE REFRESHING BEVERAGE FOR YA!
YOU'RE WORKIN' UP QUITE A THIRST.
IVY SAYS JUST TWO OR THREE MORE BIG JOBS AND WE CAN ALL RETIRE.
THEN YOU KEEP ON PLANNIN' WHILE I POUR YA A YUMMY GLASS OF LEMONADE.
IVY SAYS WE'RE GOING TO BRAZIL UNTIL THE HEAT DIES DOWN.
HEAT? YEAH, IT SURE IS HOT IN HERE!
A COLD DRINK WOULD HIT THE SPOT, I BET!
hmm?
YEAH...
I GUESS...
oh, NO... WAIT.
IVY SAID TO DOUBLE-CHECK THE ALARM SYSTEM...
ARRGHH!

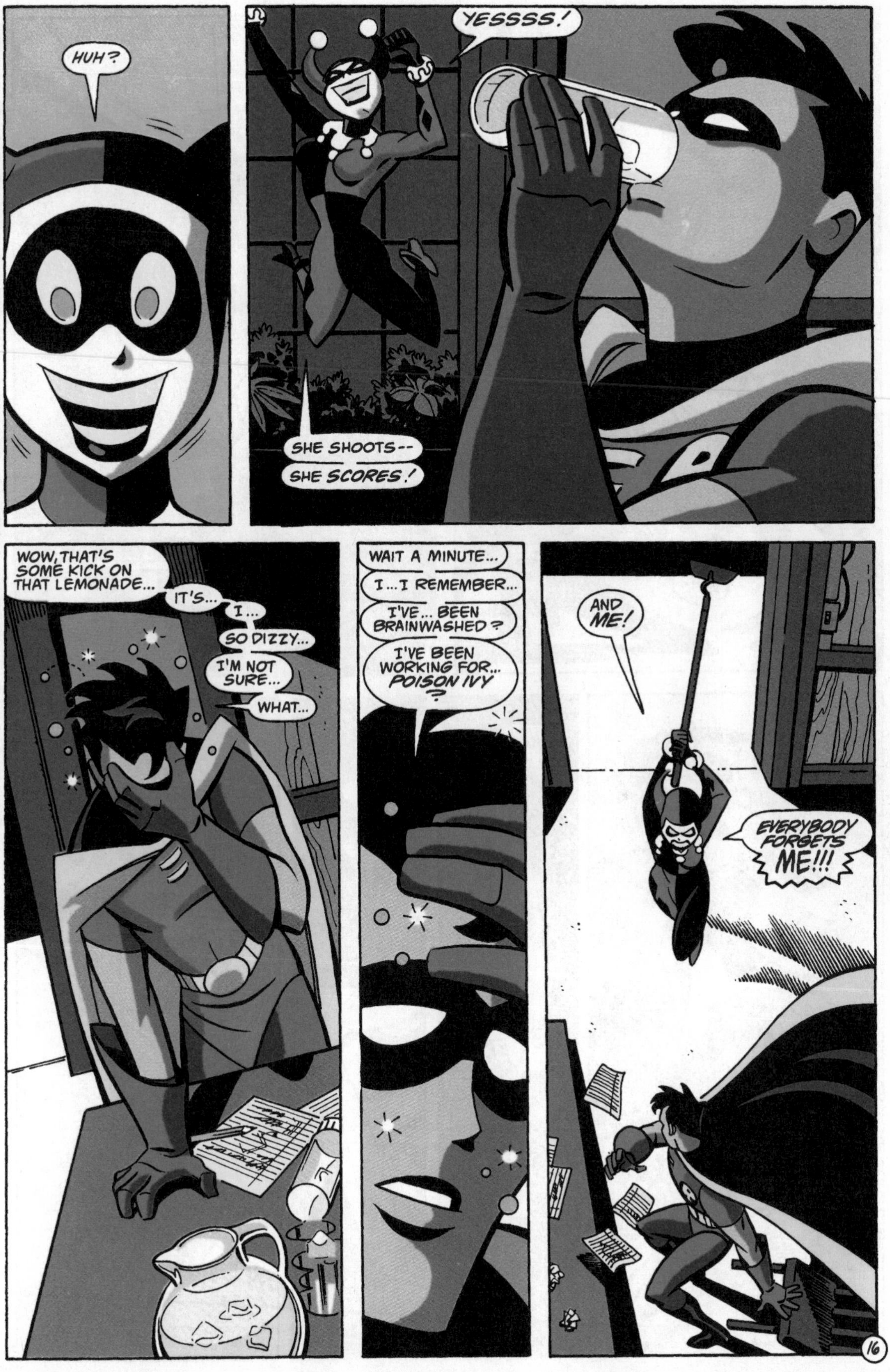
HUH?
YESSSS!
SHE SHOOTS--
SHE SCORES!
WOW, THAT'S SOME KICK ON THAT LEMONADE...
IT'S...
I...
SO DIZZY...
I'M NOT SURE...
WHAT...
WAIT A MINUTE...
I...I REMEMBER...
I'VE... BEEN BRAINWASHED?
I'VE BEEN WORKING FOR... POISON IVY?
AND ME!
EVERYBODY FORGETS ME!!!
16

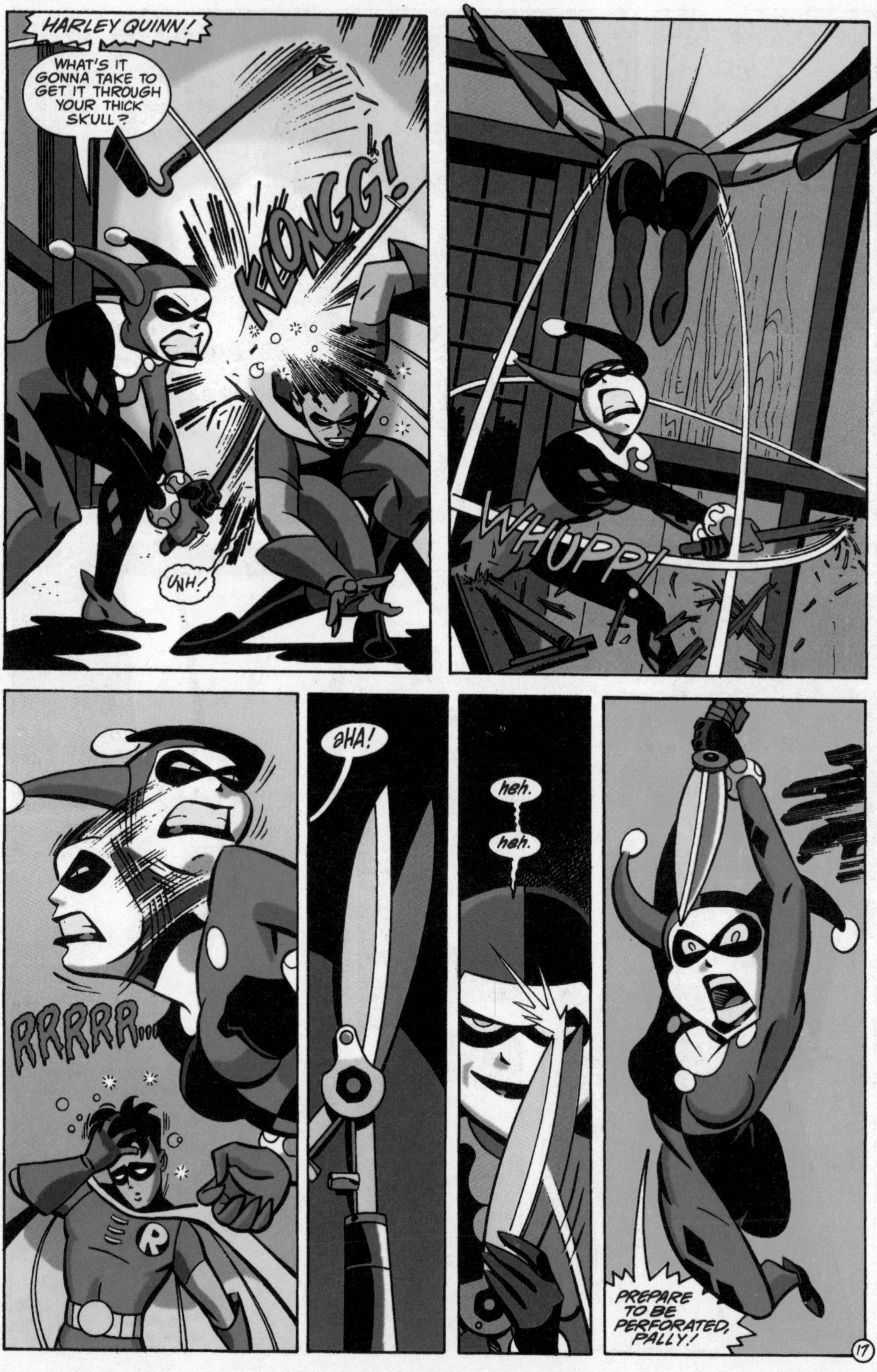
HARLEY QUINN!
WHAT'S IT GONNA TAKE TO GET IT THROUGH YOUR THICK SKULL?
KLONGG!
UNH!
WHUPP!
RRRRR...
AHA!
heh.
heh.
PREPARE TO BE PERFORATED, PALLY!
17

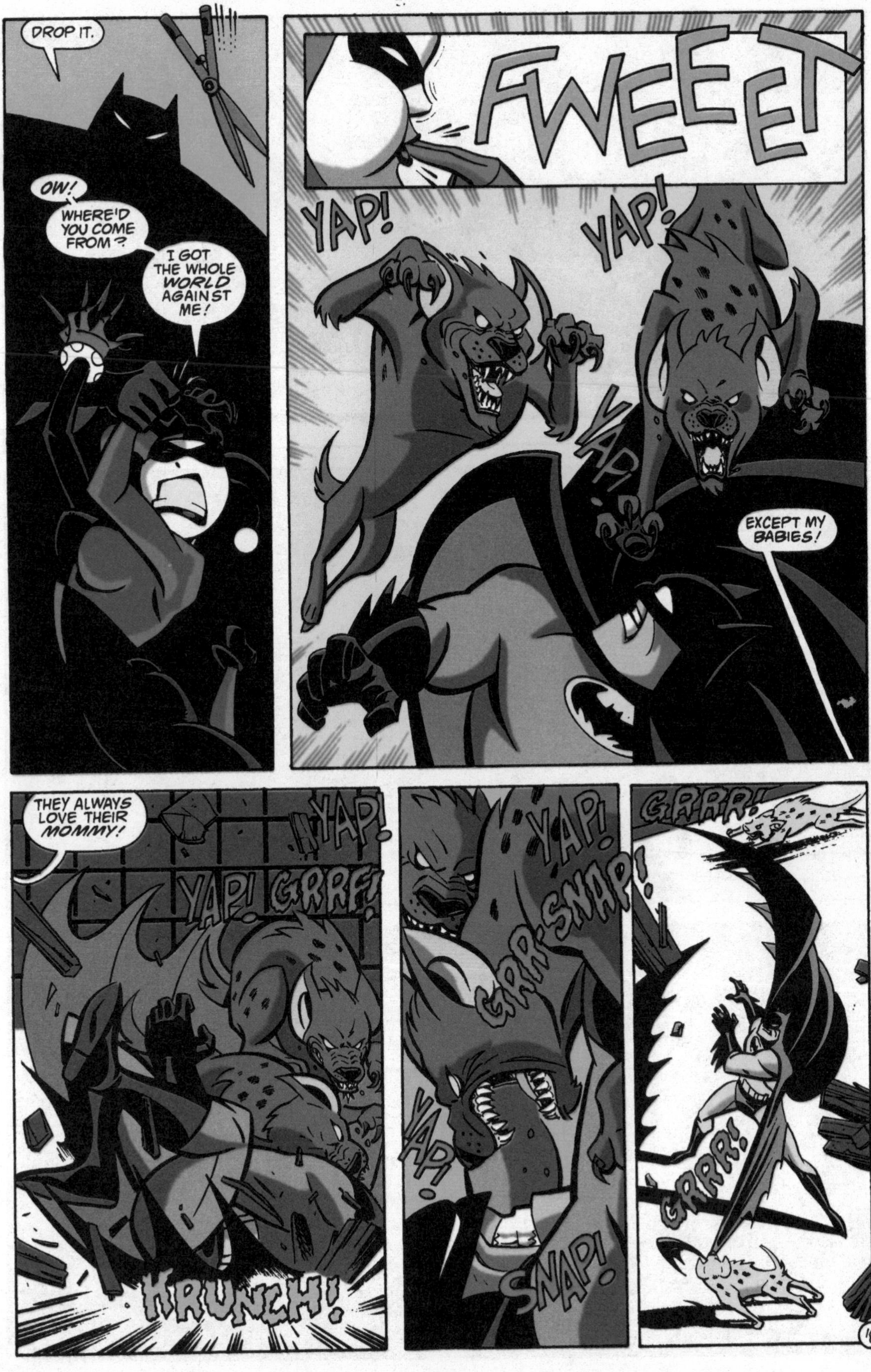
DROP IT.
OW!
WHERE'D YOU COME FROM?
I GOT THE WHOLE WORLD AGAINST ME!
FWEEET
YAP!
YAP!
YAP!
EXCEPT MY BABIES!
THEY ALWAYS LOVE THEIR MOMMY!
YAP!
YAP! GRRF!
HRUNCH!
YAP!
GRR-SNAP!
YAP!
SNAP!
GRRR!
GRRR!
18

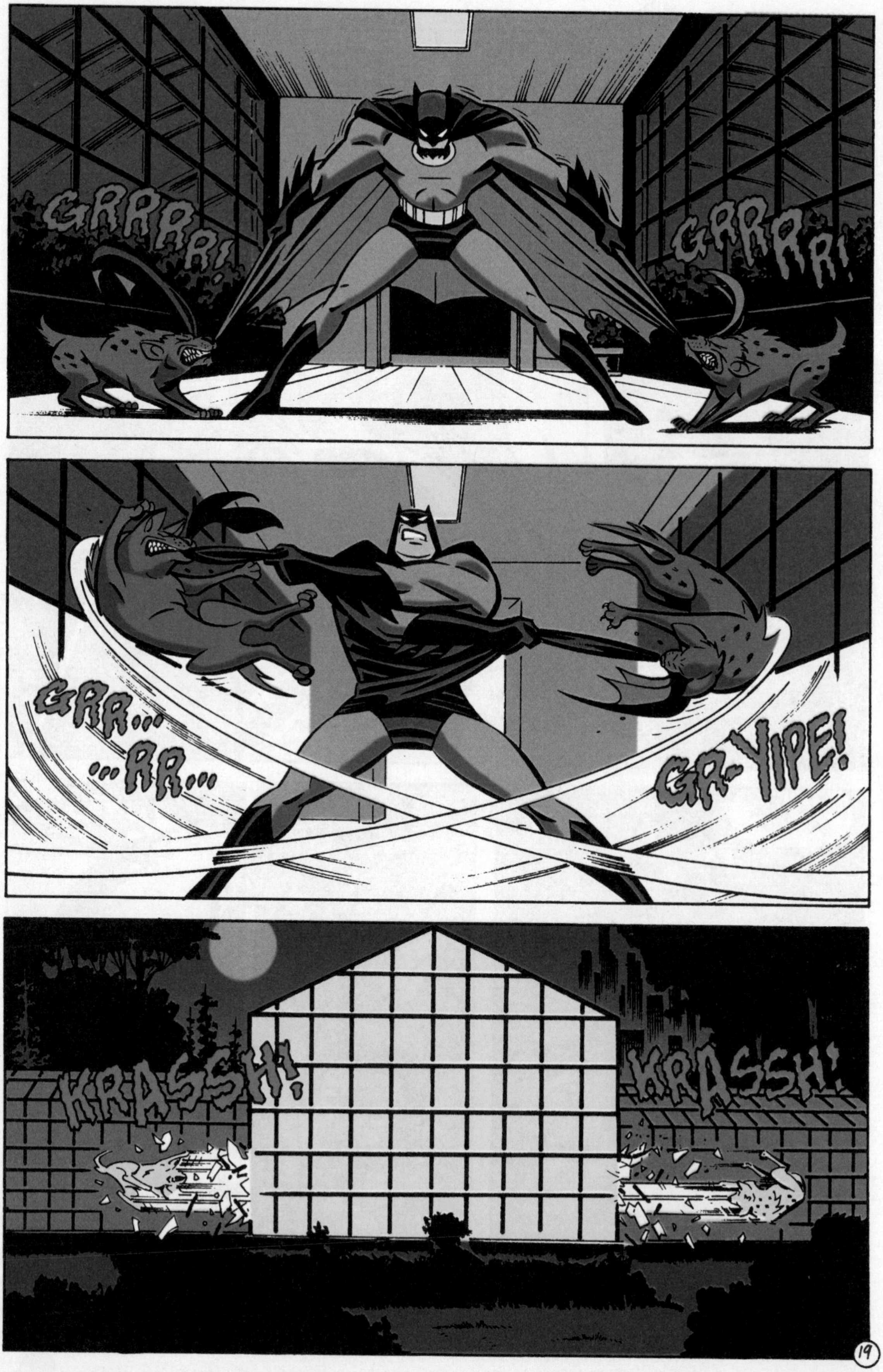
GRRRRR!
GRRRRR!
GRR...
...RR...
GR-YIPE!
KRASSH!
KRASSH!
19

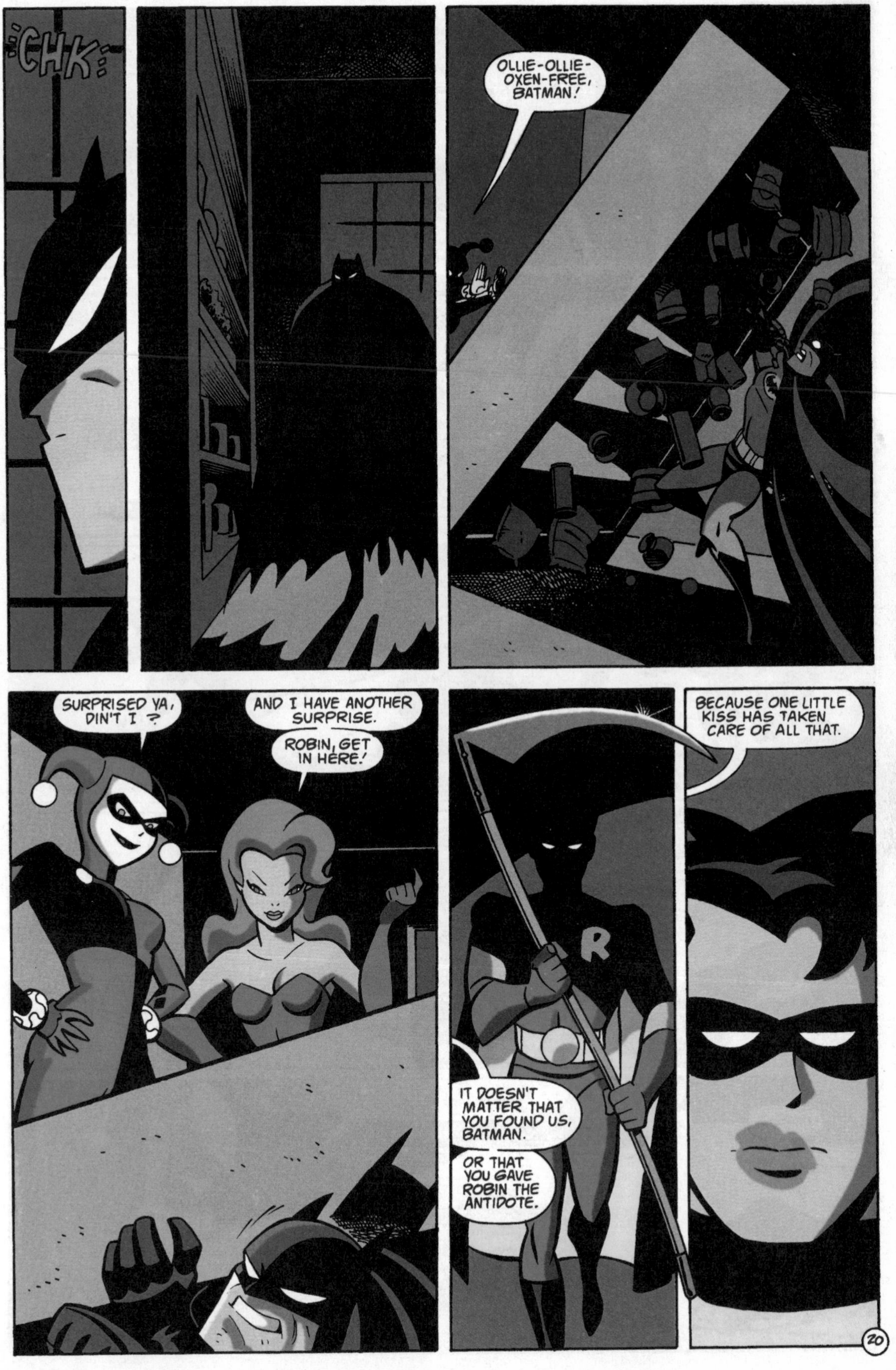
CHK
OLLIE-OLLIE-OXEN-FREE, BATMAN!
SURPRISED YA, DIN'T I ?
AND I HAVE ANOTHER SURPRISE.
ROBIN, GET IN HERE!
IT DOESN'T MATTER THAT YOU FOUND US, BATMAN.
OR THAT YOU GAVE ROBIN THE ANTIDOTE.
BECAUSE ONE LITTLE KISS HAS TAKEN CARE OF ALL THAT.
20

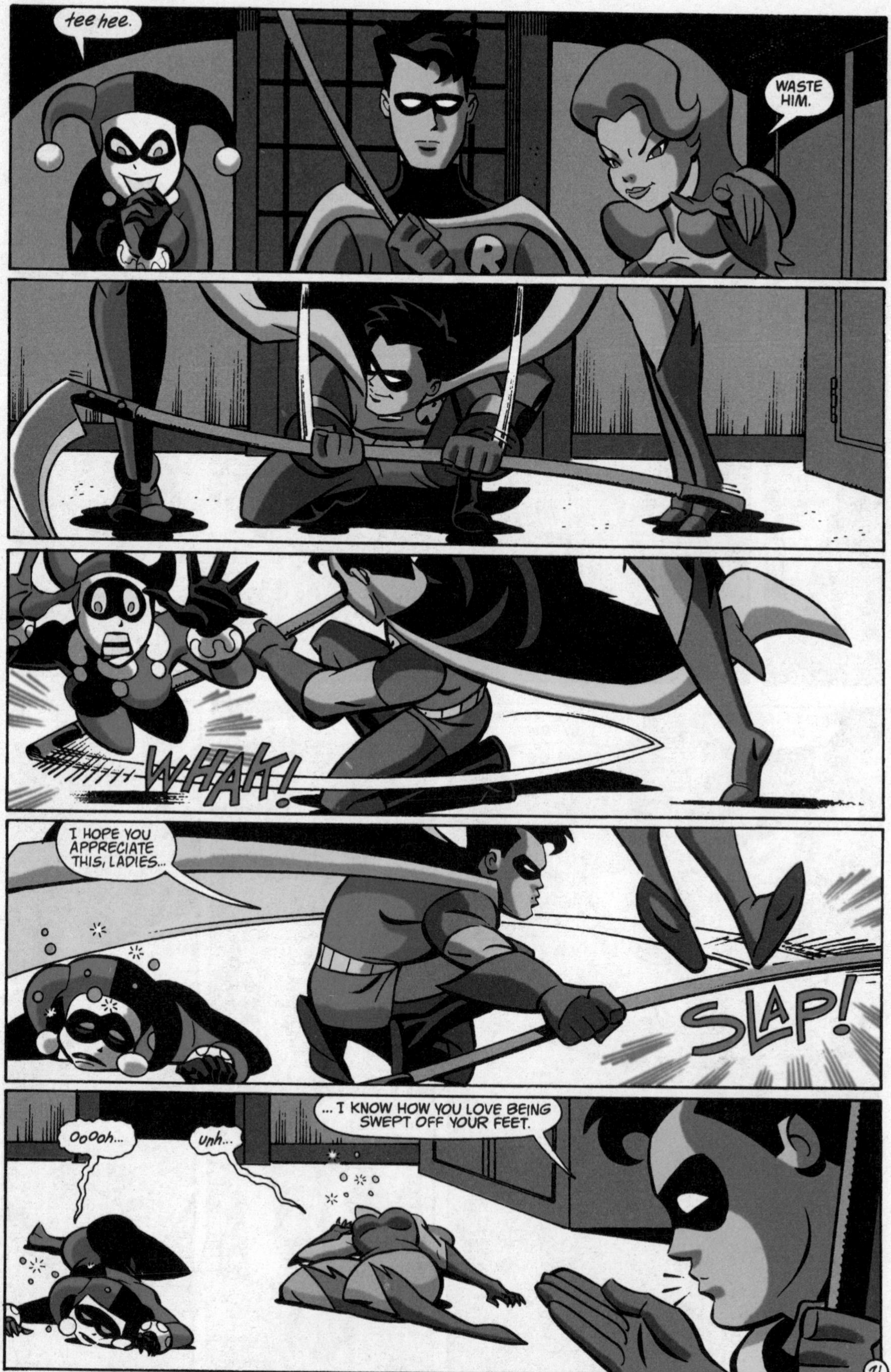
tee hee.
WASTE HIM.
WHAK!
I HOPE YOU APPRECIATE THIS, LADIES...
SLAP!
Oooh...
unh...
... I KNOW HOW YOU LOVE BEING SWEPT OFF YOUR FEET.
21

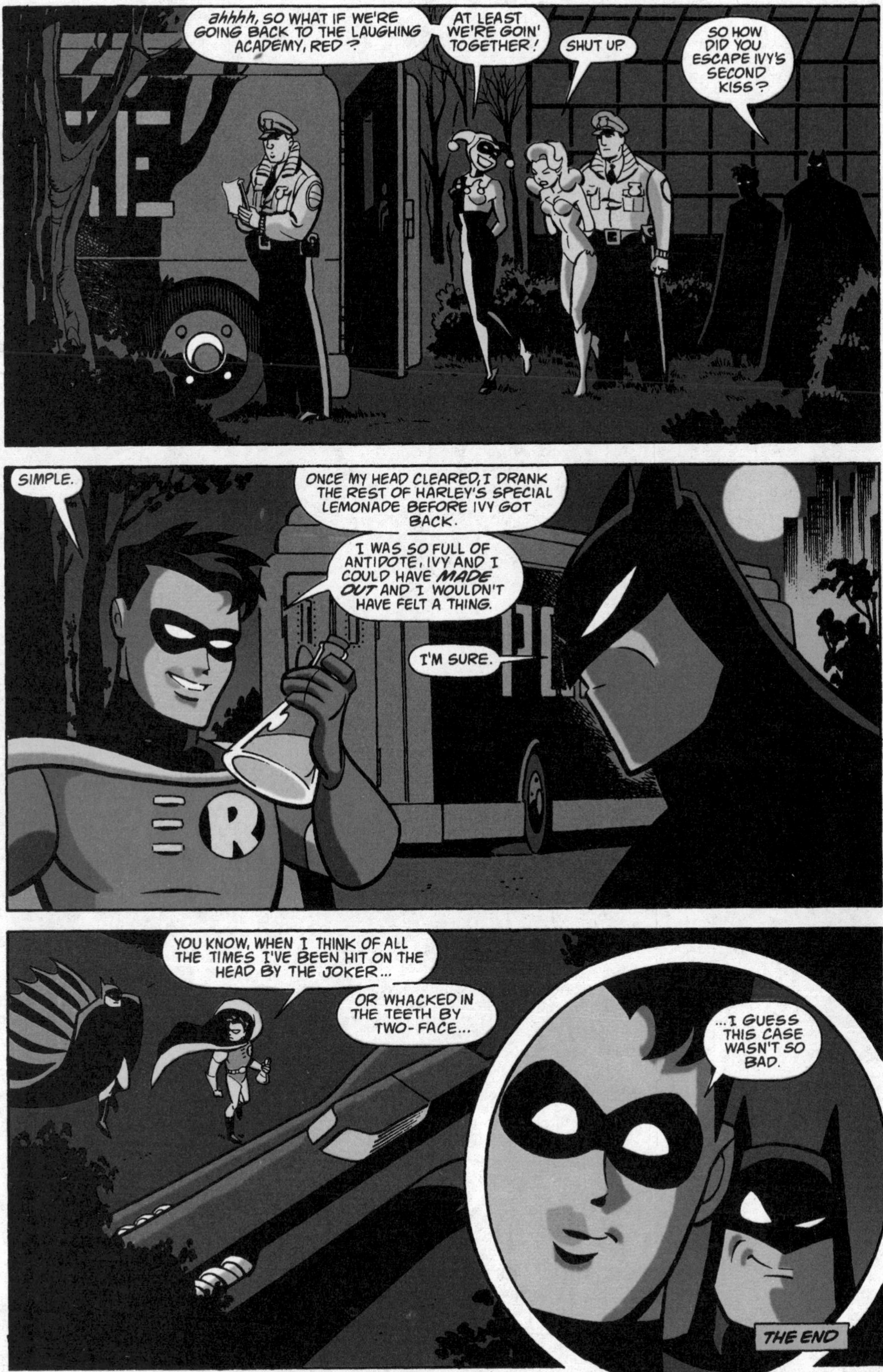

ahhhh, SO WHAT IF WE'RE GOING BACK TO THE LAUGHING ACADEMY, RED?
AT LEAST WE'RE GOIN' TOGETHER!
SHUT UP.
SO HOW DID YOU ESCAPE IVY'S SECOND KISS?
SIMPLE.
ONCE MY HEAD CLEARED, I DRANK THE REST OF HARLEY'S SPECIAL LEMONADE BEFORE IVY GOT BACK.
I WAS SO FULL OF ANTIDOTE, IVY AND I COULD HAVE MADE OUT AND I WOULDN'T HAVE FELT A THING.
I'M SURE.
YOU KNOW, WHEN I THINK OF ALL THE TIMES I'VE BEEN HIT ON THE HEAD BY THE JOKER...
OR WHACKED IN THE TEETH BY TWO-FACE...
...I GUESS THIS CASE WASN'T SO BAD.
THE END

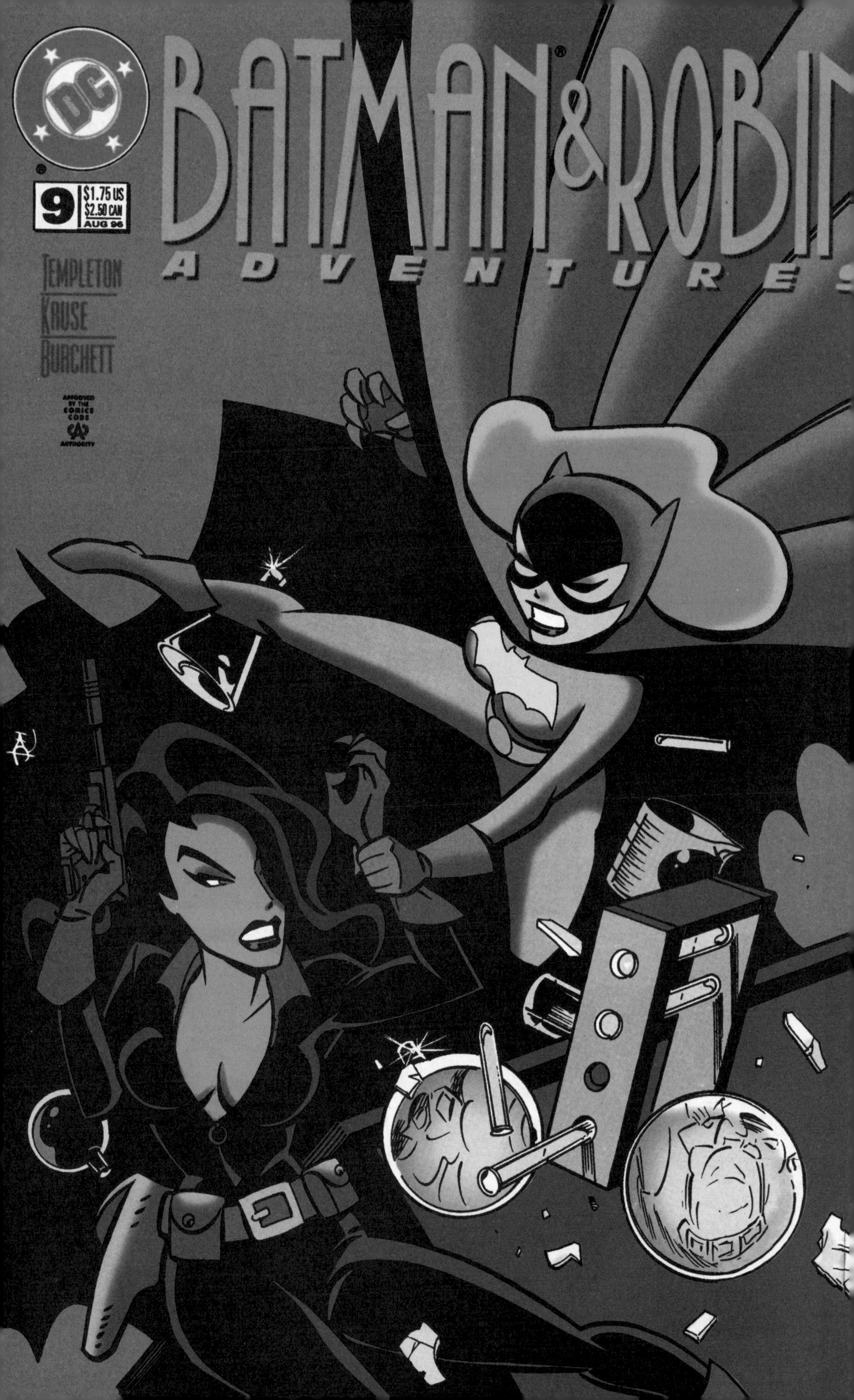
DC
BATMAN & ROBIN
ADVENTURES
9
$1.75 US
$2.50 CAN
AUG 96
TEMPLETON
KRUSE
BURCHETT
APPROVED BY THE COMICS CODE AUTHORITY

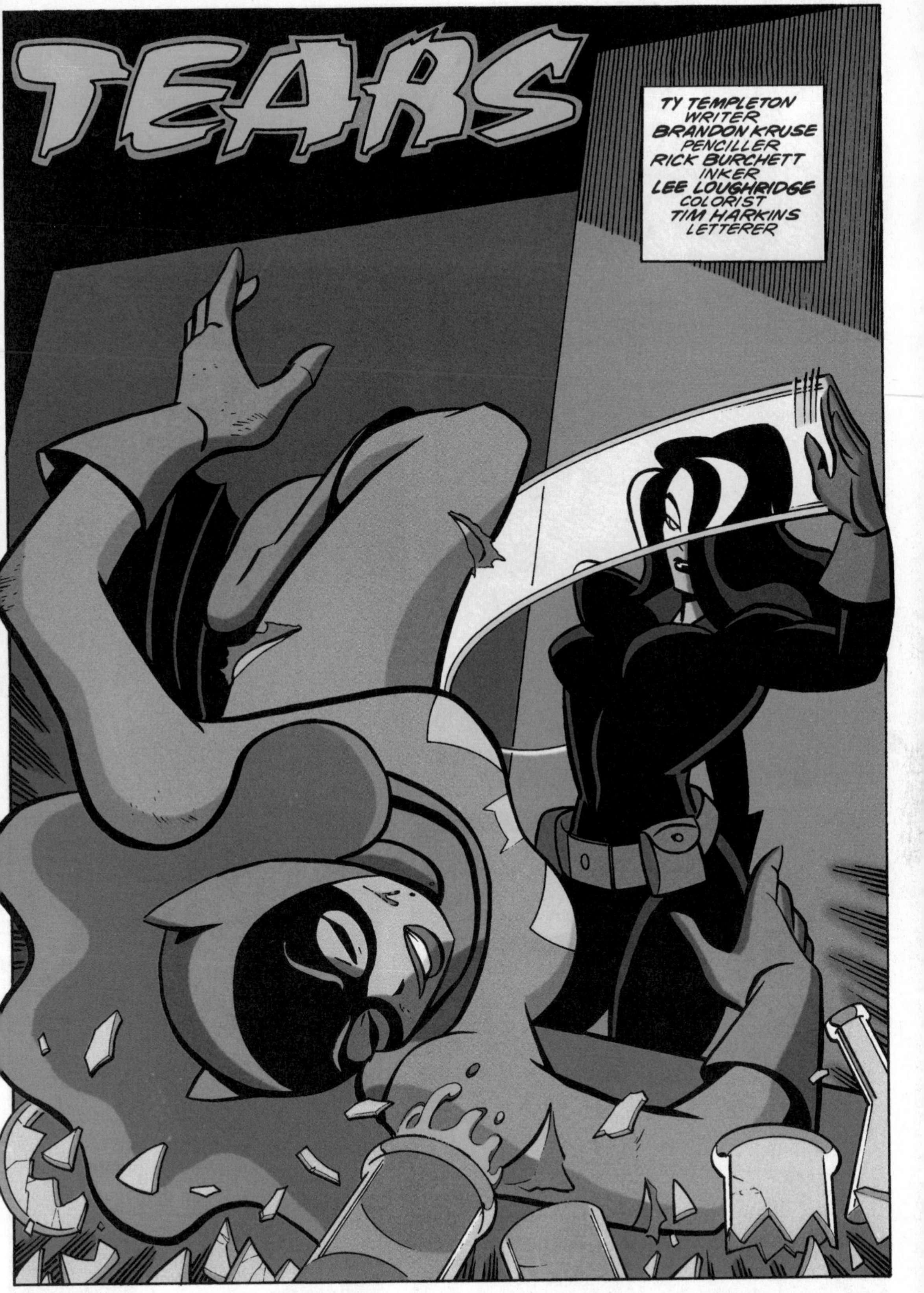
TEARS
TY TEMPLETON
WRITER
BRANDON KRUSE
PENCILLER
RICK BURCHETT
INKER
LEE LOUGHRIDGE
COLORIST
TIM HARKINS
LETTERER

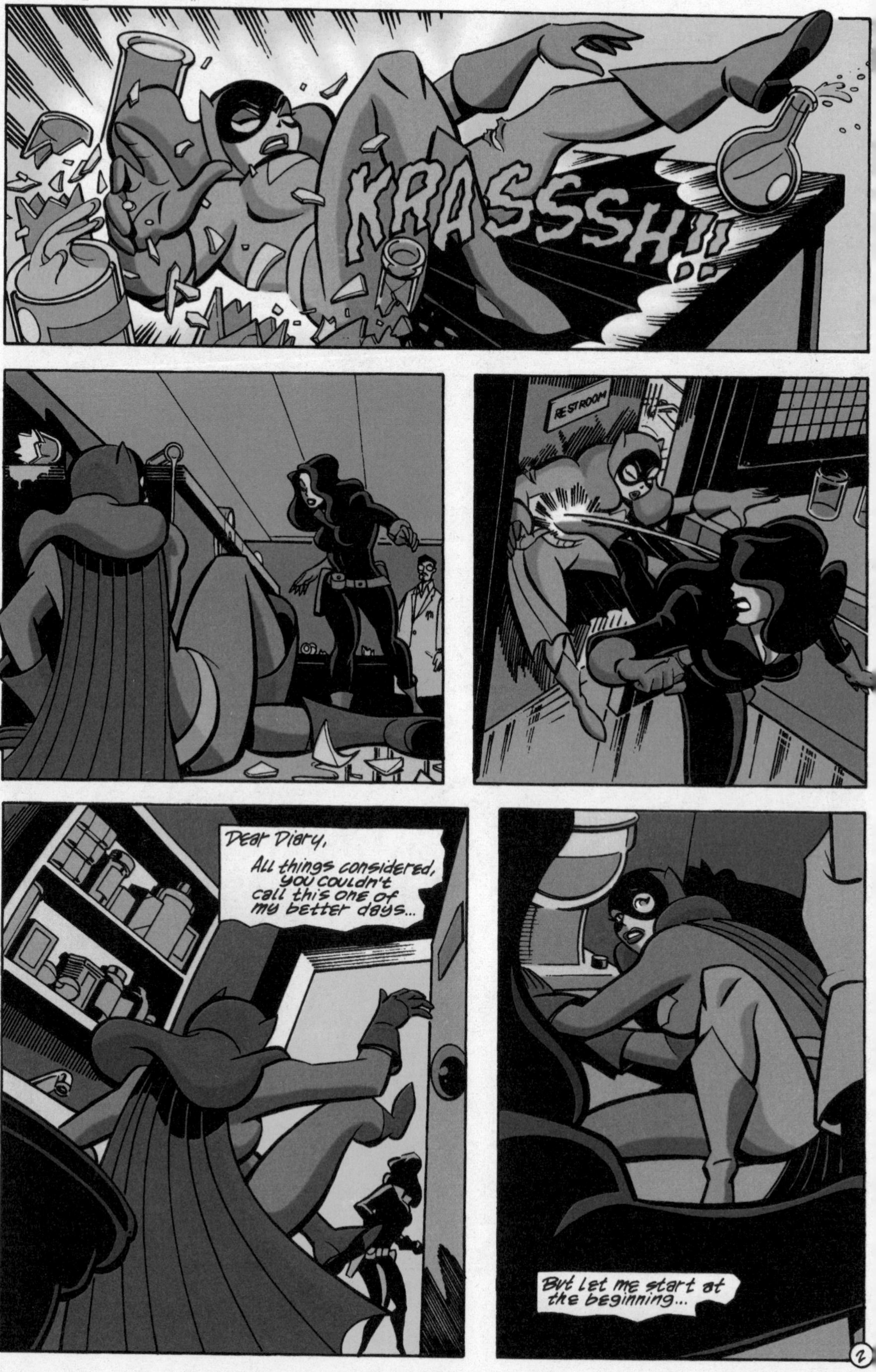
KRASSSSH!!
RESTROOM
Dear Diary,
All things considered, you couldn't call this one of my better days...
But let me start at the beginning...
2

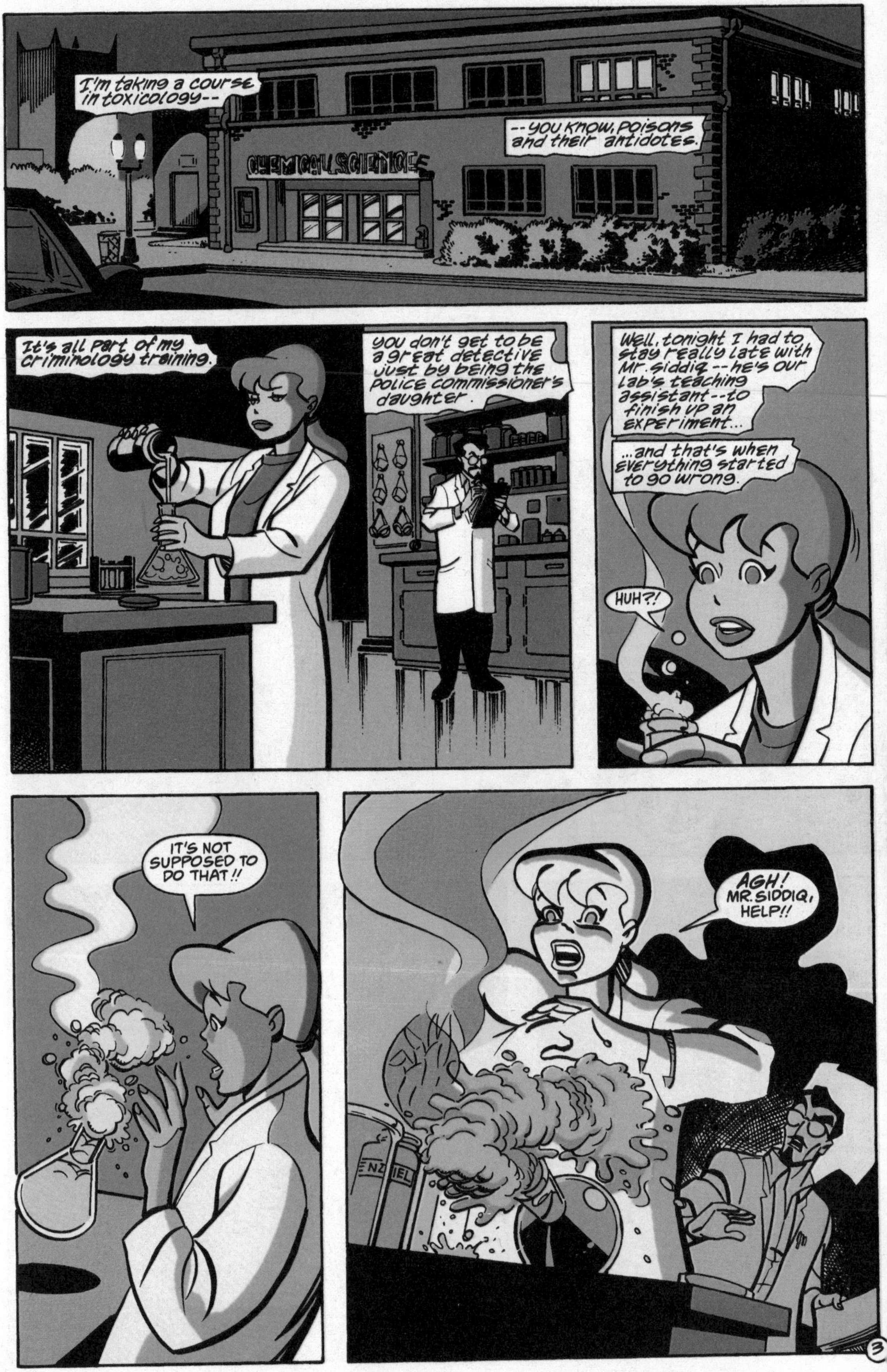
I'm taking a course in toxicology--
--you know, poisons and their antidotes.
CHEMICAL SCIENCE
It's all part of my criminology training.
You don't get to be a great detective just by being the police commissioner's daughter.
Well, tonight I had to stay really late with Mr. Siddiq -- he's our lab's teaching assistant--to finish up an experiment...
...and that's when everything started to go wrong.
HUH?!
IT'S NOT SUPPOSED TO DO THAT!!
AGH! MR. SIDDIQ, HELP!!
3

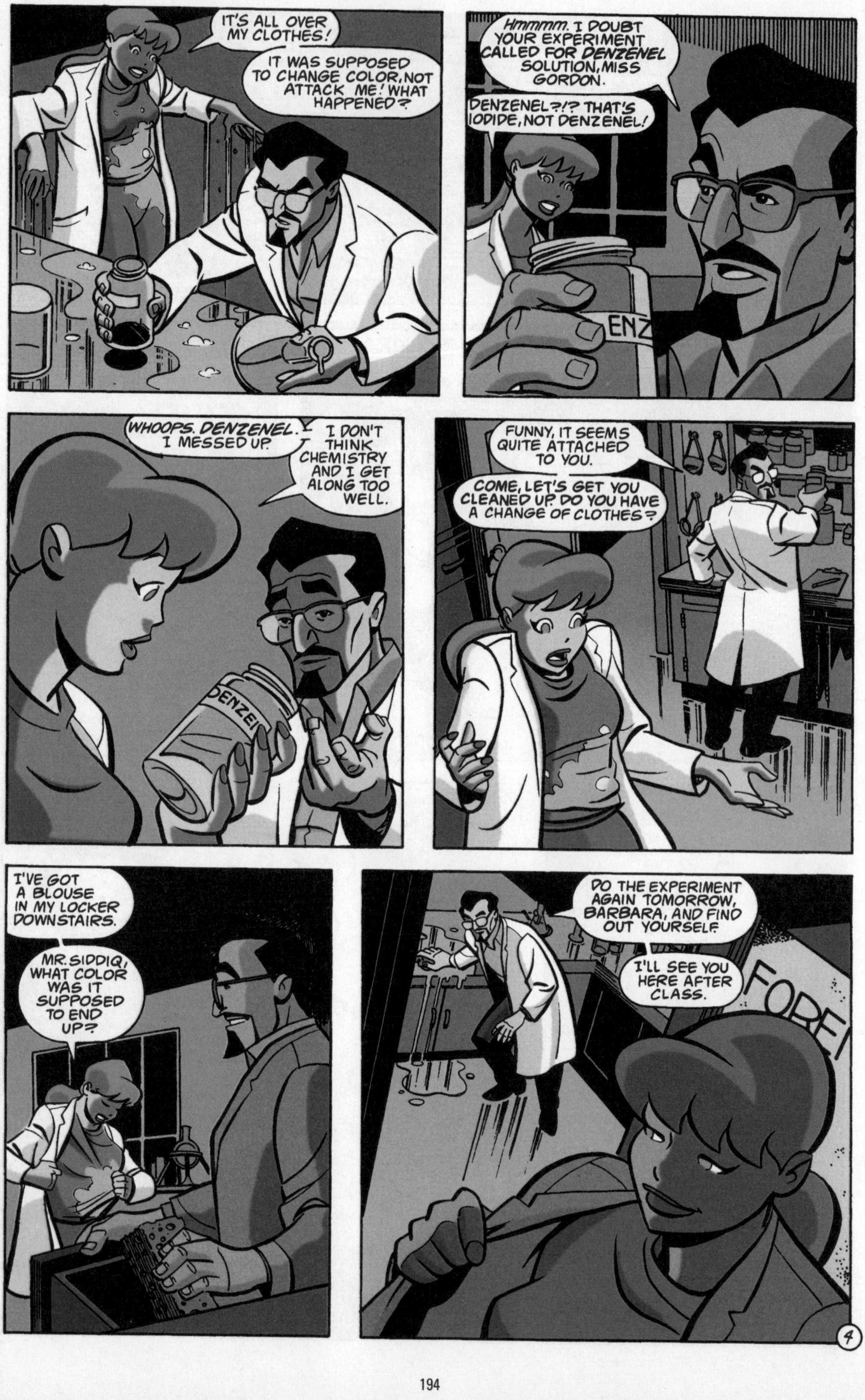

IT'S ALL OVER MY CLOTHES!
IT WAS SUPPOSED TO CHANGE COLOR, NOT ATTACK ME! WHAT HAPPENED?
Hmmmm. I DOUBT YOUR EXPERIMENT CALLED FOR DENZENEL SOLUTION, MISS GORDON.
DENZENEL?!? THAT'S IODIDE, NOT DENZENEL!
ENZ
WHOOPS. DENZENEL. I MESSED UP.
I DON'T THINK CHEMISTRY AND I GET ALONG TOO WELL.
DENZE
FUNNY, IT SEEMS QUITE ATTACHED TO YOU.
COME, LET'S GET YOU CLEANED UP. DO YOU HAVE A CHANGE OF CLOTHES?
I'VE GOT A BLOUSE IN MY LOCKER DOWNSTAIRS.
MR. SIDDIQ, WHAT COLOR WAS IT SUPPOSED TO END UP?
DO THE EXPERIMENT AGAIN TOMORROW, BARBARA, AND FIND OUT YOURSELF.
I'LL SEE YOU HERE AFTER CLASS.
FORE
4

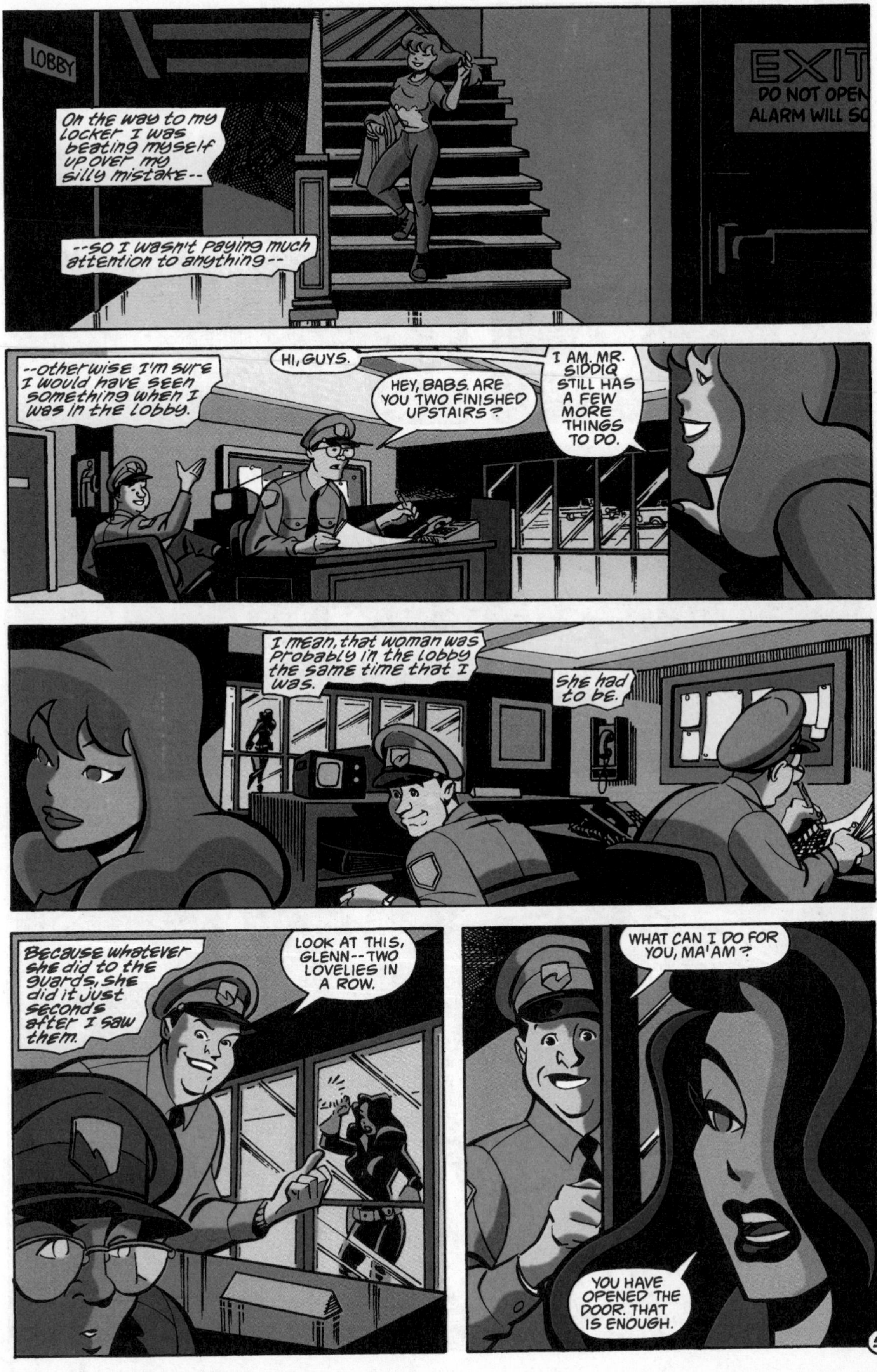
LOBBY
EXIT
DO NOT OPEN
ALARM WILL SO
On the way to my locker I was beating myself up over my silly mistake--
--so I wasn't paying much attention to anything--
--otherwise I'm sure I would have seen something when I was in the lobby.
HI, GUYS.
HEY, BABS. ARE YOU TWO FINISHED UPSTAIRS?
I AM. MR. SIDDIQ STILL HAS A FEW MORE THINGS TO DO.
I mean, that woman was probably in the lobby the same time that I was.
She had to be.
Because whatever she did to the guards, she did it just seconds after I saw them.
LOOK AT THIS, GLENN--TWO LOVELIES IN A ROW.
WHAT CAN I DO FOR YOU, MA'AM?
YOU HAVE OPENED THE DOOR. THAT IS ENOUGH.
5

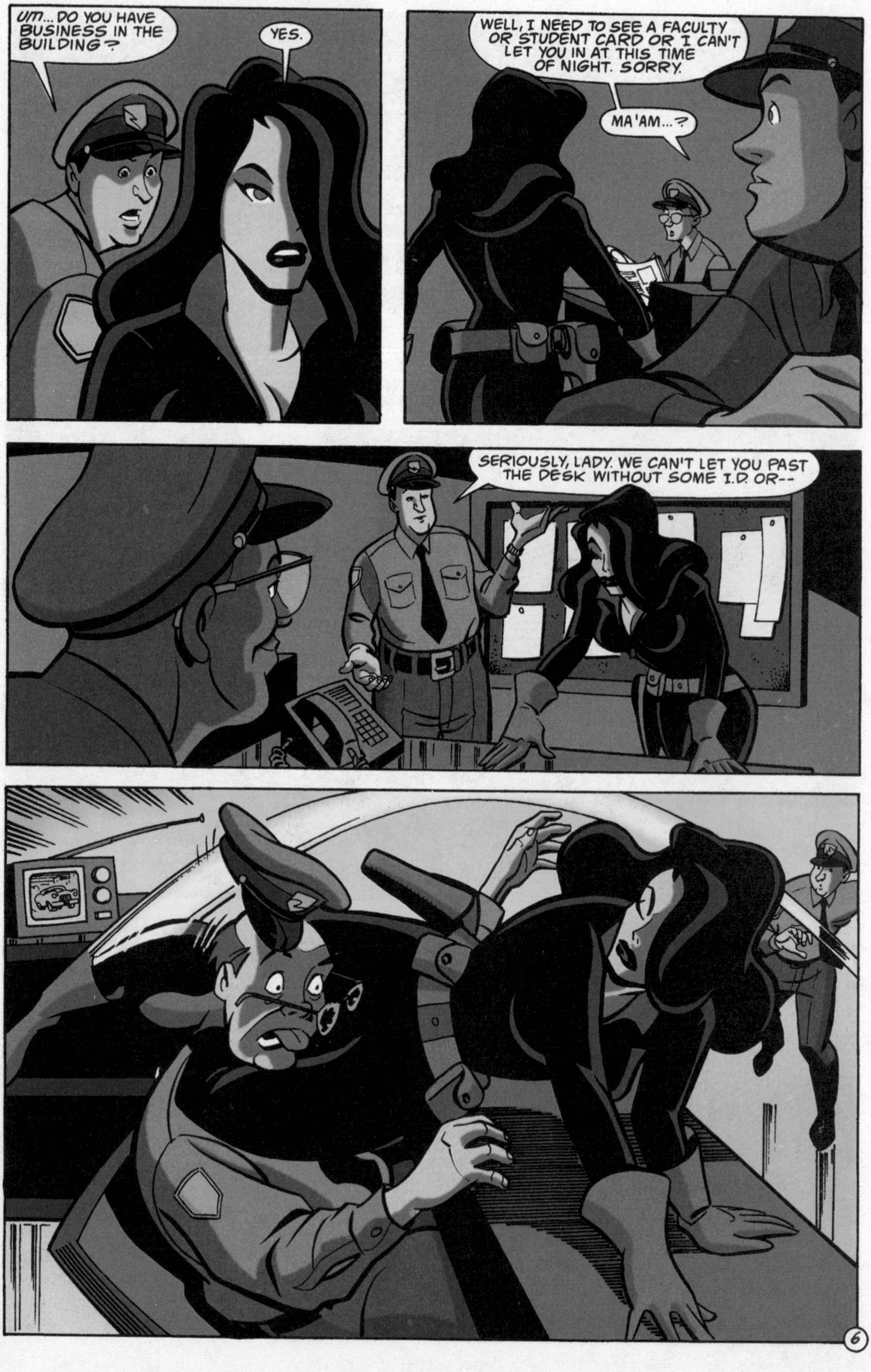
UM... DO YOU HAVE BUSINESS IN THE BUILDING?
YES.
WELL, I NEED TO SEE A FACULTY OR STUDENT CARD OR I CAN'T LET YOU IN AT THIS TIME OF NIGHT. SORRY.
MA'AM...?
SERIOUSLY, LADY. WE CAN'T LET YOU PAST THE DESK WITHOUT SOME I.D. OR--
6

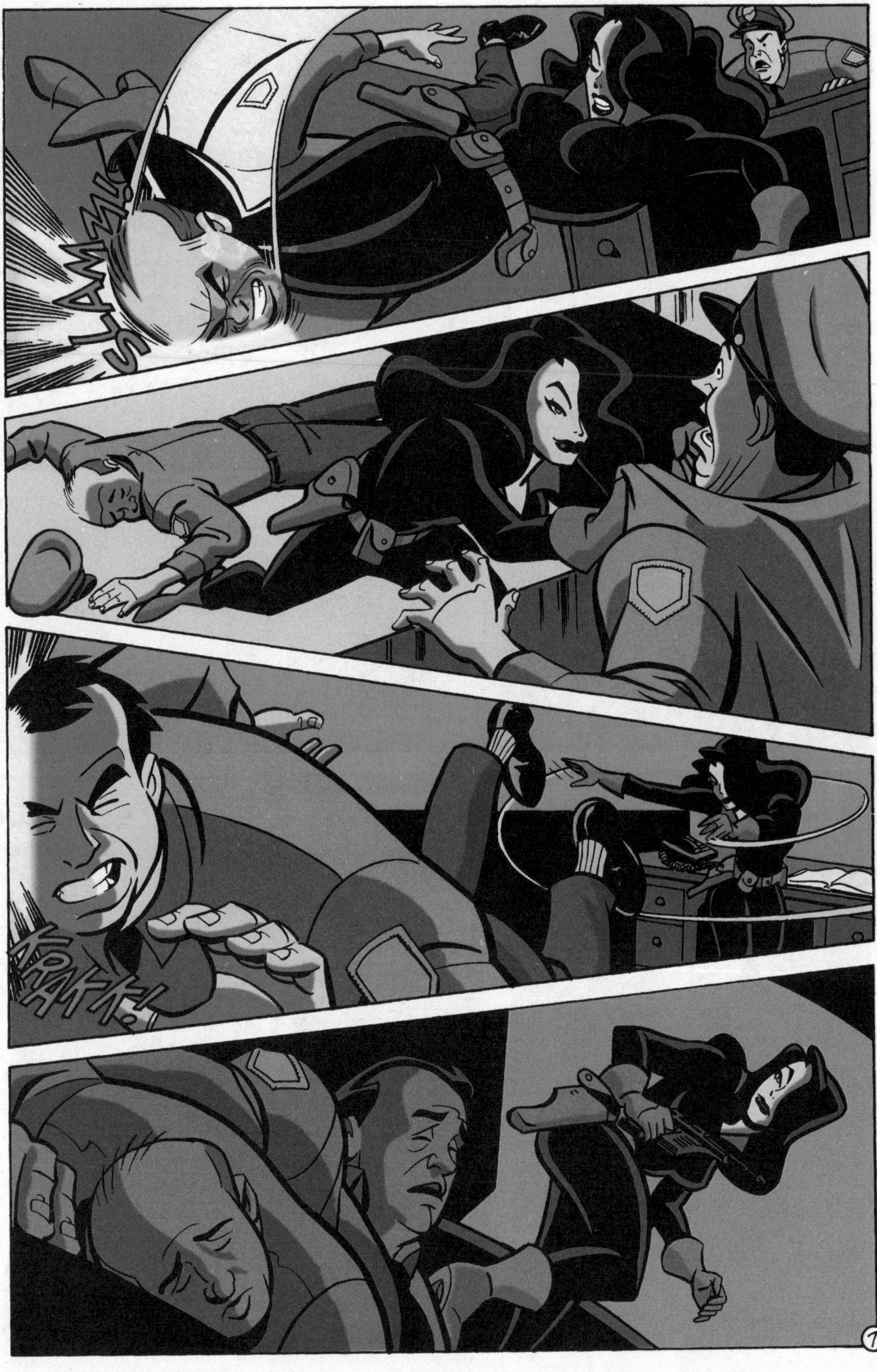
SLAMM!!
KRAKK!
7

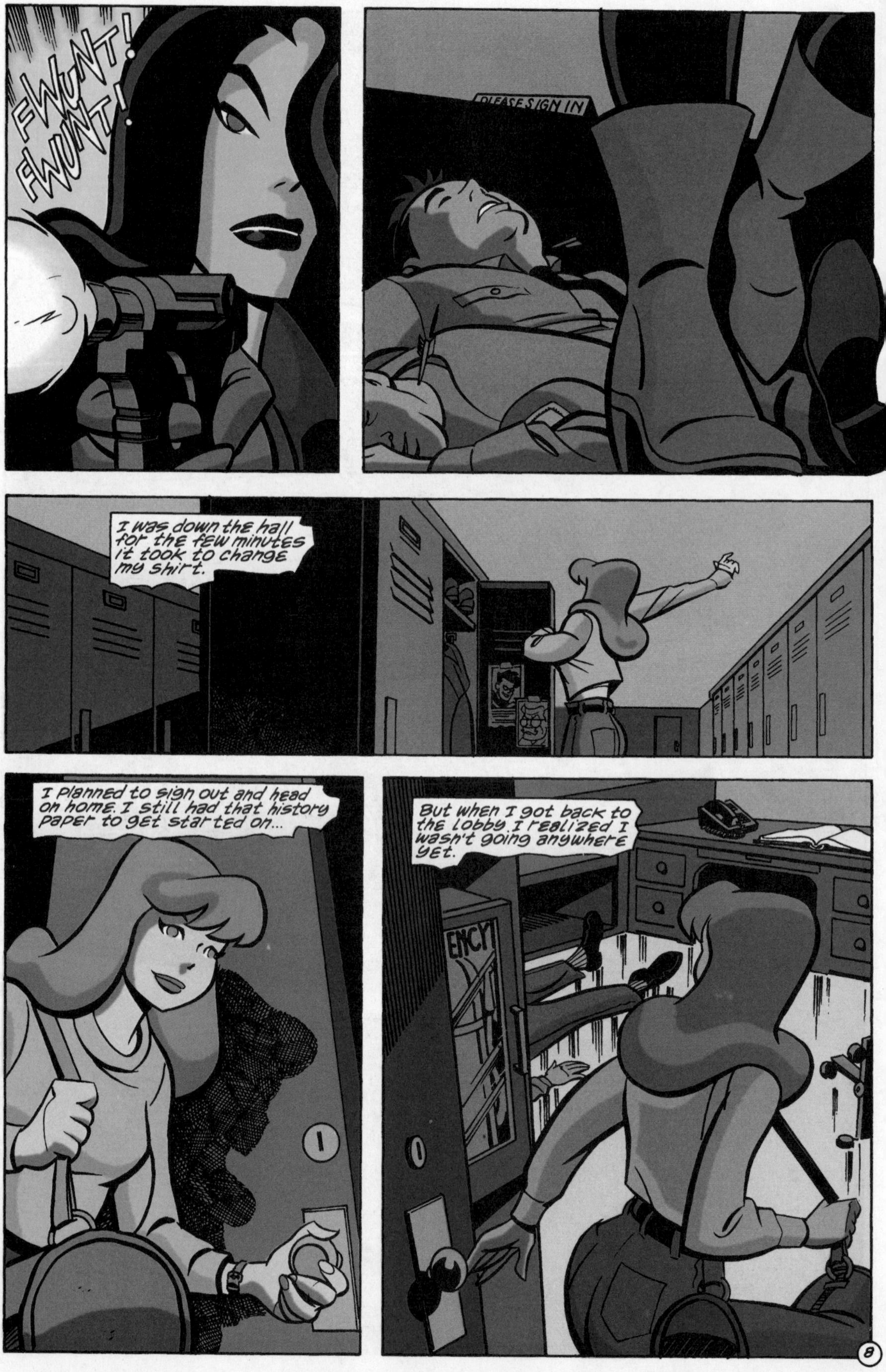
FWUNT!
FWUNT!
PLEASE SIGN IN
I was down the hall for the few minutes it took to change my shirt.
I planned to sign out and head on home. I still had that history paper to get started on...
But when I got back to the lobby I realized I wasn't going anywhere yet.
ENCY
8

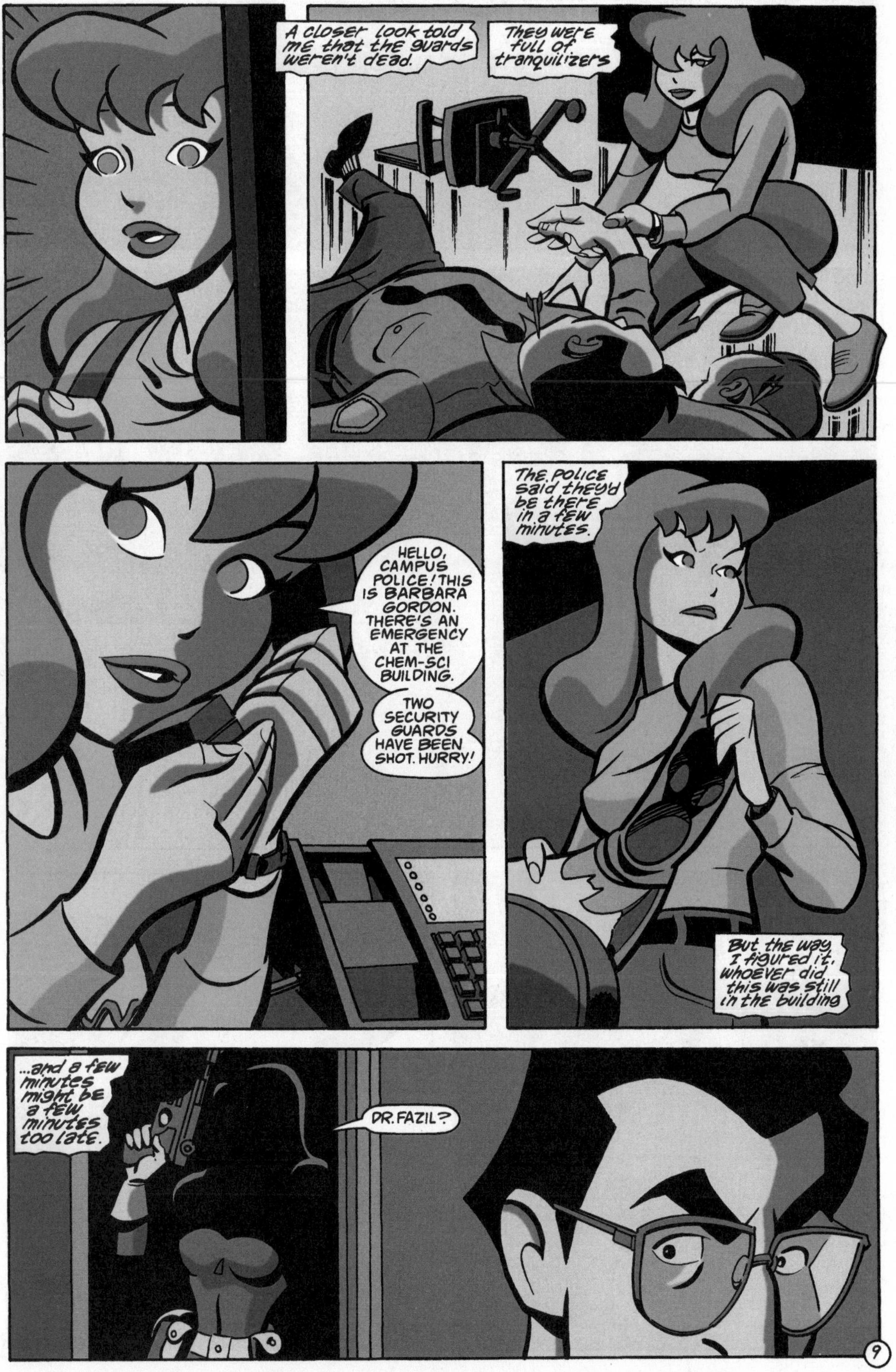
A closer look told me that the guards weren't dead.
They were full of tranquilizers
HELLO, CAMPUS POLICE! THIS IS BARBARA GORDON. THERE'S AN EMERGENCY AT THE CHEM-SCI BUILDING.
TWO SECURITY GUARDS HAVE BEEN SHOT. HURRY!
The police said they'd be there in a few minutes.
But the way I figured it, whoever did this was still in the building
...and a few minutes might be a few minutes too late.
DR. FAZIL?
9

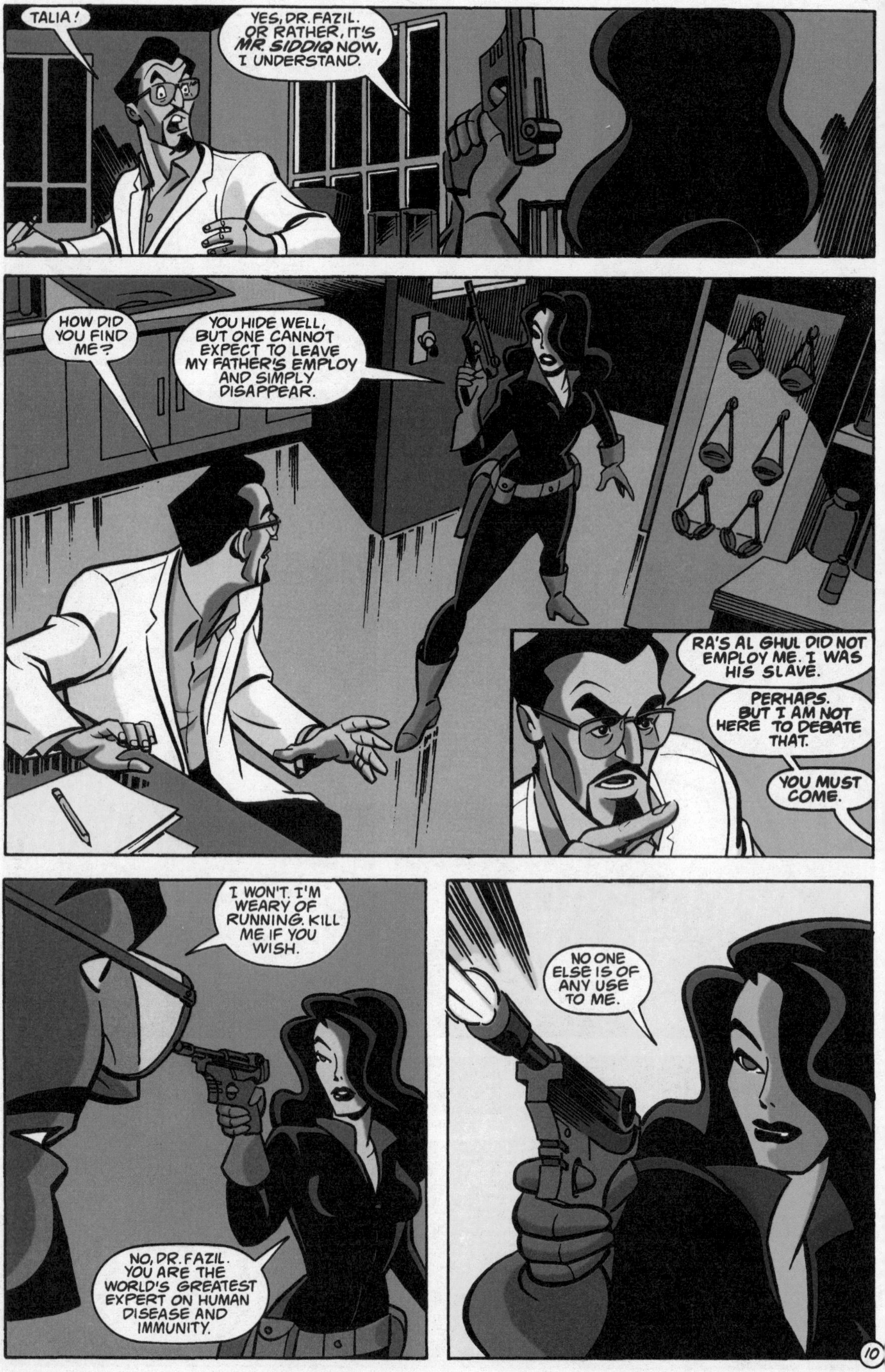
TALIA!
YES, DR. FAZIL. OR RATHER, IT'S MR. SIDDIQ NOW, I UNDERSTAND.
HOW DID YOU FIND ME?
YOU HIDE WELL, BUT ONE CANNOT EXPECT TO LEAVE MY FATHER'S EMPLOY AND SIMPLY DISAPPEAR.
RA'S AL GHUL DID NOT EMPLOY ME. I WAS HIS SLAVE.
PERHAPS. BUT I AM NOT HERE TO DEBATE THAT.
YOU MUST COME.
I WON'T. I'M WEARY OF RUNNING. KILL ME IF YOU WISH.
NO, DR. FAZIL. YOU ARE THE WORLD'S GREATEST EXPERT ON HUMAN DISEASE AND IMMUNITY.
NO ONE ELSE IS OF ANY USE TO ME.
10

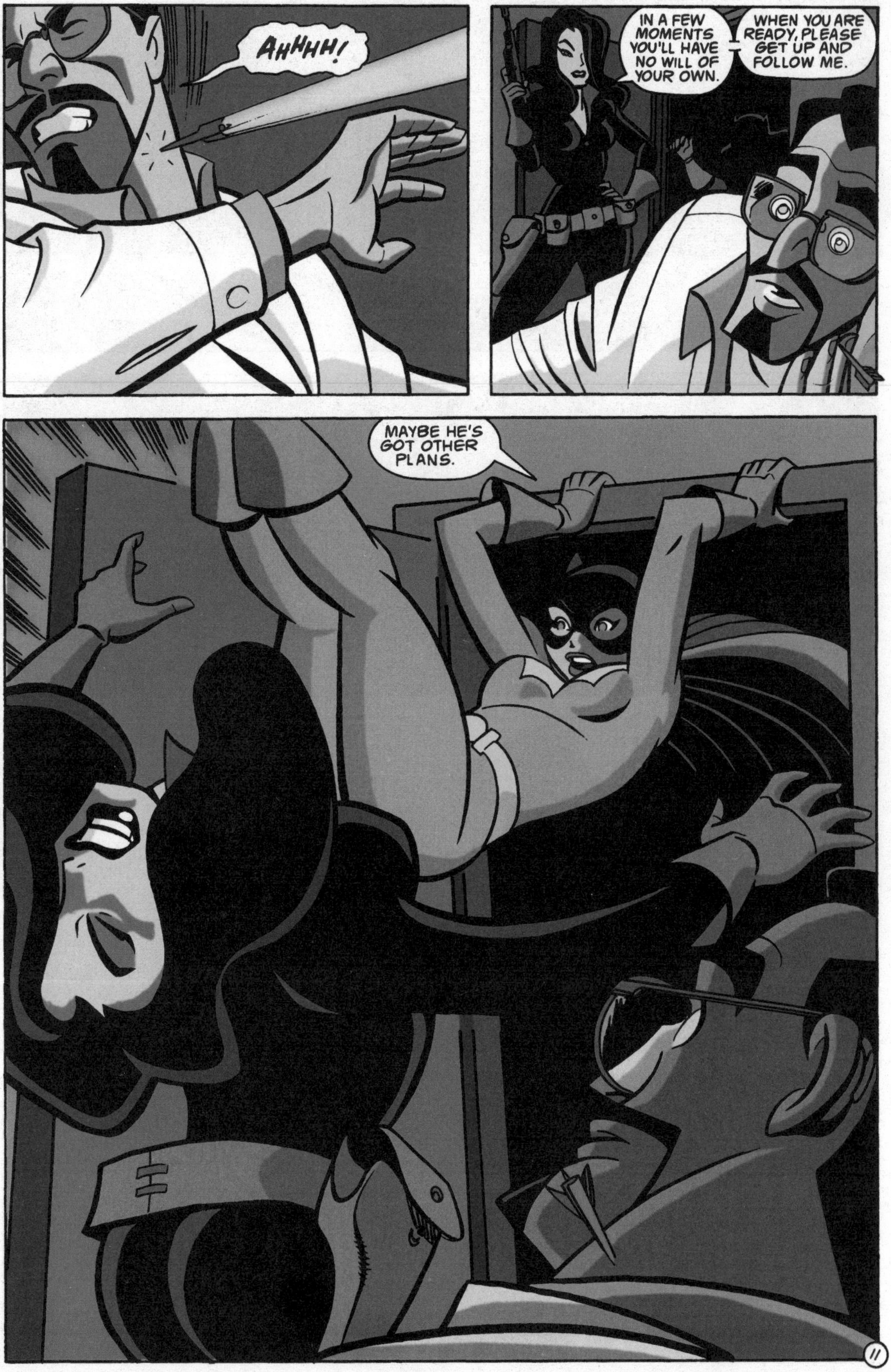
AHHHH!
IN A FEW MOMENTS YOU'LL HAVE NO WILL OF YOUR OWN.
WHEN YOU ARE READY, PLEASE GET UP AND FOLLOW ME.
MAYBE HE'S GOT OTHER PLANS.
11

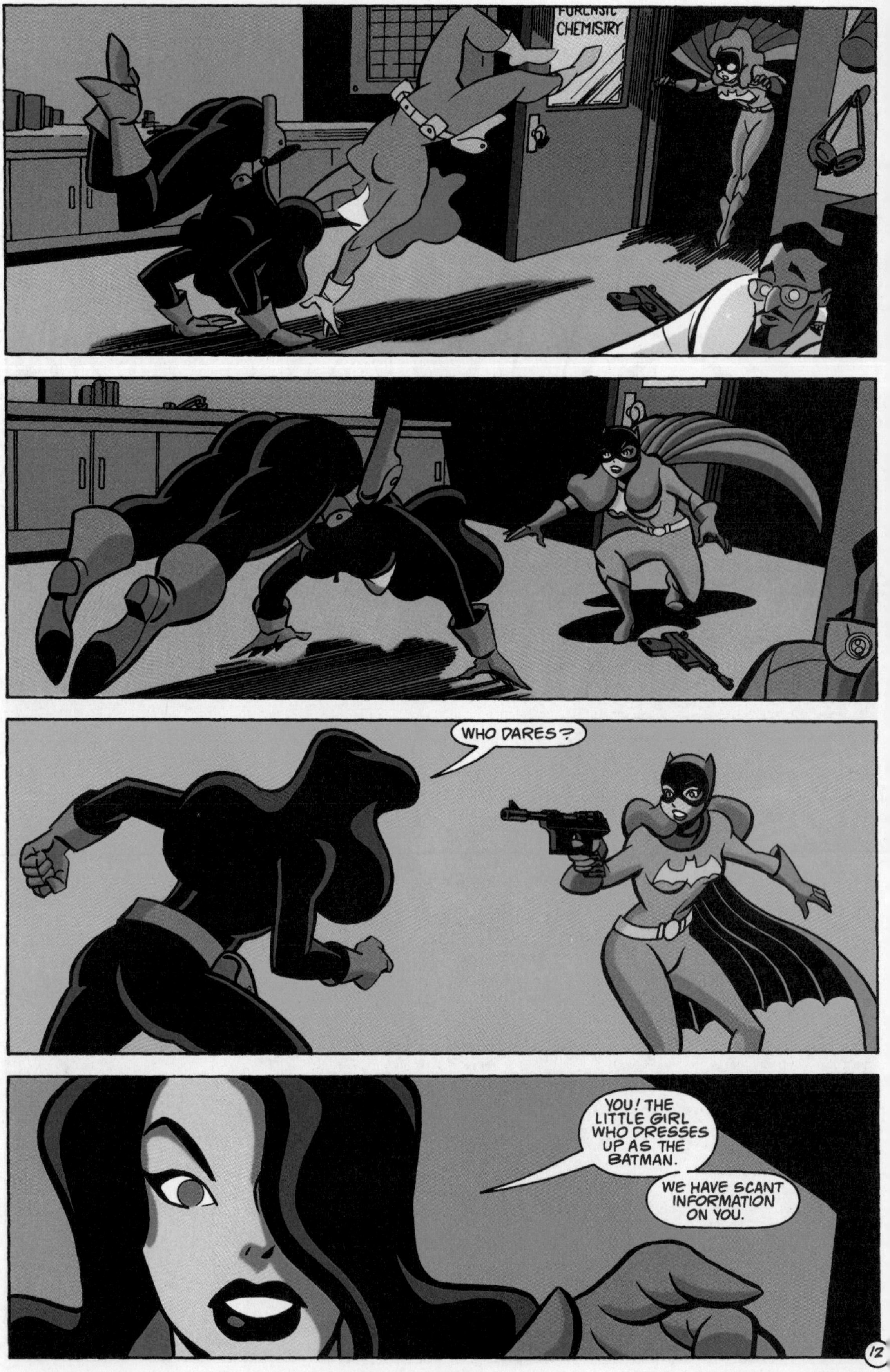

FORENSIC CHEMISTRY
WHO DARES?
YOU! THE LITTLE GIRL WHO DRESSES UP AS THE BATMAN.
WE HAVE SCANT INFORMATION ON YOU.
12

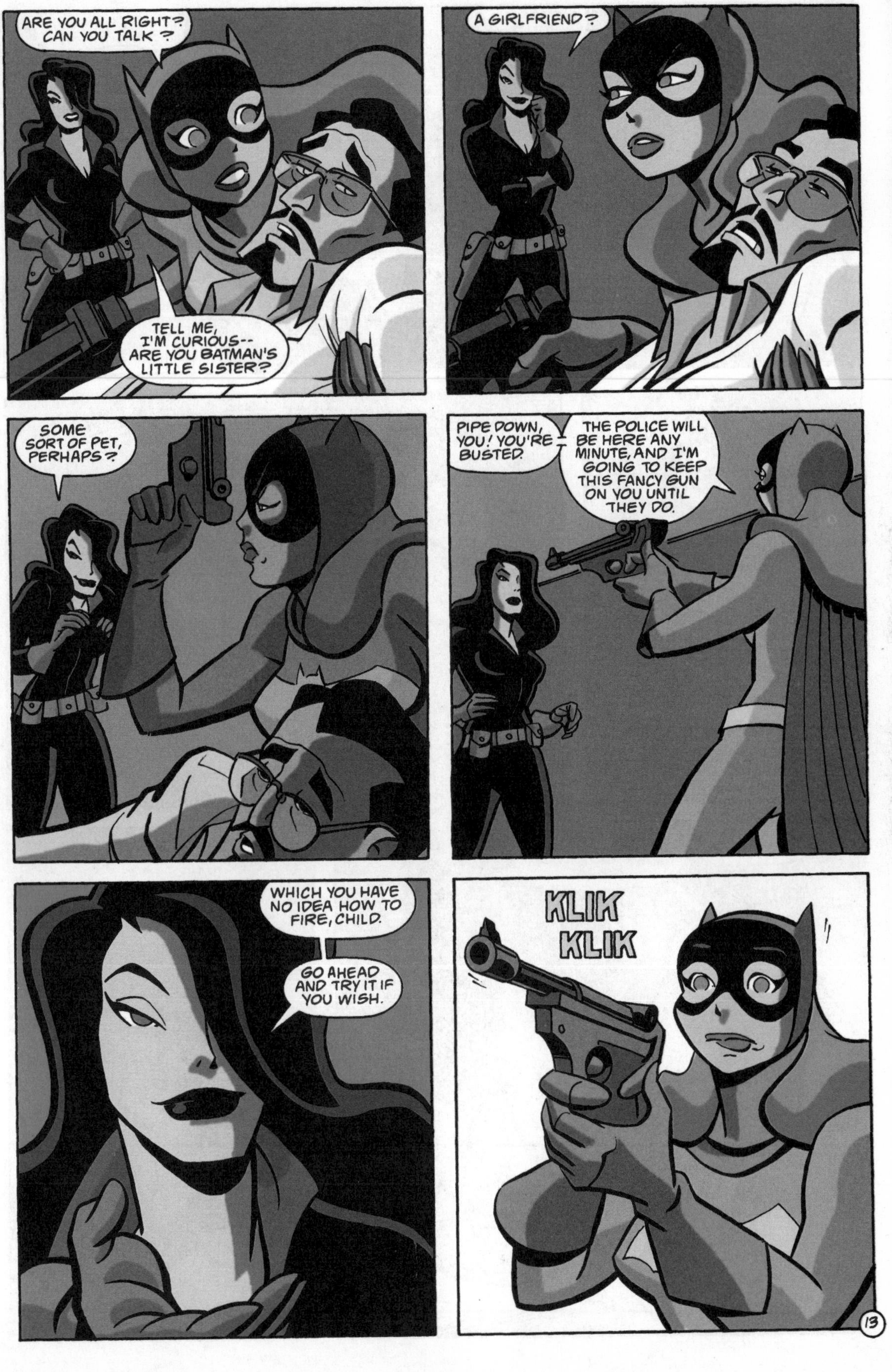
ARE YOU ALL RIGHT? CAN YOU TALK?
TELL ME, I'M CURIOUS-- ARE YOU BATMAN'S LITTLE SISTER?
A GIRLFRIEND?
SOME SORT OF PET, PERHAPS?
PIPE DOWN, YOU! YOU'RE BUSTED.
THE POLICE WILL BE HERE ANY MINUTE, AND I'M GOING TO KEEP THIS FANCY GUN ON YOU UNTIL THEY DO.
WHICH YOU HAVE NO IDEA HOW TO FIRE, CHILD.
GO AHEAD AND TRY IT IF YOU WISH.
KLIK
KLIK
13

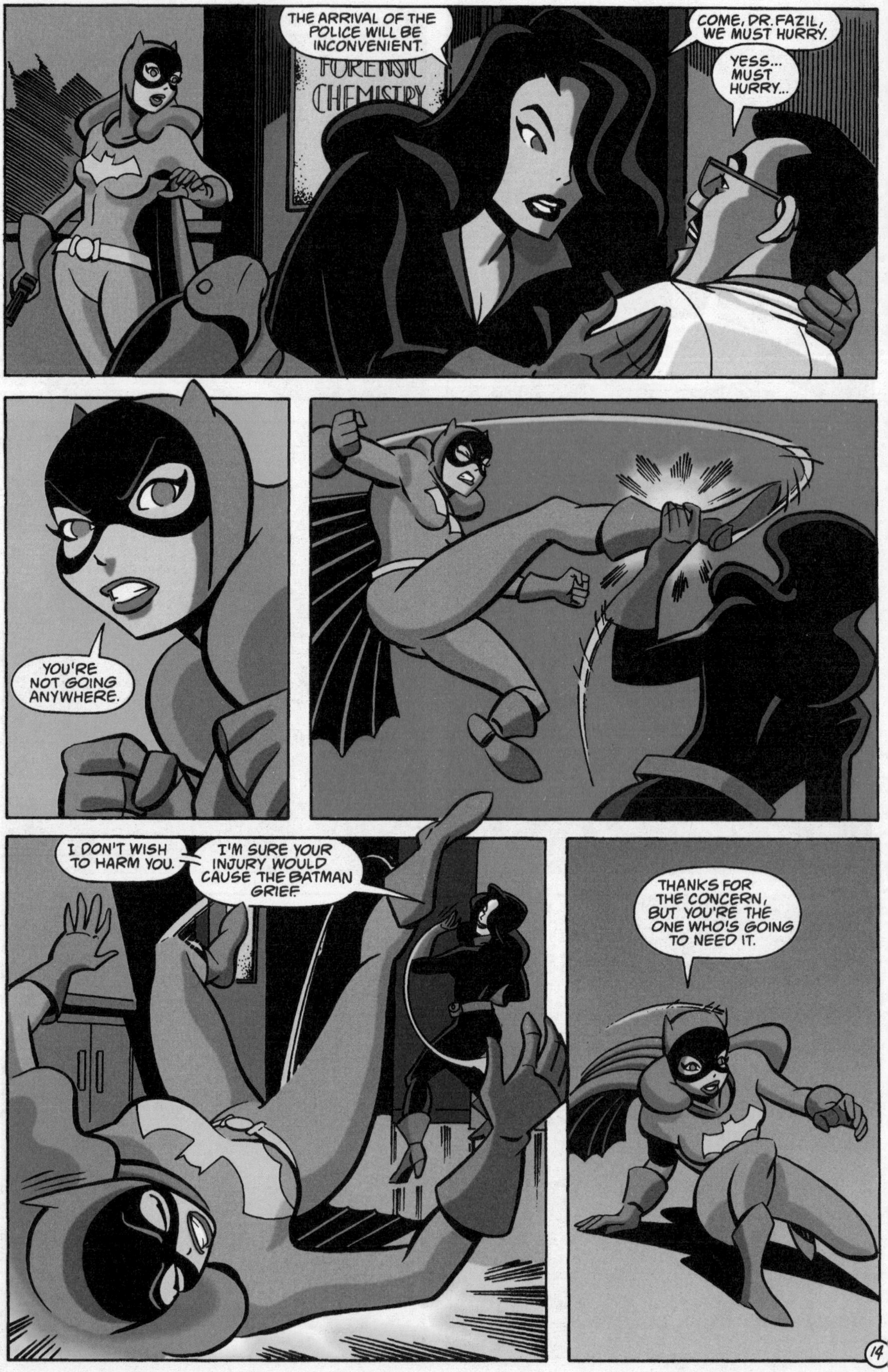

THE ARRIVAL OF THE POLICE WILL BE INCONVENIENT.
FORENSIC CHEMISTRY
COME, DR. FAZIL, WE MUST HURRY.
YESS... MUST HURRY...
YOU'RE NOT GOING ANYWHERE.
I DON'T WISH TO HARM YOU.
I'M SURE YOUR INJURY WOULD CAUSE THE BATMAN GRIEF.
THANKS FOR THE CONCERN, BUT YOU'RE THE ONE WHO'S GOING TO NEED IT.
14

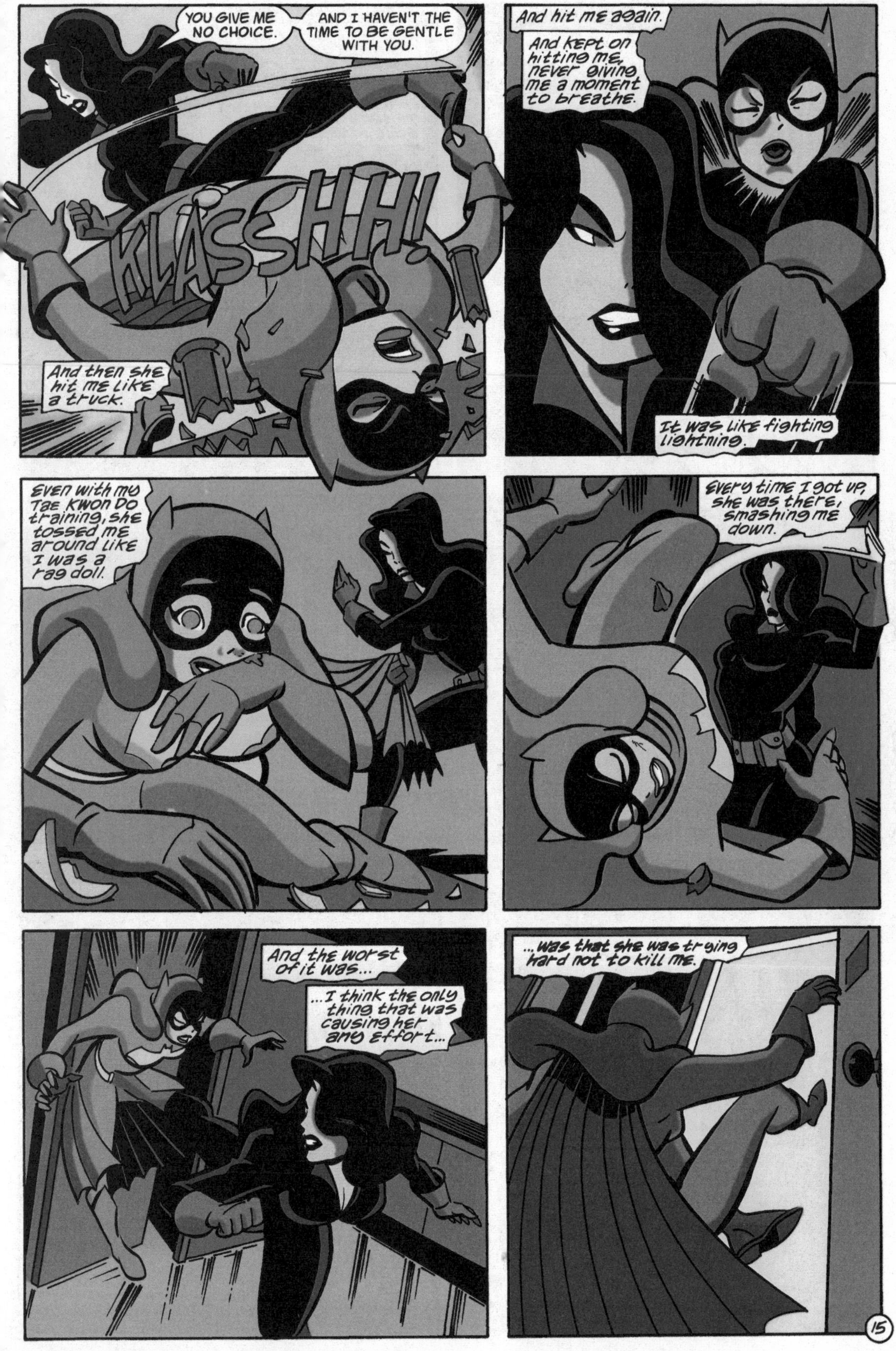
YOU GIVE ME NO CHOICE.
AND I HAVEN'T THE TIME TO BE GENTLE WITH YOU.
KLASSHH!
And then she hit me like a truck.
And hit me again.
And kept on hitting me, never giving me a moment to breathe.
It was like fighting lightning.
Even with my Tae Kwon Do training, she tossed me around like I was a rag doll.
Every time I got up, she was there, smashing me down.
And the worst of it was...
...I think the only thing that was causing her any effort...
...was that she was trying hard not to kill me.
15

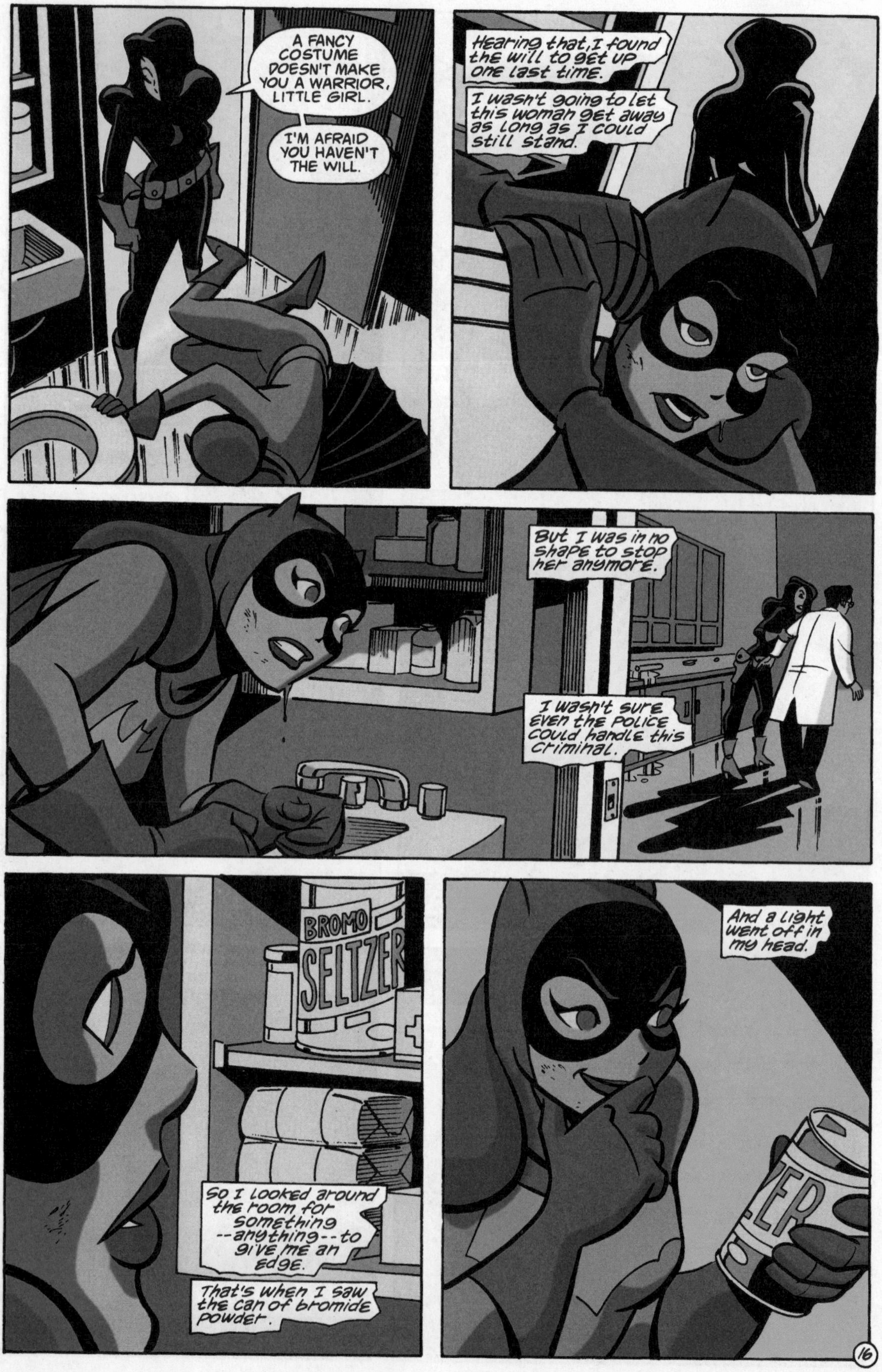
A FANCY COSTUME DOESN'T MAKE YOU A WARRIOR, LITTLE GIRL.
I'M AFRAID YOU HAVEN'T THE WILL.
Hearing that, I found the will to get up one last time.
I wasn't going to let this woman get away as long as I could still stand.
But I was in no shape to stop her anymore.
I wasn't sure even the police could handle this criminal.
BROMO SELTZER
So I looked around the room for something --anything-- to give me an edge.
That's when I saw the can of bromide powder.
And a light went off in my head.
16

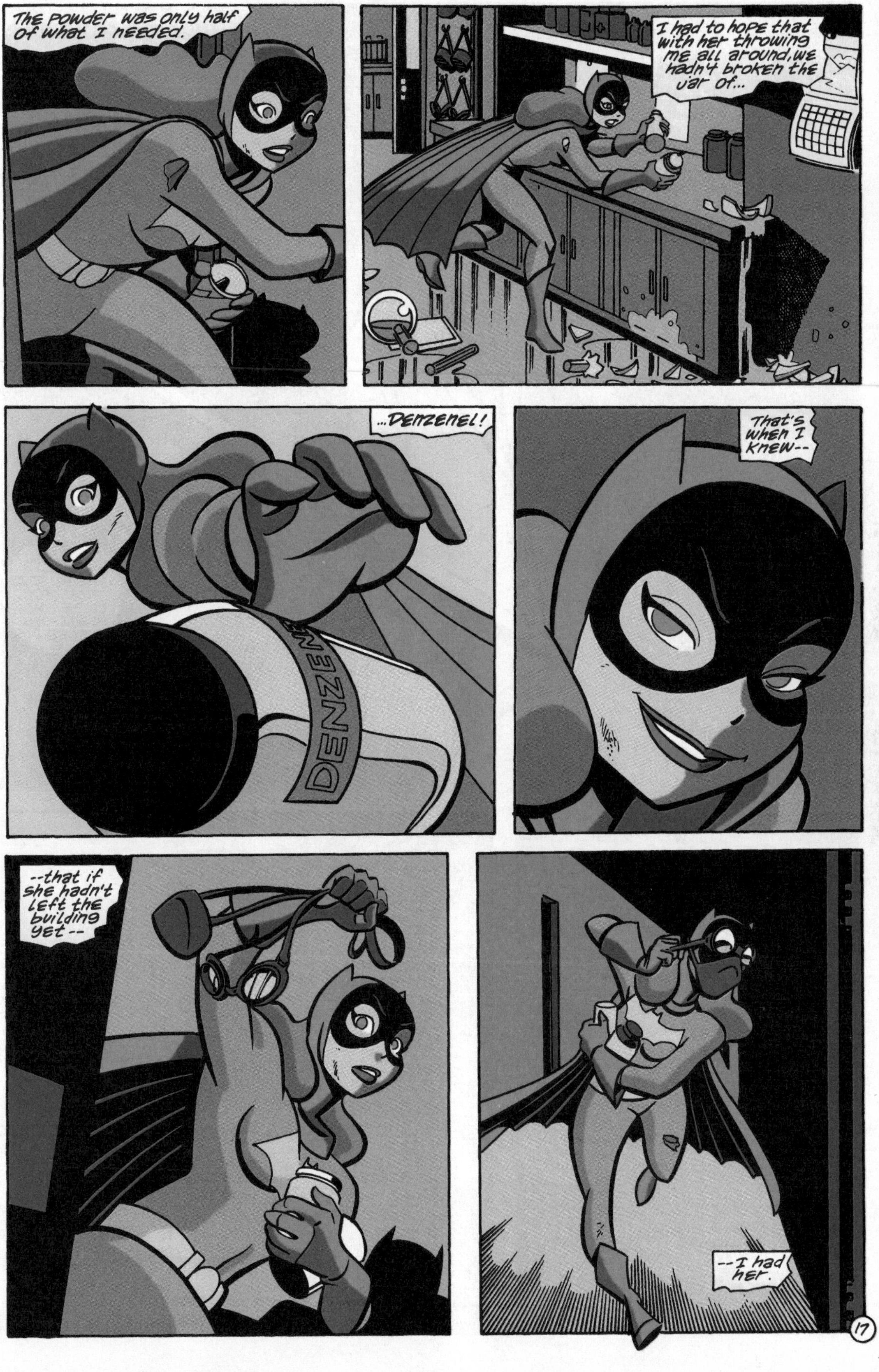
The powder was only half of what I needed.
I had to hope that with her throwing me all around, we hadn't broken the jar of...
...DENZENEL!
DENZENE
That's when I knew--
--that if she hadn't left the building yet--
--I had her.
17

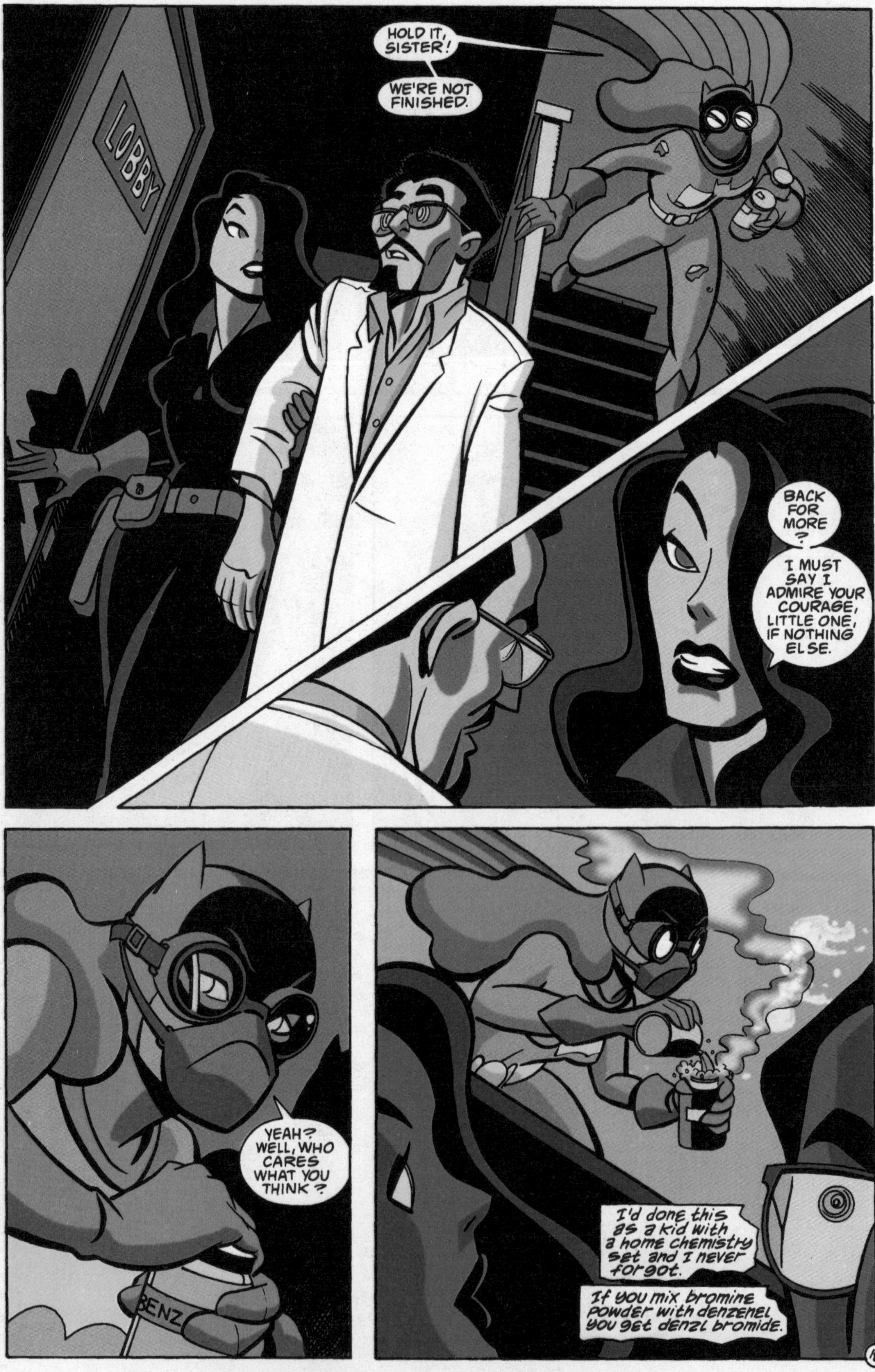
HOLD IT, SISTER!
WE'RE NOT FINISHED.
LOBBY
BACK FOR MORE?
I MUST SAY I ADMIRE YOUR COURAGE, LITTLE ONE, IF NOTHING ELSE.
YEAH? WELL, WHO CARES WHAT YOU THINK?
BENZ
I'd done this as a kid with a home chemistry set and I never forgot.
If you mix bromine powder with denzenel you get denzl bromide.
18

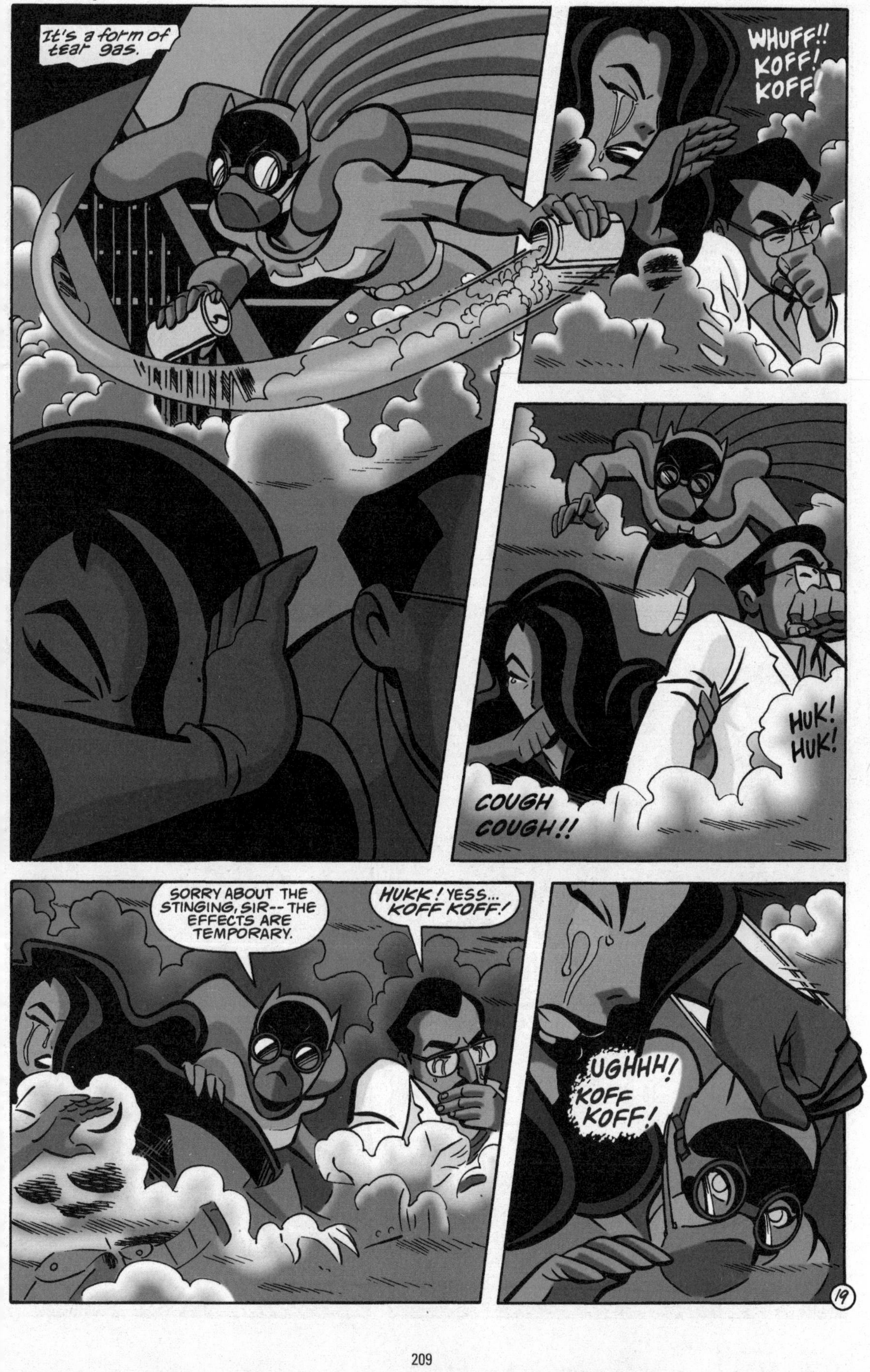

It's a form of tear gas.
WHUFF!! KOFF! KOFF!
HUK! HUK!
COUGH COUGH!!
SORRY ABOUT THE STINGING, SIR-- THE EFFECTS ARE TEMPORARY.
HUKK! YESS... KOFF KOFF!
UGHHH! KOFF KOFF!
19

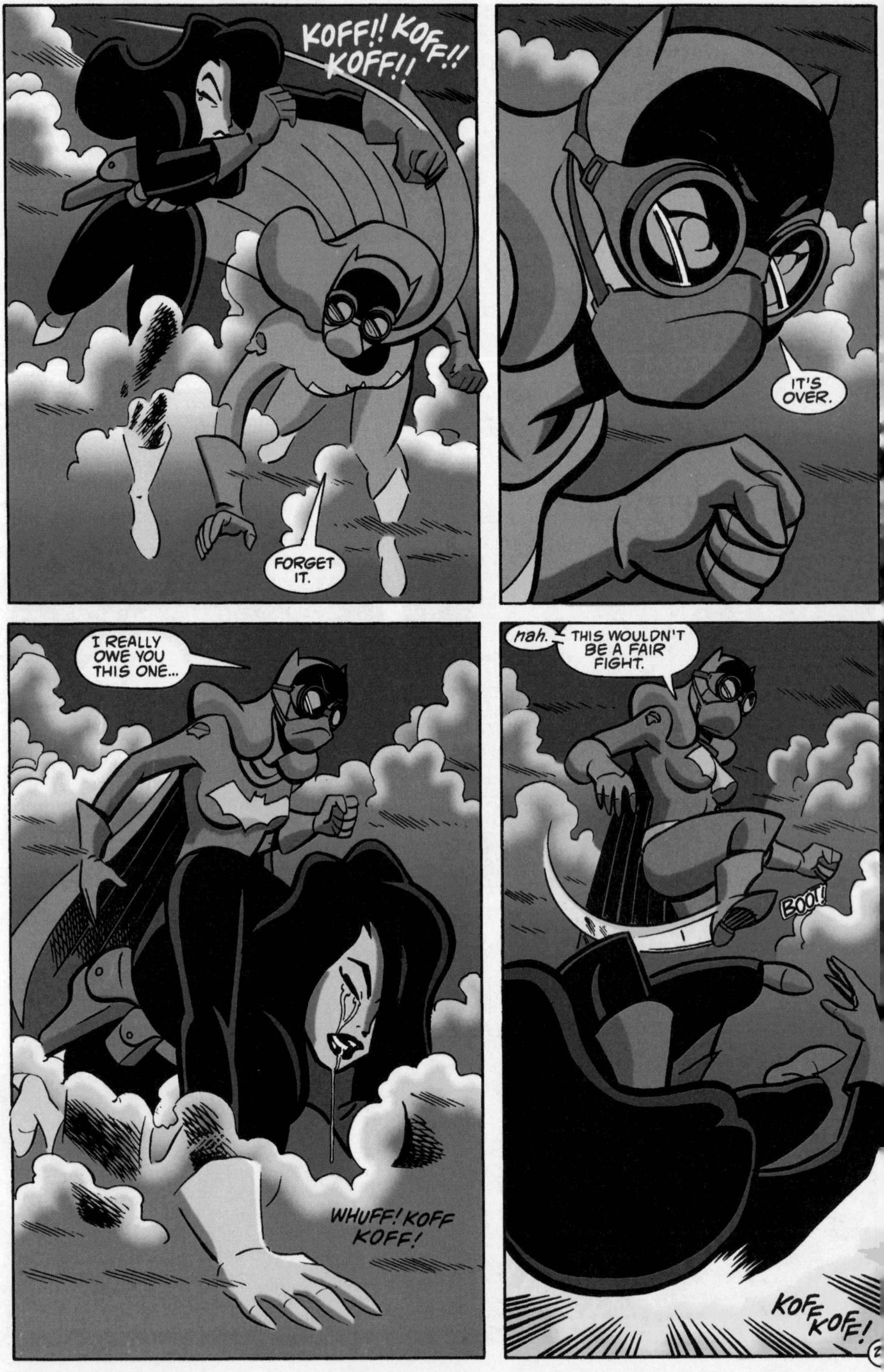
KOFF!! KOFF!!
KOFF!!
FORGET IT.
IT'S OVER.
I REALLY OWE YOU THIS ONE...
WHUFF! KOFF KOFF!
nah.
THIS WOULDN'T BE A FAIR FIGHT.
BOOT!
KOFF KOFF!

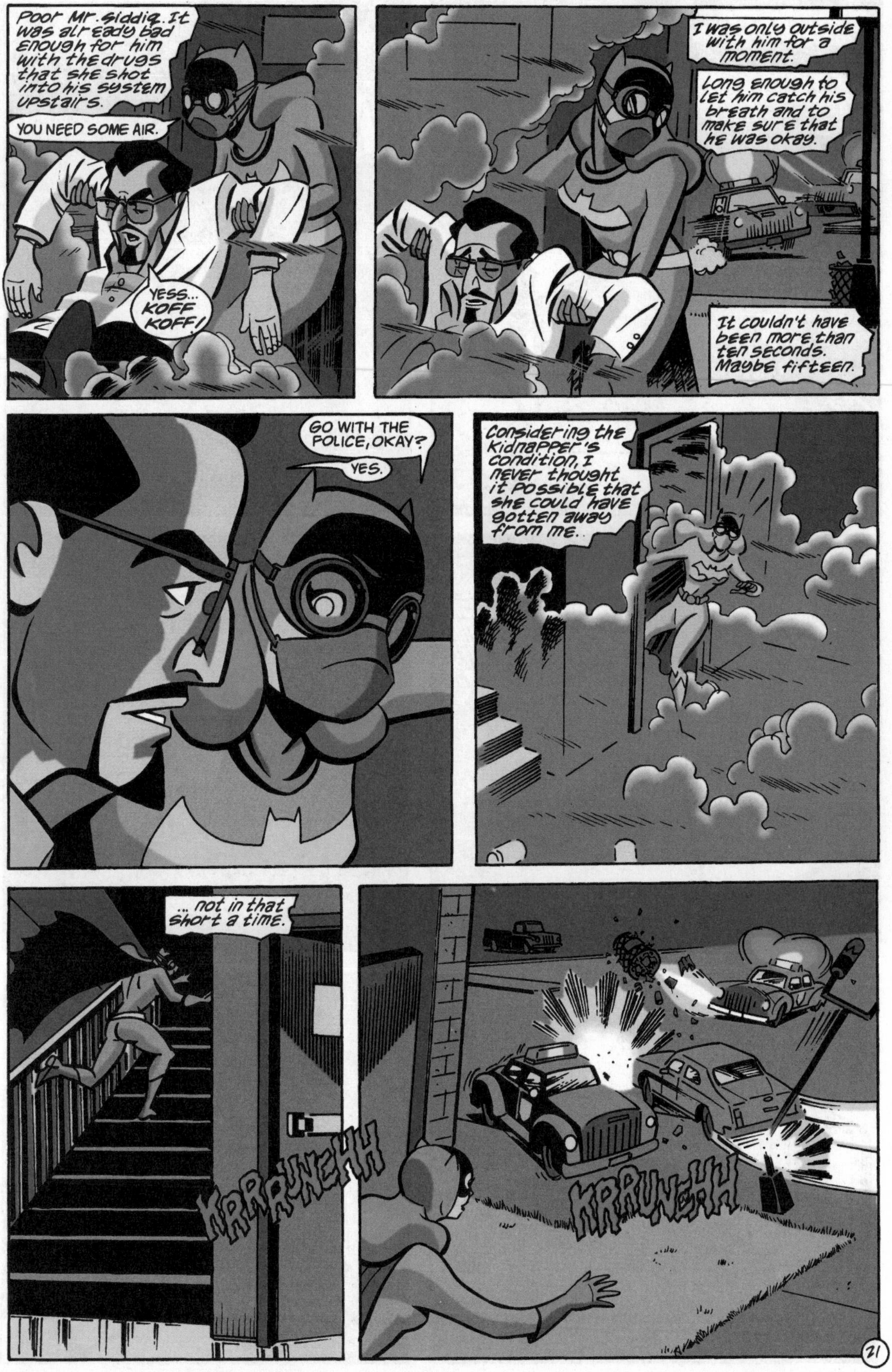
Poor Mr. Siddiq. It was already bad enough for him with the drugs that she shot into his system upstairs.
YOU NEED SOME AIR.
YESS... KOFF KOFF!
I was only outside with him for a moment.
Long enough to let him catch his breath and to make sure that he was okay.
It couldn't have been more than ten seconds. Maybe fifteen.
GO WITH THE POLICE, OKAY?
YES.
Considering the kidnapper's condition, I never thought it possible that she could have gotten away from me..
... not in that short a time.
KRRUNCHH
KRRUNCHH
21

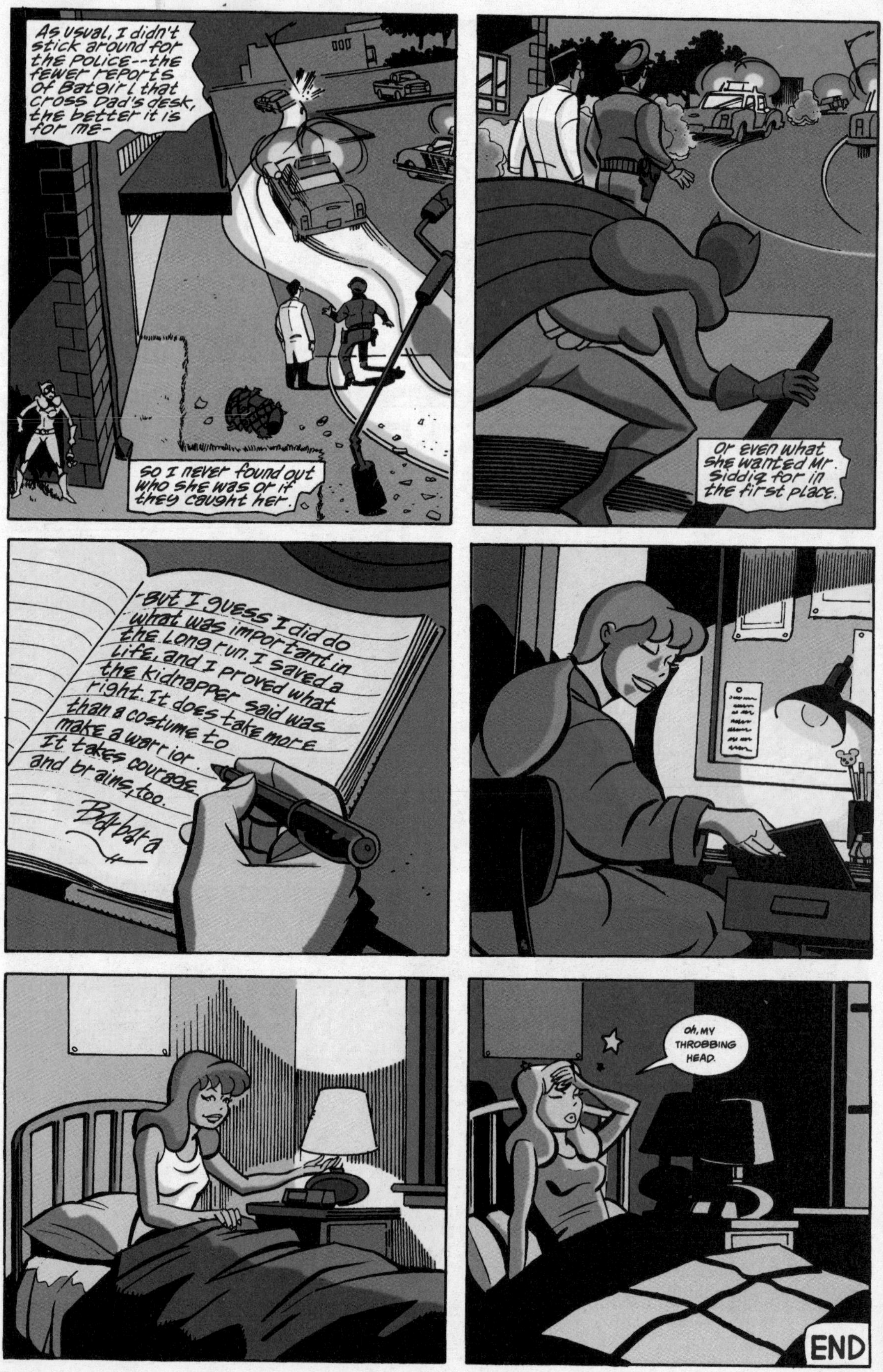
As usual, I didn't stick around for the police--the fewer reports of Batgirl that cross Dad's desk, the better it is for me-
So I never found out who she was or if they caught her.
Or even what she wanted Mr. Siddiq for in the first place.
-But I guess I did do what was important in the long run. I saved a life, and I proved what the kidnapper said was right. It does take more than a costume to make a warrior. It takes courage and brains, too.
Barbara
Oh, my throbbing head.
END

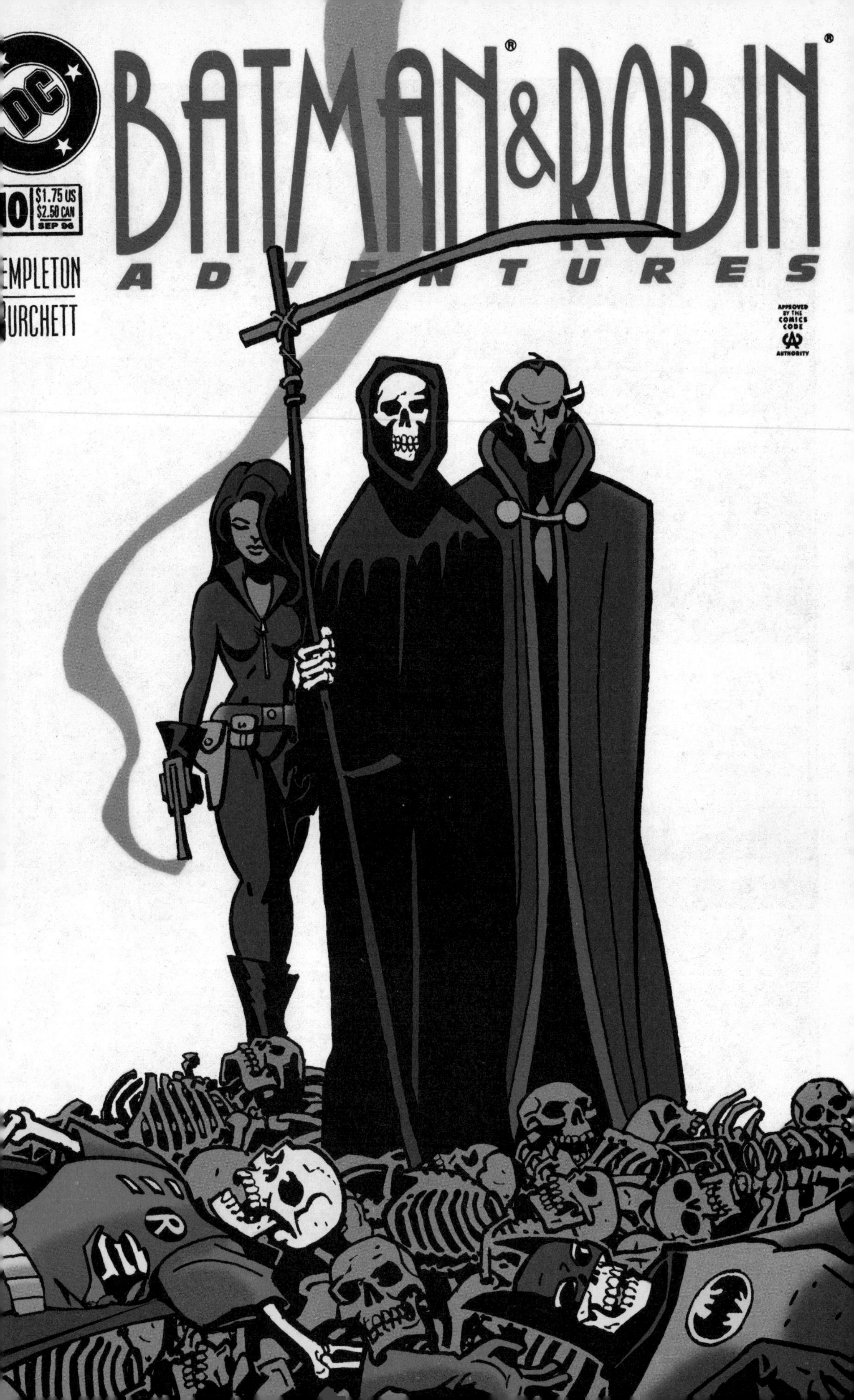

BATMAN® & ROBIN®
ADVENTURES
10
$1.75 US
$2.50 CAN
SEP 96
EMPLETON
URCHETT
APPROVED BY THE COMICS CODE AUTHORITY

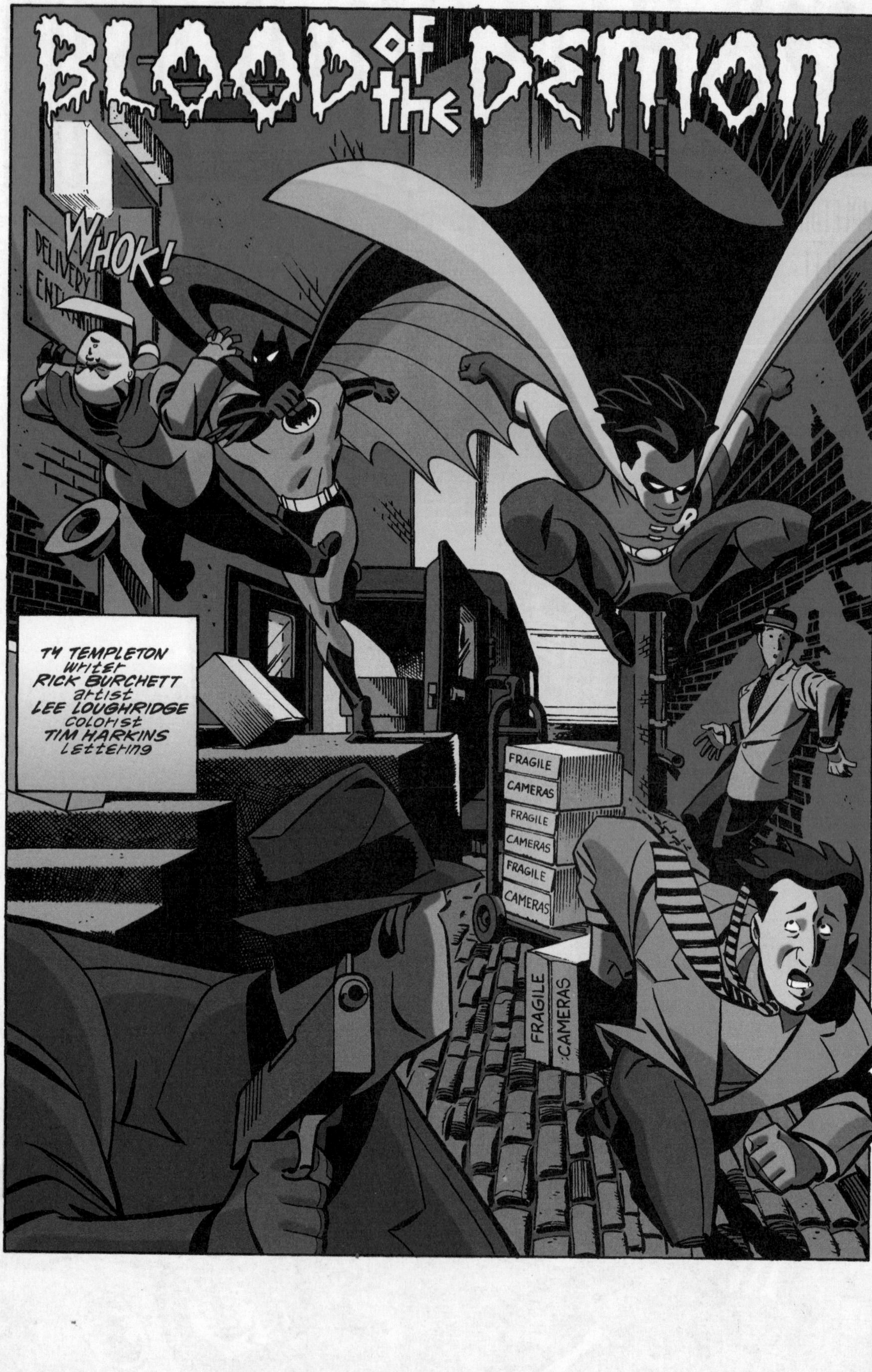
BLOOD of the DEMON
DELIVERY ENT
WHOK!
TY TEMPLETON writer
RICK BURCHETT artist
LEE LOUGHRIDGE colorist
TIM HARKINS lettering
FRAGILE
CAMERAS
FRAGILE
CAMERAS
FRAGILE
CAMERAS
FRAGILE
CAMERAS

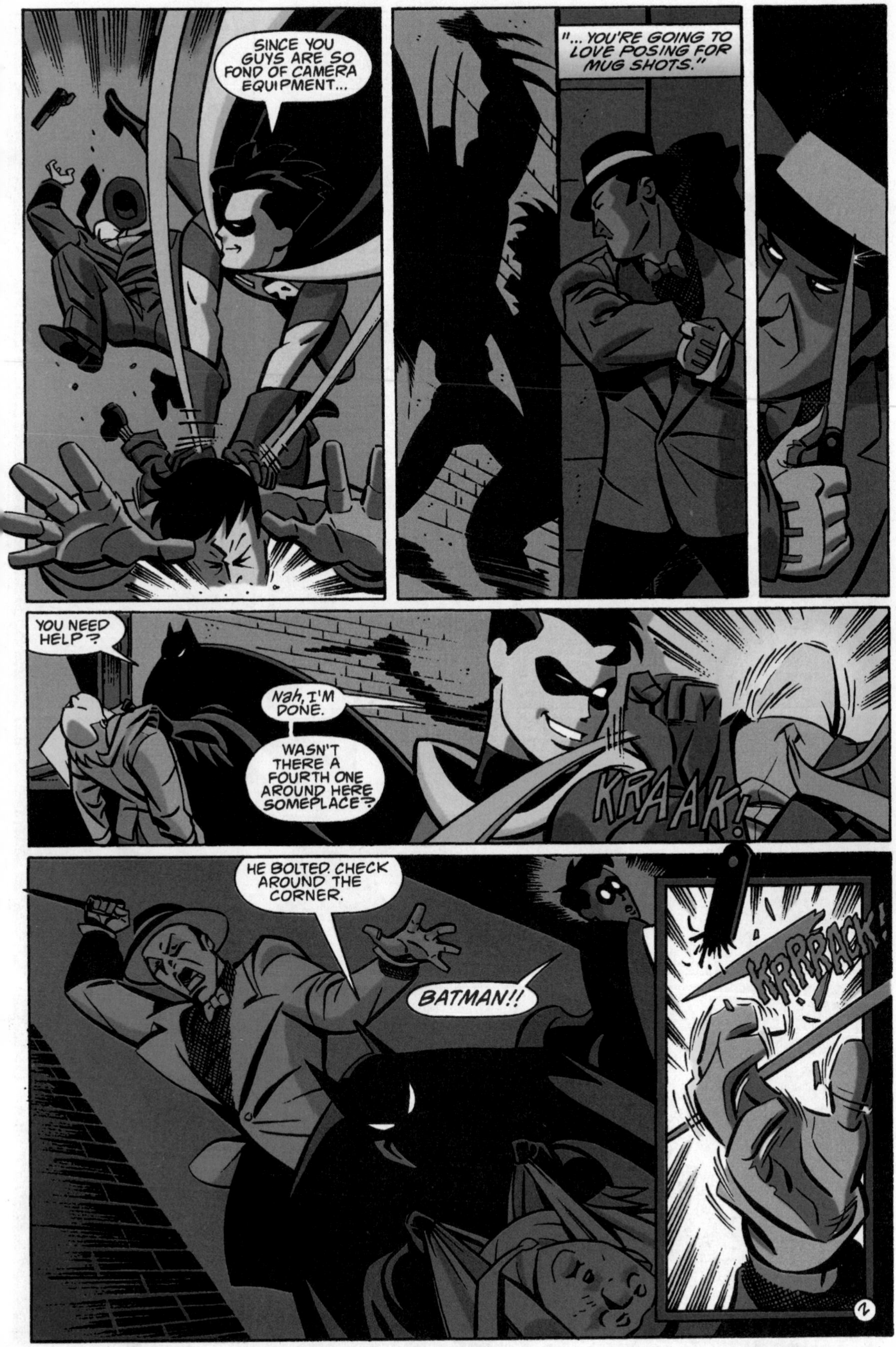
SINCE YOU GUYS ARE SO FOND OF CAMERA EQUIPMENT...
"... YOU'RE GOING TO LOVE POSING FOR MUG SHOTS."
YOU NEED HELP?
Nah, I'M DONE.
WASN'T THERE A FOURTH ONE AROUND HERE SOMEPLACE?
KRAAAK!
HE BOLTED. CHECK AROUND THE CORNER.
BATMAN!!
KRRRACK!
2

TALIA.

I KNEW YOU WERE IN NO DANGER FROM THIS FOOL, BELOVED, BUT WHY TAKE RISKS?

MY HAND!!

"BELOVED?" THAT'S NICE.

WHAT ARE YOU DOING IN GOTHAM CITY?

KRAK

CHOOSING THE LESSER OF TWO EVILS.

I AM HERE TO ENLIST YOUR AID AGAINST MY FATHER.

GO ON.

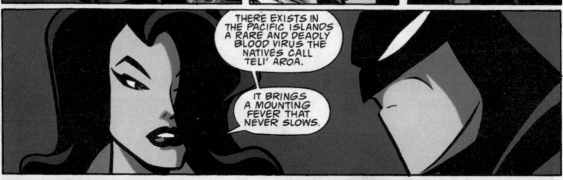

THERE EXISTS IN THE PACIFIC ISLANDS A RARE AND DEADLY BLOOD VIRUS THE NATIVES CALL TELI' AROA.

IT BRINGS A MOUNTING FEVER THAT NEVER SLOWS.

FOR DAYS, THE VICTIM'S TEMPERATURE CONTINUES TO RISE, UNTIL IT REACHES SO HIGH...

...THAT THE BRAIN LITERALLY BOILS TO DEATH INSIDE ONE'S OWN SKULL.

GROSS.

3

YES, IT'S HORRIBLY PAINFUL.

AND UNTIL RECENTLY, VERY RARE, AND IMPOSSIBLE TO CONTRACT UNLESS BITTEN BY MOSQUITOS DURING THE SUMMER MONTHS.

UNTIL RECENTLY...?

RECENTLY MY FATHER'S SCIENTISTS HAVE MUTATED AN AIRBORNE STRAIN, WILDLY CONTAGIOUS AND EVERY BIT AS DEADLY AS ITS NATURAL COUNTERPART.

...ONE YOU CATCH BY BREATHING.

GOOD LORD!

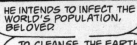

HE INTENDS TO INFECT THE WORLD'S POPULATION, BELOVED.

TO CLEANSE THE EARTH OF WHAT HE CALLS "THIS DISEASE OF HUMANITY."

YOU MUST RETURN WITH ME TO FATHER'S ISLAND IMMEDIATELY, BATMAN.

ALONE. I HAVE NO ROOM FOR THE BOY.

YEAH, SURE...

SHE'S RIGHT. I CAN'T RISK TAKING YOU WITH ME TO FACE SOMEONE AS DANGEROUS AS RA'S AL GHUL.

YOU GOTTA BE KIDDING!

THIS IS NO DIFFERENT FROM THE ROSCOE ROLLINS CASE LAST WEEK, ROBIN.

YOU STAY BEHIND.

4

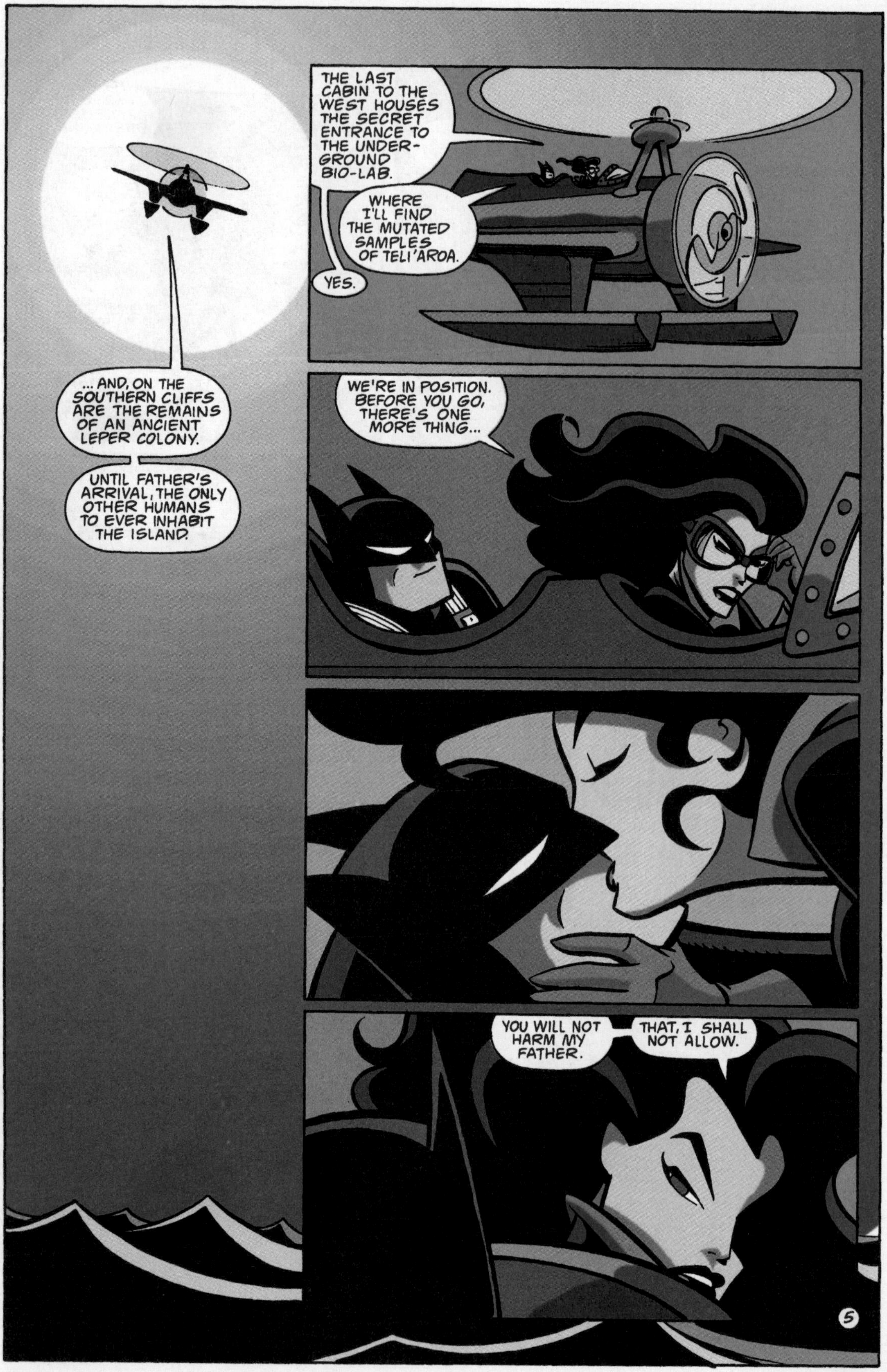

... AND, ON THE SOUTHERN CLIFFS ARE THE REMAINS OF AN ANCIENT LEPER COLONY.
UNTIL FATHER'S ARRIVAL, THE ONLY OTHER HUMANS TO EVER INHABIT THE ISLAND.
THE LAST CABIN TO THE WEST HOUSES THE SECRET ENTRANCE TO THE UNDER-GROUND BIO-LAB.
WHERE I'LL FIND THE MUTATED SAMPLES OF TELI'AROA.
YES.
WE'RE IN POSITION. BEFORE YOU GO, THERE'S ONE MORE THING...
YOU WILL NOT HARM MY FATHER.
THAT, I SHALL NOT ALLOW.
5

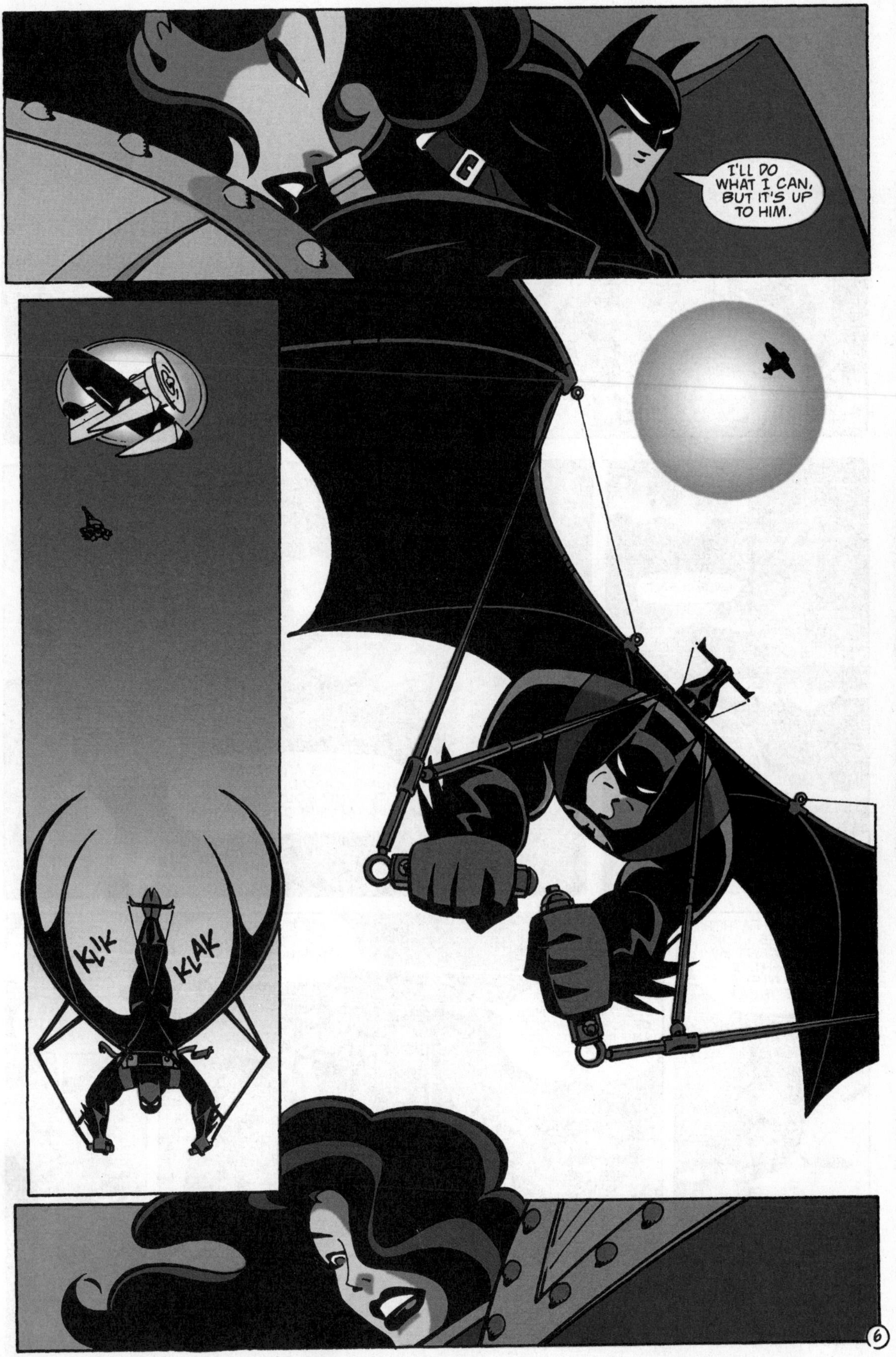
I'LL DO WHAT I CAN, BUT IT'S UP TO HIM.
KLIK
KLAK
6

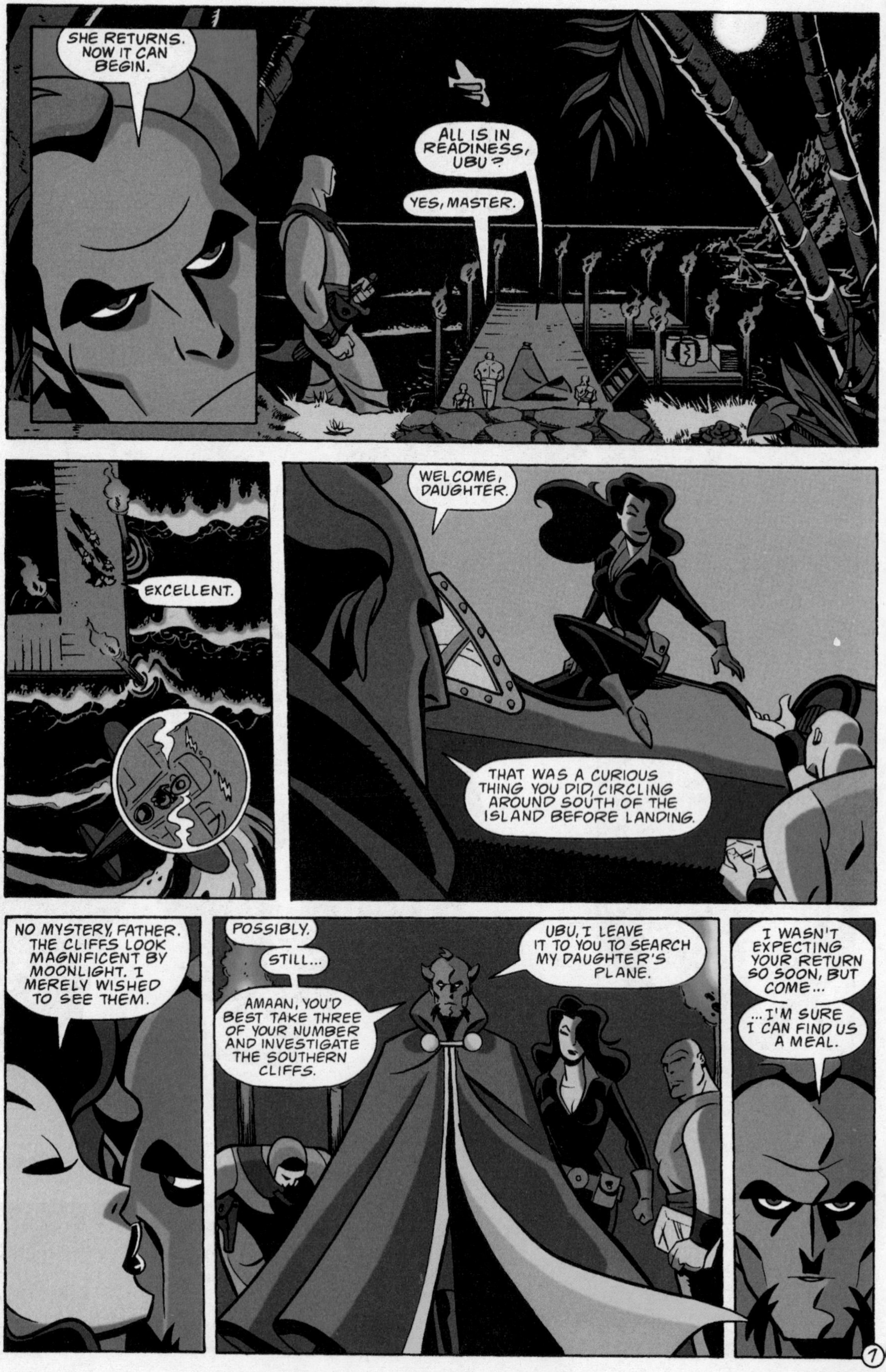
SHE RETURNS. NOW IT CAN BEGIN.
ALL IS IN READINESS, UBU?
YES, MASTER.
EXCELLENT.
WELCOME, DAUGHTER.
THAT WAS A CURIOUS THING YOU DID, CIRCLING AROUND SOUTH OF THE ISLAND BEFORE LANDING.
NO MYSTERY, FATHER. THE CLIFFS LOOK MAGNIFICENT BY MOONLIGHT. I MERELY WISHED TO SEE THEM.
POSSIBLY.
STILL...
AMAAN, YOU'D BEST TAKE THREE OF YOUR NUMBER AND INVESTIGATE THE SOUTHERN CLIFFS.
UBU, I LEAVE IT TO YOU TO SEARCH MY DAUGHTER'S PLANE.
I WASN'T EXPECTING YOUR RETURN SO SOON, BUT COME...
...I'M SURE I CAN FIND US A MEAL.
7

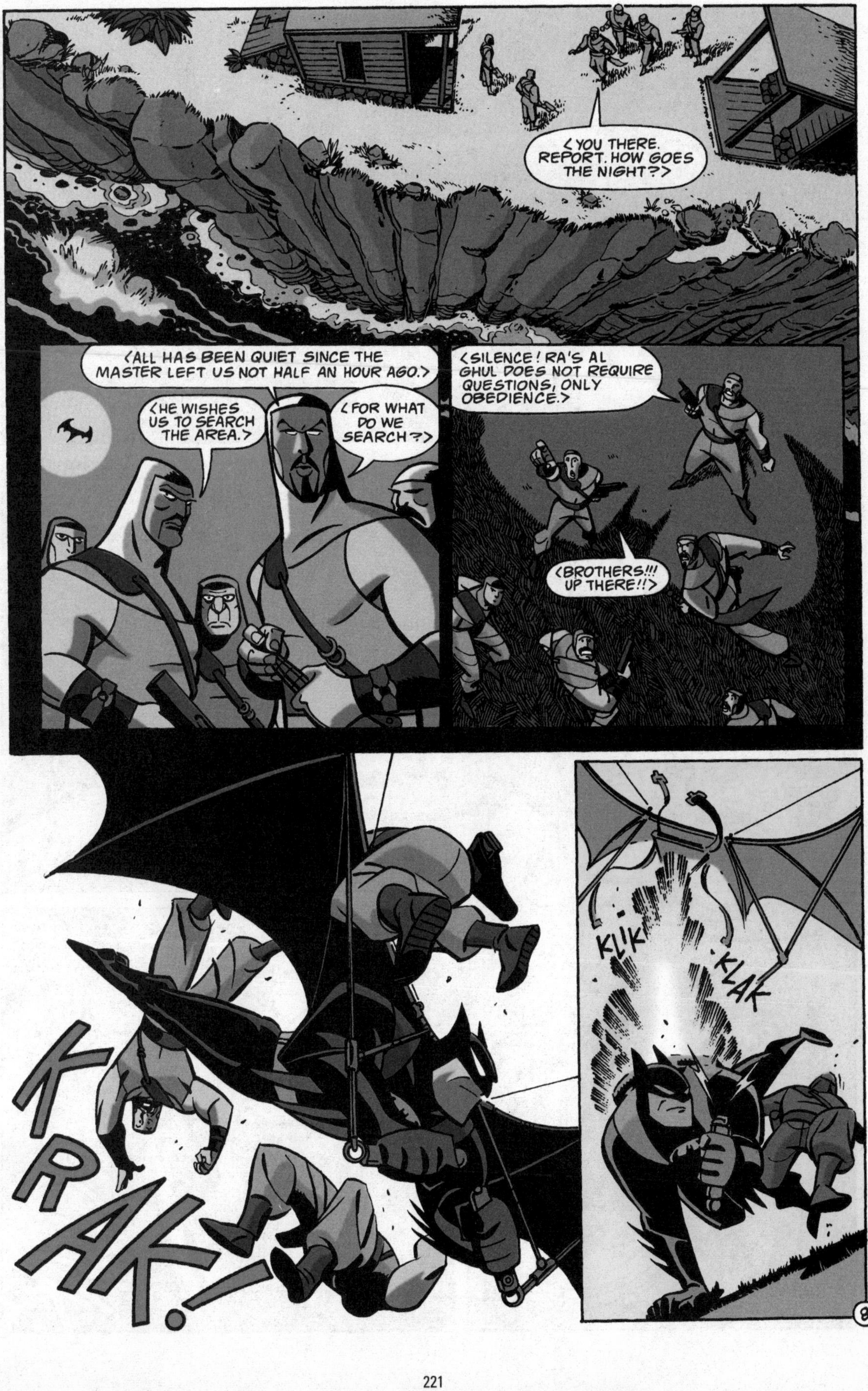

<YOU THERE. REPORT. HOW GOES THE NIGHT?>
<ALL HAS BEEN QUIET SINCE THE MASTER LEFT US NOT HALF AN HOUR AGO.>
<HE WISHES US TO SEARCH THE AREA.>
<FOR WHAT DO WE SEARCH?>
<SILENCE! RA'S AL GHUL DOES NOT REQUIRE QUESTIONS, ONLY OBEDIENCE.>
<BROTHERS!!! UP THERE!!>
KRAK!
KLIK
KLAK
8

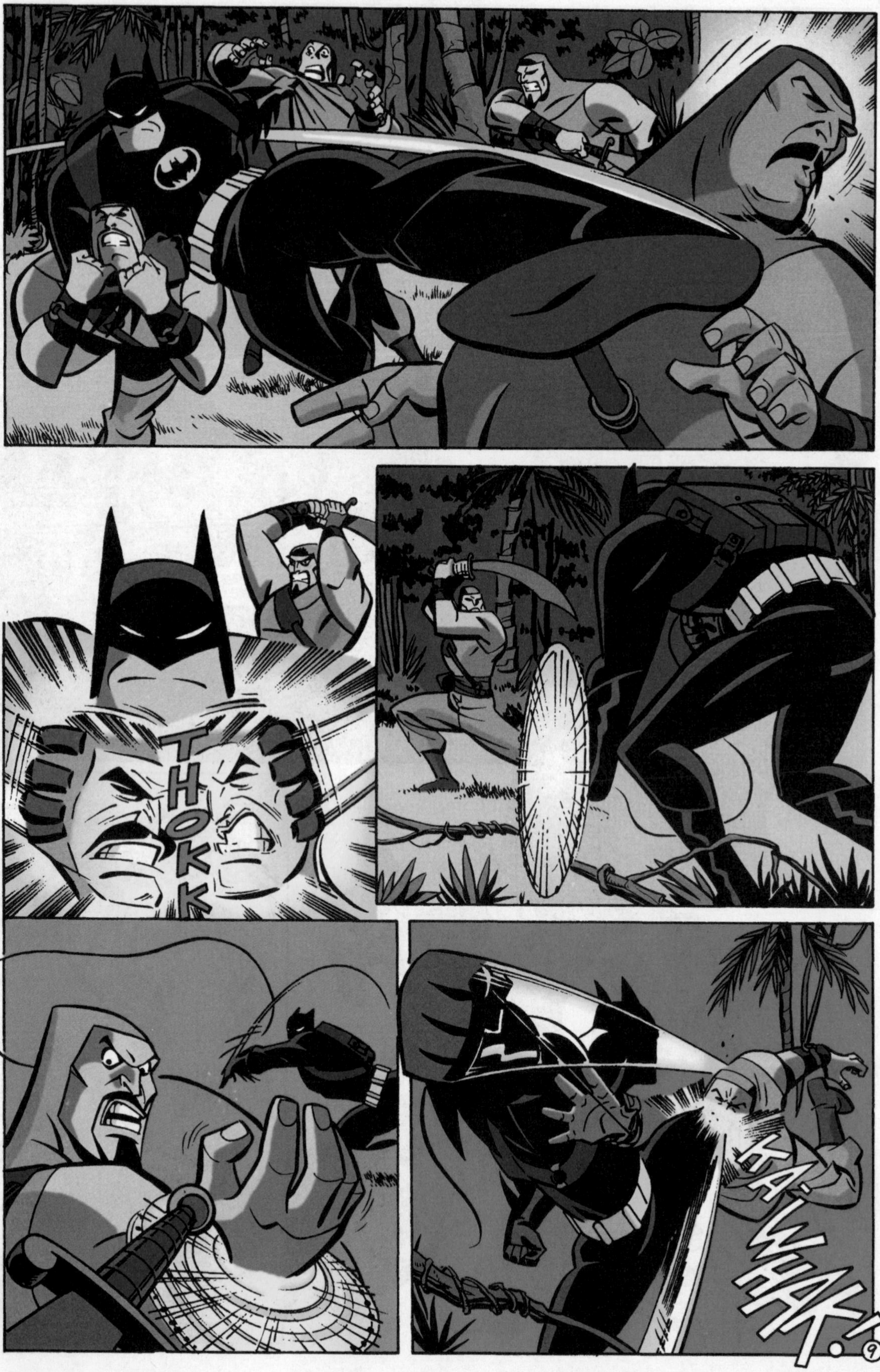
THOKK
KA-WHAK!
9

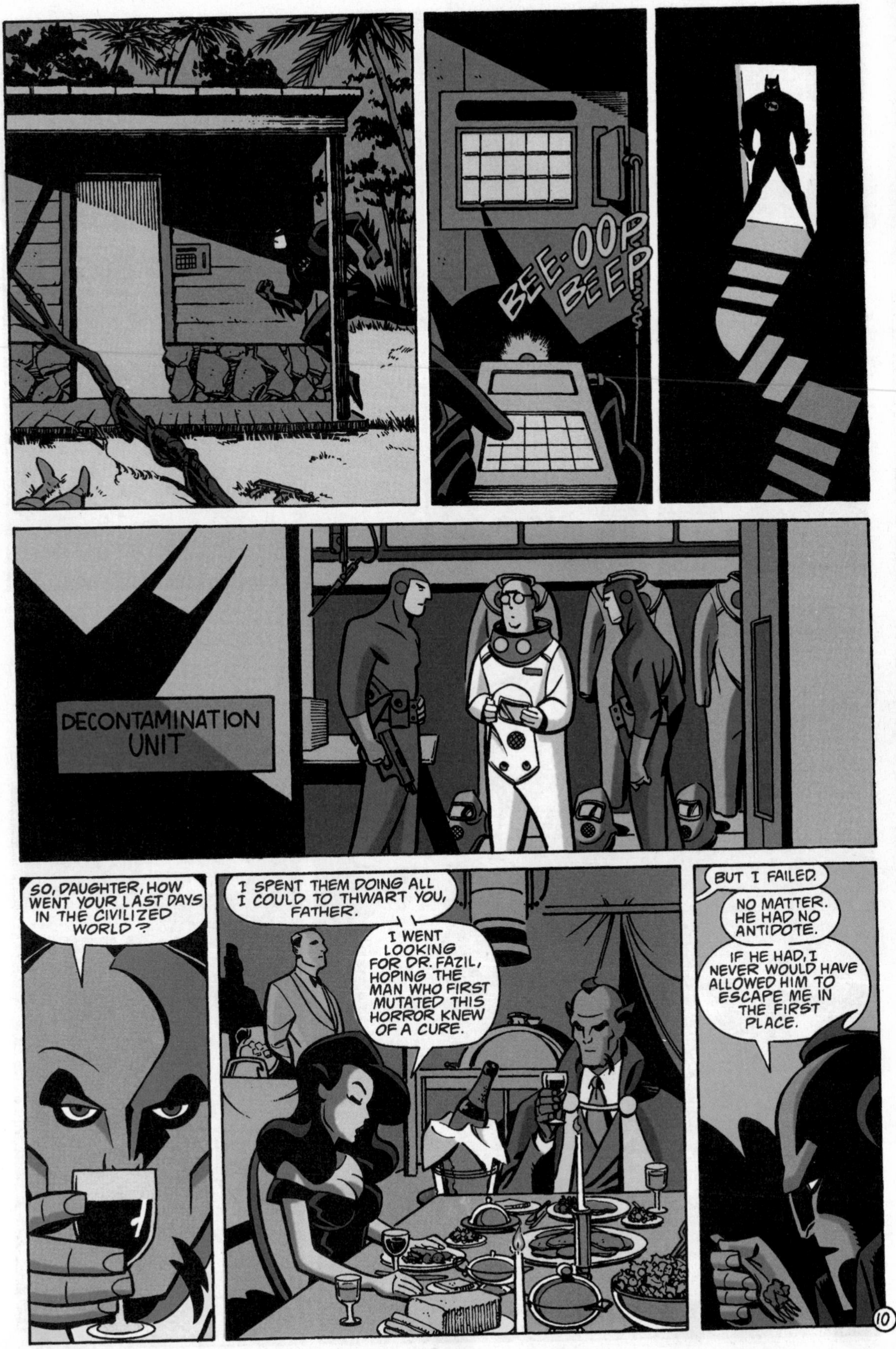
BEE-OOP BEEP
DECONTAMINATION UNIT
SO, DAUGHTER, HOW WENT YOUR LAST DAYS IN THE CIVILIZED WORLD?
I SPENT THEM DOING ALL I COULD TO THWART YOU, FATHER.
I WENT LOOKING FOR DR. FAZIL, HOPING THE MAN WHO FIRST MUTATED THIS HORROR KNEW OF A CURE.
BUT I FAILED.
NO MATTER. HE HAD NO ANTIDOTE.
IF HE HAD, I NEVER WOULD HAVE ALLOWED HIM TO ESCAPE ME IN THE FIRST PLACE.
10

FATHER...

I SHARE YOUR PASSION TO SEE THE WORLD RENEWED, TO HALT THE YEARS OF ENVIRONMENTAL RUIN...

...BUT SURELY ALL THIS PAIN AND DEATH...

YOU SEE THINGS WITH THE SENTIMENT OF YOUTH, DAUGHTER.

ALL CREATURES ARE BORN TO DIE. THAT IS NATURE.

IT IS SIMPLY BEST FOR THE EARTH IF THIS GENERATION OF HUMANS WERE TO DIE ALL AT ONCE.

WHY? BECAUSE YOU SAY IT IS SO?

BECAUSE IT IS *DESTINY*, CHILD.

CONSIDER...

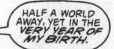

THE EARLIEST CASE OF THIS DISEASE YOU CALL A HORROR WAS RECORDED IN THE FOURTEENTH CENTURY.

THE NATIVES CALLED IT *TELI'AROA... "THE BLOOD OF THE DEMON."*

HALF A WORLD AWAY, YET IN THE VERY YEAR OF MY BIRTH.

FOR UNTOLD AGES THIS FRAGILE PLANET HAS CALLED OUT FOR MY PROTECTION...

NOW IT OFFERS TO ME THIS POTENT WEAPON AT A TIME OF GREATEST NEED.

I HAVE A DUTY TO THE LIFE FORCE OF THIS WORLD, TALIA.

THIS IS *DESTINY*.

AND IT IS UNSTOPPABLE.

11

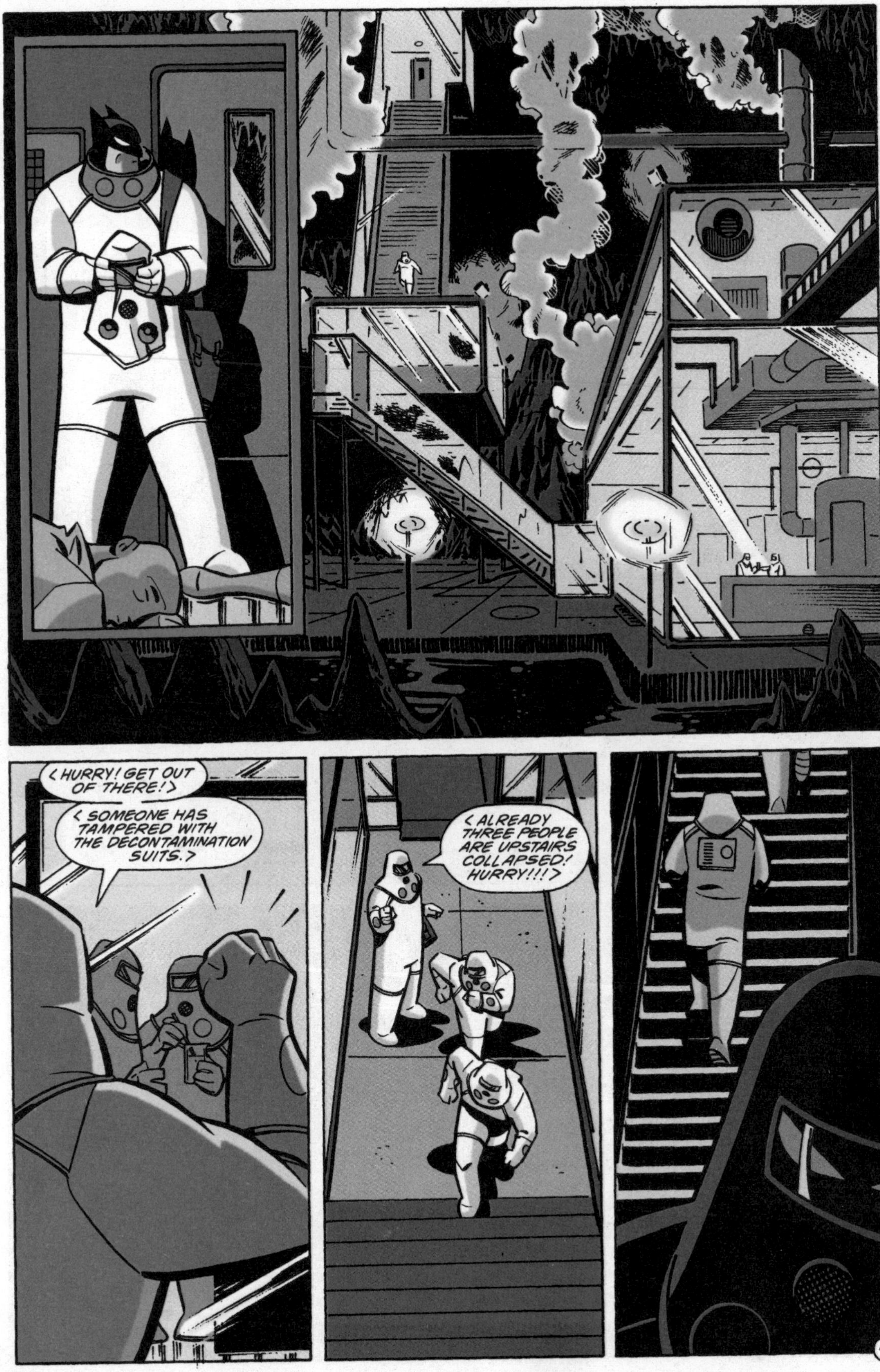
< HURRY! GET OUT OF THERE! >
< SOMEONE HAS TAMPERED WITH THE DECONTAMINATION SUITS. >
< ALREADY THREE PEOPLE ARE UPSTAIRS COLLAPSED! HURRY!!! >
12

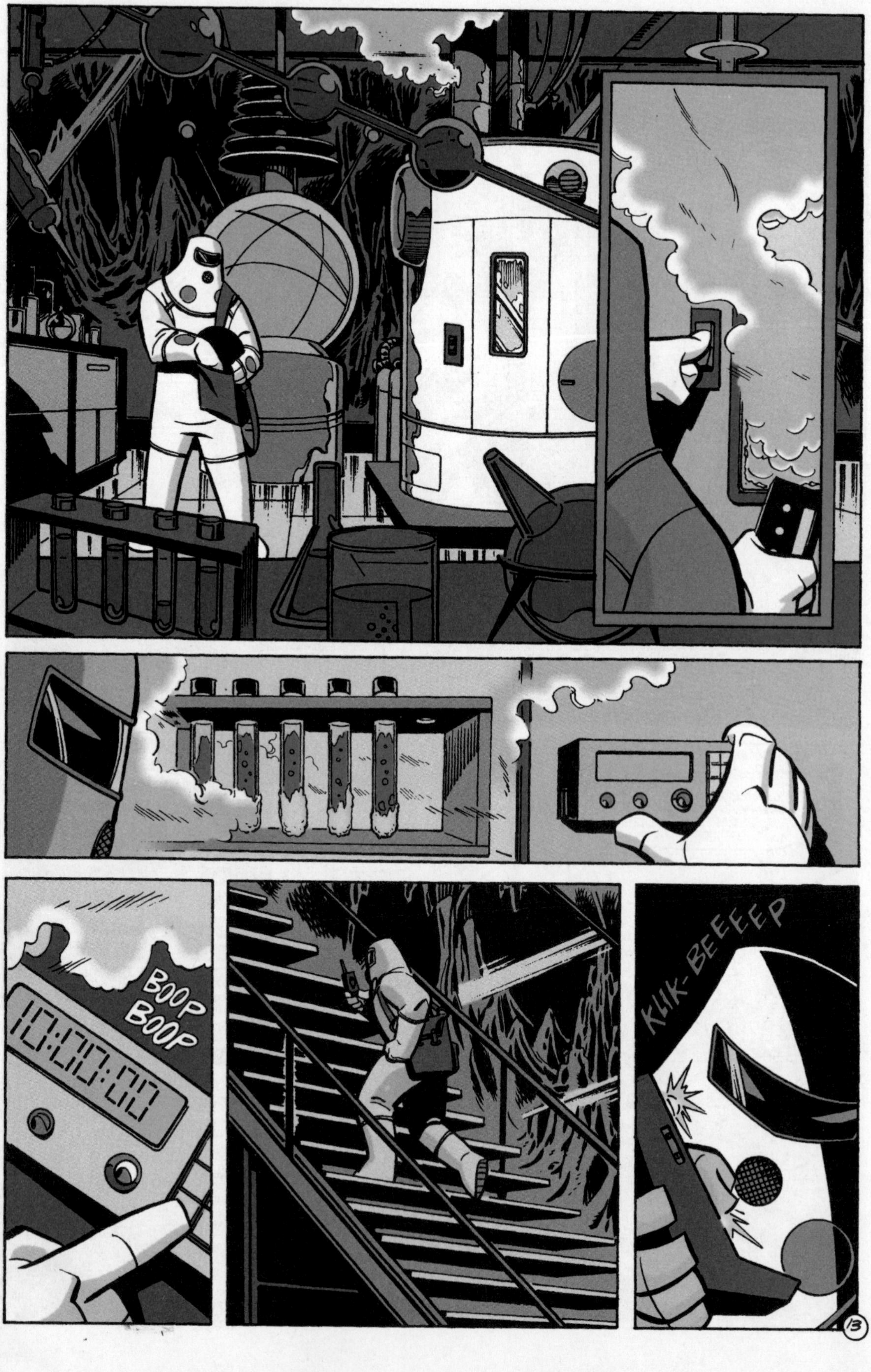
BOOP
BOOP
10:00:00
KLIK-BEEEEP
13

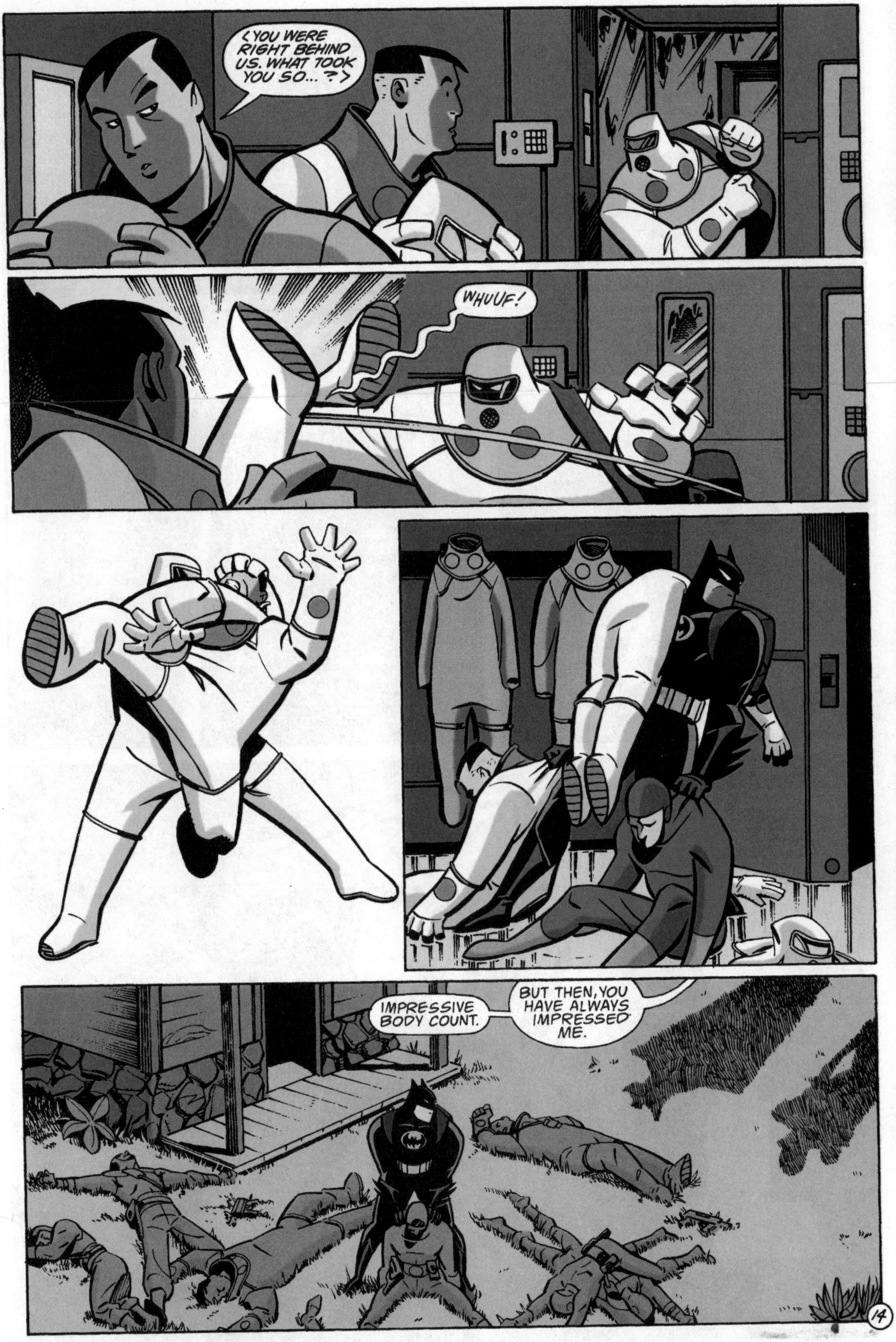
<YOU WERE RIGHT BEHIND US. WHAT TOOK YOU SO...?>
WHUUF!
IMPRESSIVE BODY COUNT.
BUT THEN, YOU HAVE ALWAYS IMPRESSED ME.
14

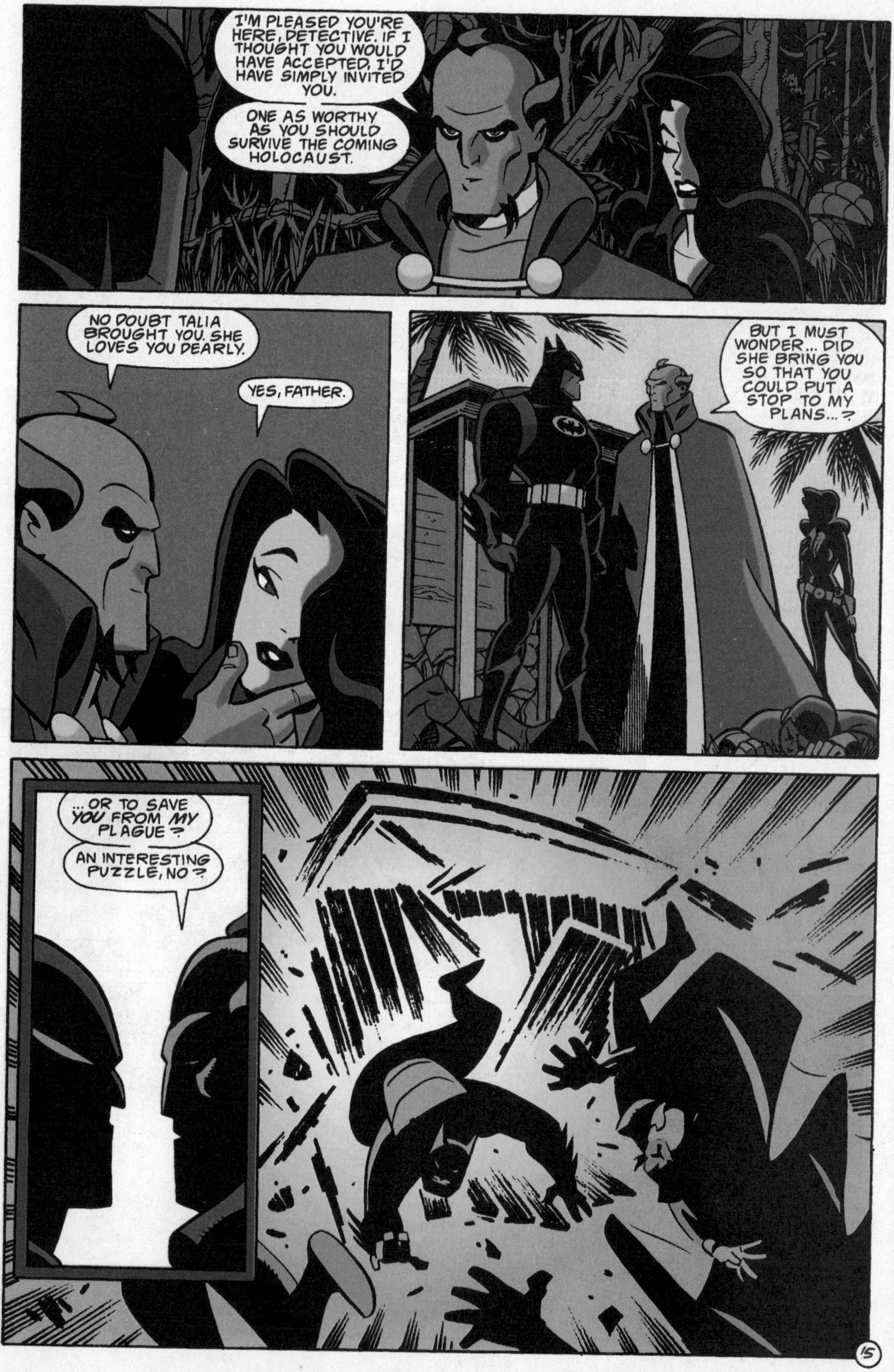
I'M PLEASED YOU'RE HERE, DETECTIVE. IF I THOUGHT YOU WOULD HAVE ACCEPTED, I'D HAVE SIMPLY INVITED YOU.
ONE AS WORTHY AS YOU SHOULD SURVIVE THE COMING HOLOCAUST.
NO DOUBT TALIA BROUGHT YOU. SHE LOVES YOU DEARLY.
YES, FATHER.
BUT I MUST WONDER... DID SHE BRING YOU SO THAT YOU COULD PUT A STOP TO MY PLANS...?
...OR TO SAVE YOU FROM MY PLAGUE?
AN INTERESTING PUZZLE, NO?
15

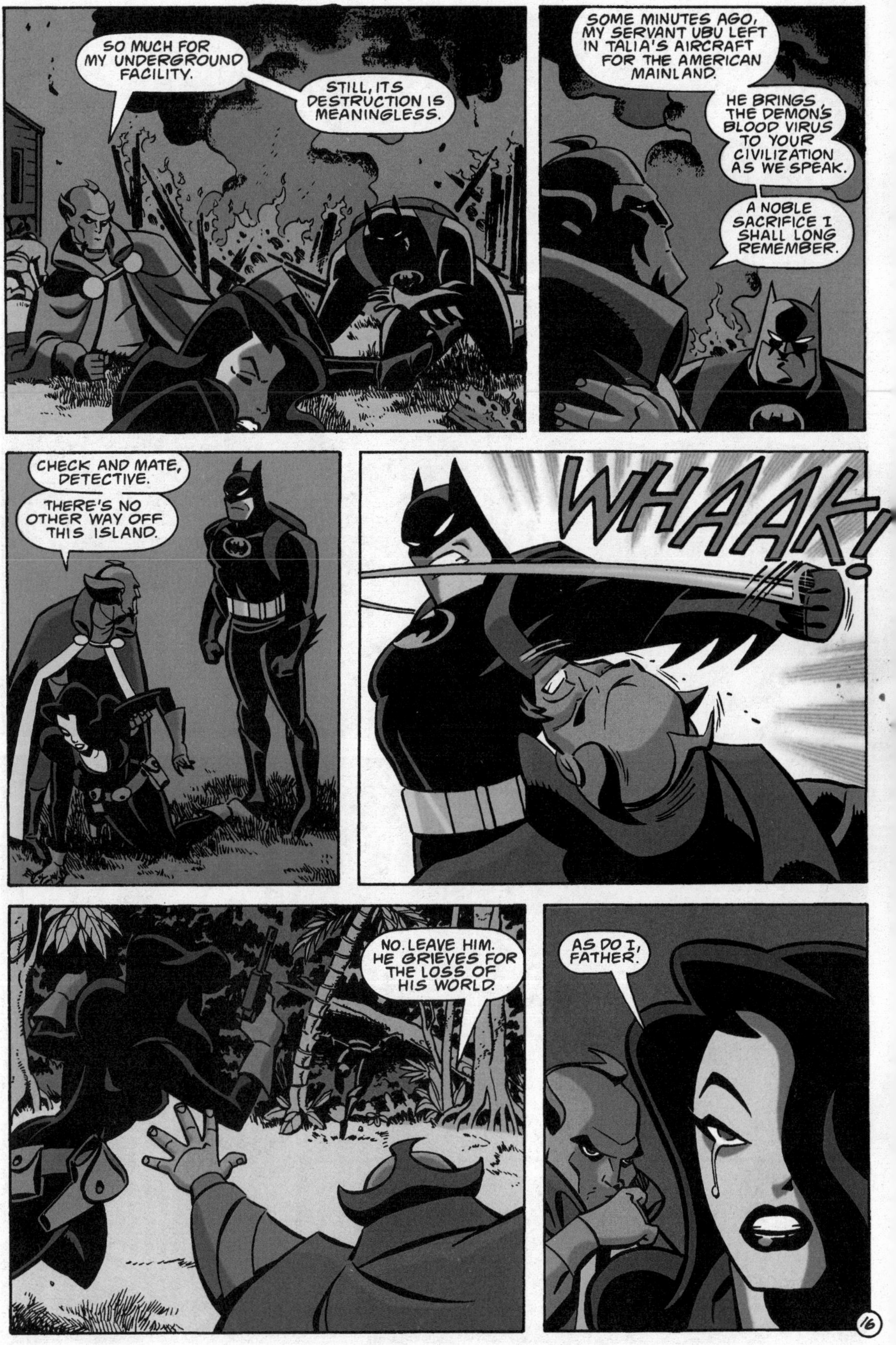
SO MUCH FOR MY UNDERGROUND FACILITY.
STILL, ITS DESTRUCTION IS MEANINGLESS.
SOME MINUTES AGO, MY SERVANT UBU LEFT IN TALIA'S AIRCRAFT FOR THE AMERICAN MAINLAND.
HE BRINGS THE DEMON'S BLOOD VIRUS TO YOUR CIVILIZATION AS WE SPEAK.
A NOBLE SACRIFICE I SHALL LONG REMEMBER.
CHECK AND MATE, DETECTIVE.
THERE'S NO OTHER WAY OFF THIS ISLAND.
WHAAK!
NO. LEAVE HIM. HE GRIEVES FOR THE LOSS OF HIS WORLD.
AS DO I, FATHER.
16

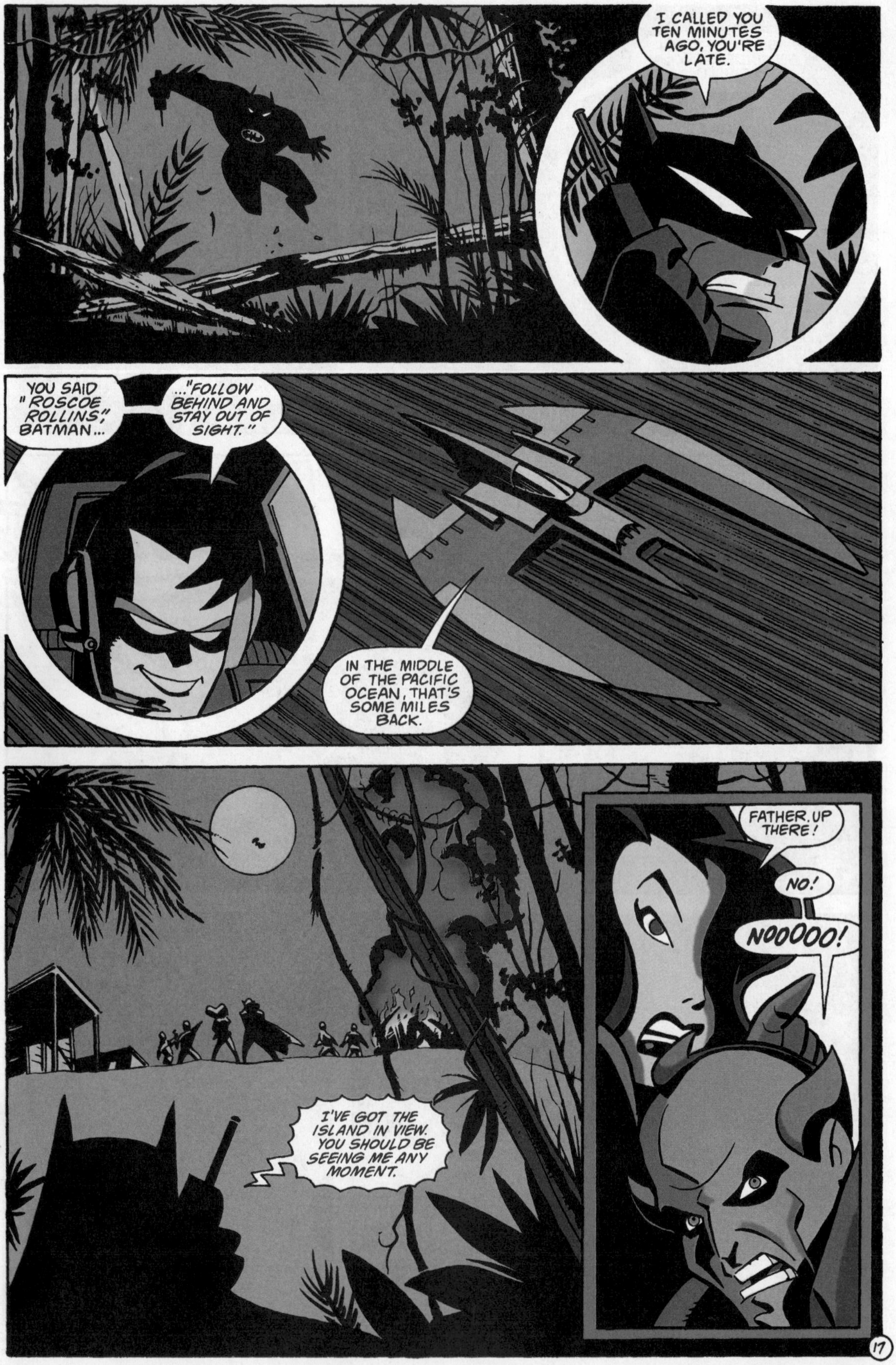
I CALLED YOU TEN MINUTES AGO, YOU'RE LATE.
YOU SAID "ROSCOE ROLLINS," BATMAN...
..."FOLLOW BEHIND AND STAY OUT OF SIGHT."
IN THE MIDDLE OF THE PACIFIC OCEAN, THAT'S SOME MILES BACK.
FATHER, UP THERE!
NO!
NOOOOO!
I'VE GOT THE ISLAND IN VIEW. YOU SHOULD BE SEEING ME ANY MOMENT.
17

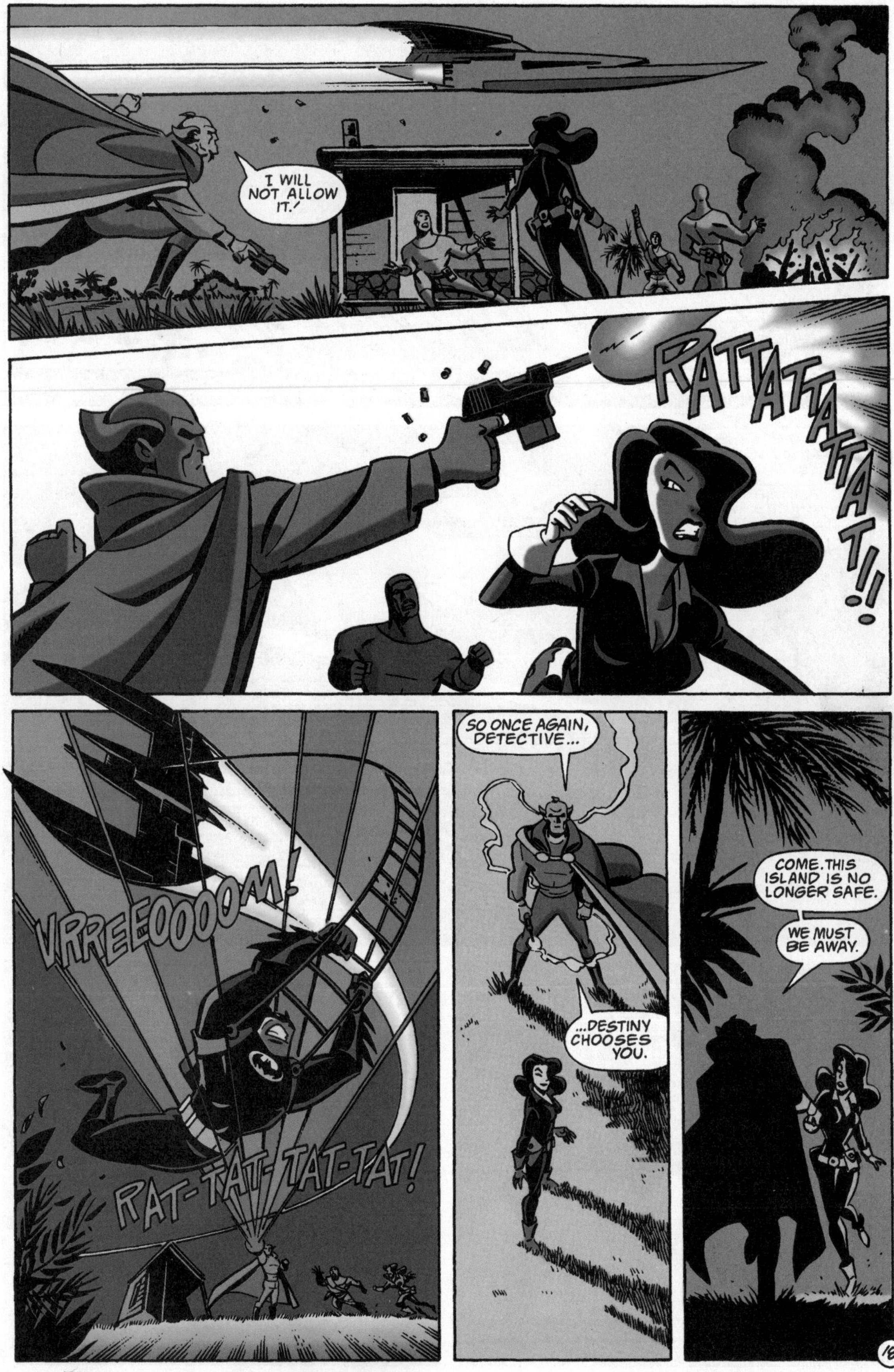
I WILL NOT ALLOW IT.'
RATTATTATTAT!!
VRREEOOOOM!
RAT-TAT-TAT-TAT!
SO ONCE AGAIN, DETECTIVE...
...DESTINY CHOOSES YOU.
COME. THIS ISLAND IS NO LONGER SAFE.
WE MUST BE AWAY.
18

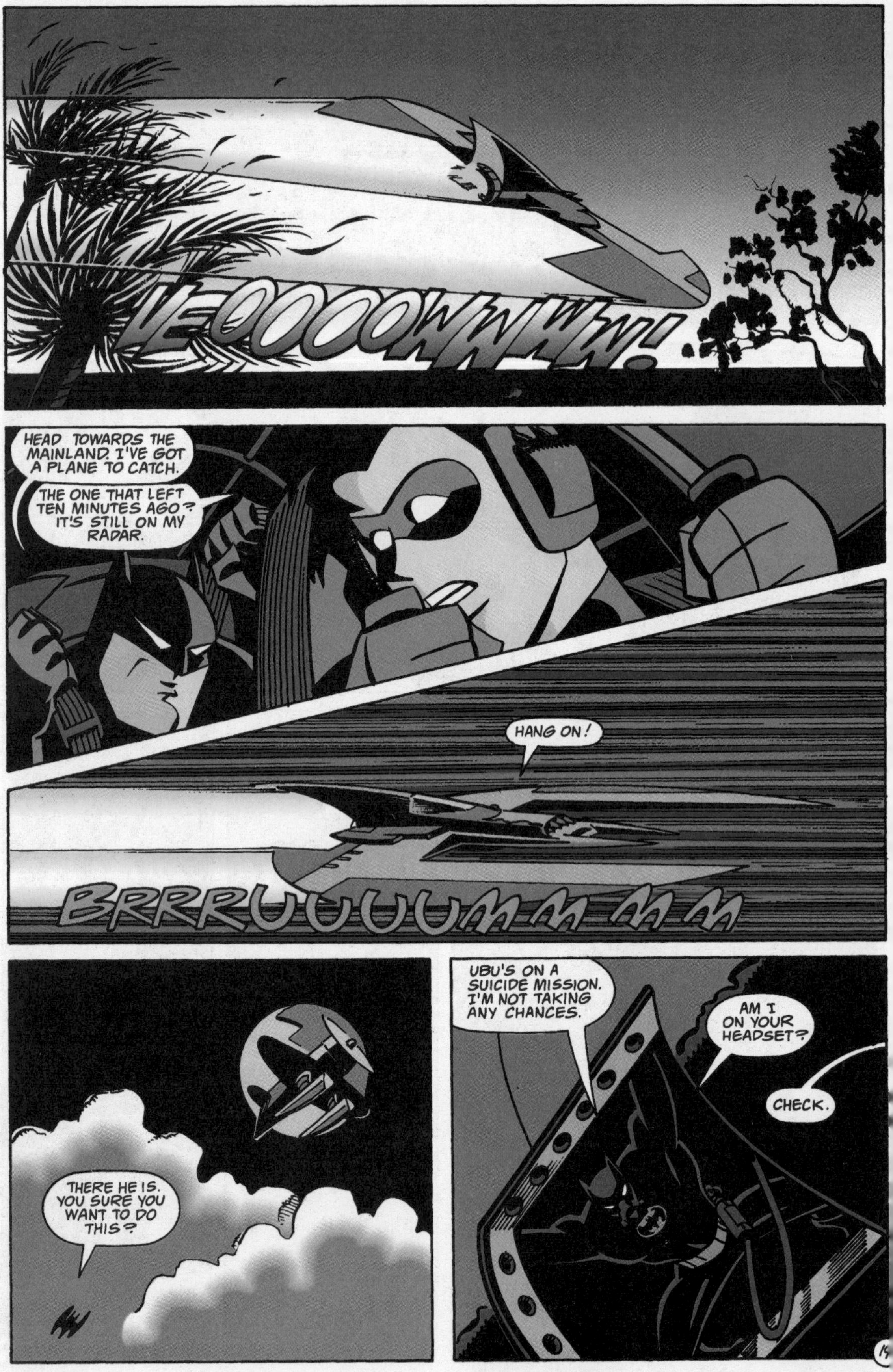
VE-OOOOOWWWW!
HEAD TOWARDS THE MAINLAND. I'VE GOT A PLANE TO CATCH.
THE ONE THAT LEFT TEN MINUTES AGO? IT'S STILL ON MY RADAR.
HANG ON!
BRRRUUUUMMMMM
THERE HE IS. YOU SURE YOU WANT TO DO THIS?
UBU'S ON A SUICIDE MISSION. I'M NOT TAKING ANY CHANCES.
AM I ON YOUR HEADSET?
CHECK.

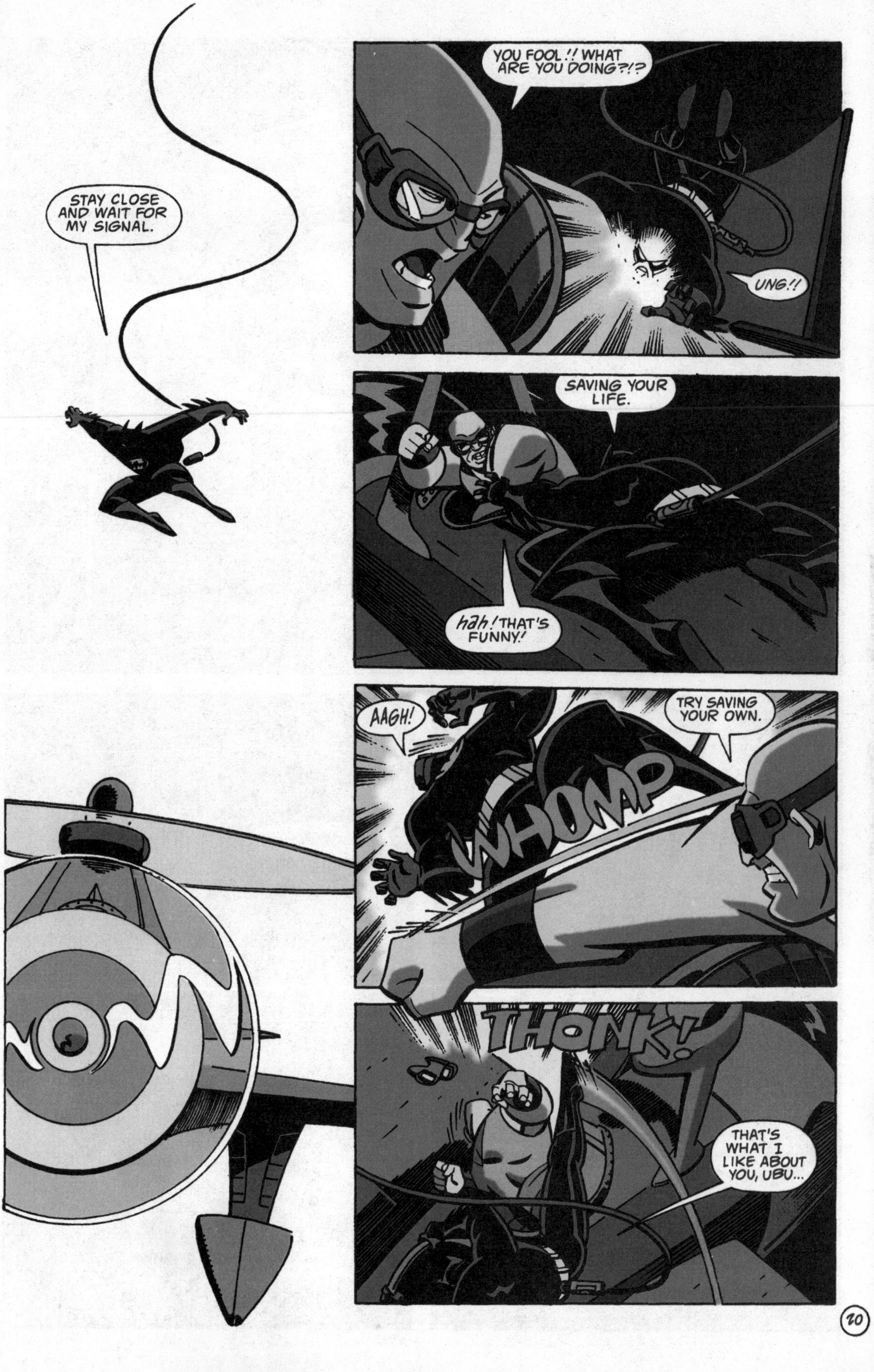
STAY CLOSE AND WAIT FOR MY SIGNAL.
YOU FOOL!! WHAT ARE YOU DOING?!?
UNG!!
SAVING YOUR LIFE.
hah! THAT'S FUNNY!
AAGH!
TRY SAVING YOUR OWN.
WHOMP
THONK!
THAT'S WHAT I LIKE ABOUT YOU, UBU...
20

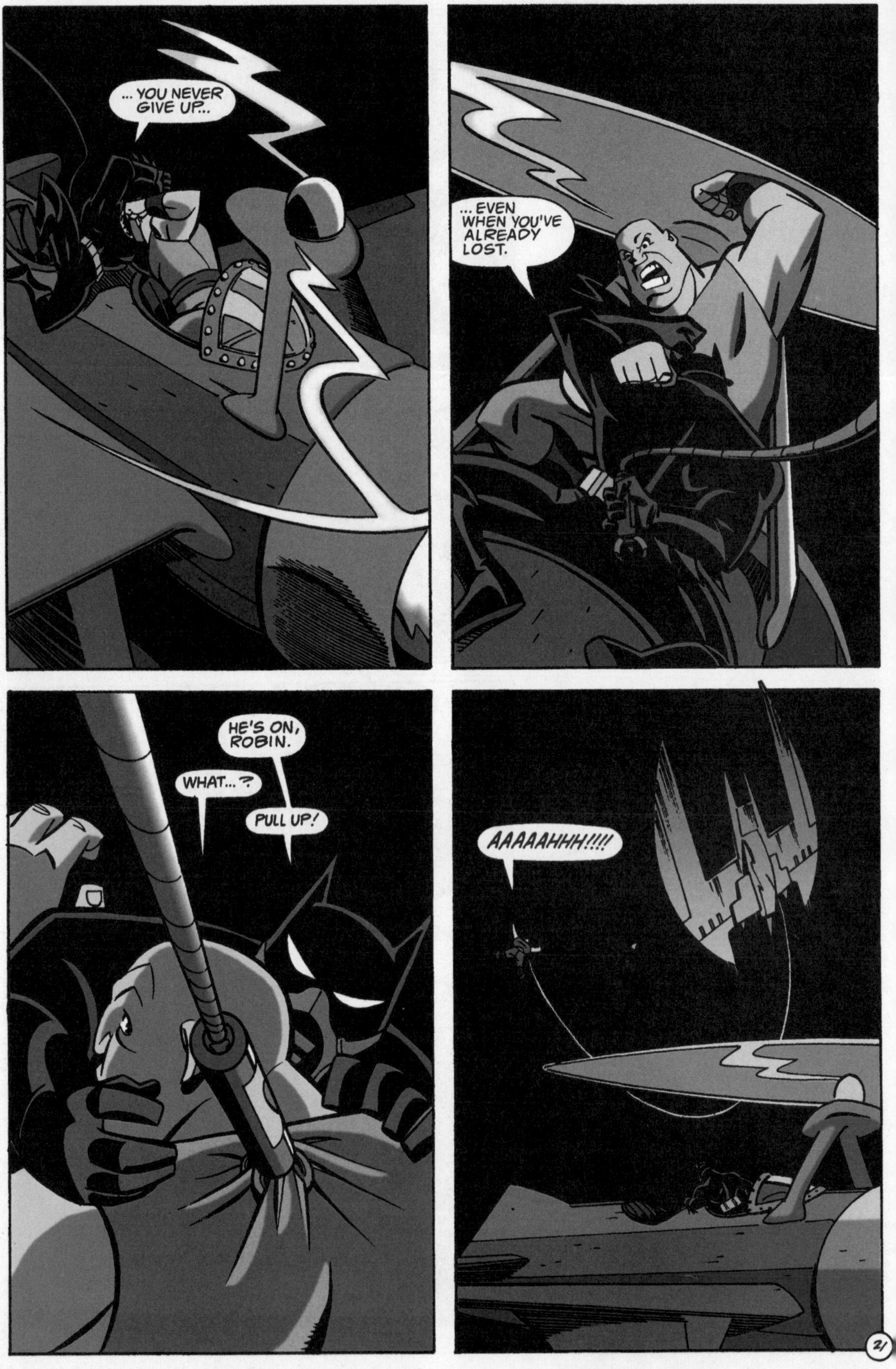

... YOU NEVER GIVE UP...
... EVEN WHEN YOU'VE ALREADY LOST.
HE'S ON, ROBIN.
WHAT...?
PULL UP!
AAAAAHHH!!!!
21

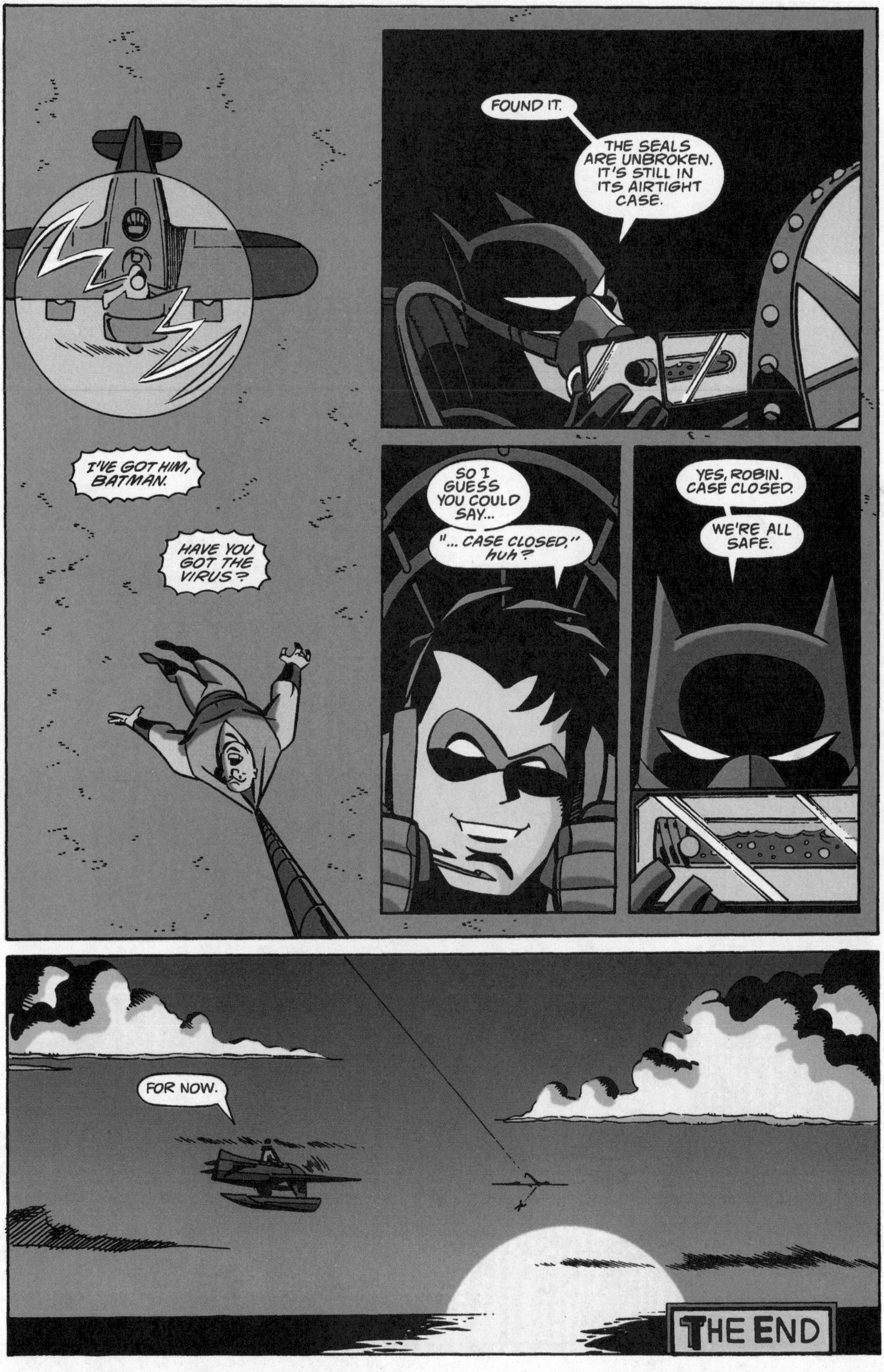
FOUND IT.
THE SEALS ARE UNBROKEN. IT'S STILL IN ITS AIRTIGHT CASE.
I'VE GOT HIM, BATMAN.
HAVE YOU GOT THE VIRUS?
SO I GUESS YOU COULD SAY...
"... CASE CLOSED," huh?
YES, ROBIN. CASE CLOSED.
WE'RE ALL SAFE.
FOR NOW.
THE END

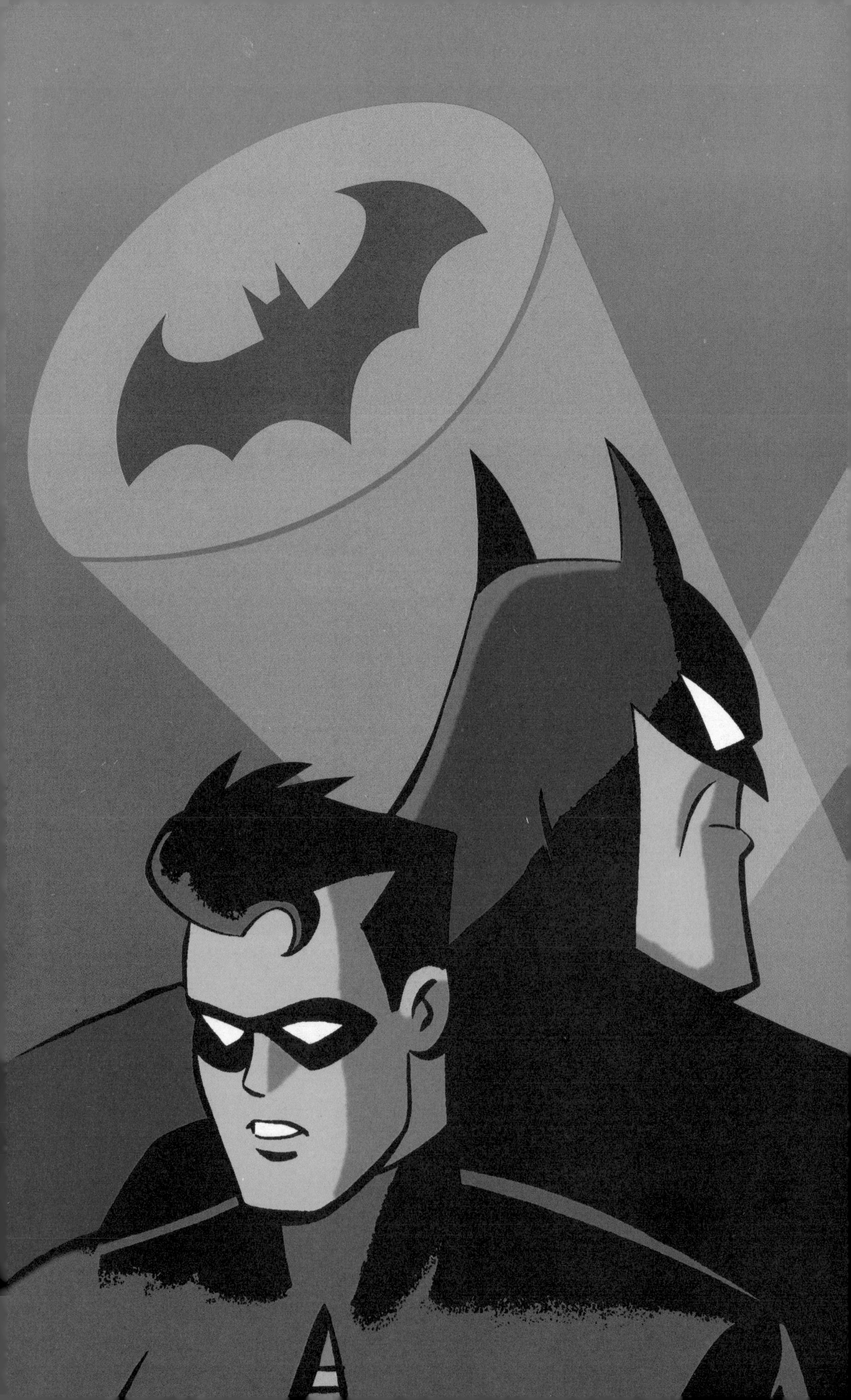

"Game-changing redefining of the Caped Crusader."
—ENTERTAINMENT WEEKLY SHELF LIFE

"A wildly entertaining ride that's been at all times challenging, unsettling, amusing, inventive, iconic and epic... one of the most exciting eras in Batman history."
—IGN

FROM *NEW YORK TIMES* #1 BEST-SELLING WRITER

GRANT MORRISON
with ANDY KUBERT, J.H. WILLIAMS III and TONY S. DANIEL

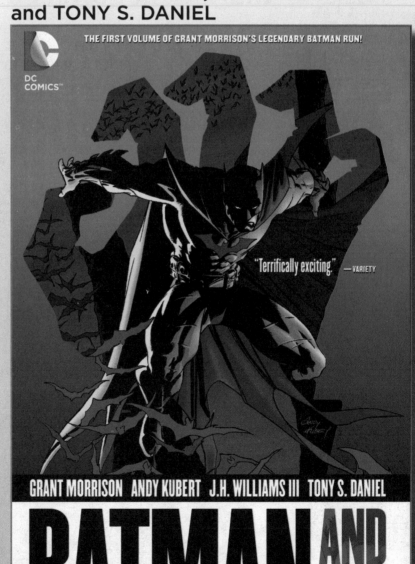

THE FIRST VOLUME OF GRANT MORRISON'S LEGENDARY BATMAN RUN!

DC COMICS™

"Terrifically exciting." —VARIETY

GRANT MORRISON   ANDY KUBERT   J.H. WILLIAMS III   TONY S. DANIEL

BATMAN AND SON

DC COMICS™

"Brilliantly executed."
—IGN

"Morrison and Quitely have the magic touch that makes any book they collaborate on stand out from the rest." —MTV's Splash Page

"Thrilling and invigorating....Gotham City that has never looked this good, felt this strange, or been this deadly." —COMIC BOOK RESOURCES

GRANT MORRISON
with FRANK QUITELY & PHILIP TAN

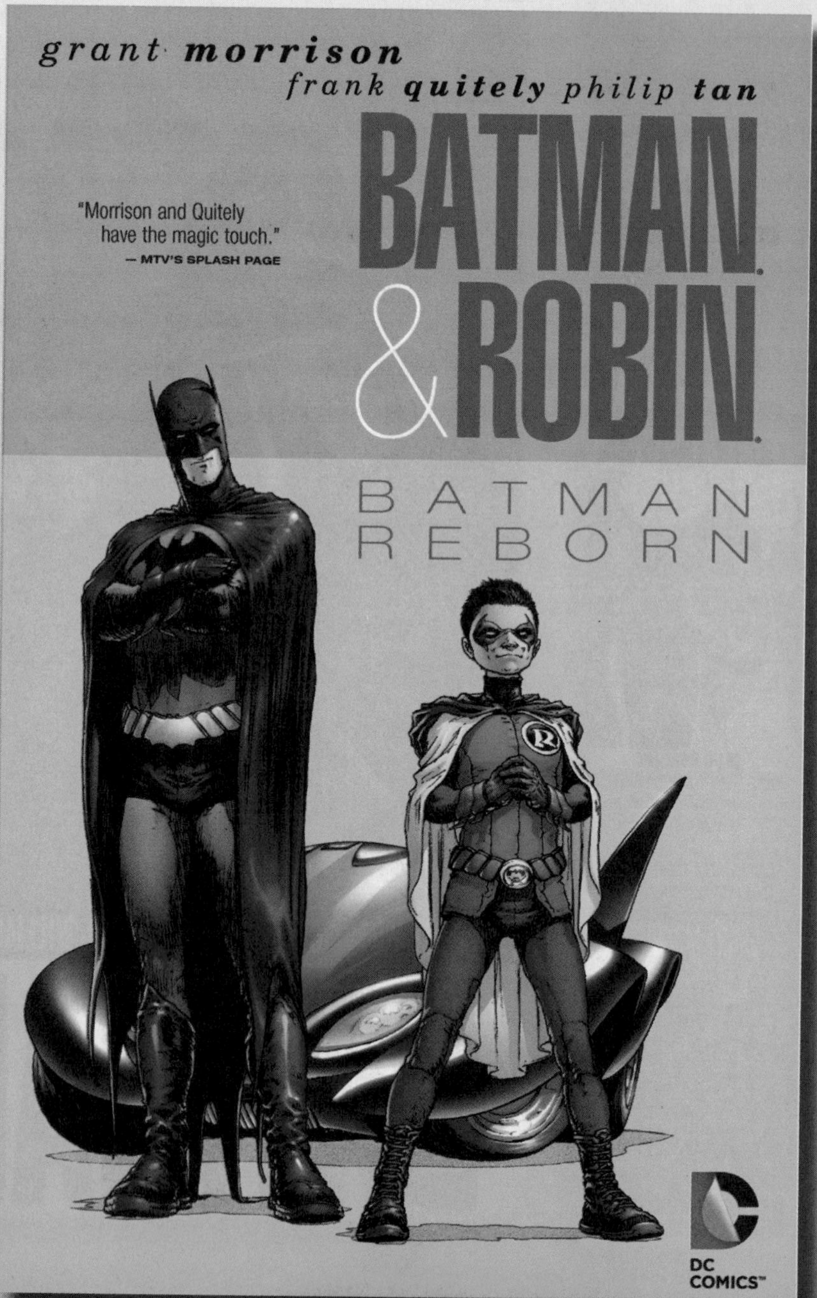

grant morrison
frank quitely philip tan
BATMAN & ROBIN
"Morrison and Quitely have the magic touch."
— MTV'S SPLASH PAGE
BATMAN REBORN
DC COMICS™

VOL. 2: BATMAN VS. ROBIN

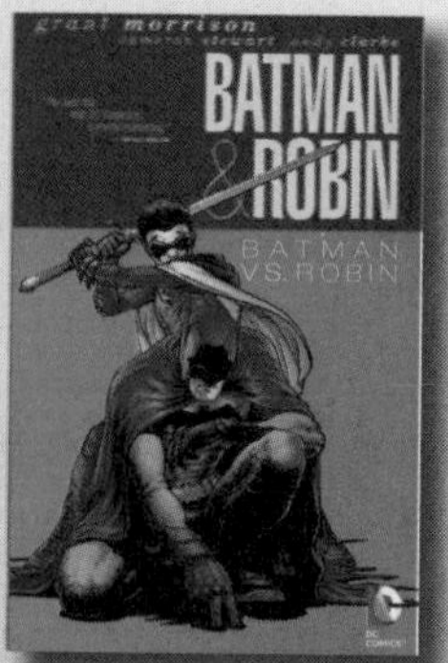

BATMAN & ROBIN
BATMAN VS. ROBIN

VOL. 3: BATMAN & ROBIN MUST DIE!

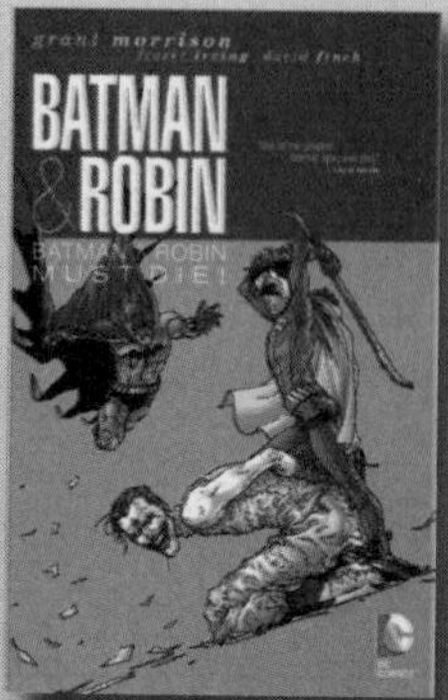

grant morrison
BATMAN & ROBIN
BATMAN & ROBIN MUST DIE!

DARK KNIGHT VS. WHITE KNIGHT

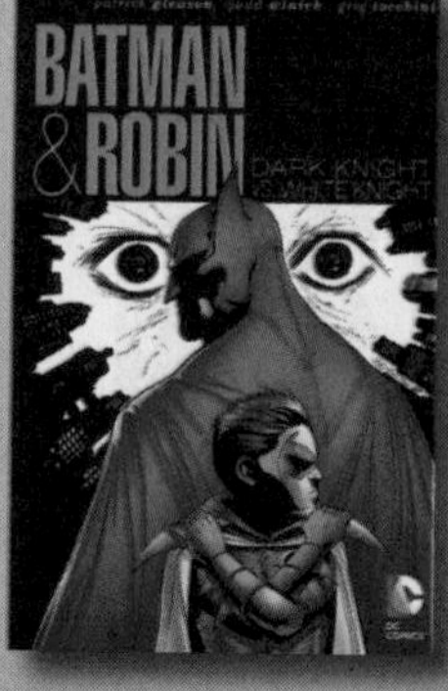

BATMAN & ROBIN
DARK KNIGHT VS. WHITE KNIGHT

START AT THE BEGINNING!

BATMAN & ROBIN
VOLUME 1: BORN TO KILL

BATMAN & ROBIN
VOL. 2: PEARL

BATMAN & ROBIN
VOL. 3: DEATH OF THE
FAMILY

BATMAN
INCORPORATED
VOL. 1: DEMON STAR

DC COMICS™

THE NEW 52!

BATMAN AND ROBIN

VOLUME 1
BORN TO KILL

"PETER J. TOMASI AND PATRICK GLEASON ARE KNOCKING IT OUT ISSUE AFTER ISSUE."
— WIRED.COM

PETER J. TOMASI   PATRICK GLEASON   MICK GRAY

DC
COMICS™

"Stellar. A solid yarn that roots itself in Grayson's past, with gorgeous artwork by artist Eddy Barrows."—IGN

"Dynamic."—The New York Times

"A new generation is going to fall in love with Nightwing."
—MTV Geek

START AT THE BEGINNING!

NIGHTWING
VOLUME 1: TRAPS AND TRAPEZES

NIGHTWING VOL. 2:
NIGHT OF THE OWLS

NIGHTWING VOL. 3:
DEATH OF THE FAMILY

BATMAN:
NIGHT OF THE OWLS

KYLE HIGGINS EDDY BARROWS